NEXT TIME, USE MA BELL!

Eric had stopped on the edge of a small valley, a tiny ravine with a grove of stunted oak trees visible below him. Eric concentrated hard, thinking of Beth; the sound of her voice, her laughter, the way she looked at him that night. *Trying to reach out to her—* :*Hey, Beth, pick up the phone. It's me, Eric, your crazy Bardic friend, calling you on the Ma Bell cellular brainwave line—come on, Beth, talk to me—:*

Someone else spoke, a low, breathy voice, a whisper in the silent recesses of Eric's mind: :*Who speaks in my dreams? Who awakens me from my slumber?:*

Eric looked around, bewildered. *Excuse me?*

:*Who is it who walks silently through these hills and calls to one who is far away? Who are you, intruder into my endless night? What are you?:*

Eric sighed. *Well, this is no weirder than anything else that's happened to me lately.* Eric carefully constructed a reply. :*Yeah, hi. My name is Eric Banyon. Sorry, I didn't mean to wake you up, I'm just passing through the neighborhood. I'm human, of course. And a Bard—at least everyone keeps telling me I am. Who are you?:*

The reply came not in words, but in the rustle of leathery wings, high above the valley, spreading to block out the moon and the stars. :*This is what I am.:*

Eric looked at the monstrous *thing* looming above him, tattered wings beating soundlessly against the sky and gulped.

The blind moon eyes, pale white, turned towards him. :*You are a Bard, human?:*

:*Well, yeah.:* Eric thought back at it.

:*Good. I am hungry.:*

MERCEDES LACKEY

BEDLAM'S BARD

ELLEN GUON

BEDLAM'S BARD

A Baen Books Original

Baen Publishing Enterprises
P.O. Box 1403
Riverdale, NY 10471
www.baen.com

ISBN: 1-4165-3282-X
ISBN 13: 978-1-4165-3282-8

First mass market unitary printing, March 1998
Fifth printing, May 2006

Distributed by Simon & Schuster
1230 Avenue of the Americas
New York, NY 10020

Production by Windhaven Press, Auburn, NH
Printed in the United States of America.

Book 1

Knight of Ghosts and Shadows

1

Tom O' Bedlam

"Selfish, inconsiderate, irresponsible—"

Maureen's voice had been rising all through this tirade; by now she was hitting A above high C, and everyone in the Faire could hear her. Eric Banyon winced, and wished she'd get to the point, since it was pretty clear he wasn't going to be able to patch up this fight.

Christ, it would be nice if she'd tell me what it is I'm supposed to have done that was so awful.

She stamped her foot, and got angrier—if that was possible—when she made no impression on the hard-baked adobe. "*Shit*, Eric, I can't *take* you anymore! You, you, you, that's all you think about! Where *you* want to go, what *you* want to do, when *you* want to screw—now—this—this—"

Now wait just a cotton-pickin' minute here—Her accusations bewildered—and angered—him. *What is this shit? I've never asked her to do anything she didn't want to. I've never gotten her into anything, she didn't okay first! So I'm doing the Faires for a while—I'm a musician, dammit, and so is she! What's the big deal about my taking a couple of gigs?*

Maureen's long red hair was coming loose from its knot; strands of it flew around her face as she gestured at the messy area back of the Elizabethan Faire mainstage. Eric presumed, however, that she was including the whole of the Faire in her gesture.

"Dammit, I have *had* it with you!" she screamed, coming into full operatic voice. "I have *had* it with your selfishness and I have *had* it with this grubby little dump and I have *had* it with you!"

"But—" he said weakly, unable to compete with a voice that could fill the Greek *without* even using the push of anger she had behind it now.

"You can just *take* this stupid gig and all the rest of it, and you can . . . can . . . keep it!" she shrieked at the top of her range, probably shattering glassware in the taverns and booths out front. "I am *leaving!*"

And with that, she threw down the bodice and skirt he'd talked her into wearing and stormed off in the direction of the parking lot, every visible inch of her pink with rage—and, in the scraps of shorts and halter she was wearing, there was a *lot* of her visible.

She nearly collided with one of the Gypsies, who was laden with costumes and couldn't see her. He half expected her to turn on the girl, but she was so angry she didn't even notice the wide-eyed dancer/musician, she just stormed on past, leaving the faint scent of scorched earth—and scorched Eric—in her wake.

He wanted to run after her, but Beth was in the way, and he'd have to bowl her over to get to Maureen in time.

Always assuming Maureen didn't deck him in full view of the "travelers" when he caught up with her.

"What in hell was *that* all about?" The dark-haired, dusty dancer put her armload of clothing where it belonged in the Costumes storage, and gave him an incredulous look. "Who was that madwoman, Banyon?"

Eric sighed, and picked the skirt and bodice up out of the dust, beating the worst of the dirt off them. "That was a . . . personality conflict," he said, choosing his words carefully. "Half of it was my fault, I guess. And the other half of the conflict was Maureen Taylor."

"*That* was your girl? The man-eating soprano herself?"

"Ex-girl," Eric replied bitterly. "At least at the moment.

She made that abundantly clear just now. She doesn't like the Faire in particular and my itinerant lifestyle in general."

"But—Eric, *everybody* knows what you're like."

"Maybe she thought that when she moved in with me I'd change? She never came out and told me that but—maybe she thought I'd settle down. Get a job. Join the Moose Lodge." He ducked behind the burlap curtain and set the costume down in a stack of others. He turned around just in time to catch Beth's sardonic expression through the open door flap. "Well, go ahead, you might as well say whatever it is you've got trying to beat its way through your teeth."

"Do the words 'fat effin' chance' translate properly?" she replied. "You've been a footloose street busker for as long as I've known you, Banyon. You're a darlin' man," she continued, slipping into her Faire dialect, "but I'd ne'er be after chasin' ye if were ye the last stallion in all of Eire. Jaysus, O'Banyon, but ye've got the wanderin' foot an' the rovin' eye, ye do, an' I'd ne'er trust ye wi' a puir maid's heart. Not t'mention the uither fairer portions of meself . . ."

"Give me a break," he said, wincing a little. "I just like my freedom."

"Yeah, and I just like to know where *my* man is once in a while." But she took a closer look at him, and her expression of irony softened to something a little like pity. Not quite—but it was at least more sympathetic. She patted his hand. "Hey, c'mon, Eric, I'm sorry. You just had a rather spectacular breakup. That was a stupid thing to say. I didn't intend to make fun of you."

"It's okay," he said, only *now* beginning to *feel* anything besides confusion and pure embarrassment. The full impact of what had just happened started to hit him. Maureen was *gone*.

Worse than that. Really *gone* this time. She'd never walked out on an argument before. Not ever. He'd always managed to get her cooled down, they'd always talked it out. Not this time. She hadn't given him a chance to get a single word in. He *still* didn't know what he'd done—but he'd sure stepped over the line somehow. And it started here, with the Faire.

Like he'd said to Beth, the Faire in particular and busking in general.

What's wrong with being a traveling musician? he asked himself angrily. *What's so important about having a mundane job? Shit, I'd rather die. I get by just fine. I did great before I got to L.A., I'm doing all right now, and I'll do okay when I move someplace else. If she wanted a CPA, she should have moved in with one.*

He pummeled his memory, trying to remember exactly when she'd first put up the storm warnings. *Okay, she was getting zoned, and I showed her the camp—that's when she just came out and asked me how long I planned on staying in L.A. with her.*

So I told her.

Damn. What did she expect me to do, lie to her? It's not like I wouldn't be coming back eventually. Why does she want a leash on me? What would she have that she doesn't have now?

He kicked at a corner of the stage, and checked for "travelers" before venturing out into public pathways. *Just what I need right now, a bunch of customers wanting to hear me play "Greensleeves" for the millionth time.*

He ducked through the burlap doorway, and into the dusty Faire "street."

I thought she'd figured out I don't like being pinned down, like the way my parents managed to pin me down for so many years. I've had my fill of being tied hand and foot, like a poor little lamb about to get his throat slit. Sacrificed on the altar of Great Art. Bullshit. No more.

I wonder if she's heading straight home to clear out her half of the apartment? Or are we going through this all again as soon as I get home? Goddammit, Maureen, you knew what I was like when you moved in with me! Why did you have to pull this shit on me now?

Beth put her armload of costumes away and changed out to jeans and a T-shirt with "Gentle Ladies of Death and Destruction™" embroidered in pink and lavender on the front.

Poor Eric. He is going to be in real deep kim chee when word of this gets back to Admin. She pulled the shirt over her head and shook out her hair. *The audience didn't know whether to listen to the show or Mademoiselle Mimi. At least he doesn't repeat his mistakes. Traci just went away. Donna married her shrink and left an invite to the wedding on his coffee table. And Kathie —the bitch—drove him out of Texas Faire. Even if that isn't the way the rumor-mill has it.*

She hung her mini-ocarina around her neck and mentally slapped her hand. It was itching for her Fender— *We have a gig Wednesday night and rehearsals on Monday and Tuesday. Stop thinking heretical thoughts! Guitars alone could get you burned at the stake by the Renaissance purists at this place, Kentraine. Electric guitars, oh horrors.*

She poked her head out into the street, and saw Eric off in the distance, shoulders slouched, head down.

Lawsy. It's hit him. Now we're going to be in for at least twenty-four hours of Gloom, Despair and Agony.

Eric slowly walked down the Tinker's Lane, past the wooden booths, decorated with colorful ribbons and cloth, where the Faire merchants were already closing up shop for the night.

Irish Hill. It's quiet up there this time of night. Nobody to bother, or to bother me. I could play a bit, get my head straight—

A few "travelers" were still wandering the Faire, gently herded towards the exit by the red-tunicked Faire Security. Mostly only the Faire folk were out in the narrow dirt streets, dancers and musicians returning from their last shows, actors carrying their props back to Lockup.

The road continued on in a marginally straight line up to the Hill, his usual post-Faire hangout. But he could see that something was happening up there, a group of Faire folk gathered around a table, the burning candles visible even at this distance Their bright costumes were now replaced by cowled dark robes. A neo-pagan Wiccan Coven was in session, and it was looking pretty serious.

Tonight is May Eve, Beltane, that's right. I'd almost forgotten. High Holy day. Lord. If you want to raise an occult ruckus, seems to me this would be the place for it. I wanted to sit on the Hill—naw, they're already in circle, I'd better not disturb them. I'll find another place to play.

He trudged up the slope to the Traveler's Road, that met the Tinker's Lane just below Irish Hill. He could hear the soft words from the Hill: ". . . Great Goddess, save our Fairesite, keep those who would destroy it at bay. This is all we ask, Great Goddess . . ." The chant faded as Eric walked down Traveler's Road towards the Wood, the dark oaks hiding the last glimpse of red-gold sunlight.

So it's bad enough that they're praying for help. I didn't know it was that grim—sounds like the death knell. Shawna and her bunch are into "the goddess helps those who help themselves," and if it's gotten to the point that all they can do is pray— He shook his head, stopped, and looked around, the familiar booths and stages of the Faire, the stubby brown grass, ancient oak trees, the shadowed Southern Californian hills rising above it all. *Damn shame. Just because some developer thinks this would be a terrific place for a shopping mall . . .*

I wish somebody really could save it. This is the best Faire I've ever seen; it's so alive, always music and laughing—But when a corporation gets something into its collective head, there ain't much you can do about it. Not when they've got all the money, all the pull they need to make whomever owned the land sell it. Possession being nine-tenths . . . and I know I saw surveyors out here Friday.

General depression piled on personal depression.

I don't know if I want to stick around and see this place turn into another shrine to McDonald's and Sears Roebuck. Maybe this is a good time to move on.

Maureen sure wouldn't mind seeing me leave L.A.

Eric sighed and continued walking, dodging three drunken travelers, two guys in shorts and T-shirts, each carrying stacked paper beer cups, at least fifteen each—and keeping their balance despite the added burden of the third member of their party, slung over one guy's shoulder, out cold.

No wonder he's DOA. Their blood must be at least sixty proof. He felt sorry for the Security guy, trying to push the three in the direction of the Faire exit. *Not my idea of a fun job.*

The Wood loomed before him now, oak branches curving overhead to create thick darkness beneath. Dark and forbidding, to anybody who didn't know it.

But it was as familiar as an old friend to Eric, who'd played there for years: on the Wood Stage, and on the streets filled with travelers and Faire folk.

His pace slowed, and he felt a pang, thinking about how this would all go under a bulldozer's blade. *God, but I love this place. It's the only place I've ever really felt at home— even when I want to escape from everything, there's that grove, hidden at the edge of the Fairesite . . .*

It occurred to him that since Irish Hill was occupied, he might want to play there for a while tonight, just get away from everybody and everything and play until he couldn't think or feel anything anymore . . .

Damn it, Maureen, everything was fine! How could you walk out on me like this?

He walked to the edge of the haybale rows that were the seats for the Wood Stage. A group of musicians was seated on the stage, playing. Eric smiled sadly, recognizing the tune even before he saw the players. *"Banish Misfortune" . . . yeah, I wish it could.*

The reality of the fight—and what it meant—hit him. He began to feel empty inside, and lost; like he'd lost more than just Maureen. Like he'd lost his way and he'd never find it again. Black despair came down on him, so palpable that he was mildly surprised that he wasn't surrounded by a dark fog like a cartoon character.

God. I don't know where I'm going, what I'm doing. Nothing makes sense anymore . . .

All of the Celtic musicians were on the stage, some still wearing their Faire costumes, others in denim jeans and sweaters. All his friends, his favorite people. Linda and

Aaron, fiddling like crazy, with Ross and red-bearded Ian pounding out the fast tempo on their Irish war drums. Judy standing over her dulcimer, the hand-held hammers moving so fast they blurred, with Jay sitting next to her, playing tinwhistle.

And four of the visiting Northerners, two fiddler girls looking like a matched set, one with short curly hair, the other a blonde; off in the back, a serious dark-haired woman concentrating on an intricate rhythm on a dumbek, and that blond bearded fellow playing the bouzouki.

Together they sounded better than any professional group Eric had heard in six years of busking, and the music was magnetic, drawing him to them. He half-reached for his flute, then sighed. *Not tonight. I can't pretend that nothing's happened, pretend to be cheerful and happy. They'll know I'm pretending, they'll hear it in my music. No, they're having fun. Better not to spoil it.*

"Hey, Eric, you crazy whistler, come down here!" Judy called to him.

He forced a laugh and shook his head, calling back to her over the loud music. "Not tonight, sweetheart, I have a previous engagement." He grinned. "Maybe afterwards."

Judy laughed and said something he didn't catch, though from the look on her face it was probably salacious. He just kept his mouth stretched in that phony grin and hurried past them, hoping none of them would decide to follow and haul him back.

"Hey, Eric," Beth hailed him from behind.

Oh shit. I didn't want to talk to anyone—especially not somebody who saw the fight.

Beth could hear Eric groan.. but he stopped, and turned to face her.

"Beth, I'm not in the mood—" he began. She shoved a flask into his long, fine-boned hand before he could finish his statement.

"Have a pull on that," she ordered. "I only heard the tail end of the fight, but I suspect you need it. Besides, we can stay here and talk about it, if you want. I may have to go take care of the rumor-mill after that ruckus."

And I want to know, because you don't usually go around making women screaming mad on purpose, Banyon, she thought wryly. *You may not think about things before you do them, but you don't screw up on purpose. And I don't think you would knowingly hurt a fly.*

Beth remembered Kathie, and how she'd used this lad to get herself into the Texas Faire, then into a pro band, then dropped him like a hot rock.

In your own peculiar way, you're the gentlest man I know. And, in your own peculiar way, the most forgiving. You forgave Kathie, and I never would have. Hell, I still haven't, and I wasn't the one who got it in the teeth.

"I'd almost rather not talk about it," he said plaintively, shaking his shoulder-length chestnut hair out of his eyes.

God, how can anyone be that pretty? *He looks like Sophia Loren at sixteen. With the appropriate male acoutrements. Very . . . nice.*

Down, girl. He's also as feckless as they come. He's no good to you or himself as he is.

"You want to live till morning?" she retorted, hands on hips. "Look, maybe I can scotch some of the worst rumors. Tongues are already clacking, and they're not being real flattering to you. Besides, you've never hesitated to talk to me before, right?" He gave her an open, vulnerable look that almost made her want to take him in her arms and give him the best kind of comfort for a broken heart.

Almost.

She continued, trying to keep her thoughts where they belonged—*out* of the gutter. "And maybe I can help you figure this thing out, keep you from getting into any more screaming break-up fights behind Mainstage . . . during the five o'clock show, no less."

His eyes widened. "You mean . . . could they hear us out there on the haybales?"

"To the tenth row, m'friend."

"Shit. Somebody from Admin is probably going to toast

my tail for breakfast." He uncorked the flask, and took a mouthful. His eyebrows rose, and he took a second.

Well, at least he appreciates my whiskey.

"Thanks," Eric said, pausing long enough to come up for air. "This helps a lot. I think Glenfiddich can cure almost anything, even broken hearts." He took another swallow, and Beth waited until he recorked the flask.

"Okay," she said, "You and Signorina Tosca seemed to be doing all right around noon—what happened after that?"

He shuffled his feet in the dust, and looked sheepish.

Too damn cute for his own good, that's Eric Banyon. He attracts too many women who think that sweet face means he's malleable. They don't look past the face to the eyes, the eyes watching for somebody who might put fetters on him. They look at the generosity, and they think he's theirs for the taking. He'll give you anything, all right; anything but himself. That part of him that he won't let anyone see, or touch . . .

"She was getting hot, I guess, and sweaty, and she wanted to know how much longer I was going to be out here. I told her all weekend. Then she wanted to know where the motel was. I said there wasn't one, and I told her about my campsite."

Oh boy, the operatic soprano hothouse-plant meets reality.

"I can hear the storm brewing already," Beth remarked sagely, since he seemed to be waiting for her to say something.

"Yeah." He took another swig, and his eyes took on their habitual expression of wariness. "Then when I was checking the schedules backstage, she wanted to know how long this was gonna go on. I told her. *Then* I said I was thinking about hitting Northern Faire in the fall, maybe stay up in San Fran after, if the busking was good. I didn't get a chance to tell her I'd be back by Thanksgiving, 'cause that was when the excrement hit the rotating blades."

Beth shook her head, and recaptured her flask. "Eric, Eric, you lovable idiot . . ." *she* took a swig. "If I was planning on setting up a fight between the two of you, I couldn't have managed it better. You probably punched every button she has."

This one is obtuse even for you, sweetie. First you let her think you're planning on a long-term relationship, then start wandering off at odd intervals, then casually tell her you may be cruising on out—without her—this fall. Banyon, you definitely take the prize.

"I don't see why," he said, obviously nettled. "She *knew* I was a street busker, that was how we met! Right at the downtown YMCA. I was playing the street; she was coming back from a rehearsal at the Pavilion. She knew *exactly* the kind of guy I am, from the minute she met me."

"Allow the Great Madame Zarathustra to read the past," Beth intoned in a cheap gypsy accent. "Tell me, in the past several weeks has she, or has she not, been making hints about how you should go do some serious auditions?"

"Well, yeah . . ." The eyes were warier.

"Has she not, in fact, set up a couple of auditions? Like the one you were telling me about a few weeks back, with that chamber orchestra?"

"Well, yeah . . ." He wouldn't look at her.

"Did you not, in fact, *go* to those auditions? *And* get job offers?" *Taking the line of least resistance, you lazy sonuvabitch. Avoiding a confrontation, and inadvertently leading her on—*

"Well, yeah—but I didn't *take* any of those jobs!"

"Which looked like what? That you weren't interested? Hell no! Like you were waiting for something *better*." Beth ran her hand through her hair in exasperation. Banyon actually looked perplexed. "Look, dummy, anybody with half an ear knows how good you are. Madame Butterfly has considerably *more* than half an ear. She figured you saw how well those piddly auditions were going, and you were gonna go for something big—and then settle down with her."

"Aw, come on, Beth—I never—I mean—she's the one that moved in, she's the one that started the thing in the first place. It's not my fault, dammit! You know it isn't! Come on, Beth . . ."

He finally wound down, and sighed. "Shit. I did let her think I was planning to stick around and take a serious gig, didn't I?"

No shit, Sherlock. "I think that's a pretty fair assessment."

He looked down at the dirt of the path for a moment, and when he looked back up at her, the haunted expression in his eyes finally made her feel a bit more sympathetic. Maybe more than sympathetic—

Hold on there, girl. Don't let that pretty face and those big brown eyes make you forget. He's the original Love-'em-and-leave-'em, Mister Drifter. He likes having no ties. Though I don't think he likes the feeling of having someone like Maureen walk out on him—they were a pretty tight little item, and the chemistry sure seemed to be there.

"I didn't mean to, Beth," he said quietly. "I didn't mean to string her along. If she'd said something, I'd have told her."

She sighed. "I believe you. I just wish for once you'd look at what you're doing before it gets to scenes like this. Holy Saints Paddy and Bride, you never do things by halves, do you, Banyon?"

She shook her head; he hung his.

"All right, now that I know what happened, I can at least see what I can do to keep your reputation out of the mud. I'll try to put in a good word for you with the Admin people, too, convince Caitlin that you couldn't avoid it, wasn't your fault." He started to turn away. "And by the way—"

"What?" he replied, lifelessly.

Come on, bucko. Keep looking down in the dumps, and I may bed you just to cheer you up. Pure therapy.

Sure, Beth, and I've got this beachfront property in Nevada . . .

"We've got another gig over in that place on Van Nuys, and we'll keep a corner of the stage warm for you. You're welcome to come on by, usual split. It's been a while—would be nice to have you back, you and that whistle of yours. "

He gave her a miserable attempt at a smile. "Thanks, Beth. I just may do that. Hey, Spiral Dance is a helluva lot better than *that* dump deserves—how come you keep going back there?"

"We have our reasons." *Which I wouldn't tell anyone unless they're one of us. Not even you, m'friend. 'Sides, I bet you wouldn't believe it anyway.*

"Oh."

Beth passed him the flask for a last swig, then headed back the way she had come, towards Woods Stage and the jam.

But as she walked down to the stage and pulled out her ocarina, she spared a last, pitying thought for the lonely figure trudging off into the dusk. *He really doesn't understand it at all. He tries, but he doesn't. Banyon, Banyon, when are you ever going to grow up?*

Beth already had her ocarina out, adding the tiny wooden whistle's voice to the jam session's version of "Kesh Jig" before she even reached the stage. Eric watched her join the others, then sighed.

Yeah, dammit, she's right. But what am I supposed to do? I can't lie. I can't. And I don't want to change.

From the stage, Beth glanced up at him, as though asking him if he wanted to join the circle of friends and musicians. He sighed again, and turned away.

No. Not tonight. I just want to be alone.

He headed farther into the Wood, where the gnarled oaks clustered closely. *Far away from everybody, that's where I'll go. The edge of the Wood and beyond. "Ten leagues beyond the wide world's end . . ."*

Most people wouldn't come back this far, past the last palm-reader's booth and the faint lingering chemical reek of the porta-johns. *Dirt and trees and me. Seems real good right now.*

It was in a small grove of oaks, set back against the hillside where Eric finally set down his flute case on a handy rock. He sat on the ground beside it, opened the case and took out the silver pieces of his flute, carefully fitting them together; as if, by taking especial care with the task, he could put his life back together again. For a moment he just sat there, the chilled metal slowly warming against his fingertips.

This wasn't the first time he'd broken up with a girl, but it had to be one of the worst. Maureen had been—nice. Not pushy. Always there for him—the way he'd tried to be there for her.

Only it was pretty likely she wasn't going to be there anymore. Until this moment, he hadn't realized what that meant in terms of loneliness. He'd gotten used to not being lonely.

God, it hurts inside, it hurts. I can't believe she's left me. I just can't. We were so tight . . .Maureen, Maureen, I'm so sorry. I didn't mean to hurt you. I didn't want this to happen.

His fingers moved gently on the familiar flute keys; remembered patterns so deep he didn't have to think about them, bringing back other memories, of music, laughter, late evenings with his friends, drinking and playing.

God, it hurts . . .

He brought the flute up to his lips, taking a deep breath and playing a soft note, hesitant. It hung in the air for a moment, followed by another note, quavering, equally uncertain.

Then the notes grew stronger, louder, more confident. He began to play an ancient Irish air, "Brian Boru." It was a melody created a thousand years before he was born, by someone else who was also mourning, hurting. Someone else who had longed after something that had been—or was it something that could never be? The tune seemed to hold all of his heartache.

The last note drifted away, fading into the darkness around him. *Damn. Is this what it always comes to, sitting alone, playing sad music? Trying to say whatever's inside me, when I can't say the words out loud? I always end up in a place like this, alone and lonely, no one in sight. Christ. Is this how I'm gonna end, too? What's the use? When am I ever going to find somebody who can hear what I'm trying to say, instead of hearing what they want me to say?*

His fingers shifted on the flute, as though of their own accord, forming the first notes of "Sheebeg Sheemore." *Yeah, old O'Carolan, now there was a modern bard. Crazy old blind guy, wandering the Irish countryside and writing melodies for his friends. Like this one. What a story, you don't even need to know what it's about to feel it. The elves of Eire, two rival groups of Faerie—kind against kind, kin against kin. Maybe even once-love against once-love, love gone sour and turned into hate*

But it's a pretty melody, not like "Boys of Ballysadare," where you can almost see the Scottish bodies piling up. I guess elves don't believe in ripping each other apart, not like us humans. Not like Maureen, anyhow. Yeah, a beautiful song, even if there's no such thing as Faerie.

He could feel the music starting to change as he stopped thinking about it; just playing, trying to take what was aching inside him and transform it into the melody. It was as though something had taken hold of his mind and body, and that something was flowing through him and the music. Like his soul was talking directly through the flute, pure, unambiguous. It was the feeling he had once in a long while, when he was playing and everything was working and it just *clicked*.

And it was happening now, as he played the O'Carolan tune, every note flawless and clear as crystal, every inflection and trill absolute perfection. But not a cold perfection, mechanical—no, this was music straight from his heart, all emotion, with no unhuman intellectualism intervening.

Eric felt a hush, a quietude, as though the grove itself was suddenly still, not a single bird echoing his flute, as though the night itself was holding its breath. As though everything that could hear his playing was *listening* to him, to the music, to what the music was saying; listening with every pore, and watching him. The ancient oak trees, branches gnarled and bent, seemed to draw closer to him, as though concentrating intently.

He closed his eyes, ignoring them. *What an illusion. Oak trees can't move. Too much whiskey, Eric, m'lad.*

He continued playing, adding all the extra trills and ornaments he'd always wanted to, but never dared try. Then he reached the last delicate run, straight down the scale, that was the end of the tune—

—and he kept going. Something inside him, all the pain and sorrow, was suddenly in the music, and he couldn't stop. It was a different melody now, his own, original. And the music was flowing through him, wild and fey, relentlessly pulling him onward.

It built to an impossible climax, a last fiercely defiant high note that seemed to shatter the still air, then—

—silence. Profound and absolute. As though the world was waiting, watching for something to happen. Nothing marred it; it was the kind of silence born of anticipation, as though a door was opening, and everything paused for a moment, expecting Someone to step through—

Eric took a deep breath, hearing a quivering echo from the trees as the last notes faded away. His heart was pounding, his fingers clenched tight upon the flute, trembling. *Damn, was that really me?*

God, I should have some lady break my heart more often, if that's what it does to my music!

Something startled him, and he sat up suddenly. For a moment, Eric thought he heard something, an answering song from the grove, not just the last echoing notes of his melody.

Then the wind kicked up, sending swirls of dust and dead leaves scattering around him. Eric's eyes began to sting from the dust—as he blinked to clear them, he saw something glinting across the grove, a brief flicker of green light.

Green light?

He felt a chill run down his back; a thrill of wonder and expectation—then his good sense kicked in and brought him right down to earth again. *Probably some Faire kids playing Jedi Knight with lightsticks on the hillside. And scaring the local rattlesnakes half to death, I'm sure. Don't they know that no one is supposed to go up into the hills? B'Jaysus. Where in hell are their parents?*

He looked down at the flute, still cradled in his hands. *I wish I had a tape of that. Damn. I'll probably never play like that, ever again.*

Eric took the flute apart, moving carefully in the dark, replacing each piece in the case by feel. There were times when he loved that instrument more than any human. He wouldn't play any better than that tonight, and he wasn't going to try.

He stood up, dusting off his jeans. *Might as well call it a night. I've got that bottle of Irish back at camp, and I think this is a good time to start on it. A real good time.*

Eric felt his way to the edge of the grove, walking with care to avoid tripping over anything, then glanced back. Something gleamed among the oak trees, another glistening trace of pale green light, as verdant and alive as spring leaves. It swirled right where he'd been sitting for a moment, then vanished. It reappeared a heartbeat later, half-hidden behind a sprawling oak tree, then faded again.

Kids. I wonder if they're playing at saving the universe? Must be too young to realize that you can't.

He headed down the dirt road towards his campsite.

Eric managed to avoid meeting anyone by carefully planning his route, but it took a lot of detours. He was tired and footsore by the time he reached the camping area, and feeling the effects of the long and stressful day inside *and* outside.

An hour later, Eric was tumbled in his sleeping bag in a faded blue tent that had seen too many Faires, groping for his bottle in the darkness.

If I make a light, they'll know I'm here. No, not tonight. Not tonight.

His hands closed on the cool neck of the bottle, and he set himself for a bit of serious drinking.

A half hour later he was falling asleep or passing into unconsciousness—with the better part of a fifth of Bushmills becoming one with his bloodstream.

And since he was the only one with a vantage point—and the only one not engaged in nocturnal activities that precluded idle observations—he was the only one of the Faire folk who noticed the activity over the hill—the verdant green glow that flickered and vanished between the trees, in the hidden oak grove he had left to sing to itself.

Eric would have chalked up the effect to the Bushmills, except that he'd seen it start *before* he took his first drink.

It was still playing its little games among the tree trunks as he passed out, and his last coherent thought was to wonder if it would continue until dawn.

2

Echoes from the Forest

"Shit! Quarter till nine, and I can't find my goddamn *socks!*"

"Damnation, Seamus, I'll ne'er be o'er thar in time! Run on wi'out me, laddie!"

Eric Banyon awoke to the absolute cacophony that was the usual "morning song" of Faire. The assorted cries and shouts of the actors and musicians in the campsite mingled with the clanking of pots and pans. The gabble of voices in a dozen conversations nearby echoed vilely in an unholy concert with the pounding in his head. He opened one eye warily, felt the bright sunlight kick him in the face, and closed the eye again.

God, I'm going to die. Please God, let me die. I think I drank too much. No, strike that—I know I drank too much.

If I'm going to die, I sure hope it happens soon . . .

He reached a hand out without opening his eyes, and felt around the floor of the tent; when his hand encountered the coolness of glass, he picked up the whiskey bottle, shaking it slightly.

No, strike that again—I couldn't have drunk too much. There's some still left in the bottle.

He opened his eyes long enough to take a healthy

swallow from the half-empty whiskey bottle. *Mmm, good old Irish Breakfast. I'll bet this is the only reason they never conquered the world.*

He swigged again, and sighed.

I think I'm going to live. Which means I'd better get on 'site.

He pried both eyes open again and crawled out of the sleeping bag, blinking blearily. Eric found his faded brown breeches on the other side of the tent, where he had discarded them last night, then rummaged through his backpack. A fresh Faire shirt, one that used to be white but now was a shade between gray and brown, replaced the one he had slept in last night. He pulled breeches and shirt on, and scratched his head, trying to remember what came next.

Feet. First, find *your feet. Then find what you put on your feet.* New socks came out of the bottom of the pack; he pulled his moccasin boots on over them without jarring his skull too much. After a brief moment of panic, he found his belt beneath the jumble of assorted props and costumes on the floor in the "storage" corner of his tent.

Eric fastened the money pouch, wooden comb, and flask on the belt, took another swig of whiskey, and he was ready to face the world again.

Well, maybe not, but I'll give it a try . . .

Taking a deep breath, he unzipped the door to the tent, stepping outside. As he expected, it was a beautiful morning, clear blue skies over the green-brown hills, with almost everyone in sight already in costume and heading into the Fairesite.

He staggered to the large water tank at the edge of campsite, and braced himself.

Here goes—

He stuck his head beneath the faucet and turned it on. The water, cold as a mother-in-law's heart, hit him like a hammer on the back of the skull, and froze him all the way down to his toenails. He was shivering when he straightened up again.

Much better. I think.

He used the metal side of the water tank as a mirror as he combed his hair, trying without success to make the shoulder-length brown mop look presentable.

Some day I'll shave it all off, honest to God. Hell, it worked for Yul Brynner, didn't it?

"Good morning, Eric," one of the dancers from the Irish show called to him from across the sink.

Some people are just too damn awake in the morning.

"Bah, humbug," he replied, somehow managing to sound cheerful enough.

Brigid, that's her Faire name, if I'm remembering correctly. Don't remember her Mundane name. He gave her a long, appraising look as she sauntered away from him with a definite swing to her hips. *Scenic. Very scenic. Lovely from the front, lovely behind, terrific dancer's legs. Well, now that I'm a bachelor again . . .*

Oh, hell. Maureen, that should be you wiggling your hips at me . . .

He watched the dark-haired dancer start towards the Main Gate with morose appreciation for a moment, then returned to his tent for his flute.

Besides, Brigid's a morning person. I could never cope with somebody who's that happy at nine in the morning, never.

He slipped the flute case into his embroidered gig bag (gift of Kathie, late of the Texas Faire, two girlfriends before Maureen) and started down the hill towards the Main Gate.

I've had my Irish Breakfast; I'd better get a real one before I fall on my nose.

Eric expertly dodged through the thickening Faire crowds, a tankard of coffee and a stack of hot sticky cinnamon buns balanced precariously in his hands. He found a quiet haybale near one of the smaller stages, and sat down to break his fast.

Three Commedia dell'Arte actors were on the stage, wearing the brightly-painted leather masks of the legendary Italian comedians.

". . . Isabella, don'tcha know you're a-breakin' my heart?"

"An' that isn't all I'll break, Harlequino!"

Eric laughed with the travelers seated around him as dainty Isabella chased Harlequino around the stage, waving a rolling pin with wild enthusiasm.

Except Isabella's hair was long and vivid red, and her voice was a little too strident.

Almost operatic.

A piece of cinnamon bun stuck in his throat.

Eric stood up abruptly, leaving the show even as Harlequino protested his innocence to the furious Isabella.

He walked through the Faire, eyes mostly on the dirt road littered with pieces of hay and sawdust. "Boothies" were briskly doing business with the crowd of travelers haggling over handmade jewelry, leather pouches, intricately-decorated costumes. Hawkers were already calling to potential customers: "Ice cold milk and hot fruit pies!" "Turkey legs!" "Beef ribs, two hundred pence!"

I don't have anywhere to go, anything in particular that I have to do, at least not until the 1:30 show. Christ. Nothing to do at all . . . except brood.

Well, if I'm going to brood, I might as well do it melodically.

He took his gig bag off his shoulder, removing the flute case. He fitted the flute together, slinging the bag back to its comfortable place at his side.

The travelers looked at him peculiarly. It wasn't all that odd to see a costumed musician walking the Faire, but a flautist was a rarity, and the morose melodies he chose were definitely out of keeping with the "merrye spirit of Olde England" that everyone else was projecting.

Eric finished a rendition of "Coleraine"—*Funny, you never think of how an Irish jig could be so depressing*— and began another slower, even sadder tune. He was so lost to the melody and his own depression, that he really didn't notice the two step-dancers that smoothly moved in and escorted him around the corner.

Until they each grabbed an elbow.

"Hey, wait a—"

"Och, don't ye be frettin', Master Eric," one of the

dancers said with a wicked grin. "We've been sent to fetch you, we have."

"But—"

"No arguments, sar, we shan't listen to them!"

"But—"

One of them carefully took the flute from his hand, replacing it in his gig bag before they hurried him through the crowded "streets."

Suddenly he realized where they were taking him. Eric's eyes widened.

"No, not the washing well!" He tried to pull free, but the two young women had him past escaping—unless he wanted to take this out of the realm of a street bit and practical joke and into a serious scuffle.

"We've brought him, Mistress Althea!"

The heavyset woman, her dark hair tucked up into a clean muffin cap, looked him over with a practiced eye. "Well, then, he does seem truly the scruffiest of minstrels. We can't have this. Before we take 'im over, first we'll need to give 'em a bath . . ."

NO, not a bath! Not in the godforsaken filthy washing well!

Mistress Althea took him firmly by the ear, pulling him over to the washing well to the vast amusement of the onlookers. "I'll get even with you for this, Susie," he whispered, too low to be heard by the mundanes.

"But not till after I've had a good chance to wash your ears," she whispered back, barely able to keep a straight face. "This'll teach you to clean up your act before you come on 'site."

Eric suffered through having a scrap of cloth, dipped in the well, rubbed over every inch of his face.

Finally, Mistress Althea pronounced him cleansed, and fit for human company. "Now, girls," she said sonorously, "do take him onward to his next stop."

My next stop? All right, who's playing games, here?

Eric let the two girls drag him onward, down the dusty road to the stage where Sunday Mass was in progress.

Father Bob wearing a Roman collar over his Elizabethan

costume dutifully blessed Eric as the girls paraded him up
to the front of Mass. "In the name of the Father, the Son,
and the Holy Ghost, Lord, who watches over fools and
children, wilt Thou see that somebody please keeps an eye
on this minstrel boy? Thank you very much, God."

Eric stared backwards at Father Bob as the dancers
pulled him away again. The priest was trying not to break
into laughter. *Yes, something definitely strange is going on
here* . . .

The two girls—Eric realized he didn't even know their
names—pulled him down the lane, past the glassblower's
booth and the stall hanging with dozens of bota bags,
directly towards the Kissing Bridge . . .

Now wait just a second—

Before he could react, they were halfway across the
bridge, beneath the colorful garlands and ribbons that fes-
tooned the wooden archway. They stopped, keeping him
trapped between them, and the two dancers kissed him
expertly, one after the other.

More than a bit bemused, Eric let them. After his initial surprise, he *helped* them.

Well, this is definitely an unusual *experience* . . .

Then they tugged his hands to draw him onward, across
the bridge and down the lane to the Laughing Fool Tavern. And there was Beth, waiting with the other musicians
by the gate.

Oh, now this is all starting to make sense . . .

The two dancers delivered him to the tavern gate, bob-
bing a quick curtsy to Beth. "An' here he is, mistress, clean
and blessed. And warmed up. As 'twere."

"Why, thank you, my dears," Beth said, her eyes never
leaving Eric's. "I do truly appreciate your efforts." She took
Eric's arm, leading him into the tavern.

"Beth . . ." he muttered, "I'll get you for this."

She let go of his hand and stepped up onto one of the
rough-hewn tavern tables, calling out for silence in a clear
voice. "M'lords and ladies, we have here a lad who has been
well and truly heartbroken, who spent last night all alone
with only a bottle for comfort . . . and we all know that

a bottle is a rather cold and miserable bedmate, not like a saucy wench!"

Eric felt himself blushing as the crowd of travelers outside the tavern cheered rowdily.

Beth smiled. "Seems he needs a hand. So, what shall we do for this poor lad, I ask you?"

"Give him to the German mercenary wenches!"

"Sell him to the gypsies!"

"Make him play us dancing music!"

Beth turned to him, her voice slightly softer. "Well, sirrah, what shall it be?" She looked him up and down. "I dare say we shouldn't get much for you from the gypsies. Too skinny, methinks. So, it's the girls, or the tunes. A spritely dancing tune, or the meaty paws of the German wenches?" Beth grinned evilly, and added in an undertone, "I'd play the tune if I were you, Eric. Karen Wolfsdottir has been yearning to get her mitts on you all season."

Eric was already reaching into his gig bag for his flute.

The first tune he played was "Banish Misfortune," as lively and cheerful a melody as he could think of. The Faire folk, seated at the wooden trestle tables, began to clap and pound the table with their tankards in rhythm with the tune, and then he saw Ian and Linda sneaking up from the back of the tavern, drum and fiddle already in their hands. *Oh, Bethie planned this one in advance, methinks! Okay, then, let's do it right!*

He leaped up on the table without missing a beat, startling the two peasants playing a game of Cathedral next to him. With Ian holding the beat steady on his bodhran drum, and Linda deftly carrying the melody for him, Eric continued to play the flute, but also began to hop and skip down the long table, to the raucous cheers of the onlooking travelers. Beth clapped her hands in glee, watching him from a precarious perch atop the tavern fence and laughing wildly.

Winded, he jumped off the edge of the table, landing in the straw next to the two giggling dancer girls who had brought him there. He stopped the tune in mid-note and grabbed the older of the two girls, the one with the long red-gold hair and wicked green eyes, and kissed her soundly before letting her go. She landed on her posterior in the thick hay, still laughing.

Eric doffed his cap at her and her companion. "I thank ye both for bringing me here," he said in his finest Elizabethan accent. "You're both lovely lasses, and I implore you to dance for us all!"

The two girls looked at each other uncertainly.

Beth called from her position on the rickety tavern fence. "Oh, and come on with you now, lasses! Show us what ye can do!"

And they did.

Eric applauded and cheered with the travelers and Faire folk as the red-haired girl helped her companion up onto the table. Then they moved into proper stepdancer position, arms linked, one foot raised with the toes delicately pointed forward.

Linda and Ian were watching him for the signal. "Athol Highlander's!" he called, then hit the first note of the rollicking Scottish jig straight on, Linda joining in a moment later with as sweet a bit of fiddling as he'd ever heard her play, then Ian tossing off a few clicks on the rim of his bodhran before settling into some serious drumming.

The girls danced down the long table, skipping and pirouetting to the shouts and calls of the audience. Then, as the tune wound to a close, they also leaped off the table, startling Eric so much that he flubbed the last note. They both laughed with him, as he shook his head in disbelief.

It only got better after that.

After several more dances and tunes (including a very bawdy Elizabethan song that sounded almost prim when sung solo, but when you sing it in a round, the words made the most amazing sentences), Eric relaxed at one of the tables. A tankard of the Fool's best was in front of him as he watched the expert belly dancer strutting her stuff to a Scottish strathspey.

Well, it may not be "period," but who cares at this point?

Beth sat down next to him, taking the mug from his hand

and draining a long draught. "Is life treatin' you better now, Banyon?"

He sighed and reclaimed the tankard from her hand. "Well, I still think telling Susie to wash me in the well was a rotten trick . . ."

"Agreed. But I couldn't let you in here with dirty ears." She leaned close to nibble on his right ear. "Do you see why?"

He took a moment to recover. "Uh, yeah."

"I'm glad." She stood up, taking his hand. "I think we've caused enough mischief for one morning. Want to take it elsewhere?"

Eric glanced up at the main trestle table, where the two dancer girls had kidnapped two Spaniards and were trying to teach them to stepdance, to the laughter of all onlookers. "Sounds good."

Beth led him behind the tavern, through the back gate and across the lane. Directly towards the Kissing Bridge.

Oh no, not the Kissing Bridge again . . .

She pulled him onto the Bridge, already populated with lingering couples. "There's only one cure for a broken heart, Banyon, and I've taken it upon myself to administer it. Don't take it personally. This is for purely therapeutic reasons only."

"Bethie—"

And she kissed him.

A significant amount of time later, he managed to find his voice again. "Uh, Bethie—"

"Mmmm?" She cuddled even closer.

"You know, I have half of a perfectly good apartment that's free for the taking, anybody could move in. And it could really use someone with a nice feminine touch—"

Beth suddenly stiffened in his arms. "Don't even think it, Banyon. Someday you may find someone who's right for you, but I'm not that lady. Don't get me wrong, I like you a lot, but let's not complicate it past that, all right?"

"Okay." He kissed the tip of her nose, making her giggle. "I just like you a lot, too." His lips moved lower, down her neck. "The offer's there if you want it, all right?"

An apologetic voice, somewhere next to his left ear, interrupted what had been a fascinating progression down the strong line of her shoulder. "Er, ah, Mistress Beth, they're about to start the Mainstage show, and Carl really is wondering if you're planning on joining us today."

"Oh, damn." Beth retrieved herself from Eric's arms, quickly straightening her costume. She gave him a wry grin. "Well, duty calls, Master O'Banyon. I'll look for you after the show."

Eric watched regretfully as Beth and her showmate disappeared into the crowd of travelers on the street. *I can never manage to hold on to that girl for more than five minutes at a time. That's all she's interested in with me. I guess some guys would like that, a lady who's just a good friend and a willing bedmate. The perfect situation, right?*

Damn.

He walked away from the Bridge, wandering aimlessly. After a while, he realized that he was back on the road above the Laughing Fool. Since he and Beth had left, the tavern had returned to its usual quiet state, a few actors conversing over a mug of ale, some "peasant women" eating lunch at another table.

Eric found himself an empty haybale near the tavern gate, sat down, and took out his flute again. He touched the keys lovingly, as the metal warmed to his hand.

Hello, old friend. Just you and me again. He remembered how he had argued with Admin over playing a metal flute at a "period" Faire. *I don't know what I'd do if they hadn't given in. I can't see doing a gig without you. I think they knew that, and decided they'd rather keep me and be anachronistic than watch me walk out.* He played an experimental run, thinking about how the red-haired dancer had laughed after he had kissed her. *I should write a tune for that lovely, something she and her friend can dance to.* He smiled as a tune began to shape itself in his mind and fingertips, a lively little melody that brought pleasant images, recollections of Faires past; of laughing girls, dainty feet tapping out an intricate highland dance, and of chilled ale on a hot Faire afternoon.

Then his spirits dropped again, and he settled down to some seriously morose music.

"Cliffs of Moher," *there's a good one. And* "Kid on the Mountain," *that's challenging* and *depressing.*

Without his realizing it, Eric's sad fluting brought in a crowd of listeners to the edge of the tavern fence. He looked up to see the travelers listening intently to him, and smiled sadly to himself, thinking: *They don't understand.* He continued to play.

Eric looked up again. Something in that mass of face-less travelers had looked strangely familiar . . .

*. . . yeah, that skinny guy, the tall blond, the one with the embroidered cloak . . . wait a minute—his cloak—*my cloak!

Eric leaped up from the haybale, diving over the wooden fence like an avenging angel. The young man in the shroud-ing cloak took one look at Eric's snarling face and ran like hell.

A matronly female customer screamed as Eric catapulted past her, one hand reaching for the trailing edge of the ankle-length cloak. Other travelers scattered out of the way as Eric pursued the young man past the astonished washerwoman at the well and right through a colorful troupe of morris men dancing in the middle of the dirt street. Angry shouts and the sound of clattering leg-bells followed them down the road.

The thief crashed through the bota-bag booth, sending the hanging wineskins flapping wildly at their tethers. Eric followed close on his tail, waving his flute like a deadly weapon. "Stop, you lousy bastard! Thief! *Thief!*"

The cloaked robber dashed under a monger's carefully balanced tray of fresh tripe and crossed the Kissing Bridge in one desperate leap. Eric vaulted after him, thoroughly disrupting the amorous affairs of the kissing couples on the Bridge.

Then he saw the kilted Scottish troop directly ahead of him, carrying their pikes at attention as they marched down the street. Eric skidded to a stop, not wanting to crash into the Scottish warriors—and their six-foot spears.

But the cloaked man kept running.

Right through the formation of marching pikesmen. Eric stared in disbelief as the nimble thief danced past the warriors and their deadly spears. Somehow he made it look simple and easy as he dodged between them. Then the thief was across, on the other side of the formation without so much as causing a single pikeman to miss a step.

Several of the watching travelers applauded, doubtlessly thinking this was part of a show. Eric just stood there, staring after the escaping thief in amazement.

Nobody should be able to do that . . .

Eric took a deep breath and ran after him, straight into the pike formation . . . and three seconds later, he found himself sprawled on the dirt with several pikes lying around him, and a half-dozen irate Scotsmen glaring at him in disgust.

Then the dark-bearded Scottish chieftain himself walked over and looked down at Eric.

"Oh, Eric, lad, you've done yerself quite a turn this time, ye have," the Chief said sadly.

"Sorry, Boss," Eric muttered, trying to stand up without much success. His ankle hurt. Not to mention his pride.

After yesterday, there wasn't anything left of his dignity to hurt.

The Chief crouched down in the dust close to Eric. "By the way," he said in a quiet voice entirely devoid of Scottish accent, "Caitlin wanted to see you in Admin. Something about the Mainstage show yesterday."

"Terrific," Eric said morosely. One of the Scots helped him stand, dusting him off. Eric thanked him, then scanned the crowd for any sign of the thief

Nowhere in sight. Damn.

So much for my favorite Faire cloak. I wonder how that little rat got past Security and into my tent?

The pikemen lined up into their formation. The Chief gave Eric one last, pitying look, a look Eric caught out of the corner of his eye as the troop of Scotsmen marched off towards their encampment.

Well. Better get it over with.

He headed for Admin Hill and the offices directly behind the large brightly-colored Faire mural.

Caitlin's a good lady; she usually understands things. I mean, she's the one who got me out of that jam last year with the Maypole dancers. They're not going to fire me . . . I hope.

Eric moved carefully through the thickening traffic on the dusty lane, past the travelers haggling with the boothies over their wares. He stepped carefully over three peasants sprawled out "drunk" in the street and doffed his cap at the bored Security guard at the office entrance.

Inside the musty, crowded office area, costumed actors and musicians were relaxing, several smoking some definitively non-period Marlboros, others drinking sodas and catching up on gossip. Eric crossed to the hanging burlap flap that was the door to Caitlin's office, and took a deep breath. "Caitlin?"

A tired female voice answered. "Come in."

Eric walked into the makeshift office. Caitlin looked up from the stacks of paperwork on the table, her ever-present can of diet soda in her hand. "Hello, Eric. Is it Fate or bad luck that you always end up in my office?"

"A bit of both, I think." He sat down on a folding chair across from her. "Does it help if I tell you that I really try to avoid this sort of thing?"

"Yes, a little. I was starting to wonder if you got in trouble just so you could flirt with me in my office." She leaned back in her chair, wearily running her hand through her short auburn hair. Her long blond wig, with the floppy hat she usually wore as part of her costume, was lying on the table near the papers.

Eric stared at the wig to avoid meeting her gaze.

"So, Eric, you and your girlfriend decided to break up, right behind the four-thirty Mainstage show yesterday. Made it quite interesting for the audience. I understand your ex-girlfriend has quite an operatic voice."

Eric winced. "Yes, she does. Great projection, too."

Caitlin almost cracked a smile. "You're classically trained too, aren't you? Somebody told me you studied at Juilliard. Is that true?"

"Yeah, I was at Juilliard. Two years." He shifted uncomfortably, a knot already beginning to tighten in his gut at the mere thought of those two years. He flashed on his last recital—

Playing better than he ever had in his life; playing his heart out. Then putting the flute down. Announcing to the panel— "Today was my birthday. Last night somebody threw rocks at my window all night long to keep me awake. This morning somebody else jammed the lock on my door so I had to climb out my window to make it here on time. I can't take this shit anymore. I'm eighteen and my parents can't do a thing about me now. Gentlemen, ladies, you can take your goddamned classical education and shove it."

And the long, absolute silence as he walked out.

Six months before I could bear to touch the flute. Eight before I could play again. Three years before I could even listen to Bach.

Damn. I really wish people wouldn't ask me about that.

Caitlin was watching him with knowing eyes. "Eric, you're a sweetheart, and one of the best musicians we've ever had here, but somehow you're always getting in trouble. I'll clear you on this one, cover you for the people Upstairs, but— try to avoid this kind of thing in the future? Just try, all right? Promise me?"

He sighed. *I don't know whether to be relieved that she let me off easy, or embarrassed because I know she's letting me off just 'cause I'm good. Guess I'd better just count my blessings.*

"Thanks. I'm really sorry about this." He stood up to leave. Caitlin's voice stopped him before he reached the door.

"Eric?"

He turned back to her.

"I know you're going through a rough time, your girlfriend walking out on you and everything. Just don't . . . leave, okay? I heard what happened in Texas, when you had girlfriend problems there. Don't just walk out on us, Eric. I'd really like you to finish out the season with us, okay?"

He nodded, and lifted the burlap flap, walking out of

the relative quiet of her office into the overwhelming noise levels of the Admin area.

So. Somebody told Caitlin about my Texas adventure. Shouldn't be surprised, I guess.

Damn it, what's so terrible about just packing up and leaving when things go that wrong? God, if I'd stayed at Texas Faire—between us, Kathie and me, we'd have had the place divided like the Civil War all over again. So I split, and now everybody treats it like some kind of sin. And Caitlin, she's acting like I'm about ready to run from Southern California. She doesn't have any reason to think that. Except—

—except, well, maybe I did think about it last night.

Okay. So maybe I have a tendency to get out while the going's good. So maybe it's not like I'm the only musician they've got. Why should I stick around anyhow? Maureen's left me, probably already moved out all her stuff from the apartment. I could leave next week, no one would care. I don't have a steady gig here, they don't need me for the show. Nothing I promised to do, just Bethie and Spiral Dance once in a while, and this Faire, and both of them could keep running fine without me . . .

Caitlin's words echoed in his mind: *"Just don't walk out on us, Eric."*

And Bethie, sure, she'll give me a roll in the hay, but nothing more than that. I may not be Mister Commitment, but I'd like more than just that in a relationship, y'know? Maybe not True Love, but—Serious Like? Honest Lust?

He left the Admin building, walking through the crowded streets. *At least Caitlin didn't throw me off the Fairesite. Thank God for that, I guess.*

He sidestepped a group of Faire children playing tag in the middle of the lane; narrowly missed a collision with a black-velveted noblewoman and her retinue.

"Oops, Milady," Eric said respectfully, doffing his cap, Lady Anne Millesford (AKA Terri Leiber of Riverside, California) just gave him a disdainful look and flounced onward.

Then he heard them, the exuberant Gaelic shouts and

keening and general noise, approaching from twelve o'clock high.

Oh, shit, I forgot about the show!

He dashed through the crowd of travelers and Faire folk, towards the Scottish parade marching past. The double line of Celtic warriors, the Chief and his household walking within the protective row, processed past the washing well as Eric caught up with them. With an expertly-timed move that he had down perfectly after years of always being late for stage shows, he ducked under the closest Scotsman and slipped into his proper position with the other musicians.

He hollered the Gaelic gibberish (that he really didn't understand) along with the rest of the marchers, the ulu-lating cries of the women echoing in his ears. As they marched up to Mainstage, he joined the other musicians on stage right. The Chief began the show patter: *We're traveling through England and Donal just up and croaked, so we're holding a party—I mean wake—for 'im.*

The frazzle-haired Dancemistress ran through the show order as Eric and the others did a last minute tuning check, ticking off the numbers on her fingers. "Jig set, two-hand reel, slipjig solo, Gaelic song . . ." She turned to one of the other dancers. "Hey, remind everyone that we're doing 'John Ryan's'—you know, 'Boom Boom'—right after the song, so everyone should line up fast." She emphasized the "Boom Boom" with a quick shimmy of her hips, and the dancers laughed. "All right, let's do it!"

The dancers ran out to center stage, grabbing partners by the hands and forming sets.

Looks so impromptu, they never guess we practiced these routines for four weeks.

Linda kicked off the tune, a lively fiddle version of "Top of Cork Road," and Eric joined in with Ian on the fifth measure.

It was a good, solid show, one of their best all season. The audience applauded and laughed at the right places, the music was at the right tempo, no one tripped or missed a step in the strathspey-reel, and—*Thank God*—none of the stepdancers sprained an ankle. *Not like last weekend, two casualties in the Saturday 11:30 show alone, not to mention the three the weekend before.*

And Maureen's comment when he told her about the sprained-ankle victims: *"Probably wouldn't have happened if they did decent warm-ups, like we do at the Chandler . . ."*

"Och, and now we'd be after hearing our fine musicians play us a tune, indeed we would!" the Chief called out in a voice that carried to the last row of haybales.

Musicians solo time. Well, here we go again . . .

Eric and the other minstrels moved to the front of the stage. "'Banish Misfortune' into 'Drowsy Maggie,' two and three," Linda called.

Eric gazed at the audience, row after row of attentive faces, waiting, watching him . . .

Bright lights, starched collar of my concert shirt scratching my neck, the orchestra ready and waiting behind me, taking a deep breath and beginning to play . . .

That damned program book: "Eric Banyon, flute prodigy, performing Dances Sacred and Profane" . . .

Then he heard "Banish Misfortune," as wicked and sprightly an Irish jig as he'd ever played, and Eric realized in dismay that the band was already halfway through the A part and he hadn't even noticed that they'd started. He tossed in a quick trill, hoping that it sounded like he had meant to join in the middle of the tune.

Linda's giving me that "raised eyebrow" look, though, I don't think I fooled her! I'll probably catch hell for this later . . .

Then Aaron gave the signal and they dived into "Drowsy Maggie," half again as fast as "Banish" and twice as lively. They ended in a flurry of wild notes, and the audience applauded enthusiastically.

Oh, that was fun. Maureen, you would have liked that one . . .

That brought a sudden pain to his gut, his throat tightening. *Damn it, Maureen, I thought you'd love the Faire, I thought we'd be terrific together, soprano and flute. You'd actually get to be close to your audience, see their reactions, how much they like your music; three feet right in*

*front of you instead of on the other side of the orchestra
pit. I thought you'd be happy here, and understand why
I love doing this, playing Faire.*

Why did you have to walk out on me?

He marched with the "Celtic bus" halfway back to the
Hill, leaving the parade formation just outside the Turkish coffeehouse. Eric waited in line at the counter, already
imagining how the sweet iced coffee would taste. Then he
reached for his belt pouch to get out some cash, and—

—and there were only the leather strings dangling from
his belt, neatly cut just below the knot.

Oh SHIT!

*Somebody stole my money pouch! GODDAMMIT, this
isn't FAIR!*

He *started* to get angry—but he ran out of energy,
halfway through "disgusted."

Flat-lined. Emotional burnout.

Eric left the line, walked slowly to a convenient haybale,
stretched out and closed his eyes in numb despair.

*What a truly revoltin' development. First Maureen walks
out on me, then someone steals my cloak, then I damned
near get thrown out of this Faire, then somebody cuts my
belt pouch. All the money that I made yesterday, busking
with Maureen and the others. Gone.*

I can't believe all of this is happening to me.

"But it could be worse."

The low male voice spoke quietly, directly into his left
ear. Startled, Eric sat up, looking around.

And realized that no one was within ten feet of him. The
closest person was a four-year-old girl who was busily smearing
baklava over her face while her mother and a friend were
watching the dance show on the small coffee-house stage.

*Terrific. Now I'm losing my mind, too. Just what I always
wanted.*

The little girl held out a sticky hand to Eric, gravely
offering a piece of straw-coated baklava. He smiled and
shook his head, then stood up.

Maureen's left me, he thought at her, as if she could hear
him. *Then someone stole my cloak, I nearly lost this gig,*

*and a cutpurse got my cash pouch. It only had fifteen bucks
in it, not the end of the world, but that was all the money
I had on me.*

Methinks I need something stronger *than Middle Eastern
pastry, sweetling. But, in the interest of the Faire's pristine
reputation, I'll get out of the way before I look for it.*

He waited until he was in the hidden grove, far from
the thick dust and crowds, before reaching for the corked
flask at his side.

Then Eric proceeded to become thoroughly, profoundly
drunk, for the second time in twenty-four hours.

*I love the smell of fresh dirt—but I wish my nose didn't
hurt.* He opened his eyes a little, and saw—

Brown.

*Oh. I'm lying facedown in it. That must be why it's a
little difficult to breathe.* Eric tried to roll over onto his back,
and failed. He tried again, then gave it up as hopeless.

*S'okay. I really don't want to go anywhere, anyhow.
I've always wanted to be a worm, anyway. Worms can
have a good time all by themselves and never know the
difference. "Oh, you're my tail? I thought you were my
girlfriend."*

He lay there in the dirt and oak leaves, imagining a
beautiful red-haired woman smiling at him. A *particular*
beautiful red-haired woman.

"Eric, I've decided it doesn't matter to me what you do
with your life, all I want is to be with you, always."

Then she leaned forward to kiss him and . . .

Dream on, Banyon.

Oh, Maureen . . .

He managed to get his head turned to one side, and
pillowed his cheek in the crook of his arm. He blinked back
tears and sniffled, startling a bluejay who had been inves-
tigating him curiously, doubtlessly wondering if all that hair
would make a good lining for her nest. *Great, I'm lying
in the dirt, completely wasted. Now I'm going to start
leaking from the eyes. I'm going to make mud to lie in. A
perfect ending to a thoroughly delightful weekend.*

"Bard? Bard? I need to talk to you."

The voice spoke softly, low musical tones, definitely male. Eric tried to open one eye to look at the guy, but decided It wasn't worth it. "Go 'way. 'M trying to meditate."

"Please. It's very serious. I would not disturb your meditations, but I must ask some things of you."

"Nothing's that serious. Here, have a drink." Eric still had his hip flask in his other hand. He blindly shoved the flask in the direction of the voice. "Feel free to join me, there's plenty of whiskey, plenty of room here on the ground. It's quite comfortable, really. If you don't mind having rocks poking holes in your body."

The voice sounded profoundly puzzled. "No thank you. But please, I must speak with you. I have many questions, and you are the only one who can tell me the answers."

"Why? Who put me in charge? Go ask Caitlin or somebody."

"Why? You must—you're the one who Awakened me." The voice became desperate. "Please, Bard —please."

Eric tried again to lift his nose from the dirt so he could see whom he was talking to, then gave it up as a lost cause. "S'sorry. I didn't mean to wake you up. I just talk to myself when I'm drinking, can't tell how loud I am, you know, just happens."

The voice wasn't paying any attention to him. "Please, you must answer my questions. Your song Awakened me last night, and I don't know how long it has been. I cannot find any of my own kind here, and . . . I heard disturbing talk, Bard. They are saying that this place will be destroyed soon. You, of all people, must know what that will do to all of us. And the others—are they still Dreaming, or has something worse happened to them?"

Either I'm more drunk that I thought, or this guy is talking about something really and truly bizarre.

Third possibility. Whatever he's doing has sent him into another reality. Bad drugs, Eric. Humor the man. "Is this part of some street bit? I'm not in on it. Maybe you should save it for the travelers, m'friend."

There was a long and profound silence, during which Eric

felt his tenuous grip on consciousness slipping even further from his grasp. *Yeah, passing out right now does seem somehow like the appropriate thing to do.*

Oh, Maureen . . .

He choked on a sob; remembered he wasn't alone, and held it in. All of it.

Stillness, unbroken by so much as the fall of a leaf. Then a single word.

"Oh."

Then someone's hands gently rolled him onto his back, removing the rocks and sharper branches from beneath him, piling leaves to create a comfortable bed for him. He tried to open his eyes and thank the stranger, and couldn't manage either.

"Rest now. Forget a little. I will find you later, when your heart is not in such pain."

Eric smiled as an unseen hand brushed the stray locks of his hair from his face. In the alcohol-confused haze of his mind, the gentle hand could only have belonged to one person.

Mmmm, Maureen, that's nice, feels good . . .

The last he heard was quiet footsteps, crunching through the dry oak leaves as the stranger walked away.

When he awoke several hours later, the sun already fading from the leafy branches above him, Eric was alone in the grove.

3

The Unfortunate Rake

Eric managed to pry one of his eyes open, and looked around blearily. *God, I feel awful. This is getting to be a habit.*

He pried open the other eye, and his head reacted with a predictable stab of pain.

Maybe I'd better think about changing my habits.

He sat up. Slowly.

Was there somebody here earlier, or did I dream that?

He succeeded in getting into a sitting position and realized that he'd been nestled in a snug little bed of leaves. *I sure didn't have the sense to do that. No, he was real. Guess he went back to Fairesite.* His stomach lurched, and he lay back down before it could turn rebellious on him.

Wonder who the guy was? I didn't recognize the voice.

He looked up at the darkening sky through oak branches above him. *Sun's setting. I must have been here for hours.*

All right, Eric. Time to return to Reality. Or, at least, the Fairesite. He made a second attempt at mobility, a successful one this time, and staggered to his feet, wincing as he bent down to pick up his abandoned gig bag. *Gods, I ache all over, just like I've been—*

—drunk all weekend.

Yeah.

Well, it seemed like a good idea at the time . . .

He beat the dust out of his breeches, and walked—carefully—back towards the main grounds of the Faire. *I wonder how badly I've managed to screw up. I did make my show before I went facedown in the bean dip. I didn't get drunk in a public place. But I wasn't making the rounds.* He sighed. *Oh well. The worst they can do is fire me. Then I will have a reason to head north.*

He entered the Faire grounds—cautiously. The boothies were packing up, carrying boxes to the cars and pickups parked in the narrow streets.

Andrea and Tom were loading up the last of their handmade costumes into Andrea's Honda as Eric walked by. "See you guys next weekend," he called to them. Andrea called out a goodbye to him; it got lost in the noise of one of the water trucks passing by, liberally soaking everything in its path with fire retardant. Andrea's Honda joined the line of cars on the dirt road leading out of Fairesite, kicking up a small cloud of dust as it chugged up the hill.

Eric walked past a small covey of actors carrying their props, ungainly stuffed hobbyhorses embroidered in bright colors, then he saw Judy, struggling to carry her large hammer dulcimer.

"Need a hand?" he asked, catching up with her.

She flashed him a grateful smile. "Thanks, Eric. You're a sweetheart."

He took the dulcimer stand and her costume bag from her hands, knowing she'd rather carry the musical instrument herself. "So . . . did you have a good weekend?"

She sighed. "If you don't count that drunken idiot who tripped over my Pass-the-Hat bowl, then threw up almost on my feet."

Eric winced.

Judy gave him a very direct look. "But that was the only bad spot in an otherwise terrific weekend. I heard you weren't so lucky."

He shook his head ruefully. "Damn, but bad news travels fast around here."

"A lot of people were really concerned about you, Eric.

I remember what happened out at Texas Faire a couple years back . . ."

He stiffened slightly. "Well, this is different. I'm handling it just fine."

Just fine, half the weekend drunk off my ass, barely managed to do my shows, didn't even play street at all. Yeah, that's really handling it, Eric.

Judy set down the dulcimer on a haybale outside the Turkish coffeehouse. "I'm meeting some folks here before heading out. Maybe play a few last tunes before returning to Mundania. Want to join us?"

Eric propped the dulcimer stand against the haybale, the costume bag next to it. "No, I think I'm going to wander for a little longer, see who's still hanging around the 'site. I'll probably see you on my way out, though."

He headed back into the main area of the Faire, not certain what he was looking for, or whom.

Looks like everyone's packing it up for the weekend. I probably should, too.

Two of the Scotsmen were lifting up stacks of pikes, lashing them down in the bed of a faded Dodge pickup.

Hope they tie those down good. I sure wouldn't want to be driving on the freeway behind them and suddenly see a dozen pikes flying point-first toward my windshield.

I can see the headlines now. Man Skewered by Runaway Medieval Arsenal? Killer Scottish Pike Strike Massacre?

Spear Today, Gone Tomorrow?

But I bet Maureen's land-tank is tough enough to handle a pike assault. I'll wager on a Chrysler any day against a Scottish brigade . . .

Oh, damn Maureen's car—*she was going to give me a lift home. I'm sure she isn't coming back to get me. I'm stranded out here.*

Terrific. One last lousy touch on a truly wretched weekend.

Maybe if I can catch up to Judy . . .

He hurried back to the coffeehouse. As he approached, he heard the faint sounds of hammered dulcimer, bodhran, and fiddle.

Well, that's a break. I probably can talk Judy into giving me a lift home.

He recognized the tune "The Butterfly," one of his favorites. Eric quickly pulled his flute case from the gig bag, and was playing along with the melody by the time he reached the jam session at the coffeehouse.

Judy was intent upon her dulcimer, hammers dancing lightly across the strings, but the four other minstrels smiled in welcome as Eric joined them.

The four Northerners, that's right. Damn, but they're really together, really tight. I'd bet my flute that they've done a lot of gigs together.

The dark-haired fiddler girl suddenly grinned impishly at the others and switched into a harmony that Eric had never heard before, beautiful and haunting. As the tune came back around for a second time, Eric smiled to himself and began playing counterpoint.

For a moment, it was almost as good as the melody he'd played in the grove, every note falling perfectly, the counterpoint transforming the music into something more than just a tune.

When it was over, the last note fading away, Judy was the first to speak. "Eric, that was *nice.*"

"Damn good playing," the bearded bouzouki player said. He pulled a flask from his belt, offering it around the circle of musicians. Eric took a draught, smiling as the Irish Mist burned with a heartwarming fire all the way down his throat.

He handed the flask back to the man, then noticed that the drummer girl was gazing at him thoughtfully. "Where do you play? Are you touring with a band, or playing concerts?"

Eric shook his head. "I do Faires, street stuff. Haven't been in a band on a regular basis in years, or played concerts . . ." . . . *since the day I walked out of Juilliard. No more. Life's too short.* "Mostly I just sorta sit in."

"Haven't you ever thought of doing something more with your music than just busking? You're a damn sight better than any flautist I've ever heard on the Faire circuit."

He shrugged. "This is all I want to do. I'm happy. That's

all that matters." He turned to Judy. "Listen, I came back because, well, my girlfriend was supposed to give me a lift home, and you know what happened with that . . ."

"You're in Van Nuys, right? No prob, although . . ." Judy glanced up at the sun, barely visible above the hills. ". . . we should start out soon. The traffic's going to be something fierce on 101."

"But one last tune, Judy?" The fiddler's fingers were twitching. "Not a Faire tune, we've been playing them all weekend. How 'bout something a little different . . . ?"

She raised her bow to the strings, and began the opening violin solo from "Danse Macabre."

And stark terror reached out to grab Eric by the throat.

Oh my God, no, please . . .

He tried, but couldn't block the memories rising up in his mind to drown him. He backed up without knowing he was moving; half fell over the haybale behind him, landing on his knees in the straw and dirt, shaking and retching, unable to think or speak.

No, it's just music, it's nothing, it can't happen again . . .

"Eric!"

"What's wrong with him?"

He heard the concerned voices, somehow distant, unreal. The only things that were real were the bright lights of the stage and the shadowy darkness of the concert hall, and the nightmare stepping out of his mind and into reality . . .

It's only a memory, it happened over ten years ago, it's not real. Dammit, it's not real!

But he could hear them, the whispering voices, could feel them closing in, calling to him, reaching for him . . .

Then he felt a *human* hand gripping his shoulder, yanking him back into the present. Judy, staring down at him with eyes that were wide and frightened, her hand clutched tight on his shoulder.

"I'm . . . I'm okay," he said weakly, looking up at her. The others were gathered around him, worried. "Probably just food poisoning from that damn Hungarian pie booth," he said, hoping that his voice sounded calm. That it didn't shake the way he was still shaking inside. "I got sick after eating there opening weekend, shouldn't have done it again today." He took a deep breath, steadying himself.

He managed to stand up, the blond bearded Northerner helping him regain his feet. "Thanks, man. This hasn't been one of my better weekends. I . . . I think maybe I should go home." He tried to grin, but by the looks on their faces, it wasn't convincing. "Is that all right by you, Judy?"

"Yeah, sure." She quickly packed her dulcimer away in its case, slung it over her shoulder. "Let's hit the road."

Judy's tiny car disappeared around the corner, leaving Eric alone on the street, the ominous bulk of his apartment building looming overhead.

Home to the concrete jungle. Maybe Maureen's upstairs, waiting for me to get home, wanting to talk it over, work things out.

Not bloody likely.

He unlocked the security door, and the children playing in the courtyard stopped to look at him curiously as he headed for the stairs. *Yes, kiddies, it's the refugee from the 16th century, home from the wars.*

Eric opened the door and walked into his apartment. He stepped into the living room, took one look, then wearily sat down on the battered couch.

No, I don't think Maureen wants to talk things over . . .

With no more than a glance, he knew she was gone. *The Beethoven statue, the Japanese flower vase, that "Ride of the Valkyries" poster with those funny little Vikings climbing all over it—she's taken all of it. All of her stuff.*

His record collection was neatly stacked on the floor next to a now-nonexistent record cabinet. He looked through them briefly—she hadn't taken a single record of his, from what he could see, and she'd even left the ones they had bought together, over the last few months.

Like she didn't want anything to remind her of me . . .

He walked into the kitchen, and saw the note on the fridge: "I took the cat. You don't deserve her. Goodbye, Eric."

Great. Terrific. At least that scrawny furball will have a good home. Now there really isn't anything holding me in Los Angeles, not even that damn cat . . .

Maureen, how could you do this to me? Why?

He sank down into a chair, his head in his hands. *Oh, Maureen . . .*

Something clicked behind him, the sound of a door closing. Eric sat up abruptly, looking around.

My God, is someone in here with me?

Eric slid to his feet, quietly moving to the dish rack and palming a large sharp steak knife.

All right. I've been ripped off twice this weekend already, and this is it—if anybody's in the apartment, they're toast!

He slipped off his Faire boots, padding silently across the living room to the closed bedroom door. The knife clenched tightly in his fist, Eric suddenly flung the bedroom door open and leaped inside—

—and tripped on a pile of his clothes. He barely managed to avoid cutting himself with the knife as he landed face-first on the floor. He sat up slowly, gingerly rubbing the new sore spot on his chin.

Oh. That's right, Maureen was the one who bought that standing wardrobe. I guess she decided to take that, too.

The bedroom window was open, the curtains fluttering in the breeze. *That must be what caused that noise. There's no one in here.*

Just to be safe, he checked the closet. As he closed the closet door, Eric had the strangest sensation, as though something was moving just on the edges of his vision. He turned quickly, but there was nothing in the room but scattered clothes and the unmade bed.

My brain is draining—it's turned to yogurt, and it's draining. I'm seeing little green men who aren't there. Bad booze, Eric.

He returned to the kitchen and opened the fridge, wondering if Maureen had cleared out half of the food as well. He reached into the freezer for one of the many identical stacked dinners of genuine frozen food-shaped plastic, and realized that the bottle of iced Stolichnaya was missing.

That was a low blow, Maureen. Sure, it was a Christmas gift from a friend of yours, but it was to both of us, remember?

Eric absently shoved the frozen dinner into the oven, turning on the gas, then leaned back against the cabinet, trying not to feel too much.

He took the carton of milk from the fridge, drinking straight from the container, as he sat down again at the kitchen table. *Well, it's not the end of the world. I've lived through this kind of thing before. I'll live through it this time.*

I always do, whether I like it or not.

His feet were chilled, bare skin against the cold linoleum. Eric reached down for his Faire boots, and—

—and his hand encountered empty air.

He looked down. No boots.

I think I'm losing my mind.

No, Eric, you're not insane, just stupid. Okay, you must have moved them and not thought about it. Absent-minded. Pre-Alzheimer's. And you drank too much this weekend . . .

He ate dinner in silence. *No Maureen, to tell me all about the rehearsals at the Pavilion, all the little inside jokes and gossip. No damn cat, even, trying to steal my dinner. This is the most depressing meal I've had in a long time.*

Eric finished the pre-packaged dinner, leaving everything on the table. *I'll clean up tomorrow. Right now, all I want is a hot shower, and a toke, and crash.*

Half an hour later, drying his hair with a towel and wearing a second one around his waist, Eric returned to the kitchen for a glass of juice.

And the abandoned frozen dinner tray had vanished. The fork and knife were missing, too. After a moment Eric realized that they were in the dish rack, dripping wet.

This is very, very weird. I don't remember washing the dishes. I hate washing dishes. And why in hell did I wash the tinfoil thingie?

He shook his head, and looked at the dishrack again, but the stuff was still there. *Okay. Too much whiskey, too much stress, and not enough sleep. But, I can cope. Though maybe*

I'd better just call it a night now before I start speaking in tongues and telling the neighbors to find Jesus . . .

He returned to the living room, and sat down on the couch. On the low table were a carved wooden pipe and a small plastic bag.

At least she didn't take the stash.

Eric filled the pipe with the fragrant weed, lit it, and smoked in silence for a few minutes.

Uncle Dan's cure for heartbroken insomniacs. When I see him I should thank him for scoring this for me at such an opportune time.

He felt his head beginning to fog; the hurt inside started to seem less important. *He always seems to come up with things I'm gonna need before I need them. I wonder if he knew what was going to happen? Wouldn't surprise me— Beth, Allie, Dan, all those Spiral Dance crazies, they're all a little strange that way.*

The pipe went out, and he stared at it in mild surprise. *Amazing how fast it goes. Huh. Just like the Bushmills last night. Now, say goodnight, Eric. Goodnight Eric.*

He took pipe and bag and tucked them carefully into the nook under the corner of the couch frame. *Paranoia never hurt. God. Thank God this weekend's over . . .*

He stood up, slightly unsteadily, and staggered to the bedroom. He had to wade through the piled clothing to reach the bed, and had barely enough cognizant thought left to pull the blanket over him before all of his sorrows faded away in a deep, dreamless sleep.

Dreamless? Well . . .

There *was* a voice in his head. Just a voice, though, and a presence that . . . comforted.

Heal, saddened one. You feel the song? It is yours; you have only to follow . . .

A non-dream like ones he'd had, a long, long time ago, when he was a child and music was spun of equal parts of melody and magic, and he could hear things in his sleeping mind that slipped maddeningly away when he woke.

Follow and find healing . . .

ᦇ   ᦇ   ᦇ

Oh God, it's morning again. Eric blinked at the bright sunlight shining through the open window. He glanced at the alarm clock on the nightstand. *Well, almost afternoon, I think. Ten o'clock. I'd better start moving or I'll miss the lunch crowd downtown.*

He stood up, stretching, and looked around the room. And found himself smiling. *Amazing. I actually feel good this morning. Almost human again.* He rummaged through the piles of clothing on the floor, and found a pair of jeans and a T-shirt that were relatively clean and unrumpled.

Time to pay the rent, I guess. Energy filled him, and he discovered he was looking forward to getting out on the street with anticipation. He hummed as he laced a pair of ancient tennis shoes on his feet, and sang a little as he slung his gig bag over his shoulder. Five minutes, and he was ready to head out.

He grabbed a leftover donut from the fridge on his way out the door, whistling "Banish Misfortune" as he strolled down to the bus stop. *This is really a beautiful morning, blue skies—well, bluish-brown, this is L.A. after all—and I feel terrific. Surprisingly good. I don't even miss Maureen—*

A lump in his throat suddenly sprang up and interfered with the passage of his donut.

Much. He swallowed donut and lump and resolutely grasped after his earlier cheer. *Dammit, I am not going to let this ruin the rest of my life!*

To his amazement, some of his cheer returned. *Wow. Instant self-psychotherapy. I wonder if it was Dan's grass?*

He saw the bus approaching the corner and ran for it, his gig bag bouncing off his side. He caught up to the bus just as the driver started to close the door, and leaped inside just in time.

Maybe this is to make up for the weekend? Reverse Instant karma?

Eric took the last seat at the back of the bus, propping his feet up and gazing out the window as the bus trundled down Victory Boulevard. *Another day, another twenty-seven dollars and thirty-three cents. At least, that's what I made on Friday. I sure hope this Instant Karma helps with the busking, too.*

He got off the bus at Broadway over an hour later, with the steep hill ahead of him, the unmarked border between the crowded, dirty downtown area and the classy and immaculate business district.

He found his favorite busking spot and set down his gig bag on the bench. It was a street corner near the YMCA, with a small outdoor cafe and a small lawn area that was terrific for relaxing and wriggling your toes in the thick grass. *Best of all, I've never had a single problem with the cops over here.*

Most of the "suits" walking past didn't even look at him as Eric set up for busking, "salting" the hat with a handful of dollar bills and quarters, positioning his sign just right: *"Yes, this is my real day job. Please support the Arts."* But a few of the businessmen and women recognized him, and smiled or waved hello. Eric smiled in response as he fitted his flute together and played a few quick notes to warm up.

Then he began busking in earnest. Light, lively Celtic tunes, with the occasional phrase of a classical piece thrown in for kicks. The serious-faced suits walking past stopped to listen; when he finished the tune medley, there was a burst of spontaneous applause, and no few of them reached into their pockets for change to toss in the hat.

Hey, not bad for the first thing in the morning. And the lunch rush hasn't even hit yet . . .

He began "Irishman's Heart to the Ladies," one of his favorite jigs. Several corporate types, apparently on their way to a meeting, stopped to listen, and one of the silver-haired businessmen kicked up his heels in an impromptu jig step. They moved on, but not before the older man dropped a five-spot in Eric's hat.

Eric doffed his cap, grinning from ear to ear at the departing businessmen. *All right! Let's hear it for that kindhearted gent and the Instant Karma!*

An hour later, as the lunch crowd thinned, Eric's energy dropped as well. He began to play slower tunes, trying to find a spot on the corner that wasn't in the bright sunlight.

Too damn hot. He stopped playing in the middle of one tune to wipe the sweat off his forehead. *L.A. in May, it shouldn't be this hot yet. This is almost as bad as Faire last year. A hundred and ten in the shade, and all of us doing shows on those blacktop stages . . .*

He mustered the strength to play another fast tune, "Fox Hunt," one of the best slipjigs he knew.

"Hey, Misty, listen! He's playing the 'Foxhunter's Jig'!"

Eric looked up in surprise at the three suits gawking at him. He finished the tune with extra energy, adding a last trilling ornament and long, intricate run, then bowed elegantly as they applauded.

The blonde woman was shaking her head in disbelief. "A Celtic musician playing on the street! They'll never believe this back home!"

"Where are you from?" Eric asked, wiping sweat from his brow.

One of the men smiled. "Tulsa, Oklahoma. We're all Celtic music fans, but had no idea that people played Celtic stuff on the streets of L.A. This is quite a surprise."

"Well, there's not many of us," Eric said. Winded by the fast-moving tune, he sat down to catch his breath. "Most everybody plays at the Faire or in bar gigs, but there's a few of us that play street as well. There's one lady, a terrific singer who lives in the South Bay, she sings traditional ballads. And a few others, like a fiddler that I know. There aren't very many buskers in this town, not nearly as many as in San Francisco, but we do all right."

"That's really wonderful." The woman smiled, then asked hesitantly, "Maybe . . . could you play 'Rocky Road to Dublin' for us? It's one of my favorites."

Eric nodded, and took a deep breath. It was one of his favorites, too—a fast slipjig that was difficult, but not impossible. He added in extra ornaments on this tune as well, and was very pleased by the wide smiles on their faces when he finished.

"Thank you, so much. You've made our trip out here something special." The woman knelt down, setting a folded bill in his hat. "I really hope we'll see you again."

The younger man handed him a business card. "If you're ever in Oklahoma, give us a call. Maybe we can help you get some gigs, introduce you to people." He also slipped a bill into the hat.

"Thank you very much," Eric said, pocketing the card. *Well, that'll be handy if I ever move to Oklahoma. God only knows why I'd ever want to do that, though.*

The three walked away, leaving Eric alone on his street corner again.

Eric picked an easy tune to play next, "Fair Jenny's," as sweet as an Irish tune could be. A man in a five-hundred-dollar suit walked by, stopped briefly to listen, reached into his pocket and tossed two pennies into Eric's hat.

Oh, that's cute. Real cute. I bet you think you're really clever, mister, tossing in your two cents worth. Give me a break. Eric sneered disdainfully at the man's retreating back. *What a twit.*

But those Okies, they were something. I wish there were more folks like that, in L.A. So good-natured and friendly . . .

Still, the local business suit types, they're all pretty much the same. They think the world is theirs. And hell, who knows, they may be right. There isn't much an individual can do against the corporations, the government, and the ones with the bucks. Not when they have the power and the cash to hold on to it.

He finished "Fair Jenny's," and began a fierce, angry rendition of "Tamlin's Reel." *Yeah, look at the Faire, it's going under because some corporation guys decided that the land would be terrific for a shopping mall. Sure, people are trying to stop them, but I'm betting on the corporation. They always win.*

Well, I've got money for groceries, and a good start on next month's rent. Might as well pack it in. Otherwise, this heat will do me in. I can just see the channel 13 news bulletin: Itinerant musician melts into puddle on downtown L.A. street. News at six, film at eleven.

Eric completed the tune, ending on a mournful, unresolved C sharp. *Yeah, that's how I feel today. Very unresolved. Though not especially sharp . . .* He disassembled the flute, and replaced it in the case. *Tomorrow, maybe I'll try the busking outside Century city, haven't played there in a few weeks. The business crowd around there is usually pretty good on tips, not like the tourists in Hollywood.* He smiled, remembering the gawking faces of the Japanese tourists, doubtlessly trying to figure out why this *gaijin* was playing classical flute next to the Chinese Theater.

He walked down to the steep hill, toward a crowd of rookie cops learning how to direct traffic on the corner below. *I've never seen so many cops in one spot in my life. But I bet somebody's car could be ripped off fifty feet away and they'd never even notice.*

Eric strolled past the Chandler Pavilion, with its endless glass windows and the huge chandeliers just visible inside. *Maureen's probably in there right now, rehearsing for "Traviata." And probably listening to that crazy guest director endlessly scream things in French. I wonder if he's figured out that none of them can understand him?*

Somehow, though, thinking about her didn't really hurt at all. He remembered when he first met her, not far from where he had busked today; a beautiful red-haired woman who listened to him play, then improvised a harmony to the old O'Carolan tune. How he joined her and her friends for lunch the next day at one of the hangouts the Pavilion people frequented, then went backstage with her, climbing around the high walkways above the stage. *God, we had fun.* Walking on Venice Beach, laughing as they dodged the kamikaze rollerskaters. He thought about the late nights they'd spent talking, singing impromptu duets, making love.

Eric tested the memories gingerly, like someone worrying at a sore tooth, and was surprised to feel no resulting heartache. *Just memories, good memories of all the times we spent together. It doesn't hurt anymore.*

He smiled suddenly, clicking his heels in a quick jig step, and reverenced to the huge Pavilion building. *Ave atque vale, m'lady Maureen. I hope you'll find someone who'll make you happy, I really do. Goodbye and good luck, my mistress of music.*

The rookie cops looked at him suspiciously as he danced past, whistling. *They probably think I'm on drugs. But I'm not. At least I don't think I am, I just feel good. As though everything is about to change for the better—*

He waited at the bus stop, and was surprised to see the RTD bus show up exactly on schedule. *Hot damn, something is right with the universe. These buses are never on time . . .*

He stopped briefly at the supermarket, picking up a sixer of Guinness, two cans of chili, a hunk of plastic-wrapped cheddar cheese, and a package of Hostess cupcakes—*Yeah, I feel like celebrating tonight. A real feast. Today was a great day for busking, and I feel terrific. I think I've even gotten over Maureen.*

But the moment he unlocked his apartment door, he knew something was wrong.

Eric glanced around the living room, and his eyes narrowed suspiciously. *I didn't leave those books lying out on the floor, I know I didn't. And my leather jacket, I know Maureen didn't take that out of the closet. It was hanging there last night . . .*

Moving quietly, Eric set the bag of groceries down by the door, and reached for the baseball bat, propped against the wall. *I thought I was just imagining things last night, but I think there really was somebody in here. And I was too zoned to catch them.*

Oh God. Maybe they're still here now . . .

He glanced into the kitchen, then crossed to the bathroom, looking inside.

Nothing here.

He pushed the bedroom door open with his foot, carefully leaning inside to look around.

The clothes were sorted. By color. And stacked in careful piles along the wall.

But his bed was a mess, and he'd made it before he left.

Oh God—whoever was here—is here—is a serious loony. He tried to remember what drugs did things to your head like that. *PCP? No. Acid, maybe. Acid and THC? Could be*— He swallowed with difficulty, and gripped the bat a little harder. *I could be in for a world of hurt here.*

He backed out of the bedroom and into the kitchen.

The drift of cold air over his feet told him that his intruder had left the refrigerator door slightly ajar. He edged over to the fridge and opened the door enough to look inside.

There hadn't been much in there in the first place—but now anything that had been left was useless. Because everything, *everything* in the refrigerator had had one neat bite taken out of it. Including the apple-shaped candle he kept in there as a joke.

If he'd had any doubts about there being an intruder, they were gone now.

Oh God. Oh God. I'm dealing with a real, genuine lunatic here.

He shut the door firmly and crept into the living room—

Where the first thing that met his eyes was his own Faire cloak, draped over a chair. Except it hadn't been there when he came in.

He felt his jaw dropping open; stared at the sweep of wool—

And a red rage swept over him. *Maureen's gone—my purse gets cut—my cloak gets stolen—and then the* bastard *that steals it follows me home and eats my food and sleeps in my bed and makes a* mockery *out of me!*

"*Get out here!*" he screamed, brandishing the bat. "Goddammit, I *know* you're in here—*you get your ass out here, you bastard!*"

Sure, Banyon. Like he's going to—a tiny, cooler corner of his mind thought—just before the young man stepped into the bedroom doorway, smiling shyly.

He was very tall, taller than Eric; he was very blond, white-blond, hair that was too silken and curled too tightly to be real. He was muscular, but slim—and he was wearing Eric's clothes.

Eric's jeans, *Eric's* favorite Faire shirt and *Eric's* black leather vest—

And my goddamn boots!

That was too much for flesh and blood to take. Eric charged him, swinging the bat. *You lousy sonuva—*

The young man flung out his hand in a gesture of warding—

And music. Hit. Him.

A wall of music. A chord so pure there were no overtones or undertones, no pulsings of harmonics. A progression of four notes of blue-white, crystalline clarity. Perfection.

Oh, he thought. *A major.*

And the floor rose up and hit him.

"Bard?" said the soft, frightened voice. "Oh please, Bard, I didn't hurt you, did I? You startled me."

I'm lying down. On my back.

Cool, slick surface under his right hand, his left lying across his stomach.

Umph. He took inventory without opening his eyes. *Hide of nauga, with a lump just under my left kidney. I know that lump. Maureen complained about it often enough. I'm lying on the couch.*

"Bard?"

With a nut-case bending over me.

Eric cracked his right eye open, cautiously. And was caught in emeralds.

Eyes, he told himself. *Those are just eyes. You can look away—*

Only he couldn't, not until they blinked, and the generously sensuous mouth under them smiled in delight and relief.

Those eyes. They're green. Like a cat's—

Ohmigod.

"Bard?" said the owner of those green, slit-pupiled eyes, touching his face, gently.

Bad drugs, Eric. Really bad drugs. Serious bad drugs. This is a hallucination.

The hallucination bent lower, his face shadowed with concern. Tendrils of that unbelievably white-blond hair fell into his unbelievably green eyes, and he tucked them behind one pointed ear in an unbelievably graceful gesture of annoyance.

He used the same hand to touch Eric's cheek—

Pointed ears?

The figment of his fevered imagination frowned, then bit his lip "Bard? Can you speak?"

Pointed ears?

Another touch, the concern deepening in the hallucination's eyes. But the almost-caress was no hallucination though it was the lightest of feather-strokes.

Pointed ears? Like—an elf?

Ohmigod. Eric blinked; then blinked again. *Ohmigod. Either I've gone crazy, or there's an elf coming on to me in my living room.*

He squeezed his eyes shut. *Please God, let it be crazy, and I promise I'll never do drugs again . . .*

4

The Faerie Reel

Eric opened his eyes, and wished he hadn't.

The elf was still there.

Please, God, don't let this be real. This has to be a drug flashback. It just has to be.

"Bard?" Again, that soft, hesitant voice. It bordered on timid. It was *certainly* diffident. "Please, talk to me, tell me you're all right. Bard?"

It's not real. I'm just seeing things. There isn't an elf in my living room. I'll close my eyes, and when I open them again, he'll be gone, or he'll be a rubber tree, or maybe a unicorn. Eric shivered, his head throbbing, and closed his eyes again. *If he's still there—I won't think that. This isn't happening. If there isn't an elf, if it's all in my head—*

It has to be in my head. If it isn't in my head—those nightmare things—were—

Real. No. Oh God. Please, no. Not again. I can't face them twice.

"Bard?"

I can't even face an elf. Maybe if I don't talk to it, it'll just go away.

The hallucination sighed deeply, and said something that Eric couldn't understand, a brief phrase in a language that was liquid and musical, even if it did sound like a muttered curse.

A hand traced a delicate line down Eric's cheek; rested on his shoulder.

He shuddered away from the touch. *Just go away, please . . . don't be real.*

Then an electrical shock slammed into him; he'd gotten hold of a live wire once, helping set up for a gig, and this felt exactly like that all-too-unforgettable incident. Eric yelped and somehow managed to leap into the air from a prone position, levitating in midair for a brief moment before landing again in a painful heap on the couch.

He glared accusingly at the hallucination, who was smiling broadly, his grin bright with relief. "Oh, good, you weren't hurt at all! I was . . ."

That was all the elf had time to say. Eric was goaded past being afraid. The creature froze at the rage in Eric's eyes, and then he gurgled as Eric reached over and grabbed him by the throat.

The next exciting thing Eric experienced was the unmistakable sensation of having his face flattened against plaster as he slammed against the far wall of the living room. With a groan, he slid down to the carpeted floor.

He did not want to move. Not at all.

Not for four or five days, anyway.

His head rang with the impact and with a strange polyphonic harmony. *This can't be a hallucination,* he thought dazedly, tasting salty blood where he had bitten the inside of his cheek. *It hurts too much.*

"Bard?"

Oh God, he's still here.

"Please, Bard, you have to stop attacking me. I don't want to hurt you anymore."

Eric turned over—slowly—then blinked a few times, as the room spun wildly around him. "Yeah," he muttered thickly, "I don't want you to hurt me anymore, either."

He pulled himself up into a sitting position, and shook his head to stop the ringing in his ears, then looked at his unwelcome house guest.

Eric stared in fascination as several identically-blond elves moved towards him from across the room, then slowly reformed into a single figure that knelt down beside him.

"Let me see," the figure said, and lightly touched Eric's forehead. Eric winced at the sudden pain that lanced through his head, front to back.

"This is my doing. I shall take care of it," his imaginary visitor said quietly. To Eric's surprise, the pain began to recede as a soft melody (somehow as close as the wall, and as distant as the moon, simultaneously) echoed lightly in his mind.

If anybody ever puts that in a bottle— he thought; then he wasn't thinking, just listening. Listening to music that seemed to be becoming a part of him. Like the very first time he'd ever listened to anything on a really good pair of stereo headphones only better. Enchantingly better.

It's like Bach, all the layers of voice, building together.

Finally, the music faded. Eric sat up with a pang of regret, feeling as though he had just awakened from a long restful night's sleep. The elf was looking at him with those large, emerald cat's eyes, eyes that were darkened with concern.

This cannot be real. Scratch that. It can't be what it looks like. So what would it be if it wasn't what it looks . . .

Maureen. She's getting even with me. And she must know a bizillion people over in the studios.

Those ears—

The delicate ears, curving to a graceful point—*They have to be fakes, like what those Faire kids all dressed up in wolfskins were wearing last season.* Eric wondered if the tips would come off if he pulled on them . . .

"Try it," the creature said in a voice suddenly cold and steel-hard, "and I'll knock you on your backside again, Bard or not."

How did he know— "No thanks, I think I've had enough of that," Eric said hastily. He carefully stood up, gingerly touching the side of his face that had impacted so resoundingly with the wall. To his surprise, it was slightly sore, but didn't hurt. Much.

The elf helped him walk back to the couch, and Eric sank down onto the squeaky cushions with an audible sigh. The elf sat beside him.

"This is not going as I had planned," the elf said, looking at him out of the corners of his eyes. "You are not cooperating, Bard."

Take a different angle. Yah. It's not "real" because this has to be some kind of trick. "My name's *not* Bard," Eric snapped. "Who the hell are you, when you aren't breaking into people's apartments and bashing them into walls?"

The elf straightened, pride written in his stance and expression. Eric's blue jeans and Faire shirt looked incongruous on him, like a polyester business suit on King Arthur.

Okay, so he's an actor, at least. Pretty good one, too.

"I am Korendil, warrior and mage, second to Prince Terenil, leader of the elves of this region."

"Uh huh," Eric replied dryly. "I'm Eric Banyon. Street busker. What the hell are you doing in my apartment?"

The hair could be his, could be a wig. Ears are latex. Eyes—contact lenses. You could even do the funny pupils that way; that's what they did in "Thriller." Korendil, Terenil, they sound like somebody lifted those names right out of Tolkien. And yeah. He didn't read my mind, he read my eyes. I looked at his ears—he's gotta know that the first thing anybody would think is, "Are they real?" And he's too smart not to figure I'd try to yank on them.

"I followed you here," Korendil said, some of the pride draining out of his stance. "I followed you from the place-of-festival."

Cute. "Place-of-festival" instead of "Fairesite." Oh, you're good, fella. But I'm not that stoned, no matter what Maureen told you about my habits.

"You followed me, huh?" Eric sat back and rubbed the sore side of his face. "Why?"

"I was trapped in the Node-Grove, the magic nexus at the place-of-festival, trapped by our enemy, Terenil's and mine, the traitor we once harbored in our midst."

"You expect me to believe elves have traitors?" Eric laughed. "Come on! You'll have to do better than that."

Korendil glared. "You, who play 'Sheebeg Sheemore' with such feeling, how can you be such a great fool as *that*?"

"Watch who you're calling a fool, buddy," Eric growled. *He's got the script down good, that's for sure.* "Just what is this guy supposed to have done to you?"

"He caught me unawares and bound me in sleep in the oaken grove. Until you Awakened me."

"Say what?" *Whoever wrote this script sure has a weird imagination. And Maureen sure gave him a lot to work with.*

Korendil leaned forward, earnestly. "You Awakened me, Bard. With your song. two nights ago.. And you freed me from imprisonment in the grove."

Music, wild and fey, the trees bending closer to listen, then that moment when everything had clicked, *that moment . . .*

And how the hell did he know that? Maureen wasn't there. There's no way he could know what happened Saturday night.

Okay, wait a minute. He was at the Fairesite, he stole my cloak. He probably talked to people who know me, knew I tend to slink off to that grove to be alone. Hell, he probably was hiding in the trees and listening to me!

Bastard. You almost had me falling for it.

But I didn't hear or see anyone, and I would have. Wouldn't I?

"You're stoned, mister," Eric said slowly. "Yeah, I played in that grove on Saturday night, but I didn't do any more than that."

"But you are a Bard—and Bards are the greatest of mages. Bards control the magic of creation, the magic only the most skillful of High Adepts can use. Even untutored, you are a greater mage than I or even the Prince. Untutored, you can break the spells of lock and ward simply by wishing for freedom as you play."

I wanted freedom—and—

Damn, he's good. He almost suckered me in. I wonder where Maureen found this guy? The annual Screen Actors Guild Christmas party? "You still haven't said why you followed me home."

"It is a long tale—" Korendil looked at him doubtfully.

Eric spread his hands wide. "I've got nothing but time. Humor me."

The elf cleared his throat, and took on that proud posture again. "Once we lived freely in this land," he said, his words sounding as if he was reciting some chronicle. "We came here from across the sea, seeking freedom from fear even as your kind sought it. We spread farther and faster than your kind, and were well settled by the time they came upon us again. We welcomed them. Our groves were scattered among the humans' dwellings, and we lived in peace with them. That changed; in the way of humans, so swiftly that we were taken unawares. You humans began to build with cold iron in this valley, more and more as the years went past, and slowly our people were cut off from each other."

Eric shrugged. "So? What's that got to do with anything?" *Logic; let's have some logic here. How'd he do what he did to me? How do you fake magic?*

"We have been cut off from the Node-Grove, the nexus the source of all our magic, by the walls of cold iron you humans have built. That has weakened our power, and—"

"So move," Eric interrupted. "Do what everybody else does. Head for the suburbs." *He's SAG, I bet. Using some kind of special effects. Bet Maureen can just wiggle her hips and have forty techies begging to do her favors.*

"We are *tied* to our groves," Korendil explained, as if to a particularly stupid child.

Eric bristled a little, and Korendil continued, apparently not noticing. "Without the magic of the Node-Grove, most of us are bound to the groves where we anchored ourselves in your world. We cannot travel far from the home-trees without much pain and further weakening. Only those of the High Court, who need no anchoring to dwell on this side of the Hill, remained free to move. They could not, and would not, leave the others."

Eric was only half-listening, sizing the guy up. *He could be a martial artist. He's got the build for it. That would sure account for him being able to toss me across the room. And if Maureen gave him her key, he could have been in and out of here all he wanted.*

"Uh huh," Eric said vaguely, shifting his weight so that the couch creaked. "So, they're stuck. What's so bad about that?"

"What's 'so bad,'" Korendil said acidly, "is that when elves are cut off from each other and the source of their magic, they fall into Dreaming."

The capital "D" was as plain as if Korendil had written the word.

"Dreaming what?" Eric replied, interested in spite of his anger at the trick being played on him. *Whoever came up with this should write a book. It's better than half the fantasy schlock I've picked up lately—like telepathic horses, or ancient Aztec gods invading Dallas.*

"Dreaming . . . it is a—" Korendil groped for words. *This part must not have been in the script.*

"It is a state," he said, finally. "A state in which only 'now' is important. There is no memory of the past, or thought of the future. All that matters is existence and amusement."

"Sounds like half the kids hanging out at the malls," Eric replied, uncomfortably aware that Korendil was describing something very like his own life.

"And that is where you find them," Korendil said, nodding. "In the malls. What little magic they have left to them, they use to help steal what they want. Things of amusement, entertainment, and clothing that catches their fancy. Surely you have seen them, and yet never noticed them, nor noticed that they are not to be seen outside of your malls."

God, what a concept! Eric suppressed the urge to laugh. *Mall-elves! Tolkien invades Southern California! Christ, it's as hokey as a Saturday-morning cartoon show! Like that one I saw a while back—what was it called? Jewel?*

Damn, but this guy should really write a book!

"Even the Prince has been lost to the weakening of magic," Korendil continued sadly. "Even he has begun to give up all hope. So—I turn to you, Bard Eric, and I offer you your heart's desire."

Eric crossed his arms over his chest, and put his feet up on the scarred coffee table. *Okay, this is too clever and*

too consistent to be some lunatic's private fantasy. So let's
hear the pitch I'm supposed to fall for. "And just what is
that?" he asked.

If he has a Taser up his sleeve, that would account for
the electric shock too. I think I've got you figured out, fella.
I'm willing to play the game through before I throw you
out. Make you work for your money.

"I offer you," the elf said, proudly, "a cause to fight for."

"What?" Eric laughed aloud. "Go around playing reveille
for all your little mall-elves?" He shook his head. "I'm a
flautist, not a trumpeter."

Korendil's eyes darkened and narrowed. "No," he said
coldly. "Have you heard nothing in the past three days? The
place-of-festival is doomed—and all magic for this Valley
originates there at the Node-Grove. Bad enough that my
people are lost in Dreaming, but if the nexus is destroyed,
all magic here will die. My people, unable to flee to a new
source, will fade and die. And you mortals stand to lose
as well—mark you. The Node-Grove is the reason for
Hollywood and all that is associated with it being located
here. If the Node-Grove is destroyed, *your* connection to
magic and creativity will be lost, and the dreams and hopes
that make your short lives worth living will be destroyed
as well."

You slipped up, fella. One minute you're talking for-
soothly, and the next, about the Industry. Uh huh. Gotcha.

Eric laughed in the impostor's face.

"Sure," he said, deliberately sneering at him. "And I'm
the only person in the whole of L.A. who can help you.
Right. Where'd you get this idea, anyway? Some script you
couldn't sell? Well, you can't sell it to me, either."

"You mean—" Korendil looked aghast. "You mean you
don't believe me?"

Still playing the part. He's good, I'll give him that.
Wonder why I never saw him at Faire before this?

"Damn straight I don't believe you—and even if I did,
I don't see anything in it for me." He shrugged. "And you
can tell Maureen I said she's not gonna be playing any
games with my head anymore."

"But—the magic here is one of the reasons you play so well," Korendil cried, his face twisted with anguish. "You respond to it, and it responds to you, don't you see? You're a true Bard, like Merlin, like Taliesen—"

"Like bullshit," Eric interrupted. "You can tell Maureen that I didn't find her little trick very funny, and I didn't fall for it. I hope she paid you a bundle—you earned it, that's for sure. But, no matter what she told you, I'm usually in pretty good control of my reality. And I don't like this kind of practical joke, mister. So you can just pack your act up and get the hell out of my life."

"But I'm not—" the phony elf started to say.

"Bye," Eric said, wriggling his fingers. "You'll pardon me if I don't get up. I've had kind of a strenuous day."

Korendil rose from the couch—

Probably a dancer, too. Maybe he's in ballet. Too tall to get a lead part, though; he must be six-five if he's an inch. Wonder if he's gay? It sure seemed like he was coming on to me for a while.

I wonder if that was part of Maureen's little game, too? Would it make her feel better about the breakup if she found out I was into guys?

"I will be back," the elf-actor said, making the words a promise. "I will be back. I will convince you somehow, Eric Banyon. That, I swear!"

Eric shrugged. "Just don't expect Maureen's key to work again. I'm having the locks changed."

The elf wrapped anger and frustration around him like a cloak, and glided out the door, which—despite Eric's assumptions—did not slam shut behind him.

Christ. What kind of an idiot did she take me for, anyway? A few special effects and a fairy tale, and I'm supposed to fall for it. Hell, he wasn't even dressed like an elf, he—

He was wearing my clothes!

Shit! And he took them with him!

Bastard!

Eric sat up slowly, feeling a residual ache in too many places. *Christ, Maureen, why did you have to do this to me? I never thought you'd stoop so low—*

—or that you hated me this much.
The elation he'd had earlier was gone.

What did I do to make you hate me like this?
He looked around the living room, seeing only the empty places that used to be filled with Maureen's posters, her Beethoven, all the other reminders that someone else lived here. *Funny. Most of the things that made this place look like a home instead of Howard Johnson's were hers. Everything I care about you could put in a couple of backpacks.*

If I died tomorrow, nobody'd miss me until the rent was late.

Helluva note.

From the high of the afternoon he slid abruptly into one of the lowest lows he'd had in a long time. He rubbed his eyes, as the silence around him oppressed him further still.

I can't stay here alone tonight. I can't. If I do, I'll go crazy, or drink everything in the apartment, or do something equally stupid. Maybe I should call some people, set up a jam.

Wait a minute—

There's Spiral Dance, they're playing in Studio City tonight. Beth wanted me to join them, the usual split. Hell, the money would be good, and I sure don't want to stay here tonight, staring at the ceiling, listening to the water pipes play percussion solos.

His throat felt tight, and he shivered.

Maureen is probably in Westwood tonight with her Pavilion friends, drinking wine and laughing about that idiot flautist she walked out on.

Eric closed his eyes tightly, fighting off the impulse to bury his face in the couch pillows.

Dammit, I am not going to cry. I'm going to get off my ass and play a gig tonight, make some cash, drink a few with Beth and the Spiral Dance folks. And have a good time. I sure did the last time I did a gig with them.

He thought back to his last gig with Beth Kentraine and her wild crew of folk-rock musicians—which had climaxed with Beth launching herself, Fender and all, from the stage and landing on one of the tables, much to the surprise of the customer sitting there.

She didn't even make the table rock. God, she's crazed.

He began to smile, and his depression slowly lightened. *Yeah, I'm up for that. Old Celtic melodies with electric guitar and trap set. Black leather and studs, and Bethie's dark velvet voice, singing an ancient, gentle Irish air.*

Oh, they're crazy, but fun-crazy, terrific to play a gig with. Now they might have taken that pointy-eared joker seriously.

That's a good reason not to get tied up too closely with them, though. There's something kind of weird about them— like how they cancel a gig if someone has a bad feeling about it. All that weird shit. Like too many people at Faire, acting like their characters are real. Caught up in some reality I don't understand.

Hell. They got a right. Beth and the Spirallers are good people, damn fine musicians. Even if they are a little weird.

That's it. I'll go gig with them tonight.

He pried himself off the couch, and headed into the bedroom to look for his gig clothing. His black leather boots, his least-faded pair of jeans, a dressy shirt, bright red with little fake-pearl buttons. *Yeah, that's me: Eric Banyon, the hottest rock-flute player in L.A., and a snappy dresser too.*

I really wish that SAG guy hadn't walked off with my leather vest, though. That was pretty cheesy, taking off with my clothes. And my Faire boots.

Damn it, Maureen, that was a low trick! But I'm not going to let your stupid games spoil my life, or even one night.

Eric retrieved his cloak from where the actor had left it, draped over one of the chairs. He fastened the brass clasp at his throat, then walked over to where his gig bag was lying on the chair.

And stopped at a tug on his throat. *Something isn't right—*

He looked down. The cloak was six inches longer than it had been the last time he wore it.

But it used to fit me perfectly, exactly ankle length. I don't—wait, that pointy-eared actor was at least six-two, closer to six-five, and I'm five-ten. Could he have had somebody add more material to my cloak, make it longer so it would fit him right?

Eric examined the hem of the cloak, and shook his head in disbelief.

Nope. No sign of anything added. Not even that the hem got let out. It's just longer. Besides, how in the hell could he have matched the plaid lining?

Okay, okay. It's wool. Wool stretches. He got it wet, and it stretched. Let's get real about this.

He let the cloak fall, trying to ignore the fact that it was dragging on the floor with every step he took. *I'm not going crazy, it's just that somebody is playing mind-games with me, messing with my head, and dammit, Maureen, it isn't funny!*

Screw that. I'm going to play a gig and enjoy myself.

Eric slung the gig bag over his shoulder, and stopped, one hand on the doorknob.

Okay, the cloak got stretched—but how in hell did that guy fit in my jeans?

Don't ask, Banyon. Just—don't ask.

Deliberately whistling a jazzed-up version of "Banish Misfortune" with determination, he locked the apartment door behind him.

The RTD bus bounced and swayed along Van Nuys Boulevard, the driver honking angrily at someone who was blocking the street in rush-hour traffic.

Eric added that syncopated rhythm to the tune he was composing. He smiled at the elderly woman in the seat across from him, who was glaring silently at him as he whistled another brief snatch of melody then quickly scribbled the sequence in his notebook.

That's what I like about L.A., everybody is so friendly . . .

Eric leaned against the grimy window. His depression was gone, just as quickly as it had descended. Everything seemed somehow brighter, touched by the red-gold of the sunset, the wisps of multicolored clouds overhead. The Hollywood hills were a reassuring presence on the right.

All those rich Industry people, just waiting to discover a talented musician like meself—

Ahead, Burbank and Pasadena vanished into the thickening brown-blueness of the sky, the last glint of sunlight reflecting off the distant antenna towers capping Mount Wilson, high above the Valley.

Looking down at the street, Eric watched the moving crowd: the shoppers, weighed down by packages; the high school kids walking in clusters, like some modern kind of herd animal. A policewoman directed cars as a broken traffic signal flashed its single red light forlornly.

I don't know what it is, but I like this city. Of all the places I've lived, or just wandered through, I really like L.A. the best. Sure, it's crowded, and smoggy, and dirty, but there's such a feeling of life to it. Maybe it's the dreams— all the hopes and dreams of all the people who live here make this place come alive.

The little old lady on the opposite seat suddenly gasped with surprise. Eric stood up quickly and looked out the window as two motorcyclists, both wearing skintight red-and-white racing leathers, arced past the bus, barely avoiding the cars ahead of them. One motorcyclist dropped down on one foot, the bike banking sharply, then gunned the engine and followed his friend down the boulevard.

The elderly woman muttered something about hooligans and reckless drivers, and transfixed Eric with a dark accusing look, as though all of this were his fault. But Eric barely noticed, watching as the bikers disappeared into the late afternoon traffic.

They're crazy. But beautiful. I wish I could do things like that with a motorcycle. Though that's not too likely, not unless I could find a bike that somehow drives itself! But they really are beautiful to watch. Like dancers.

Eric sat back down in his seat, looking out the bus window. Even through the glass, he could hear the pounding beat of a rap song.

A group of kids were breakdancing on the sidewalk. Eric

watched in disbelief as one boy moonwalked backwards, flipped over into a handstand, then rolled to the concrete in a tight backspin. The kid vaulted back up onto his feet, moving aside so one of his friends could take his turn on the pavement.

Damn. Another thing I wish I could do! He laughed silently at himself. *"If wishes were fishes we'd walk on the sea."* They *make it look so easy, but I'd probably kill myself if I tried any of those stunts.*

A white limousine pulled in between Eric and the sidewalk, blocking his view of the street dancers. Eric tried to peer over the top of the car—

But his gaze was caught by a movement inside, and he saw a man in the back of the limo, gazing out the open window. An older man, silver hair, strong features—

I've seen someone like him before, somewhere. I know I have. The curve of his jaw, the high cheekbones—God, he looks familiar . . .

Then the man looked up, and saw that Eric was watching him. Their eyes met; Eric was unable to look away, trapped by the intensity of the man's gaze.

Green eyes, clouded emerald—falling into a bottomless pool of water. Jade mirrors reflecting the shadowed night sky. Something watching, wanting, reaching out and reaching in—taking hold—taking possession—

Eric turned away from the window with an effort, shaking his head. *What in the hell is wrong with me?,* he thought desperately. *I know what it is. He has the same eyes as that actor, Korendil, that so-called "elf," the same leaf-green eyes. No. I'm seeing things. Or else they've both got the same optometrist.*

Against his will, Eric slid back to the window, and stared down at the man in the limo again. The man, gazing up at the bus window, smiled—but it was a smile edged in frost. The emerald eyes caught him, drew him in close, and refused to let him go.

Eyes—

Reaching up and through, touching intimately, examining everything, no matter how secret—echoes of scornful laughter—something foul and slimy where no one should ever be able to go—shame—violation—stripping everything away, all the illusions, all the delusions, leaving a rag of self for all the world to see . . .

A wave of dizziness hit Eric like a wall, blocking out everything except the feeling that the world was spinning around him, and there was nothing he could hold onto, nothing that was still him. He clung to the window, his mouth dry, bile in his throat, and clutched for *anything* that was real.

Nothing I've ever done has made any difference to anyone; *nothing I do is ever going to* make *any difference. I could throw myself in front of a semi, and no one would care. I wouldn't even rate more than three words in the obit column.*

This was more than depression, this was despair, bleak, cold, hopeless.

Nobody would ever miss me. Maureen wouldn't. My landlord wouldn't. The Faire wouldn't. Beth might wonder where I vanished to—for about five minutes. Then she'd forget about me. They'd all forget about me. I might as well never have lived.

Despondency weighed heavily upon his soul, and sent his heart plummeting downwards.

Nobody gives a damn about me, and nobody ever will. I've never done anything worthwhile. I've never done anything right. I might just as well take that dive and get it over with—

When he looked out the window again, unable to keep from shaking, the white limo was gone. Nauseated and sweating, Eric closed his eyes and leaned against the cool glass, breathing unsteadily.

Christ. What's happening to me?

I think I'm losing my mind. God, I'm better off dead . . .

He concentrated on the feeling of the glass against his forehead and closed his eyes until the nausea passed. When he opened his eyes again everything had changed.

The breakdancers were still lounging on the sidewalk, but now they were gathered around an elderly man like hyenas around a helpless gazelle. Eric stared in horror as one of the youths shoved the old man hard against the wall, sending him sprawling facedown on the pavement, where they proceeded to strip his pockets, riffling through the fallen bag of groceries spilling out onto the sidewalk. A gray-haired shopkeeper watched in silence from behind the dubious safety of his glass storefront, then turned away. Even the pedestrians on the street carefully looked the other way as they walked past.

What in hell is going on here?

Everything is so gray, so unreal . . .

Even the Hollywood Hills, instead of their usual green-brown dotted with houses, seemed to have faded. The sky had darkened to a sullen gray. No one on the street laughed. or smiled, or even looked as though they were enjoying life, or were glad to be alive.

They looked more as if they were enduring the last few moments before their own executions.

Eric trembled and closed his eyes, turning away from the window. *God, what's happening to me?*

A burst of laughter and applause drew his attention back to the window. Eric saw the breakdancer bow to the gathered crowd, as the elderly man, still carrying his bag of groceries, bent down to put a dollar bill in the cardboard box next to the dancers' tape player.

The bus lurched into movement again, slowly rumbling down the boulevard, as Eric stared at the receding sidewalk and the breakdancers. *But I know what I saw—*

The despair was fading, almost tangibly.

It's the drugs, Eric. Serious drugs. Definitely too much in one weekend.

He shook his head, hoping to clear it. *First a gay elf, then Svengali in a limo, then a remake of 1984. Shit. I hope I can get my act together for the gig tonight, or Beth Kentraine is going to kill me.*

5

Parcel of Rogues

The club's name was "Diverse Pleasures," but Beth and the band just called it the Dive. *Not to the manager's face, of course, but then even the manager must have a hard time justifying this place. Cheap and pretentious, that's this joint.*

Eric edged his way past the noisy crowd at the bar, trying not to inhale the overly-redolent aroma of cigarette smoke, cheap whiskey, and cheaper perfume—*No wonder this place doesn't have roaches; they have too much self-respect to hang out here*—and narrowly avoided colliding with a barmaid carrying an overloaded tray of drinks. Eric smiled apologetically at her, but the bleached-blonde just sighed, casually sidestepping the drunk reaching for her thigh from the closest table.

Sure wouldn't want her job, either . . .

Eric quickly escaped to the relative quiet of the backstage area, and the small offices that served as warmup rooms for the bands that played the Dive.

Beth was tuning the Fender, the guitar propped carefully on her knee. She looked up, surprised, as Eric walked into the cluttered room, then grinned. "Hey, you made it! I was hoping you'd show tonight." The smile faded. "Dan's got the flu, so we're down on electric bass tonight. Allie can try to cover with the DX7, and Jim says he'll just pound the hell out of the drums, but three people isn't much on stage, y'know?"

"Yeah, I know." Eric sat down on a packing crate next to her. "How much time till we're on?"

"Twenty, twenty-five. It's a good crowd out there, for a Monday night. Bo promised to turn down the TV when we go on."

"That's nice of him. Not that anybody would be able to hear a damn thing once we start playing, anyhow." Eric fished his flute case out of the gig bag, quickly fitted the pieces together. He played a practice run, and Beth grinned, echoing the line on the guitar. Even in the relative quiet of the back room, he could barely hear the trill of the unamplified electric guitar, but caught the touch of bluesy ornamentation that Beth tossed in with the run.

"Even without Uncle Dan, it should be a good gig tonight," she said, setting the guitar down. "We'll do a sound check in fifteen, okay?"

"Okay." Eric stood up, his fingers moving absently on the flute keys, then set the flute back down on its open case. "I'm getting a drink, I'll be back in a few."

"Sounds good." He started towards the door, and Beth called after him. "Hey, Banyon!"

He turned. "Yeah?"

"Thanks for showing up tonight. I *really* appreciate it. Honest to God."

He nodded, a little embarrassed by the look on her face. *Beth Kentraine, looking grateful, like she actually needs me. I've never seen Beth look like that at anyone ever before. She's always in control of the situation, always knows what she's doing. Probably the most "together" person I know. One helluva lady . . .*

A real changeling, too. Today, hard-rock lady, yesterday—

Oh yeah, yesterday. Standing on the Kissing Bridge with Beth Kentraine in my arms, now that was the one nice sideline to the afternoon. I wouldn't mind it if that kind of afternoon became a permanent part of my life.

He felt a twinge of pain. *I liked that. I liked that a lot. But that's all she wants. A casual fling. That, and another permanent person in her band. Not necessarily another permanent person in her life.*

And I could never go to bed with someone who only feels sorry for me.

At least tonight, I feel useful. Eric flagged down one of the barmaids, requested a Scotch and water, watched as the brunette shimmied back toward the bar. *It feels right. And I'm glad I came. This should be a good gig tonight.*

When the barmaid returned with his drink, Eric found a quiet corner of the club, sat back, and took a look around at the crowd. The Scotch burned a comfortable path down his throat, relaxing him, wiping away the last vestiges of stage fright.

I always feel nervous before a gig, don't know why. God knows I've only done a few hundred performances, so far. But I don't think that'll ever go away.

Someone walked past him, laughing lightly at her companion's words. Eric caught a glimpse of bright eyes, iridescent green beneath a tangle of black curls, before the young woman vanished onto the crowded dance floor with her friend.

Eyes, glowing; like a cat's, emerald green—

No way. It can't be.

How many people in this town are going to the same damned optometrist?

Eric stood up, moving towards the dance floor. The rock rhythm held them all in thrall. Even as he pushed past the swaying bodies of the dancers, no one even glanced at him. He moved in closer to one of them, a slender woman with a riotous mane of black hair, lost in the beat, trance-dancing with an inhuman grace.

Her ears . . .

Just visible through the dark curls. Delicate, curving, *pointed* ears.

What in hell is this, anyway? Some kind of fad?

He looked around the crowded club, the gathered circles of dancers on the floor, the tables with clusters of drinkers, laughing and talking. He began to count them, the different ones—

The clothing, wild and costumey; the hair done in more styles than he could count, like off the set of a sci-fi movie. The glitter of Jewelry: incredible jewelry, rings, belts, necklaces, and things he couldn't define, like the dragon, with emerald eyes just like its wearer's, that perched on one dancer's shoulder, wings wrapping over her neck and shoulder and tail down her arm. Or the necklace that turned into a breastplate of chains that turned into a belt studded with thumbnail-sized gems.

This was *not* the Dive's usual Monday-night crowd. Oh, they got some flashy customers, maybe as many as half a dozen—but half the club?

My God. They're real. Or I'm nuts. Or both.

He stopped looking for them and began looking *at* them.

They move very gracefully, that's for sure. Terrific dancers.

He noticed something else. *You can spot them by the faces, too. Oval faces, fine cheekbones, sharp chin, and those eyes . . .*

He stared at one table after another, silently tallying up the numbers.

Half the people in this club look like Korendil. Elves. Maureen couldn't have gotten to this many people. One, but not dozens. Oh god. they're real.

This club has been taken over by elves.

I wonder if the management knows that they're catering to non-humans? He shook his head, afraid to believe what he was seeing.

That's it; I'm going crazy. I'm losing my mind. Instead of pink elephants, I'm starting to see green-eyed elves.

But there's a shopping mall here in Van Nuys, only a block away from this club. One of those older malls, where they decided not to cut down the trees but left them standing, a whole grove of old trees—oak trees—

What if I'm not crazy? What if that guy was telling the truth?

What if there really are elves, living in Los Angeles?

What if I'm completely utterly insane, and all this is my delusion?

I think I'd rather be insane. I think.

But—they're so . . . beautiful—

He started shaking, and had to hold onto a support pillar for a moment to keep his knees from giving out under him.

Beth is going to kill me. I'm supposed to play the gig tonight, not have a nervous breakdown. Shit.

Eric found an empty chair, and sat down heavily, draining his Scotch in a single swallow.

Okay, so what if the club is filled with refugees from Middle Earth? I have to play a show. Right, Banyon. The show must go on. Afterwards, you can go crazy. Offstage, preferably.

He set the empty glass down on the table and headed backstage.

Another thrilling night at the dive. Beth adjusted the Fender's strap, wishing that the band could find a better weekly gig than this club. *It helps pay the rent, and we can use the practice, but I really wish we could find a better gig.*

Maybe there'll be a rich promoter sitting out there tonight, scouting for talent.

She sighed. *Might as well wish for Eric Banyon to permanently join the band. That's about as likely.*

I shouldn't think that way about him. Oh hell, I shouldn't, but it's true. He doesn't seem to think twice about getting involved with any of his lady loves, but try convincing him to take on any other commitment, and he runs like hell.

He's a damn fine flute player. I just wish he'd get his act together.

If he ever did—

No. Beth, you'd be crazy to get involved with a man like him. Give him your heart, and he'll probably leave town the next day.

But, if he ever did get his act together—

She glanced at her watch. *Strike that . I just wish he'd get in here!* "Sound check!" she called to Allie and Jim, who were carrying the DX7 out from the practice room. She followed them out onto the stage, the Fender's pickup line coiled in her hand. *Dammit, Banyon, where are you?*

She saw his face, the mop of unruly shoulder-length brown hair backlit by the dance-floor lights. He was walking quickly through the crowd toward the backstage door. For one moment, it looked as if he was glowing.

Right, Beth. Saint Eric. Fer sure.

She blinked again, and the glow was gone. She shook her head, made a mental note not to try the house brand of Scotch again—

Probably has diesel oil in it—

—and headed for the stage.

The Dive's overworked electrician/sound engineer was checking a mike cable as Beth stepped up onto the stage. "Bo, we've got our flute player with us tonight, we're using the AKG mike for him. I think I wrote down the board settings last time," she said, plugging the Fender's cable into the appropriate socket. Bo nodded, jumping off the edge of the stage and heading for the sound board controls.

Beyond the darkened stage, the crowd was only a blur, lit by the colored glow of the dance floor and the occasional flash of a cigarette lighter. The noise of Spiral Dance setting up their equipment was lost beneath the pounding beat of whatever Top Forty dance-rock song was currently playing over the speakers. No one even glanced up at the stage.

Well, let's see if you can still ignore us when we start playing, hey?

At least there's a good crowd tonight. I don't know what pulled them in, but it's almost twice our usual Monday night crowd. And they're all dancing.

This should be a terrific gig . . .

Eric hurried onto the stage, flashing a quick smile at Beth. "Are we ready?" he asked, moving in front of the fourth mike, where Dan usually stood.

What the hell. Let's see what the crowd really wants.

She glanced up at Bo, half-hidden in the shadows, and he gave her the thumbs-up signal. The Top Forty song ended, and the dance-floor lights faded away. The stage was still unlit, leaving most of the club virtually pitch black, completely dark.

Now, let's have some fun . . .

Beth moved close to the microphone. "Ladies and gentlemen . . . we *are* Spiral Dance."

Behind her, Jim began the drum line to "Missing You," starting softly, then gaining in intensity. Allie followed him on the synth, minor chords building up to an impossible climax.

Beth hit the first notes on the Fender, just as the lights came up on the stge, blindingly bright. A moment later, Eric dived in with the descant, leading right into the first verse.

Lovely bit of work there, Banyon—

Then she leaned in close to the mike, and let the song pour through her. Hard rock, her voice nearly breaking on the high notes, but strong, the strongest she'd sung in a long time.

> "Too long, too many nights,
>   no reason left to try,
>   Too far to go to see a glimpse of light.
>   Don't tell me you don't know,
>   don't give me reasons why,
>   I don't care, 'cause I'm missing you tonight . . ."

Beth could hear Allie and Jim, their voices blending perfectly with hers on the chorus. Then she glanced up at Eric, who nodded. *All yours, bucko—*

Second verse, and Eric took the solo.

Eat your heart out, Ian Anderson! Beth couldn't help but grin as the flute solo, first low and breathy, then building to a wailing intensity as Eric caught the melody line, caught the audience and took them with him, high with the music.

The shouts and whistles after the solo almost drowned out the words of the chorus. Beth caught a glimpse of Eric, grinning like crazy, as the crowd cheered wildly.

Damn, but that was good!

The floor was overflowing with people dancing, some just standing by their tables instead of fighting for space by the stage. And one young man, very tall with flowing silver-blond hair, just standing near the edge of the stage, not dancing. Just staring at Eric.

It's hard to see with the stage lights, but it almost looks as though his eyes are glowing green—no, that's impossible, must be a trick of the lighting. Ye gods, I'm seeing everything in fireworks tonight.

She shifted position just a little, and caught a glimpse of something in his expression before the crowd swirled between them.

Need.

She started. *Ye gods—was he— No, scratch that. It wasn't sexual. Or at least it mostly wasn't sexual. Not that Banyon isn't a honey by anybody's standards—*

But this was something—desperate. What has our whistler been up to?

The song finished with a sudden chord, and the lights cut abruptly.

The applause was deafening, and she dismissed the question from her mind.

This is definitely turning out to be a fantastic gig . . .

As the lights came back up, Beth gestured to Allie, who began the first notes of "Come by the Hills," an old traditional air.

> "Come by the hills, to the land
>   where fancy is free . . ."

This song was as gentle as the first rock song had been wild. Eric joined her on the first chorus, the flute weaving a bittersweet counterpoint around her voice. Then he took the solo again, a delicate melody line, beautiful and fey, and aching with unspoken longing.

It was hard for her to see the crowd, past the blinding lights, but something was happening out there—

They're not dancing, they're not walking away to the bar, they're just standing there. Standing, and listening, and swaying with the music. Some of them holding hands, and all of them looking up at the stage, at us, at Eric. Like they're in some kind of a trance.

This is definitely the weirdest crowd we've played to in a long time.

Then a flash of movement out on the dance floor; a pair of gracefully dancing figures whirled elegantly across the floor, and the crowd moved back to give them room. *Looks like some kind of waltz, but not quite—not ballet, either, but it's close. Damn, but they're good! I wish I could find out who they are—I'd love to see them dance when I don't have to concentrate on the music. They're truly lovely.*

Slowly, other dancers joined the pair on the floor, until all Beth could see was the beautiful swirling patterns of color and movement, strange and wonderful. Something about their flowing clothing caught her attention for a moment.

God and Goddess—you don't buy that stuff off the rack! At least not at J.C. Penney's. This is not our usual draw. Not by a long shot. What in hell happened tonight? Did we just get discovered by the Rodeo Drive crowd?

What's happening to us tonight? We're so hot, the energy is so damn good, it's incredible. It's more than just having Eric jamming with us—it's something else, something that I don't quite understand—

Four songs later, though, she didn't care about understanding anything. *All I want to do is sit down. Just for a few minutes.* She glanced around, and saw that Allie and Jim were also looking faded, though Eric looked like he could keep going on all night.

One corner of her mouth quirked up in a lopsided grin when she picked up on that.

Damn him, he probably could!

She signaled Bo, then spoke clearly into the mike "We'll be back after a break." Then the stage lights darkened mercifully.

The break room seemed like an oasis of calm after the set onstage. Beth propped the Fender against one of the packing crates.

"I think I'm going to die," Allie moaned, and slumped down on a wooden chair. "That far left stage light has been shining right in my eyes all night. I can't see anything except purple and blue spots."

"I'll tell Bo," Jim said, leaving the room.

"How are you holding up, Bethie?" Eric asked, sprawled on the floor.

"They're really a demanding crowd tonight," Beth replied thoughtfully. "Really alive. I feel like they're taking everything we can give them and then a little bit more."

And they seem to be focusing on you, my friend, though you're too modest and unassuming to notice it. I really wish that you would join Spiral Dance for more than an occasional gig. Especially if all the gigs could be like this one.

"I think I'm going to die," Allie said, staring at her hands. "There's spots crawling all over my skin."

Beth reached over and mussed Allie's hair good-naturedly. "Close your eyes. hon, you'll live. I played an all-night gig once, with bright green lights shining right in my eyes. I thought everyone in the audience was an H.P. Lovecraft Cthulhuoid after that."

"I'll get you a wet paper towel," Eric offered. "You can lay that over your eyes, maybe that'll help."

"Anything," Allie said mournfully. "But I won't guarantee that I'll still be alive by the time you get back."

Eric opened the door, admitting a blast of noise and cigarette smoke, then closed it behind him, shutting out the bedlam outside.

Beth eased herself to her feet. "I'm going after a beer, Allie. Want anything from the bar?"

"Some Guinness to pour over this poor musician's grave," the keyboardist said solemnly.

Beth couldn't help but laugh. "All right, I'll snag you a Guinness. I'll be right back."

She stepped into the hallway, waiting a moment as her eyes adjusted to the dim light. *And my lungs adjust to whatever in the hell is in the air tonight. Smells like weed—God, I sure hope the cops don't bust this place while we're playing! That's all we need. A police record would be a real boost to our careers.*

Someone was standing near the entrance to the hallway silhouetted by the flickering light from the dance floor. He caught at her wrist as she walked past.

"Excuse me," Beth said, trying to be polite as she disengaged her arm from the stranger's grasp.

"Hey, pretty lady," the man said, his voice low and hoarse. "You sing real nice."

"Gee, thanks," Beth said, attempting to move around him. "You'll hear some more in a few minutes." *Who is this guy? Jeans, boots, leather jacket—one of the usual crowd, and drunker than hell.*

Wonderful. This is just what I need right now—

His hand tightened on her shoulder, refusing to let go even as she pried at his fingers. "Hey, we can go out back, have some fun, smoke a little. I've got some fine stuff, nice and dusted. You'll like it."

Smoke? With this guy? And pigs fly, my friend . . .

. . . dusted? Shit, he can't mean—Oh God, get me out of this! He's talking about PCP!

"I don't think so," Beth said carefully. *This guy's eyes are so dilated, he probably shouldn't be able to walk.* "That's really not my scene. Listen, I've only got a few minutes before we're starting again . . ."

She glanced down the hallway. *No one in sight. Shit. And this guy is dusted, I could break his arm and he'd never feel it. I can't handle this alone—*

Before she could move, the man suddenly shoved her away from him, knocking her off-balance into the wall. "Whaddaya mean, not your scene? You don't like me or something?"

Oh shit.

The man moved closer, blocking Beth's line of escape. She pressed back against the wall, looking for anything she could use as a weapon. *Nothing in sight. Terrific. What now, Kentraine? If I break his instep with my heel he won't even blink. If I give 'im a knee, he might get angry.*

"Come on outside with me. We're going to party, right? Have some fun." The man's fingers gripped her upper arm tightly, digging in. Beth knew she'd have bruises from that by tomorrow morning.

If I get to see tomorrow morning. If I live that long. He's drugged out of his mind! If I shout for help, who knows what he'll do? And if I give in, go outside with him—

Lord and lady, get me out of this!

Eric moved quickly through the crowd, trying not to drip water from the paper towel in his hand, and trying not to look intently at the people around him as he walked past.

Yeah, don't stare at the elves, Eric, it isn't polite.

I know I'm going crazy now.

Well, everybody thinks that musicians are crazy anyhow, right?

He dodged a drink-laden customer, staggering in the direction of the johns, and saw a vivacious redhead, eyes made up like a pair of iridescent butterfly wings, laughing merrily with some of her friends. Green-eyed, of course.

Damn, but there's a lot of green-eyed people in the club tonight . . .

"Bard?"

Eric froze in mid-step. *I know that voice.*

No. It can't be him again. It can't. I can't deal with this.

"Bard? I must speak with you."

Eric steeled himself, and turned to face Korendil. The elf-actor was staring at him beseechingly, that impossibly blond hair cascading over his shoulders . . . *and my leather vest! Damn it, he's still wearing my clothes!*

Be nice to the man, Eric. Or he'll probably knock you into another wall.

"Uh, hi," Eric said eloquently, very aware of the water dripping from the paper towel onto his jeans. "The name's Eric, by the way. Remember?"

The blond man nodded quite seriously. "I know, Bard. I heard your name at the place-of-festival, when the beautiful witch was trying to aid you. And you told me again this evening."

Beautiful witch? Do I know any beautiful witches? Who is this guy?

"Please, listen to me, Bard. I know you did not wish to see me again, but you must hear my words." *The—elf. He is. He's an elf*—spoke earnestly, his green eyes pleading with Eric's, reaching out to him . . .

Green eyes—can't look away—that man in the limo—

Eric broke away from Korendil's gaze with an effort, shuddering at the memory.

What's happening to me? I thought nobody could be hypnotized against his will!

"Look," he said, trying to think of a way to get out of this conversation. "I'm in the middle of a show, I can't talk right now."

Korendil gestured at the hallway to the break room, and the back door beyond, where Beth was standing, talking to some guy. "Bard Eric, can we go outside to speak? Just for a few minutes?"

Eric shook his head. "Not 'Bard Eric.' Just Eric. And no, I don't want to go outside, I have to be back onstage in a few minutes."

And if I have to talk to you, I want to do it where there's witnesses. In case you decide to slam me into a wall again.

The elf—*nope, dammit, he's as human as I am, it's just makeup and F/X*—looked at him in shock. "Do you think I would purposefully hurt you? I would never do so, I promise. But I need your help. We all need your help."

He really means it. "You're serious about this, aren't you? You're an elf, and somebody's trying to kill your people, and you need me to help you?"

Korendil nodded, gravely earnest. "Will you help us? Even as we speak, our enemy is marshaling his forces, preparing to destroy that which gives us life itself . . ."

Eric tried to keep a straight face. *Come on, Eric, you've got a few friends with—unusual—realities. This guy's no worse than any of them. Besides, he's trying to be nice, and you should be nice right back to him. Instead of laughing in his face, and then calling the cops*

"I don't know, I need some time to think about all of this, really." *Yeah, just get away from him, that's the first step in dealing with a loon—*

Something doesn't feel right. A ripple of honest-to-God fear—fear with no cause—rolled down his spine. *Something is very, very wrong—*

Eric glanced over the elf's shoulder, and suddenly what he had seen a moment before registered. Beth, cornered by a man near the back door, glint of shiny metal—*oh shit, he's got a knife! He's holding a knife on Bethie!*

Korendil's eyes widened just as Eric gathered a breath to shout for help, and the blond man whirled—stared—

Less than a microsecond, Eric would have sworn to that. *Surely* not enough to have seen what was happening, much less think of anything to do. Yet suddenly he was crossing the distance between them and the hallway in a few quick leaps.

Eric dashed after him, pushing people out of his way. *How in hell did he get through the crowd so fast?*

He skidded into the hallway, just as the blond *actor-elf?*—dived between Beth and the stranger, shoving the man away from her. Eric caught a glimpse of her frightened eyes, then the man with the knife was on his feet again, facing Korendil, hissing words almost too low to hear.

". . . mess with me, mister, you don't . . ."

The words suddenly faded away, as the man stared up into Korendil's eyes. They seemed momentarily frozen, all of them: Beth, crouching back against the wall; Korendil, gazing in the man's eyes; and the stranger, the knife only inches from Korendil's face, not moving . . .

What in the hell is going on here? That guy's still holding the knife, but he's not moving, just standing there, staring into Korendil's eyes. My God, isn't he going to do something before the guy goes for his neck?

Then the man dropped the knife suddenly, the blade clattering on the floor. He staggered backwards, hitting the wall and sliding down into a sitting position, blank-eyed and shuddering.

Eric stared at the man, who was clutching his hand and whimpering, as Korendil moved to Beth, his voice quiet and concerned. "Are you all right, Lady? Did he harm you?"

Beth was shaking her head, wiping tears from her eyes. *Bethie crying? I've never—oh shit, that guy's about to—*

Eric shouted a warning as the man on the floor suddenly moved for the knife. "Korendil, look out!"

The elf turned just as the man lunged with the knife.
Freeze-frame.

A flash of fire—no, a rope of fire—

Next frame.

Fire coiling, lashing out at the man's wrist—

Music up.

A burst of melody, a discordant B-flat minor that could
break your eardrums—

Resume speed.

—as Korendil's fist slams into the man's face, and the
surprised look on his face as he falls—

And the thought, lingering in Eric's mind: *That can't be
real. But it wasn't a special effect. That was* real.

*I've gone crazy, the whole world is crazy. I've completely
lost it.*

The stranger twitched once and then was still, sprawled
unconscious on the floor.

Eric was suddenly aware of the dripping paper towel,
forgotten in his hand. The blond actor—*actor?*—held Beth
gently in his arms, murmuring something as he brushed
away her tears. Beth was trembling, her hands shaking
uncontrollably.

The break-room door opened suddenly, and Allie looked
out blearily, blinking at the dim light. "What in the hell?"

Her eyes widened as Beth, half-carried by Korendil,
staggered unsteadily into the break room.

"Beth?" She focused on Eric as he walked past her. "Eric,
what—"

"I don't know, some guy attacked Beth," Eric said, watching as Beth, with Korendil's help, sat down on a packing crate.
"He's out cold on the floor. This guy decked him."

Beth, her face in her hands, tried to push Korendil away
from her. The blond man shook his head, said something
too low for Eric to hear and rested his hand on her shoulder
again.

For a moment, Eric thought he could hear a faint
melody, echoing from somewhere in the room.

Very classical, sounds maybe like a variation on the third
Brandenburg Concerto—

Why am I thinking about music at a time like this?

"Beth?" Eric asked hesitantly, sitting on his heels at her feet, and looking up at her anxiously. "Are you okay?"

She nodded without looking up.

Then Beth took several deep breaths, and spoke quietly. "It's all right, I'm okay," she said. A moment later, her voice was stronger. "Allie, could you tell management that there's an unconscious sonuvabitch lying in the hallway? They'll probably want to call the cops."

She's starting to sound like herself again. Eric tried to banish the image of Beth Kentraine, crying, barely able to walk. *She's Bethie again, she's okay now. Thank God.*

Allie nodded silently, and walked out of the room. Eric shifted uncomfortably, looking at the way Korendil's hand was still resting on Beth's shoulder. "Listen, uh, Korendil, I, uh—" *Might as well spit it out.* "Look, Korendil, I still think you're crazy, but—thanks for being here."

He wanted to say something more, but the look in Korendil's eyes stopped him short. Eric left the room quickly, but he could feel Beth's and Korendil's eyes intent upon him as he closed the door.

The L.A.P.D. officers hauled the man away, slumped between them. Eric watched from the edge of the hallway. *Damn, but whatever that guy Korendil is, he sure knows how to deck somebody in one punch.*

And whatever he did to disarm the guy—

No. That wasn't real. You can't hit somebody that way, not with fire and music. It didn't happen.

Doesn't matter what I thought I saw. It wasn't real. It didn't happen. It's a drug flashback or something.

Or something.

Eric glanced at the half-empty dance floor, and noted the cluster of people over by the club's restrooms.

Amazing, how many people suddenly had to go to the bathroom when the cops showed up. Eric snickered to himself. *Sure hope they didn't clog up the toilets with all the stuff they were flushing down 'em—*

He walked towards the break room at the end of the

hall. He stopped outside the closed door, hearing quiet
conversation within.

". . . what I can't understand is how anyone could profit
from something like that. I mean, they'd lose the magic,
too, right?"

Beth's voice.

*She's talking to that loon about— Oh, terrific. He's
probably telling her how I have to be the Great Savior of
Middle Earth. What did I do to deserve this?*

He opened the door. Beth and Korendil looked up. "Hi,"
Eric said awkwardly, wishing he had knocked first. Beth and
Korendil were sitting very close together on the packing
crates.

Too close.

"Bo thinks we should start up real soon," Eric continued, noting the way the elf's—*actor's!*—arm was around
Beth's shoulders. "Take everybody's mind off all of the cops
that just came through the club."

Beth disengaged from Korendil and stood up, dusting
off her black pants. "Sounds good." She smiled at Korendil.
"I'd like to talk some more, Korendil. Maybe after the
show?"

Eric felt something tighten in his throat, at the warm
way Beth and Korendil were looking at each other, so
intense and intimate.

Damn it, it's her life, none of my business—

But he's an elf! Not even human!

*No, he's an actor, with good makeup, contact lenses, all
of that. He's just another guy. Another six-foot-five guy,
blond, built like a dancer, and handsome. Even if I don't
swing that way, he's damn handsome. I can see why she
likes him.*

*It's none of my business who Beth Kentraine gets involved
with—it's her life, not mine.*

*Maybe it's just that I'm on the rebound, but it hurts,
the way she's looking at him—*

"Eric, perhaps you could join us?" Korendil ventured,
gazing at him with an intent, worried expression. "I would
speak with both of you, if possible."

*Oh, great. Now the loon wants to flirt with Beth and
drive* me *nuts at the same time. Very economical.*

I can't handle this.

"Maybe later," Eric said, wishing he was anywhere else
but here. *Even Juilliard. At least when I was there, I had
reasons for thinking I was crazy.* "But we have to do the
show now." He started towards the door, not looking back.

*Maybe if I wish for it hard enough, this guy'll go back
to Oz or the North Pole or Santa Monica or wherever he
came from. It's worth a try.*

*I just don't want to think that I've gone completely,
utterly insane, that's all—*

—and I don't want this to be real.

6

Give Me Your Hand

"Wait a minute, Banyon."

Eric turned slowly, unwillingly. *I don't think I'm going to like what's coming.* "Yeah, Beth?"

She pushed her dark, ragged bangs back out from her eyes with a tired gesture. She looked wrung out.

Not surprising.

And preoccupied.

Which doesn't bode real well, either.

"I want to talk something out with you. Now. Just for a couple of minutes. I have this bad feeling that you're going to vanish the minute we finish the show."

Eric warily glanced at Korendil, then sat down on a crate. "What did you want to talk about?"

Beth sighed, giving Korendil a sidelong look. "What do you think?"

They've been talking about the elves, and that "Eric the Bard" bullshit. Damn it, Beth, how did you let him sucker you in so fast? I thought you were smarter than that!

"Uh, I don't know what he's been telling you, but—"

"You don't?" Her lips tightened. "Then you're dumber than I thought, Banyon."

He bristled. "Oh come on! You don't really believe this

92

guy, do you, Bethie? I mean, look at him! He has to be an actor. And those ears are fake, I know it—"

Eric reached out his hand towards the tip of one of Kory's ears, showing through the blond curls.

The fake elf held up his right hand in a graceful, but dangerous gesture of warning. There was a steely glint in his green eyes, a definite challenge, as clear as if he'd spoken aloud.

Touch my ears and you die, white boy.

Eric hesitated, suddenly remembering the pain he'd felt earlier this afternoon as his face met the wall at high speed.

He coughed, and turned his own gesture into a shrug.

Well, maybe I won't demonstrate how the ears are just a latex special effect . . .

He turned to the only other—marginally—sane person in the room. "Beth—listen to me. You're not a ten-year-old, or a member of Hobbits Anonymous. You can't really believe what he's saying. There's no such thing as elves. Or magic. Or any of that crap."

Beth leaned back, crossing her legs and surveying him with a faint smile on her lips. "Really? Then how do you explain what Korendil did to that creep in the hallway? How do you account for three-quarters of the people out there in the audience tonight? Have you taken a *good* look at some of those outfits? At the way they look?"

So she's seen them, too. "I don't know, maybe they all just showed up from a cast party on the Universal lot. It's a helluva lot more believable than a nightclub full of dancing elves." Eric shook his head, trying stubbornly to break through Beth's conviction. "I just don't believe in Santa Claus, the tooth fairy, or elves. As far as I'm concerned, this guy is playing a practical joke on all of us. I think Maureen paid him to do it; she's got enough connections. And she's always been a bit jealous of you. She'd be perfectly happy to get both of us with her prank."

"I told you he'd be difficult to convince, Lady Beth." *That* was from Korendil.

Eric gave him a dirty look.

The elf sighed, ignoring it. "For a Bard, he has a very closed mind."

That's it! *I'm sick of hearing that word!*

"Goddammit, I am *not* a Bard!"

The actor turned to face him. His voice was very soft, yet it demanded attention. "Then what are you?" he asked simply.

Eric was silent for a moment before speaking. "I don't know. I'm a musician. A reasonably-talented street musician. Sometimes I'm a composer. I don't know if I'm any good at it. And besides that?" He shrugged. "Not much else."

"No." Korendil shook his head solemnly, but with stubborn conviction. "You are a Bard. You must feel it, the magic that flows when you play your music. Everyone else can."

Midnight, alone in the grove, playing "Sheebeg Sheemore," then the music taking over, a melody strange and wild, as the trees bend down to listen—

Korendil continued relentlessly. "You can heal and harm and create with your magic. Glimpse the distant past or—" His voice suddenly took on a tone of desolation.

"—touch the future . . ."

The bleakness of the last three words threw Eric into the waking nightmare of that moment on the bus—

Los Angeles, grayness everywhere, no life, no joy, only misery like a living thing, dragging everything down, destroying all hope—

He shook off the clinging weariness, shook off the despair. *How can he do this? How can he reach into my thoughts and know exactly who I am and what's happened to me? That's not possible. Nobody can do that. That's— magic.*

Fear made him clench his jaw; made him try to deny that last thought.

No. This can't be real.

But—

The rope of fire—the music—

I wasn't stoned. I saw it, back there in the hallway. I

wasn't stoned on the bus, or this afternoon at the apartment. It was magic. And it was real.

I can't keep pretending that it's all fake. There's too many things that have happened, too much to disbelieve. It's real, as real as I am.

And if it's real—

Then so are my nightmares.

Oh shit.

Eric sat down slowly, before his knees went. "Okay," he said weakly. "You know. I don't know how you know, but—yeah, I saw the future. At least, I think it was the future, It was horrible "

Korendil nodded sadly. "You probably saw what would happen if the magic nexus was destroyed. Now do you see why that must not happen? *That* is what this city will become."

Eric shuddered, thinking of the desolation on the faces of the people in his vision. "When I saw that—there was a man, watching me from a limo. An older guy, with silver hair, and green eyes like yours—"

Green eyes, reaching inside where no one should see, violation, a hand that fouls all it touches—

"Perenor." The elf's voice was a whisper of apprehension threaded with pain.

Eric looked up at Korendil, startled. "What?"

Korendil's eyes were clouded, his face as still and pale as a death mask. "His name is Perenor. He was one of us, and now is our greatest enemy. Where did you see him? When?"

Perenor. I won't forget that name.

Eric shivered, remembering the despair, the hopelessness that had almost pushed him over the edge. "I saw him on Van Nuys Boulevard, this afternoon. It was weird it was like he recognized me, somehow he knew me."

Knew me, and tried to take me apart at the seams—and he knew every button to push. Every twitch. Whatever else is going on, I wasn't imagining that—it was real! What that bastard did to me, it was real!

Korendil's green eyes were troubled with things Eric

couldn't read. "I did not realize that Perenor knew of your existence. Perhaps he felt the magic in the place-of-festival when you awakened me, and decided to seek you out. Perhaps it was an accident—but I cannot believe that. If Perenor knows of you, then you are in great danger, Bard. He will hunt for you, knowing that you are the only one who can stop him."

*The only—hey, wait a second—*His horse sense reared and snorted in alarm. "What do you mean, the only one? You've got other people who are going to help you, right? I mean, you're pretty flashy with the magic, mister—"

"—Not compared to Perenor," the elf said, resignedly. "My power is nothing to his. Believe me, Bard Eric, the little power I have is insignificant beside even your own, untutored as you are. That is why we need you so very much."

Beth gave him a look.

Like— "Turn him down, and I just may decide never to speak to you again." Thanks, Beth.

"Even if I *do* help you," he said, trying to keep from sounding like he was ready to dive under one of the crates, " you don't expect me to take on this guy by myself, do you?"

Korendil gazed at him with rising hope and eagerness. "Then you will help us?"

He froze. *Oh shit. I just said that, didn't I? Me and my big mouth.*

Well, if I'm going to back out of this one, better do it quick.

He started to open his mouth, started to search for words to extricate himself without Beth disowning him—then stopped again, struck by something he wasn't certain he understood. A feeling that whatever he chose or said at this moment was incredibly important. And a feeling of conviction.

What if I am a Bard, like this guy says? What if I really do have some kind of power that his people need?

What if I'm the only one that can help them?

If that's true, and I walk away from this guy, I'll be doing the worst, lowest thing I've ever done in my life.

I can't live with that.

Eric looked away from those too-bright eyes for a moment. "I—I don't know," he replied, haltingly. "I mean, I'm just Eric Banyon. I'm not some great hero out of the legends, here to save your ass. I'm just a busker, a wandering musician . . . God, it's hard enough for me to stick around one place long enough to finish a run of Faire, let alone fight a Crusade! Aren't there any other bards around who can help you?"

Korendil shook his head, wearily. "No. Not one. Either they do not believe, or they do not have the power to aid us. And most of the elves are Dreaming, trapped in despair and apathy. Even the great Prince, our leader, is lost to Dreaming. It may be too late to save them, I don't know. But if you will help me . . ."

He gazed at Eric now with pleading, and something akin to worship.

Or awe. Great. Now I've got an elf who's convinced that I'm the Second Coming of Christ. In addition to whatever it is that he wants me to do.

This really is too weird for words. Even If I really do believe him, I'm still not certain I can deal with this . . .

"So, what are we going to do?"

Eric and Korendil both glanced up in surprise.

Beth Kentraine stretched, standing up slowly. She looked at them questioningly, hands on her hips. "Well? What are we going to do about this?"

"We?" Eric repeated.

"Yeah, bucko. *We.* Did you think I wasn't going to get involved in this? Get real, Banyon."

She smiled, but her eyes were distant, looking off at someone, something that wasn't in the Here and Now. "When I was a kid, a friend of mine told me about elves, how they were real. How he'd seen them, talked with them, how there were maybe even a few of them living in California. I believed him, he'd never told me anything else that wasn't true, no matter how strange it had sounded. I used to dream about them—but I never really thought I'd see one."

She turned her gaze back to the present; looked from

Eric to Korendil and back again. "Now, I *have* seen them. Now I *know* they're real—hell, there's one sitting right here in front of me—and I hear that they're in real trouble. What the hell do you expect me to do? Of *course* I'm going to help." She grinned. "Just try and *stop* me, Banyon."

Before Eric could speak, there was a sharp knock at the door. "Hey, guys, are you in there?" They could hear Bo's anxious voice through the thin plywood. "We've got a crowd waiting out here, and they're getting tired of the canned stuff. Are you going to start up soon?"

"Just a sec, Bo!" Beth called to him. She turned back to Eric and the elf. "We'll talk more after the gig, right?"

"Right," Korendil said, glancing at Eric.

Yeah, right. Terrific. Now Beth's involved in this lunacy, too. I don't know if this is going to be dangerous or not— I don't want her to get hurt—

He followed her out the door, heading for the stage, thinking furiously.

I've got no idea what this is all going to cost. Or even what or who we're going to have to face—like that Perenor guy. He really did mess with my mind; a little more and I would have been playing tag on the Ventura Freeway. What could he do to Bethie?

This could be worse than dangerous. I don't want to think of him doing something like that to her.

But as she took her place in front of her mike, he looked at the straight line of her back, and sighed with resignation.

I know her. There is nobody in the world that can out-stubborn Beth Kentraine. Once she's made up her mind, she won't budge. There's no way I'll be able to convince her to stay out of this.

Terrific. Three of us committed to this idiocy: me, an elf, and a rock singer. Against God knows what. Shit. We should be committed.

Maybe we should get some cards made up: The Unholy Trinity. Weddings, Bar Mitzvahs and Parties. Worlds saved, only a modest additional fee—

    ❧   ❧   ❧

The Porsche banked sharply around the curve, barely touching the dividing yellow line, then swerved back for the next turn. A professional race-car driver might have taken that curve at a tighter angle, but no one else.

The engine purred as the driver downshifted for the canyon hills that rose stark and shadowed above the accelerating car. The lights of the city reflected off the glistening black paint, glittering against the windshield's glass, brighter than the stars in the night sky above Mulholland Drive.

Another turn, at a speed that most would consider reckless. A policeman would have called it illegal. But for the driver, it was only skill, reaching for the edge. Perfectly controlled. Flawless.

A test of excellence.

Ria Llewellyn clenched black-gloved hands on the steering wheel, ignoring the strands of blonde hair flying haphazardly in the wind from the Porsche's half-open window, concentrating on the road, and driving at the limits of her abilities.

Damn him!

The Porsche banked around another tight curve. For a moment, the sports car skidded towards the edge of the canyon, the steep stone wall blurring past, only inches away from the Porsche. Then Ria tightened her grip on the steering wheel, expertly bringing the car back to the center of the twisting canyon road.

Right in the middle of the goddamn board meeting. "Ria, I need to see you. The Japanese restaurant in Studio City, one hour."

And when I ask him what in the hell is so important I need to leave a critical strategy session at ten o'clock at night, all he says is "Korendil has escaped . . ."

She sighed, brushing long blonde hair back from her face with a gesture of annoyance. *As if one person—even a warrior of the Old Blood—could make a difference in this. I told him we've secured the land, it's already signed for, nothing and no one is going to stop it now. Definitely not a fool who's spent the last ten years asleep under an oak tree . . .*

Like the rest of those fools. Unable to see the real world around them. Living in Dreaming—hell, living in shopping malls! When everything they could possibly desire is so close, within their reach—

Like Mother, in that commune somewhere—Mendocino? Marin? I don't remember. Not that it matters, I never see her anyway. How could she give up everything that Father could offer her—for that? What a sham she is, to preach about caring, then walk out on us before I was even in kindergarten. And what did she get? Tie-dyed T-shirts, drugs and "love." "Love," what a joke, what hypocrisy.

It's all escapism, hiding from reality. That's all these fools are doing. Like Mother.

Except now, it's too late for that. They're going to lose everything. Even if Korendil is free, it's too late for him to do anything.

A wailing siren interrupted Ria's thoughts. She glanced into the rearview mirror, and saw the flashing red-blue lights of the police motorcycle, close behind her.

A motorcycle cop, on Mulholland at night? Unusual. A bit of bad luck that he spotted me. But it doesn't really matter; it'll take only a moment to be corrected—

She pulled over to the side of the road, waiting for the helmeted policeman to dismount from the white police-model Kawasaki. His boots made sharp crunching noises on the rough gravel as he walked towards the black Porsche.

"Good evening, officer." Ria smiled at him through the open window.

How pleasant. A handsome motorcycle cop. That curly brown hair would be quite attractive if he let it grow out a little longer·and got rid of that mustache. Why do all the policemen in L.A. have mustaches?

"Your driving license and car registration, ma'am. I'm writing you up for reckless and exhibitionist driving—"

"Here's my license." She reached down to the black purse on the seat beside her, removed the license from her wallet and handed it to him.

"This says your name is"—he glanced up at her over the

edge of the laminated piece of paper—"Arianrhod Llewellyn? Is that correct?"

She smiled, gazing into his eyes. "Absolutely correct."

Brown eyes, ordinary, very human. But reach beyond, brushing past surprise and disbelief, and you can touch, and take control, and change—

Brief struggles, like a small bird fluttering in my hand, trying to escape. They always try to escape, never realizing that it's already over . . .

The cop stared at her blankly, unable to look away, Ria's driving license trembling slightly in his hands. His right hand edged towards the .38 holstered at his hip.

No. You are mine, now. Be still.

Ria surveyed the man standing beside her, motionless. *Unfortunately, I do not have time for you tonight, even if you are a handsome, obviously virile man. But, if I ever see you again—*

She released him, breaking the spell. The officer shook his head slowly, dazed. "I—I, uh, I'm just going to give you a warning miss. Please drive more carefully."

"Thank you officer." Ria smiled to herself as the cop walked unsteadily towards his parked motorcycle.

Remember me. Dream that one day I will call you.

A pity that Father needs to speak with me tonight. That man could have proved to be an interesting . . . diversion.

She waited until the cop had left, then started the Porsche, driving through the shadowed canyon. At Laurel Canyon, she turned left, and a moment later the lights of the Valley were visible before her, scintillating jewels against the darkness.

Beautiful, but I would rather be back in Century City, finishing up the contract for the meeting tomorrow—

Dammit, Father, why tonight?

Ten minutes later, she parked the Porsche in front of the entrance to the restaurant. The valet opened the door for her. His eyes brightened when he saw the folded bill she handed him with the keys. "Make sure nobody scratches the paint."

"Yes, ma'am." His eyes followed her, hungrily, as she

strode to the restaurant door. She smiled to herself and gave her hips a little extra twitch, just for his benefit. She could feel the heat of his eyes on her as she reached for the lacquered black door handle.

Dream on, little man. Only—this dream costs more than you'd ever want to pay.

She stepped inside, glancing around the entrance. A distinguished older man rose from his seat near the koi pond, and moved gracefully towards her.

"Good evening, dear," the silver-haired man said, and she leaned close so he could kiss her cheek. "You're looking especially lovely tonight."

She offered him a hint of icy smile. Enough so that he could read her annoyance—not enough so that he could read how *very* annoyed she was.

He took her arm to lead her towards the back of the restaurant. "Kyoshi's holding a table for us. Have you had any dinner yet?"

"Not really."

Damn him, he really wants something from me, I can tell. Of course, he'll never just come out and say it. We'll have to go through this whole dinner routine first. "Some sushi, maybe. And hot sake would be wonderful. It's been a rough day."

"You'll have to tell me about it." He maneuvered them to the table, isolated behind a colorful paper screen and a small stand of potted bamboo.

"Sake, Kyoshi," he instructed the waiter standing patiently beside the table, "and a tray of sushi to start with."

Ria sat back in the chair as the waiter hurried away, and surveyed her father thoughtfully. Was it her imagination, or were there faint lines at the edges of his eyes? Probably not—he was never less than perfect.

As always, his silver hair was immaculately barbered, carefully masking the tips of his long, slightly-pointed ears. But nothing could disguise his eyes, the cold emerald-green, slitted black pupils.

At least my eyes are human. I suppose I should thank Mother for that.

A twinge of something, not quite concern, touched her briefly. *He looks tired. This Korendil affair must be worrying him more than I thought. Unless it's something else that he wants—*

I suppose I might as well start the game myself.

"As much as I enjoy seeing you, Father, I must admit that tonight isn't the best night for this. Did I tell you that we're about to sign the investment deal? Twelve million in paper, tomorrow at noon. My execs are still at the office, hammering out the details. And I'm sure they're wondering just what was so important that their boss had to disappear immediately."

To see her father—

His green eyes glinted with hidden amusement. "I'm sure they have faith in you, my dear. They probably just think you're closing another deal, right now."

"Am I?"

Her father smiled. "Perhaps."

You bastard. Games within games, even with your own daughter.

I know what he sees. His beautiful little girl. A corporate executive. Half of the Old Blood, half human. Not quite his equal in power, but damn close. Someone he can manipulate and control, and use in his games.

But you taught me not to trust others, Father. To believe only in myself, and what I can do, and never let anyone past my guard. So of course as I grew older, I realized that included you as well. You never put that variable in your equation, did you?

Now you think you can snap your fingers and I'll come running to help you—

It'll snow in hell first.

The sushi arrived, with two small ceramic containers of hot rice wine. Ria and her father were silent as the wine was poured, a brief respite in the verbal fencing match. Parry, riposte. Feint and feint again.

Ria sipped the steaming-hot wine, then dipped a piece of octopus sushi in the small bowl of soy sauce beside her, savoring the unusual texture.

And waited for her father to make the next move.

Which of course, he isn't going to do.

Perenor sampled another piece of sushi, then mixed more green wasanabe horseradish into his soy dipping bowl. "Try the crab, my dear, it's really quite excellent tonight."

He's trying to bait me. And, damn him, he's succeeding. I don't want to spend all night sitting here, making polite conversation, trying to figure out what he wants from me. Not when I've got twelve mil in paperwork sitting back at the office.

She heaved an obvious sigh, and gave her head a little shake. "All right, Father. Why are you so concerned about Korendil? What does it matter if he's free? He's just one person, and he isn't going to awaken the Dreamers, or desert them to rouse the High Court; he can't do anything against us. He isn't even one-tenth of the mage that you are."

The silver-haired man was silent for a long moment. There was an indefinable expression in his emerald-ice eyes. "Ria, what would you say if I told you that there was a Bard in Los Angeles? A true Bard, with all the abilities of the ancient Bards?"

"I'd say that you've been drinking too much sake," Ria said flatly. "There are no more true Bards. Taliesen was the last one, and he died a thousand years ago." She pondered that a moment. "Well, perhaps O'Carolan. But he was a drunkard, and he never used his magic."

Her father picked up another piece of sushi, a pale-orange fantailed shrimp, and gazed at it thoughtfully. "You shouldn't discount what I say so quickly, Arianrhod."

Ria stared in silence at her father.

It's true, then.

A Bard, in Los Angeles. A true Bard.

But that's impossible—

"All right, you've found a Bard." She shrugged. "And Korendil is free. That still doesn't add up to any danger that *I* can see."

"You still don't understand, do you?" Perenor said tersely. "Korendil is the one who found this Bard, somehow—or the Bard found him. This one has great potential—too great.

I saw that when I encountered him, recognized his power, and touched the boy's mind. I've taken steps to neutralize him. but I want to be rid of Korendil before he brings any other players into this game. And for that, I need your help."

Ria almost laughed aloud. *Why, father mine, you're not feeling inadequate now, are you? A little bit of self-doubt, here? Is that why you needed my help so many years ago, to trap Korendil in that grove?*

You are getting older, even for one of the Old Blood— you wouldn't happen to be getting weaker, as well? You power fading, even as mine grows in strength? Now, that would be an amusing thought—

"I imagine I could help you with this, Father," she purred. "Of course, I would like to know what's in this for me . . ."

Perenor's fist slammed down on the table, rattling the sake bottles. The young couple at the table across from them glanced up at them in surprise, then carefully looked away.

He leaned forward, speaking in a low whisper. "Don't play games with me; and don't forget, daughter, exactly what is at stake here. This is our chance to finally rid ourselves of any who might thwart us. To avenge ourselves on those who cast me out, who refused to acknowledge you. And to gain such power, power as you've never dreamed of it—"

"I have power," Ria said, cutting through his words. "Power in the humans' world, true, but it's good enough for me. I have my business, and money, and control in this city. Why should I help you? What does it matter to me what happens to any of the Old Blood? They're fading now, they're no threat to anyone, least of all to me. I see no reason to exert myself, to involve myself, just because you want to amuse yourself with another game."

He leaned back a little, his eyes glittering, and toyed with another piece of sushi. "Even if, with a little 'exertion,' you could win immortality?"

Breath failed her momentarily. "What are you talking about?"

Perenor shrugged. "I thought you knew. You . . .

inherited . . . certain gifts from me, Ria, but you *are* half-human, after all. Eventually, you'll grow old and die."

An unpleasant smile passed briefly across his lips.

"I'm sure," he continued, "that I'll still be alive to see it. That, of course, is one of the reasons I suggested that we purchase the Elizabethan Faire land. I was thinking primarily of you, my dear, though, of course, I will gain a few benefits from this as well. Once we have control of the nexus, you'll never have to worry about this again. The power itself will hold time at bay and keep you young."

He reached out, touching a strand of her pale blonde hair with mocking tenderness. "You're so lovely, such a remarkable child. I truly would hate to see you grow old, see your beauty wither away."

She tasted the bitterness of being outmaneuvered. *I'm sure you would, Father. I know I'd feel just the same way, if you were the one who was aging and dying.*

Very well; for now, our goals are the same. But, when this is over . . .

She laughed lightly. "Father, of course I'll help you. I, I just thought this was part of your fight against the Old Blood, and that was why you wanted control of the magic nexus. To avenge what they did to you, so many years ago. I never dreamed it was more than that . . ."

Perenor leaned back in his chair, a faint and satisfied half-smile flickering across his handsome features. "Well, now you know." He glanced at his watch. "There's time enough to deal with this tonight. I know where Korendil is—this shouldn't take very long."

The silver-haired man tossed several bills onto the table, then stood, extending his arm to his daughter. "Shall we?"

"Of course."

But I won't forget this evening. And, once we control the nexus—

—we'll talk again of power and promises, Father.

7

Beware, Oh Take Care

*Korendil, Knight of Elfhame Sun-Descending, squire of
the High Court, Magus Minor, and Child of Danann—
Fine titles, but will any of that aid me now?*

Korendil sighed, gathered borrowed hope about him like
his borrowed finery, and stepped out into the crowded hall
of the place called "Diverse Pleasures." Hope was such a
fragile thing—and it rested upon such fragile mortal shoulders.

He watched the young Bard, Eric, follow the lovely witch
to their places on the stage. Such frighteningly fragile mortal
shoulders . . .

The Bard hardly looked his part. Taliesen—or so Korendil's elders had told him—had been as skilled with blade
and bow as with his harp. Eric was small and thin, with a
face that would have been sweet, had it not been so wary,
so marked with distrust. A very attractive young man—

But *not* a warrior, nor anything like one. And just now,
a hesitant man, one uncertain about what he had just agreed
to.

A very *young* man.

Korendil knew exactly how he felt. Korendil was a very
young elf, scarcely two hundred years old as the mortals
counted time. There was only one younger than he in all

of the High or Low Courts of Elfhame Sun-Descending and
Elfhame Misthold, and that was his cousin to the north.
There were too many times when he was uncertain; too
many times when he felt a fool. Especially of late.

But I cannot just give up. I cannot allow this to happen—

He glanced about at the Dreaming elves, scattered
through the crowd like so many exotic butterflies. *I could
conjure my own garments,* he thought absently, while counting the number of elvenkind who had somehow gathered
here, and marking those who seemed by their eyes to be
the least lost in Dreaming. *I would not look so out of place
in them here. Then I could give Bard Eric his property back
. . .* He recalled the Bard's resentful stare when the young
man thought that Korendil was not aware of his glances.
They take possessions so seriously, these mortals—

*But if I did that, I should only need them again before
I left—and besides, I have already altered them to my own
use. Would that I knew them well enough to conjure dupli-
cates. I suppose I could try kenning them now, so that I
could duplicate them later.*

He took stock of himself, first, and decided against the
idea.

*A distinctly foolish notion. I am no kind of a mage, not
really. Subduing that madman expended enough of my magic
as it was. I have little power to waste on kenning. Not if
I am going to have any hope of Awakening any of the
others.*

*Perhaps the Bard's music will help. That is surely what
drew them all here this evening. Although he scarcely seems
to believe it himself.*

Korendil smiled to himself, remembering Eric's shocked
expression when he had first seen the warrior-elf in his
place-of-dwelling. *So young, so eager to disbelieve. Would
that this Bard was a Taliesen, older and powerful, ready
and willing to do battle with our Enemy. But if Bard Eric
was as skilled as Taliesen, Perenor would have learned of
his existence before this, learned of him and taken steps to
dispose of him . . .*

No. Better this way. At least now, I can have hope that he will quickly learn what he must do to save us. And perhaps, if we are very careful, Perenor will not be able to find us.

He moved out of the little space by the hallway and into the milling crowd. His goal was a table near one wall, with three brilliantly-costumed elfmaids on tall stools about it, like three bright tropical birds upon their perches. Two of the three he knew, both of the High Court: Variel and Mayanir, sisters; and both—at least ten years ago—Awake enough to *know* what was happening to them.

Awake enough to have begun to fear.

And that was before the danger to the nexus, he thought soberly, easing between two chattering groups of mortals who seemed as oblivious to the presence of elvenkind as the elves were to them. *If there are any that I can Wake— surely that will be Val and Mai.*

Loud, discordant laughter made him wince as he passed the bar. His sensitive hearing was suffering in this place. *I cannot see how the Bard can tolerate it. The mortals' world seems to have changed so very much in ten years— but then, that is the way of their world.* He sighed. *And the world of Elvenkin is different as well. I cannot say that either of them have changed for the better.*

He politely declined the advances of a very drunk mortal woman, one with too much flesh crammed into too little clothing. Moments later he declined again—with more grace, and a touch of sympathy—the advances of a shy and bespectacled young mortal man. *He* was equally drunk, but Kory could read in him that he had so indulged out of unhappiness, and in an attempt to bolster his nerve.

These mortals were all so rawly open. It was hard to move among them and feel their thoughts and emotions jostling his mind as their bodies jostled his.

And so few of them were here out of joy. *That* was the saddest of all.

The elves were still, deep pools of silence in this jungle. Too silent—but a relief from the screeching of the mortals. Unless you needed, as Korendil needed, to rouse them.

Finally he reached his goal, the three elfmaids poised beneath an overhead spotlight. *In other times they would have been lit softly by their own magic. But that was before the magic was choked off by so much cold iron about us.* He stood beside the table, patient in the shadow, waiting for one of them to notice him.

None of them did.

Their eyes were bright but vacant, like all the others he'd seen here this night. They sipped at drinks, listened with half an ear to the music playing, and giggled conversationally to one another, weaving a circle of attention that closed them inside and Kory out.

He decided to violate protocol. "Val—" he said, touching her blue-silk-clad arm, sending a little tingle of carefully hoarded power from himself to her. *"Val—"*

She blinked, turned very slowly, and looked into his eyes. She blinked again, and licked her lips. "Hi," she said, uncertainly. "Hi. I know you—don't I?"

"It's Korendil, Val," he replied with emphasis, trying to get her to focus on him. "Kory. You certainly do know me. "

"Oh, yeah," she said, blinking again. "Hi, Kory. You haven't been around for a while. Have you been away somewhere?"

He reined in his temper, and refrained from swearing. *Is this the depth to which we've sunk?*

"Perenor and that half-Blooded daughter of his trapped me in the nexus grove," he said as forcefully as he could. "It's been ten years, Val."

"Oh, wow," she said, a little more interest stirring in the back of her eyes, focusing a little better on him. "Ten years? Gods. That long? Like—you were trapped?"

"Yes," he replied fiercely, fighting with Dreaming for her attention, spinning out his feeble magic to try and pull her back to something like the maid he had known. "That long. Val, listen—" she started to gaze off past his shoulder and he touched her arm again to bring her back. *"Listen.* This is important. The nexus grove is in danger. Someone is going to destroy it un—"

"Ladies and Gentlemen," Beth Kentraine's voice called

over the babble of the crowd. *"We are Spiral Dance. We're back and ready to rock!"*

Kory cursed in every language he knew. The moment the first note resounded, he lost Val completely. She was off her stool and onto the dance floor; every word, and even his existence, completely forgotten.

He tried again, with another elf he recognized. Eldenor a warrior of the High Court, who currently sported a purple mohawk and a black leather jumpsuit so tight he must have magicked it on.

Eldenor was alone, sitting in a two-person booth near the bandstand; his eyes fastened on the Bard, drinking in every note the young man played. When Beth began singing a traditional Celtic tune, and Eric built a foundation for her voice to soar over, Eldenor's eyes began to take on a glow of *here-ness*. A sense that he was at least focusing on something. Kory slipped into the other side of the booth.

"Eldenor?" he said, when the other took no note of his presence.

"Yeah?" The eyes didn't waver from the bandstand.

"Eldenor, don't you remember me?"

"Shit no, man."

Kory closed his eyes, asked for patience, and tried again. "Eldenor, it's Kory. Korendil. You helped train me. To be a warrior. Remember?"

The eyes flickered briefly from the stage to him, returning to the stage. "Oh, yeah. Kory. You went away."

Kory reached out and seized the other by the elbows, sending power in the kind of shock he'd used to rouse the Bard this afternoon. "Eldenor, I *didn't go away*. I was *imprisoned*. By Perenor and his daughter—" The shock brought only the barest of responses, and Kory lost his temper. *"Damn you, Eldenor,"* he cried, shaking the other. "This is important! The power nexus is going to be destroyed!"

As if to underscore his words, the lights flickered briefly. Kory sensed that a storm had begun outside.

Eldenor shook his head, and looked at Kory, a faint hint of puzzlement in his expression. "Hey man, chill out," he said. "Nothing's all that important—"

Then Eric began playing a solo, and Kory lost him completely.

He tried several more, but all with the same lack of result, and all the power he used to try and shock them back into an understanding of their peril vanished without a sign of any reaction. They were so drained of magic that it just trickled into them without making an impression. Any glimmer of hope began to fade before despair, and the depression that failure after failure left him with. *How can this be, that they are so completely lost? What has happened to them in the ten years since I was imprisoned?*

The lights flickered again just as the band finished the Celtic song, and flickered a third time as they began a rock number. And in the moment between those flickers of light, Kory caught a familiar lift of a head, a high, proud profile—and his heart raced.

Blessed Danann. He's here. My prince—

He shoved his way through the crowd, paying scant heed to those who swore at him or cast angry glances in his wake. He fought to reach the table at the rear where he'd seen that glimpse of majesty—

Only he reached it to find just how ruined the majesty had become.

Kory could feel something dreadfully wrong as he forced his way between packed chairs to the table at the back where the Prince was sitting alone. He knew that the *wrongness* went deep when he saw the way the Prince was sitting, slouched down in his chair, with his eyes blank and his hand wavering a little as he reached for his drink.

But when he recognized just what it was that Prince Terenil was drinking he froze in horror. Dark brown, effervescent—

Coca-Cola.

There was a pitcher of the stuff on the table, and it was three-fourths empty.

An elf could drink any five mortals under the table. An elf could shrug off the effects of most of the drugs that left mortals paralyzed or insane. But this—this stuff that mortals imbibed with such careless ease—*this* was another thing altogether.

Caffeine. Soft drinks, coffee, tea.

To the Old Blood it was deadly.

It enhanced Dreaming; induced hallucinations. Destroyed will and removed the elf that indulged in it from any semblance of reality.

And Prince Terenil, the pride of the High Court on this side of the Hill, was sitting in a mortal nightclub, his eyes glazed, his hands shaking, and most of a pitcher of cola plainly inside him.

Kory was not even certain that he could hear the Bard's music, much less Feel his magic as the others so clearly did.

He had thought he had seen despair at its worst when he had first awakened, and heard the talk of the place-of-festival. How at the festival's end the place would be leveled, the groves of oaks destroyed—including the one that anchored the magic nexus to this side of the Hill. He had thought that there was nothing that could possibly be worse—

Until now.

He looked at the ruin of his liege and lord, and wanted to howl his despair to the four winds.

Instead, he sat himself carefully by Terenil's side, and used most of the last of his magic to try to touch the Prince's mind.

By Danann, I don't know if I can even find *it, much less touch it!*

He could only imagine one reason for Terenil falling to this state. The Prince had given up any hope of Awakening his people. It must have happened soon after Kory, his friend and closest advisor, had fallen prey to that traitor Perenor, and vanished from the ken of the elves. Perhaps that vanishment itself had triggered the Prince's fall.

"My lord?" he prompted verbally, holding his despair at arm's length.

The Prince gave no sign that he had heard.

Blessed Danann—is there anything left of the warrior

*that once held us all in awe? And if he has sunk so low—
what hope is there of saving the rest?*

"My lord, it is Kory. I've returned to you, my lord."

The Prince stared at his hand, and slowly raised the glass
of sparkling poison to his lips.

And drank.

Kory restrained himself from slapping the foul stuff out
of his hand, and spoke again, as gently as he could.

"My lord, I have news. I have found a Bard, a human
Bard. A true Bard, and one of such power as I have never
seen. He has agreed to be our Champion, my lord. He has
said he will help me Awaken the Dreamers and save our
magic."

Still no sign that Terenil even knew he was not alone.

"My lord, I did not leave you willingly. The traitor
Perenor imprisoned me in the Grove, after his daughter had
lured me there and struck me down with trickery. This Bard
that I have found—he loosed the spells of lock and ward,
and woke me out of my spell of slumber. He freed me from
Perenor's power, and he is untutored! Just think, my lord,
when I have taught him to use his Gift—"

Terenil made no response, none at all.

If Kory had been alone, he would have put his head
down on the table and wept.

I still may, he thought, swallowing hard. *Only let me be
by myself—and I shall weep and not be ashamed. Oh my
lord, my beloved lord—*

"We have a chance, my lord. With the help of this Bard,
we have at least a chance."

He stood, as Terenil continued to stare at his hand, the
one holding the glass. Blinking slowly, but showing no other
sign that he was still conscious.

I cannot stay here, and still remain sane, he whispered
to himself. *Perhaps I should go and wait for the Bard to
complete his work—*

He began to make his way back across the room, when
he felt eyes upon him. Eyes with power behind them,
watching him with scarcely-concealed venom and contempt.

He stopped, as the lights flickered once again; stopped

and turned, scanning the room with all his senses, looking for the one who radiated such power and menace.

The enemy obligingly displayed himself; moving from the shadows to the edge of the dance floor. The light fell clearly on him, flickering blues and greens illuminating his malicious smile.

Kory's despair was quickly forgotten in a wash of something far more personal.

Fear.

Just as there was no mistaking the Prince, no matter how low he had sunk, there was no mistaking *this* face. Carefully arranged silver hair, hooded, brilliantly green eyes, high cheekbones—and power coiled within, power that showed Kory's magics to be the amateur efforts that they were.

Perenor.

Exiled traitor from Elfhame Sun-Descending. Showing himself arrogantly to the young elf who had been his prisoner for so many years, and now was the only functional Champion in the mortals' world.

The supremely powerful, saturnine elf had avoided elvenkind since his banishment. Perenor hadn't even gone after Kory himself; he had sent his daughter, Arianrhod, to lure him into his hands.

But here he was—and there could only be one reason that he showed himself so plainly.

He *knew* that Kory had escaped from his imprisonment.

And he was hunting for him.

Kory stood silent, staring at Perenor, unable to look away.

And he knows I'm here. He's searching for me. He knows that I escaped, he knows about the Bard, and he's here, searching for both of us—

As he stared at Perenor, the older elf's eyes continued to scan across the crowd, until they rested upon the object of their hunt.

Perenor smiled at Kory.

:Good evening, Korendil. What a pleasant surprise to find you here.:

Kory froze; and found a single phrase echoing frantically around in his head, a phrase borrowed from mortals—

Oh shit—

∾   ∾   ∾

Eric stood silently on the stage, the flute held lightly in his hands, listening to Beth Kentraine's warm, rich voice, singing the lyrics to an old Gaelic song. To his annoyance the lights flickered again, briefly plunging the Dive into darkness, cutting off a half-second of the music as the PA system blinked off and on again.

Great. The thunderstorm must be playing games with the electrical grid. I sure hope we don't have a blackout in this club. That's all we need—ten million drunken idiots trying to run for the doors. And who knows how many drunken elves doing whatever it is drunken elves do in the dark.

The dancers on the floor didn't even seem to notice.

Hell, don't worry about it, Eric. Worry about the solo coming up next verse instead. Bethie's already given me The Look.

This is the next-to-last song. Thank God. Just a little more, then we'll be done for the night, I can crash—

—go home, drink a few, and think about all of this. About Korendil. An elf, for Chrissake, asking me to save his people.

I'm still not certain whether I really believe all of this or not. Maybe I'll just wake up tomorrow morning, and all of this will have been a dream . . .

Yeah, right. Not bloody likely.

Eric lifted the flute to his lips, a quick breath before the phrase. *It's a beautiful song, needs some nice ornamentation. I'll just play with it see where it takes me . . .* He closed his eyes and began to play.

The notes were pure and clear, a delicate line slowly growing stronger, like a kite tugging at the string, trying to break free. *A little more, holding that high C for just an instant longer, then letting go, falling away, fading. Good. Now Beth is taking the vocal line again—*

He opened his eyes, blinking at the sudden brightness of the stage lights. *I like that song. We've been doing a lot of the old trad tunes tonight, more than Spiral Dance usually does. Last gig, we only did two slow ballads, the rest was hard rock. Tonight, it's almost half and half. Very strange.*

He looked out over the audience, seeing the colorful costumes past the glare, the dancers moving in swirling, regal patterns amid the colored lights. *No, not strange at all, not for tonight. The whole evening has been like this, mysterious and—and magical. Well, I guess that when half your audience is non-human—*

—strange things are bound to happen.

I wonder where Korendil is? I can't see him out there in the crowd.

Thinking of the elf made him flush slightly, uncomfortably. *Maybe I should apologize to him. I've been a real bastard to everybody, these last few days. And I took a lot of that out on him. Sure, I thought he was a nut case, but still, I could have been more polite about it. Of course, he did steal my clothes and he did knock me into a wall, but still—*

Then he heard it. A soft whisper, a strange female voice, low and breathy, barely audible.

:*Bard. Look at me.*:

Eric immediately glanced up at Beth, singing with her eyes closed, intent upon the last verse of the song. *Bethie? No, she's not even looking my way. Must have been somebody else—*

A faint whisper, lightly pulling at him, like—*Like a kite on a string—*

:*Look at me, look at me . . .*:

He looked out at the crowd, too far away for a low whisper to carry that distance. *What in the hell? Who said that?*

God, no. I'm starting to go crazy again—

Then he saw her, at the edge of the stage. Watching him. *Oh my.*

Red silk. Tailored, expensive, and very tight around the right curves. Blond hair, slightly curly, perfectly framing that face, those vivid blue eyes.

What is someone like her doing at The Dive? She looks like a fashion model, the kind of lady you see in Westwood or Beverly Hills, escorted by some handsome guy wearing a five-hundred-dollar suit. Not the kind of lady you see alone in a sleazy nightclub in Van Nuys!

She's beautiful. Very beautiful.
And she's staring right at me.
Oh my God.

Eric forced himself to look away, trying to remember
what song he was supposed to he playing. *Oh yeah, the
Gaelic song. Right. Shit, where are we? Last verse?*

He saw Beth looking at him, puzzled. Then her eyes
moved past him, to the woman standing in the shadows.
Beth's eyes narrowed.

The song ended, just as Eric remembered what key it
was in, and was about to start playing again. He stopped
himself, just in time.

*Terrific. What's happened to my brain? I think it's turned
to guacamole. Thank God, we've only got one more song
in the show. I don't think I could deal with anything else
tonight.*

A moment of applause, then Jim started the intro for
the last song, a subtle, light pattern on the rim of the snare
drum. Beth joined in a moment later: rough, resounding
chords on the Fender. Then Allie on synth, a quick run,
leading into the melody. Eric smiled at the intensity of the
music, fierce and demanding, building with each moment.
Damn, but I like this one.

Then Beth's voice, breaking through, taking over . . .

> "Starlight and shadow, end to begin,
> Balancing, changing, losing to win.
> Make the choice, take the chance,
> Reach for dreams and more.
> And in that moment you will know
> The spiral dance won't ever let you go!"

First solo was Allie on synth, starting quiet, then letting
it rip into a jazz run, her fingers moving almost too fast
to see over the DX7's keyboard. The audience roared as
Jim took the next solo, pounding on the drums like a wild
man, his hair flying, looking like it was glowing in the glare
of the stage lights.

He's wrapping it, about to hand it to me—now!

Eric hit a high D, a rasping trill, wailing descant down the scale. A moment later, he heard Beth echoing the flute line on the Fender, following him down. He smiled to himself, starting a fast jazz break, which she caught and held. Then they went into a counterpoint, the electric guitar and flute fighting each other, each striving to hit harder, higher, then finally blending on the last note, harmonizing matching each other perfectly. Eric tossed in a final trill, unresolved, a ringing defiant cry.

The last note faded into silence.

The lights suddenly cut out, leaving them standing in shadow. A moment later, the screams and cheers of the audience began reverberating around them.

Now that was a nice bit of work . . .

The lights came back up. From across the stage, Beth grinned at Eric, then leaned closer to the mike. "Thank you, and good night."

The stage lights faded down again, to be replaced by the normal club lights. Eric wiped the sweat off his forehead, glancing back to see Beth hugging Allie and Jim, then starting to help them disassemble the stage gear.

A terrific gig. I should play with Bethie and the Spirallers more often. This was a fun night. Definitely weird, definitely wired, but fun.

Eric looked out at the club, the emptying dance floor.

I wonder where Korendil is? I thought he'd be here, waiting for us at the end of the gig.

Oh, what the hell. I'm too tired to deal with all of that "Save the universe" stuff tonight, anyhow. Might as well pack it up and head home. Maybe I can hitch a ride with Bethie—

A soft murmur, insinuating into his thoughts.

:Yes. You are the one.:

Eric looked around in surprise. *Say what?*

Shit. I'm hearing voices again. Dammit, I had myself convinced that I'm not crazy. This isn't fair.

"No. It isn't. Look at me."

Slowly, he turned to the side of the stage, to the blonde woman that he somehow knew was still standing there.

He dazedly shook his head. *Who is she? I wonder if—if she—she looks like she might want to meet me. Talk to me. Maybe—maybe she does . . .*

Eric walked several steps towards her, then hesitated. *I'm imagining things again. This time, instead of an elf, it's a beautiful blonde, making eyes at me from across the stage. Reality check, Eric. You are* not *her type.*

But her eyes—blue eyes—it's like she's calling to me—

He took another step, and another, moving towards the blonde woman, unable to look away from that electric blue gaze.

Blue eyes—reaching out to me—drawing me to her—

Something was wrong. Eric tried to remember what it was. *Something about being on the bus, looking out the window, and—something—trying to remember—this has happened before. Hasn't it? I—can't remember—*

Then the woman smiled, and held out her hand to him.

:Look at me, Bard. Look at me, and dream . . .:

Eric stepped off the stage, his eyes never leaving hers for a moment. He took her hand in his, and touched her fingertips to his lips. He was not certain if it was his thought, or hers, that echoed through his mind, low and seductive, beckoning.

:Yes—you are the one—:

Kory glanced around the shadowed alley, the rain misting down on the dark asphalt, turning everything before him to gray.

I must lead the traitor away from here, away from the Bard. If he realizes that Eric is here—if he realizes that Terenil is here—

Eric undefended, Terenil completely lost in Dreaming. Blessed Danann, how did everything go so wrong so quickly?

The alley was dark, even to elven eyes, but promised a path to safe retreat.

If I can lead him off, then lose him, I can come back to this club and spirit the Bard away to safety.

He could feel the traitor behind him, the menace, the carefully controlled anger—and above all, the power.

How is it that he has such power when the rest have been magic-starved into Dreaming? How—

Oh. Fool. He was High Court, and not tied to the groves. And he has his daughter. She must be keeping him very . . . prosperous. I wonder if she even realizes that he's using her— using all of us—

Anger surged in him, and lent speed to his feet. The heavy rain flattened his hair into his eyes, and soaked him to the skin in a few moments. He ignored the clammy, clinging fabric, ignored the chill.

I have fought in worse circumstances. I have fled in far worse.

He stumbled against something he hadn't seen in the darkness, and went to his hands and knees. He picked himself up immediately, but the power that was Perenor behind him had gained a few precious yards.

If he catches me, that will leave Eric open to him. He uses the mortals, that was the whole centerpiece of his defiance of Terenil; uses them, and discards them. He would take Eric and twist him—turn him into something foul and shadowed, as evil as himself—

Gods. Not the Bard. Anything but that.

The icy rain slashed at him, and he stumbled again on the slippery pavement. Then a flash of lightning from above showed him the end of the alley.

The *end* of the alley.

A *dead* end. All too literally, a dead end.

The passage ended in enormous loading-dock doors set into the otherwise blank wall of a two-storied building. To Kory's right, another blank wall. To his left, a building with some few windows set too high above the street to reach from the ground, and a few feet of tall privacy fence.

If I had a minute, I could climb that fence, vanish into the maze of this city.

I don't have that minute.

Kory whirled, just as he heard the slow, deliberate footsteps behind him, putting his back against the wall of the building.

Perenor had brought his own light with him. It illuminated

him softly, and Kory saw that he hadn't so much as a single drop of rain marring the careful arrangement of his hair or the expensive gray suit. He was making it quite clear that he had power to spare. Power to *waste*, if he chose.

He extended a finger and lit Kory in merciless detail as well. Kory was all too clearly aware of how he looked: hair straggling in soaked, tangled strands dripping into his face and down his back, clothing plastered to his body. He drew himself up proudly, anyway—

Pride is all I have left.

"Well, it *is* young Korendil, after all," Perenor said, his voice subtly mocking. "You used to have better manners, youngling. Aren't you going to offer me a civil greeting?"

He is going to kill me—and destroy everything with me. Unless I can keep him occupied long enough for Eric to finish the show and leave—and when he leaves, the others will follow. Perhaps. But "perhaps" is all I have . . .

I must give Perenor something to amuse him, to delay him long enough for Eric to escape.

"We did not have a civil parting, Lord Perenor," he replied as coldly, and dispassionately, as he could.

He may kill me now, but I won't let him take Eric and the others as well.

Perenor shook his head. "Ten years asleep and no wisdom learned in all that time. Korendil, you disappoint me."

I am not going to answer that—except with this—

He used the last of his power to Call his sword. In an instant, the shimmering weapon was in his hand, ready for battle.

Perenor laughed. "Korendil, that is exceptionally foolish even for *you*—"

And the elf-mage extended his hand again—and the sword vanished in a shower of sparks from Kory's hands, leaving him staring stupidly at the air where it had been. Then Kory moved, drawing light and power from the air, condensing it into a weapon and hurling it at the traitor.

The older elf easily warded off the attack with a single gesture, a snap of his fingers. The magic dissipated harmlessly, leaving Kory and Perenor in the glimmer of witch-light, staring at each other.

Perenor's smile faded, and his face darkened, a moment of calm before the fury.

Kory swallowed. *I think that maybe I don't amuse him any more* . . .

8

Smash the Windows

"Enough of this, Korendil."

Perenor's voice was icy. When he spoke again, it was not aloud, but in the silent speech of the elvenkin. :*Korendil, don't be too much of a fool. You know you cannot fight me. Give up now, and I will make this painless and quick.*:

Kory flung his response at the traitor's mind, ringing and defiant. :*Never! May you rot in the humans' hell first, betrayer of our people—*:

Perenor shook his head in mock-sadness. :*As you wish. You know, Korendil, you would have been wiser to stay in the Grove, lost in your dreams.*: He raised his hand slowly, his green eyes incandescent with resonating power.

Kory edged along the wall, knowing there was no escape, but unable to simply stand motionless like a frozen rabbit waiting for the strike that would kill him. His foot slipped on the wet asphalt, and he fell backwards over a garbage can, landing on his knees in the spilling refuse. The lid of the can clattered loudly in the silence.

No! I cannot die on the ground like an animal! Is there nothing I can use as a weapon, enough time to—

Kory sensed the burst of magic an instant before the blinding light and heat surged towards him.

Oh Gods, NO!

He groped for anything to shield himself, anything, and recoiled at the touch of Cold Iron. Then, disregarding the soul-scorching pain that lanced through his hands, he grabbed the metal object and desperately hurled it towards Perenor.

A silent explosion . . .

. . . as the trash can lid shattered into a million shards of light, impacting with the force of Perenor's magic.

Kory blinked, then looked up to see Perenor warding his eyes with his hand, trying to see past the glittering snow-fall of multicolored light-specks. *Oh, thank Danann, I'm still alive—for at least another ten seconds—*

He scrambled to his feet and picked up an abandoned piece of wood, not as long as his elven sword, or as balanced, but embedded with several short, blood-colored spikes on one end. By the icy twinge through his trembling hands, he knew that the pointed metal prongs were iron, possibly the only thing that Perenor might fear.

:I will not be easy prey for you, Perenor.: With a weapon in his grip, he felt the warrior's fury rising within him as he cast the challenge at the elf-lord. *:Come and fight me, if you dare."*

Perenor smiled, as if approvingly, and conjured his own blade, the bright elf-metal reflecting the lightning ripping through the skies above. *:I am pleased, Korendil. At least you will give me a bit of sport before you die . . .:*

Without warning, he struck at Kory, the sword arcing down towards him.

Kory rolled under the edge of the blade, somersaulting up onto his feet. *I can't let him touch this stick—that sword will cut through it instantly, and then I'll be unarmed again—*

He countered, slashing at Perenor's face with the filthy board. The elf-mage dodged back, and Kory kicked the fallen trash can into his opponent's path. Perenor tripped, falling hard on the wet ground.

Now—while I have a chance—

Kory ducked in close, bringing the spiked wood down sharply. But Perenor reacted instantly, his sword moving up to block.

The blade sliced through the wooden board like paper, then the stroke continued. across Kory's exposed leg—

Kory's scream echoed in the silent alley as he stumbled back, half-blinded by the pain. *Oh gods—oh gods—* he felt the slick hardness of the wall against his back, the warm wetness coursing down his leg. He tried to fight off the dizziness and overwhelming pain, but it was all he could do to stay on his feet.

He shook his wet hair out of his eyes, frantically tried to make them focus on where his foe had been. Perenor was lying on the ground, the elven sword beside him. *He's not moving. Please, Danann, let him be dead! If one of those pieces of Cold Iron—*

Then Kory saw his enemy stand up and reach for the killing sword on the ground next to him. Perenor limped slightly as he shifted towards Kory, and he was no longer immaculate.

At least I did that much . . .

Perenor's clothing was filthy and he was dripping wet. His face was a mask of fury as he turned towards Korendil.

Kory tried to muster anything, a last burst of magic, *anything,* but all he could do was stand there, fear coiling in his gut, watching his death approaching, one slow step after another.

Perenor smiled, and raised the sword for the fatal blow.

:*No! Korendil*—:

Fire, green and gold, blossomed around them.

Kory shielded his eyes against the blinding brilliance. When he could see again, Perenor was sprawled on the pavement again, but this time he was looking up with sudden uncertainty and fear visible—for a brief moment— in his eyes.

Kory followed Perenor's gaze to the far end of the alley, where another figure stood, vibrant green light still flickering around his hands.

"Leave the boy alone, Perenor."

The newcomer stepped out of the shadows, the witch-light reflecting off his golden hair and pale features.

∾   ∾   ∾

Prince Terenil.

Awakened, alert, ready for battle—

—by all the Gods, it's him!

The Prince smiled at Perenor, who was staring at him in stunned surprise. "I'm the one you want—right? The one who named you outcast, who banished you from the Elflame and the High Court." He drew the blade sheathed at his side. "Now is your chance to avenge yourself. Fight me."

He's awake, he was only pretending to be lost in Dreaming, and now he's going to fight Perenor! He lured Perenor into this, he must have!

Perenor nodded slowly, painfully picking himself up off the gravel. Kory watched silently as the two elven lords moved to face each other across the dimly-lit alley, swords at ready.

Another wave of dizziness washed over him. He glanced down, and saw the blood dripping from the long gash in his thigh. He quickly ripped away part of his shirt and bound it tightly around the wound, clenching his teeth against the throbbing pain.

When he looked up again, Perenor and the Prince were circling each other, each waiting for an opening, a chance to strike.

Even Perenor is no match for the Prince. He never was, which is why he fled into exile rather than face him the last time they met. Another minute, and Terenil will finally defeat the Traitor—

Then fear and dread tightened a fist around Kory's heart. The Prince's hands were shaking.

No—

As he watched, Perenor feinted lightly, and the Prince responded clumsily, leaving his own side wide open to a killing thrust.

Oh no—no—

But Perenor did not take the opening, only smiled and feinted again.

This—it can't be happening! My lord, my liege—

He's—he's falling to pieces. And Perenor's playing with him! Oh gods—he's going to kill the Prince!

In that instant, Terenil slipped on the wet pavement, and Perenor lunged, swinging the flat of his blade against the Prince's head.

Prince Terenil collapsed, crumpling on the ground; Perenor kicked the Prince's fallen sword away from him. As Kory choked on a sob, Perenor reached down and took Terenil by the hair, and forcibly turned his former liege over onto his back.

The Prince stared blankly upwards, unseeing, his body shaking uncontrollably, convulsively—

—like a man caught in the throes of drug withdrawal. Tears joined the rain on Kory's face.

Perenor set the edge of his sword against the Prince's throat. "What an amusing evening," he remarked conversationally. "I've wanted to kill you for some time, Terenil, but I never thought it would be this easy."

:NO!:

The weak burst of magic that hit Perenor was scarcely more than a flicker of light, but the elf-lord looked up nevertheless.

At Kory, standing against the wall, his hands trembling. :No. You can't kill him. I won't let you.:

"Really?" Perenor smiled humorlessly. The renegade elf raised his sword, pointing the weapon at Kory. "And do you really think you can stop me?" His eyes narrowed, bright with eldritch power.

He's going to—

Oh SHIT!

Kory dived for the fence as the wall exploded outward in the spot where he had stood; hauled himself over the top, and tumbled down again on the opposite side. He gasped in pain, feeling something snap inside his chest as he landed hard on the ground.

Just run—keep running—

The backyard of someone's house, shadows of trees, a low hedge. Kory vaulted over the bushes and out onto the darkened street, the pain blinding him to anything but the need to run, keep going—

Sweat was stinging in the small cuts on his face and

hands, where he had fallen and hurt himself before and not realized it, and he could barely breathe against the stabbing pain in his chest.

Something's broken inside—a rib—can't catch my breath! Just . . . keep running—

At the corner, he glanced back once, and saw Perenor close behind him, running at a light, steady pace.

If I can keep him after me, maybe the Prince will be able to get away. If I can keep running . . .

Oh Gods, it hurts!

Another alley, the glimmer of streetlights, far ahead. *I can't lose him by running, he'll just track me down with his magic. And I won't be able to run much longer.*

He'll chase me until I fall, and then he'll kill me. And he'll go back and finish off Prince Terenil, and then he'll find Eric, and—

—no! I won't let him win!

Cold Iron. That would block his magic. He wouldn't be able to find me, but he'd waste a lot of time trying. Perhaps even enough time for the Prince and Eric to get away.

A glimpse of movement on the street ahead, a large vehicle that Kory could smell even at this distance. He doubled his speed, running desperately, and gathered the last of his strength, channeled it inward, reaching inside, changing—

A small silvery cat, running painfully on three legs, suddenly leaped up at the passing garbage truck, landing in the back among the reeking trash.

The searing touch of Cold Iron, burning through his fur, his skin—

Oh Gods! I can't—the pain!

He clenched his teeth on the feline scream trying to escape from his throat. *This is far better than what Perenor intends to do to me—*

The silver-haired cat shrank away from the side of the truck, and found a large plastic bag among the refuse. Moaning faintly, the cat collapsed upon the plastic, barely moving.

But it watched with large, frightened green eyes as Lord

Perenor stood alone on the corner, staring in silent fury at the empty street before him.

This sure has been one helluva night. Beth Kentraine flipped down the clasps of the Fender's case, then lugged it toward the open back door to the club, and the waiting Jeep beyond. Allie and Jim were already standing in the rain next to Jim's pickup, quickly loading the last of the trap set into the back.

"Beth, we're heading out," Allie said, seeing her walking across the wet asphalt towards them. The keyboardist looked intently into Beth's eyes. "Are you—are you going to be all right, Beth? Bo said you told the police you didn't want to press charges against that guy."

"No, I don't." Beth managed to keep her voice level. 'They booked him on public drunkenness and felony possession"—*God, the man was carrying a virtual pharmaceutical business around in his jacket pockets*—"And I really don't want to get involved in a court case. He didn't hurt me, Allie. Really, he didn't."

Just scared the living daylights out of me, that's all. And he would have done a lot more, except Kory came to the rescue.

Kory—I've never met anyone like him before. Never seen anyone who could do what he did, fighting off that bastard.

And he's gone. He left without even saying good-bye . . .

Is it just bad luck, or do I always fall for the flakes? The Eric Banyons and Korys of this world, the guys that vanish at the first possible opportunity. Leaving me standing out in the rain, literally.

And Eric—

It's hard to believe what Kory said. Eric Banyon, a Bard? Sure, he's a terrific musician, but Eric's so feckless, such a . . . a twit. He can't even balance his own checkbook. How in the hell is he supposed to save the L.A. elves?

And, speaking of Banyon . . .

"Allie, are you and Jim giving Eric a lift home? It's almost midnight, and I think he's missed the last bus across Van Nuys."

Allie shook her head. "I haven't talked to Eric since we finished the gig. I think he's back inside the club."

Figures. He's probably expecting me to remember that he's stranded. "All right, I'll check on him. And I'll see both of you at practice on Wednesday, okay?"

Jim grinned. "You bet. This was a *wild* gig tonight, hey?"

"Yeah." *And stranger than you know, m'friend.*

Beth walked back inside the building, shaking the icy droplets of rain from her short hair. *Rain in May. Terrific. If this doesn't dry out in the next couple days, the Faire is going to look like a mud-wrestling competition. Not to mention the fact that I'm going to have a helluva time getting home tonight if I don't leave soon . . .*

She walked into the break room and picked up Eric's gig bag, still lying on one of the packing crates. A moment later, she found his flute, abandoned on one of the stage speakers.

What in hell? Eric never leaves this flute alone for a minute, never. What's going on here?

She put the flute in the gig bag, slinging it over her shoulder, and looked out at the shadowy, smoky club. Most of the crowd had left soon after the band finished their show, but a few were still on the floor, dancing to the beat of the canned music.

Banyon shouldn't be too hard to spot in all of this. He's probably soaking up a last free beer, knowing him. I still can't believe he left his flute onstage. She moved along the edge of the stage, scanning the crowd.

Then she saw him, standing on the far side of the room, talking with someone, a woman she didn't recognize.

Who in the hell is that lady? And what is Banyon doing with her?

Beth stared at the vision of blonde, tailored perfection, laughing at something Eric apparently had just said, her hand resting on his with obvious familiarity. And Beth felt a peculiar emotion rising within her. *He's making time with Miss America, that's what he's doing.*

Jesus C. Frog, I'm not getting jealous of Eric Banyon, am I?

No, not of him. Of her, maybe. She looks like everything I could never be—beautiful, rich, poised, and elegant. I probably shouldn't even bother to ask him about a lift home. She looks like she'd be more than willing to take him anywhere.

No, I should ask, just in case. Maybe he's trapped in a conversation with this woman, waiting for someone to bail him out. Expecting me to show up any minute to rescue him.

Yeah, right. Sure he is, Kentraine. And you're Princess Di.

Well, I should ask him anyhow . . .

She walked around the dance floor, sidestepped the gyrating bodies of the two mohawked dancers, wove a path around several others merrily rolling across the floor. As she moved closer, she realized that the woman was even more beautiful than Beth had originally thought. *Lady, you sure know how to make every woman in the room feel real insignificant, don't you?"*

Even her voice is lovely, Beth realized, now close enough to hear the blonde's low contralto.

And to see the way her fingers were tracing little patterns on Eric's hand.

I can't be jealous. That's Eric Banyon, Eric "I'm a twit" Banyon. It's not like there's anything between us, more than just friendship—

—so why do I want to kill the bitch?

Beth walked uncertainly towards the pair, and stopped a few feet away. Neither Eric nor the blonde woman noticed her. *What in the hell, am I invisible or something?*

"—No, I've never been to the Elizabethan Faire, Eric, but I think that's really a marvelous idea—"

"Hey, Eric," Beth said uncomfortably.

Eric glanced at her. For a stunned moment, Beth thought he didn't recognize her. Then he smiled. "Oh, Beth, hi. I thought you'd left already."

"I wanted to make sure you have a ride home first." *Something is really strange here. He's not quite looking at me, or her, or anything. If I didn't know better, I'd say he's had too much to drink. But Eric's not like this when he's drunk—he never gets this strange, distant look in his eyes—*

He gets silly, that's what he gets. Or he gets morose. And he can't be stoned, either, or he'd be snoring at her feet, or panting at them like a cocker spaniel in heat. You can set your watch by the fifteen minutes it takes Eric Banyon to pass out after he gets stoned.

There's definitely something weird going on in the three brain cells residing underneath all that hair.

"Thanks, Beth, but I'll just catch the bus."

Beth's voice tightened with annoyance. "Eric, the last bus went by half an hour ago!" *You fool, don't you ever look at your watch?*

No. That's not it. There's something else going on here. I don't know what it is, but . . . something about this lady is making the back of my neck prickle. That predatory little smile, the greedy way she's looking at Eric. Something is very wrong—

"Oh, I didn't realize it was that late." Eric said after a moment, and smiled vaguely at her. "I guess we should go, then." He turned to the woman beside him. "I—uh, I'm leaving now. It's really been nice talking to you, Ria—"

The vixen gave him a warm, seductive look. "I've enjoyed talking with you as well, Eric. If you'd like, I—" Her lips curved invitingly. "I could give you a lift home . . ."

Like hell you will, lady!

The blonde looked up suddenly, as though she had heard Beth's thoughts. Her eyes met Beth's, intense and calculating.

Where did Eric find this wench, anyhow? God, but he looks wasted. Too many drugs, Banyon. I'd better get you out of here.

Beth took Eric's hand firmly, and was startled at the chill of his flesh, the way his hand seemed nerveless against hers. "Come on, Banyon, we're leaving."

:Do you really want to fight me for him, little sister?:

Beth blinked, not certain if she'd heard the woman speak, or had just imagined the words. *No, she didn't say it, I didn't see her lips moving at all. She didn't say anything.*

Then—who did?

I didn't take any drugs!

"Banyon?"

Eric had a remarkably stupid look on his face, one that Beth recognized from too many evenings of seeing him passed out drunk at Fairesite.

Banyon, what in the hell have you been drinking? Sterno?

Well, you can sleep it off. Assuming we don't get caught on the road. Woodley Park is probably already flooded from this storm—

"Nice meeting you," Beth called over her shoulder, starting to walk away with Eric in tow.

A delicate hand descended on her shoulder. Beth felt the elegantly lacquered fingernails digging in, even through the thickness of her leather jacket.

"I think you've interrupted a private conversation," the blonde said softly, her contralto voice rich with barely concealed menace.

"No, I think that Eric and I are leaving now," Beth retorted, with just a hint of steel in her voice. *Get your mitts off me or you're going to lose them, Blondie.*

"Are you?" the bitch smiled, her fingers tightening on Beth's shoulder. "And what makes you think that he wants to go with you?"

Beth glanced at Eric, who was staring off into space, completely oblivious to everything and anything going on around him. *Banyon, what is wrong with you? And why in the hell am I defending your virtue?*

No. I know why I'm doing this. I know what this "lady" is, I can read her loud and clear. Man-eater. She wants to take the Banyon-boy under her wing, amuse herself for a while, suck him dry, then spit him out again. And laugh as he falls apart.

I won't let her do that to him. He may be a real schmuck sometimes, but he's my friend.

"Because I'm his friend," Beth said, surprised at the way Blondie was gazing intently at her. *Like she's trying to burn a hole though me with those eyes. If she stared at me any harder, she'd probably go cross-eyed.* "Besides, he thinks I'm cute."

"Does he? So, tell me, dear, just how do you get that particular kind of hacked-off-with-a-knife look with your hair? I've never seen anything like it before, even at my coiffeur's in Beverly Hills. I'm sure Eric finds it very attractive."

Why you bitch!

"Try hacking your hair off with a knife," Beth retorted. "And, you know, I really do like your remarkable color of blonde, while we're on the subject of hair styles. Do you use Clorox to get that effect, or just hair coloring? It's really *you.*"

The woman's eyes darkened. "My dear, you're treading on very dangerous ground."

"So are you, lady." Beth smiled, showing teeth.

The woman shrugged. "Be that as it may, I do think Eric enjoys my company more than yours. Don't you, Eric?" She favored the flute player with a winning smile.

"Uh, yeah, sure," Eric said dazedly, staring at the flickering colored lights of the dance floor.

What in the hell is going on here? Beth gave the bitch a stiletto glare. "Listen, Blondie, we're leaving, and I'm taking Banyon here with me. I won't let you take advantage of my friend, who's obviously too drunk off his ass to fend for himself. You've struck out, so why don't you go find some other happy hunting ground? Like, in another county?" She bared her teeth again. "Maybe you'd find somebody more your type on Hollywood Boulevard. Or do you prefer to work in Santa Monica?"

For a moment, Beth thought that Blondie was about to haul off and swing at her. *Just try it, and you won't know what hit you, lady. I'd love an excuse to knock you flat on your derriere.*

Then the woman's eyes narrowed.

:*No. Not that. I'm going to do something very, very* special *instead—something you'll never forget, you little bitch—*:

And she smiled, her eyes locking with Beth's.

Blue eyes—icy blue, so cold, so . . . murderous. As if she's trying to reach out somehow—trying to do something—

Beth felt a chill run down the back of her neck, a warning tingle. *Those eyes, so cruel, reaching—*

She gave herself a mental shake, and glared right back.

Well, I hope the silly bitch gets a migraine, staring at me that way.

Beth broke eye contact first, shrugged, and saw a visible ripple of surprise run through the other woman.

What the hell? Did she expect me to run away screaming, just because she gave me a dirty look? Honey, I've had nastier looks from my landlady.

"Come on, Banyon, we're leaving. It's been a long night, and you need to get some sleep before heading off to work tomorrow, right?"

"Work?" he repeated dully, looking from her to the other woman.

"Yeah your day job, remember?" She glanced at the bitch, still staring at her in shock. "Buenos nachos, Blondie. I hope you enjoyed the show."

The woman's astonished expression faded into something else: a thoughtful speculative gaze. Then her eyes widened, looking at something beyond Beth.

Beth turned to look, and stopped short.

There was a man standing on the other side of the dance floor, a silver-haired man wearing an expensive, stylish business suit.

Well, it *had* been an expensive suit. Now the trousers and jacket were stained and torn, dark with mud. Blood trickled from a small cut on his cheek, mixing with the water dripping from his hair, plastered against his face and ears.

His *pointed* ears.

Equally unmistakable was the burning fury in his green eyes, seething as he stared at Beth and Eric. Especially as his gaze rested upon Eric Banyon.

Green eyes, like Kory's. He's an elf, one of them—

No, that look in his eyes, such hatred and fury—I've never seen anything like that before. He's not like Kory, not like the dancers, there's something about him that just feels wrong. *I don't know what it is, but—*

—Jesus H. Christ, I think I'm in trouble—

The blonde started and crossed the dance floor, hurrying towards the bedraggled silver-haired man. "Father! What happened to you? Are you all right?"

Her dad? That figures. They definitely look like two of a kind. Like a couple of exotic snakes.

She turned to Eric standing openmouthed next to her, and punched him lightly on the arm. "C'mon, Banyon, I'm taking you home."

He looked at her as though seeing her for the first time. When he spoke, his voice sounded distinctly puzzled. "Bethie? I thought—"

"That's the problem with you, Eric. You don't think. Look, I want to get home before dawn. Let's go."

"Yeah." He shook his head. "I just—I just feel funny—"

Terrific. With my luck, he's going to end the evening by throwing up all over the inside of my jeep. Wonderful.

Why in the hell do I bother with him, anyhow?

Because—because he's my friend. And it was hard enough watching that bitch Maureen tear him apart, let alone standing by while somebody else repeats the performance. I wish Banyon had common sense. Or better taste in women.

Though I have to admit that on looks alone, Blondie really is a class act—

"C'mon, Eric, let's go." She gave him a push in the direction of the door, then glanced back at the two across the room. And froze.

They were watching her. And Eric.

I've never seen such hatred in anyone's eyes before, such venomous hatred. And menace, like all they want to do is see our blood leaking out all over the floor.

Sudden fear crawled up Beth's back.

He's an elf. I don't know what she is, but she's obviously with him.

Maybe they do want to see our blood all over the floor . . .

Kory told us about his enemies. No, his Enemy—an exiled

elven lord, by the name of Perenor. An older elf, silver-haired.

Silver-haired.

Like this guy, staring at me from across the room. Who looks like he wants to vivisect me and Banyon.

Oh shit.

What—what if Blondie wasn't just trying to lure Banyon into her bed? What if she was trying for something else?

And—

And where in the hell *is Kory? I haven't seen him since—*

Everything clicked in her mind at once.

Oh holy shit!

Beth grabbed Eric's hand and pulled him bodily towards the front exit. She looked back over her shoulder, and saw the two start across the dance floor. Heading towards her, towards them, striding purposefully through the last of the Monday-night crowd.

Beth signaled frantically at Bo, who was standing at the bar, talking with the barkeep, and pointed at the pair coming up behind them. Bo raised an eyebrow curiously but nodded and said something quietly to the bartender who stepped out from behind the counter, wiping his hands on a cloth.

At the front door of the club, she took a moment to glance back. Bo, with the barkeep right behind him, had stopped the bitch and her dad and was speaking with them, the words lost in the noise of the blaring Top Forty dance music.

Thank you, Bo. You'll keep 'em busy for a few minutes, at least . . .

She shoved Eric out the door, steering him around the corner to the jeep, parked in the side alley.

"Bethie?" Eric looked at her, very bewildered, the rain dripping down his too-handsome face.

"Just shut up and get in the car, Banyon!" She pushed him headfirst into the jeep, tossed his gig bag in after him, slammed the door shut, and dashed to the other side of the vehicle. *Christ, this can't be happening to me.*

No. It's real. That guy is after Eric, maybe after me, and he's definitely after Kory—who has vanished. I have a real bad feeling about this—

She turned the key in the ignition, and the Jeep's engine rumbled into life. *Thank God, the Beast is actually running this week. I want out of here, right now!*

Someone stepped out from the edge of the building, silhouetted by the jeep's glaring headlights.

Oh shit, it's him!

Beth slammed the jeep into gear and shoved the emergency brake off. *Baby Beast, don't fail me now!*

And a blinding flash of light hit her right in the eyes.

The world vanished into white, images searing into her retinas, impossible colors and shapes. Beside her, she heard Eric Banyon moan softly, incoherently. *Something about D minor . . . What the hell, Banyon?*

She cursed and rubbed at her tearing, aching eyes with one hand. *Can't see, can't drive—God, I can't believe this is happening to me!*

Then she heard the quiet footsteps on the gravel, moving towards the parked jeep.

Christ! I am not staying around to see if he can do something besides fireworks!

She hit the gas, unable to see, but praying. *Oh Lady, take pity on us. Whatever happens, I'm not going to stop. Either we're going to get away, or Eric and I will be splattered all over Burbank Boulevard, but I'm not going to stop. Gods, get us out of this—*

She tightened her grip on the steering wheel, expecting to feel the bone-crushing impact at any moment—

A split-second later, her vision cleared. Beth glimpsed a gray-suited figure diving to the side of the alley, barely managing to get out of the way of the accelerating vehicle, just as the jeep bounced off the edge of the sidewalk and onto the street.

Hah! Almost, but not quite, you bastard!

A red sports car screamed to a stop only inches from her, and Beth yanked the wheel hard, the jeep spinning wildly in a half circle across the wide street. Then she had control of the vehicle again, and floored the gas pedal.

She glanced at her passenger, white-faced and shaking in the seat next to her. His fingers, clenched tightly to the dashboard, looked like they would need to be pried off with a crowbar.

The Noble Bard gulped audibly as Beth took another turn at a reckless speed, putting all the distance she could between them and the Dive.

And the elf-lord that tried to kill us.

Beth laughed, and Eric looked at her like she was crazy.

Maybe I am. But, by the gods, we're alive!

9

The Pleasures of Hope

"—and I still don't understand why you were talking to her in the first place. Anyone, even someone as dense as you are, Banyon, could have figured out that bitch was pure trouble."

Bitch?

Eric blinked, looking around his apartment in bewilderment.

Beth locked the door behind them, then tossed him the key. He caught it unthinkingly and replaced it in his pocket.

How did we get home? It seems like five seconds ago, I was standing onstage at the Dive—

Beth peeled off her dripping jacket and hung it in the closet next to the front door. "—and of course, *I'm* the one who has to bail you out. Jesus, Banyon, don't you ever think before you get into these situations?"

Bail me out? What is she talking about?

"I've never been in such a shitty situation in all my life, and it's all *your* fault. What was that bitch's name, anyhow?"

Eric realized that Beth was looking at him, apparently expecting an answer. "Uh, who?" he asked uncertainly.

"The bitch. You know, the ravishing blonde. The one who cornered you after the show." She glared at him. "*The maneater,* Banyon. What was her name?"

Eric shook his head. "I don't know who you're talking about."

Why do I feel so—wet? He glanced down at himself, and did a double-take, startled.

His boots were completely soaked, his jeans wet to the knees.

When he looked back at Beth, she was sitting on the floor, pulling off her boots and socks, then dropping them in a damp pile on the carpet. He averted his eyes as her pants quickly followed.

Beth stood up, rubbing her hands together. "Christ, I think I froze my patooties off. Can I borrow some sweats for the night, Eric? A blanket would be great, too. I expect that couch gets rather cold at night."

For the night?

What in the hell is going on here?

"Uh, yeah, sure," Eric said, more than a little confused. "There's a stack of clothing in the bedroom, on the dresser. Help yourself."

As Beth vanished into his bedroom, Eric looked down at his drenched clothes then around at the familiar apartment. Slowly, methodically, he hung his Faire cloak on the hook on the back of the door to dry.

What in the hell happened to me? What happened to my mind? I've never blanked out like this before, no matter what drugs I'd been doing. The worst I've ever done was fall asleep in the middle of the bagpipe practice.

He sat down, prying off his boots and socks. After a moment's consideration, he peeled off the wet jeans as well. Beth emerged from the bedroom, wearing a blue pair of sweatpants and a worn Faire shirt that were both several sizes too large for her.

"Hey, Banyon, I thought you might want these." She tossed an armful of dry clothing to him. He caught it—jeans and shirt—and pulled the pants on, fastening them quickly.

"Thanks, Bethie." Eric picked up the wet clothing, draping it over the kitchen chairs.

How the hell did we get soaked? Where have we been?

A few feet away, Beth sprawled out on the living room

couch, closing her eyes wearily. "I'm glad we managed to get here. For a while there, I wasn't certain if we could get down Hayvenhurst Street. I still can't believe how fast the streets over here flood during a storm. A foot of water in less than an hour. Christ." She opened one eye to look at him, and smiled tiredly. "Thanks for the offer of crash-space, Eric—I'd never have made it back to Tarzana."

"You're welcome," he said. *I really don't remember inviting her to stay over. Not that I don't want Beth here, it's just I don't remember inviting her. And—*

And I don't remember how we got home, either.

He sat down in one of the armchairs, trying to think. *Okay, we finished the show. I was standing on stage, and then—*

—and then, here we are, in my apartment. In Van Nuys. Half an hour's drive from the Dive.

And I don't even remember walking out of the club. What was I drinking tonight?

God, just thinking about this is making my head ache—

"So, what was her name, Banyon?" Beth asked again.

He looked up in surprise. "Whose name?"

"Don't tell me you've forgotten her already?" Beth's eyes were intent upon him. "The Blonde Bombshell. The one who was crawling all over you after the show. Christ, I thought she was going to devour you without ketchup, right there on the dance floor."

"Bethie," Eric said slowly. "I don't know if you're going to believe this, but I don't remember a damn thing about any blonde woman."

No, I do remember something—blue eyes, icy blue, smiling at me. A voice. A voice in my head. "Dream of me, Bard . . ."

Who did those eyes belong to? The same person as the voice?

And why can't I remember what happened tonight?

This is definitely too weird for words.

Beth was staring at him, sober and very thoughtful. "What do you remember, Eric?"

He thought about it for a moment. "I remember playing

the gig," he said carefully. "That bastard that attacked you during the break. And then talking with you and Korendil. And—you buying into Korendil's little war. Me too. Then we played the second half of the show, did the last song, and—and that's it. I don't even remember unlocking the apartment door just now. Honestly, I don't. Bethie, I think I just lost an hour of my life. And—and I know I didn't drink anything, not even during the break. Well one Scotch, before the gig. That's all. I didn't do anything, uh . . . recreational. And I'm not drunk now. Just . . . very, very confused."

Beth spoke quietly. "You know, this is starting to make sense, if those two were working from some kind of a plan. First, they do something to get Kory out of the way. I don't know what, but he disappears. Then they come after you, messing with your mind, trying to get you to leave with La Chic Bitch. Then, when I interfere and they think we're going to escape, they try to kill us both—"

"Somebody tried to *kill* us?" Eric's voice squeaked on the word. "Holy shit, Beth, what happened tonight?"

She ignored his words, apparently lost in thought. "Or, at least, I think they were trying to kill us. Probably they were after you. I suspect I was just an afterthought."

"Oh, that's *terrific*. That's just *wonderful!* Christ, Beth, what have we gotten ourselves involved in?"

Beth didn't answer for a long moment. "I don't know Eric. When Kory told us about this whole thing, how he needs us to help save the elves, I never thought—I never thought somebody would try to *kill* me."

She sighed. "Eric, I guess you don't remember this, not if that woman was screwing magically with your mind, but this elven guy—I think it was the Lord Perenor that Kory told us about—he did something, and I m pretty certain it was magic. He threw light at me, blinded me, and I nearly crashed the Jeep." She was shrinking in on herself with each word. "It was . . . real scary, Eric. Scarier even than when mom and dad and I were grabbed by accident by the Greek cops."

Why, she's trembling. Oh, Bethie—

He moved closer to her, gently taking her hand. "Listen,

you must have done something right. I mean, we're alive, aren't we? You got us out of there alive and in one piece." He grinned weakly. "You know, that's pretty impressive, come to think of it. I wish I could remember it."

She smiled tremulously, but it faded. "And I'm also real worried about Kory. He never came back after the show—"

"Hey, I wouldn't worry too much about Korendil," Eric said, giving Beth's hand a reassuring little squeeze. "He seems like a pretty tough guy. Hell, he took care of that drunken idiot that came on to you, and knocked me all over the room this afternoon, too. I think he can take care of himself all right."

Beth snuggled closer to him. "I know. It's just I've—I've never had anybody try to kill me with magic before. When it was happening, I didn't have time to think about it, or be scared, I just reacted but now, thinking about it, I feel kinda . . . spooked."

"Hey, it's okay." He smiled. "I'd probably be scared shitless, if I could remember what happened."

"Yeah." She rested her head against his shoulder. "Eric you're not going to back out on Kory, are you? I know, we didn't expect anybody to try to kill us, but he's counting on you to help him."

"No. I gave my word that I would help him."

And I will. I know that now. Whatever's going to happen, I won't walk away from him. Especially after this.

Beth smiled up at him. "Have I ever told you you're one helluva guy, Eric Banyon?"

"No, not that I can recall."

"Well, you are. And—and I might as well tell you the truth now. You should know this. I'm a practicing witch, Eric."

He looked at her in disbelief. "You're practicing to be a witch?"

"No, I *am* a witch, silly. All of us in Spiral dance are. That's part of why we're together in the band—we're trying to combine our music with magic, reach out to people, make a difference. Music gets to a helluva lot more people than rhetoric."

Bethie? A witch. Makes sense, actually. And explains a lot of stuff about her. Well, it explains the things she never would explain, or talk about. The other witches I've met, like that group out at the Texas Faire, there were a lot of subjects they just wouldn't talk about, either. "Well, if you know witchcraft, Bethie, couldn't you have just done something back to Perenor when he attacked us?"

"I wish I could've. But witchcraft doesn't work that way. It's a—oh, shit, it's a pattern, a way you start thinking. Like Zen or something." She crossed her eyes, and waved her hands languidly. "Like, man, you *go* with the *flow*—" When he laughed she continued, a little more seriously.

"It's not fireworks and special effects. I've never seen anything like what that guy did to us before tonight. I can't do that kind of stuff—and, to be honest, I don't know exactly what he did. But I sure don't ever want to be on the receiving end of *that* ever again."

"I hate to say it," Eric said, shifting slightly to put his arm around Beth's shoulders, "but if we continue helping Korendil, and try to save the L.A. elves, we're probably gonna see a lot more of that kind of fireworks."

"Yeah, don't remind me, I've already thought about it." Beth sighed, leaning back. "All I can say about it is, well, that Perenor guy may be real flashy with the magic, but I'd like to see how he'd feel about getting bonked by a good old-fashioned baseball bat. 'Cause that's what I'd like to do to him, next time I see him."

"Yeah, me too." Eric smiled, his fingers toying with Beth's punk tail, a single long curl of dark hair. "Though I wish I could remember that blonde woman. I mean, she sounds like she was real interesting—"

Beth swatted at him. "She must've been. I practically had to drag you away from her."

"Hey, I wasn't the one making eyes at Korendil earlier in the evening—" Eric waited for Beth to laugh, then he saw the way she was looking away and biting her lip pensively. "You really like him, don't you?" he asked quietly, obscurely disturbed.

"He's . . . really something. I've never met anyone like

him before. It's not just that he's cute—which he is, he's one of the handsomest men I've ever seen—but there's also an intensity to him, and such openness, honesty—"

He swallowed, trying to sound more easygoing about this. "Yeah, I understand that. He's a really special guy—tall, blond, and with pointed ears. Who could resist him? Especially the ears!"

Did that come out as bitter as I think it did?

"Eric—" She pressed her fingertips to his lips, trying to get him to shut up, but he shook his head and continued.

"Beth, you know I'd rather see you get involved with someone who's more your type like, a human being—but if you really want Korendil, that's fine." He took a deep breath. "Really, it is. Besides, I hate to be tied down anyway, right? I hope you'll be happy. I know I won't stand in the way. In fact, you'll probably never see me—*mmmph!*"

Eric had to shut up then, because Beth was kissing him. A very serious kind of kiss that nearly knocked him off the couch, both from imbalance and the surprise of having a double armful of Beth Kentraine in his arms.

"Uh, Bethie—" he managed, when she pulled away long enough for him to catch his breath. "I didn't invite you over for this. I mean, I don't want you to think that I—"

She only smiled and kissed him again. "Methinks the gentleman doth protest too much," she said teasingly, running her fingers through his damp and still-tangled hair.

"It's just-mmmf," he said eloquently, as Beth kissed the corners of his mouth, working her way over to his right ear.

He sighed, then gave up any pretense of resistance as her deft fingers began undoing the buttons of his shirt. *Oh well, when have I ever been able to deter Beth Kentraine from whatever she wanted to do?*

Not that I'm objecting too much to this.

Not that I'm objecting at all . . .

He carefully unfastened the laces of her Faire shirt. Then he moved his hands lightly over her skin, pausing lingeringly at the ticklish spot over her ribs.

Beth, resting her cheek against his shoulder, toying with

his shirt buttons, suddenly stiffened in shock, realizing where
his hands had stopped. "Eric Banyon, you wouldn't—"

"AAAAAR! There's no mercy for you, wench!" he growled
in his best bad pirate imitation, and began tickling her
unmercifully.

She laughed, twisting and trying to get away from him.
"Eric, no, don't—let me go—ack!" Beth tried to pull free
but he wouldn't let her go, holding her closely in his arms,
tickling and kissing her until he couldn't keep from laughing
either.

The laughter faded to silence, and a calm expectation
that Eric had never felt before. *It's as if I knew we'd
reach this point, someday. Like I've known that all along,
since the day I met Beth. It's just—I never realized it until
now.*

Beth's dark eyes met his. She was smiling gently. He
wondered if perhaps she was thinking similar thoughts. *Her
eyes are so serious, and . . . somehow open, defenseless. That's
how I feel—as if there aren't any facades or masks between
us, no more lies or half-truths. Just Eric and Beth . . .*

She leaned forward to kiss him, a light kiss, barely
brushing his lips, but somehow that made the kiss more
intense, more intimate and passionate, than anything before.
It's like that kiss is a promise—a pledge—

Eric called upon the last bit of rational thought left to
him, wrapped his arms around Beth and lifted her up. She
laughed softly as he carried her to the bedroom, and carefully closed the door behind them.

"Mmmm, Beth?" Eric reached out, gently touching her
bare shoulder. "Beth, you awake?"

"Ummf;" she muttered, turning slightly in his arms.

No, guess not.

He sat up slowly, looking around the shadowed bedroom.
Pale sunlight filtered through the blinds, and he could hear
the beginnings of rush hour traffic on the street below.

Beside him, Beth Kentraine was still asleep, curled up
against him with one arm outflung across the sheets.

She's so lovely when she's asleep. That little smile on her lips, as if she's dreaming of something wicked. She's beautiful when she's awake, too. When she's happy or sad, frightened or spitting like an angry kitten . . . she's still beautiful. I think I could fall in love with her, given half a chance. I wonder if she knows that? And I wonder if she feels the same way about me . . .

Eric moved closer to Beth, wanting to kiss her, then shook his head. *No, she had one helluva day yesterday between that scum who attacked her during the break and Perenor coming after us later. I should let her sleep.*

He smiled to himself, thinking about last night. *I could get very used to this, real easy. Playing street by day, Faire on the weekends, evening gigs with Spiral Dance, and nights with Bethie—*

Except she said she doesn't want to get involved with me, when we were talking at Faire. She doesn't want anything serious.

Well, maybe after last night, she'll change her mind.

It's just—I feel that she's a part of my life, now. With everything that's happened to us, I think that if she said, "Well, it's been fun, Eric, see ya around sometime," I'd just want to die. I've never felt that I needed someone so much before.

He sighed, and smoothed Beth's short mane with his fingers.

I need Bethie. I can't just let her walk away from me. I can't—

He stopped in mid-thought, hearing something from the living room. *What was that?*

Eric listened, at first hearing nothing but the distant traffic noises. Then he heard it again, a faint, low scratching noise, coming from the front room.

What in the hell could that be? Giant mutated Angeleno mice?

He stood up quietly, trying not to awaken Beth, and reached for a pair of jeans, folded on the dresser. Eric padded out to the living room, and looked around, trying to pinpoint the source of the sound.

Then he saw the small cat crouched upon the window

ledge, peering at him through the dirty glass. The cat's pale silvery fur was stained with blood, its green eyes shadowed with pain.

Oh, you poor thing. What could have happened to you? You look like you were hit by a Mack truck—

Eric opened the window, and the cat half-fell into the room, crawling a few feet before it collapsed on the carpet, shivering and panting.

I'll wake Beth up, then call the vet. There's one on Sherman Way, we cant take this little guy over there right now.

The cat looked up at him with large, pain-filled eyes, and then—

And then—

Blur of chords, sounded on an out-of-tune organ by a musician pushed so far past exhaustion that he no longer heard what he was doing, no longer cared, no longer really knew—

Eric blinked.

There *had* been a mutilated tomcat on the floor.

Not now.

He stared, not able to really understand what he was seeing. It had been a cat. Now it was Korendil, lying at his feet.

Korendil, looking very different from the confident warrior who had rescued Beth from her attacker, or the eloquent speaker who had tried to persuade Eric that his story about L.A. elves was no trick. Even different from the shy, diffident creature who, in the end, had pleaded with Eric to help his people.

This was a Kory who had been through a meat-grinder.

He lay in a twisted, bleeding heap on the carpet of the bedroom, and panted, like the tomcat had panted; and his green eyes were glazed with pain. Not surprising, since his leg was slashed from crotch to knee, at least an inch deep. He was bruised and burned, and cut in a dozen places, and he shook like an aspen leaf.

"Holy shit. Korendil?" Eric's voice sounded incredibly loud in the sudden silence.

At Eric's words, Kory raised his head. He looked up blankly, then focused on Eric. "Blessed Danann—" he gasped in a hoarse whisper, his expression warring between relief and pain. "You're *safe.*"

As if he hadn't dared hope for that.

"Oh my God!"

Eric glanced back to see Beth standing in the bedroom doorway, wearing nothing but a startled and horrified expression. "Christ! What happened to him?"

"Perenor—" Kory's words were barely audible. "He knew that Eric awakened me—knew that we were at the place-of-music. I had to draw him away from you, from both of you, he was going to kill you—"

He started to rise—tried to—and cried out in agony. Both of them reached toward him involuntarily. Kory stared at them, his eyes wildly dilated with pain, his hand outstretched, like a drowning man reaching for a lifeline.

"*Help me,*" he whispered, with what sounded like his last breath.

Eric and Beth touched his hand at the same moment.

Music.

Broken music. Music wounded; music dying.

Eric shuddered as the room faded from around him, to be replaced by something else, an aching pain, a silent scream of agony, and music—

Once, in his first year at Juilliard, one of Eric's teachers had described Johann Sebastian Bach's works as "building cathedrals with melody."

This was a cathedral that had been shattered by an earthquake, or the ravages of a bomb. The soaring arches cracked. The upreaching vaults crumbling. The flying buttresses—falling.

Dissonance. Broken chords. Savaged counterpoint. More of it fading with every moment.

More of it trailing off into nothing, into dissolution.

Dying.

No!

He reached out, reached in, plunged into the midst of it, and began trying to hold it together somehow. He saw, then, how the music was trying to repair itself; how the threads of melody reached for the broken lines, trying to patch them into some kind of a whole again.

But I can do that—

He eased himself into the consort; gave the fading music a strong foundation to rest on, solid chords, the way he played a foundation for Bethie's voice to soar—

He heard her singing at that moment, wordlessly, but outside the whole. She was lending her support to the music, but from outside. It would be much better if she could weave herself into the melody from within—

He reached out without really thinking about it, and caught her up and brought her in. There was a gasp of surprise that might have been his own, then she was with them, singing strongly, confidently.

Three of them now; three songs that were part of a greater whole. The two songs that were himself and Beth moved to bracket the wounded one, lending it power, keeping it from fading, from faltering, filling in the places it couldn't—quite—reach.

It was like . . . like doing a gig, with one member having an abysmally bad day. Picking up for him, filling in for him, supporting him.

The third song gathered strength from them, began to join with them—closer—stronger—

Like playing a gig? No, not anymore. This was like the Pachebel Canon, with three voices interweaving, braiding in and out of each other, taking joy from one other and giving it back again, until Eric could no longer tell where his song ended and the others began.

Until they were one song.

*And suddenly the music took fire, and now it was Bach again, in the Toscanini transcriptions—*no, Beethoven, the Ninth, all the counterpoints fusing in to the one harmony—*no, Dvořák, Mannheim Steamroller, Mahler, Clannad, Rachmaninoff—*

Emerson, Lake and Palmer. Tchaikovsky. Vangelis. Prokofiev. Kitaro. Everything and everyone and none of them at all. It was Eric setting the melody, and the others following with variations of their own. He couldn't tell where it was going, only it was glorious beyond anything he'd ever heard before—

—pure, untainted, unalloyed song—a melodic joy that raised him to a height he'd never dreamed of —

And then threw him back into reality.

Oh my God, what was that?

Eric shook his head slowly. He blinked, seeing nothing but pinwheels and blobs of light, like he'd been staring into spotlights too long. His eyes couldn't focus, and he couldn't seem to catch his breath, either.

"Holy shit," he said, after a long moment of silence. "What the hell was that all about?"

"I'm . . . not sure." he heard Beth say faintly, from beside him.

He blinked again, and finally some of the light-show effects cleared away. *Thank God. I can't deal with that when I'm tripping on a liquid dose—I sure as hell can't deal with it when I haven't even had a cup of coffee yet.*

Eric heard the faint sound of something breathing raggedly, and looked down. Kory was lying beside him, sprawled on the floor, his eyes closed and his face gray with exhaustion. He still looked like he'd been through a major war, and come out the loser.

There was a dark, scarlet stain under his leg, soaking into the cheap puce carpet.

The landlady's gonna love that. So much for my cleaning deposit . . .

God, how can I think about something like that when Kory's bleeding to death in front of me?

Get your brain together, Eric. First, a bandage, something to tourniquet that wound—

Beth reacted first. She snatched at an old T-shirt, lying on the floor, went for Kory's leg—and stopped short, looking at the slash in the elf's jeans in disbelief.

The long, hideous slash in his leg was closed. Still nasty-looking, but closed as neatly as if it had been sutured and healing for about a week.

A week, not a few minutes.

But I saw that wound. He was bleeding like a stuck pig, his leg cut halfway open. Something like that just can't vanish!

Eric stared at Kory's leg.

It's impossible.

Finally he looked up, and Beth's eyes met his across the sprawled body of the elf.

"Eric" she whispered in tones of awe. "Eric—we healed him."

"Excuse me," he said, hearing his own voice shaking, "but he doesn't look healed, he looks like hell—"

"It doesn't happen all at once, idiot," she retorted, already sounding more like herself, with a touch of good-natured annoyance in her voice.

"But—"

"Look at his leg, Banyon! Look at all that blood and tell me that we *didn't* heal him!"

He looked at the blood soaking into the tacky carpeting and felt himself pale. He swallowed.

"Look," he temporized, "let's just get him patched up and in bed, okay?"

Beth gave him a sharp look. "What, don't you like the idea that you could have healed somebody, Eric?"

The curious tone of her voice made the words come out that he had been thinking—not words he'd have spoken under other conditions.

"Yeah," he said slowly. "That's the problem. Maybe I like it too much."

Beth caught his thoughtful gaze, and nodded. "Yeah. I know what you mean." She bent down, and carefully got a grip on Kory's shoulders. "You get his feet. We'd better get him into the bedroom."

Eric sat gingerly on the edge of the bed, looking down at Korendil.

The elf. My elf. The one who practically got himself killed, saving my worthless hide.

Why would anybody do something like that for me?

Kory seemed to be peacefully asleep. There were dark

blue smudges under his eyes, bruises and cuts still visible on face and neck. He was so pale, he looked transparent.

My God, this is real. *He got trashed bigtime. He can get hurt. He can die . . .*

Kory's golden curls spilled over his pillow and half over his face. He tossed his head and murmured something in that liquid language of his. Eric reached forward and stroked his forehead, automatically trying to sooth him back into pleasanter dreams—

And froze, fingers still tangled in Kory's silky mane.

What am I doing?

Before he could pull away, Kory opened his eyes, and Eric felt as if he was trapped in that emerald gaze. He only shook himself free when Kory touched his hand.

"Bard?"

"Just seeing if you were all right," Eric replied. *I'm trying to be nice to a friend, that's what I'm doing. A friend who damn near got himself killed to protect me. That's all.* "Korendil, please don't keep calling me 'Bard.' It doesn't seem right." Deliberately, he finished the motion he'd begun, smoothing Kory's hair out of his eyes.

God, Kory has great hair. I know chicks that would kill for a head of hair like that.

"Would you call me 'Kory,' as you do in your thoughts?" The elf smiled hesitantly. "My friends call me that."

Eric smiled back. "Sure, if it makes you happy. I'd rather be your friend, anyway, than have you treat me like some jerk up on a pedestal." *I would, too,* he thought, resting his hand on Kory's shoulder. *Jesus H. This guy almost died to keep me safe. What did I ever do to deserve that?*

Eric patted the shoulder awkwardly. "You just get some rest, Kory. You aren't in any shape to rescue a cockroach in distress right now."

"And what will you be doing?" Kory's eyes followed him as he got up and moved toward the door.

"Well, Beth thinks she's got a way to keep the bad guys from sniffing you out, so she's gonna do her thing when she gets back with her stuff. Then we're gonna go talk to a friend of hers who might know something. We're kind of short on information. It seems that the Bad Guys know everything about us, and we don't know jack about them."

Kory sighed, shifted a little, and tried to suppress a wince of pain. Eric saw it in his eyes anyway, and moved back beside him.

"Are you sure you're gonna be okay?" He reached toward Kory's shoulder again. "You want one of us to stay with you?"

The elf lifted his own hand with a visible effort, and took Eric's. "No. I shall be well enough. Truly, Eric, I will. What I need now is to sleep. But—thank you. Thank you for everything."

For what? "Hey, you tried to keep those guys from killing me last night, and now you're thanking *me?*"

"You saved my life this morning," Kory replied simply. "Without being bound to do so, by anything but your word to help save my people. Yes—"

Eric shivered, caught in the grip of emotions he didn't recognize and didn't understand. *He's right, I guess. It's just, well, I couldn't let him lie there and bleed to death. I couldn't.*

It's funny, though—the way he's looking at me right now, it's more than a little embarrassing. Like I'm everything in the world to him. God, if he was a girl, I'd want to kiss him—

Hell, I'd do more than just kiss him. I'd—oh God—why am I thinking these things? About a guy?

"—yes Eric. I do thank you."

Kory let his hand go, and the moment passed. Eric hesitated, then brushed Kory's hair out of his eyes again. "Okay, guy," he said, gently. "Your thank-you is accepted. And I'm thanking you, too, for trying to save my ass last night. Now, just get some sleep, okay? You leave the fighting to us for a while."

Kory smiled, and closed his eyes. Eric patted his shoulder once more, and retreated from the bedroom before something else he didn't understand could happen to him.

He sat down on the living room couch, his head in his hands.

I don't understand this at all. What's going on in my

*head? Why am I feeling this way about him? He's an elf,
for Chrissakes, not even a human being!*

God, I think I need a drink.

Or several.

Or maybe I'll just finish the whole bottle—

10

Fighting for Strangers

"Three parts coffee, two teaspoons sugar, one part Bushmills . . ."

Eric measured out the whiskey, then threw another splash of it in the mug for good measure.

After everything that's happened in the last twenty-four hours, I definitely need a little Irish Breakfast—

"Isn't it a little early in the morning for that?"

Eric looked up at Beth, standing in the kitchen doorway. He shrugged. "Not all that early, by my standards."

"Methinks you drink too much, Banyon," Beth said, settling a grocery bag down on the counter. She gave him a thoughtful, measuring look; then in a lightning-quick change of mood, tweaked his nose playfully, and kissed him—a warm "hello" kiss.

For a moment, Eric hoped that the kiss might progress into something more than that, but Beth pulled away and shook her head, touching his lips with a fingertip. "Duty calls, bucko. First this, then we'll go talk with my friend, then there's the "Save the Faire" rally this afternoon. I'm thinking that we might be able to find out a little more about who's doing what, and where we can throw a wrench into the works." Something intense burned for a moment at the back of her eyes. "I'm sure looking forward to messing up their plans."

"They," of course, is Lord Perenor and the blonde, who I still can't remember. He let go of her reluctantly, and picked up his Irish coffee which was warm and potent, but a poor substitute for Beth. *Damn, but I wish Beth had less of a sense of responsibility, and more a sense of, well,* timing.

Beth turned away from Eric, opened the shopping bag, and reached into it as the brown paper rustled.

"What's in there?" he asked, leaning over her shoulder to peer inside. It was quite a jumble.

Looks like a lot of Baggies of herbs, some books, and— a knife? Nasty-looking piece of work, that. Probably street-illegal; it must be at least a foot long.

"My bag of tricks." Beth nudged him out of the way, then rummaged through the bag and tossed Eric a bright red apple. He managed to catch it without dropping the mug of coffee. "And breakfast, too. A better breakfast than *that.*" She nodded at the doctored coffee. "How's our patient?"

"Sleeping, last I checked. He's a lot better, amazingly better, really." Eric bit into the apple in his best *Tom Jones*-eating-scene imitation.

Beth took the long-bladed dagger from the shopping bag, and slipped it, still sheathed, under her belt.

He put a little more soul into his next bite.

She ignored him.

He sighed theatrically.

She continued to ignore him, and poured a glass of water from the tap, then carefully shook out three shakerfuls of salt into the water.

He gave up, took a swig of coffee, and returned to the apple without the additions from *The Joy of Sex.*

"What are you doing?" he asked as he sat down at the kitchen table.

She wore a little frown of concentration as she held her hand over the top of the glass. "This is to set up a protecting circle. Then I'll meditate for a while, try to reinforce the idea that nobody's here, not us or Kory."

He accepted that without a blink. A week ago he'd have been snickering into his apple.

But a week ago he hadn't been tossed around the room by magic, or watched a creep get trashed by magic, or——or helped heal somebody by magic.

So——I guess I'm getting used to this. This "circle" sounds like a good sort of thing to do. I'm glad Beth knows how to build this kind of stuff. I guess "build" is the right word. I just wish I understood how it works.

Beth unsheathed the long dagger at her belt, stirred the water with the blade of it, then resheathed it and began walking around the living room, flicking drops of water with her fingers at the walls. "This is the actual protection part," she said, as if she had overheard his thought. She flashed him a smile. "Witchcraft 101, Banyon. Salt and water are very strong protection against things you don't want around. You draw the circle with the consecrated salt water, making sure you do the doors and windows——"

"Hey, I've never had a girlfriend who'd do windows before," Eric teased. Beth gave him a look of acute suffering, then continued. "I don't know whether or not you believe this'll work, but figure it's like chicken soup—can't hurt. I believe, and I'm the one who's setting it, and that's what counts."

She stopped at the window, sprinkled water on the glass, then drew the dagger again. Eric munched on the apple, watching closely as Beth traced a pentagram over the glass, then moved to the next window, repeating the action.

Definitely looks weird. Huh, I should talk. But——you know, somehow this whole routine is just like Beth. Sharp as a knife, always knows what she wants, and more than a little weird at times. I guess that's a part of what makes her so terrific. His mind drifted back to the astonishing events of the previous night—what he could remember of them. *Like she was last night. She's such a complex woman, sometimes so strong and independent, sometimes sweet and cuddly beyond words. Just looking at her makes me think about——*

Eric hid behind the coffee mug, glad that Beth was

occupied with the window, and didn't see how he was blushing. *God, that's all I ever think about. I just look at her and want to drag her back off to bed again. It's something in the way she smiles, the way she looks at me—*

His thoughts faltered a little as a memory of green eyes superimposed itself over the memory of brown.

What really seems . . . bizarre . . . was that Kory was looking at me the same way. So serious, honest—like he'd never lie to me, never intentionally hurt me. And like he was worried about me. The careful way his hand touched mine—

Eric shook his head, trying to dislodge the uncomfortable memory and the equally uncomfortable feelings it was causing. *I don't understand it. Beth, sure—I've liked her for a long time, and I could see us getting together, that it could work. But—Kory? He's an elf—and a guy. I shouldn't feel that way about him.*

But—

I do feel that way.

God, what's going on in my head? Why am I feeling like this—about another guy?

"Hey, Eric—"

Eric glanced up. Beth had finished trickling water around the living room, and was standing at the bedroom door. "I'll need some quiet for this last bit," she said. "Don't come into the bedroom, or open any doors. It'll just take a few minutes, okay?"

"Sure," Eric replied, taking another swallow of his Irish coffee. "I'll just stay put out here."

"Thanks." Beth headed into the bedroom, and closed the door behind her.

Too many strange things have been happening lately, that's what's going on with my mind. And what I'm feeling about Kory, that's just part of it. Everything's so completely weird right now. Like that big gap in my memory. Like the woman Bethie was telling me about, the one I can't remember—

He closed his eyes for a minute, as something like a twinge warning of headache-to-come hit his forehead.

Unbidden, an image rose in his mind of a beautiful blonde woman holding out her hands to him.

:Bard—are you thinking of me?:

Eric opened his eyes, startled, and glanced around the empty room, suddenly disoriented. *What the hell? For a minute there, I thought someone was talking to me.*

But I'm alone. There's no one here but me.

Must be a TV show in the next apartment.

Then he heard the voice again, low and seductive, as if someone was speaking right into his ear.

:No, I am here, Eric.:

Eric blinked, and his disorientation grew. *Say what?*

:Close your eyes and dream of me, Eric, and I will come to you—:

He closed his eyes obediently, and then saw her clearly. Blonde hair, cascading over her bare shoulders. Blue eyes, bright as sapphires, and blood-red lips curving in a smile. She was naked, gloriously nude, and the sight of her made his breath catch.

:I have not forgotten you, Eric. I cannot forget you. You are a longing that I cannot deny, a fire in my blood. Dream of me, think of me for just a moment more, and I will find you. And we will be together—:

She moved closer to him, smiling. From a distance, Eric thought he could hear music, a quiet melody slowly building in strength, and another voice, softly chanting.

> "By salt and water, blade and Will
> None shall harm, or wish ill
> Upon those within this circle round
> That wish with my power, I have bound."

What's going on here?, he thought fuzzily. *Why do I feel so strange?* He tried to focus his eyes, to stand up, but something seemed to be clouding his thoughts and his vision, slowing everything down to a crawl, turning the world into flitting shadows and impenetrable darkness.

:Do not think, Eric, just feel. Close your eyes, and I will find you—:

Caught by her words, Eric closed his eyes again. Then he felt the touch of her hands upon him, and forgot everything else. She was running her hands down his chest, her breath warm against his skin—*Beth? No, she isn't Beth, Beth's in the other room. Who—*

The distant chanting voice faded away, barely audible over the pounding of his blood. All that existed was his unseen lover, her body entwining with his, warm flesh like silk beneath his hands. Lips, touching his in the darkness, a kiss that made his heart beat even harder. Coherent thought fled before the rising fever in his blood, the longing and the need—

And the silent voice, whispering in his thoughts.

:Dream of me Bard. Just a moment longer, and then I will be with you—:

:Yes—: Eric heard himself answer. *:Yes, I will, I am waiting for you—:*

He could feel her silent laughter, the richness of her thoughts, drawing closer to him, reaching for him. *:So close—another moment—and—*

Then Beth's voice, loud and disrupting.

"By the innermost fire, grant me this desire
As I will it, so shall it be!"

Like a door banging shut, something slammed down between Eric and the other. He caught a brief snarl of rage, of frustration and thwarted desire, before the whispering voice faded into silence.

Eric opened his eyes, and blinked.

What in the—did I just doze off, or what?

Christ. That—that was quite a daydream. I haven't had a dream like that since I was a teenager and I swiped Jeff's father's Playboy.

He looked around the living room, and slowly shook his head. *Jesus. You'd think that after last night, I couldn't be thinking about sex, at least for the morning!*

A moment later, Beth walked out of the bedroom, carrying the cup and knife. She glanced at him, then walked over to the table setting the implements down and looking at him closely: "Are you okay, Eric? You look kinda pale."

"I'm just a little tired." He shrugged, then grinned wickedly at her. "Didn't get enough sleep last night, I think."

She hugged him, and mussed his hair good-naturedly "I bet. Maybe I'll let you get some sleep tonight." She breathed into his ear. "But don't count on it."

He caught Beth's hands, drawing her to him for a lengthy kiss. "Do we really have to go to that rally? I can think of a better way to spend the afternoon."

"Absolutely," she said. "Besides, our patient is still soundly asleep in the bed. I wouldn't want to disturb him."

"Didn't he wake up when you were chanting?" Eric asked.

Beth looked at him strangely.

"Eric—I didn't say anything out loud," she said after a moment's pause.

Yeah? Then what did I just hear?

Oh no. The universe is getting weird on me again. God, I hate this. Like daydreaming about that blonde, just now. Or how I felt when I was with Kory, earlier this morning. I can't deal with this stuff, really, I just can't—

"Does—does Kory look okay? Is he sleeping all right?"

"He seems to be fine," Beth said. "I guess these elves are pretty tough. But I'm thinking that maybe we should move him to my place, later—I've put some serious protections on it over the years. A lot more than I can do in a few minutes over here." She glanced at her watch. "Listen, if we head out now, we can catch my friend at home, and still get to the rally in time. I want you to meet this guy— he's the one who first told me about the L.A. elves."

"Sure," Eric said, standing up. "Who is this friend of yours?"

"Oh, you'll like him," Beth assured him, as they walked to the apartment door. "He's as crazy as we are. He has to be—he's an animator."

Phil *always* made Beth smile, no matter how serious the situation was. Today was no exception.

"Beth, sweetling, it's good to see you again." The deceptively frail-looking old man hugged her, then stood back a pace and looked at her intently. "You're looking good, honeybunch—there's a nice glow in your eyes, and jeez, you're in terrific shape. Keeping yourself busy, I hope?" He gave Eric a speculative glance.

Eric, of course, began to blush.

Oh, Banyon, I can't take you anywhere.

"I'm doing fine, Phil," Beth said, kissing his weathered cheek fondly. "This is Eric Banyon, a friend of mine. Eric, Phil Osborn. We're here because of another friend of ours, who isn't doing fine."

"Well, come in, sit down, and tell me about it." Phil ushered them into the small apartment, then vanished briefly into the kitchen, returning a few moments later with three cans of Coke. He handed them each a can, then sat down in his favorite old overstuffed armchair.

Beth saw the way Eric was staring at the living-room walls, decorated with animation cels and original sketches, and smiled to herself. *Well, we've lost Banyon for a while, I think. I know how I was the first time I saw Phil's apartment.*

"Our friend is one of the elves," Beth began, sitting down across from Phil on the couch.

Phil started, then settled back in his chair, a look of speculation on his face. "So you finally got your wish, hmm, honeybunch?" He lowered his voice for a minute. "Should we be talking about this with your young man here?"

She sighed. "He's in on it. In fact, he's further into it than I am."

"Oh." Phil considered that for a moment. "Something tells me your experience wasn't entirely pleasant."

"Most of it wasn't pleasant at all, Uncle Phil." She frowned, and haltingly began detailing the entirely bizarre events of the night before.

And it feels like it was a year ago.

"So things are going pretty badly for all the elves," she concluded. "I guess you must have known some of that. Poor Kory got more than his share of getting dumped on, though."

"Who did for him, honeybunch?" Phil ran his hand

thoughtfully through his thatch of gray-white hair. He was taking her story entirely at face value. Hardly surprising; he was the one who'd told her all about the elves in the L.A. hills when she was a child—and convinced her that they were real when she'd grown up.

"He told us it was an elf called Perenor. He *seems* to be part of the bunch trying to destroy the L.A. Elizabethan Faire site, the magic nexus." She took a swallow of Coke and leaned forward. "I remembered the stories you used to tell me, and I thought maybe you might know something that would be useful about Perenor, something we can use to stop him, or something we can do to bring the other elves out of Dreaming so they can get out of here before the nexus goes."

Phil frowned unhappily. "I hadn't heard about this until you told it to me—but then, the elves are so locked up in Dreaming right now I couldn't shake most of them loose with dynamite. So, somebody is figuring on destroying the magic nexus? That's serious bad news, Beth. Very, very serious."

"I know, Phil," she said, patiently. "That's why we're here. If there's anything you know that might help us—"

"Beth says that you know a lot of the L.A. elves," Eric said from across the room, where he was looking at a framed cel of Snow White.

Phil raised white eyebrows abruptly, so abruptly it looked as though they'd jumped halfway up his forehead. "So you weren't B.S.-ing your old Uncle Phil. This *is* another Believer. Well, well . . ." He turned slightly to get a better look at Eric. "So, Beth told you that I know something about the elves, hmm? Well, that's very true. A lot of them were my friends. Back in the early days, when I first started working in the Industry—did Beth here tell you that I created Defender Duck? He's still my favorite character. Saving the world from Fascism and duck-hunters everywhere—"

"Phil," Beth interrupted carefully, "You were telling Eric about the elves."

"Oh, that's right. Where was I?" He suddenly smiled, a sly, mischievous smile, like a little boy who's just gotten away with something.

Eric was looking at Phil with the stunned expression of someone who can't reconcile what's before his eyes with what he knows.

Is he seeing something I don't?

"Why don't you tell Eric everything you've told me? That way we'll have a different perspective on things."

Phil smiled again. Beth began to suspect something. What, she wasn't sure, but she began to suspect Phil of trying some kind of complicated game on them. "Well, I started in '38 with Warner, then moved over to Disney."

"Uncle Phil—"

"I'm getting there! It was years later—I was working right here in Burbank on the studio lot—when I saw my first elf. We were watching the dailies for one of the early color features—you know what dailies are, don't you, young man?—and I noticed that someone was sitting a few seats over from me, somebody I'd never seen before. I figured he was one of the execs, dropping in to see what we were working on, but then—"

The old man's eyes brightened, and softened with remembrance. "Then, when they turned the lights back on, I saw him clearly. He was very tall wearing the strangest clothing, with lots of golden hair, curling all over his shoulders. No one, mind you, especially not an executive, wore long hair in those days. My God, he looked just like Snow White's Prince Charming, the way I wanted to do him. Jeez, what a travesty that was. See, the Old Man had this thing about long hair on guys—he'd've just as soon put crewcuts on the Greek gods!"

"Uncle Phil—"

"Right, the guy. He just sat there, looking up at me and smiling. And the most peculiar thing about it was that no one else seemed to see him. It was like he wasn't there. That's when I saw the ears, and I had it figured: either he was an elf, or I was drunk. And I *wasn't* drunk, at least not that day. He saw me looking at him, and he kept smiling at me. And then . . . and then he leaned real close to me, and whispered, like it was a big secret: 'Nice work on that last scene, Phil. But you got something wrong—a unicorn's hooves are supposed to be silver, not gold!'"

Phil's cackling laughter rang through the room, and Eric smiled, slowly. "Well, that was the first time I saw Prince Terenil. I wanted to talk with him some more—after all I'd never seen an elf before—so l just told him right back, 'Look, whoever heard of pastel unicorns, anyway? It's artistic license!' He laughed, and said we ought to go talk about it. I tell you, I was just about to bust out with excitement. I mean, me and an elf! We got some sandwiches from the commissary and sat under the trees on one of the backlots, just talking. Talking about everything—animation, art, elves, humans. Turns out he was a real cartoon fanatic—thought it was amazing how we created living characters out of nothing but voices and blobs of paint. We had a lot in common, for an animator and an elven prince." He shook his head reminiscently. "He really liked the Duck. You know, that Duck was sure my fav—"

"Uncle Phil" Beth said warningly, having finally figured out what was going on. "You can put on that senile act with everybody else, but it isn't going to work with me."

The old man raised his cola can to her, not looking the least bit repentant. "Okay, sweetling. Yeah, those were the days. We used to meet a couple times a week like that, sitting in a backlot, eating lunch, and talking." Phil's eyes clouded suddenly. "Until the big layoffs, that is."

He sighed, and leaned back in his chair. "That was a bad time, for me. for a lot of people in the Industry. Leila— my wife—she was alive then, and working days in a department store. We were all right for a while, living off her salary and our savings, but then money started getting tight. Just when I thought I was gonna have to go back to being a security guard, Prince Terenil showed up on the doorstep, with a leather pouch in his hand. Honeybunch, did I ever tell you that Leila could see the elves too? Wonderful woman, Leila. God, I miss her."

He fell silent for a moment, and just stared sadly off into space, so sadly that Beth didn't have the heart to prompt him. "Best thing that ever happened to me, was Leila," he said softly. "She really was. God, I miss her—"

The old man's eyes were so lost, so infinitely lonely, that

Beth finally had to pretend to examine her Coke can, overwhelmed by the feeling that she was intruding on something very private.

Phil cleared his throat, and took another sip of his cola. "Yeah, she could see them; she and Terenil had a real thing about keeping me from not going off into a gloom about the layoffs. So Terenil showed up. He said he had a sudden craving for a piece of Leila's pecan pie—but after she'd fed him, he said, 'It's about time I returned a little something for your hospitality.' He opened that leather pouch up over the kitchen table, and then there were all these sparkling stones on the formica. A dozen little gems. I thought my jaw was gonna come off, and Leila—she started crying, and hugging him . . . He would never tell us where he got them, just that he didn't steal them. Leila sold them to a jeweler, and we had enough money to live on until the studios started hiring animators again."

You never told me that story before, Uncle Phil.

"It was right after that he took me over to the Elfhame side of . . . whatever. What they call 'under the Hill.' My, now that was different." His eyes had lost their sadness, and were focused on something infinitely lovely, but very far away.

"Did you ever meet Perenor?" Beth asked.

The animator nodded, but his cheerful smile faded. "Oh, I definitely did, Beth. That was quite an afternoon. Prince Terenil and I were at the Elfhame Grove, you know, the one where they all used to meet and party. We were eating oranges and talking—that was when most of the San Fernando Valley was still orange orchards, Beth, years before you were even born—and suddenly Terenil stands up. He has this intent look in his eyes, like he's listening to something, even though I can't hear anything but the birds in the trees around us. Then he starts off through the trees. I didn't know what was going on, but I followed him."

Phil's lips thinned to a hard line. "And there, on the edge of the oak trees, is this handsome silver-haired elf, with a human boy. They're just sitting there, not doing anything that I can see; but the boy has this look on his face like he's drugged out of his mind. And Terenil starts shouting at this other elf; about how that's forbidden magic, that Perenor's hurting the boy and he doesn't even care. Perenor just shrugged. So Terenil just grabbed the boy and stormed off with him. And Perenor gave me this look like he wanted to rip Terenil apart, but wouldn't mind killing me instead, so I ran and caught up with Terenil."

The old man stared down into his Coke can, as if searching for an answer that wouldn't come. "That boy was in a real bad way. Like he was lost somewhere inside himself. Like those kids they call 'autistic,' now. I took him home to his parents, didn't tell them about the elves, just that I'd found the kid wandering in the orchards. His parents told me that he'd been a normal child, no, more than normal—really a special kid, a bright little penny, with a singing voice that you couldn't believe. But he couldn't speak, or hear, not after that afternoon with Perenor. And, months later, I came back to see if he was doing better and found out that the kid had been hit by a car. He was walking across the street and the driver honked and the kid couldn't hear it." Phil paused, taking a long swallow of his soda, as if he was washing away something bitter.

"Later, I heard that Terenil had exiled Perenor from the elven community. All I heard of him after that was a few years later, that he had found himself a human girlfriend, and they had a child, a little blonde girl. Arianrhod, I think that's what her name was. Terenil told me about her, about how she was going to inherit human and elven magic, but I don't remember exactly what he said. It's been a good many years."

A little blonde girl—yes, that makes sense! That's the bitch who was with Perenor last night. His daughter—

Out of the corner of her eye, Beth saw Eric shudder slightly. *Maybe he's figuring it out too, or remembering something of what happened last night in the club—damn, but that Perenor and his daughter are a nasty set of people.*

"You don't know anything else about Perenor, or maybe his daughter? Something about them that might help us?"

Phil suddenly grinned, raising his can of Coke meaningfully. "Sure. Just take 'em out for a glass of cola, and you'll take 'em out, fast enough."

Beth just looked at him. "What do you mean?"

The animator sipped his soda, then looked at the can thoughtfully. "It's something that Terenil told me about, years back. Caffeine. It's just a minor stimulant for us, but for the elves, it's a deadly and addictive drug. In small amounts, it acts like a trank, sends the elves into Dreaming, even if they're okay before they down it. Enough of it, and they'll die from overdose."

"Well." Beth thought about that for a moment. "That's useful information, though I don't know how we can hold Perenor down long enough to pour some coffee down his throat." *Though I'd sure love to do that to you, you murderous bastard—*

"Besides, I don't know if it would work on his daughter, since she's half-human." Phil shifted in his chair, glancing at Eric. "You're being very quiet, young man."

"Just thinking," Eric said, obviously subdued. "They're holding all the cards, aren't they? The people who own the Faire site have already sold it to a developer, it's going to be turned into condos, and that'll destroy the nexus.

Perenor's masterminding that, somehow. I mean, he may be a powerful elf-lord, but he's got a corporation doing his dirty work for him. How can we stop that? You don't stop corporations with magic, I don't care how good you are."

"That's one thing that doesn't make sense to me," Phil mused aloud, "that Perenor wants to destroy the nexus. After all, the loss of magic would hurt him as well as the others. He'd fall into Dreaming, just like them, and then when his magic ran out, he'd fade. And then, what the loss of that magic would do to Los Angeles—"

"What would it do?" Eric asked. "I mean, it would just hurt the elves, right?"

Phil shook his head. "Unfortunately, that isn't the case, young man. You don't realize how much we depend on that magic here. That's why the film industry, and most of the music industry, are located here. That magic nexus gives the elves what they need to live, but it also powers human creativity, the human soul. Without it, we might as well build cars. Because our films would have all the soul of a Chrysler, all steel and Fiberglass."

Eric looked at him with a puzzled expression on his face. Phil turned the can around in his hands, thinking. "You know, there's already places where the magic has died—look at downtown Detroit, where the druggies are stealing the aluminum siding off the walls of houses. Think of the Jersey Turnpike. If you lived there, your imagination, your soul, would wither and die. Think about it."

Beth *did* think about it. *Maybe that's why I'm still living in L.A. this place has so much potential, so many creative people, all trying to do something meaningful. That's the magic that means the most, the magic of the human heart. If that magic dies—*

"Now, what I want to know," Phil continued, "is how Perenor will benefit by destroying the nexus. I think I'll go out and do a little research. Most of the elves I know, like Terenil, are trapped in Dreaming. But maybe one or two of them are coherent enough to talk to me."

"Meanwhile," he said, glancing at Eric and Beth, "I do think that you should talk to these corporation people. See if they understand what they're doing. Without making yourself sound like loons, of course. I'd really hate to have to spring you out of a mental institution, Bethie."

"I'll try to stay out of trouble, Uncle Phil." She grinned. "And we're going to a protest rally at the corporation headquarters this afternoon. I'm hoping we'll find out something useful." *And, with any luck, we'll find a way to stop those bastards—*

Eric looked up at the towering building, the opaque glass window exterior hiding everything within. *Anything could be going on in there, and we'd never know,* he thought, gazing skyward.

So, this is the home of Llewellyn investment corporation, the guys who bought the Faire land—I wonder if it's as intimidating on the inside as it is from out here?

All that stone, that glass—it made him think of . . . prisons. Buildings like this were meant to trap, to hold, to *clutch*—

He looked resolutely away from the intimidating facade. *Caitlin's inside, talking with some of their execs. She's really doing her damndest with this. She, of all the Admin people, really cares about what happens to the Faire.*

He glanced around at the rest of the protestors, looking to see if any of them *glowed* in that peculiar, silvery way the old animator did. Was that strange, magical light just something that only people who knew elves had? And why was he beginning to see it around people *now?*

That question triggered another. *I wonder if any of these people know that there's more at stake than just an Elizabethan Faire site? Do any of them know about the magic nexus?*

Near him the motley group of Faire people (some wearing mundane clothing, others in their colorful Faire garb) milled around uneasily. Beth was several feet away, talking with some of the dancers from her Faire show.

It's strange, I know so many of these people, but here I am, feeling as though I'm standing out here all by myself. It's not that anyone's excluding me, or deliberately not talking to me. It's just that I feel like I'm on the outside, looking in.

He felt odd, uncomfortable—and obscurely unhappy. He wanted to get a little distance from the crowd—but he didn't want to leave them, either.

It's funny, I never thought about it, but I guess that's how I am with Faire people in general. The L.A. Elizabethans, the Texas folks, everyone else I've ever played shows with. I know so many people, but they really aren't friends. Not really.

He swallowed, not liking the direction his thoughts were taking. *Maybe this is what Beth was talking about over the weekend, about how I never commit to anything.*

But I don't want to get hurt—

"If I don't let them get close to me, they can't hurt me." Yeah, that's true, but look at where I am now. Standing alone in a crowd.

The building seemed to loom over him, gloating at his unhappiness. He could almost hear it in his mind—

Then he *did* start to hear a strange, slithery voice in the back of his head.

"See," it seemed to say, *"see how utterly insignificant you are? See how utterly meaningless this all is? Why, you can't even call any of these people a friend, not really— and what good are friends, anyway? Will they buy you power like this?"*

Friend . . . The only one I feel close to at all is Beth, and maybe a few of the musicians. Like Aaron, that crazy fiddler, over there on the sidewalk with a few of the other Irish.

But somehow he couldn't bring himself to join them. *Now that I think about it, I guess this is how my life has been for a long time. Years. Always moving on before I can make any friends, get to know anybody real well. What kind of a life is that? No commitments, sure, but no real friends, either. Even my girlfriends, it's always ended with me leaving town, moving away. I don't know why, but that's how it is . . .*

"And that's the way it will always be," the voice said in his ear. The building loomed silently, staring at him with a thousand cold glass eyes.

But *that* hit his stubborn streak. *That's just my own paranoia talking. And hell, maybe I can change that. Right now. I'm needed here, to help Kory with whatever it is he needs me to do. Save the Faire land, save the elves. And, after that? I don't know. But maybe—maybe Beth would want me to stay here. And Kory—*

He shuffled his feet. The very thought of Kory made him uncomfortable in a different sort of way.

I don't know what to think about Kory. Already, I feel like he's a close friend of mine, even though I've only known him for a few days. And, yeah, there's something else going on there, something I don't understand. It feels good, but—I don't know. I like him in a way that definitely is more than "just a friend." I don't know what's going on there, I just don't. How can I feel that way about a frizzy-haired elf?

Eric shook his head, looking out at the gathering crowd. *Better not think of it now. Looks like everything's about to get started here.*

Caitlin walked out from the entrance to the Llewellyn building, with a business-suited man at her elbow. She stopped at the top of the steps. "Okay, everybody, they've agreed to hear our grievances. We're going inside in an orderly fashion—not like the Noon Parade, youse guys! Go into the conference room on the right side of the lobby and sit down. Some of their executives are going to talk with us there."

Eric joined the throng of Faire people moving toward the large double glass doors.

This place looks normal enough inside. Dozens of suits, but that's to be expected. God, my imagination is working overtime. What did I expect? Sorcerers in gray-flannel robes?

Then he glanced around the busy lobby, and saw *him*.

An older man, tall, distinguished, talking with another businessman by the receptionist's desk. Perfectly normal, except—

Except for the tips of his ears. *Pointed ears,* showing through the immaculately-groomed silver hair.

A flashback of memory hit Eric like a slap in the face.

Sitting on the bus, looking out the window at the limo. And that man, that man with the green eyes—

Green eyes, emerald ice—gazing at me—and reaching—reaching—

Oh shit, it's him! That's Perenor!

Eric ducked back through the crowd, trying to put as many people and as much distance between himself and the Elflord as possible. He tried to signal to Beth, but she was already walking into the conference room with some of the other Rennies

He looked around quickly, trying to spot anything he could use for cover. *In another minute, everybody will be in the conference room. And I'll be out here in the lobby, with* him *standing less than twenty feet away. Shit!*

God, get me out of this!

11

Are You Willing?

The boardroom was silent except for the whisper of turning pages. Ria watched as her executives leafed through the copies of the proposal before them, her face a carefully controlled mask.

This one should be a shock for them. Linette typed it up off my notes only ten minutes before this meeting. Right after my little lunch with William Corwin.

They don't realize it yet, but if we can muster the cash to take advantage of it, this'll be the greatest coup I've accomplished yet.

The dark-haired man seated next to her was the first to speak. "This is a surprise, Ria. Are you sure we want to go through with this?"

She nodded. "Believe me, Jonathan, this one's worth it."

Jonathan Sterling, Ria's V. P. for Acquisitions gazed down at the proposal in his hands, a faint frown between his eyebrows. "It's just—well, Ria, if we pursue this, we'll be overcommitting on capital. Negative cash flow for at least a month, and some serious interest charges from our creditors. If this doesn't pay off, and pay off big, we'll lose a lot. I just think it's too risky."

Oh, Jonathan, you're the only one who's willing to be honest with me. The rest of them are too scared. But you're not telling me anything I don't know already. Ria Llewellyn shifted in her chair and tapped the papers stacked before her with a lacquered nail. "True. It's risky. I know that. What I need you to tell me is—can we commit the cash right now? Because if we're going to do it, it's absolutely critical that we purchase the Corwin stock before the end of the week."

Jonathan gave her a curious look. "You know something we don't," he said, a flat statement.

From the far end of the table, she heard a low mutter, *sotto voce.* "Oh great, here we go again, another week of working till midnight."

Ria spoke quietly. "Yes, I do know something you don't. And, you're right, Harkness, it probably is going to mean another week of working late." She raised her voice slightly. "I especially appreciate all of you staying late last night to finish that purchase proposal. Believe me, there'll be a solid bonus for that. And another, when—not 'if,' gentlemen, *when*—we pull this one off."

Ria continued, very aware that every eye in the room was upon her. "The reason we need to invest in Corwin Systems right now is because they're about to be purchased by National Technology, as part of National's bid to take over the West Coast market share. When that happens, Corwin's stock will double, possibly triple. We, and our represented clients, stand to make a very, very healthy profit. That is, of course, highly confidential information, gentlemen." She leaned back in her chair, waiting for their reactions.

Her executives—

My little worker bees—

—just stared at her, blinking. Jonathan was the first to recover. "Ria, how do you know that?"

She smiled. "The usual sources, Jonathan."

"That's amazing," Harkness, Director of Accounting, said in a barely audible voice, "if it's true."

"Of course it's true," she said coolly. "My sources are impeccable, and they're never wrong. As you should know by now. And we stand to make a killing on it. Harkness, do you have some good, trustworthy people who can handle the accounting end of this? I'll also need several analysts to run projections for the next couple days. Mitchell, if you don't mind, I'm pulling you and Susan off the stock futures project and onto this. Jonathan, I want you to find them some good assistants from your office."

Ten minutes later, Ria called the meeting to an end. The executives, already talking eagerly among themselves, began to trickle out of the boardroom.

They took it in stride. Good people, my execs. I think they're starting to expect the impossible from me. Which is fine . . .

She began gathering up her paperwork from the table. *This should generate more than enough profit to cover that Faire land purchase. It looks like we will have to take a loss on that. The price was just too high—I still can't believe it, over ten million for seven acres that weren't even good commercial property. But Father insisted that we purchase it; just so we can bulldoze it, 400-year-old oak grove and all.*

Father will be pleased—they should begin construction on the site in another few weeks. She straightened, as a thought occurred to her. *If we use that purchase as a tax loss, I won't even have to take it out of his investment accounts. He'd fight me over that, just to have a fight going, and I don't have the time to waste.*

She slipped her neat stack of notes on the meeting into her leather portfolio. *He should be quite happy, in any case. Everything is going so well. Especially with the company. I wonder if he envisioned this, all those years back when he suggested that I consider business school?*

She glanced around the silent boardroom—her boardroom—and smiled cynically. *He probably knew exactly what would happen, that sneaky old bastard. I imagine he just wanted someone to manage his investments for him, so he wouldn't have to bother. I knew he was well off, but that was something of a surprise. Quite a considerable fortune—*

And every penny of it gained by business practices even I would consider questionable. I wonder if that sticks in

*his craw, knowing I've made more money than he ever did,
and I never even had to kill anyone to do it? Just by using
my wits, and a little sorcery here and there to . . .what
were the lyrics to that song last night? "Throw the odds
in my favor . . ."*

She could see the face of the young Bard without even
closing her eyes, clear and precise as a photograph. Lips
pursed over the mouthpiece of his flute, soft, dreaming eyes
half-closed in concentration, stage lights sharply defining the
delicate arch of his cheekbones—

*Throwing the odds in my favor. Oh, if I had that Bard
beside me, I'd do more than just that. I don't know why,
just can't stop thinking about him.*

She recalled the touch of his hand on hers, the dark depths
of his eyes, and shivered with self-indulgent pleasure.

*Father can't go beyond seeing the Bard as a pawn,
someone he could use and toss away—but there's so much
more there, so much potential. And there's something about
him that just—I don't know what it is, but it draws me
to him. Power calling to Power, perhaps. Perhaps. . . .*

Her thoughts drifted off for a moment, and she called
them to heel sharply.

*Besides, if all the legends are true, and I could convince
him to join me—with my magics as a half-Blood sorceress,
and his Creation magics, working together in tandem, there's
nothing we couldn't do. No one could stop us. Not even
Father.*

She analyzed her memories, paying close attention to the
way he had looked at her in that shabby club, and the way
he had responded to her this morning when she had tried
to pinpoint his location. He had been so immediately . . .
overwhelmed.

*He finds me attractive. That's no great surprise. But does
he feel the same way I do? Does he realize the potential,
the power that every touch of our hands creates?*

*Most of the men I've known are so . . . callow. Espe-
cially the humans. I have to agree with Father; I can't see
them as anything more than tools. But the Bard—he has
such latent power. Even just thinking about him—*

She put her hand against her flushed cheek, trying to calm her thoughts.

I can't stop thinking about him. I have to find him somehow. He was thinking of me, earlier. I would have been able to go to him, but something interfered, I don't know what. But he'll think of me again, I know he will. And then—then I'll be able to find him—

Ria replaced the rest of her papers in her leather brief-case, then sensed a whisper against the sigh of the air-conditioning as the door of the boardroom opened, and the presence of someone standing behind her. *Jonathan. I wonder what he wants?*

She turned, giving her veep a warm smile. "Well, Jonathan. You look like you have a question for me."

He glanced around the boardroom, waiting until the last briefcase-toting exec had left. His voice was very quiet. "Ria, do you know what you're doing?"

She shrugged. "Of course."

Jonathan's voice was even lower when he spoke. "Ria, you know what I mean."

"No, I don't know what you mean," she said impatiently, closing and locking her briefcase.

He rested his hand on hers, not letting her walk away. "Insider trading, Ria. That's what I'm talking about. I know you had lunch with William Corwin this afternoon."

She shook her head. "No, Jonathan. It's not what you're thinking. There were five other people at the table besides William and I. We never even talked about his company."

But he thought about it, quite a lot. Poor William, that decision to sell was on his mind all the way through the lunch meeting. I couldn't help but overhear it, feel how it weighed on him so heavily, knowing that there'll be lay-offs after the sale. Overhear it, hell—he was broadcasting so loud, it was almost deafening. I do feel for him, so con-cerned about his employees, so conscientious. An admirable businessman, William Corwin.

"Five witnesses?" Jonathan repeated carefully, amazed; then he flashed her a smile. "Well, Ria, if you're involved in something illegal, I have to say that you do this kind of thing very well. And I'm glad I'm working for you, no matter how you find your information."

She patted his hand. "You're the best person I have, Jonathan. But I can't reveal my secrets, not even to you."

"Oh, why not?" He grinned. "If I knew your tricks, then I could start up my own company from a ten-thousand-dollar investment, and have corporate assets of fifty-five mil in less than five years."

Ria was so startled, she only stared at him for a brief moment. Then she laughed. "Oh, Jonathan, how did you ever manage to find that out? There's no one still working here who was with me in the very beginning."

"I have my secrets, too," he said, smiling. "When I'm working for a sharp cookie like the lovely Ms. Ria Llewellyn, I have to keep on my toes. Or else you'll—"

His words were lost as Ria stiffened suddenly, overwhelmed by a roar of noiseless sound, a silent inner klaxon as every magical warning went off simultaneously in her mind.

There's someone near me—someone with such raw power—not Father, it's a different signature—

Gods, he's in the building, moving towards me, closer every second!

"Excuse me, Jonathan," she said breathlessly, picking up her briefcase and hurrying towards the door. "I've got to get back upstairs right away."

Yes, get upstairs to my office. I've used it for sorcery before, the shielding should protect me from whoever this is—God, he's strong! Who in the hell can this be?

She moved past Jonathan, ignoring his startled stare, through the doorway and into the carpeted hallway. Ria stopped for a moment, scanning the building with her inner sight, trying to find the intruder.

He's very close—moving closer every moment—he's only a few feet away from me right now!

She turned, and saw him.

Eric ran blindly down the first corridor he saw.
I have to get out of here before he sees me. I can't let

him do . . . that . . . to my mind again. I can't. And if he tried to kill me and Beth last night, God knows what he'll try if he sees me now—

There's a stairway sign at the end of this hallway. Maybe I can hide upstairs for a few minutes, wait until he leaves the lobby, then get out. Maybe—

The door at the end of the hallway opened, and a woman stepped out into the corridor, carrying a briefcase. A stunningly beautiful blonde, dressed impeccably in a black silk dress and heels. Eric thought he saw an expression of sudden fear twisting those features, but couldn't be certain.

Then he recognized her, and his breath caught.

That's her. The woman from my dream—

She looked up and saw him, and her eyes widened with surprise.

Eric stopped, right in the middle of the corridor, staring at the woman in disbelief.

:Eric? Is—is it really you?:

The voice was gentle and low, barely a whisper in his thoughts.

Eric couldn't move, just looked at her, bewildered. *How can this be? I—I only dreamed about her—how can she be real?*

She smiled, and held out her hand to him. *:Eric, you came here to find me, didn't you? You came here for me. . . . :*

Eric felt his heart skip a beat, seeing the transformation that smile created in what was already an extraordinarily beautiful woman. Without thinking about it, he moved closer toward her, toward that outstretched hand, the beckoning smile.

She touched his hand, and he felt something akin to an electric shock run through him. *God—what's happening to me? I can't think straight—it's so hard to think at all—*

:You frightened me, Eric. I thought I would have to defend myself from some unknown menace, and it was only you.: The voice in his mind spoke lightly, teasingly. *:Let's go upstairs, to my office.:*

:Yes,: he answered silently, *:that's . . . a good idea—:*

He let her lead him back into the lobby, into the elevator.

Upstairs, where their feet trod noiselessly on the thick velvety chocolate carpeting, she drew him towards a closed office door; past a male secretary working at his desk, past a young executive who was staring at both of them in astonishment, and into her office.

Inside, a single lit lamp cast shadows on the dark mahogany desk and bookshelves, the elegant leather-upholstered chair and couch. She held tightly on to his hand, not letting go for an instant, looking at him with such longing in her eyes. *:I never dreamed—I never thought this would happen—oh, Eric—:*

She moved closer—within inches of him—then kissed him. For a moment, Eric couldn't think, with the woman's silk-clad body molded against him as his arms closed around her in a tight embrace.

Then a coherent thought flickered briefly through his mind. *No. That was only a dream. I don't know her, I've never seen her before, I don't know what I'm doing here . . .*

But something was speaking stronger than that last whisper of sanity. And then he couldn't think of anything at all except the woman who was in his arms, in his thoughts, everything fusing and fading into a silent song that only they could hear.

Music—two melodies, interweaving, very different but counterpointing perfectly, rising toward some unknown, impossible resolution—

She broke away from him suddenly. Eric reeled back several steps, thoroughly shaken by both the fierceness of the music and the passion of the kiss.

Wow. 220 volts, definitely. If this is a dream, I don't want to wake up, ever.

He blinked, tried to recapture his breath, his balance. *Maybe—maybe that wasn't a dream. She recognizes me, knows me. What if that daydream was real—what if she really was searching for me—*

The blonde sat down slowly on the leather couch, "The music," she whispered, then looked up at him, her eyes mirroring shock and some indefinable emotion. "What are you doing to me? I don't understand—why can't I let go, why can't I think of anything but you?" Her eyes darkened dangerously. "Is this a game to you? Playing with my mind? Is that why you came here today, to amuse yourself by turning my world upside down?"

He shook his head and spread his hands. "I came here because of the protest rally. For the Faire site. That's all. I—I'm one of the Faire buskers. I've never—I don't even know your name." His voice faded to an incredulous whisper. "I thought you were only a dream . . ."

She was silent for a long moment. "You didn't come here to find me," she said at last. "You're here because I'm the President of Llewellyn Corporation. Not because of . . . me." Her voice tightened, and her face became an expressionless mask. "You don't have any understanding of this at all, do you? Of the games within games, the chess pieces moving across the board." Now she looked at him sharply. "Or do you? Did you think you could use me?"

Eric blinked again, his mouth dry. *What's she talking about? A chess game Who—or what—does she think I am?*

Well, you're here, Eric, in her office. The office of the President of Llewellyn Investment Corporation. Here's your chance to make a stand, try to do something meaningful for a change. Fight for the Fairesite, and Kory . . .

He cleared his throat awkwardly. "No I didn't think— I mean, I don't want to use you, I didn't know that . . . this . . . would happen." He felt his face warming. *Oh, terrific, now I'm blushing, too. I really wish I could keep from doing that.* He shoved his hands down into his pockets, feeling awkward and very much out of place. "I just wanted—"

Come on, Banyon—don't let her bullshit you into talking mundanities. Hit her with the real *reason why the Site has to be saved.*

"Look," he said, taking his hands out of his pockets. "I know why you bought the land. You're planning to destroy the magic nexus. And that'll kill the L.A. elves. You can't do it." He crossed his arms, gazing at her defiantly.

"So you came here to plead for your elves?" She laughed, her voice brittle. "How quaint."

Eric flushed. *She's only laughing at me now. She thinks I'm a fool.*

The blonde woman moved to her feet instantly. She reached out, taking his hand. He let her. "No, Eric, I don't think of you as a fool. Untrained, unknowing, ignorant of your potential, perhaps, but never a fool."

She drew him toward the couch, still holding his hand. "Sit down, Eric, and I'll tell you the truth about all of this. "

Hesitantly, he sat down next to her. *The truth? Her truth, or the real one? I don't know if I should trust or not—*

—but how can I not trust her, when she looks at me with those eyes—blue eyes, calling me—

He brought himself back to reality with a jolt, realizing that he had been drifting away. *I can't make any sense out of this—everything is so confusing right now—God, it's hard to think straight—*

The blonde woman smiled across at him, her fingers lightly touching his. "I—I don't know where to begin. Who have you been talking to, Eric? Korendil?"

He nodded dumbly.

The woman sighed. "Poor Korendil. He means well, but he really doesn't understand what's going on. But you can, I think." She traced a pattern on the back of his hand with one fingertip. "Eric, I'll tell you my secret. You're the only on who knows this, other than those of the Old Blood. I'm half-elven. My father is of the High Court, a warrior-mage. My mother was a human with magic potential, like yourself. That's why, when I first saw you in the nightclub I knew we had to be together. I'm sure you could feel it, too. Power calling to Power—"

The woman at the Dive—the one I couldn't remember—it's her . . .

He closed his eyes for a moment, and frowned, trying to bring the memory back. Standing on the stage, and—and then—

"Listen to me, Eric. The elves, they're not like us. You can grow into your power, your potential. You can redefine your focus. They *can't* change."

The woman, standing across the room, holding out her hand to me—

Her voice took on an insistence, a weight, that made her words sound like they had to be true. "Through the years, they've become more and more isolated, trapped within their groves. The humans have taken their territory, Eric, and molded it into a different world, one in which the elves cannot exist."

And everything—everything was so strange, so unreal— like I could reach out and touch reality, brush it aside like a curtain—

"And the nexus—well, because of the prevalence of Cold Iron in the humans' cities, and the way that the elves are only tapping into the nexus now through Dreaming, it's become—polluted. It is going to *die*, Eric; die or go bad. If it dies, there'll be no magic left here at all, not for you to draw upon when you play your music, not for any of us. If it goes bad—" She shivered. "Nothing, only desolation and despair. So, my father and I devised a plan—to direct the magic through a new nexus."

"A new nexus?" he asked. *If the magic dies, I'll never feel this way again, like I do now, or I did, that night in the grove—as if the world is wide open before me, all the chords and harmonies mine to change, to control—I'll never feel like that again—*

But Kory said that his enemies were going to destroy the nexus. He never talked about anything like moving it.

"Korendil doesn't know anything," she said, as if hearing his thoughts. "He's been asleep for a long time, Eric. He doesn't know what's going on at all. We have to create a new nexus, or the magic will die or be lost to us forever. We have to, or watch everything worth having become corrupted."

"But if you do that—the elves will still die, won't they?" he protested, weakly.

Faint scorn colored her voice. "Think about them, Eric. You've seen them, last night, in that nightclub. They're already dead. Lost in Dreaming. Nothing can save them now. What you're seeing is only the last moment before they fade away completely. Even the High Court elves, the ones who do not need the nexus to live, they're all lost to Dreaming as well. The only reason Korendil isn't in Dreaming is because he's been spellbound for so long. They can't be saved, Eric; they're terminal patients in the last days of their illnesses. Korendil won't—can't—admit that. But I think it would be kinder to them to pull the plug, to let them go. Korendil is the only one worth saving, and Korendil is High Court. He doesn't need the nexus. When he sees it's hopeless, he can save himself."

Unbidden, the images of the green-eyed people-elves—in the club last night drifted into his mind. Lovely, yes, but . . . as mindless as any brain-dead stoners. Maybe she was right—

"This—" he said faintly, "This sounds like you're doing the right thing, but you also tried to kill Kory last night. What you're trying to do doesn't justify something like that—"

Her face hardened, her eyes turning to blue ice. "You're right, it doesn't. *That* was my father. He hates Korendil and Terenil, for reasons that I don't really understand. And I don't agree with him, or his methods." Her eyes softened again; the vivid blue of the sky at twilight, on a perfect spring night. "But—but if you would help me, Eric, we could accomplish this without my father's interference. No more harm to anyone, just what we have to do—change the nexus."

"Change the nexus—" he whispered, caught in her eyes.

"And if you help me now, there's so much more that I can do for you, Eric. You're a brilliant musician, you should be playing on better stages than some rundown dive in the Studio City. I have friends in many places—you could have the kind of music career most people only dream of, the recognition and money you deserve. It would be so easy—"

Her blue eyes, intense and alive, held his gaze.

:*So easy, Eric—all you need do is reach out your hand and take what you want.*:

He couldn't seem to look away from those eyes. *I—I don't know what to think. She's . . . so beautiful—and those eyes, looking right into me . . . All I want to do is say yes, say I'll never leave her again—*

But—Kory and Beth—I can't abandon them. I promised I would help them. I can't go back on that, either.

I don't know what to do—what to think—

She squeezed his hand gently. "Don't make a decision now. Just think about it, okay?" She stood up and moved to the large desk, quickly writing down an address on a notepad. "This is my home address." She handed it to him; for a moment, her expression was suddenly very vulnerable. "I'll— I'll be there; tonight, if you want to come over and talk."

Eric took the piece of paper, and slipped it into his jeans pocket. He smiled shyly. "You know, I—I don't even know your name," he said.

"Ria." She moved closer to him. "Ria Llewellyn."

"I'll, uh, I'll see you later, Ria," Eric said awkwardly, distinctly uncomfortable under the intense gaze of her eyes.

"I'm certain you will," she said, walking with him to the office door.

Ria shut the door, then leaned against the wood, closing her eyes and smiling. She had to exercise every bit of control to keep from laughing aloud. *Oh, what incredible luck! I can't believe it. I thought I'd never see him again, and he walked right into my office! It's almost enough to make me believe in Fate—*

Young, untrained, and very malleable. Not to mention a few other perks, like those wonderful dark, dark eyes. He's really quite handsome. And, ah, definitely interesting enough to hold my attention for a long time . . .

She tingled all over, with excitement, arousal—and Power. *He'll come tonight, I know he will. And when he arrives at the door . . . let's see. I'll greet him myself, doubtlessly give him a warm little hello kiss, which he'll return with interest, and— and then—oh, what the hell, we probably won't even make it all the way to the bedroom. Probably shouldn't even try. I'll introduce him to the jacuzzi and the waterbed afterwards . . .*

Then a chill of doubt froze her. *But—but what if he changes his mind? What if he never shows up?*

She shook her head, stubbornly. *No, that's impossible. He has to be there tonight. No man has ever walked away from me, ever. He'll show up tonight, I know it. He will.*

She smiled to herself and stretched luxuriously. *He is so very delicious. I've never felt such . . . anticipation . . . before. I just can't stop thinking of him—*

A sharp knock at the door interrupted her thoughts. "Come in," she said brusquely, and walked back to her desk and took her place behind it.

The door opened. Ria frowned as her father prowled into the plush office. He crossed to the mahogany cabinet without even glancing at her.

"We need to talk, Ria," Perenor said, removing a bottle of Scotch and a glass from the cabinet.

He always thinks he can just stroll in here and take charge! My own dear, sweet Father— "I just had a very important meeting, Father, and I really don't think this is a good—"

"An important meeting? With the young Bard, perhaps?" Perenor smiled, and raised the glass of Scotch to her in a toast. "You're definitely my daughter, Ria. You never let an opportunity pass by, and you're quick to take . . . advantage of a situation. I'm impressed."

Despite herself, Ria flushed. "It's none of your concern Father." *None of your damn business, either. I know what you'd do with Eric if you got your hands on him—and that's why I'll never let you near him.*

"Oh, but it is my concern." He took a slow draught from his glass. "When my own daughter consorts with the enemy . . . By the way, Ria," he said, giving her a cursory glance, one tinged with the faintest hint of contempt, "your clothes are in quite a state of disarray. Perhaps you ought to rebutton your blouse. You mustn't allow your employees to see you as anything less than immaculate, true?"

Ria met his gaze squarely, not even glancing down at her attire. *I know what you're doing, you old snake. Trying to unnerve me, take control, as always—*

"And you might want to consider, ah, shielding your activities from those of us who are sensitive to such things,"

Perenor continued. "It's quite distressing to be interrupted in a business conversation by the realization that my daughter is seducing a Bard several floors above me."

Damn him, he's doing this deliberately! Trying to fluster me, to get me off-balance—I won't let him! Two can play at this, Father. "It's no worse than some of your own . . . amusements," Ria said silkily, allowing no hint of emotion to leak into her words. "I've never complained about your choice of companions, even when some of them are distinctly . . . distasteful. Especially the ones who aren't even human or elven—"

Perenor's hand tightened visibly on the whiskey glass.

No—you don't like being reminded of your own perversions, do you? But I think I know where this little game of yours is leading—and no, I won't let you get control of Eric. No matter what you say or do.

"That is not the question here," the elf-lord said coldly. "The fact is that you are playing a very dangerous game, with a young man—a young human man—of unknown potential. You're playing with fire—"

Ria shook her head. "I know exactly what I'm doing, Father. Believe me, I do." She smiled, noting the way his eyes had narrowed thoughtfully. "Unlike you, I don't believe in destroying my opponents. Not when there're more . . . satisfying ways of winning."

Her father was silent for a long moment, swirling the Scotch in his glass. Then he spoke, very quietly, "He's dangerous, Ria. So is Korendil. After I find Korendil, I will deal with this Bard of yours, I assure you of that."

Her back stiffened; her head came up. *Like hell you will, Father!*

"Don't touch him," she said in a voice like ice. "If you do—"

Perenor smiled.

She tightened her jaw at the sight of that poisonous smile. *As though he just scored a major victory, that old bastard—*

"Of course, my dear," he said smoothly. "I didn't realize you were so . . . concerned about this Bard of yours. I never thought you would become so attached to him so quickly."

"Attached? Hardly. It's just—he'll be very useful to me," she said, carefully choosing her words. "That much potential is far too valuable to be wasted, Father. I didn't make this company what it is by squandering profitable property on mere amusements."

She hid a smile as her own dart scored, and Perenor's back stiffened. "And he'll be safely under my control, no danger to you or anyone. I'll make sure of that."

Yes, he'll be mine, mine to control, and to use, possibly even against you, Father dear—

"How do you intend to control him?" Perenor asked idly, sipping from his drink. "I would think that controlling a Bard, someone of such unfathomable power, might even be beyond your capabilities my dear."

She shrugged. "I lied to him."

"What did you tell him?" Perenor glanced at her over the rim of his whiskey glass.

"That we're moving the nexus. That the magic is fading, and if we don't do something, it'll die. Technically, that is true—though it won't happen for at least another thousand years. And when that does happen, it's likely that the magic will simply find another weak point in the veil between the worlds through which it can flow easily. Creating a new nexus. Or so you instructed me, Father dear."

Perenor smiled. "Not bad. But what if he learns the truth?"

"After tonight, nothing will matter to him but me."

Her father laughed, honey with gall. "You have a lot of confidence in your abilities, daughter."

"I think both of us do. And with good reason." A thought suddenly occurred to her. "What did you mean, Father after you *find* Korendil? Don't you know where he is?"

Perenor cleared his throat uneasily, not meeting her eyes. "Actually, I don't. For some reason, I can't seem to locate him. It's more than possible that he didn't survive the night, of course. Very likely, in fact. He would have bled to death from those wounds in a few hours."

Oh my. Father dearest, have you, of all people, actually fumbled something? Certainly, Korendil is dead—unless he's alive, and somehow hiding himself from you. Oh, this is amusing. I never thought I'd see the day that you'd admit you were incapable of anything.

"Not that it matters," her father added, a little too hastily. "There really isn't anything Korendil can do against us. My only concern was that young Bard, though if you feel you have that situation well in hand—"

Ria smiled. "Believe me, I do." *In more ways than one, Father.*

Perenor drained the last of his Scotch, setting the glass on the cabinet. "Well. That sounds quite definite." He raised an eyebrow at her. "I may visit you, Ria, after tonight, just to see what you do with this young prodigy."

I'll bet you will. And I bet you'd like to get your hooks into him as well. Believe me, I intend to leave him much more . . . intact than he would be after some time in your tender hands. I have more in mind for this Bard than simply to use him once and cast him aside. My plans are much more . . . permanent.

She realized her father was scrutinizing her with a very speculative gaze. "What if he doesn't show up?" Perenor asked bluntly.

She froze for a moment, *Would he—*

No. No man had ever walked away from me.

"He will. I know he will. He doesn't have any choice in this."

No choice at all, she thought, realizing at that moment that this young man was drawing her as much as she was drawing him, *Which she hardly dared admit to herself, much less to her father.*

No, he has no choice. Not any more than I do. There's something pulling our lives together, binding us—Power calling to Power—

Whatever happens, he's mine. And no one, not even my father, is going to stand between us.

He has to come to me tonight. I know he will. He has to—

12

No Irish Need Apply

Eric stared through the grimy window, as the RTD bus chugged painfully up the hill over the Sepulveda Pass to the Valley. Even though it was still early in the afternoon the traffic was already slowing to a turtle's pace, creeping along the freeway through the smog-shrouded hills.

His mind felt just as smog-shrouded. *Nothing seems to make sense anymore . . .*

He leaned against the glass, gazing down at the cars creeping past the bus.

Only a few days ago, everything seemed so . . . normal. I was busking days, playing different gigs nights, Maureen and I were still together, life was fine. Now, in less than three days—

He sighed, and rubbed the back of his sweaty neck with his hand. *Now there's two women in my life. And one elf.*

How did my life get so complicated so fast?

Eric wedged himself closer to the glass and closed his eyes.

Ria Llewellyn. Even her name is magical. What a combination. What an incredible combination. Corporation president, a half-elf, and one helluva lady. Not to mention staggeringly beautiful. She's like something out of my dreams. It's hard to believe she's real.

But there's something about her—

He recalled the odd light, the predatory chill in her eyes when he'd left her, and shivered involuntarily.

There's a funny intensity there when she looks at me. Like a cat, a cat that's got a mouse trapped, and is thinking about playing with it instead of eating it. It's damn scary—like I'm nothing to her, only a toy, or a tool—

A car honked right under the window, but the sound seemed to come from another world entirely. As if the world that held traffic jams and the world that held Ria Llewellyn couldn't possibly be the same. He replayed the scene with her over and over in his mind, concentrating on it, trying to sift some kind of meaning out of it, but all he got were contradictions—

—like that other way she looked at me, like she's just a child, only wanting someone to hold onto, someone who'll take all the pain away. So lost, so vulnerable. It took everything I had to keep from taking her in my arms right then, trying to comfort her. It's like someone hurt her once, hurt her real bad, and she's never admitted it to anyone; maybe not even herself.

He chewed his lip with frustration. *God, I can't make heads or tails out of it; one minute she's about to take a piece out of me, the next, she's like a little kid—*

And yet another facet of memory focused.—*Then she changes again—she looks at me with that little bedroom smile, those come-hither eyes, teasing—inviting—brushing her hand against mine—*

He blushed, and pillowed his head into the crook of his arm, hoping no one in the bus was watching him. *I don't understand that, either. Sure, I'm always making a fool of myself in front of women, but she—she's really something. All I want to do when she smiles like that is drag her off to a cave somewhere. That's not like me, usually. I try to be a little more . . . dignified about my sex life.*

And everything about the meeting was washed in a kind of glowing fog. The more he tried to concentrate on some memory-fragment, the more the memory slipped into a haze. *It's so hard to think straight when I'm around her. It's like everything is wrapped in gray fuzz, I don't know where I am, what I'm doing, what to think.*

And that led him back around full circle, to last night and this morning. Those memories were as clear as crystal, everything sharp-edged and diamond-cut. *That's sure not like the way it is with Beth. With Bethie, I always know what's going on.*

Or, at least, I think I do—

He pondered that, and concluded ruefully that maybe he didn't know what was going on between himself and Beth.

She's got me going too, I guess. I mean, I thought we had something special, something really nice. Maybe even something permanent. I think she understands me, better than anybody else. After all, she's kinda like me, she's a gypsy too. I make my way playing street and gigs—she works in TV. A production manager is always between gigs, moving from studio to studio; or on hiatus, like she is now. She understands how it is.

But when he'd looked for her in the lobby, she'd been gone.

She didn't even wait for me, back there at the Corporation. Just left without me.

Maybe she thought I'd already taken off—after all, I did kinda vanish from the protest meeting. But she didn't even leave a note with the receptionist—

It had been like the time his mother had forgotten to pick him up from school. He'd stood on the curb forlornly for an hour, clutching his flute, watching for the car that never came—until one of his teachers took pity on him and took him home.

Another car—or the same one—honked again, and this time he jumped. *Well, that really doesn't matter, I guess. What matters now is what I'm going to do. I just don't know who to believe, Kory or Ria. Which of them is telling the truth?*

Korendil—what he'd said—the *elf* believed his own words, that was the truth, anyway. But how much of the truth?

Kory—I really don't know what to think about Korendil

either. Everything is moving so fast, too fast to figure out. I like him—he's a friend, like no other friend I've ever had—

But there's something about him that makes me feel so . . . uncomfortable. The way he looks at me, like I'm everything he ever dreamed of, the answer to all of his prayers. It's more than a little embarrassing. And whatever it is that Ria's got—that magnetism, that . . . allure—he's got it too . . .

God, why am I thinking that? Maybe it's just that he got himself so trashed trying to keep Perenor away from me and Bethie, or the fact that we healed him, but—I feel so—

He gave himself a mental shake. *Confused. That's how I feel. All of this is so confusing, Kory, Beth, the magic—Ria—*

He clenched his fingers in his hair. *God. Magic. I can't disbelieve in it anymore. What we did this morning to heal Kory, me and Beth—it happened, it was real, as real as I am. Which means that it all is true, the elves, the magic, everything. It must be true—I am a Bard. Whatever that means. And—and if that's true, then what happened, all those years ago, it was real, too—*

He shivered, huddled close against the window. The memory came back, as clearly as if the living nightmare had occurred just the night before.

He was standing on the stage, the bright lights making everything look so distant, out-of-focus—the orchestra was beginning the first notes of "Danse Macabre."

Then he began the opening solo.

And the music—suddenly it was so strong, so powerful, better than he'd ever played before; everything coming together and clicking into place and perfect—

Then—

Caught in the spell of the music, he began to shiver. The weird melody called up his nightmares, the things of childhood; the things that lurked under the bed, behind the closet door, and waited for the light to be turned off—

He felt unfriendly, hungry eyes on him—looked out of the corner of his eye at the wings—

—and saw them.

The watchers in the darkness of the theater, the creatures detaching from the shadows. Unnoticed by the audience, gliding toward him like cloaks of liquid night, hands outstretched, reaching for him—

He stood there, frozen in place, not believing what was happening—

Then flung the flute away and ran, ran—his throat so choked with fear he couldn't even scream—just whimper—

He opened his eyes, and clenched his hands on his knees to stop their trembling. *I ran all right. Ran like hell. The conductor was horrified by the kid prodigy freaking out backstage; my parents were freaking out almost as bad as me. Two years of psychoanalysis, of everyone telling me that it wasn't real, it didn't happen. I just imagined it. Two damn years being told I was crazy that night. Then the kids at Juilliard found out about it—*

More years of taunting, tricks with things being hidden in his closet. with "practical jokes" and attempts to scare him into another fit of hysterics in public. Notes addressed to "Loony Banyon." Getting on the mailing list of every nuthouse in the country. Good old Chuck Marquand, the second-best flautist at Juilliard, setting up phony appointments for Eric with the local shrinks.

Beginning to doubt his own sanity.

But—if all of this is real, then that was real, too—those things, *staring at me with such hunger and need, they were* real; *creatures that shouldn't exist but did, all because of me.*

Because of me—

Because I'm a Bard.

Christ.

He tried to laugh at himself. *You know, I really wish somebody else could've been picked for this honor. How did I get so lucky? Anybody else would be better for this. Like Bethie; she'd be perfect. She's got it all together, knows what she wants to do; she never falters or feels like she can't cope.*

He gritted his teeth to keep from shivering. *I do, all the time. I'm not the right one for this, for whatever it is I'm supposed to do. I feel like I'm being pulled in all these directions, with no idea which way I want to go. Everyone wants so much from me—*

But he needed answers, and the only place he was going to get them—was from himself.

I'll figure this out for myself, that's what I'll do. I'll make my own decision, and stick to it. That's it.

He glanced out the window, and leaped to his feet, diving for the rear exit of the bus. *Shit, I missed my stop!*

Eric stumbled down to the street, and looked around sourly. *Oh well. It's only a few blocks back to the apartment. I'll live.*

He trudged across the intersection, sidestepping several kids on skateboards. *With the way my luck has been lately, I'm likely to get run over by a rollerskater in Woodley Park. What else could possibly happen that would complicate my life even more than it is now?*

Strike that. I don't even want to think about anything that might complicate my life!

Eric started down Sherman Way, past the sprawling Post Office building. Ahead of him, he could hear the faint roar of a cargo plane taking off from Van Nuys Airport only a few blocks away. *Probably one of those big World War II bombers. I think some of those pilots are still living through the war, the way they fly those big clunkers. Not living in reality.*

Hell, who am I to talk about living in reality? Me, the Bard, with my best friends the witch and the elf. Some reality, Eric.

He coughed a bit as a junker growled past, burning more oil than gas. More had happened to him in the past week than had happened in the last year—

And it had taken some of the starch out of him, that was for sure. He was sweating by the time he reached his apartment; hot and tired, and a little gritty.

He'd never noticed quite how much of an eyesore the tacky old pink building was. He couldn't help but contrast this—and the steel and chrome sleekness of the Llewellyn

Building. And Ria Llewellyn's office—no plastic couch with a lump in it for her. Nothing but the best . . .

So what could she possibly see in *him*? Grubby little busker, no money, no muscles, nothing a woman like that couldn't have just by snapping her fingers—

Maybe she saw the same thing that Beth and Kory did. *Whatever that is.*

He unlocked the security door and trudged down the hall to his apartment, suddenly wanting both of them around. Needing them. Badly.

I need a sanity check. I need to find out how much of what she said is true—and why she's so hot on me—

But as he unlocked the door of his apartment, a voice spoke from the shadowy living room before he could call out.

"They are not here, Bard."

A voice like broken music.

He opened the door; slowly, carefully.

There was an elf sitting on his living room couch.

Blond, like Kory, and long-haired; but his hair was unkempt and neglected, dulled and brittle. Tall, gaunt, with lines of pain etched around his mouth and eyes. And the eyes themselves—

If Kory's eyes were crystalline emeralds, and Perenor's clouded jade, this elf's eyes were reflections of the sea on a moonless night. Deep gray-green, and haunted, they gave Eric the feeling that something too terrible to think about moved beneath the surface. Ancient eyes; anguished eyes.

Eric tried to speak, and found he couldn't get his mouth to work until the elf looked away. "W-which one are you?" he stammered, as he shut the door behind himself. "And where are they?"

"I do not know," the elf replied, again in that beautiful, ruined voice. "They had departed before I arrived." He raised a wing-like sweep of eyebrow at Eric. "I took the liberty of removing the blood from the carpet. Dangerous, to leave it there, and not just for Korendil."

Eric could feel a thousand unspoken, fear-ridden questions behind the elf's calm facade.

"Yeah, well, we weren't thinking about that—"

"No. I would imagine—from the amount—" The elf's eyes closed briefly, and the pain-lines about them deepened.

"Was the boy badly hurt?" he asked, his voice a harsh whisper.

"Yeah," Eric began. "Perenor really trashed—"

The elf opened his eyes, and sea-fire raged in them. Eric flinched away from his fury.

"*Danann*—if he is dead, I swear by my honor I will—"

"He's okay—" Eric stammered, interrupting him. "W-w-e healed him. Me and Beth—"

The elf stopped, frozen. "You. Mortals. You healed him. And you put no binding upon him?" A darker emotion lurked in those gray-green eyes, roiling with restrained violence.

Eric blinked. "Say what?"

"No, I see that you did not." The fire died in the elf's eyes, and he slumped a little. "No Bard would, I think. It was not all Dreaming, then, what the boy said of you. Korendil is wiser than I." He pondered that for a moment, then placed one hand on his chest and bowed, with a smile of self-mockery. "Bard Eric Banyon, you see before you all that is left of Terenil, prince of Elfhame Sun-Descending. I would ask for your help."

Eric felt his jaw slipping. "*My* help? But—"

The elf rose and walked a little closer, and now Eric could see that he was dressed incongruously enough, in stained, scuffed, deep-scarlet leather. Like Robin Hood, only in red. Eric's jaw slipped a little more.

"Well . . . that is less than the truth," Terenil admitted. "I came to search out Korendil; I could not sense him nor trace him with magic, and I feared—"

Eric felt a chill, if Terenil could find his way to the apartment, how long would it take Perenor? "How did you know he was here?"

"The blood," Terenil replied. "Suddenly I could sense the blood. But when I arrived, he and the witch had already gone. I was not certain what to think; especially after I found the blood and . . . those—"

He nodded his head toward the chair next to the door. On it were the ravaged and bloodstained garments Korendil had been wearing. Eric eyed them mournfully.

My best Faire shirt—and my boots—

"It was only moments later I heard your footsteps. I still cannot sense him, therefore she must be shielding him. If he has been hurt, *that* is just as well—"

"Yeah," Eric said vaguely. *They're not here—so they must be at Beth's place. That means he was in good enough shape to move.* Jealousy cramped his throat. *No wonder she didn't wait around for me. Why should she? What am I, compared to him? What have I got that he hasn't got more of? And on top of it all, he's an elf. What'd that old guy say to her? "You've finally got your wish"? She's been looking for an elf like him for years . . .*

"Bard—I still need your help." The elf broke into his unhappy thoughts. "Please—help me."

"Why?" Eric spat, suddenly angry at the whole race of elves. *Yeah, I can guess what Beth is doing, now that she's found her elf. They're probably—*

"Because—" Terenil's shoulders sagged. "Because no one else will," he said raggedly. "Those few of my own who are not lost themselves have given *me* up for lost. Even Korendil. I—I failed him, last night. I failed him . . ."

Eric's anger ran out of him. "Hey," he said awkwardly. "Like, it wasn't your fault. You aren't in real good shape, y'know?

Oh shit. That's it—that's probably why she had to move Kory in a hurry. He was in lousy shape, and she didn't want to risk Perenor tracking them down. Maybe that blood . . . well, whatever. That's probably why she didn't wait.

Though I really wish she'd left me a note . . .

"And whose is the fault, then?" Terenil asked, his voice rough with self-accusation. His eyes caught Eric's for a moment, just as Kory's had—

Thoughts ran wild in his head, with an underscoring of lament, dirge to something lost past recall.

Korendil vanished; more of the Low Court falling into Dreaming by the day. Those of the High Court who had

*not gone north to Elfhame Misthold or under the Hill, had
slipped hopelessly into Dreaming themselves. Without
Korendil to rally the High court remnants, to help him—
it was useless to struggle on against the Dreaming for he,
who should have been able to protect who was responsible
for protecting them, was helpless, helpless . . . Only a Bard
could have saved them—and Perenor had seen to it that
there would be no Bards here.*

*So why not give up, give in, let dreaming take him too?
They were all doomed. Better that he would not be capable
of witnessing or understanding the end . . .*

Despair too profound even to register as pain nearly
knocked Eric to his knees. Only once had he ever run across
anyone who lived with anguish like that. An ex-'Nam vet
named Tor, up at the law school at Stanford, who used to
let Eric stay with him between Faire weekends, feed him
and give him crashspace on the dorm floor when the busking
got too thin—

And who used to get drunk with him when the pain was
too much, and neither of them wanted to get stoned alone.

*Wonder what happened to Tor? It's been years. Did he
ever get out to Colorado like he always said he wanted to?*

He answered Terenil's despair with Tor's own words.
"Sometimes shit happens, no matter what you do. Sometimes all you can do is try and keep yourself in one piece,
so you can figure out what happened, and figure out how
to keep it from happening again." *Yeah, you had the right
idea, old friend—*

He was rewarded by seeing some sanity come back into
the Prince's expression.

"I have done poorly at even that," Terenil replied bitterly.

Eric cocked his head to one side, and took a really close
look at him. *Well, he looks pretty strung-out, but he doesn't
look drugged. And hell, enough people have written me off—
too many times—I'm damn sure not gonna slam the door
in his face.*

"It happened," he said. "Not even one of you incredibly powerful magical type elves is going to be able to

change the past. So, how can I help you out, your Highness?"

Terenil raised his eyes to meet Eric's, astonishment erasing some of the pain-lines.

"You'll help me?" he said incredulously.

Eric shrugged. "Sure. Why not? I think you deserve help. I don't know that I can help you much, but whatever I can do, I will. I told Kory I'd do what I could for the elves, and last time I heard, you hadn't turned in your union card."

The gratitude in Terenil's expression was as hard to face as his rage had been. Eric *had* to turn away from it—and to cover his lapse of manners, picked up the ruined clothing and looked it over, hoping to find some sign it could be salvaged.

"It is beyond repair, I fear."

The voice was right in his ear, and he jumped, dropping the shirt. "Y-yeah, it's pretty totaled," he agreed. "I mean, I don't grudge it, but—how come he had to take my clothes?"

And how the hell *did he ever fit into them?*

"Because, Bard, we cannot *create* with our magic. Alter easily. Copy, yes—if we know the article intimately. But not create. Only a Bard or a very powerful Adept can create something from naught but power."

"Okay—but why *my* clothes?"

"He would have been rather conspicuous without them," the Prince said dryly. "Being as he was bespelled wearing his armor—and so woke in the same condition."

"Lots of people wear armor on the Faire Site," Eric objected.

"Armor like *this*?"

The Prince straightened, gaining at least two inches in the process—and began to glow . . .

Eric closed his eyes; the Prince's outline wavered in a way that was making him slightly ill— and besides, he was hearing music again—

Slow, majestic chords; a massive pipe organ, like the one in that chapel in the Santa Cruz hills—

The music faded, and he opened his eyes—and lost his jaw entirely.

The Prince looked like a Prince now; clad head-to-toe in some fantastic suit of gold and scarlet enamel, chased and filigreed and articulated so finely Eric had no doubt that Terenil could dance in the stuff. It made the armor in the movies look modest and restrained. Not to mention bulky and awkward.

Terenil favored him with an ironic half-smile.

"Yeah, I see." Eric swallowed. "I guess he would have been kind of conspicuous."

"And he was bespelled ten years ago. The only clothing he could replicate—assuming he could spare the magepower, which I do not think he could—would have been bell-bottomed jeans and leisure suits, Bard Eric; or High Court garb, Equally conspicuous."

The idea of Kory in a polyester leisure suit made Eric splutter with laughter. When he looked up again, Terenil was back in his scarlet leather.

"I guess—I guess I don't mind so much," Eric admitted. "Not when you put it that way. But—" He surveyed the blood-stiffened boot in his hand with regret. "I'll miss my boots. Be a while before I can afford another pair."

"If you will permit?" Terenil took the boots from him, held them in front of his chest, and frowned at them.

A quick, staccato chord—

The moccasin boots were gone. What was in Terenil's hands was something else entirely. Eric had lusted after the famous "Faire boots," tooled and decorated, hand-made, custom-fitted boots, for years. *These* made *those* look like his worn-out moccasins. Brilliant scarlet, and embellished with tiny metallic gold sunbursts—

Like Terenil's armor.

"Not your colors, I do not think," the elf muttered, and as a strange little fluted melody played behind Eric's eyes, he watched the tint deepen to wine, watched the sunbursts vanish, to be replaced by a simple vine and leaf pattern, all in silver, threading from the sole to the top.

"Here," Terenil said, with a touch of pride, holding the boots out to him. "In simple things, at least, it seems I have not lost my abilities."

Eric took them. *This is it. I have gone around the bend. I am no longer operating in this reality—*

Nevertheless he kicked off his sneakers and pulled the boots on. It was almost with relief that he found them to be miles too big.

Thank God. Reality. Next, I find out I'm wearing Baggies on my feet, and that he hypnotized me.

"They're—"

"Indeed, I expected. They are, after all, copies of *mine*." The elf knelt for a moment, and ran his hands down Eric's legs—

The feeling of Terenil's hands upon him was disturbingly sensual.

Christ! First Kory—

Then the leather *moved*, tightening around Eric's calves and feet until the boots might have been painted on him. He'd have jumped, if Terenil hadn't been holding his ankles.

Jesus H—

The elf stood and straightened. "Now do they fit well enough, Bard Eric?"

Eric swallowed hard. "Uh—yeah, sure."

Too weird for words. Definitely.

I'm almost afraid to think what could happen next . . .

The Prince hailed a cab at the curb, directing the driver to some place in Beverly Hills. Eric was too bemused to note the address. He kept expecting his boots to turn back into Baggies, or into his old, ruined pair.

All this talking about magic—but these are real; I can touch them. And Kory being healed was real, too. It's not talk, it's not F/X. It's happening.

The cab stopped. Terenil produced a fifty from nowhere (literally), and handed it to the driver, who opened the door for them. Eric found himself stepping out onto a driveway that looked like it went on for miles.

The cab pulled away, leaving them standing beside a wrought-iron gate with more security hookups than Eric had ever seen in his life.

Terenil idly placed his palm on one of the mysterious

black boxes, and Eric heard a complicated burst of twelve-tone—

And the gate swung open.

"I have the feeling that this isn't your house," he said, nervously. "Are we going to get arrested for breaking and entering in the next five minutes?"

Terenil raised his eyebrows again. "Are you more concerned with the impropriety of appropriating someone else's property, or the possibility of being caught at it?"

"Being caught!" Eric said promptly, with a grin.

"You should have been born one of us." The Prince pushed the gate completely open and beckoned to Eric to follow him. "The owner of this manse is an old friend of mine. He is currently in Eire, and will be for some months. He has left only one caretaker, who is surfing, and will not return until sundown. I have convinced the alarms that we hold the proper keys. There will be no police here."

The driveway *did* go on for miles, white and glaring under the afternoon sun "So why are we here?" Eric asked, following the scarlet figure up the hot stretch of concrete. "I have the feeling you've been here before."

"I have," Terenil sighed. "Often—though not for this purpose, precisely. I came here when I . . . needed a place. . . undisturbed."

Eric flashed on a glimpse of one of the elves last night, sitting in a corner stoned out of his wits. He nodded to himself. *Yeah. Being an elf isn't going to keep the cops from hassling you by day if they think you're blitzed.*

"So why are we here now?" Eric persisted.

Terenil moved off the white desert of concrete and onto a path of tastefully arranged stones. " We are here, Bard Eric, because we need a place undisturbed. A place of combat, and this manse has such within it."

Place of combat?

"What's wrong with the park?"

They had reached a portico of rough-hewn redwood beams. Terenil played his trick with the door, and it, too, swung open at a touch. He strode inside as if he knew exactly where he was going.

He said he did.

"This a place where we will not be conspicuous," Terenil said carefully, leading the way through the tiled entry and down a birch-paneled hallway. "My abilities are not . . . what they were. I cannot make us 'invisible,' engage in combat, and hold my memories in your mind, all at once. Two of the three, yes, but not all three. Here."

He touched another door and motioned Eric to precede him, and Eric found himself in a dojo.

Who the hell's house is this, anyway?

"Why do I need your memories?" he asked in confusion, as Terenil shut the door behind them.

"Because, Bard, I need very badly to regain my skills' in fighting, both by blade and magic—and to do so, I need an opponent." He tapped Eric's chest with an outstretched finger. "You."

"Me?" Eric's voice squeaked.

"Indeed. "

The elf-prince placed his hand on Eric's forehead before Eric could scramble away.

The world vanished with a shout.

13

False True Love

"In truth, Terenil, this is indeed schizoid," Eric said dubiously, taking his stance where the elf-Prince pointed.

"I don't think I like it. I feel as though I am me and you, too. It is quite weird facing myself like this."

"I would imagine," the elf agreed; he moved to about twenty feet away from Eric, and stood with his legs braced. He shook his hands to loosen them, and flexed his fingers. "But giving you my memories is the only way in which I shall face an opponent of equal strength and skill. I used to spar thus with Korendil—"

"Well, he's in no shape to do that right now anyway." Eric shook his head to try and settle all the alien thought-patterns. They kept floating around inside his skull, intruding when he least expected them to. Strange patterns, somehow delicate, yet fraught with an intensity he had never—

Oh shit, first I start talking like him—now I'm starting to think *like these pointy-eared jokers, too!*

"Am I going to keep this shit in my head forever, or can you get rid of it when you're done?" Eric asked plaintively.

"Without my sustaining the memories, they will fade and quickly," Terenil assured him with a faint smile. "I am just as pleased to be facing you, in truth—Korendil is no kind of mage, and Perenor is both warrior and mage. If I am to confront him again, I shall need my skills at both."

"Well, how'm I supposed to know what to do?"

"You do not," Terenil said, with just a hint of maliciousness. "You simply react—"

He pointed his finger at Eric.

And suddenly a there was a burst of trumpet-blare, and a bright glowing ball was hurtling straight for him.

Shit!

Eric yelped and dove for the floor.

"Interesting, though not particularly effective," the Prince observed. "Granted, I would not have thought of that."

"But—" Eric protested from his position on the mat.

"Dodging will not help you a second time, Bard—"

This time two of the orange balls of flame were coming at him. He threw up his hands in a pathetic attempt to ward them off—

And one of those *other* memories stirred. Without understanding what he was doing, he reached for . . . something. And when he had it, he twisted it into a C major arpeggio, strong and resounding.

And a ball of red flame intercepted Terenil's two, consuming them.

"Excellent!" the Prince laughed. "And I would not have thought of *that*, either!"

"What's *that* supposed to mean?" Eric panted, getting to his feet.

"You have my memories of working magic—but you use your own powers. Like so—"

Roar of brass. Lightning lashed down where Eric stood—

Except that he wasn't standing there anymore. He'd dodged again, and that something inside him acted. He heard a musical run like a trombone cadenza, saw he was sending a streaming lance of fire—*like a flamethrower*—straight at the Prince.

Who deflected it (*crash of cymbals*) but not easily.

Hey, I'm not doing too bad at this! Eric Banyon mage-warrior, just like something out of Tolkien! Hah, take that, Prince Terenil!

Then Terenil got serious.

After a few moments of being chased around the dojo, Eric began searching—frantically—for those strange memories, calling them up on purpose instead of being used by them. He began fighting back..

The Prince was grinning.

And while Eric wasn't exactly *relaxing*, he was beginning to see what was going on. There was a distant source of energy, of power, that he could touch, use.

The nexus—

And he could do things with this power. After several more exchanges, he began to see the patterns, the relationships between what he *heard* in his mind's ear, and what was actually happening.

"Couldn't you have made yourself a robot or something?" he squeaked, when a lash of fire came a little too close and he realized that Terenil was not holding back.

"A simulacrum would not have free will, Bard," Terenil replied, dodging Eric's return volley. "It would be like fighting a mirror. Not good enough. I *do* like your evasive maneuvers, by the way. Perenor will never expect me to drop to the ground to avoid a flamestrike."

"Hey, whatever works, y'know?" Eric yelped again, as a little tongue of lightning snuck around behind him and connected with his rump—

I'm gonna charge you for these jeans, you pointy-eared creep!

He fired off a series of things like Roman-candle balls (*staccato burst of clarinet*), none of which connected. But the attempt forced Terenil to move rather briskly, which at least was *some* comfort.

At least I'm giving him a run for his money—

Then Terenil hit him with the Big One.

A thundering D minor chord from a double orchestra—

A whirling wall of light descended on him.

And the memories momentarily deserted him.

He had *no* idea what to do, how to counter the thing—and there was no place to run from it. He reached in desperation, gathering everything be could find and throwing it—

A major.

The wall stopped, not two feet away from him, held there by the glowing shield he had somehow erected between himself and it.

"Enough," said Terenil, and the light vanished. Eric stumbled backward a few steps, and when he reached the wall, collapsed against it and slid down it.

He was sweating, and exhausted, and panting hard to catch his breath. It was no compensation to see that the Prince was in the same shape.

"You did very well," Terenil said, lowering himself down to the floor beside Eric. "*Very* well. Better than I had anticipated. Forgive me; I forgot that you are not a trained sorcerer there at the end. I had not intended to use that bit of magery on you; it is far more powerful—even when muted—than I would ever have used in practice against anyone but an experienced magician."

"Oh," Eric replied, feeling somehow deflated. "That's why I sort of lost everything. So you stopped it?"

"Why . . . no." The Prince gave him a peculiar look. "You did."

Eric had hardly enough time to get his breath back before Terenil had him done up in a copy of his own scarlet-and-gold armor, facing him with sword in hand. The armor turned out to be no more uncomfortable than a set of motorcycle leathers Eric had once tried on. The sword, however, felt very strange, and very alien in his hand.

But the actual sparring proved to be easier than the stuff Terenil had been putting him through up until then. The memories he needed *here* were simpler; physical memories only. He could relax, put his mind in neutral, and let his body take over. It was kind of fun, actually—

Until it got to be work.

Then hard work.

Then *painfully* hard work.

Finally Terenil called a halt, and made the armor go away. There was a low bench at Terenil's side of the dojo; Eric sprawled on the floor with his back braced against it, head thrown back, eyes closed, getting his wind back.

I'm sweating like a horse. I don't think I've ever worked this hard before in my life.

"Here." He felt the familiar chill of a metal can in his hand, and didn't stop to wonder where it came from. Terenil had magicked it up somehow, of course—

I'm beginning to take this magic stuff for granted, like microwaves and telephones.

"Thanks," he said; fumbled for the pop-top, and took a long pull, all without opening his eyes.

Yeah. Nothing like a Coke, sometimes.

"And here." Eric opened his eyes at the tap on his arm. Terenil had done the thing with the fifty-dollar bills again he held out two to Eric. "I will not leave with you," the Prince said. "And you will need a cab, true? Just be very careful not to spend these in the same place."

Eric took a good look at them, and realized they had exactly the same serial numbers. He raised one eyebrow at the elf.

"As I told you," Terenil said shrugging. "We cannot create only copy."

And I'll bet the Treasury Department would love to talk to you about that . . .

"So," Eric said, after his second swallow. "What's with all this? Why did you suddenly decide you wanted to take Perenor on again?"

The bench creaked as Terenil settled beside him. Eric opened his eyes. The Prince looked as completely exhausted as *he* was; hair dripping sweat, the leather tunic gone, muscles trembling with a little weariness. He was slumped over, elbows on his knees, hands wrapped around his own can of soda, looking at a point on the floor between his feet.

"Because I must," the Prince replied. "You know, you came very near to defeating me, Bard. More than once. I am not what I was."

"I'm not Perenor—"

"Precisely." The Prince sighed. "If I were to meet him as I am at the moment, the result would be the same as last night. All that saved me then was Korendil's luring him away from me. If Perenor has a weakness, it is that he prefers a moving target to a defeated one."

Eric couldn't think of anything to say. Except— "But you'll still challenge him anyway?"

"I must," the Prince said simply. "For the sake of the others."

You've seen them, Eric. Lost in Dreaming—I think it's kinder to pull the plug.

Maybe not exactly Ria's words, but certainly the sense of them.

"What makes you think you can do anything for them?" he asked bluntly. "I mean, I've seen them—"

And I saw you. A real brain-dead stoner, last night . . .

Terenil winced, as if he had heard the thought. "I do not know that I can, I only know that I must try."

It was Eric's turn to wince away from the conviction in his words. He covered it by draining his cola—and as soon as he put it down, there was a second, water beading on its sides, on the bench beside him.

Yeah, so maybe he can't handle his drugs. But he's not so gone that he still can't think beyond himself. He wants to do something meaningful, even if he isn't actually capable of carrying it off. And what have you done with your life, Banyon?

Not much.

"What's with this thing between you and Perenor?" he asked.

The Prince tossed down the last of his soda and magicked himself up another can. "Hate," he said. "That is what is between us." He grimaced. "One of the two emotions that we are taught to avoid at all costs . . ."

"Huh?"

Terenil pulled damp hair behind his ear, and turned his head a little to look at Eric. "We are virtually immortal, Bard. Our lives are measured in centuries, not decades. That can be as much curse as blessing. Firstly, we are few in number. Secondly, strong emotional ties bind for *centuries*, not mere decades. Your legends call us light-minded and frivolous in our affections—but think you for a moment.

Suppose you have a love that turns to dislike. But you are tied to the place where that love dwells, and there are perhaps a few hundred inhabitants of that place. Try as you will, you must see that love *every day*. For the next *thousand years*. Unless one of you finds a way to leave." He shrugged. "So do we avoid both love and hate, granting either *only* when there is no other choice."

"So, why are you and Perenor—"

"A fundamental difference in the way in which we see you and your world, Bard. It began when we journeyed with Maddoc of Wales, knowing there was another land at the end of his sail. We left because we were being crowded by humankind. *I* thought, and the Queen, that if we could establish ourselves and put down deeper roots than those we had aforetime, we could coexist with your world. Share it, despite your use of Cold Iron."

"Sounds like a good idea to me," Eric offered tentatively.

"So it has proved, most places. It was only that here, I misjudged in placing the nexus. Or perhaps—" He looked up at the wall opposite himself, frowning, then shook his head. "I cannot recall. It may be that Perenor urged the placement there. He may have been working against me even then . . . Well, our Queen took a group north to establish Elfhame Misthold; I remained here with a second, smaller group, mostly of Low Court elvenkind who must be tied to physical *places*. I established Elfhame Sun-Descending. Then Perenor began showing his true motives."

"This was how long ago?" Eric asked.

"Before the Spaniards." Terenil frowned again. "Perhaps . . . ten to fourteen of your centuries. Time does not hold as much meaning for our kind."

Jesus, I guess not! Eric stared at a being who looked no more than forty years old, and felt a little stunned.

"So. We had found a place for a nexus; the Queen's Bard—a human, like yourself—opened it and created the anchoring point for it, and the Queen and most of the High Court had gone on up northwards. Then Perenor began spreading his poison. Why, he said, should we be subject to the vagaries of humanity? Why should we allow *their* lives to rule what *we* did? We had magic at our disposal; our lives were infinitely longer—why should *we* not rule *them* ?"

Terenil took a swig from his can, and tightened his lips, angrily. "He did not mean only to rule—he meant to enslave. I could see that—and fortunately, so could most of the rest. And that was enough to keep him in his place for many years."

"God." Enc shuddered at the notion of having Perenor as "Master."

Somebody who can read your thoughts, and touch the innermost part of you . . .

"Jesus, Terenil, how the hell did you guys see through him? And—I mean, why didn't you just go along with him?"

Terenil gave him a lopsided grin. "You humans make poor slaves, Bard. Your own history should teach you that. Soon or late, you rise beneath your chains and go for your masters' throats. We had *all* seen enough of history to know that. And . . . there was still another reason. Of all the wondrous things we can do, we cannot *create*. Our 'culture,' if you will, is made up of what we have borrowed from you humans. And a slave generally is very poor at creation. After all, why should he create anything, when it is his masters that have the benefit of it, and not himself? There are deeper reasons, too, but these will suffice."

Enlightened self-interest. It never fails. Eric chuckled to himself.

"So, there was mistrust of Perenor on my part, hatred on his. Your people moved to this valley—and then it all began to fall apart for us. You moved too quickly for us to be aware of what was happening. We learned too late that you were trapping us in mazes of Cold Iron, cutting the groves off, one from another. I and those of the Lesser Court who were mages worked to find a solution—for without an Adept, which we did not number among ourselves, we could not reestablish new ties to the nexus, or move it elsewhere. I was so preoccupied with this that I did not watch Perenor. Finally I learned that he was working forbidden magic against the humans, draining them to his own use. I caught him in the act—"

Terenil stopped, wiped the back of his hand across his eyes, and finished his soda in a single gulp.

"I caught him in the act of draining a child. A child who *would* have been a Bard. I realized then that he had probably been doing this evil for as long as humans had been within his reach—and that he had destroyed our chances of moving the nexus by destroying the children who could have grown to be Bards. That is when I exiled him."

"But he didn't leave."

"Not so. He did, for a brief while. He found a human woman who *could* have been a great magician if she had chosen to train her powers, and fathered a child upon her—yes, Bard, that *is* possible, although it requires the intervention of magic. He raised that child himself, training her in sorcery and elven magic. Human magic—it is very rare, but it is powerful. Perhaps because it is buttressed by all the potential of your brief lives . . ."

Terenil brooded down at the floor until Eric got tired of waiting for him to pick up the story again.

"Then what happened?"

"Oh. Then he returned to challenge my rule again." He discarded the can he was holding, and magicked up still another. "That was not all that long ago. I fought them for days, with young Korendil at my side. Korendil. He was—is—*my* best hope, you know. He has scarce two centuries, yet there is such wisdom and courage in him—he amazes me. Sometimes he frightens me—he is so like a human—so passionate. I have tried to warn him from passion, from caring so deeply—"

"The fight," Eric prompted.

"Oh, aye. We fought them and drove them out again, though not without cost to both worlds. I was badly exhausted. We roused things across the Barrier that were best left sleeping, and the battle itself started a fire, the one that burned out Bell Canyon." Terenil looked at him, and blinked. "Are you old enough to recall it?"

"I read about it." Eric said, half to himself.

"I thought I had banished them. I thought . . . I don't quite remember. Danann, it all fades, it all blurs . . . Then

Korendil vanished, and left me the only one of the High Court still aware, with all the rest of Sun-Descending lost in Dreaming. To try further seemed . . . so futile. Perenor gone, the girl-child gone, Korendil gone. Nothing left— enemies, friends, all gone—"

Too late Eric heard the slurring of his words, the rambling. He had seen the familiar red-and-white cans they were both drinking from—but the *meaning* of those soft drinks had not occurred to him.

Caffeine. Terenil had downed at least three cans of Coke as they'd been sitting there, and was working on the fourth.

"—nothing left," the Prince murmured. He looked up as Eric got to his feet, but didn't seem to recognize him. His eyes were glazed and unfocused, his hands shaking.

"Mortals," Terenil said sadly. " 'Don't open your heart to mortals'—that's an old saw, and I told Korendil that, over and over. They die and they leave you. Leave you alone. Don't you, Bard? You always leave us, no matter what we do—"

The elf's head sank; his hand loosened and the empty can of Coke fell from it, to roll around on the floor. As Eric watched, Terenil slid from the bench to curl up in a drunk—or Dreaming—stupor on the floor.

The cab ride home was very depressing. Sunset was grayed-out by haze tonight; in fact, the whole world seemed grayed-out and lifeless. Eric had never felt so alone.

God. Maybe Ria's right, maybe it's better to pull the plug on them. Even the best of them can't stay straight for a single afternoon.

He rethought everything Ria had said, compared it to what Terenil had told him. He couldn't see any flaws in what she'd told him about *herself*, and she'd admitted that her father was doing things she didn't approve of. And yet— yet it didn't feel quite right, as if she was telling the truth, but not *all* of the truth.

I need Beth, I need Kory. I have got to talk to them.

The cab pulled up outside the tacky pink apartment building, and pulled off as soon as Eric paid the driver. He hadn't asked the cabby to wait, but he had been figuring he'd just duck into his apartment, change his shirt, grab his flute, and warn them he was coming.

He got the first two done inside of a couple minutes— but when he called Beth's apartment, all he got was her answering machine.

"Beth?" he said, when the recording ran out. "Bethie, it's Eric—are you there?"

There was no answering *click* of the phone being picked up.

He went blank for a moment, then took a deep breath and went on. "Beth, some stuff happened back at the demonstration, some pretty heavy stuff, that's why I sort of bugged out on you. Beth, I'm on my way over, I've got to talk to you and Kory real—"

Click. Dial tone.

He hung the phone up carefully, and stood there for a moment with his gig bag dangling from one hand. His mind just wasn't working; he just couldn't picture what could have happened that she wouldn't *be* there.

Oh God—what if they're in trouble, and I was out fooling around with Terenil. What if Beth didn't make it here? What if she got arrested back at the Llewellyn Building—

Strike that. Terenil said she was shielding Kory. So she took him from my place. They were together then, and I'm pretty sure she wouldn't leave him alone. Which means they're still together. In her apartment. And they're not answering the phone.

Which means what, Banyon?

He thought about them, closing his eyes the way he had when Ria had tried to . . . contact him—

He blushed at the memory. But he tried it anyway reaching out with that *something* he'd been working with, thinking very hard about both of them. It seemed like there was a "Bethness" and a "Koryness" that were both tied into him somehow, a tiny touch, as though they were both resting a hand on his shoulders, and that he could follow that to the real people.

It worked; he started to see very vague images against

the blackness of his closed eyes. But not that vague. *Beth and Kory—together—*

Anger flared and banished the images from his mind, and he could not recapture them. He struggled for a moment to calm himself down, but every time he tried, he could see them—

You've been played for a fool, Banyon. All that talk about "commitment," being a team, and the first thing Beth does when she gets Kory alone is jump into bed with him. Damn her!

His hurt and jealousy settled into a burning lump in his throat and the pit of his stomach. He clutched his flute against his chest and struggled to breath slowly.

I ought to—

No, violence never got him anything. Violence wasn't the answer.

I could be wrong. This could be my own lousy imagination. I have a dirty enough mind. I can't stop thinking about how Kory is such a hunk, how Beth must be attracted to him. That's probably all this is—just me and my over-active imagination.

He trembled with suppressed anger and with indecision. *I ought to go over there, and see for myself. I could be wrong. But if I'm right—*

The cab ride into Tarzana was accompanied by a growing rage, and an increasing sense of betrayal. He had taken long enough for a shower and a change of clothing, trying to wash some of his unhappiness and anger away. It hadn't worked, and he spent the ride in silence, his throat aching, his flute case clutched in both hands. By the time he reached Beth's apartment building, he was no longer sure of *anything*.

"You'd better wait," he told the cabby as he passed him the change from the first of Terenil's fifties. "There's a good chance I'll need you right away."

The cab driver shrugged, pulled out an SF book, and kept the meter running.

He'd been tempted, back there in his own place, to throw the money in the trash and send the boots after.

But Terenil hadn't been the faithless one, the Prince had tried (*noblesse oblige?*) to make up for the damages that had been inflicted on Eric. *He* hadn't strung Eric along; he'd been honest with him.

"Don't open your heart to mortals."

Yeah, guess not. Don't trust them with the real truth, either.

Still, Terenil had been fair to him. So he had put the boots on and stuffed the cash in his pocket and called another cab.

He ran up the clattering wooden stairs, stairs that led up the side of the building to Beth's second-floor apartment. He was so knotted up inside it felt like he was going to have to double over any minute. He knew where to go; he'd been here before. He headed straight along the balcony until he reached the end and the last doorway. He started to pound on the door, but it swung open at his first knock.

"Eric, if that's you, I'm in the kitchen," Beth called from somewhere beyond the half-open wooden door. "If it's not, you're in trouble, whoever you are."

He froze, hand on the door handle. He really didn't want a confrontation.

I could go away now, and never know—never have to face what's been going on.

No. I have to know. He pushed the door open, shoving it a little harder where it caught on the carpeting.

Beth's voice floated down the hallway past the living room, guiding him. "Eric, I'm sorry I didn't pick up the phone when you called, but we were bus—"

He stepped in through the door of the tiny yellow-painted kitchen and stood staring at her from within the frame of the door. She was standing beside the window in a T-shirt and a pair of cutoffs, her hair plastered wetly to her head, as if she had just washed it. He caught a whiff of shampoo-scent as she turned. She took one look at the expression on his face, and froze in mid-word.

He felt his mouth twitch, and shoved his hands angrily down into his pockets. *Busy? Yeah, I'll bet you were busy.*

Before he could get a single word past the hard lump

choking his voice, Korendil (wearing nothing more than a towel draped negligently around his waist) strolled in through the other door—

The one leading to the bedroom.

The elf's long blond hair hung in damp, dripping ringlets, and there were beads of water on his shoulders.

Looks like he's sure made a full recovery.

Kory didn't seem aware of Eric's presence at all; he moved easily, gracefully, showing no signs of any of his injuries, and no hint of lingering weakness.

"Beth—" Kory made a caress out of the word, and leaned over, embracing her, to give her a very warm, very sensuous kiss. His mane of hair hid their faces, but Eric had no doubt that she was enjoying it. *She* had both her arms around him, returning the embrace—oblivious to Eric still standing there.

Like I don't mean a thing to her.

He started to turn to go. The gig bag knocked against the doorframe, and Kory broke off the kiss, pivoting quickly to face him, his hands coming up in a gesture of either attack or warding. Eric backed up a pace.

Korendil's wary stance relaxed when he saw who it was— but then he saw Eric's expression, and frowned in puzzlement.

"Yeah," Eric said slowly, ignoring the elf. "It looks like you were busy, weren't you? Too busy to even think about me."

"Eric—where were you?" Beth asked, pulling self-consciously away from Korendil. "You just vanished on me. I looked for you, I really did."

"Uh-huh." He sniffed, and swallowed, and couldn't clear the lump from his throat. "Yeah. I had to . . . I saw Perenor, Beth. He was in the building. I was scared shitless, Beth—" He blinked his burning eyes to clear them. "Why didn't you wait for me?"

"I had to move Kory before my protections wore off . . ." Her voice trailed off and she looked away from Eric.

"Sure." Eric shifted his weight uneasily, feeling as if his skin were off and all his nerves were screaming. Korendil began toweling his hair, carefully not looking at Eric.

Eric's insides knotted up. Korendil—God. A hunk by anybody's standards. *Christ, why should they give a shit about me? Beth doesn't need me—not with him around. Okay, he needs this Bardic magic crap. So he's nice to me. Big deal, he's nice to me so he can use me, just like everybody else.*

"So, what happened?" Beth asked, too casually. "A lot," he replied. "I ran into the lady that runs the corporation. Literally. Her name was Ria. Ria Llewellyn."

Out of the corner of his eye he saw Kory stiffen at the mention of that name.

"A very nice lady, a very *blonde* lady, a very *sensible* lady. She had a lot of things to tell me. Things that made a lot of sense."

More so now than they did then.

"Eric?" Korendil said very softly. Eric wouldn't look at him.

"So, all things considered. I guess I don't need to stick around. You look like you're doing fine without me. Maybe you guys had better find yourselves another Bard, huh? Maybe a girl this time." Now he looked at the elf, or tried to. His eyes burned and blurred and he couldn't really see. "Yeah, that would be kind of nice for you, Kory. I . . . it's been real."

Eric pivoted and ran down the hall, down the stairs and out to the cab He flung himself into the back seat, and fumbled in his pocket for the piece of paper Ria had given him.

They can find another sucker. It's time I started looking out for myself.

He rubbed the back of his hand across his burning eyes, sniffling, until he could read the address. But he couldn't— the letters and numbers wavered and he couldn't make them out properly.

And he thought he could hear someone calling his name.

"Here—" He shoved the paper and the second fifty at the driver. "Can you get me there?"

"Eric! Eric, wait!"

The driver glanced at the paper. "Hey, no problem. What about your friends?"

He gestured at the apartment building. Beth was pelting down the stairs, Kory behind her, both of them waving frantically at the cab.

"They aren't my friends." Eric said, huddled into the seat cushions, holding his flute to his chest. "Let's go."

14

My Darling Asleep

The wind whispered through the trees, ruffling the surface of the swimming pool, rising and falling like a soft melody. Eric touched the cool metal of the flute to his lips, smiling to himself. *It is like a song, a little dancing air. Very Irish, come to think of it . . .*

But although he waited, fingers poised, no melody came to him; only a vague yearning and a sense of indefinable loss. He took the flute away from his lips, and moved his fingers restlessly and soundlessly over the flute keys as he looked out over the garden and the crystalline water of the pool.

He sat down on a marble bench near the water's edge, with the leafy fronds of a palm tree shading him from the bright Southern California sun. To his side was the sprawling expanse of Ria's house

—No, her mansion, definitely a mansion. I've never seen a place like this before. It just proves what Ria says is true, that we can accomplish so much with our magic, working together—nothing we can't do—

But the silent flute mocked that bold statement.

So why can't I think of any new tunes? It's like there's an emptiness inside me where all the melodies used to be. I haven't be able to write a new song in days.

Eric sat up suddenly.

Days?

How long have I been here, anyhow?

He set the flute down in his lap, trying to figure it out. *I arrived here last night—no, it was two nights ago, last night we went to Maxwell's for dinner. Or was it three nights ago? It's hard to remember.*

The more he tried to remember the signposts of the passing days, the more they eluded him. *I haven't really been doing much of anything, just listening to her CD collection on that fantastic stereo upstairs, exploring the library, and—and sleeping. I don't think we've gone to, uh, sleep, anytime before 5:00 A.M. for the last few nights.*

He blushed, just thinking about it. *Ria—she's—she's really—quite amazing that way. I wonder how she manages to get through the day without falling asleep at her office? I know I couldn't live on the amount of sleep she's getting. Two hours a night? Three? Forget it. I usually need at least seven—*

An inexplicable chill crept down the back of his neck. *That's funny; now that I think about it, I seem to be sleeping more than I usually do. And still feeling tired all the time. Shit, you think with all the napping I've been doing, I wouldn't be feeling anything but wired.*

Hell, that doesn't matter. What matters is that tune I wanted to play, the one that keeps slipping away from me. Maybe if I just play something I know, rather than something of my own, it'll come to me by itself.

He brought the flute to his lips again, took a breath, and began to play the old Irish air, "Come to the Hills." He stopped after several bars, and looked down at the flute in consternation.

What in the hell is going on here? I sound awful. It's just . . . notes. Nothing special. Like there's no life to it, no magic. Dead.

I've never sounded like this before in my life . . .

Something more subtle than a recognizable sound distracted him. Eric glanced up, to see the sliding glass door open quietly. Ria stepped out into the garden, wearing a dark blue dress and carrying her high-heeled shoes in her hand.

She glided towards him. "Hi, handsome," she said, leaning down to kiss him. "I couldn't bear the thought of you here all by yourself, so I decided to come home for an hour or so. Want to do something interesting for lunch?"

"What did you have in mind?" he asked, standing up.

She gave him a wicked look. Eric laughed, and pulled her into his arms for a lingering kiss, flute and music totally forgotten.

Ria touched her fingertip to his lips. "Now, now. Behave yourself, love. I have to be back at the office for a one o'clock meeting. Otherwise, I know *exactly* how I'd like to spend the afternoon."

"Better be careful, beautiful," he murmured against her faintly-scented blond hair, kissing her beneath her right ear. "Or you'll wear me out."

She pulled away from him suddenly. "Don't say that, Eric."

Say what? Why is she looking at me like that?

Ria took his hand in hers, her expression changing so quickly he couldn't be sure he'd seen what he *thought* he'd seen. "I was thinking of something else. My father is inside the house. I wanted to know if you'll join us for lunch or not."

"Hey, why not?" He picked up the flute lying on the marble bench. "Let's do lunch with Daddy."

Ria watched her father with veiled suspicion, as Perenor speared a piece of pineapple with his fork, and slowly raised it to his lips. His eyes never left Eric, who was busily sawing the last of the meat off a chicken thigh.

"Delicious, Ria," the older man said, coolly. "I always knew you were talented—a brilliant businesswoman, a gifted Adept; it seems you make an excellent pineapple chicken as well. What more could a man ask for in a daughter?"

I'm sure you could think of something, Father dear. Like a daughter who wouldn't prefer to see her pet Bard carving out your tripes instead of a piece of chicken? "I'm glad you approve, Father. You know how much I enjoy having you visit here."

Eric glanced up, as if hearing something other than the spoken conversation, then smiled hesitantly. "I like the chicken too, Ria. I didn't know you could cook this well."

She smiled back at him, the adoring look in his dark eyes warming her even from across the table. "Thank you, love."

He bit hungrily into a piece of chicken. "Though I can't figure out when you had the time to cook this. I mean, you've been at the office all day, and I know you didn't do this last night—"

"Don't worry about that, Eric." Ria refilled the wine glasses, then sipped hers thoughtfully. *I still haven't spotted the reason why Father wanted to come over today. He said he was curious about Eric, but it has to be something more than that. If he wants something from me, I'm sure he'll tip his hand soon enough—*

Her eyes narrowed, as she noted the intent way Perenor scrutinized Eric. *I know what he's thinking. But if he so much as touches Eric, I'll Challenge him, right here on the spot. And in my home, I hold the distinct advantage, especially now . . .*

Perenor pushed his plate away from him. "Truly excellent, Ria. I should come by here for meals more often."

"That would be nice, Father," she replied lightly. *Next time, maybe I'll serve some steak with amanita mushroom sauce—or roast beef with aconite instead of horseradish.*

Eric rose and began gathering several dishes in his hands. "I'll just run these into the kitchen—"

She gestured for him to sit down again. "Oh, Eric, leave it be. The servants will take care of it."

"No, it's all right, I don't mind." He balanced several glasses precariously on a plate, then carefully moved toward the kitchen.

Perenor glanced at her speculatively as Eric disappeared through the doorway. "You're doing quite well with him, Ria. I'm impressed."

She leaned back in her chair, giving him a patently false

smile. "Why, thank you, Father. I'm rather pleased with how things are going, myself."

He chuckled. "I am, too. What are your plans now?"

"Now, as in the rest of the afternoon, or the indefinite future?" She drained the last of her wine glass, watching him over the edge of the crystal.

"You know what I mean."

She shrugged. "Business as usual, I suppose. Why do you ask?"

What exactly do you want from me, Father?

"It's just—I was thinking of taking a little vacation, now that everything else is . . . taken care of. A visit to the High Court at Misthold. I was wondering if you and your . . . consort might want to join me."

Curiouser and curiouser. Just what are you planning, Father? "Sounds like it might be fun. We haven't been to Court in years. Is there any particular reason why you want to go now?"

Perenor's eyes were distant, as if looking at something only he could see. "Now that everything is under control here, I thought I might—"

So that's *the game you're playing this time, Father! I should've guessed—*

"No." Her voice was sharp and icy. "Absolutely not. If you want to do a power play in the High Court, you're doing it without my help, or Eric's. I'm not risking everything I have just so you can amuse yourself."

He stood up angrily. "You don't understand, Ria. It's the only thing that matters to me. *You* have influence and power over the mortals—that's all very well, but it's meaningless. They're nothing but pawns. It's only winning over those with *power* that matters."

She firmed her chin stubbornly. "I told you no, Father. I mean it. I helped you with the Faire purchase because there was something for me to gain. I have no interest in the High Court, or my full-blooded elven cousins. You can pursue this on your own, if you're determined to do it. I won't risk myself or Eric."

"It's not *your* help that I need," Perenor said quietly,

but with implicit threat. "Just your pet Bard. I don't need your help, or your permission . . ."

Oh, really?

She called a small amount of Power, and raised a careful shield; not quite a Challenge, but something to let him know she wasn't to be trifled with. "I won't let you use Eric. Not for this, or *anything*. He's mine." She calmly met his furious gaze, the first hot tendrils of Power writhing around her hands, clenched beneath the table. *Push me any further,* Father, *and we'll see what happens next—*

"I found some cookies—" Eric stopped dead in the doorway, a plate of cookies forgotten in his hands, staring at Perenor and his daughter. She registered his presence, then dismissed him, ignoring the Bard for the moment, keeping her senses trained on her father.

There was a moment of tense expectation. Ria's eyes held Perenor's, unwavering, waiting. *The instant I sense him drawing Power, I'll strike. He must know that. If he does—*

Perenor's lips curved slightly, a tiny smile, and he bowed ironically to his daughter. "Not now, daughter," he said lightly, then walked to Eric and took a cookie from the plate. "We'll have to continue this discussion at a later date, Ria," he added. "I need to take care of some business. May I borrow some tapes from your video library, my dear?"

"Of course, Father," she said. Her eyes never left him as he walked to the stairway. *Every day, it seems, we come closer and closer to a final confrontation. But, somehow, we avoid it each time. What is going to happen when we can't avoid it any longer?*

I wish I knew what was going on here. Eric set the dirty plates down on the counter and wiped his hands on a nearby dish towel. *For father and daughter, those two argue a lot. Not that I blame Ria, her dad is kinda opinionated. I've never felt quite comfortable around him, either. Something just makes me feel—oh, I don't know—like I don't want to be near him any more than I have to—*

Something nagged at the edge of his memory. Something . . . important. Something he couldn't quite recapture. *Green eyes, like Perenor's—looking up at me with such pain—and blood on my hands, blood on silvery blond hair, on the carpeting—*

He dismissed the image. *That's ridiculous. Must be from one of Ria's videos. I don't know anybody with silver-blond hair.*

He spent several minutes trying to figure out how to start the dishwasher, then gave it up as hopeless. *The servants will take care of it, like Ria said.*

Servants? That was odd. There wasn't anyone here in the kitchen. *And—I've never seen any of them. Not a single person in this house other than Ria and me. But the house is always immaculate, spotless; the gardens well-tended, everything in terrific shape. I wonder if they work late at night or something? Maybe when we're already in bed.*

That's just one of so many things that I don't understand—

He wiped the counter clean with a sponge, then turned, hearing a sound behind him.

Perenor stood watching him from the kitchen doorway, several videocassettes held negligently in one hand. The older man smiled. "And how are you doing these days, boy?"

"Just fine," Eric said, his throat strangely dry. "Where's Ria?"

"Oh, she's already on her way back to the office," Perenor replied. "I just wanted to talk to you for a few minutes before I leave, too."

"Uh, sure," Eric nodded. *What is it about this man that makes me feel like I want to run away, as fast and as far as I can?*

Perenor walked several steps closer. "We've never really had a chance to talk, you and I. That's a pity—I'd like to get to know you better."

"Ria—Ria's told me a lot about you." *A lot that I wouldn't repeat in polite company. She sure doesn't like you very much, even if you are her father.*

"I'm sure she has," Perenor said, his voice sounding amused. His eyes met Eric's, brilliant green. "Now, let's—"

—green eyes, like ice, deep pools of emerald nothingness.

Everything fading, disappearing into that void, falling in, consumed, ashes and dying flames.

He was having trouble breathing—seeing—hearing—

And music, a strange warped polyphonic sound, rising up around him. It set claws into him, dragging him in, touching where no one should touch. He could feel it dismembering him, pulling away pieces in its claws, pieces of himself. He was losing himself, falling; feeling everything whirling away into nothingness—

No! Let me go!

Everything being wrenched out of him, everything he cared about, everything he loved—

Eric reacted instinctively, drawing upon a half-forgotten memory.

A clear burst of chord, a strident A major thrown up like a shieldwall, shoving the hungry void away from him; a flash of light and sound, illuminating the shadows.

The warped music shattered into a thousand notes, falling away into silence.

He leaned against the counter, panting, his heart pounding.

Oh God—oh God, what was that?

He blinked several times, completely disoriented: the room was blurring around him, everything hazy, things melting into each other.

When he could see again, Perenor was standing very close to him, but the elf-lord's eyes were wide with astonishment and disbelief. His hand, with its elegantly manicured fingernails, still rested intimately on Eric's shoulder.

He took a deep breath, then another. "Don't—don't touch me," Eric said unsteadily, shoving Perenor's hand away from him. *"Don't touch me."*

Perenor stared at him, not speaking. Then he turned, and strode away. A moment later Eric heard the front door slamming shut behind him.

Eric collapsed against the counter, trying not to shake. *God, what's happening to me? I feel like everything is falling to pieces around me. Nothing to hold on to, nothing I can understand.*

He staggered into the living room, and sank down onto the plush couch. *I'm losing it. I'm really losing it. I'm so tired, it's all so crazy. Nothing makes sense anymore.*

Eric stretched out, closing his eyes, the velvet of the couch soft against his cheek. *It's easier not to try to think, not to worry about anything. Just let everything drift—just fall asleep, and it'll all be gone when I wake up—*

—busking in a New York subway, trying to ignore the rancid reek of stale urine from the restroom across the tunnel, looking down at the handful of coins in his flute case. Sag of despair.

No, that's not even enough to pay for another night at the Y, much less a meal and a bunk.

Out of the echoing tunnel, that hateful, unforgettable voice, loud above the dull roar of the crowd.

"Well, if it isn't Loony Banyon—"

Looking up. That face. Those greedy eyes. Chuck Marquand, the second-best flautist at Juilliard. Looking at him, and smiling; a smug, self-satisfied smirk

"It's been a while, Eric." A laugh; a braying, triumphant laugh. "You know you look like hell."

Eyes that raked over his clothing: the dirty jeans, layers of plaid flannel shirts against the cold.

"Poor old Loony. Here. Let me help you out." He reaches into the pocket of his thigh-length leather jacket, fishes out a bill. Drops it in the case. "For old time's sake, Banyon."

I should take that money and stuff it down his arrogant throat.

But it's a twenty, lying there among the dimes and quarters.

He can't reach down to pick it up. He can't move. Instead, he starts playing again, a fast version of a Mozart sonata.

Chuck laughs and walks away.

The notes fly faster and faster, until the music and the subway are one blur, invisible behind the veil of tears, inaudible over the clanging noise of the trains and the laughter of the pedestrians.

Twenty dollars means a place to stay for the night. A

hot dinner. A bus ticket that'll get me out of this miserable city.

I should've rammed it past his teeth.

Oh God, what have I turned into?

Choking on sobs, gasping, the flute sliding from his hands, that damned twenty burning a hole in his flute case.

Crying . . .

"Eric? Are you all right?"

He opened his eyes. Ria was standing over him, a concerned frown on her beautiful face. Eric sat up slowly, his head aching.

From clenching my teeth in my sleep, yeah.

"I'm—I'm fine."

"No, you're not. You were having a nightmare, weren't you?"

He nodded hesitantly.

She sat beside him, and touched his shoulder gently. "Talk to me, Eric. Tell me about it."

No. No, you wouldn't understand—

"Yes, I would," she said, very softly, and moved over closer on couch next to him. "Eric, I care about you, a lot. If something or someone has hurt you, I want to know."

She does. She cares, I know that. It's just—I can't talk about that, not to her, not to anybody—

:*Eric. Please. Talk to me.*:

Okay. Okay. I will.

"It was years ago, Ria." He buried his face in his hands. "Not long after I quit Juilliard. I was busking from city to city, barely making enough to live. I was busking the subway. It was November, and cold. I looked up, and there he was. Chuck Marquand, who was second chair back in the orchestra—standing there in his fancy suit, his leather coat, laughing at me. And then—shit, he'd always hated me, I don't know why—he . . . he gave me—" He felt the tears beginning to trickle through his clenched fingers. "He gave me money, and God, I've never hated myself so much in all my life—I took it, I needed the money so badly—"

He rubbed his eyes fiercely with his knuckles, looked

up at her, and managed a wan smile. "Hell, I can't believe a dream is affecting me like this."

She didn't answer, she only looked at him with those wide blue eyes, bright with tears.

"It was one of the most awful times of my life," he continued, after a long silence. "I was starving, but I wouldn't go back to my parents, and I couldn't get even a McDonald's job. And then Chuck, humiliating me like that—I wanted to die, I just wanted to crawl away and die—"

"I—I know how that feels," Ria said, very quietly. "All those times when I was a child, when we would go to the High Court and my father would talk about me like I wasn't even there. His half-blooded daughter, not a *real* elf. The little mongrel. How useful I would be, when I grew into my Power. That was all he cared about, that he'd have a half-human sorceress to use in his little games."

"Ria—"

She's crying. I've never seen her cry before.

As if hearing his thoughts, she dashed away her tears angrily with one hand. "It's all in the past, Eric. You're never going to have to busk on a streetcorner again, ever. And my father—he knows he can't use me now. I won't let him."

"It's not in the past, if it still bothers you," Eric said slowly. "Like that rat, Chuck Marquand. I can't forget him. You can't forget what your father did to you."

When Ria spoke again, her voice was remote, distant. "You know, I used to be scared, when I was a kid, that I'd grow up and be just like him. That I'd enjoy hurting people." She glanced at him, tears trickling unnoticed down her face. "I don't. I don't like hurting people. But sometimes you don't have any choice—"

"Hey, you've never hurt me," Eric said, carefully brushing the tears from her cheeks, his own tears forgotten. "You've never been anything but wonderful to me, more than I could ever imagine. Even if you do look like a raccoon right now, with all of your makeup dripping down your face."

She hugged him tightly. "Oh Eric. I don't know how I lived before I met you." She smiled, despite the tears.

"I'll never hurt you, Eric. I promise, whatever happens, I won't hurt you. I just—I just hope you'll understand someday—why I do what I do. And—and that you'll never leave me."

"I won't leave you Ria," he whispered. "I love you."

Eric turned the page, trying to read his novel, but unable to concentrate. *It's like I've forgotten something, and it's nagging at the back of my mind. Something, can't remember what it is—*

:Bard! Bard, can you hear me? Eric?:

He looked across the room to where Ria was seated at her desk, poring over a set of contracts, a pair of wire-rimmed reading glasses delicately perched on her nose.

"Ria?"

She glanced up and smiled. "Yes, love?"

Eric shook his head, slightly bewildered. "—Uh, it's nothing. Sorry I disturbed you." *I could've sworn somebody was talking to me, calling my name—*

He opened the book again, and took another slow sip of Scotch from his glass.

Then an image came to his mind: the moon shining clearly down on the lonely hills, the chitter of crickets, the night air cold and crisp in his lungs, with the faintest scent of the ocean. A perfect night for a walk—

A walk—yeah, that would be nice. I love walking through this neighborhood, all the huge houses, fancy cars in the driveways. That's a terrific idea. I should've thought of it earlier.

He set the book down, finishing the last of the Scotch. "Ria, would you like to go for a walk outside?"

"Not tonight. I have to finish these contracts for tomorrow. But you should go out, if you want to."

"Okay." He stood up, stretching slowly. "I'll be back in a bit."

He left the library, and detoured to the bedroom for his jacket before heading downstairs. *It'll be nice to get outside. I've been spending too much time indoors, the last couple of days.*

Eric unlocked the front door, then stopped, just as he was about to step outside.

There's someone out there. I can't see them, but I know it—somebody hiding in the shadows.

Then a figure moved into the pool of light beneath the driveway lights. A smallish young woman with black hair cut very short and punk. She just stood there for a long moment, looking at him.

Like she knows me—

He blinked, then smiled, remembering. *Oh, right, that's Beth Kentraine. We used to play gigs together, do shows at Faire, that kind of stuff. I wonder what she's doing here in Bel Air?*

And then he saw someone standing next to her, a haggard young man with wild blond hair that curled over his shoulders. *That's funny. He looks familiar, too. That cloak he's wearing—I've seen that before, too. Kinda like my boots, in a way.*

"Eric—" Beth said. Her voice cracked. "Eric, what's happened to you?"

He just looked at her, unable to understand her. "I don't know what—"

"You don't know?" She walked closer, and he could see the tear-tracks down her cheeks. "We didn't know what happened to you, whether you were alive or dead. You abandoned us, Eric. Why didn't you come back?"

Abandoned her? Say what?

"We were worried about you, Eric," the man said, stepping closer. Eric could see the tips of pointed ears showing through that mop of hair. *So he's an elf, like Perenor. Jeez, that's weird—why is Beth Kentraine hanging out with an elf?*

"Look," he said, trying to be patient. "Beth, I don't know what you're talking about. I haven't even seen you since that last Faire show. And I'm sorry that I missed the gig at the Dive, but I never promised you I'd show up—"

She stared at him, her hands curling into fists.

Whatever shit she's on, I hope I never get talked into trying it!

"Beth, take it easy," he said soothingly. "It's okay. I'm alive, obviously, and I'm doing fine. If that's all you came here to find out, then I think—"

"No Bard—you do *not* think. You are not thinking at all," the young man said quietly. "You are caught in your own kind of Dreaming, and you went into it willingly."

He glared at the interloper.

Just who the hell do these two think they are?

"Listen, Beth, it's nice to see you and all, but I'm a busy guy, y'know?" He turned, and glared aggressively at the strange elf. "And you, mister, I don't even know who you are, where do you get off talking to me like that?"

They just stared at him. *Like they're seeing a ghost. Or something that isn't real. What's going on here? Who is this guy, anyhow?*

"Eric?"

He looked back to see Ria standing in the hallway directly behind him. "Yeah, Ria?"

"Who're you talking to?" She walked closer, resting her hand on his shoulder.

Then she glanced past him, and her eyes narrowed dangerously. And he heard something—something deep inside his mind. In Ria's voice. :*Well, well. Uninvited visitors. I should've guessed— Korendil and the little witch, both here to take Eric away from me. Or did he call you here? Well, that doesn't matter right now—:*

Ria raised one clenched fist, her mouth set in a furious line, eyes burning with anger.

Music, in a minor descant, starting from absolute silence and building to a thunderous roar in the space of a single heartbeat . . .

The blond elf reacted instantly, grabbing Beth by the wrist. Before Eric could blink, they vanished, both of them, as though they had never been there at all.

What in the—

Eric turned back to Ria, and was startled by the venomous look in her eyes. He fumbled for something to say. "Ria, I don't know what you're thinking, but . . ."

Her voice was icy. "I know exactly what you were doing,

Eric. Don't bother lying to me. I should never have trusted you."

"But I didn't—"

"The first time I turn my back, there you are, consorting with my enemies! I should have guessed you would do something like this, you traitorous bastard! *Damn* you, Eric Banyon!"

She stalked away from him. After a moment, he hurried after her. In the hallway he caught up to her, taking her by the shoulder and turning her towards him. "But Ria, I didn't *do* anything!"

The look in her eyes stopped him in his tracks.

:Traitor. Deceiver. Snake. I bring you into my life, give you everything you could ever want, and this is how you repay me? I want to throw you to the sharks, drop you out of an airplane at thirty thousand feet, use your guts for clothesline. Nobody *plays me for a fool, Eric.:*

He backed away from her, into the dining room.

You know, I think she's really mad at me—I'd better do something quick to calm her down—

Before he could speak, the porcelain vase on the table exploded into shards, right before his eyes; closely followed by the table itself, which splintered and burst into silver and red flames.

Maybe it's too late for that—

He backed towards the kitchen, unable to look away from the fury in her eyes, even as the house fire alarm began to wail shrilly.

"Now, Ria, don't do anything hasty . . ."

"Oh, don't worry about that Eric." She gave him a smile that chilled his blood. "I intend to take my time with this."

Amidst the roar of flames and the noise of the fire alarm, Eric heard a faint melody, gathering strength and speed with every split second—

Oh SHIT!

He dived to the floor, just as the entire contents of the china cabinet assaulted him from above. Dozens of dishes shattered around him, jagged shards drawing blood from his face and hands. Eric rolled to his feet, sliding through the doorway onto the linoleum floor of the kitchen—

—Where every appliance was whirring at high speed. Eric didn't stop to look, he continued his home-run slide toward the living room, bouncing down the three steps and landing in a heap on the ornate Persian rug.

Oh God—she's trying to kill me!

He had time for a brief thought—*this can't be happening to me*—before the rug attacked him.

Eric screamed hoarsely as it wrapped around him. He struggled to free himself, feeling the thick rug pressing tighter and tighter against his face, choking him; then he pulled free and kicked the rug away from him, gasping for breath.

Eric glanced back to see Ria, standing in the doorway. "Was this what you were planning all along?" she hissed. "To worm your way into my confidence, then use everything against me?"

"Ria," he gasped, "I don't—you don't—"

"I'll teach you what happens to people who double-cross me, you bastard!" She slammed her hand down, the sound barely audible above the raging cacophony in the house.

Pain hit Eric like a fist, doubling him over, making it impossible to breathe, impossible to do anything.

Music, disharmonic chords, tearing at me—have to stop it, stop her, break free, get away—

HELP ME!

He *reached*— He reached—and touched something. Something dark. Something deadly. It wanted to come to him—and he opened a door to it.

The pain vanished instantly, as a darkness moved into the shadows of the room, itself a shadow, gliding from nightmare into reality. He took it all in instantly: the sudden stillness, as though the entire world had stopped moving for a moment; the creature, gaining substance and strength with every moment that passed. The ghost-hands reaching toward Ria, and the look of absolute terror in her eyes.

And he realized that he had called this thing—and it wanted Ria.

It's going to—No! Not—not her! Leave her alone!

The creature turned sightless eyes toward Eric, and suddenly he could feel its not-thoughts, inside him, one with his pulse. Hunger and need, hunger and need, and aching emptiness—

No. Not her, and not me. Go away!

He pushed at it, at the thin fabric of chords that was the creature, and felt it unraveling beneath his touch, dissolving into nothingness. When it was gone, he looked up at Ria.

She was still standing in the doorway, clutching onto the door jamb, visibly trembling.

"Ria? Ria, are you okay?"

She shook her head once, not looking at him.

She—she doesn't look like she want to kill me anymore. That's something, at least.

Eric stood up painfully. His flute case was still on the living room table; he picked it up slowly. He walked past Ria standing silently in the doorway, and out the front door. Outside, the cold air seemed to slap him in the face, a sober awakening.

What now?

I don't have money for a taxi, and I'm sure the buses don't run in this neighborhood.

Eric looked back at the house, wondering if Ria would try to stop him. Plead with him not to leave, maybe. He waited a moment, then sighed.

Not likely, Eric, not after that last bit of fireworks. I think I really scared her.

I sure know that I scared me.

Damn. Helluva way to break up with a lady.

He glanced at the lightless hills around him, and began trudging down the long driveway.

I guess I'm walking home tonight.

15

Tamlin's Reel

Well, maybe this wasn't the best route for getting to the Sepulveda Freeway—

Eric looked around at the shadowed hills rising around him, the darkened landscape with only a hint of the moon peering through the clouds for illumination. *I don't think I'm lost. I mean, I kinda know where I am. Somewhere between Bel Air and the San Fernando Valley—*

He snorted. *Yeah. That's most of Southern California. Face it, Eric, you're lost.*

Eric kicked at a rock, and squinted at the sky. *Might as well keep walking. Sooner or later I'll have to hit a street, or a housing tract. The Hollywood Hills don't go on forever, after all.*

But I must be the only guy in the world who's stupid enough to try and hike over them at midnight—

He walked carefully down a dry stream bed, sidestepping the rocks, the wild growths of shrubbery and trees. *A sprained ankle, that's just what I need to make this night the epitome of stupidity.*

He followed the stream bed up the next incline, stewing at himself, and staggered as a wave of disorientation hit him, a feeling like—like everything had been wavering out of focus, and now was back in again. *Yeah, I sure wasn't thinking, when I started on this little hike. Or using my brain earlier tonight, either. That—that thing that I called, when I thought Ria was going to kill me—that could've munched both Ria and me, then gone off to eat the rest of Bel Air for dessert. Real bright, Eric. I'm just glad Beth and Korendil were far away when I did that cute stunt.*

He sighed, and stumbled over an unseen rock. *They're probably real ticked at me, anyhow. I sure didn't give them a warm reception when they showed up.*

I didn't give them much of a reception at all—

He slogged through another stretch of scrub oak, using his flute case to push the low branches out of his way. *I'll call Beth when I get home, and apologize. I don't know what I was doing, treating them like that. They probably think I was stoned off my ass or something, don't know what.*

Or something—

He fought off another sudden wave of dizziness. *That was really strange, how I didn't recognize Kory at first. Must've been the bad light outside. It's like, I was just thinking about that whole little incident just now, and I remembered that it was Kory standing there with Beth. Too weird for words, Eric.*

The scrub oak caught at him, clawed at him. He barely noticed. *Hell, its been a weird few days, since that scene at Beth's, Tuesday night. I guess it's none of my business who she sleeps with. It's just that, well, it hurt. But then again, I guess I hurt them by running off like I did. And, whatever else is happening between all of us, they're my friends, so they were worried when I didn't surface after a day or two. Good friends, those two. I wonder how they tracked me down so quickly?*

He sighed, glancing up at the pale aurora glow of moon through the clouds. *Must be way past midnight by now. I've been walking for ages, or at least that's how it feels. Damn it, I knew I should've just walked down through the streets, instead of trying to shorten the hike by going through the hills. Stupid Eric.*

A lone owl hooted somewhere off to the side. *If he hadn't been so stupid, maybe he could be curled up next to Ria,* without a care in the world. *I wonder what Ria's doing right now, back at the house? Is she worrying about me, like Beth and Kory were worried, or is she glad that I'm out of her life?*

Things had been so good with Ria until this evening. *She's— she's really something. But I don't know if I love her or not. There don't seem to be any real connections between us—*

Connections. Ties. Commitments. He'd never wanted them before and Ria had offered him a life without them. But somehow now that seemed an awfully empty way to live.

The way I feel about her—it's not the same way that I feel about Bethie, or—or about Kory, I guess. I do care a lot about those two, it's a little like being really good friends, but more so. Like . . . family. Like we all belong together. *Even with Beth, now that we've well, spent a night together. And Kory—God, but I still* don't *know what to think about him! But it's not this kind of, uh, fiery emotional stuff that I felt with Ria. Like everything was intense—*

Too intense. Unnaturally so. And the, the sex, too, that was something. But . . . too much, somehow. That was very strange— Ria's very strange, that way.

He shook his head, then cursed under his breath as his hair caught on a branch. Wincing, he tugged it free. *I don't know what to think about that lady, or the last few days. Bizarre. I only walked out a couple hours ago, but already all of it feels so unreal. Like it wasn't really me, it happened to somebody else.*

As if it all was just a dream—

The more he tried to focus on it, the more unreal it seemed. *Maybe it was a dream. It sure feels that way. Like I've been completely asleep for the last couple days—*

A pair of clouded jade eyes gazed at him sardonically from memory. *Oh, shit. Maybe I was asleep. I know Perenor can play games with people's minds, like what he did to me on the bus—what if Ria was doing the same thing to me? She's one helluva good sorceress, I learned that for a fact. Yeah, that was almost the* last *fact I ever learned, that's for sure.*

And maybe that's why it's so hard to remember what I've been doing for the last few days, why it was so hard to think when I was in her house.

A memory of blue eyes interposed itself over the green. Blue eyes, wet with tears. *But she said she loved me—*

Yeah, well, different people show love in different ways. Maybe she didn't realize what she was doing to me. Or maybe she did, but she thought she was doing the best thing for me. I don't know.

He felt as if his mind was going in circles. *No wonder Kory and Beth were so pissed at me, when they saw me at her house. They probably figured it out right away: Eric following Ria around like a lapdog, tongue hanging out, without an original thought in his useless brain. Jesus. I have been acting real brainless lately, haven't I?*

Stupidity runs rampant in the life of Eric Banyon . . .

He swallowed hard. It seemed like all he was doing lately was messing things up. *Well, I hope Beth and Kory will forgive me. I'll definitely call them as soon as I get home.*

A sudden thought made him stop dead in his tracks. *Hey . . . maybe I don't have to wait till then. I'm a Bard, I'm supposed to be able to do all of this magical stuff. The only times anything magical has ever happened, it's been an accident, when I wasn't trying to do anything. Maybe I can do something deliberately, for a change. Intelligently. Use this weird Gift of mine to get in touch with Kory and Beth.*

He had stopped on the edge of a small valley, a tiny ravine with a grove of stunted oak trees visible below him. Eric concentrated hard, thinking of Beth: the sound of her voice, her laughter, the way she looked at him that night on the living room couch. *Trying to reach out to her— :Hey, Beth, pick up the phone. It's me, Eric, your crazy Bardic friend, calling you on the Ma Bell cellular brainwave line— come on, Beth, talk to me—*

Someone else spoke, a low, breathy voice, a whisper in the silent recesses of his mind: *:Who speaks in my dreams? Who awakens me from my slumber?:*

Eric looked around, bewildered. *Excuse me?*

:Who is it who walks silently through these hills, and

calls to one who is far away? Who are you, intruder into my endless night?:

He sighed. *Well, this is no weirder than anything else that's happened to me lately.* Eric carefully constructed a reply, sending it out blindly to the unseen speaker, *:Yeah, hi. My name is Eric Banyon. Sorry, I didn't mean to wake you up, I'm just passing through the neighborhood.:*

:What are you?:

What? Eric looked around in surprise. *What am I? That's one helluva question.*

He thought about it for a moment before answering. *:Well, I'm human, of course. And a Bard—at least, everyone keeps telling me I am. Who are you?:*

The reply came not in words, but in the rustle of leathery wings, high above the valley, spreading to block out the moon and the stars. *:This is what I am.:*

Eric looked at the monstrous thing looming above him, tattered wings beating soundlessly against the sky, and gulped.

Oh shit—I didn't need this, not tonight, not after everything else that's happened.

The blind moon eyes, pale white, turned towards him. *:You are a Bard, human?:*

:Well, yeah,: Eric thought back at it, trying to keep his mouth closed as he looked up at the bulk of the creature effortlessly aloft in the air above him, its sinuous neck craning down towards him.

I've never seen anything like this guy before, not even in my worst nightmares—I don't know if I should run like hell, ask him if he likes to play canasta, or what! What do you do with somebody who's a hundred feel long, aside from anything he wants?

:Good. I am hungry.:

Eric blinked once. Shock and sudden fear coursed through him as the creature's words registered. *Uh oh—I don't think he's talking about doing margaritas together at Que Pasa, here—*

The creature suddenly plummeted toward the ground, toward him, falling from the sky like a stooping hawk. Eric didn't stop to think, he just ran; right down toward the only cover in sight: the grove of twisted trees below.

A whisper of foul stench slid past him, a hiss of breath and wings passing directly overhead; then the sound of claws, tearing through the rock where he had stood, until the stones screamed in agony.

Eric dived into the scanty cover of the trees, feeling a strange tingle over his hands as he grabbed on to an aged oak and cowered behind it. *This—this is an Elf Grove, like the place at Fairesite. I can feel the magic, feel the life in the trees themselves. But there's no elves here—*He tried to catch his breath, looking around unsteadily.

:*No, there are not,*: the oily voice murmured. :*Perenor summoned me here to despoil this Grove, and I have long since devoured the last of the Old Blood that resided here. But I am yet fortunate, for now you have arrived, a young Bard—*:

:*Hey, can't we talk about this?*: Eric protested, glancing up through the leafy branches at the creature, now hovering a hundred feet above him. :*I'm not really much of a meal for you. Kinda lean and stringy, y'know? Wouldn't you rather munch out on a horse from the Equestrian Center or something?*:

:*I am not interested in simple meat, Bard. I prefer the taste of one with Power, such as the Old Blood. Such as yourself.*:

Oh, terrific, Eric thought crazily. *Of all the monsters I could've run into, I get the guy with the gourmet palate, a connoisseur.* He tried again, a different tack. :*Look, you really don't want to do this. I mean, I'm going to put up a fight. It'd be a lot easier just to call it quits, right?*:

He looked up as the huge creature soared past overhead, and ducked back into the shelter of the tree as several droplets of something foul and indefinable sizzled down through the leaves beside him.

:*Why should you fight me, Bard? Why should you fight at all?*: The voice in his mind was icy, mocking.

:*I know you, young Bard. I can see who you are, reflected in the light of your own Power. You have always drifted, letting the winds of Fate direct your life, letting others make your decisions for you. You have never cared about anything—now, you do not care enough to run from me, do you? You do not care about anything at all, even your own life . . . do you?:*

Eric leaned back against the gnarled trunk of the tree, breathing hard. *It's—it's doing something to my mind—it's so hard to think straight—confused—*

:Come out of the Grove, Bard, where I can see you, away from the shrouding wisps of dying Elf-magic. Let me control your life, let me take away the necessity of decisions, the painful choices. All you have to do is step away from the trees . . .:

Eric shook his head slowly, waves of despair and desolation washing over him. *Yes—I should just let everything go. It doesn't matter, I don't matter—I'm never going to do anything meaningful, anything that's going to make a difference. I might as well just let it all go—*

:Yes,: the voice whispered. *:Yes. Abandon all the pain that is your life, let the dark oblivion wash it away. Come to me now, Bard.:*

:Yes—yes, I will—:

Eric began walking toward the edge of the grove, the moonlit hillside beyond. In his mind he could sense a dark exultation, and a dreadful, anticipating hunger.

Then an image flitted across Eric's mind, of Beth Kentraine standing on the driveway, tears wet on her cheeks. "You abandoned us, Eric . . ."

He stopped, one hand resting on a low-hanging branch. "Beth—"

:Come to me, Bard, come to me now—:

Anger raced through him like an electric charge, erasing the haze that the creature's spell had cast upon him. *:Yeah, that's what you want, isn't it? Eric the Bard, your little midnight snack strolling right down your throat? Well, let's try it the other way—how 'bout me having some Cajunstyle blackened monster for a change?:* He leaped back into the sheltering trees, just as he felt and heard the creature's roar of hatred and frustration.

Then the grove exploded into flames around him.

Holy shit!

Eric rolled to the ground, trying to beat the fire off his jacket. *Oh God—I'm going to fry in here if I don't do something quick—* Gasping for breath, he fumbled desperately with the clasps of his flute case.

He shoved the pieces of the flute together, then glanced up through the burning branches, just in time to see the winged form arcing down toward the grove for another pass.

But the creature landed instead, crashing through the flaming trees. The huge clawed hands, the tentacled mouth dripping slime, all blindly lashing about, searching for the Bard.

Who was sprawled in the smoldering leaves, less than twenty feet away.

Oh God—oh God—it's trashing the Grove, trying to find me. If I run, it'll zero in on me in a few seconds. There isn't anything else I can hide behind. And if I stay here . . .

Eric brought the flute to his lips, and played for all he was worth.

"Banish Misfortune." *Oh, God, please, if there's any resident deity around here, get me out of this!*

The first notes were inaudible against the screaming fury of the monster, the trees shattering in its wake, and the crackling of the raging flames. Then the descanting melody broke through, stilling all to silence; even the crackling fire dimmed down to mere flickers of flame.

It's—it's working, something's happening—

He clambered to his feet, still playing the Irish tune, and moved toward the crouching monster. The pale moon eyes were turned toward him, transfixed.

I'm holding it, somehow. Now what can I do with it?

If I let it go, it'll kill me, just like it killed the elves, and probably every hiker and jogger that's been through these hills in the last few months. I guess—I guess I have to kill it. Now, while I'm holding it trapped.

A memory: he and Prince Terenil in the dojo, and lightning scorching down, barely missing him.

That wouldn't have killed me, though it sure would've

been worse than sticking my finger in a light socket. If I do that, but with everything I've got behind it—

I"m sorry. I wish I didn't have to do this.

He raised his hands, and called the lightning.

Scream of tortured violins. The sizzling roar shook the ground around him, followed by a reek of stinging ozone.

For a moment, Eric couldn't see, blinded by the smoke and light—

:FearTerrorPAIN . . . fading, fading . . .:

When he could see again, the winged monster was lying motionless, its eyes open and staring. Eric covered his nose and mouth with his hand, overwhelmed by the reek of burned flesh and smoke.

Is it—is it dead?

:Bard—come closer—:

Involuntarily, he moved forward, caught in the dying creature's gaze.

:Yes—if I must die, trapped here by a hated enemy, unable to fly from this valley and slain by a mortal, then at least I will take you with me, into the shadows.:

Falling into darkness, falling, dying, everything fading—NO!

Eric wrenched free of the creature's dying mind with an effort, shaking. The monster shuddered once, and was still.

He stood there for a long moment, clutching his flute with fingers that were too numb to feel it. *I think it's really dead, now. Christ.*

Eric staggered away from the huge corpse, away from the smoldering oak trees, to the open grass. He glanced back—

—to see the monster's body changing, dissolving into something else.

The wind kicked up, sending the dead ashes swirling away from the barren trees, scattering the pile of dead leaves and ragged black plastic sheeting. The plastic crackled in the wind, like the snap of leathery wings.

It's—it's really gone. I killed it. God.

He managed another few steps before falling to his knees, unable to walk; retching his guts out, trembling in every limb, and covered in ice-cold sweat.

Oh God, oh God—I've never been so scared. But it's dead, it can't come after me again, it's dead, it's dead, it's gone, it's dead . . .

Eric stood on the top of the ridge, the wind running invisible fingers through his long hair. The lights of the San Fernando valley glittered beckoningly before him, the winding road through a sedate tract of houses leading down to civilization.

I'll be home soon. Only a couple more miles to go, thank God; I've never wanted to see my apartment so much in all my life.

I'll get home, wash some of this soot and dead monster slime off of me, and then call Beth and Kory.

Using the telephone, this time.

Christ, I feel like hell . . .

He walked past the darkened houses, down to Ventura Boulevard. Even at this hour of night, there was still traffic on the street, cars passing him by, occasionally slowing down to look at him.

Yeah, I probably look terrific right now. And smell great, too. Eau de fried monster. Really lovely.

After what seemed like an eternity of trudging along the city streets, Eric finally reached his building, and started up the stairway to his apartment.

Then, on the top stair, he hesitated.

Ria—she must've known where I lived, or she could find that out, real easy. I wouldn't put it past her to know exactly where I live, my bank account number, the sock drawer where I keep my cash, everything. What if—

Eric, you're getting paranoid.

Yeah, but I want to stay alive, too.

He gazed at the locked door for a long moment.

Okay. Maybe I'm not going to open the door just yet. Maybe I should drop in on Beth first. I don't think Ria would've figured out where she lives, at least not yet. Especially if Beth's got that magical shielding up around her place—

Damn it, this isn't fair! All I want to do is go inside,

take a shower, and sleep! Why did my life have to turn out this complicated?

Eric reached for the door handle, then shook his head. *No. I'm not going to push my luck.*

Then how in the hell am I going to get to Beth's, at this hour of the night?

He looked down at his aching feet, and sighed. *Oh well. It can't be more than seven or eight miles away.*

Here I go again . . .

Eric didn't know what time it was when he finally hiked around the last corner and saw Beth's apartment building in front of him *But it must be getting close to dawn. God, my feet hurt. If Beth isn't here, I'm just going to fall asleep on her doorstep, I don't care if her landlord calls the cops or not. I'm so tired—*

He found a last burst of energy and jogged up the wooden stairs, two at time. He hesitated before knocking on the door.

What if she doesn't let me in? We didn't exactly part on the best terms, earlier this evening.

She has to. I don't have anywhere else I can go.

He rapped sharply on the door, waited, then knocked again. *She's probably asleep. I'd better keep knocking, give her a few minutes to wake up.* He was about to knock a third time, when the door suddenly opened.

She stood, haloed by the hall light behind her, wearing only a long nightshirt, her dark hair tousled, her dark eyes wide with surprise. *Beth, how could I have left you? God, that was stupid. I—I feel so good, just seeing you now— just being here—*

She reached for the door, suddenly, and Eric knew that in another half-second she was going to slam the door in his face.

"'Beth!" Eric blocked the door with his foot. She backed away from him, then whirled and—

—and ran. He shoved the door open and stepped into the apartment, seeing her stumbling away towards the living room.

"Beth, don't run away from me!"

She turned, angrily, and he saw the tears on her face. "Me. run away? What in the hell do you think *you* did?"

God, she looks awful. Like she hasn't slept in days. And there's white hairs in that black frizz of hers that I've never seen before. A finger of cold trailed down his backbone. He ignored it, moving towards her.

"Look, I know I was acting stupid earlier." Eric began reasonably, "But I'm back, aren't I?"

"Yeah, you sure are," she said bitterly. "Hooray for you." She sat down on the sofa, reaching for a half-empty bottle of beer, refusing to look at him.

It's Kory. That's what it is, it's Kory. Oh God, I've lost her before I ever had her, and it's my own stupid fault.

"Beth, listen. I—I need to know—are you in love with Kory?" He swallowed painfully. "If you are, it's . . . it's okay, I'll just leave now. I don't have anywhere to go, but that's never mattered before. Are you?"

She stared at him, as though she didn't understand what he had just said, then laughed—only it wasn't much like a laugh, it was more like a cry of pain. "Why should you care, after what you did? And why should I tell you?" She clenched her fist, pressing it to her temple, face contorted with pain.

Then, suddenly, she sagged with defeat, and swigged from her bottle. "Not that it matters, anyhow."

She's never talked like this to me before, ever. What's happened since I left? Then something else she had just said sank in, along with a low heavy feeling in his gut. "What do you mean, it doesn't matter?"

Her words were muffled behind the bottle. "Kory's gone, Eric. He—he gave up hope, these last couple months since you left us. He completely lost hope, and now he's left me." She trembled, the beer bottle loose in her hands, close to spilling. "He left me—"

"Why would Kory—" Eric began, then stopped short. "Months? *Months?* What are you talking about?"

She glanced up at him, her dark eyes empty and cold, with something brittle and about to shatter at the bottom of them.

"We spent two months looking for you, Eric," she said tightly. "Trying to fight Perenor's people without you, to stop them from destroying the nexus. But we couldn't do much, not by ourselves. God, we tried. Kory wore himself away to *nothing*, trying. We *knew* they had you—at least for a while. But he couldn't find any trace of you, nothing. We— we thought they'd killed you."

She choked back a dry sob. "Then one night Kory heard you playing, somehow—so we knew you were alive, and roughly where you were. That's what led us to you, your music. Otherwise we'd never have known what happened to you."

Eric sank down to the couch, his legs refusing to support him. "No. That can't be true. I've only been gone for three days—"

Think, Banyon. All those old Celtic ballads about people being trapped in the land of Faerie, spending a night dancing in an elven circle, then waltzing home to find out that ten years have gone by. That's what happened to you.

Holy shit.

That's what Ria was doing to me . . .

He took a deep breath, and another, trying to get his mind back into first gear. *Not in neutral. Wheels spinning, but not going anywhere. That's where I've been for the last* two months.

Two months.

"Okay," he said at last. "Okay. So I lost a bit of time. But why did Kory walk out on you?"

Beth shook her head slowly, her voice ragged with despair, every word tearing at his heart. "You still don't get it, do you?" she said dully. "It's been months, Eric. They bulldozed the Fairesite three weeks ago. It's all over."

The bottle fell, a stream of beer cascading into the carpet, as Beth buried her face in her hands, sobbing. "He gave up. We knew, the last day, we knew when it happened. He just sort of . . . folded in on himself when the bulldozers hit the first tree. And he gave up. There's nothing left. No hopes, no dreams. Nothing. It's over, the elves are going to die, Kory's going to die—he knew he was going to die, so he left me, so I wouldn't have to watch him, see him die slowly, fading like all the others—"

Eric moved closer to her, gently putting his arm around her shoulders. "Oh, Beth."

She looked up at him, her face streaked with tears. "But I know he's dying, I can *feel* it; I can feel him dying a little at a time. It hurts, Eric, it hurts so much—" He held her tightly against him, feeling the dampness of her tears soaking through his shirt.

Every word felt like a knife in his heart, but nothing hurt as badly as the knowledge that he was the one responsible for the whole disaster.

If I hadn't walked out on them—God, Beth, how could I have done this to you, to Kory? I didn't know—oh God, I'm sorry, I'm so sorry—

She cried until she had no tears left, dry sobs shaking her body. She cried herself into absolute and utter exhaustion.

And all he could do was hold her.

He carried Beth into the bedroom an hour later, after she'd finally cried herself to sleep in his arms. Eric set her down carefully on the mattress and pulled a blanket tenderly over her. From the doorway, he glanced back at her; the gleam from the streetlight outside filtered through the bedroom curtains, casting long shadows on her tear-stained face.

Eric walked back to the living room, his thoughts in chaos. On the living room table was a bottle of Irish whiskey, half-empty; he picked it up, opened it, and took a long draught.

Time for drinking and thinking. In that order. I should probably take a shower, get some of this filth off of me, but I'm too depressed.

He sat down on the sofa, the bottle clenched in his hand. Across the room, the television was on, with the volume turned all the way down. Eric crossed over to the TV, and raised the volume just enough so he could hear and not awaken Beth.

Black and white shadows flickered across the screen. *A 50's science fiction film. Terrific. Something mindless to watch while I get drunk.* He sat back down on the couch, wishing the whiskey would take effect faster. *I want to be really drunk, really soon—*

God. How could this have happened? Why didn't I realize what was happening? I still can't believe it—two months.

Kory's gone, and maybe he's already dead. I don't even know where he is, even if I knew how to help him.

Ria and Perenor—they've won. Last game of the night, all the cards on the table, and they've won.

He drank another swallow of the whiskey, the fiery liquor burning a track down his throat.

It's over. There's nothing Beth and I can do.

A tiny voice spoke into his thoughts, an echo of his own grim thoughts, and the creature he had fought earlier this night: *Yeah. You can wallow in self-pity. Get drunk, get stoned, get trapped under a Faerie hill, wipe the world away. That's what you can do. Like you've been doing for the last two months. You can go on doing absolutely nothing. You're really very good at it.*

Eric stopped, the bottle of whiskey half-raised to his mouth. He hesitated, and his hand wavered, then he slowly set the bottle back down on the table.

No. No more. This time, I'm going to do things right. I don't care if it's hopeless—I'm not going to give up again. I've spent too many years running away from problems and commitments. This one I'm going to face.

There's a beautiful, wonderful lady asleep in that next room, a lady who cares a lot about me. I'm not going to fail her. And somewhere out there is a frizzy-haired elf guy, a guy both of us care about, who depended on me—

And I let him down.

But I won't do that again. We'll find him, and we'll make this work out right.

If we can find him.

If he's still alive.

Something deep inside him refused to give up, revolted

at the idea of Kory being gone. *He has to be alive. I won't believe he's dead. If he was, I think . . . I think I'd know, somehow. I don't think anybody, not even Ria, could keep me from knowing that.*

He glanced at the television screen, where a handsome blond hero was blowing away a killer tinfoil robot with some kind of ray gun. *I wish everything was that easy. If I thought it was, I'd pick up a .45 from a neighborhood pawnshop and go hunting for Perenor. But that won't accomplish anything, other than probably getting me killed. I remember real well what he did to Kory.*

The hero-actor posed and gestured like a wooden puppet, somehow more artificial than the tinfoil robot. *God, but that movie is awful. Really bad. Not "so bad it's cute" bad, but just pathetically bad. It's not even funny. Doesn't have any magic to it at all.*

No magic . . .

Is this what all the movies, all the music, are going to be like now? So . . . lifeless? Like the same old stupid plots, replaying over and over again?

That's something terrific to look forward to. If I fail at this, if I can't do something to save Kory and the elves, I'll never be able to sit through a movie, ever again.

Hell, why am I thinking about movies? If I go after Ria and Perenor and blow it, I'll be dead. Perenor would kill me with all the hesitation and moral consideration of somebody swatting a fly. I'd—I'd like to think that Ria wouldn't try to kill me, but I know better than that.

The images on the television changed from scrolling end credits to the early morning news, and a video clip of firemen and police officers clustered outside a burning building. Eric suddenly tuned his ears into what the announcer was saying, curious. "... and in Van Nuys, firemen are still battling a blaze that broke out roughly an hour ago . . ."

Eric blinked, looking at the flames rising from the ugly pink apartment building. *I really feel for whoever lives there. That place looks just about totaled.*

Who'd want to live in that ugly—pink—oh my God, that's my apartment building! My home is burning down!

Holy shit!

He stared in shock at the television set, and the green flames rising from the pink apartment building. *Green and pink, really lovely. I think I'm going to be sick—*

Wait a second, here. Green *flames?*

Suddenly he recalled another set of green flames. Magic flame. When he and Terenil had dueled—

But Terenil wouldn't have done anything like this—

Even if he *could* have.

Which left—

The only other two creatures in this city capable of wielding that much magic power.

Ria.

And Perenor.

He rose to his feet, so angry he was shaking. *Damn you! Damn you! Haven't you done enough to me? Haven't you got it all? Do you have to turn my apartment into a bonfire? Why in hell can't you leave us alone? I'm no threat to YOU!*

He didn't even realize he was screaming the words at the top of his lungs until somebody began to pound on the wall from the apartment next door.

And he didn't care.

"Damn you, Perenor! Leave us alone!"

16

Whirlwinds of Danger

"Damn you, Perenor, leave us ALONE!"

Someone coughed behind him. He turned to see Beth blinking sleepily, staring at him from the bedroom doorway. "Yo, Eric," she said conversationally, in close to a normal tone of voice. "Could you scream a little quieter? I was asleep for the first time in three days."

Someone pounded on the wall.

"And I think you woke more people up than me." She glanced past him, at the television set, and her eyes widened. "Hey, isn't that—"

"Yes," he said wearily. "Perenor just torched my apartment. Excuse me, I think I'm going into the bathroom to bang my head against the wall and cry."

He started to walk past her, both hands buried in his hair. "Everything's gone to hell. Kory may be dead, the nexus is destroyed, and everything I own except these clothes and my flute just went up in smoke. That's it, I can't take it anymore."

He pivoted and slammed his hand against the wall. "Dammit, they've *Won!* Why are they doing this to me?"

A strange expression crept across her face and Beth caught him by the arm. "No. Eric, that's not it. That doesn't make any sense. If those bastards have really won then they wouldn't have any reason to still come after us, would they?"

He shrugged, and ground his teeth. "I don't know. Maybe they're just bored, and ruining our lives is more entertaining than watching soap operas. Maybe it's just Ria, wanting to get even with me for walking out on her. I don't know." He glanced back at the television set, expecting to see another glimpse of his life going up in smoke, and froze.

It was a different news clip, with a photograph of a pretty dark-haired girl, smiling at the camera. ". . . and in the South Bay another victim of the 'East Side Slasher' was discovered last night. Octavia—"

Martinez. Octavia Martinez. Eric completed the thought before the announcer was two syllables into the girl's last name. *Octavia, "Tavy" to her friends, a fifteen-year-old who's already a virtuoso on the cello—gifted and bright, lead cello in her school orchestra—*

It was as if he had known her all his life. The details of her short lifespan flooded into him too fast to really comprehend.

How can I know this? What's going on with my head?

But he knew her, he *knew* her. Even though they'd never even matched eyes in a crowd, much less met. *Tavy, a beautiful young girl, already an incredible talent, so happy, always laughing, loving life so much, her music bringing joy to everyone who heard her—*

". . . and police are intensifying the search for suspects and now believe that the killer may be using trained attack animals, such as pit bulls, for these murders." A series of photographs flashed onto the screen. "Already the Slasher has claimed seven lives since the first murder in the East Los Angeles area three weeks ago."

The words faded away beneath the images forming in Eric's mind, the still photographs changing to visions of people, alive and vibrant. *Michael, yeah, he was an artist, worked in advertising, with a real gift for making his artwork come to life . . . Sandy Chelsea, solo vocalist with the Master Chorale . . . Danny, only eight years old, but already well-known as an actor, doing voiceovers for cartoons . . .*

All of them people he knew as well as his closest friends—and had never encountered in the flesh. *How can I know all of this? I've never heard of these people in my life, I've never even seen photographs of them before!*

"Eric—Eric, are you all right?"

He opened his eyes and saw Beth watching him with concern. "Beth, all of those victims . . . I know them. They were all like me, all of them able to do the things that I do . . ."

"Bards?" Beth looked at the television screen, now showing a commercial about vacation homes in the mountains. "All of them were Bards?"

Eric moved to the couch and sat down heavily. "That is what's going on. Perenor. He's killing off everyone with the Bardic Gift." He looked up at Beth, who was staring at him, wide-eyed, her sleep-rumpled hair standing up like a cartoon character's. "You were right, there must be some way that we can hurt him still, or he wouldn't have any reason to do this."

"Yeah. If we could just figure out what—" Beth stopped in midsentence, then reacted. "Christ! This means he might try for Uncle Phil, too!"

For a moment, Eric couldn't remember who Beth was talking about, then an image flashed into his mind: the elderly man with the house full of artwork and animation cels, and how his eyes had shone when he looked at Eric—no, not his eyes, but something behind them, something that was a part of him, reaching out to Eric like an old friend, speaking to a part of himself that answered in harmony. "Yeah, Phil—Beth, he's got the Bardic Gift, too."

"Of course he does," Beth said tersely, disappearing into her bedroom. Eric could hear the sound of drawers opening and clothing being flung out. Beth's voice drifted to him through the open door. "He's an animator, after all—you just look at his work and you know that there's more going on there than just blobs of paint on transparency cels!"

She reappeared a moment later in jeans and sneakers, pulling a sweatshirt down over her torso. "Come on, we're leaving," she said, picking up his flute case from where he had set it down on the table. She gave him an impatient look. "Well?"

"Hang on a sec, Beth—"

He had to close his eyes; the vision overlaying the *real* world of Beth's apartment was too confusing to sort out otherwise. *Images: a sleepy little street in Burbank, the pale yellow house, the first glints of sunlight reflecting off shadowy water, an old convertible parked on the street. And a feeling of cold and calculating intent, of gathering will force, and—*

"Holy shit, Beth, I think Perenor's doing something there right now!"

She didn't say anything, just grabbed him and ran.

What if I'm wrong? What if I'm completely crazy, if all of this is just delusions? What if I'm imagining that Perenor is at Phil's house, planning to do something awful to the old guy?

How do I know if what I'm feeling is real? That I'm not completely crazy?

His mind might doubt, but his gut *knew*. This was for real. The cold feeling in the pit of his stomach intensified as the jeep careened around another corner. He glanced at Beth, and saw that her knuckles were clenched tight on the steering wheel. *She feels it, too. Something awful is happening—*

Beth floored the brakes. The jeep skidding to a stop in front of the little yellow house, nearly ramming into the parked convertible. Before Eric even got out of his seat, she had vaulted out of the Jeep and was halfway to the front door. She pounded on it several times, calling out Phil's name, as Eric grabbed his flute and hurried across the lawn to her.

"He's not answering," she said shortly, and reached into a potted plant for a hidden key. Eric followed her as she hurried to the side gate and into a backyard filled with assorted junk and pieces of furniture, past a swimming pool murky with fallen leaves and debris. "Beth, if someone sees us doing this, we could get arrested—" Then Eric stopped, staring at the back of the house.

Or rather, what *used* to be the back. After a giant had reached down and ripped off the wall and roof. Pieces of splintered wood and plaster were scattered everywhere.

I have a bad feeling about this—

Eric tore his eyes away from the devastation, to see Beth Kentraine already vanishing through the remnants of a sliding glass door. "Beth, wait! You don't know if—"

Shit, she's already gone inside! He glanced at the carnage around him, then swallowed and followed her in.

If possible, the inside of the house was in worse shape than the outside. Eric saw the Snow White cel that he had admired, lying on the floor practically at his feet, shredded. *With all of that slimy black gunk smeared all over it— slimy—like that* thing *that I killed last night—oh shit! Beth! Where in the hell is she?*

He ran into the next room, feeling as though every nightmare he had had as a child was upon him, every screaming terror resonating down his nerves. And he saw Beth, kneeling on the filthy floor, not moving, just staring at—at—

Eric turned away and retched onto the destroyed carpet, falling to his knees, shaking helplessly. *Oh God—oh my God—*

When he could, he looked back at Beth, still motionless on the floor, holding the old animator's hand. He managed to stand and took several unsteady steps towards her, then sank to the filthy carpet beside her, staring down at Phil Osborn's face.

And tried hard not to look at anything other than that wrinkled, surprisingly peaceful face; not at the ruined body, opened like a butterflied shrimp, ripped flesh and exposed internal organs glistening in the dim light, blood spreading slowly into the carpet around him. Eric felt the wetness soaking into the knees of his jeans, and clutched his gut, trying not to throw up again—

—then Phil's eyes opened, looking right up at them, and he nearly lost it one more time. *Christ. He's still alive. They did* that *to him, and he's still alive. Oh my God . . .*

"Beth." The old man's voice was a whispery thread, his eyes glazed and very bright. "Beth, listen to me."

"I'm here, Uncle Phil," Beth said softly, kneeling close to him. She rubbed at her eyes with the back of one hand, and Eric saw the blood and tears and undescribable filthy smearing together across her face. "I won't leave you."

"Beth, you can stop Perenor. That's why he's—" Phil gasped, his chest heaving. "Stop him, Bethie. I know you can do it."

We can? How in the hell are we supposed to stop somebody who would do this, turn another person into a piece of sushi?

Then the old man smiled, looking at something beyond Eric and Beth, something only he could see. "Leila . ."

The room faded from around Eric, as a slow rising chord echoed through his mind. *Power, clear and strong as a river, reaching out for something—a brightness, an intensity, shining like a beacon from within—and from far away, the hint of another Power, different, yet the same, reaching toward the first.*

This is what a Bard is, he realized dimly. *This quiet strength and power, the force of creation held by a living being, power shining so bright, almost incandescent.*

—and the distant melody, drawing closer, strengthening the faltering notes of the first. Then the two joining—

—then fading, fading . . .

And gone.

The aged, agonized eyes focused on nothing, then ceased to focus at all. Beth sobbed quietly, Phil's bloodstained hand still pressed against her cheek.

He's dead.

That—that was him. Phil. A Bard. Is that what I am, too? What I look like to Kory—and Ria?

Eric swallowed, feeling his nausea rising again. *And she and her dad had me in their clutches for two months. They could've done this to me at any point, exactly what they did to Phil. Christ.*

He edged closer to Beth, resting his hand on her shoulder, wanting to comfort her, but not really knowing how. *What do you say to someone who's just seen an old friend murdered—hell, taken apart like a laboratory frog! What good are words now?*

"Eric."

Beth's voice was low, it barely penetrated through the clamor of his thoughts. Then she spoke louder, stronger. "Eric, I don't want to leave him like this. I don't want anyone to see him. Not the cops, not anyone."

He nodded, understanding what she was saying, even though he wasn't certain what she expected him to do.

"All right. Stand back a bit, Beth."

She bent low and kissed Phil's bloodless lips briefly, then stood up.

Okay. This time, I'm going to do it right. For Beth. He removed his flute from the case, fitted it together, then brought it to his lips. He closed his eyes, concentrating.

Slow notes, a quiet melody, then building in intensity, filled with aching pain . . . "O'Carolan's Farewell to Music," a fitting tribute to a murdered Bard, someone who held power in his human hands, who created life with ink and paint.

If there's a heaven, this old guy is headed straight for it. Or wherever it is that we Bards go when we die.

Through his closed eyes, Eric saw a bright spark of light, then a burst of green flame. He opened his eyes, watching as the crackling eldritch fire consumed the old man's body. When nothing was left but a fine dusting of ashes on the floor, Eric let the fire die away.

Strange. The floor isn't even scorched. But the fire was hot, hot enough that I could feel it from here. And hear it, the snapping flames—

For a moment, Eric thought he heard something else, a faint slithery sound, like a water hose dragged along concrete. Then there was silence again, except for the sound of Beth crying softly.

He touched her shoulder gently. "Beth, we'd better get out of here. If some neighbor calls the police . . ."

She stood up, still gazing down at the small heap of ashes. "Thank you, Eric," she said quietly.

Eric put his arm around her as they walked to the bedroom door. In the ruined living room, Beth bent to pick up a shattered photograph frame. The picture that fell out was a black-and-white of a younger Phil and a lovely dark-haired woman. She caught it before it touched the slimed carpet, rolled it up and slipped it into her jacket pocket.

Outside, the first hints of sunlight were breaking through the clouds overhead. There were only moments left until true dawn. Eric and Beth, walking in silence, picked a careful path through the debris on the swimming pool deck.

"Beth," Eric began hesitantly, "when Phil called out to Leila, did you see—"

He stopped, feeling as if someone was standing just behind him, peering over his shoulder. *Somebody very close, close enough to touch . . .*

Then he screamed as something wet and oily coiled around his ankle, yanked his feet out from under him, and dragged him backwards. He thrashed, trying to free himself, and caught a glimpse of something. Something huge and dark and dripping, topped by a rearing equine head with glittering red eyes and distended fangs. Then the thing slammed him down on the concrete, knocking the breath and wits from him. His flute case went flying in one direction as he was yanked in another.

Toward the pool.

"Beth!" he shrieked, hearing her scream echoing behind him. Then the water closed over him, black and icy cold, as icy as the scaled flesh against his bare skin. He struggled against that inhuman grip, already knowing it was hopeless, trying to reach the surface to breathe, feeling the darkness closing in around him as every second ticked past.

God, please, just let Beth get away, don't let it get her, too—

Then the clawed hand thrust him up into the open air, and Eric gasped for breath gratefully. Then he saw why the creature had surfaced, and his heart stopped beating for an instant.

Beth!

She stood like some fantasy art heroine, her clothing soaking wet and clinging to her, a piece of wood splintered to a sharp point clenched in her hand. He could see where the tip was stained with blood and a foul ichor as she danced

closer along the slippery rim of the pool, trying for another
stab.

"Beth," he yelled, "get your ass out of here!"

Then Eric screamed again as the piece of wood sailed
within inches of his nose to embed itself in the creature's
eye. With a shriek that rent the air, it flung Eric onto the
concrete and sank beneath the pool's surface.

Eric just lay there for a long moment, choking and
gasping, and concentrated on some serious breathing.

Oh God. I'm still alive—

Then he realized Beth was pulling him away from the
water's edge. "I'm-I'm okay," he gasped hoarsely, trying to
sit up.

She held on to him tightly. For a moment, he thought
he could hear her voice, even though her face was pressed
too closely against his shoulder for her to speak.

:I thought I'd lost you again, lost you—Oh, Eric—:

"I love you too, Beth," he whispered.

She kissed him, then helped him to his feet. "At least
you don't reek quite so much now," she said dryly.

A noise behind them made both of them turn. The
opaque water of the swimming pool was roiling with darkness, seething as though something was thrashing below.
They glanced at each other, then Eric scooped up his flute
case and they ran for the gate. And didn't stop until they
were in the Jeep. Beth sent it accelerating onto the west-
bound Ventura Freeway.

*It must be dead. How could anything live after getting
drilled through the eye like Beth did to it?*

*Then again, how can anything like that be alive in the
first place?*

*Kory gone, Phil dead, the nexus destroyed—God, I wish
this was a bad dream and I could wake up.*

Fat Chance, Banyon.

He looked across the seat at Beth, and realized that her
hands were shaking on the wheel. "Maybe you should pull
over for a minute."

She took a deep breath and shook her head. "No. I'm okay.
It's just—how long do we have, Eric, before Perenor tracks

us down and kills us? He obviously hasn't forgotten about you. What can we do against a guy who summons creatures like that swimming-pool thing to take care of his enemies?"

Or that winged monstrosity that tried to eat me last night in the hills— "I don't know. Go on the offensive, maybe?"

"Offensive against what? If we go anywhere near him, he'll swat us like flies, Eric!"

He thought about it for a moment. "What about the nexus? Maybe there's still something we can do about that."

"Okay," Beth said after a long pause. "Let's go out to Fairesite."

They bulldozed the site three weeks ago.

Even knowing what to expect, Beth was still shocked and horrified by what she saw.

They didn't just destroy it, they devastated it. I've never seen anything like this before done with such . . . maliciousness. Like they didn't want to leave one single paving stone next to another.

She looked out at the desolation, seeing in her mind's eye what once had stood there . . . *Over there, that was the Mainstage, where now there's only a heap of splintered wood . . . Irish Hill, they practically leveled it completely, there's nothing left except some scattered straw . . . the old Wishing Well, they just left the concrete foundation broken, didn't even bother with removing the pieces.*

There's nothing left here but dirt and chips of wood. Nothing at all.

She reached down, picking up a piece of what had once been a bright green ribbon, now torn and dark with mud. She straightened and saw Eric, moving towards what had been the Wood.

The Wood Grove. That's where Kory said the nexus was, within the circle of ancient oak trees.

Oak trees, torn out of the ground, lying like mutilated corpses on the dusty ground, dead—they've destroyed it completely. There's nothing we can do here.

Uncle Phil murdered, and now Kory is going to die, too, if he isn't already dead—

Pain ripped through Beth, making her clench her eyes closed to keep from crying aloud. Pain like someone stabbing her in the heart—

—or the soul. It's over. Kory must be dead or dying, it's hopeless.

Eric's still picking over the mess, walking through the fallen trees, looking around. Doesn't he realize that there's nothing we can do, nothing at all? Why doesn't he just give up?

Ria disappeared around the edge of the ruined Wood, into the hilly area beyond. Beth followed hesitantly, not certain where Eric was going. *That's what used to be the end of the Wood, there's nothing beyond there, nothing except a few more oak trees—*

Beth climbed carefully over the bulldozed trees, trying to spot Eric. *There's still a few oaks left standing, by the edge of the Wood. And—*

She felt her heart leap with sudden hope, seeing a cloaked figure sprawled beneath one of the oaks' spreading branches. Then she ran forward to where Eric was standing, looking down at the motionless man.

It's him, it's Kory!

Now she could see him clearly, that wild blond hair spilling over his shoulders, mixed with dirt and blood and tears. His slack face streaked with tears and mud, his jeans and Faire shirt the same no-color.

And the six-pack of empty Coke cans on the ground next to him.

Beth slowed to a stop, and stared at the shiny red cans in horror. *But that—that's poison to elves—*

—oh my God, no!

She fell to her knees next to Kory, seized his hands and touched his face. still damp with tears. His hand was icy cold in hers. She moaned, deep in her throat, and began patting his cheeks, trying to get a response. When nothing happened, she searched frantically for a pulse. "Kory, please, no, don't be dead—"

She looked up at Eric, who was staring down at Kory in stunned silence. "God *damn* you, don't just stand there, do something! Use your magic! You're a Bard, this is what you're supposed to do! Help him!"

He swallowed, and stepped back a pace. "Beth, I don't think—"

"I don't give a shit what you think, Banyon—you're going to play that fuckin' flute now or I'm gonna ram it down your throat!"

"Beth, I don't know *how!*" he said, shouting to be heard over her rising voice. "The fire—that just came! This is *complicated.*"

She forced herself to calm down, and took a deep breath. "Okay. Let's think this through. I think maybe we need a—a spell of some kind. Maybe what you played to wake him up would work again."

He knelt beside her and opened the flute case. "I think—I think maybe I played 'Sheebeg Sheemore.' That's a spell?"

She took a *very* deep breath and seized his hand, flute and all. "A spell, Eric, is a *process,* and not a *thing.* A spell makes you concentrate your energy on a goal. 'Sheebeg Sheemore' is about elves, isn't it?"

"Yeah, but—"

"It worked last time, didn't it?"

"Yeah, but—"

"If you don't start playing," she said softly, clenching her jaw to keep from screaming at him again, "that flute is going to be shoved where you won't like it."

She turned away from him as the first notes sang out into the sunlight, searching Kory's face for a flicker of life, any sign that he was being drawn back—

Nothing.

The last notes died away, and nothing had changed—except that maybe the pulse beneath her fingers was a little weaker.

She was about to round on the musician and demand that he try something else, when Eric began "Tamlin's Reel." He followed that with "Tom O'Bedlam."

One tune after another poured from the flute, the different melodies filling the stilled air, and now Beth could feel the desperation under the notes, the frantic fear that mirrored her own so exactly that she trembled beneath the double burden. And still nothing happened, nothing changed—except the sun rose a little higher, and the wind stirred Kory's hair and dried the tears on his face.

Eric could feel Beth's desperation, it was a match for his. So he *tried*, poured his soul into his playing, tune after tune, note after note, everything Celtic he knew—and nothing, *nothing* happened. Finally he ran out of things to play, and dropped his aching arms.

He's going to die. Kory's going to die, and there's nothing I can do to stop it—

Kory's face was as slack and lifeless as before. Eric could feel the life in him; could *see* it if he looked just right— flickering, fading . . .

Dammit, I healed him, there has to be some way to channel this power right! There just has to be! Maybe—maybe it's me. I'm not making the right connections. If a spell is a process, it probably has to convince my subconscious. Which means it has to be simple. And something I can relate to.

Simple—well, the Celtic tunes are sometimes simple enough, but do I really relate them to what I have to do? Maybe I'd better get down to my own roots.

So what do I want to do?

I want to put Kory back together. To put him back the way he was. To come out the way he was.

None of the tunes he'd played so far addressed that need.

Which may be why they didn't work. He frowned, clenched his hands on the flute. *I need something clear, something simple. I've got to make this come around right—*

Then it came to him, with those words. It all came together, making such a perfect pattern that he was blinded by the clarity of it.

He closed his eyes again, made himself very still inside, and *reached*—

—and played.

He felt Beth go still for a moment, then felt her reaching out to him; heard her begin to sing.

"She danced on the water and the wind—"

He stopped. She sang another word, and faltered. "Eric? What's—"

"That's *wrong*, Beth," he said around the flute mouthpiece. "Not the pagan version—the original. The Shaker hymn. You said we needed a spell; well, that's a spell. It's about returning to balance, to what you were and what you were meant to be."

He heard her swift intake of breath, and began the tune again. She let him play it through once, then joined him on the second round.

> " 'Tis a gift to be simple,
>   'tis a gift to be free,
>   'tis a gift
>   to come 'round where we ought to be—"

Yes. That's it. He could feel the power rising now, dancing around him, following the lead of his music—and hers—echoing the simple tune.

> "—and when we find ourselves
>   in the place just right,
>   'twill be in the valley of love and delight."

Now he could feel the fading flicker that was Kory gaining strength, reaching for the power. He twined it once about the elf, twice, three times, verdant and living, tying him in vines of melody, anchoring him to *here* and now.

Beth poured her heart into the song, into the words. Eric could feel *her* strength, a dark fire joining his own power.

> "When true simplicity is gained,
>   to bow and to bend
>   we shan't be ashamed—
>   to turn, turn, will be our delight.
>   Till by turning, turning,
>   we come 'round right."

But that wasn't enough. Not yet. Kory was not a simple creature, a one-dimensional cartoon elf. He had depth and breadth and heights Eric couldn't imagine—

So Eric called to the power and the music, and reached for Kory with it.

Touched.

No doubt; this was the Copland transcription from "Appalachian Spring." Building on the original melody, weaving in and around it, calling in images as well as melody. Thunderstorms in the mountains. A quiet, secret stream. Song of a single bluebird—and the haunting cries of hundreds of skeins of geese. A towering oak. A tiny violet, hidden in fallen leaves. Oboe carrying the melody with him, a second flute making it a round, clarinets laughing a harmony—

—then the strings—

Come back, come home, come round right—

—weaving a braid that turned to a circle that turned, turned, turned—

He couldn't hear Beth anymore, but she was in there too, making the song a prayer, an outpouring of love and passion.

Now the music was returning to what it had been, each part dropping back to join the flute-line, the melody, the simple line; joining it and reinforcing it. "*—till by turning, turning, we come 'round right—*"

When they all were *one*, Eric played it through one last time, slowly, with all the emotion he could muster.

Silence. And he opened his eyes—

—and saw Kory, gazing up at him with those brilliant, leaf-green eyes—

Alive.

17

Rocky Road to Dublin

Eric had time for one coherent thought—*He's alive!*—before Kory lunged for him, his mailed hands closing tightly around Eric's throat.

He tried desperately to pry those metal-clad fingers off his neck without success. Kory lifted him right off the ground by the neck and held him dangling with his toes just brushing the dirt.

"Kory—" Eric wheezed, gasping for breath.

"You human bastard," the elven warrior hissed, his green eyes incandescent behind the golden sheen of his helm. "I wasn't hurting anymore, I was beyond that, everything was so peaceful. so painless, and you brought me back! I'm going to rip you apart, mortal!"

Eric was suddenly aware of Beth pulling ineffectually at Kory's arm, trying to get him loose—

And beyond her, a circle of elven observers watching in silence.

Just . . . watching. Just curious, mildly interested. Like it's vaguely entertaining, watching one of their own strangle a human.

Then he heard the sound of clapping hands, and a few scattered comments.

"A little higher, perhaps . . ."

"His technique is a little sloppy, don't you think?"

"Could be—"

"Well, Korendil is out of practice, after all."

Oh God, Eric thought as everything began to blur and fade around him. *I'm going to die to a chorus of remarks from an elven peanut gallery, murdered by my best friend. This really isn't fair.*

Kory's not like them, he wouldn't do this, just stand by and watch somebody get killed—

—if he wasn't the guy trying to kill *me!*

With a last burst of energy Eric kicked wildly at Kory, connecting with one graves-clad leg; hitting the elf's knee just above the metal plate. Kory's hands loosened from his throat for an instant, and Eric slammed his fist into the side of the elf's helm, connecting with Kory's lower jaw and lip. As Kory staggered back, Eric fell to the ground, choking and gasping for air.

He didn't stop to try and reason with Kory; he just rolled away in the soft dirt and grabbed his flute out of the dust where it had fallen. Somehow he ended up back on his feet, facing the furious elf.

Who still looked like he wanted to rip Eric apart limb from limb.

I could play something, use my Gift against him—but what in the hell would that accomplish? I'm trying to save his miserable life, not kill him myself!

Before either of them could move, Beth Kentraine stepped between them, her hands on her hips. "All right, guys," she said in a voice like ice. "Enough of this. Kory, what in the hell do you think you're doing?"

Kory wiped a trickle of blood away from his mouth. "Stand aside, Beth. I intend to destroy that traitor."

"Wait a second," Eric began to protest. "I was just trying to keep you from killing yourself, you stupid—"

"So you brought me back," Kory finished, glaring at him. "I never should have trusted you, Bard. The first chance you had, you ran away to our greatest enemy, willingly placing yourself in her power. Leaving us to die. *Now,* now that it's too late, you've brought all of us out of Dreaming.

Why? So we can die in agony as the last magic of the nexus fades away to nothingness? Did she teach you to savor the pleasures of another's pain?"

"Kory—I didn't—I mean, there's got to be something we can do—" Eric stammered, backpedaling before the look of hatred in Kory's eyes. *Maybe this wasn't such a good idea. It isn't just that he was mad that I left. He's not going to listen to any excuses. He wants to hurt me; really, seriously hurt me—*

"There is something that *I'm* going to do," Kory said levelly. "I'm going to kill you, Bard."

Oh my God—

As Kory advanced towards Eric, Beth interposed herself between them again. "Kory, no. Whatever you do to him, you'll have to do to me first. I won't let you touch him." She glanced at the small circle of elves, also garbed in bright metal and peacock-colors.

"Eric's not with Perenor. He wants to help you. And Eric's the only Bard here, the only one who can help you."

"If Korendil believes the human must die, then we will stand beside him," one of the elves said. "It is you who should not interfere, mortal woman."

"Oh, fuck off," Eric heard Beth mutter under her breath.

From the edge of his vision, Eric saw two of the elves edging closer to her, trying to circle behind her.

I can see exactly where this is going now. Godammit, Beth, why do you always have to fling yourself into these situations, trying to save my ass?

I thought I was doing the right thing. Maybe I wasn't.

Forget the excuses, Banyon. There aren't any excuses for what you did by walking out on these people. Just because one of them happened to be sleeping with a lady you love—

I guess I'd better face the music.

Eric pushed Beth gently to the side, and moved forward to stand in front of Kory. "Okay, I'll admit it. Running off to Ria was a real stupid idea. And everything that's happened since, it's really my fault, because you were counting on me to be there to help you. Well, I'm here now. And either you can kill me, or we can try to figure out a way to keep you guys alive. It's your choice, Kory." He managed a weak grin. "Though I'm sure you can guess which of the two *I'd* prefer that you chose."

Kory only stared at him, his hands within the gauntlets clenching and unclenching slowly. Eric realized that his own hand, the one that had hit Kory in the face, was throbbing with pain. *That doesn't matter. Nothing may ever matter again, depending on what this guy chooses to do. If he decides he'd rather kill me than let me try to save his skin— well, I'd rather be ripped apart by Perenor's pets. To go into the final darkness, like Phil, but know that Kory sent me there*—wanted *me dead. And didn't forgive me . . .*

The despair in the back of Korendil's eyes hurt worse than his hand—hurt worse than *anything* ever had before.

He swallowed hard and tried to meet those bleak eyes, and the pure fire of hate in them. *At least, if he kills me, I won't have to watch him die later, when the last of the magic fades away—*

Eric winced inwardly, but did not look away. *That's really a comforting thought, Eric. Sheer brilliance. No wonder Kory has no faith in you at all.*

He tried to find courage in himself—somewhere. *But he should have faith in me. I'm going to get them out of this mess, if—if it kills me. It's mostly my fault that this all has happened. They were counting on me. And I failed them.*

He felt a despair to match Korendil's, chilling his heart. *Right. I failed them. So I shouldn't be surprised if Kory decides to deep-six me after all—*

Then, to Eric's immense relief, Kory nodded. "I do not think you did this out of evil intent, Eric." The elf warrior's voice was weary. "So I will not harm you. Leave us now. Let us fade away in peace." He turned and began to walk away.

"So that's it?" Beth said angrily. She ran after him, grabbing him by the shoulder and forcing him to look at her. "So long, and thanks for the memories? Like hell, Kory!" Eric could hear the pain in her voice as she continued. "I love you, you idiot elf! I won't leave you here to die!"

Eric bit his lip, feeling a different kind of pain tearing

through him. *She loves him. I knew that, really I did, but hearing her say it—*

"And Eric may be an idiot, too, but he's a Bard, and I'm sure there's something he can do to *help* you, if you'll just let him. If you're willing to try something other than suicide or Bard-murder. God, why are all the men in my life such fools?"

Kory didn't answer, he only stared deeply into her eyes for *far* longer than Eric liked. And then he nodded again, slowly—and leaned forward and kissed her. As the kiss lengthened, Eric felt the seconds ticking by, each like a sharp stab into him with every heartbeat. Finally, Beth moved away from Kory, gasping a little.

The elves were watching with the same detached interest with which they had viewed the fight.

She loves him. That's obvious. Christ, why did I get myself involved in this? Saving his life just so Beth—

He stared down at the dirt at his feet, his throat so choked he could hardly breathe, and never realized that Kory was walking towards him until the elf stopped right beside him. He looked up, startled, and saw Kory was just standing there, looking at him soberly. Very close. *He looks like he's going to say something—maybe an apology for nearly tearing my throat out? That would be kinda nice, actually. Even if I was a schmuck, it still hurts to swallow.*

Or maybe something about Beth, how the best man—elf—won, but let's still be buddies, hey?

Oh hell, he's my friend. And If Bethie wants him—

Then Kory placed a gauntleted hand on each of Eric's shoulders—and kissed *him*.

Eric's startled exclamation was muffled, and his first reaction was to—

—to slide his arms around Kory's shoulders, to draw him even closer, to lean into the kiss, to hold him tightly and never, ever let him go—

—then Eric pulled free of Kory's embrace, trembling.

He turned away from the puzzled and hurt look in Kory's eyes, towards where Beth was standing several feet away, her expression undecipherable.

"I'm—I'm sorry about abandoning you, Kory," Eric said, valiantly trying to gather his wits around him. "I—I was a schmuck. An idiot. I promise, I won't let you down again." He ventured a look at the elf out of the corner of his eye.

God, no one should look that good.

"I accept your apology," the elf said, faint, courtly formality accenting his tone. Then a ghost of a smile drifted across his face. "And I promise, Bard Eric, that I shall never try to throttle you again." He glanced at the other elves. "Well, if we are to live, I suppose we should start by trying to find a solution to this situation. Shall we?"

For the first time, Eric actually *looked* at the elves around him. And gaped in surprise.

Unimaginably bright colors, glittering armor and sheathed weaponry, thigh-height boots embroidered with fantastical designs, flowing capes over tunics, multicolored skirts and breeches. *Like taking the best of the Faire costumes I've ever seen, then making them a thousand percent better.*

Although some of them were dressed more like the types seen on Melrose Avenue, studded black leather and dyed mohawks forming an unlikely contrast to the ornate garb to the others.

And Kory—

Well, at least he isn't still wearing my clothes— Eric thought, gawking at his friends.

Kory—no, *Korendil* was garbed like a character out of King Arthur's knights, clad head to toe in golden-hued armor, intricate with blue enamel inlay and gemstones. His blond hair cascaded down over a cloak the color of the sky at midday. There was no mistaking the regal look in his eyes, either: the look of a lord of the High Court of Faerie.

Eric felt terribly shabby. And grubby.

Next to him I look like one of the beggars out of Monty Python. Dirty and rumpled from walking all night, all slimy from fighting monsters, still damp from being dragged into a swimming pool—and he looks terrific.

No wonder Beth has the hots for him.

I could really hate these elves, given half a chance—

A lovely silver-haired elf woman, clad in flowing blue silk

with a sheathed sword slung over one shoulder, stepped from the small circle of Faerie still gathered around them. She kissed Kory fondly. "Young Korendil," she said, "we, the mages and warriors of the High Court who remain here, pledge you now that we will follow your guidance and that of this human Bard, though death be the end of it."

"Val," Kory began, looking suddenly awkward and very young. "I don't know what to say—"

Another elf, a broad-shouldered figure in skin-tight black leather, his purple mohawk falling rakishly over one ear, clapped Kory on the shoulder. "Then say nothing, Kory. But you will lead us into battle."

"Eldenor, you're my *teacher!* You should—"

"We are all that is left of Elfhame Sun-Descending," the elf said in his low, resonant voice. "Our enemies have nearly succeeded in destroying us. You and the Prince were the only ones who saw our danger. And now we do not know if Prince Terenil is still alive. But you are here with the Bard you brought to aid us." Eldenor grinned. "Even if you were ready to kill him a few minutes ago."

"Kory," Eric began hesitantly, "I don't know what I can do, but if you just tell me what, I'll do it."

He does look kinda overwhelmed. But I know he can lead this motley crew, if anyone can. And figure out what we can do to solve all of this. If we can.

He resolutely pushed his doubts away. *No. We have to solve this. There's too much at stake here. Kory, he's my friend. Maybe—maybe he's even a little more than that, I don't know. But I do know that I won't let him die.*

Kory was looking around at the devastated grove. "This is what must be remedied. Unless we do something soon, despite what you have done with your magic, Eric, we shall fall back into Dreaming, and then die. That is why we came here, to the last lingering wisps of magic."

"Wait a minute," Beth said suddenly. "Something just occurred to me . . . if the magic is all dried up, then where is our minstrel boy getting his juice from? Eric?"

Eric shrugged. "I've never thought about it before but you're right, I must be drawing it from somewhere." He closed his eyes, replaying what had just happened in his mind, how he had reached out . . .

. . . *and called the power, called it, drawn it from—* "From Ria's house," he said at last, opening his eyes. "It's coming straight from her place in Bel Air. I guess I can tap into it, just because"—he felt his face warming, and tried to quell his embarrassment before it became too obvious— "because, uh, I was so, so close to her, for so long. They must have moved the nexus there somehow."

"That makes sense," Beth said thoughtfully. "That's a terrific way to keep everything under lock and key: kill the old nexus and plant a new one in your backyard."

"She is an accomplished sorceress," Kory acknowledged. "With her father aiding her, I do not doubt that she could redirect the nexus, once its focal point had been destroyed, since of course she would not be able to create a new nexus from nothingness. This must have been Perenor's intent all along, to have all the magic of this region at his disposal."

"But there's one thing I don't understand," Eric said hesitantly. "How can you pick up a nexus and move it around L.A. like this? I mean, what is a nexus, anyhow?"

"The nexus is only a tiny gap in the veil between this world and the world of our kind, Bard," a flame-haired elf woman explained. "It must be small, or it would weaken the veil. To create such a thing is beyond the skill of all, except—"

Except—

Terenil, sitting around the dojo after that workout, drinking and talking. ". . . and the Queen's Bard, a human like yourself, created an anchoring point for the nexus . . ."

A human Bard. Like me.

This *is what I can do. This is how I can save Kory and his people.*

His mouth suddenly felt very dry. *Except that Perenor and Ria have already taken control of the nexus. Which means I'll have to fight them for it—fight Ria—*

"Kory," he said, slowly, looking at his feet, "I can create a nexus. Creative magic, that's what Bards do. That's what the Queen's Bard did when you first came here—"

Only I'll have to fight Ria to do it.

He looked up to see Beth watching him. "'Bout time you figured it out. Banyon," she said quietly. "Think you can handle it?"

Eric took a deep breath, then another. Kory and the elves were watching him as he spoke. "I—I don't know. I'm really not very good at this magic stuff, at least not yet. I mean, I don't even know what I was doing, I just sort of did it off the cuff. By accident. Improvising. But this is something that, if I screw it up, we probably won't get a second chance—"

"I think you can do it, Eric," Beth said. "But we've got another problem. Even if you can do this whole schtick no sweat, do we want you to put the nexus back here? This place is going to be turned into condos in another couple months. Doesn't seem like the best place for a magic nexus, next to the hot tub and laundry rooms, y'know?"

"She is very right," Val said thoughtfully. "We need another place for the nexus, one which is not close to the humans' dwellings, so rife with Cold Iron. And one that is nearer to those of the Lesser Court, trapped in their groves. A place that will be safe for many years to come."

Good luck, finding a place like that in L.A. This place is so overpopulated, even the mosquitoes are having a hard time finding a place to breed. Everything that's not Federal or State land is going to be developed into housing, sooner or later.

—Federal or State land—

That wide, empty valley, with the oak trees growing among the tall grass. Federal land, that no one can touch. An elven grove in the Hollywood Hills. And a dragon, starving to death because no one came near enough to eat—

—that area wouldn't be so great, it's still too close to the city. But maybe if we go a little further east—

"How 'bout Griffith Park, in the Hollywood Hills? There's a lot of land up there where nobody goes except maybe the real compulsive hikers. That might be a safe place for the nexus."

Kory glanced at Beth, who nodded. "That's a real solid

idea, Eric. Griffith Park will never be turned into houses or shopping malls, not so long as the city stands. I can't think of any place that would be nearly as good." She gave Eric a wry grin. "Now you'll just have to do your magic stuff, bucko, and we're back in business."

Eric hesitated as that dark thought reoccurred to him. "What about Ria and Perenor? We know that the opposition isn't going to let us do this without a fight. I don't think I can do all of that, restore the nexus *and* hold off two sorcerers." *Ria and Perenor, they need the nexus, or they wouldn't have gone to all of this trouble. They need it bad enough to kill for it, that's for certain. To kill Phil, and all those other potential Bards—*

Ria. She used me, manipulated me—but there's still part of me that cares about her, that needs her.

If Ria comes at me again, throwing everything she has at me—one of us is going to die. We can't fight like that again, and not kill each other. But could I really bring myself to kill her?

Could she kill me?

Eldenor clasped Eric's arm strongly, breaking into his thoughts. "We will guard you, Bard. We will keep any from harming you as you work the Magic. Trust me—as you will fight to save us, we will battle to protect you." The muscular elf glanced down as Eric winced in sudden pain. "Korendil, it seems that your stubborn skull is as thick as ever. Come see what the Bard did to himself trying to knock some sense into you."

"I think it was the helmet, actually," Eric muttered, as Kory carefully took Eric's hand in his own. Beth moved in closer to look. Eric saw her eyes widen at the sight of his hand, bruised and bloody, two of the fingers already purpling and swollen. Kory tried to bend the fingers, and Eric bit back a yelp.

Damn, but that hurts!

"This is because of my foolishness, Eric," Kory said at last. "The place of magic is nearly drained, but let me see if I can mend what my stubbornness has wrought."

The elf closed his eyes, cradling Eric's broken hand in both of his; and this time, when Eric heard the first stirrings of melody, he *knew* what was happening. The gentle interweaving of melody, somehow touching him; invisible fingertips tracing over his hand, through his hand, knitting together the broken bones, the torn flesh. He was not surprised to hear Beth singing distantly, silently, part of the magic as well.

As the melody faded, Eric looked down at his hand and flexed the fingers lightly, the fingering pattern for "Sheebeg Sheemore."

That's what this is—the two rival groups of elves, just like in the O'Carolan song. Except this time, we're playing for keeps. It's not a song, or a Bard's vision. It's life and death, and not just for them—for me, and for Beth, too.

God. It's so scary that it's almost beautiful.

But I still wish I could wake up, and all of this would just be a dream—

Terenil floated in the vast *nothingness* of Dreaming. No pain, no hunger—just oblivion.

Soon enough he would trade this oblivion for another—when the last of the magic ran out, when his whole being thinned and faded away. He had been in Dreaming longer than any of the others of the High Court; would he be the first to die? He hoped so, when he found the will to hope.

And what would it be like, this ending? A last fading into nothingness? He had only had enough will left to come here, to the place where Elfhame Sun-Descending had been born, and then he had lost himself in his Dreams. No time to wonder, no chance to fear. The humans claimed elvenkind had no souls—If that were so, then there would be no knowing that the end had come. It would simply come, and Terenil would be no more.

No more pain, no more sorrow.

And Perenor would have won at last.

Something in him stirred in rebellion at that thought. Stirred, and struggled to wake, struggled to prod him to action. Spurred him to *listen* when the first thin strand of melody sought him in the darkness.

He listened—and it found him, fastened on him; a melody deep with meaning and rich with magic. Bardic magic, he had never hoped to hear again

To turn, turn, will be our delight, till by turning, we come 'round right—

It turned about him, twined about him, fed and nurtured his heart in ways he had never known were possible.

'Tis a gift to be simple, 'tis a gift to be free, 'tis a gift to come 'round where we ought to be—

Without knowing how the magic had reached within him, he found himself recalling his first days in this brave new land, when Maddoc had led them all out to Gwynedd. How he had stood upon the shore of this western sea and breathed in the salt air, feeling that there was nothing he could not do in this new Elfhame.

The memory was vivid, more clear than it had been for years, decades, centuries.

And when we find ourselves in the place just right, 'twill be in the valley of love and delight—

This *had* been the valley of love and delight, rich with peace and promise. And he had been lord of it all—

And you can be again, the music whispered. *Turn, turn, turn again. Return to what you were—what goes around, comes around, good as well as evil.*

But I can't— he protested weakly.

But you can, it replied. *Turn, turn, return again—*

I'm dying. This is a death-dream. There was no magic left; Korendil's Bard had deserted them, and there was no hope. This was death's final illusion before dissolution—

—but it was a sweet illusion. *So be it. I die in dreams and Dreaming.*

He gave himself over to the music; stopped fighting it. And it turned him, turned him—

Returned him.

Till by turning, turning, we come 'round right.

There was no transition between Dreaming and waking. One moment he was lost in the Dream and the music, the next—

Terenil blinked in the harsh sunlight. He was standing,

tree-sheltered, in the shade of a gnarled old native oak on the edge of what had once been the nexus-grove.

I'm not dead. That was his first thought. His second— *I'm well. Whole. I have not felt like this in—*

—in far too many years.

Then he chanced to look down at himself. And stared.

My armor—

His gold and scarlet armor glistened as if new-burnished, new-made. *He* had not been able to conjure it so since the last time he had defeated Perenor. And since that humiliating episode in the alley, in the rain, it had been dull, stained—as if the stains upon his honor had translated themselves into his armoring.

But that was by no means all. For there was none of that *hunger* that had devoured him of late, that craving for the dark poison of the humans' creation. He felt young—strong—

Movement beyond the trees and the glint of sun on burnished gold and azure warned him to hide himself behind the tree-trunk. Shame kept him there, as he overheard young Korendil's converse with the Bard. Not once was there mention of him—

Because they have learned they cannot depend upon me. I failed them once—I, who should have led them. I lost myself in drugged Dreaming; failed their trust, and the vows I made to them.

Bright Danann, what have I made of myself?

Shame kept him trapped, huddled behind the tree-trunk, as the last of the High Court consulted with the humans and planned their next move. He waited, numb and paralyzed, as they separated into two parties—the humans and Korendil going for the girl's vehicle, the rest going to seek out any one of the Lesser Court of Faerie who might yet be awakened.

He watched as they vanished on their two missions.

And a slow tear etched its way down his cheek.

The distant thread of music tugged lightly at her thoughts, barely audible, but slowly gathering in strength and power—

Ria Llewellyn leafed through the thick report and idly jotted down several notes in the margins. She was seated at her desk, relaxed, a cup of fresh-ground coffee at her right hand next to the sheaf of papers. *Jonathan did a good job with this. He always does. If anybody could keep this company running other than myself, it would be him. But I think his estimate on the interest rates is a little too optimistic. He'd better check on that before we meet with the investors on Friday.*

Music, weaving a subtle pattern of words and melody, speaking deeply without disturbing the surface of her thoughts: "—*turning, turning, we come 'round right*—"

She quickly scrawled a reminder in her desktop calendar about the meeting with the stockholders next week.

I'd better make sure Linette has arranged something with the caterers for this. Lox and bagels, maybe?

Suddenly, Ria was *aware* of the faint melody, building into a profound harmony, drawing inexorably towards some unknown conclusion—

She stopped writing abruptly, listening intently to the distant music that only she could hear.

Flute, and a woman singing—

Realization hit her like a physical blow.

That's Eric! *What in the hell is he doing?*

Ria *reached* out, trying to touch something happening far away, a world away from the glass-windowed office building overlooking the city.

And drew back quickly, sensing more than just Eric and the human witch; the presences of other elves, slowly awakening from their Dreaming stupor.

No! It can't be!

But it was true.

He's doing it. He's awakening the High Court!

She remembered the look on his face as he had left her last night, vanishing from her house into the hills like a modern-day Thomas Rhymer. *After nearly killing me. I can't forget that, either. How he summoned that soul-devourer, unleashed it upon me*—

I've never been so frightened in all my life.

Ria shivered in spite of herself. *Father told me about those creatures, but I never thought I'd see one. I still can't believe that he was able to control it. I was certain that . . . thing was going to kill both of us.*

But he banished it, somehow. And then he left me.

Left me, and didn't come back.

She bit her lip, truly unhappy for the first time in years. Even worse, there was no remedy.

I should never have let him go. I could've stopped him, by force if need be. Letting him leave was a mistake. We could have worked it out—I know he was happy, living with me.

She twisted her pen in her hands, the cool, matte silver no comfort. *I haven't been able to stop thinking about him. From the moment I saw him, back in that sleazy bar, I knew he was meant to be with me. We were . . . so good together. It's my fault he ran away; I was so angry that I frightened him into summoning that creature.*

Now I don't think he'll ever come back to me; at least not of his own free will.

She closed her eyes in pain. And saw, in her mind's eye, the bulldozed valley, oak trees lying like felled warriors. And Eric, his brow furrowed in concentration, playing the silver flute.

Awakening the Faerie.

Why is he doing this? He must know that Father won't let him save the elves. He's signing his own death warrant, there in the ruined Grove.

Unbidden, another image rose in her mind: Eric, sprawled in an alley, blood staining his white shirt and jeans, his dark eyes empty and lifeless.

And Perenor, walking away and wiping the traces of blood from his blade, walking away without even a backward glance—

She choked. *No! No—I don't want that to happen. Even if he walked out on me, I don't want to see him dead.*

Oh, Eric, how can you be doing something this foolish? I know what you must be planning—once the Faerie are awakened from Dreaming, you'll try to reestablish a nexus.

But Father won't let you do that. If you were to succeed, we would lose control of the magic. Father has planned this for too many years, plotting to avenge himself upon the elves and win control of the magic of this area.

And—I can't let you do this either. Because if you succeed, I'll grow old, and die—

A secret thought whispered in the recesses of her mind: *That wouldn't be so terrible, if you have someone like Eric to grow old with, to share everything. Even dying. That's a very . . . human way to live.*

But I'm not human.

She clenched her fist, crumpling the papers under her hand.

I can't let him do this. I can't let him take control of the nexus.

But if we fight again, like we did last night, one of us is going to die . . .

The silent music continued to resonate within her mind, the power flowing into Eric, then out, answering his unspoken, unconscious will. And calling an answering echo from herself.

We are still touching, Power calling to Power, even though he walked out on me. I wonder if he realizes that? Like it or not, we are bound together by more than just emotions. Killing him would be like killing part of myself.

How could I live with myself, knowing that I've murdered the only man I may ever love?

What am I going to do?

The clock on her desk ticked away the seconds as Ria buried her face in her hands.

I don't want to kill him. There has to be an alternative.

Something occurred to her suddenly, a possible solution. *I can offer to send the elves across the veil, to the Faerie Lands. With the nexus at my disposal, I could do that easily. Then there would be no deaths, no need for Eric to attempt to create a new nexus, no reason why he couldn't stay with me, live with me forever—*

Another voice spoke silently into her thoughts, a voice she recognized instantly. :*Ria?*:

She could see him in her mind, an angel of shadow, infernally handsome and darkly angry. :*I know, Father. I can hear the Bard's magic. He's probably going to make an attempt on the nexus after he brings them out of Dreaming.*:

There was a brief pause before Perenor spoke, and his words were as cold as the darkness between the stars. :*You know what we have to do, Ria.*:

:*Yes. And I'll help you, but on one condition, Father.*: She took a deep breath. :*You'll let me try to deal with them in my way. Without any killing. I'll make sure that we keep control of the nexus. And—you won't harm the Bard. I want him back.*:

Ria felt her father hesitate, if only for a fraction of a second, before he answered. :*Agreed, daughter. The nexus is what's important; much more than anything else. I'll contact you again as soon as I know where they're going.*:

The light touch of his mind faded. Ria opened her eyes slowly, looking out the window at the hills.

Does he mean that? Or was he only saying that so I would help him?

It doesn't matter. We've been building to this for a long time, Father and I. A final, decisive confrontation. If he tries to harm Eric—

I'll kill him.

I love Eric. And I won't risk losing him again.

18

Come Now or Stay

Beth squeezed back against the apartment door and let the other two precede her. Eric first, battered, filthy, and mangled, with bruises darkening his throat—then Kory looking thoroughly exhausted.

Riding in the Jeep wasn't easy for him. Too much Cold Iron; guess I should have gotten one of those little plastic Korean cars. He was in pain most of the ride. He'd never have managed if he hadn't had his armor to insulate him.

And there's too damned much unfinished business in here.

She closed the door and leaned back against it. "Well?" she said. "Talk, you guys. The tension in here is sharp enough to shave with."

Eric eyed her doubtfully. "Talk?" he faltered. "What about?"

She threw the double lock on the door—the one only she had ever been able to juggle open successfully. "You're trapped, guys. No getting out." She leered. "You're in my power."

Eric sagged down on the couch. "Oh come on, Beth— get serious."

"I am." She flopped down in her favorite papasan chair. "We've got the misunderstanding translated. Now—let's get personal things straightened out among the three of us."

Kory started to sit in the recliner—and Beth had a sudden vision of what all that metal would do to the leather upholstery. "Kory!" she yelped, and he froze; halfway between sitting and standing.

"Without the hardware. Please."

He flushed, and looked pleadingly at Eric. "Bard?" he said hesitantly.

Eric's head snapped up, his eyes wide and startled.

"Please, Bard—I—" Kory's flush deepened. "I have no magic left."

Now it was Eric's turn to blush. "Shit, Kory, I'm sorry— I—oh hell—" He fumbled his flute out of the case, and ran through a quick rendition of "Banish Misfortune." Two verses and a chorus later, Korendil eased down into the recliner clad in nothing more harmful than silk.

High Court garb, Beth was certain of it. *One look at him, and half the producers in the Valley would be on their knees to him offering him contracts.* She grinned to herself. *And the other half of them would be offering him their—ahem. This is* not *the time. We've got a race of people to save, and if we can't get our act together we won't be able to.*

But oh—he looked *wonderful*. Flowing azure silk, velvet, and gold trim, and jewelry of gold and sapphires; his golden curls tumbling into those incredible green eyes . . . and that body under all the finery . . .

Dammit, Kentraine, get your mind on business!

"Guys—"

"Kory—" Eric said, at exactly the same moment. And blushed again.

She bit back a giggle. *Ye gods, he's got a low blush-factor.* He looked at her uncertainly.

"Go on, Eric," she urged.

He blushed even redder and hung his head, staring at his flute. She looked over at Kory out of the corner of her eye. He was collapsed bonelessly in the recliner, eyes half-closed.

"Kory?" Eric said, very softly. "Kory? Listen. Please don't call me 'Bard.' Please?"

"But it's what you are," Kory replied, without looking up at him.

"Yeah, I know that's what I am—I mean, now I do. For a while there, I didn't seem to know much of anything. But the way you're saying it, it's like we aren't friends anymore." The sadness in his voice penetrated Kory's weariness, and made him open his eyes wide.

Beth held her breath as the elf flowed up out of the recliner and slowly took a single step toward the musician.

"Are we friends, Eric?" Korendil asked. "Are you doing this now, finally helping us out of guilt or—"

"Kory," Eric said urgently, finally looking up and meeting the elf's eyes. "Kory, please. Yes, I know I've done some really stupid things, how the hell could I not feel guilty about that? I nearly killed you—"

Kory took another step toward him, and towered over Eric, his face gone utterly still.

Eric kept his eyes fixed on Kory's. "But it's not just that. I mean, that's not all. I . . . like you, Kory. I thought you liked me, before I messed things up. I want you to like me again. I never had any friends like you and—and Beth before. People who really give a damn about me. And if I screw this one up—" He clenched his jaw against *something*. Beth thought—*tears?*

"Kory, I'm scared. I don't know what I'm doing. I *know* what's going to happen when we try to fix the nexus. It's obvious they're going to try and stop us—and they aren't gonna do it halfway. Any of us could end up—I mean, I don't want to die—but it won't be so bad if—if—I know I've got friends again. If—if it isn't alone—"

Korendil reached down, took Eric's hands in his, and pulled him to his feet.

Oh gods, Kory, don't kiss him again. He doesn't know how to deal with that at all . . . hell, I barely know how to deal with that!

But the elf only put one hand on each of his shoulders, gazed into his eyes and said, huskily, "You have friends, Eric. Friends who will die beside you, if need be. Two, at least; Beth—and myself. Is that enough?"

And it was Eric who made a strange little sound in the back of his throat and threw his arms around the elf. Kory hugged him back—but carefully, breaking off the embrace when Eric pulled away.

But Eric didn't pull completely away, not like he'd done back at the Faire site. He kept his hands on Kory s shoulders, and his gaze locked with Kory's—and Beth began to feel as if they were reaching some kind of a deep, wordless understanding.

It was a little uncomfortable. *I feel like a Peeping Tom or something,* she thought; she rose to her feet, and began edging toward the kitchen. *Maybe if I go fix some herb tea or some—*

She stopped, because Kory's hand was on her elbow. He drew her towards the two of them.

Then Eric's arm was around her waist, and—she was part of a three-way embrace that was *so* warm and intimate that she had to close her eyes and hold her breath.

Oh gods, oh gods—don't ever let this stop—

"Beth," Eric said, slowly, as if he was thinking out every word. "I'm sorry. I screwed things up for you, too. Beth, I never meant to hurt you. I—I'm sorry. I guess I'm saying that a lot. I—I guess I've got a lot to be sorry for."

"I think," Kory replied softly, and very carefully, "that we should all agree to forgive each other and let the past bury itself. We, all three of us, delivered soul-wounds, whether we meant to or no. I am as guilty of that as you are, Eric. No matter that I did so out of ignorance—the hurt was there, I saw it, and I did not try to heal the hurt in time."

Beth *saw* the image in Kory's mind, the moment in the kitchen when Kory walked in and kissed her—saw through Kory's eyes the hurt, the betrayal in Eric's expression.

She blinked, and felt a stab of guilt at her own actions—that she had been so angry at Eric for vanishing at the demonstration that she had flaunted Kory in his face.

"Me too," she heard herself saying, her voice gone husky. "I didn't think you would care so much about Kory and me. And—I wanted to hurt you, Eric. It was stupid and childish, and I did it anyway."

"So—can we three find forgiveness in each other's hearts, do you think?" Kory finished.

She looked at Eric—

Eric was crying, and nodding. So was Kory.

So, she discovered. was she. She squeezed her eyes shut again, and hugged them as hard as she could. Within milliseconds, they had responded.

And . . . *something* stirred.

After years of raising the Cone of Power in Circle, Beth knew the sensation when Power began moving. And this was Power; a Power uniting the three of them, binding them, weaving them into a three-stranded braid of love and faith and strength that nothing would break short of death.

My gods. No. Yes. Jesus Frog on a pogo stick—

This isn't possible. It can't work.

Why not? she asked herself as the power continued to bind them into the whole. *A tripod is the most stable configuration there is. A three sided column bears more weight per inch of surface than a square one. An equilateral triangle is the prime geometric shape—*

It's crazy, that's why.

She wondered if Eric was hearing the power-flow as music. She cracked her eyes open a little, and saw his beatific expression and figured that he was. *What the hell. So it's crazy. I'm crazy.*

She immersed herself in the binding.

The power faded—as it was inevitable that it should do. Reality intruded itself, and with it, certain discomforts. *Like Kory's damned armor digging into my*— "hate to break this up," she said, a little hoarse from the emotional overload, "but you're leaving chain-mail imprints on my chest, elf."

Kory chuckled, and let her go. She opened her eyes—and gasped.

Jesus H. Frog—

Her jeans and T-shirt had somehow been transmuted; now she was wearing something like a fabulous cross between Faire garb and her stage gear. Flowing black silk shirt and breeches, tight black leather tunic and thigh-boots and gloves, all trimmed and studded in silver.

Kory, clad again in his armor, was splendid enough—but *Eric*—

He *had* been disheveled, filthy, his hair straggling into his eyes; bruised, and generally looking as though he'd been through the tumble cycle on a dryer. With rocks and mud and razor blades. The only thing about him that had looked worth saving had been a pair of burgundy-leather Faire boots—and *those* had needed cleaning badly.

That had been a few moments ago. But now—

Now he was clean, as immaculately groomed as Kory, and clad head-to-toe in an elven Court costume of silk, satin, and soft sueded leather, all in a rich wine color trimmed in silver.

But as Beth looked at him in wonder, she realized that there was something more changed than simply clothing—there was a look in his eyes. A stability. As if he'd finally found himself.

Like . . . he's finally grown up. He's what I never dared hope he'd be. That's why the power—the binding. There was pain there, and a self-knowledge that wasn't far from pain. Maturity and depth. And not even a hint of bitterness. He looked like a Bard, every inch of him.

Is this what Kory saw in him, all this time?

Kory had switched back out of his Court gear and into his armor, as Beth's chest could attest.

They looked incredible. Beth caught her breath at the realization of how much she loved both of them.

"Jesus," she said, half in awe, half in an attempt at flippancy. "I'm locked in my apartment with the two most gorgeous hunks in the Valley."

She expected some kind of response to that out of Kory—but it was *Eric* who went to one knee; then kissed her hand, and replied, looking to each of them with a grin, "Nay, lass, ye've got it backwards. I'm locked in your apartment with"—he dropped the accent—"with the two most wonderful people in the universe."

Kory reached down and brushed his cheek lightly with his fingertips, then held out the hand to help him to his feet again. Eric took it.

She saw that look creep into their eyes again, and realized that it would be all too easy for them to mesmerize each other for the rest of the morning.

"Okay, you sexy things, we'd better get our rears in gear," she said. "Eric, would it help if you had musical backup that's equally used to being *magical* backup?"

Eric stood by the apartment window, half-listening to Beth on the phone, half-embroiled in the endless questions that refused to leave him alone.

". . . yeah, Allie, I know, you're supposed to be at work at noon . . . I thought it was hopeless, too, but we've got a chance now. Eric came back last night."

In the street below, the rush-hour traffic was just starting. As Eric watched, an ivory limousine glided past, disappearing into the apartment complex's parking lot.

A white limo? Where have I seen one of those lately?

Those crazy guys from the Mad Hatter booth who showed up last weekend on Fairesite in a limo? No, theirs was a black stretch model, I remember that now.

Besides, that was months ago, remember?

He glanced back at Beth, now dialing another number. And Kory, soundly asleep in the recliner.

He looks so . . . peaceful, sleeping like that. Even with that one silly curl that keeps falling over his eyes, every time he shifts a little.

Eric resisted the impulse to walk over and brush that curl back into place. He glanced back at Beth, and saw her watching him with that familiar, speculative, thoughtful gaze.

Well, at least Kory's getting some rest. I wish I could fall asleep like that. I feel like I haven't slept in days. Which isn't too far off the truth, actually.

It looks like all of this is gonna work. The band and the elves are meeting us at the donut shop, then we'll head up to the hills. And me—I'll do whatever it is that I'm supposed to do.

God, I have never been so scared in all my life.

Beth hung up the phone, and walked back towards Eric and Kory. She bent over the sleeping elf, and kissed him tenderly. "Hey, handsome. Time to go."

Kory's eyes opened instantly, and he gazed up at Beth. She smiled, and lightly pushed that errant curl, the same one that Eric had wanted to fix, away from Kory's eyes. Then she walked over to the wall, where a guitar case was propped against a cabinet.

Beth picked up the guitar case and cradled it lovingly. "This," she said with the air of a mother showing off her firstborn child, "is my twelve-string acoustic guitar, hand-built by John Mello, a terrific guitar luthier up in Berkeley. It cost more than I'd care to mention—but I'd been earning good money for a while, and I figured it was well-spent on this baby." She patted the case with a fond, possessive smile. "*Now* I'm glad I got her. We're going to need every edge we can get. The others'll be bringing their best stuff as well. Believe me, Eric, you're going to have the finest backups you've ever imagined." She slung her purse over her shoulder and hefted the guitar case in her other hand. "Well, gentlemen, shall we?"

I'm starting to think this might really work. That maybe we can really make this happen—

"Let's hit the road," he said, turning away from the window.

A faint burst of melody flickered across Eric's thoughts, a brief flutter of distant, discordant music, almost too low to be heard, as he walked back to pick up his flute from the couch.

Then all he could hear was Beth's terrified scream as the living room suddenly exploded into roaring flames.

Jesus H.—

Eric stumbled backward against the wall, one hand flung over his eyes as the fire leaped up before him. Everything around him was burning, green light glowing in weird patterns.

The couch ignited before his eyes, instantly charring and crumbling into gray ash. Eric backed up along the wall, choking in the thickening smoke.

Can't—can't see the others—oh God—

His path to the door was already blocked by green flames, burning even brighter as they encircled him.

Green fire—it's Perenor! He's trying to kill us all!

Eric saw Beth trying to open the closed window through

the flames, the frame already buckling from the heat. Then she raised her guitar case and smashed the glass. The noise was barely audible over the sound of the crackling flames.

At least Beth can get out of here, escape before we all turn into kabobs. And maybe Kory—where in the hell is he? I can't see him through the smoke—I can't see him through the smoke—

His eyes watering too much for him to see anymore, Eric tried to feel his way along the way—and stopped, sensing the fire, only inches away from him in every direction.

And the malevolence directing the blaze, the intense hatred that fueled the flames.

The hatred, directed at Eric.

:And so it ends, Bard—:

Then someone crashed into Eric with a tackle worthy of a professional football player, slamming him to the floor. He felt himself being physically lifted and hurled through the air, to land in a smoldering heap next to the shattered window.

Kory shoved him through the rough glass, to where Beth was standing on the ledge outside. Beth and Kory both held on to Eric as he choked, trying to catch his breath, wiping the tears from his eyes with a sooty hand.

"I'm—I'm okay," he said at last. Without speaking, Kory and Beth helped him to the corner of the building, where they jumped down safely onto a parked pickup truck.

Eric glanced back at the upstairs apartment, as the windows burst from the heat, the green flames licking hungrily at the walls and roof.

This guy is definitely playing for keeps. That was too close.

He was suddenly aware of Beth's voice, next to his right ear.

". . . that sonuvabitch, that was my books, my records, my art, dammit, all of my costumes, my *Fender* guitar, that bastard just burned up everything I own! Christ; Eric, he did this to *both* of us! God, I am going to *kill* that fucker!" She raised the guitar case like a sword, ready to hack away at anything before her.

Eric glanced at Beth, ranting furiously, filthy with soot, her hair singed at the edges; and Kory, next to her, who for once genuinely looked like hell. *I can't do anything about all of that stuff upstairs, but—but this—just like what Kory did earlier, only more specific—*

He closed his eyes and concentrated on a thin thread of melody, "Oh, the Britches, They Have Stitches," and *imagined—*

All of us, looking just fine, damn Perenor's eyes.

This time, he could feel the music weaving around them, the Power taking shape beneath his hands. A moment later, he opened his eyes—

And looked across the parking lot to where a tall, silver-haired man was standing next to a white limo. Watching them.

Calmly, slowly, Perenor began to walk towards them.

Eric just grabbed both Kory and Beth by the hands and ran for Beth's Jeep parked twenty feet away. Beth vaulted into the driver's seat as Kory and Eric scrambled into the back, Beth shoving the key into the ignition and cranking the engine hard.

Perenor only continued walking towards them. Even from a distance, Eric could see the smile flickering across his lips.

Christ, he's playing with us, he knows he's going to get us, no matter if we try to run—

The Jeep's engine suddenly sputtered into life, and Beth snapped the emergency brake loose, hitting the gas hard. The vehicle virtually leaped forward, heading straight for the parking lot exit.

Maybe we can get out of here before he fries us all—

Then Eric noticed the dark fire burning in Beth's eyes. Uh-oh.

"No, dammit," Beth said from between clenched teeth. "I'm tired of running from this guy. I am tired of this guy, period".

"Beth—!" Eric yelped, but she yanked the wheel hard, simultaneously flooring the gas pedal. The Jeep's tires screamed as it accelerated.

Heading straight towards Perenor.

Eric saw Kory's wide-eyed expression of disbelief as the elf looked back at him in shock, then Perenor was directly ahead of them.

Oh God, she's going to hit him straight on—

Eric winced, expecting the impact at any second. *She's gonna—But this guy deserves it—what he did to Phil, and the others, he deserves to die like an animal, like roadkill—* He forced himself to look up, wanting to see the look on the elf-lord's face, to see him die. *To see how you'll react to being cut down, you bastard, just like all the people you've killed—*

And then he saw Perenor *smile*, as with a contemptuous flick of his wrist, he vanished. The Jeep careened directly over the spot where he had stood.

Beth barely slammed on the brakes in time to prevent crashing right into a parked van. The Jeep squealed to a stop, and the three of them just sat there for a moment, staring at each other.

"I knew it couldn't be that easy," Kory said at last. "We had best go to meet the others quickly. I am certain that will not be Perenor's last attempt to thwart us."

Yeah. He's got too much riding on this to let us win. Him and Ria both.

Ria—

What am I going to do, if she tries to kill me? What if I can't bring myself to fight her?

What if I can't handle the magic, if I can't create the new nexus?

Then Kory will die.

Oh God, please, no.

Yeah, I'm scared. If I blow this, there won't be a second chance.

And what if . . .

At this hour of morning, Whoopie Donuts was virtually deserted, except for the bored man in a dirty white smock wiping the counter with a rag. Eric walked in with Beth and Kory, glancing around to see if any of the others had arrived yet.

Just us so far.

This was a great place to meet. I wonder if sugar donuts can have a positive effect on Bardic magic? A cup of coffee will probably help, at any rate.

Eric reached out with his thoughts, touching the small bit of magic he had created while they were in the Jeep under Kory's direction. *A disguise spell. To make Kory look like a normal guy, sans armor and sword. Double-Oh-Seven, eat your heart out.*

They walked up to the counter, where the proprietor barely gave them a cursory look before jotting down their order.

When the man pushed two cups of coffee and an orange juice across the counter to them, Eric picked up the Styrofoam cup and sipped gratefully, feeling the strong drink heating him all the way down.

Down to that cold lump in my stomach, right next to the butterflies.

Stay cool, Eric. It's okay to be nervous. After all, I've never saved the elven race before. This is a first.

The only other patrons were two women, seated at one of the plastic tables across the room. Eric glanced idly at them, then realized they were staring at Kory.

As if they could see him as what he was, not a myopic teenager in a blue T-shirt and jeans.

Oh well. So much for the disguises. Great idea, Kory.

One of the two looked as if she was going to stand up. Then (amid the squealing of tires that sounded, to Eric's tired ears, vaguely like horses) the rest of the elves arrived.

Eric peered through the glass door and saw Val: a beautiful, silver-haired woman wearing a stylish blue linen dress, stepping out of a white Corvette—

No, an elf-woman, regal with years beyond counting, garbed in blue silk, standing beside a white stallion that butted playfully at her hand as she moved away from it, striding toward the glass door of the donut shop—

This is definitely too weird for words.

The man at the counter glanced up as Val and Eldenor walked into the shop, then went back to polishing the

Formica. But if anything, the two women's eyes were even wider.

And Eric caught a flicker of light about them. Not silver, like Phil's had been, but a sweet hint of green. Not the green of decay, like Perenor's, but playful green, like sunlight shining through the ocean waves.

With unseen depths, living power welling up from below.

Sonuva—Hey, maybe it's not the disguises that are the problem here—

Eric took a good look at the two, trying to figure out who—or what—they were.

And why they're in here right now, with us—

The fiftyish, coffee-skinned woman, her silver hair coiled in an elegant braid, was watching them with a faint, knowing smile. Next to her was a young girl, maybe fifteen, with short brown hair and a skin-tight black leather jacket that would make any biker turn green with envy. Eric winced, seeing the safety pins visible in her ears as the kid turned her head, eyeing all of them suspiciously. Especially Eric.

That older lady—I feel almost as if I've met her before. That calm, quiet way of looking at the world, like she understands people, and knows she can handle anything.

But that kid—if I saw her on the street, I think I'd run; just so she wouldn't have enough time to stick a knife in me. What are those two doing together? They're the unlikeliest pair I've seen in a long time.

The kid leaned over and whispered something to the woman, who nodded.

"Hey, who are you guys?" the girl called from across the room.

Eric, Beth, and Kory exchanged glances, then Beth smiled.

"We're in a play," Beth said, absolutely straight-faced. "It's a remake of *West Side Story.* Set in Tolkien's Middle Earth."

"Oh, come on, don't give me that shit," the girl said, with narrowed eyes.

"Kayla," the older woman said reprovingly.

The girl shrugged. "Hey, it's the truth. She's bullshitting

us." The kid looked up at Beth with a wicked grin. "Don't get me wrong, I sure wouldn't expect you to tell the truth— like why you're wandering around Los Angeles with a group of elves. Is Sauron in town or something?"

"Much worse," Beth said, very quietly. She glanced at Eric. "Banyon, why don't you go get us some more donuts or something, while I talk to these ladies?"

"Sure," Eric said. He waited at the counter behind two of the other elves, each of whom produced a fifty-dollar bill to pay for their breakfast.

There sure are lots of those fifties floating around in this elven community. I just hope this guy doesn't look at the serial numbers—

"What's a bearclaw?" Eldenor asked another elf behind him, in a low voice.

The second shrugged. "I don't know. Does sound familiar though, doesn't it?"

Donuts in hand, Eric sat at the edge of the one of tables, where two of the High Court, as brightly colored as tropical fish, were catching up on gossip for the last ten years. They smiled at Eric as he sat down with them, but continued with their conversation.

Eric glanced down at his donut, and wondered for the thousandth time what he was doing here.

It never changes. Even now, when I'm probably about to get myself toasted for these people, I'm not really a part of their group.

He bit into the donut, liberally dusting himself with powdered sugar. *It's just like Faire, all over again; I'm on the outside, looking in.*

Then Korendil sat down across from him, an eclair in his hand. "Bard—Eric, rather—have you tried one of these? The proprietor says they are quite fine, in truth—"

"No, thanks." *Chocolate eclairs really aren't my scene, I'm more into powdered sugar, really . . . Hey, wait a second—ohmigod—chocolate!*

Eric swatted the confection out of Kory's hand, just as he was about to bite into it. The eclair skidded across the floor, as Kory stared at him.

"That was a chocolate eclair," Eric explained quickly hoping that Kory would wait for the explanation before swatting him. "Chocolate has some caffeine in it. I don't know if it's enough to affect you or not but I didn't want to take the chance."

Kory just looked at him for a moment, then he reached across the table, squeezing Eric's sugar-dusted hand gently. "Again, you are guarding me from harm, Eric. I must learn more of the ways of this human world, or you will have to spend all of your time protecting this foolish, headstrong elf."

"That's okay," Eric said, past the lump in his throat. "You've saved my ass more than a few times, yourself. We'll just have to keep looking out for each other, that's all."

They both looked up as Beth, a Styrofoam cup of coffee in her hand, slid in next to them. Eric leaned past her to look at the empty table where the two women had been seated. "Is everything all right?" he asked.

Like, are those two going directly to the cops to tell them about the loons in the donut shop, or what?

"Everything's fine," Beth said, adding some extra sugar to her coffee. "Turns out those two are the same kind of people as you are, Eric. Well, sort of. They're Healers. I let them know that we're heading into some rough stuff, and Elizabet promised to keep her ears open in case we need her help. Which, with any luck, we won't."

"That little punkette was a Healer?" Eric tried to reconcile the two images in his mind, and came up with a complete blank.

"Kayla is Elizabet's apprentice, Beth said. "And pretty damn good at the trade, from the sound of it. She's a nice kid."

A nice kid? Are we talking about the same girl? The one with the pins in her ears?

Then again, Beth does tend toward the black studded leather herself—

What the hell. If things turn out bad, we'll need their help, in a big way.

But it is one hell of a coincidence that they just happened to be in here eating donuts this morning—

"Beth!"

The other three members of Spiral Dance entered the shop, starting towards them.

Eric felt a tight fist closing around his gut. *Everybody's here. This means we're going to head over to Griffith Park and actually do this thing.*

And Ria and Perenor may try to stop us. Or, if we're lucky, they won't.

Personally, I'm not betting on that kind of luck.

He glanced at Beth, talking animatedly with Allie and Jim, and at Kory, sitting so close beside her.

At this point, I don't really care if she dumps me for him. Not now. I just want all of us to live through this. That's all I care about right now.

I'll worry about the rest of that later.

Afterwards.

19

Twa Magicians

Eric tried to relax; tried to pretend that it was just another gig. After all, the setting wasn't that different from Fairesite—

Hell, I've even played a couple of weddings out here. Not with the Dance, though, with a pickup band—

Beth was tuning that exquisite twelve she was so proud of, fussing over it as if the least little discordance would throw everything out of whack.

And how do I know it wouldn't?

Allie had a little battery-powered Casio synth; state-of-the-art, and capable of producing anything but an omelet. She was giving Beth her pitches; she'd tuned Eric just a couple of minutes ago. The girl looked sleepy and uncertain.

Like maybe wondering about our sanity?

Like maybe I'm wondering about our sanity.

Dan had his bouzouki and was noodling bass runs; he was the only one of the Dance who didn't look nervous. But then again, Uncle Dan was probably stoned to the gills. Jim kept running his finger around the rim of his bodhran, trying *not* to stare at the elves.

Which was pretty hard even for Eric, who was kind of used to them by now.

The little valley-meadow they'd chosen for the new nexus-point cupped the sunlight and held it, and the bright colors of the elves' costumes and armor shone with ironic festiveness in the golden light. They'd made a circle around the band, Val casting it once, Beth once, and a third elf (in brilliant purple- and copper-trimmed robes) the third and final time.

Now the elf-mages had stationed themselves on the perimeter, facing outward; the elf-warriors just outside the perimeter, swords drawn and alert. Kory was right in front of them, his back to Eric, his blue and gold armor shining with a faint, gilding aura of light, a haze that made him look a little unreal, even to Eric, who had given him the magic that made him glow—

He looks like a special effect. Even with that bit of blond fur escaping from under the edge of his helm.

As if the thought had reached him, Kory turned and looked over his shoulder at Eric. And smiled.

That smile is enough to stop anybody's heart. Eric managed a faltering grin in return, and Kory turned back to his watch; scanning, Eric was somehow certain, with more senses than just five.

He realized that Beth had finally stopped tuning, and turned to her, his flute suddenly weighing in his hands like a pipe of lead. He swallowed. "Ready?" he asked.

She nodded, and the other three members of the band gathered around her. "How about you?"

He couldn't read her dark eyes this time. "About as ready as I'll ever be, I guess . . ."

He closed his eyes and brought the flute up to his lips. *Better start it fast, Banyon, before you lose whatever courage you've got left—*

"Banish Misfortune"—it was the first thing that came to his fingers. Just like diving into water, he slid into the starting descant, tossing in his usual trill on the B, landing solid on the E sharp. He tried to concentrate on the melody, on feeling the power, and on finding a way for it to come to him—

Nothing.

Oh, the magic was *there*, he could feel it, he could even pull it to him—but the source was still Ria's. He couldn't seem to make it come to him *here*.

Maybe a different tune.

He tried "Tamlin's Reel," "Smash the Windows," "Kid on the Mountain," "O'Carolan's Farewell," all with the same complete lack of success. The band followed him faithfully, taking the changes with him like they'd been playing together for decades, like they could read his mind. And the magic was *there*—

But just out of his reach.

"Sheebeg Sheemore," "Tom O'Bedlam," "Rocky Road to Dublin"—song after song, jigs, reels, everything.

Nothing.

Eric began to feel angry and frustrated, and his anger increased, until he could scarcely hear what he was playing, scarcely sense the magic through the red haze of emotion.

But a gentle touch on his arm startled him, cooled the rage, broke him out of the downward spiral of trial and failure. He jumped, and ended on a squeak, and the band faltered to a halt behind him.

"Eric?" Kory's green eyes graced him with concern. "Eric, you are not reaching the magic."

"I *know*," he muttered. "I'm trying, but—"

"You try with that which is already created, already old— but you are a Bard, Eric. Master of the creative magics. Try what you Called me with." As Eric tried to figure out what the elf was getting at, Kory smiled again. "In the Grove, Bard. What you used to reach me, and break the spells of Lock and Ward."

"You mean 'Sheebeg Sheemore'? Kory, I *tried* that already—"

"No." The elf shook his head, his eyes bright under the shadowing helm. "No, that was what you played that awakened me. Play what you Called me with, what you used to unravel the spellbindings."

"I—"

I sort of segued into something else, something original. God, I was more than half drunk—

More like three-quarters drunk, now that I think about it—
I remember it—I think. But what if I remember wrong?
I sort of segued into something else.

"Kory " he faltered, "I—"

The elf laid one armor-clad finger across his lips. "No, don't say it. You will succeed, Eric. I know this."

Korendil's eyes seemed to be seeing right into his mind, just as they had this afternoon. Gazing into his heart, so open, understanding him, trusting him in a way that no one ever had before.

:—*Eric, my friend*—:

Kory smiled, and took his hand away. Still smiling, he backed up, one slow, careful step at a time, never taking his eyes from Eric's. Eric raised the flute to his lips as Kory reached the perimeter of the circle—

—never taking his eyes from Kory's.

He was shaking so hard that his teeth rattled against the mouthpiece, and the first three notes he produced were so aimless that he barely held back a sob of profound despair.

He saw Kory's lips move, soundlessly.

:*You can, Eric. I know this, as I know you.*:

And Eric's fingers found the melody.

He closed his eyes then, overwhelmed, as it began to flow without any real thought or planning on his part. In moments he was lost to it, within it, more completely than he had ever been in his life.

He could see the spell he was weaving now, just as he had seen the one that brought Kory back from the brink of death, lost to Dreaming. Saw it begin to build a lattice-work of power, an anchoring-point for the new nexus, a framework to stabilize the rift in the curtain between the Worlds, a patterning that would hold it open forever.

When that framework was complete, his music would pierce that wall, and let the magic flow through. And he knew from the fragility of the net he wove that if his concentration wavered the slightest bit, it would all collapse—and there would be no second attempt. Eric knew he'd never manage to achieve this level of concentration, of power, ever again.

But already the magic he was calling from Ria's strong-hold was fading, weakening.

Terrific. I'm running out of juice.

Running out, like a stream trickling away to nothing, drying up.

He wavered—and the memory of Kory sprawled uncon-scious in the dust of the ruined Grove rose up in his mind. His throat closed, and he braced his shoulders, and poured forth a defiant, liquid run. *No! I won't let them—him—die!*

So he played with all his heart, forsook the fading stream of power, and spun the shining strands of his spell out of the fabric of his soul.

As the world faded from around him—except for the music, the spell, and his own fierce determination.

The Porsche accelerated past the open metal gate, past the park rangers standing beside their pickup truck, a pair of young men who eyed the crazy lady driver, her blond hair flying with the wind through the open window, with appreciative glances.

But Ria scarcely noticed. Her thoughts were far away with a particularly scruffy minstrel. Eric, who even now was standing in the knee-high grass, intent upon his music, as the first stirrings of Power swirled around him in scintil-lating light.

Even without trying, I can see him, touch him, feel his thoughts. Feel the bond between us, living Power calling to Power. How could Eric ever have left me, knowing that there is this between us?

A silent voice interrupted her thoughts. *:Ria?:*

Concentrating on the twisting road, and on the presence of the Bard, in the hills far above her, Ria bespoke a wordless reply. *:I'm tracking them, Father. They're in the park, away from the main road.:* She spun an image of the valley, the gathered elves surrounding the Bard, and sent it swiftly to Perenor. *:If we park on the other side, their steeds will not detect our approach.:*

:Good.: Perenor's mental voice was tinged with satisfac-tion. *:I will meet you there.:*

Her lips tightened as his voice faded. *I still don't trust him, even if he promised not to hurt Eric. I know how much his promises are worth.*

If I can just have enough time to speak, before the elves try anything stupid—

Eric will listen to me. And he'll understand. It'll be easier this way; I'll just send the Old Blood back under the hill, to the Faerie Lands. If they weren't such fools, they'd have fled as soon as they realized they'd lost, instead of lingering here to die.

Her hands were clenched tight on the steering wheel. *Before now I didn't care whether they lived or died. I wouldn't have deliberately tried to harm them, even though the temptation is definitely there, especially after so many years of living with their contempt for me, the half-breed. But now it's not worth it. I'll help them, even Korendil, if only so that I'll never have to deal with them again.*

So they'll never interfere in Eric's and my lives, ever again.

Ria carefully eased the Porsche off the winding road and parked on a barren, flat strip overlooking a small valley. She stood on the rough gravel gazing down at the grassy vale, as a white limo stopped beside her.

Perenor stepped from the car and leaned back through the open passenger door to say something to his driver. He closed the door, and the limo pulled away, heading hack in the direction of the city.

Ria's father was dressed in a business suit, immaculately tailored as always. As she watched his outline shimmered briefly. A moment later, he stood in full armor; armor that shone dully, like blue glass or blued steel. He had his sword sheathed at his side.

"You won't need that, Father," Ria said slowly. "Remember your promise to me? You agreed not to harm any of them, not unless my plan doesn't work."

Perenor chuckled dryly. "You forget, my dear, how thick-headed your full-blooded cousins are. If nothing else, this may impress them a little. I expect they look rather shabby—it has been several lean months for them since the nexus was destroyed. If they see how much Power I can command at this moment, they may listen to reason. I can sense all of them including your Bard, down there."

He gestured at the valley below them. "Shall we join them?"

Ria nodded, following her father down the grassy hillside.

I don't think I can trust him. I think he's going to try something, as soon as we're close to the elves.

And he's going to expect me to help him. Because the elves will attack me, as well as him, and he probably thinks that I'll have to fight, if only to keep myself alive.

Except—I won't.

She stumbled a little and cursed her high-heeled pumps—then, recklessly, changed them to flat, glove-leather boots.

It'll be a risk, because the elves won't know that I don't intend to fight them. And I might get hurt. Or killed. But if I raise Power against them, I've lost. Because Eric will never trust me again.

Yes, it's dangerous. But I can't risk losing Eric, not after everything that's happened between us, not the way I feel about him.

Her father strode along ahead of her, the heavy armor encumbering him not at all. She picked her way through the weeds carefully, and noticed how he looked neither to the right nor the left; simply trod over everything in his path.

And after I've sent the elves across the veil, back to the Faerie Lands, when there's nothing more that can stand between us, Eric will make a choice. And if he wants to walk away from me again, I won't stop him. Or coerce him. I want him to choose to stay with me of his own free will.

And he will *choose me. He has to. How can he deny what is between us, the way his Power is reaching out to mine, even now?*

Through the sparse trees she saw the circle of elves, the human musicians, and the young man with the flute. Even at this distance she could feel the power of his music; a melody that resonated through her, a power that made her hands tingle and her heart ache.

He's so beautiful, with the magic shining through him like a beacon. I'll never let him go again—

As Ria paused on the hillside, gazing at the Bard, Perenor strode forward impatiently. She caught up with him at the edge of the trees. The elves saw them, and moved closer together, forming a living barrier between them and the musicians.

"Eric!" Ria called, but the Bard did not move or even look at her. He seemed entranced, lost in his music, oblivious to everything around him.

One of the elves drew her sword in a swift, fluid movement. Ria set her hand over her father's sword arm as his hand reached for the sheathed blade.

:No. You promised me, Father.:

Perenor gave her an askance look. *:Of course, daughter. But I doubt you'll be able to convince these fools of anything.:*

:But let me try, at least.:

He nodded cursorily, and stepped back a pace. Ria took a deep breath, the narrowed eyes of the elves intent upon her.

"We don't have to fight," she said, pitching her voice loud to be heard over the music of the band. "There's no need for bloodshed. I'll help you, transport all of you back to the Faerie Lands. It won't matter anymore that we control the nexus, you'll be safe. All I want is Eric."

An elf in blue and gold armor stepped between her and the young Bard.

"Touch him, sorceress, and I'll kill you," Korendil said quietly.

Ria restrained the impulse to summon the lightnings and burn that insolent look from the elf's face. "There's no need for that. I won't hurt him. He'll be happy with me, I can assure you. And all of you will be safe, far from this place."

Another, in green and silver, raised his visor and looked at her with an expression full of irony. "What makes you believe that is what we want?" Eldenor asked calmly. "Why should we flee this land that has been our home for so many years? What right do you have to demand this of us?"

Perenor spoke, very softly, before Ria could answer. "The right of the strong over the weak, Eldenor. Of the master over the slave." His voice grew in strength, filled with hatred and madness. "The right of the one who was unjustly banished, cast from his place among you, and has dreamed of the moment when all of you shall lie lifeless in pools of your blood—"

An invisible fist reached out and gripped Ria, ripping through all of her carefully-constructed defenses, through the layers of *self*, to the wellspring of her powers, her innermost being. She screamed, caught helplessly in the whirlwind, as her life and magic drained away.

She fell to her knees, controlled by forces beyond her imagination. A last thread of coherent thought battled through the waves of pain, the maelstrom of power surrounding her.

He—he planned this for years. When I was a child, too young to stop him, he set this up. Knowing that he could do this to me at any moment he chose—

And he's mad. Completely insane.

He's going to use everything against them, and kill me, to destroy the elves.

And then he'll murder Eric—

NO!

Beth focused on her fingerings like a mantra; kept her eyes squeezed shut to keep her attention on one thing.

The music.

Caught up in the melody, Beth could feel the currents of power dancing around her, tendrils of magic like a living creature, weaving and darting in strange patterns.

This—this is almost better than sex. Witchcraft never felt anything *like this.*

She smiled. Her eyes were still closed, and she concentrated on the music. Her hand moved lightly upon the guitar, fingerpicking a quick-running counterpoint to complement Eric's melodic line.

Lovely work, Banyon. For a while, I wasn't certain if this was going to play, but this sounds—feels just right. Like everything is coming together, fusing, creating something new and wonderful—something truly enchanted.

Then she heard something else, a distant noise like pieces of metal clanging together. Beth opened her eyes, looking past Allie and Jim, towards the edge of the circle.

And her heart stopped beating.

The sunlit meadow had been transformed into something from one of her nightmares: a shadowy glen surrounded by billowing black fog, from which half-glimpsed creatures appeared, attacking the elven warriors, then fading away.

Beyond the elves she could see another figure in bluish-silver armor, battling sword against sword with Eldenor; and a blonde woman, kneeling motionless on the ground.

Somehow, in a way she didn't quite understand, Beth could sense the flow of power between Perenor and Ria, as the elf-lord drew strength and will from the sorceress.

Perenor. And his bitch daughter. They've found us—

And the bodies, littering the ground: Val, the lovely silver-haired elven woman, with claw marks across her face and throat, an armored swordsman, his turquoise breastplate nearly buckled in two, as if some immense force had crushed him like an insect in its grip.

They're working their way past the defenders, trying to get at us—at Eric—

She realized that she had stopped playing, and forced her fingers to continue, even as Perenor's sword bit deeply into Eldenor's side. The purple-mohawked warrior staggered back, into the murky depths of the unnatural fog.

Something, a creature that Beth's mind refused to admit could exist, reached out and dragged Eldenor back into the darkness.

Not even the music could mask his screaming.

Oh God—please, no—this can't be happening—

Her hands were shaking so much she could barely hold on to the guitar, much less play the chords. As Eldenor's screams faded, Perenor looked across the meadow at the band.

His jade-green eyes met Beth's through the slits of his helm. He moved toward her.

Then Korendil was between them, sword raised, forcing Perenor back with a wild flurry of blows.

For a moment Beth thought that Kory had a chance, that he could defeat the elf-lord. Then Perenor recovered his balance and counterattacked.

She could barely hear the music over the clashing of blades, the combatants' harsh breathing, the distant howling of the mist-creatures and the war cries of the elves; as Perenor forced Kory back a step, then another, and another, all the time moving closer to the band.

Edged steel clattered in strike after strike as Korendil fought grimly. From his stance, and his desperation—and from the strange magic that seemed to bind her, the elf, and Eric together—Beth knew that he *knew* he had no chance, but he refused to give up or falter—

Perenor feinted high, then came in at Kory's side.

Kory swung low, trying to shove Perenor's blade to the side, but not fast enough, recovering a split second too slowly.

Beth saw the opening, even before Perenor pivoted and brought his sword around in a fierce, whirling arc—

Oh God—he's going to kill him!

—and the blade sliced through Kory's armor.

Kory made a strange sound, a choked gasp, as the sword cut halfway across his torso. Beth saw him slip to one knee, then fall silently to the damp grass.

No—please, God, no—

The sounds of the battle, the horrific snarling of the monsters, all were nothing compared to the noiseless screaming in Beth's mind, the convulsive pain that gripped her heart.

Oh Goddess, no—Kory—he can't be dead—he can't be.

Perenor braced his foot against Kory's chest and yanked his weapon free.

Sobs tore her chest; her throat ached from holding back a scream. *No—please, no, anything but this—*

Perenor looked up; looked straight *at* her—

And smiled, a smile that froze the scream in her throat turned the tears on her face to ice.

He took one slow, deliberate step toward her, smile widening as she backed up a pace.

You sadistic bastard—you won't take me without a fight!

She stopped playing; reversed the guitar and took its neck in both hands, her tears now as much of anger as sorrow.

You got Kory—but you'll have to go through me to get Eric!

He licked his lips slowly, sensuously. And with a start, she heard a low, ironic voice in the back of her mind.

:That can easily be arranged, mortal child. Especially if you propose to fight me with nothing but that foolish piece of wood—:

"Indeed?"

The new voice rang out over the sound of the fighting like a trumpet-call, startling Beth so much she nearly dropped the guitar.

The fog parted—and through the rift came another armored figure. Gold armor, with touches of brilliant scarlet, so brightly polished it hurt to look at it. The stranger raised his visor—

Beth gasped. *Terenil. But—*

"So, High Lord Perenor has taken to slaughtering children, has he?" Terenil said contemptuously. He glided confidently through the tangled knots of fighting, around the fallen bodies, with no sign of his *ever* having been the wreck Beth had seen after Eric vanished—

—except for the sad and haunted look in his eyes; the look of someone who has seen himself in the mirror and found only self-condemnation for what was there.

He stopped, just for a moment, beside Beth; caught up her hand and pressed it to his lips.

:Forgive me, child.:

Before she could react to that, he gave her an odd half-smile, turned on his heel and took Kory's place between Perenor and the band, pulling his visor down as he did so.

Suddenly a golden blaze of light flared up around him as he brought his sword up to guard position.

Perenor snapped his own visor down and his blade up—
and an answering glow of cold blue sprang up about him.

Beth couldn't tell which of them moved first; they
seemed to spring at each other simultaneously, blades and
magic clashing in an exchange of lightning-quick strokes.

Unlike Kory's fight, or Eldenor's, this one involved both
sword *and* Power. Which, since Ria was channeling magic
to her father, made it two against one.

*By the gods, if I can't do anything else, I'll see if I can't
fix those odds!*

There didn't seem to be anything but fallen bodies off
to her left. Beth edged slowly past the band, out of the
circle, never taking her eyes off the sorceress. All of *her*
attention seemed to be on her father.

*Funny, if I didn't know better, I'd swear she was fighting
against him. That strained expression on her face—*

Whatever she was doing, Ria was *not* watching the puny
mortal witch making her way toward her, guitar neck still
in both hands.

Just a few more steps—

The fighters were evenly matched, even Beth could tell
that. Neither one drove the other back for more than a step
or two, and always ground lost was regained in the next
exchange of blows. Terenil gave Perenor no openings at all;
Terenil could find none in Perenor's defenses—

*Which means if I deep-six that bastard's magic
source*—She was almost within reach. Then she *was*
within reach. The sorceress stared blankly ahead, apparently oblivious to Beth's presence, or anything else happening around her.

Oh my beautiful guitar—you're all I've got left—

Gods. She raised the instrument over her head. *This is
for Kory, you—*

Ria turned suddenly, and stared right at her.

Beth froze.

There was a flicker of something unreadable in the
blonde woman's eyes before she closed them.

:*Damn you, witch, DO IT!*:

Beth brought the guitar squarely down on Ria's head with

a splintering crash and a jangle of strings. The woman folded soundlessly.

Beth whirled, expecting that now, *now* she would see Terenil take the upper hand—

—only to watch in horror as Perenor snaked his blade around Terenil's guard, and ran him through.

Beth screamed.

Terenil went to one knee. Perenor's blade embedded in his chest—and looked up into his enemy's face. As Perenor stood, seemingly frozen, Terenil reached for Perenor's sword arm—

And pulled himself toward the dark elf, impaling himself still further on the blade lodged in his chest.

And while Beth watched, he grabbed Perenor's shoulder, hauled his enemy within reach of his own blade, and drove his sword into Perenor's side.

Terenil cried out something—a word Beth didn't recognize a war-cry, perhaps—and the last of his sorcerous power surged up his blade and into the body of his enemy.

At Beth's feet, Ria began to stir, rising to her feet—

Oh shit—

Perenor's body jerked, convulsing impossibly—and the energy lashed from him in a visible arc into the body of his daughter.

Ria shrieked, clutched her head with both hands, and fell.

Terenil folded around the blade lodged in his chest, the light fading from him, as Perenor toppled to the ground beside him.

Christ!

Beth shook off her shock; ran to Terenil's side and knelt there—but as she opened his visor, she could see that the Prince had gone far beyond anyone's reach.

But—but he's smiling.

He's smiling—as if he's having a peaceful dream. Oh gods, Terenil—

Terenil—what about Eric?

She lifted dazed eyes toward the band—but her eyes fell on Kory instead.

KORY!

Before she realized she had moved, Beth was on the blood-soaked ground beside him. His skin was as cold as the metal of his armor as she cradled his face in her hands, silently begging for him to live, but knowing, *knowing* . . .

She heard his voice through her tears, a last dying whisper in her mind.

:Beth—my love—:

Then silence, like the emptiness within her soul.

No—God, no—it can't end like this—please, I love him, I can't live without him—

20

Banish Misfortune

God. Eric felt like he was about to float away. There didn't seem to be much of him left—it was mostly part of the delicate weaving of the spell, threads of luminous gold, emerald-green, sapphire-blue. What there was of him had become a wispy and transparent ghost in the heart of the structure.

Hang in there, Banyon. You're almost through. You can't let them down now, not when you're so close—

Spiral Dance's music wove around and around the outside of the spell, making it stronger, turning the threads into cables with a greater tensile strength than braided steel—but their efforts weren't what created it in the first place. And their efforts wouldn't be what created the new nexus.

He was so tired—

Don't think about being tired. It's not that much more. Just reach out—touch the veil—and call the magic—

The melody had long since slowed; not a lament, not quite. This had too much hope and promise to be a lament. It was a longing though, a heart-song of yearning. And it lacked only a handful of notes to complete it.

Only Eric could play those notes, the key that would complete the spell and bring the magic.

I can't. There's . . . nothing left . . .

321

Oh God. I . . . have . . . to—

From somewhere he found a last little drop of strength, a last breath. And played.

At the first note, the veil thinned beneath him. At the second, the spell-structure suddenly *focused* on him, on the thinning spot he touched.

And at the third—

He hadn't been quite sure what to expect—a fountain, a river, a waterfall? It was like none of these things. Instead, it was like opening a window to the sun into a blacked-out room. For a moment all he could do was feel the warmth and life flooding back into him, replacing everything he'd spent in the spell. Like one sun-blinded, he stood in the pressureless flood of power and gasped, unable to sense *anything* beyond the light.

Then, as he felt more and more solid, he began to see things, somehow; or sense them in some other fashion. He could hear, all over the city, the minds of all the Lesser Court elves; he heard them waking out of Dreaming, heard them calling to one another in incredulous joy. Voice after voice in his mind, all joining with the song-spell he'd created, elaborating on it and making it stronger.

My God, he thought in wonder. *We did it—we really did it!*

Then he felt the pain. Not his—but around him. Close. Very close.

God! It doubled him up. *Death. There's somebody dead. Lots of somebodies. And lots of dying. I have to wake up out of here.*

Please—not Beth. Don't let it be Beth—

He began pulling his way up out of the spell; it was hard—and he was exhausted. Power was all around him, a glowing mist, and it would be so easy just to stay—

No!

He broke through, finally; felt the real world settle around him, forced his eyes to open.

And his heart just about stopped.

There was blood *everywhere.* Spattering the grass, sprayed across the clothes of the shocked musicians—

Oh shit—

Splattered on *him*.

And bodies. Graceful, attenuated elf bodies, sprawled around the perimeter of the circle, so much dark blood soaking their slashed and singed costumes and armor that they *couldn't* be alive.

There were a few of them moving; one or two still standing. None in blue-and-gold armor.

Oh shit. Kory!

The strangled sob told him where to look: just on the periphery of his vision, to his right. Beth, cradling a red-streaked blond head in her lap, crying like her heart was broken.

Oh God, Kory! No!

He took one step and—inadvertently reached out with the magic that still surrounded him, even as he stretched his hand out toward them. And as his sixth sense touched them, he knew that, appearances to the contrary, Kory was *still* alive.

But he wouldn't be for long. Not without a miracle.

Or magic—

And if I do nothing, he'll die. My rival. I don't have to do a damn thing.

And how could I ever compete with him?

He could *feel* Kory slipping away; *see* the elf losing his fragile hold on life.

No! Dammit, NO!

It was like grabbing the trailing hem of a garment that was sliding over a cliff-edge; he caught and held the tenuous essence that was "Kory," and hung on to it with his teeth gritting at the pain it caused him. Recklessly he gathered the magic around himself; recklessly he flung it at his . . . his friend. Without pausing to wonder how much this was going to cost him, Eric wrapped himself in the healing spell, with a touch of the "Simple Gifts" magic he'd worked to such good effect before. Hoping that some of this would spill over, touch and help the others—but focusing the power on Kory.

Live, you frizzy-haired sonuvabitch! Goddamn you anyway, live, you idiot elf!

He was jarred out of the spell when his knees gave, and he found himself panting on the blood-speckled grass, hands clutching his flute so hard they hurt. He looked up, quickly, his heart in his throat, afraid he would see failure.

And Kory, lifeless on the blood-stained grass—

Beth was still sobbing, her face buried in her hands, but Kory's chest was moving, slowly rising and falling.

The elf opened his eyes just as Beth seemed to notice his movement. Their eyes met. Kory's expression was one of confusion, Beth's of disbelief.

"Kory?" she whispered.

Then they were embracing, crying and laughing, kissing one another, and holding each other as if they'd never let go.

Eric felt like crying too, but for a far different reason.

Okay, Banyon, you knew this was going to happen. So, how much do you care for them, anyhow?

Enough to give them each other, to get out of their way and let them love each other in peace?

His hands shook; his throat knotted.

Yeah. Yeah, I guess I do. Shit, what could I give her? I haven't got anything but the clothes on my back and the flute. And Kory—maybe this'll pay him back for when I ran out on him before.

Hot tears splashed on his hands as he quickly took the flute apart and stowed it in its case. His stomach tightened as he lurched to his feet and shoved the case away in the gig bag still slung over his shoulder.

Okay. This is where the hero's best friend saddles up and rides off into the east—so the hero and his girl can ride off into the sunset.

But it hurts so much, dammit, it hurts—

No one seemed to notice as he walked to the edge of the clearing. Eric glanced back once over his shoulder, wanting a last glimpse of Beth.

They were still kissing, so lost in each other that if the big earthquake hit right then they probably wouldn't even notice.

'Bye, guys. Be good to each other, okay?

Someday, maybe, I'll . . . get in touch.

Maybe.

ᔟ   ᔟ   ᔟ

A delicate cough jarred Beth and Kory out of their clinch. She looked up, startled, to see two people standing over her—the Healer who had been at the donut shop—*Elizabet? Yeah—Jesus Cluny Frog, what is* she *doing here?*

—and her young protégé (looking *very* green and nowhere near 'as tough as her would-be image).

"Elizabet?" Beth faltered.

"You weren't exactly inconspicuous," the woman said serenely. "If my instincts are right, you have roughly twenty minutes before the reports of fireworks going off in this area bring in the police. I think you need a little help cleaning up—unless you don't mind doing your explaining from the inside of a jail cell. In which case, I hope you have a good lawyer. You'll need one."

"Oh Christ—" Beth got to her knees, and ran a blood-smeared hand through her hair. She looked around, bewildered.

The monsters were dissolving, exactly the same way Eric had described the "dragon" disintegrating: falling to bits, becoming heaps of dead leaves, old trash, and thin, noxious liquids. But the elves—

"Beth?"

"Yeah, Allie?" she replied, distractedly.

"Beth, I can't—I can't look at this anymore—"

"Lady, I'm blowin' this taco stand," Jim said abruptly from next to Allie. "Color me history."

Beth stared at her two band members, both of whom were wide-eyed with shellshock, and visibly shaking.

We all look like—like we've been through a war. Which, I guess, we have.

Allie moved towards Beth, as though she was going to hug her, then glanced down at her hands, wet with blood. She looked up and her eyes met Beth's, tremulous and afraid. "I've—I've got to get out of here, Beth."

Beth saw Dan across the glen, bouzouki in hand, already making tracks toward the park entrance without a single glance backward.

"Yeah, sure, you'd better get going—" Beth said slowly.

It occurred to Beth, as Allie and Jim hurried away, that the unity she'd always felt with the rest of Dance, even when they were all arguing over something, was completely gone. She felt nothing as they hurried away, not even a ghost of regret.

I think the band just died. Requiescat in pace.

Maybe they saw a little more magic than they were ready for. Talking about going out there and saving the world, no problem. But watching people die for it—

Big problem.

Not that I blame them. I don't know how I'm able to deal with this. This place looks like a slaughterhouse. At least . . . at least, it's over.

She looked around, quickly, searching for Kory, and saw him kneeling beside a body in golden armor—armor whose scarlet trimmings matched the scarlet blood smeared over it

Oh God—he doesn't know about Terenil—

She stumbled across the grass toward him, and went to her knees in the blood-sodden weeds. Kory looked up at her, his green eyes brighter for the tears in them.

"Beth?" he whispered. "Why—why is he smiling?"

She took Kory's hand in hers, and told him.

Korendil concentrated for a moment, and his armor blurred and softened—and in a moment more he was clad again and in the blue trews and shirt he had "borrowed" from Eric. After a moment's consideration, he sent his sword after the armor.

Surely there will be no more fighting now. And this is far less conspicuous.

He knelt next to Elizabet, watching as the woman rested her hands against Narya's shield-arm. He could sense the bones knitting together beneath Elizabet's gentle hands. Beside her, Kayla was tracing a fingertip down a razor-thin cut along the warrior's cheek, the wound visibly closing behind her touch.

These two are truly amazing, truly gifted. If they hadn't found their way to us, I think we would have lost even more people. As it was—

He swallowed, looking at the once-peaceful meadow. *As it was, too many of our people died. And I was almost among them.*

If it had not been for Eric—

He was all I dreamed he could be, and more. Even now I can feel the strength of his nexus; the limitless pool of magic welling up, like water from a mountain spring.

And he saved my life.

"I wish there was some way we could repay you," Kory said quietly, as the Healer helped Narya to her feet.

"We don't accept money," Elizabet said simply.

Kory looked up as someone rested a hand on his shoulder, and saw Beth gazing down at him. :*Beloved?*:

She answered aloud, her voice thin with weariness. "We'll need your help to . . . take care of the bodies, Kory."

He nodded, rising to his feet.

It was a simple spell, one that the youngest child-mage learned: to Call Fire. There were no words for this moment, as he, the surviving elves, and the three human women watched each lifeless elven body dissolve into smoke and ash.

At last he stood, gazing down at Perenor and Terenil, still locked together in death.

Perenor, I can consign to the flames, easily enough. But my Prince—

A low moan distracted him; he saw the Sorceress stirring weakly, trying to move. He began to reach for his sword with his magic, but the dusky Healer spoke first. "No. Let me see her."

It was long moments (Kory's fingers aching to clench onto the hilt of his blade, wanting to summon the weapon into existence and quickly finish off the evil creature) before the Healer spoke again. "She's no danger now. That backlash nearly killed her—as it is, her mind is like a child's." She looked up; ebon-dark eyes met his. "You want to repay me— then give me this woman's life. Kayla and I will take care of her, and I'll try to mend her shattered mind."

Kory hesitated, his hand still twitching restlessly. From behind him, he heard Beth's voice, silently pleading with him.

:There's been enough blood here for one day, Korendil. Let them take her.:

Grudgingly, he glanced down at the semi-conscious blonde woman, half-curled on the ground.

Indeed, Beth speaks truth. Perenor is dead, and the nexus is restored. There is no need for this woman's death, other than my desire for vengeance.

And that is not enough reason to kill her.

"Very well. Though Eric, who has lost more than any of us to this sorceress, may wish differently—"

Eric—

Kory suddenly realized that he had not seen Eric for the last hour.

Where is he? What has happened to the Bard?

He saw that Beth had had the same realization.

"Goddammit," she said, looking around frantically. "What could have happened to him? He was here, I know he was all right, Perenor didn't even touch him—"

"He Healed the blond hunkola here," Kayla said. "I could feel it; it was right when we were driving up the road."

"And now he's gone." Beth slammed her fist into her palm. "Dammit, Banyon never thinks before he does anything! Come on, we've got to find him!"

"And how do you know he wants to be found?"

Kory and Beth both looked at Elizabeth. "What?" Beth asked, obviously puzzled.

Elizabeth shrugged. "From what I saw in the donut shop this morning, I'd say the young man is in love with you, Beth. But you care for Korendil. That's obvious as well. Perhaps you should just let him leave, if this is what he wants."

"But I don't want him to go! I love him too, that stupid whistler! And he knows that!"

The Healer shook her head. "I think you have to make a choice, Beth."

Kory watched Beth waver; then her mouth tightened with resolve.

Is she choosing between us? Or, is it as the Bard assumed, and the decision is already made?

My heart is caught by this mortal woman, but how can she choose one of the Faerie over another of her own kind? And when the other is a Bard? There is no comparison between us: I, a lowly warrior with some paltry skill at magery, and Eric, a human Bard whose power shines through him like sunlight through the leaves!

She will choose to love him, of that I am certain. And I will be alone again.

But I love them both, my dark-eyed human witch, and the Bard who saved my people.

I love them.

But I have done enough harm to them, embroiling them in this war. If I leave now, perhaps they can return to what their lives were before. In time, I do not doubt they will forget me—

Kory's dark thoughts were interrupted by Beth grabbing his arm and dragging him to the parked jeep on the far side of the meadow.

He could not bring himself to break her agitated silence until they were both in the vehicle and he had shielded himself against the jeep's Cold Iron shell. "Beth?" he ventured from the passenger seat, as she started the engine. "Beth, perhaps I shouldn't go with you. I'm not certain that is wise. Perhaps you should talk with Eric alone—"

She didn't answer, just floored the accelerator. Kory sat in silence, wanting to ask her that final, unspoken question, but not daring to speak.

Not until he saw the bright metal gate of the park firmly locked against all traffic, and the peculiar black-and-white car parked beside it.

"Beth, stop!"

The brakes squealed noisily as the jeep screeched to a halt. A mortal garbed in dark blue, walked swiftly towards them. Kory recognized the pistol in the man's hand from the many television shows he had seen through the windows of the electronics store near the Elfhame Grove.

"You, in the jeep! Neither of you move an inch."

The man's voice seemed strained, as he circled to Beth's side of the jeep, holding the tiny weapon at ready.

We must look somewhat unusual, compared to this man's bland clothing. Beth is still dressed in High Court finery, and I in Eric's garb, and both of our persons are thoroughly stained with blood.

The sight of blood does seem to unnerve many of these humans.

"You're Bethany Kentraine?"

"Yes," Beth replied carefully. "But—"

"Miss, just step out of the car, slowly. We want to ask you some questions about the disappearance of Philip Osborn and an explosion this morning in Tarzana. You there, just stay where you are, no fast moves. Miss Kentraine, you have the right to remain si—"

Kory was uncertain what was happening; but the look on Beth's face, that he understood instantly.

She is very frightened. But she will not do anything against this man, for reasons that I cannot understand.

But the power of the new nexus is still flowing strongly through me—it is scarcely an effort to reach out lightly and—

The policeman froze, one arm still raised in midair.

Beth turned and stared at Kory.

Kory shrugged. "I think we can leave now," he said, breaking the awkward silence.

"I think you're right," Beth said at last. She got out of the jeep, walked around the frozen policeman, and opened the park gate.

She climbed back into the jeep and sat there for a moment. "I guess—I guess I can't go back now. You know, it's kinda funny—I just thought that we'd save your people, stop Perenor and Ria, and then—then I'd go back home to my apartment, and in another couple weeks the show would come off hiatus and I'd be back at work again—"

"I'm sorry," Kory said softly. "I never meant to ruin your life, Beth. I never even meant to change it."

Beth sighed. "No, it's okay. It's just . . . a shock, that's all." She turned the key in the ignition. "Doesn't matter. Besides, we have a Bard to find. God only knows what trouble he's in already—"

∾   ∾   ∾

A lock of hair flopped into Eric's eyes. When he pushed it out of the way, his fingers came away sticky and wet.

He stopped, halfway down the hillside, and stared at them.

Red. Blood. Christ, I'm covered with blood.

Nausea hit him, and he rubbed his hand frantically on the burgundy-red silk of his breeches.

Funny, I don't feel tired. Just sick.

He realized in another moment why—the invisible, but omnipresent flow of magic all around him, radiating out of the new nexus. It was restoring some of what he'd put into its creation, a little more with every moment that passed. And if he closed his eyes and listened with his "inner" ear, he could hear the elves, more and more of them Waking again . . .

Well, that's one good thing you've done with your life, Banyon. He sighed. *I sure's hell don't need the cops stopping me for looking like a Faire loonie who just slaughtered half his troupe.*

Okay, disguise time. Then I can stop at the restroom by the gate and get—he swallowed his nausea—*cleaned up.*

A moment of concentration, and he was, to all outward appearances, just another skinny guy in red T-shirt and jeans. He continued his scramble down the hillside, practically stumbling down onto the hiker's path that would take him to the entrance.

For such a bright, clear day the park seemed completely deserted. He didn't see anyone until he was nearly at the entrance—but when he got within shouting distance of the cement-block restroom building, he was suddenly very glad he'd done his little disguise trick. Because there were an awful lot of cops in the park, all of a sudden.

He concentrated very hard on being inconspicuous. It must have worked, because although they were stopping anyone over the age of consent, and even a few kids, they didn't stop him.

Once inside the restroom, suddenly the most important thing in the world was to get the blood off—

He threw up a couple of times too.

He was still needlessly, neurotically sloshing icy-cold water from the sink over his head and arms when Dan staggered in the door, bounced off a stall support, and came to rest clutching the sink next to him.

"Oh God," the musician moaned. "Bummer, bummer. Not again. Not ever again. Blood. All that blood. Oh God . . ."

"Dan?" Eric whispered.

The other began to babble.

Eventually Eric made out some of what had happened, and a partial roster of the dead. Val and Eldenor.

And Terenil; Eric recognized him from Dan's description—and Dan was coherent enough at that point that Eric got a fairly good idea of just how the Prince had met his end.

That was when *he* began to cry.

Dan didn't seem to notice.

"Just before then one of those things got past the guy in black—just about reached us. Got my coat." He turned enough so that Eric could see the rent torn in the sleeve of his jacket. "Allie broke her Casio over its head. Man, that was too close. No more."

He finally faced Eric, and the flautist could see that Dan's eyes were white-rimmed, his pupils dilated. Dan, unflappable Dan, was half-mad with fear.

Christ. If he goes out there like that, *the cops'll be on his ass and they'll throw him where the sun don't shine.*

Maybe I can do something about that.

Eric concentrated, calling out of memory the soft notes of "October Winds," an old Irish lullaby. And when he thought he was ready, he reached out with the soothing notes and wrapped Dan in them.

When he opened his eyes again, Dan was standing there with a silly little smile on his face, a glazed expression like he'd just done some of his own best weed. When Eric moved a little, he seemed to snap out of it, although his expression still seemed more than a bit glazed.

"Hey, Banyon, long time, no see—you gonna—oh, that's right."

"What's right, Dan?" Eric asked quietly.

"We broke the band up." Dan shook his shaggy head. "Allie's job. Beth's—not enough time, man. Not enough t' get us outa the Dive, anyway."

Eric shrugged, feeling his heart contract at the sound of Beth's name. "You know how it is."

"Yeah. Glad I ran into you, anyway. Well, later!" The bassist strolled out as if he hadn't a care in the world.

Yeah, Dan. Later. Couple years, maybe. Eric sighed, and slicked back his wet hair. *Now if I could just self-administer some of that oblivion I just gave you—*

He had just enough change in his pockets to get him to the Greyhound station on Riverside.

If I had a choice, where would I go? he asked himself, staring at the weekday crowd hustling past him in the bright sunlight. *San Fran, I guess. That's about fifty bucks. Plus some eating money, some clothes, a toothbrush. Make it an even hundred. And only one way I know of to get it—*

Hell, why not.

He opened his case at his feet, got himself positioned right there on the street corner so that the cops couldn't hassle him for blocking traffic, and fitted the pieces of his flute together.

Okay, world. Bard Eric needs a hundred bucks. Let's see if you'll oblige him.

The magic was still there, after all—still flowing freely around him. Potent magic—

But I won't play games with their minds. I'll just give them the most beautiful music they've ever heard.

Only . . . nothing Celtic.

So he closed his eyes and started in on an Andean tune, one Simon and Garfunkel had popularized: "El Condor Pasa." The minor air suited his unhappiness, his loneliness—

From there he went to classical; Tchaikovsky, Liadov, all the melancholy Russians. He could feel a crowd gathering; sensed their appreciation. After playing for about half an hour straight, he ended the session with the "Frog Galliard."

> *Now, oh now, I needs must part;*
> *Parting though I absent mourn,*
> *Absence can no joy impart;*
> *Love once fled can ne'er return.*

His eyes filled; he held the tears back with an effort.

> *And although your sight I leave,*
> *Sight wherein my joys do lie,*
> *If that death doth sense bereave,*
> *Never shall affection die.*

When he finished, and wiped his eyes, and looked down—there was fifty dollars in bills and assorted change in the flute case.

Okay. One more try.

Maybe—maybe just one Celtic tune—

He closed his eyes again, and began "O'Carolan's Farewell to Music."

The tune that old Turlough played for his patroness, Mrs. McDermott Roe, when he returned home to die.

When the last note had died away, he opened his eyes just in time to see a man in a dark business suit standing up after setting something in his case. The man's eyes were bright—and as he averted his face and hurried away, Eric saw tears escaping from them to trickle down his cheek.

And lying on top of the rest of the money was a fifty-dollar bill.

Eric stared at it, then stared after the man's retreating back. *I wonder if I should check the serial—*

No. Let it be. Thanks, friend; whoever, or whatever you are.

An hour later, and he was sitting on the bench of the station, a ticket in his pocket, backpack on his back. Now he was really dressed in khaki jeans and a clean T-shirt (thanks to the army surplus store); the fancy outfit was carefully folded away in the bottom of the pack with his change of underwear, towel and toothbrush. The only things he was still wearing were the boots. Somehow he couldn't bear to take them off.

Terenil—I'm sorry. I wish I hadn't thought so badly of you. You were a hell of a lot better man than I am.

Even if you weren't human.

The waiting room was more than half empty.

His life felt entirely empty.

So now what? he asked himself dully. *Go off to San Fran and busk, I guess. Work the run of Northern Faire. I could probably busk up there until it's time for Texas Faire. After all this time they'll probably have forgotten what an idiot I made of myself . . .*

He closed his eyes, shutting out the dreary, plastic waiting room, and hunched a little farther down on the bench.

Funny, the stories don't ever say what happened to the hero's best friend. The Prince and Princess were married and lived happily ever after—and Sir Joe went off to . . . open an inn or something?

His eyes burned.

Probably went off to die in a ditch someplace. Of a broken heart, no doubt.

So far he'd been doing okay on the strength of feeling self-sacrificing and kind of noble—but it was beginning to wear thin.

Oh God, I miss them. If this isn't a broken heart—

—if it isn't, it's a damned good imitation.

What in hell am I supposed to do with my life now?

Something warm and wet trickled out from under his left eyelid, and he wiped it away with the back of his hand before anyone could notice.

I can keep from messing their lives up, that's what I can do. I can get far enough away so that they won't be able to find me; so they can concentrate on each other.

His other eye leaked, and he sniffed; and covered both up by rubbing at eyes and nose as if he was having a hay-fever attack.

Dammit, Banyon, act like an adult for once.

Suddenly he felt weights settle on the bench on either side of him. Which was *usually* a prelude to a bus-station mugging.

He gave up feeling martyred in favor of survival, and cracked his eyes open surreptitiously so he could size up his presumptive attackers. *Oh shit, that's just what I—*

"Eric?" Kory said softly, his eyes mirroring care and concern.

Eric went numb. All that he could think was, *Shit, he's still wearing my clothes—*

"Hey, Clint," said a voice behind him; he turned to his left, quickly. Sure enough, it was Beth.

"You figuring on riding off into the sunset?" she asked quietly.

"Y-yeah," he said, after a long moment of silence. "I kind of figured that maybe it was better that way, you know?"

"I thought," Kory admonished, "that you were going to think about how your actions affected others before you did anything."

"Yeah, but—"

"Didn't you ever think about how we would feel when you vanished?"

"Well, I—"

"We felt," Kory told him, "abysmal. Bereft, in truth. Dreadfully, dreadfully lost and alone."

"Y-yeah," Eric stammered. "But—"

"We felt like hell, Banyon," Beth said. "We thought we'd finally gotten everything on the right track, and we looked around, and there was this Eric-shaped hole in the air. And no Eric."

"But—"

"Great conversationalist, isn't he?" she said in an aside to Kory.

"We haven't given him much chance to really say anything, beloved—"

Right, guy, leave me the odd man out, and make sure you remind me about it! Dammit, you frizzy-haired creep, why don't you rub it in a little more!

"*Damn,* you, why don't you just leave me *alone?*" he cried, as heads turned all over the bus station. "You've got what you wanted! The magic's back, the elves are safe—you've got everything I promised you! And you've . . . got . . . each—"

He couldn't bear it any more. Eric lurched up off the bench and stood with his back to them, his arms crossed tightly across his chest to hold the misery in, fighting to keep the tears from coming again. "You've got places here, things to do. Beth's got her career. Kory, you're a hero, you could probably take the Prince's place if you wanted it. You've both got everything you could ever want."

"But we don't, Eric," Kory replied from right behind him, as gentle hands rested on his shoulders. "Truly, we don't. Not without you. Eric—we love you."

For a moment, Eric couldn't speak, or think.

What? Does he mean that?

"Me?" he faltered. "W-we?"

A second set of hands joined the first, and turned him so that he had to look into their eyes. As always he was caught—and held—by Kory's emerald gaze. "Eric—"

:Eric, look into my heart. I love you no less than I do Beth. And she loves you no less than she loves me. No more, and no less.:

With a last, valiant effort, Eric tried to make his mind work again.

"What Kory's saying is that he thinks it could work with us; that we'd make a pretty tight little trio." Beth gave him half a grin. "I agree."

He clenched both his hands into fists, trying to resolve the conflict inside him into an answer. He looked from Beth, to Kory, and back again.

I love her.

And—God—I can finally admit it to myself. I love him, too. Like he said. No more, no less.

How in hell can I deal with that?

He opened his mouth to deny it all—but what came out was a hoarsely whispered question. "Can—can it really work?" he whispered.

Kory's eyes were very bright. "We'll never know if we do not try, will we?"

"We've all learned a few things lately," Beth added.

"Including one of the hardest—how to admit you're wrong and take your lumps." Her expression remained deadly serious for about three more seconds, then she grinned. "Except you aren't allowed another apology for at *least* a month, Banyon. So—what do you say?"

He opened his mouth; closed it. Opened it again. Looked for an answer.

And found it in their eyes.

"I—I love you," he whispered to *both* of them.

And was caught up again in one of those magical three-way embraces.

Tears came, and this time he didn't try to stop them. *You don't fight tears when you're happy. And God, if I'm dreaming—don't let me wake up.*

Beth giggled finally, breaking the mood.

"What's so funny?" he asked, sniffling a little.

"This is so much nicer without all the armor."

Kory chuckled, and finally Eric joined him, freeing an arm long enough to wipe away his tears of joy.

"So, Banyon, where are *we* going?" She loosened her arms enough so that they could look each other in the face without going cross-eyed.

"I was heading for San Fran," he said slowly. "But—I thought—I mean you've got a job and all—"

She shook her head. "Not no more, babe. We damn near got arrested in the park. I think they want me on suspicion of being a drug-producer, or something like that. And they think I did for Phil; there's an APB out on me."

"They *what?*" Eric felt stunned. "Aren't you—don't you want to tell them the—oh."

"Exactly." She shrugged. "So, methinks the life of a footloose street busker may not be so bad for a while. I don't think I could deal with jail, really. I have this . . . problem with confined spaces . . ." She went a little quiet for a moment, then turned a faint smile back toward Kory. "So, Korendil, know anybody in San Fran?"

"A distant cousin—"

"Is he an elf or a faer—"

Kory interrupted her with a grin of his own. "Finish that sentence, Beth Kentraine, and you will surely regret it."

She feigned shock. "Gods be praised, the pillar of sobriety has developed a sense of humor!" She raised an eyebrow at him. "I was only going to ask if he was involved with humankind. If he is, he could be useful. I've *heard* the busking was good up there, but there's busking and there's busking."

Eric tried the idea of the three of them living and busking together on for size, and found it felt wonderful.

Perfect, in fact.

He held the other two closer—and they responded instantly.

No, I don't ever want to wake up.

"San Fran, then," he said. "If it's all right with you. Only . . . Kory?"

"Hm?" the elf replied contentedly.

"Could you *please* give me my clothes back?"

Summoned to Journey

*Dedicated to the memory
of the victims of the Loma
Prieta earthquake, October 1989,
and other victims of natural
disasters around the world*

1

The Mountain Top

Leaves whispered in a breath of breeze, as the early morning sun crept across the hills of San Francisco. A starling perched on the eaves of a four-story townhouse chirped in blissful appreciation of the sun on his back, the gentle breeze, the perfect Northern California morning. This house on a hill had a wonderful view of the Bay and the famous Bridge which was not being sufficiently appreciated by the two-legged being below him. There was still fog on the Bay, though it had crept down the hill just before dawn; the towers of the Bridge rose above the downy sea of fog like the towers of lost Ys. Sun shone out of a near-cloudless sky, making the pearlescent fog glow faintly.

Clank.

"Sonuva*BITCH*."

The starling fluttered its wings in startlement and gazed warily down through the green leaves at the odd, blond-haired, pointy-eared creature that had made both noises. Korendil, Knight of Elfhame Sun-Descending, Magus Minor, Envoy to Elfhame Mist-Hold, and firstborn Child of Danaan beyond the Sundering Sea, let out another paint-blistering oath that frightened the starling above him into flight.

Korendil, Knight of Elfhame Sun-Descending, was not communicating well with the hot tub.

He considered kicking it, remembered that he was bare-footed, and thought better of the idea. He leveled an angry glance at the recalcitrant object instead.

"I primed your pump," he said to it, resentfully. "Thomas *swore* to me that your motor is repaired. I saw to it that the heater was working myself. *So why will you not perform?*"

It would all be so much easier if Beth and Eric would permit him to attend to these things by magic—there would be no need for pumps or heaters or other arcane mysteries of Cold Iron and electricity. The ancient (as these things were reckoned in California) cedar hot tub would be even now bubbling merrily away, heating for the house-warming/Faire Opening party tonight. But no, they had flatly forbidden any such thing, even so simple an act as kenning and reproducing a paltry few fifty-dollar bills to ease their way.

"We have to keep a low profile, Kory," Beth kept saying. "The Feds are looking for us. There are things we can do, and things we can't do—passing fifty-dollar bills with the same serial numbers and having appliances that work without being plugged in are a couple of things we can't do. It wouldn't surprise me to know that the Feds have caught on to the elven trick of money-kenning. If the Feds found L.A. bills up here, or heard about some strange people who don't seem to need electricity, they'll be on us like fleas on a hound."

"But I do not understand why these Feds should be looking for us—" he had said, puzzled. "There was nothing for them to find in Griffith Park."

"They don't have an explanation for what happened to—to Phil," Beth had replied, her voice breaking a little, as it always did when she spoke of the old animator who had been her friend. "They don't have one for what happened to my apartment, either—or to Eric's. They don't like things they can't explain. Eric and I are the common links to all three places, and right now they'd like nothing better than to trump up some kind of charge that all three of us were involved in a drug ring or something, just to get the mystery off the books."

"And you know they were looking for Beth when the fight at the park was over," Eric had put in, mildly. "I doubt they've given up on that. Especially if they have a warrant."

Kory had shaken his head, unable to understand such blind thinking—but he had been forced to agree to abide by his friends' rules. It had been hard, though, especially this past winter when it had become so hard to earn money, and Beth and Eric had gone about with long faces, sometimes quarreling out of worry. He had feared for all of them, then, and not from these "Feds." He had feared that love would turn bitter in their hearts, that they must regret ever seeing him. It had been hard to keep from working magic then, and he had only refrained because he had known they *must* feel it was necessary, since they had gone to such elaborate lengths to keep their names from appearing in any official records.

Take this house, for instance. Officially, it belonged to Greg Johnson, a friend of Eric's, and inherited from Greg's maiden aunt who had lived here most of her seventy-two years. But Greg was something Beth called a "computer wizard," although Kory had never once seen the glow of magic about him, and he was so wealthy by mortal standards that he already *had* a dwelling he much favored. This townhouse, although it had been lovely in its day, full of glowing woodwork, with a garden even an elven lady would have been charmed by, had become neglected over the years. Greg had kept it locked and boarded up—until a friend of a friend of a friend had directed Eric to him with their tale of woe, and their acute need for housing they need not furnish references for.

They lived here rent-free—the bargain they had struck being that they would restore the place to its former glory. And there were many, many things that Kory could do there that Beth and Eric had not frowned upon. Though why it should be a bad thing to reproduce a bill of paper money, and a good thing to reproduce a sheet of walnut paneling, he was not certain.

He had only to stroke a piece of the woodwork with his magic, whispering to it, instructing it to recall its beauty—

and gouges or insect-holes would vanish, carving reappear, forty years of paint peel away, and the wonderful carved moldings of seventy years ago would shine forth as if newly oiled and newly hewn.

Only. Hmm. Well, Eric understands that it is a strain for me, if Beth does not. Since he was not a major mage, the cost to him in terms of exhaustion, personal energy and stress was high, especially when working alone. But he was no longer working alone; Eric could use his Bardic magery to tap into deeper sources of energy, and feed them to Kory, and the toll was not as high as it would otherwise have been.

Beth didn't understand what he was doing; Eric, in whom the magics of Bards ran deeply and strongly, saw it, but could not yet replicate it. That would come, in time, Kory had assured him. Eric had laughed, and retorted that he was in no hurry—what he could do already scared him enough!

It was simple enough, really. Every made thing held within it the memory of what it had been like when it was first created. Learning that was part of kenning, the means by which the elves (or Great Bards) studied a thing to replicate it. Once Kory had kenned something, he could not only reproduce it, he could repair it, by building upon that memory. That was how he had restored Eric's boots after the Battle of Griffith Park—the boots that Prince Terenil had created for him—

Now it was Kory's turn to swallow grief; Terenil had been more than liege, he had been that rarest of things among elvenkind, who chose their bonds carefully, for they would bind for centuries. Terenil had been a friend.

Well, none of this was making the hot tub function.

He stared at the dark wooden tub with resentment. He had repaired the wood magically, after Beth had salvaged it from someone else's discard heap. Thomas Crawford, who repaired appliances when he was not busking at Faires, had fixed the motor in return for a pair of magically-made boots like Eric's. Kory had traded many pairs of boots and leather pants and bodices for other work done on the house—for Faire folk were an eclectic lot, and many of them, like

Thomas, worked at the kind of odd jobs that would have been the lot of a tinker in the old days. And *all* of them coveted Eric's boots and leather trousers. Kory himself had seen to the heater, since it was of ceramic and glass, copper and aluminum, and not made of deadly Cold Iron. So *why* would it not work?

He was more than half tempted to turn his magic loose on it anyway, and Beth's tender sensibilities be hanged. But he knew what she would say if she saw it. She'd already given him the lecture once.

"People are curious at housewarming parties. They prowl, they poke, they look into things and ooh and ahh. And if they see something that's working without being plugged in—they're going to talk. And when they talk, the Feds will hear about it."

Well, perhaps if he made it look as if it were operating in a normal fashion . . . leaving it plugged in and not functioning correctly was dangerous. But if he plugged it into a socket that wasn't working and *then* magicked everything, no one would know the difference. Not even Beth.

He found the end of the cord, and picked it up, intending to pull it loose and plug it into one of the outdoor sockets he and Thomas had determined was dead and not worth the reviving—

And it came up loose in his hand, the plug plainly lying in the middle of the path.

He flushed with embarrassment, glad beyond words that there was no one here to have witnessed his humiliation. The episode with the microwave popcorn had been bad enough; the encounter with the vacuum cleaner that he had mistaken for an Unseleighe monster was worse. He would never have been able to live *this* down.

Still blushing, he took the cord to a socket he knew very well was live, and plugged it in—and was rewarded immediately by the Feel of electric power flowing through the cord under his hand, and the hum of heater and pump beyond the screening evergreen bushes. When he returned to the tub, the eddies in the water told him that all was well, and the water would be ready for soaking when they returned from the Fairesite. He stood up, then, and basked in a little glow of self-congratulation. He was no Great Bard, but he had, by Danaa, done his share to make the house—and especially the gardens—into wonderful places. He had not restored the gardens to their former manicured state. He had, instead, created a miniature version of the kind of wilderness-garden often found Underhill; a place full of hidden bowers, little moss-lined nooks, home to flowers and birds in all seasons, and green in all seasons too. One could travel from the house to the hot tub without ever once coming under the neighbors' curious eyes—which, given that Beth had insisted that this be a "clothing optional" tub, was no small feat.

Kory himself was looking forward to his first soak in this marvelous piece of human ingenuity. Beth had introduced him to the wonders of hot tubs at an odd meditation-place just south of here, in the city called "Santa Cruz," and he had been an instant convert. Wonderful stuff, hot water . . . that marvelous invention, the shower, for instance—

A shriek from the windows above made him jump, as startled as the starling had been earlier. The shriek was feminine, and followed by a curse as paint-blistering as his own had been.

"Korendil!"

He looked up, guiltily; Beth leaned out of the bathroom window, head covered in soapsuds. "How many times do I have to tell you?" she not-quite-shouted, *"The hot water runs out!"*

He blushed as scarlet as he had earlier. Like Beth's other maxim, "It works better when you plug it in," he kept forgetting that. It was easy enough to forget, when he was always the first one awake because he needed so little sleep, and the hot water tank usually recharged long before either of the other two was awake enough to even think about showering. He shrugged and grimaced elaborately, then sent a tiny surge of power to the reservoir of cold water in the half-basement. Fortunately, the new hot-water tank (traded by a contractor for three pairs of boots) was not Cold Iron either.

A cloud of steam gushed from behind Beth, out through the open window, like a bit of fog that had escaped the rest down in the Bay. Beth's head disappeared with a muffled exclamation; Kory waited a few moments to allow her to complete her shower, warm her body, and cool her temper. Then he returned to the house, following the tunnel he had created by asking the evergreens to interlace their branches above the path that ended at the lower entrance.

The townhouse was four stories in height, which had made Beth a little nervous in light of the recent earthquake. Kory had done his best to make the place as flexible as he could, given that he was working with materials and a plan that had been built nearly a century ago. He and Eric had removed every vestige of load-bearing brick and plaster, and had replaced them with conjured wooden siding on the exterior, and conjured wooden paneling within. He had worked on the supporting joists until they were supple but incredibly tough, gradually transforming them into something very like ancient briar; the whole dwelling *should* flex in a quake, but should not tumble down.

He really did *not* want to test that, however. With luck, they never would have to.

The bottom story was little more than a workshop and laundry-room. The workshop was new; he and Eric had added it. Kory smiled, recalling all the hours he and Eric had spent here, readying the house. They had strengthened the bonds between them, working together silently, sometimes with magery, and sometimes only with their hands. *Nesting*, Kory thought fondly. Domesticity suited the formerly footloose Bard. Not that he'd ever admit it.

The second story was public rooms, entered from below by the interior stair, and from the main street by a staircase to the front door. First from the front of the house was a huge room that Beth referred to as "the living-room," which had been the single change they had made to the interior layout. They had knocked down walls between what had been a room Greg called "the parlor," used only to entertain guests, and a dining room, to make one huge room. It was a place Kory found very comfortable, full of light and air, and overstuffed futon-chairs and sofas. Behind that room was the kitchen, which Beth had pronounced "hopelessly outdated." It too had been remodeled. The only things he had not been able to ken and reproduce had been the appliances. Fortunately, after he had seen all the work they had done up until that point, Greg had willingly bought those. Opposite the living room, on the opposite side of the entrance-hall, was the "media room," with the overflow of Greg's electronic toys: two televisions, a stereo, three kinds of tape players and a VCR machine. In back of the "media room" was a storeroom, still packed with wood, aluminum nails and wooden pegs, and the rest of their building supplies.

The third story was all living quarters; four bedrooms, including one master bedroom; two bathrooms. The fourth story had been servants' quarters in the days when the house had been built; once again he and Eric had removed walls to make bigger rooms, four of them. One was a library, with floor-to-ceiling bookcases. One held their music and musical instruments. One was Eric's retreat from the world, and one was Beth's. When Kory felt the need for peace, he generally went out into the garden. Rain, fog, chill—these things meant very little to one of elven-blood. More important was being able to Feel the power-flows, to tap into the magic welling up from the nexus-points into Underhill.

Those here in the north had never been walled away, as they had in the south, in the place the mortals called Los Angeles. But they were not as strong, either. The elves who had settled Elfhame Mist-Hold were a different sort; less used to wielding powerful magic and much more used to blending in with the human world. Kory's cousin for instance—Arvindel—he who had been second-born to the elves who had settled here on this western coastline—*he* actually worked among the humans, and no one the wiser. He was a dancer in the Castro District, and many were the humans who yearned after him when seeing him dance.

And Arvindel—he of the varied and capricious appetites—often indulged those yearnings. And just as capriciously dropped his conquests, afterwards.

"Fickle," Kory had teased him.

"Overfond fool," Arvin had replied, and half serious, more so than Kory. There were no few of his own kind who looked askance at this close liaison with short-lived humans, may-flies, who would fade and die in the blink of an elven eye. . . .

Kory shuddered away from the thought. *This is no day to worry about trifles like the future,* he told himself. *Particularly when a year ago you thought you had no future, and a scant few months before that you were spell-locked and Dreaming.*

Time, which normally had no meaning for elvenkind, had set its seal on him, if he was thinking in terms of "months" and "the future." Well, a pox upon Arvin, and upon anyone else who thought ill of him because of it!

He ascended the staircase, to emerge in the kitchen just as Beth, head wrapped in towels and body enveloped in an enormous white terrycloth bathrobe, descended from the bathroom above. She shot him a look, he spread his hands in apology. "I crave your pardon, my lady," he said, bowing a little to her, as he would to a lady of his own kind, "I fear I am but an airhead."

Her mouth quirked in a smile, despite her attempts to keep that same smile from emerging. Finally, she laughed. "Elves," she said to the air above her head. "Can't live with 'em, and there's no resale value."

Seeing that he had been forgiven, he shamelessly collected a kiss; a long, slow, sensuously deep kiss. She pushed him off—regretfully—a moment later, however. "No, you don't," she half-scolded. "We'll never get to the Fairesite at this rate. Have you eaten?"

He nodded, then added, with a wistful expression, "But that was before dawn. I fear I may waste of famine e'er we reach the site—"

What he really *wanted* was to watch her work the microwave; an arcane creation that fascinated him endlessly—and which he had been forbidden to touch after popping all of their twenty-five packets of microwave popcorn in a single evening.

She raised an auburn eyebrow at him. "Where are you *putting* it all?" she asked, incredulously. "If I ate as much as you do, I'd look like the Goodyear blimp!"

Having no answer to that, he simply shrugged. She busied herself for a moment at the refrigerator, then put a plateful of frozen sausage-biscuits into the microwave. She set the machine, then stepped aside to towel her hair dry while they heated. Kory leaned back in his chair, admiring her. He liked her very much as a redhead; it was a good color for her. A pity that the change had been mandated by their attempts to fool those "Feds" that were haunting their footsteps. A pity too that she could no longer sport those "cutting-edge" hairstyles she had favored, as well. In an attempt to change her silhouette completely, Kory had told her hair to become auburn and curly, and had instructed it to grow—very fast. She now had a mass of red curls that reached to the middle of her back (which she complained about constantly), and she made him think of tales the older Sidhe told of Ireland and the fabled mortal beauties of old. He'd made a new Faire costume for her which included an embroidered leather bodice and boots to match, in black and silver, with a pure linen skirt and loose-woven silk blouse of lovely forest green. Since she had been well known in Faire circles for only making the briefest of concessions to the dress-code, this should throw off hunters as well.

He had made Eric's hair into a mane of raven black; for the rest, the changes the young Bard had wrought in himself were enough to confuse pursuers. He no longer indulged in drugs or overindulged in alcohol, and he had added muscle in rebuilding this house. The result was something quite unlike the vague-eyed, skinny, sickly-looking creature Kory had first encountered. And in *his* new Faire costume, which matched Beth's except that the colors were burgundy and silver, instead of black, he was quite an elegant sight. Kory's own garb was of a piece with theirs, in scarlet and gold. The embroidered patterns matched, as did the placement, making it very clear to anyone who saw them together that they were an ensemble. Since neither Beth nor Eric had ever worked in a formal group at the Faires, that, too, should help to confuse things.

When they went out street-busking—which was how they had been paying for items like food and other necessities—they all wore their Faire boots and shirts, with jeans. The effect was striking, and caught quite a bit of attention for them down on the Wharf. Kory was quite proud that he had contributed in a material way to their success as buskers.

Danaa knew that his playing certainly wasn't outstanding enough to do so. He was competent with drum and bones, but nothing more. And his singing voice, while pleasant, was not going to win any prizes either. Beth and Eric outshone him completely in both areas.

And when Eric exerted his full power as a Bard—coins and bills leapt into their hat.

Eric, however, was inclined not to use his power in that way unless it were direst emergency—as it had been during the first month of their escape from Los Angeles. He felt that it was a cheat, that people were not rewarding his skill as a musician, they were being hypnotized into giving him largesse. Kory silently applauded such a decision; it said a great deal for Eric's growing sense of ethics. Beth sometimes seemed exasperated when he said things like that, but she also seemed to be pleased, if in a grudging way. Kory wondered often about Beth—how she could be so honorable, and then turn to and display an equally high ethical callousness. Eric just said that it was her television background, as if that explained it all.

Beth shook back her wild mane of curls with a grimace. "I can't get used to this," she complained. "It's just so weird, having all this hair—" The microwave *beeped* then, and she pulled an oven mitt over her hand and took out the plate of biscuits.

Kory grinned. "'Tis that, my lady, or be recognized. Wigs, they might expect—and hair-dye and curls. But not such a length, and obviously yours. True?"

"True," she sighed, and put the plate down on the table, snatching a biscuit for herself and biting into it. "Very true. And I'm the one who keeps harping on the fact that we have to be underground. I just wish I knew another way of making a buck without coming out of hiding besides busking—everybody in L.A. *knows* I'm a musician, and somebody is bound to have let it leak."

"But they aren't lookin' for a trio," Eric yawned, shuffling sleepily through the door, and enveloped in a robe even larger than Beth's. "And they're a lot more likely to look for you with a rock-group than with a busker." With all his newly-acquired muscle hidden beneath the bulky cloth, he looked as frail as he used to actually be. He kissed Beth between yawns, and gingerly picked up one of the biscuits, juggling it from hand to hand until it cooled off.

"That's true," Beth acknowledged, hugging him, and then pushing him into a chair. Eric was not a morning person in any sense of the word, and had been known to wander into furniture until he actually woke up. He smiled sleepily at Kory, who mimed a punch at him.

"Are you going to be awake enough to ride?" the elf asked him as he ate half the biscuit.

Eric nodded, and reached for the cup of coffee Beth was handing him. "With enough of this in me, I will be," he said, after a swallow. Kory sniffed the tantalizing aroma wistfully; one mouthful would have put *him* in a stupor; one cupful might actually kill him—but it smelled so good.

Beth handed him a mug of cinnamon-hibiscus tea, which smelled nearly as good, and did not contain any of the caffeine that was so deadly to his kind. "He'll be fine, Kory," she said cheerfully. "He's ridden up behind me plenty of times, you know that. You'd be amazed at what a good grip he has when we're going sixty-five."

"I still wish those things had seatbelts," Eric muttered, but Kory suspected that Beth hadn't heard him. He took another biscuit. "Are we changing here, or at the site?" the Bard asked.

"The site," she replied, trying to get a comb through her hair. "I've got passes for us through the Celts as 'Banysh Mysfortune,' the name we auditioned under. So don't tell anyone your real names unless they're somebody I already cleared, okay? Even if you think it's one of your best friends and they think they recognize you."

Eric shook his head, and knuckled an eye. "I think you're being overly paranoid, Bethy, but if that's the way you want it . . ." He shrugged. "I don't have any best friends but you guys anyway—and if any of my old girlfriends showed up, I'd just as soon have an excuse not to recognize them. Are we doing the Celtic shows?"

Beth nodded; one of the first people she had contacted after their initial flight had been the head of the Celt Clan, a very resourceful gentleman, as Kory had seen when he'd met them at a Berkeley hamburger place. Evidently people in San Francisco—some of them, anyway—took the appearance of fugitives from the law on their doorstep in stride. He had been their chiefest help—had "networked," was the word Beth used—gotten them in touch with others, and within a few days they had been settled into this townhouse and began putting new lives together.

At first, transportation had not been a problem; the BART system ran everywhere they wanted to play, and Kory could ride in the metal trains and buses, even though it was sometimes less than comfortable. He had rather enjoyed walking home from the stores with his arms loaded down with bags. It had been an entirely new experience. And, at first, things had been too precarious for them even to think about doing Northern Faire—making the house livable was taking up all the time they had to spare from street-busking. But as Faire-season loomed nearer for the second year of their tenure here, and Beth had realized that they could make a substantial amount of money if only they could *get* there, she had become increasingly anxious to find some sort of transportation that could take them outside BART's magic circle.

Oddly enough, it was Kory who had provided that. He had reminded her that most autos were too painful for him to ride in. Then he had mentioned, wistfully, that it was too bad that horses were no longer common—he could have called up a pair of elvensteeds for them in a trice.

Beth had narrowed her eyes in sudden speculation, but it had been Eric who had said, as if a memory had suddenly surfaced, "Elvensteeds? But what about that white

Corvette I saw Val driving? The one that was a horse, except it wasn't a horse—"

"Elvensteeds can counterfeit anything," Kory had said without thinking. "They will not stand up to much of an examination, but they can counterfeit the appearance." Then he had hit himself on the side of the head, in a gesture unconsciously borrowed from Eric. "But of course! I can call us elvensteeds, and ask them to counterfeit us cars—"

Beth had shaken her head. "Too conspicuous—and there's always the chance that somebody would try to mess with them in the parking lot, and then what?" She'd bitten her knuckle in frustration. "No, what I wish is that we had some way to get a pair of bikes."

"Bikes?" Kory had said, as Eric blanched. "You mean, motorcycles? But the elvensteeds can counterfeit those, as well!"

"The parking lot—" Beth had protested.

"Well," Eric had put in reluctantly, "we could leave them and get off and walk and they could go hide themselves. People would think we'd gotten rides or hitched, and the ones who saw us ride in would just think we'd put the bikes inside one of the Admin buildings or something. Then when we needed them, Kory could call them in again. And it wouldn't be that conspicuous for us to have bikes around here, not like a car, anyway; I know lots of buskers that have bikes." He'd gulped. "There's just one thing; I can't ride."

Beth had shrugged. "So, ride behind me. Kory? You think you can pull this off?"

He had nodded. "I can copy enough of Thomas's Ninja to make ours pass, I think. I know a way to keep them from being meddled with in public places. And I can conjure us leathers, easily enough." Beth had rolled her eyes at that, but had agreed, taking safety as a prime consideration. Kory had taken advantage of the situation to conjure leathers in "their" colors: burgundy and silver for Eric, scarlet and gold for himself, and black and silver for Beth. She had made a face and muttered something about the leathers being anything but inconspicuous, but she wore them anyway.

So their problem had been solved; and if they always arrived dry even when it rained, that could be chalked up to the San Francisco weather patterns, that would have one side of the street drenched and the other bone-dry.

"Then let us wear leathers," Kory said with relish. He loved the outfits; loved the way they felt, as if he was donning armor for a joust, or hunting garb for a wild ride. Eric sighed, ate another biscuit, and headed back up the stairs to change.

Beth took the time for another large cup of coffee; Kory finished his tea, reached for a bit more Power, and clad himself in his leathers between one sip and the next, planting his helmet on the table next to him with a muffled *thud.*

Beth shook her head. "I can never get used to you doing that," she complained.

"Hazard of living with elves, lovely lady," he said, standing up, and tucking the helmet under his arm. "If you'll excuse me, I'll go fetch the steeds from the garage."

"Thanks, love," she said, blowing him a kiss as she turned to run up the stairs. "For that, I forgive you for running out the hot water."

He grinned, and trotted back down the kitchen stairs, taking another path than the one that led to the hot tub. This one wound around the edge of the privacy fence and ended at the tiny garage occupying an otherwise useless odd-shaped corner of the garden.

It wasn't much of a garage; it would have been barely big enough for a sub-compact car. It held the two elven-steeds quite comfortably, with plenty of room for them to transform into their normal forms if they chose. Kory's steed matched his colors of scarlet and gold; Beth's twinned her black and silver. Kory had based them loosely on the Ninja models of what Beth called "murder-cycles," but he had made up a style-name—"Merlin"—and a company—"Toshiro." That way, if people thought there was something wrong with the way the bikes "should" look, they could blame it on the fact that they'd never heard either of the company or the model. The names were private jokes; a merlin was both a small falcon, and the use-name of one of the greatest of Bardic Mages, although few humans these days seemed to realize that Bardic connection. And "Toshiro" was for the human who had created many great movies of Japanese culture, movies that Kory had often watched in the long hours of the night when Beth and Eric still slept.

He wheeled them out one at a time, setting them up in the street in front of the street-side door, and waited for Beth and Eric. They came out quicker than he'd had any right to expect; Beth on the run, stuffing her hair down into the back of her jacket, with the bags containing her costume, his, and their instruments slung over her shoulder. Eric followed more slowly, locking the door behind himself and, as always, settled himself behind Beth rather gingerly. Although Kory couldn't see his face, he had the feeling that Eric wore a look of grim and patient determination.

Poor Eric; he never felt safe on these pseudo-metal beasts. Kory wondered if he'd have felt any better if they had been in their proper horse-shape.

Probably not.

He looked over at Beth, her face hidden behind the dark windscreen of her helmet, and nodded. She handed him his bags; he stowed them safely in the saddlebags on the "flanks" of his steed. Although these elvensteeds needed no kick-starting at all, they always kept up the pretense that they were real bikes by going through the motions of starting them.

Of course, with an elvensteed, there was never any nonsense of struggling with a motor that wouldn't quite catch. . . . The bikes roared to life with twin bellows of power; Beth let out a whoop of exuberance, and shot off into the lead. Kory followed, grinning happily. Beth had needed this for some time; to get back into the Faire circuit, to see old friends without worrying if the mysterious "Feds" were going to catch them—and she especially needed the party tonight.

For that matter, so did he. He hadn't had a celebratory party in—

Danaa, is it that *long?*

High time then.

An odd humming reached his inner ears, a musical sound that accompanied a trace of magic energy; he leaned over the handlebars of his bike and smiled as he traced it forward. Eric was humming—

So was Beth.

He laughed aloud, and popped a wheelie.

It was going to be a most excellent day.

2

As I Walked Through the Fair

Eric Banyon kept his eyes shut tightly through most of the ride, his stomach lurching with every turn. He joked with Beth and Kory about his fear of riding; he never let them know how real that fear was. At one point in his life he had actually envied some motorcycle maniacs who had stunted their way past a bus he'd been riding; now that memory seemed to belong to another person entirely.

I was high, he told himself, *or drunk. Or both.* There were drawbacks to going clean and sober.

Or maybe it was so simple a thing as the fact that something that looked easy when you had no prospect of engaging in it—well, relatively; as opposed to, say, piloting a 747—became something else entirely when you *had* to do it.

And the simple truth was that Eric had been terribly sheltered in this one aspect of his life. He had never once owned a vehicle of any kind. As a child, he'd been driven from place to place by his parents; as an adult he'd cadged rides or used public transportation. He *did* have a driver's license, which he'd taken care to keep updated, but he'd obtained it by taking the test on a dare, when high on a combination of grass and mescaline. He had no memory of the test, or even whose car he had taken it in. Like many things that he'd done back then, it had seemed a good idea at the time.

Kory had a license—kenned from his, with Kory's picture substituted for his own. So long as no one ever asked him to produce his at the same time, there should be no trouble. Kory *could* drive; he could probably drive anything, Eric suspected. Or ride wild mustangs or pilot a 747. In all likelihood, no one would ever even think of stopping Kory, he was just that competent.

Or even if they did, he or Kory could probably play head-games with the officer to make him give them warnings and ignore the licenses. The "Obi-Wan-Kenobi Gambit," they called it. "These are not the elves you're looking for—"

Eric had never once driven anything that he remembered. He may have driven any number of times that he didn't remember; there was a great deal of his life that was lost in an alcoholic or drug-enhanced fog. But now that he was sober and staying that way, he had no intention of being at the helm of *any* vehicle when Beth and Kory were around to drive it. Hell, he wasn't even certain he knew how to start these things! Let them deal with the motorcycles— even if Beth did drive like a graduate of the Evel Knievel School of Combat Driving. He'd stay a passenger, unless, of course, it was a dire emergency and both of them were incapacitated.

Not bloody likely—I hope, he thought, and clung a little tighter to Beth's waist as she rounded a curve and the bike began to lean. The elvensteeds weren't metal; Beth had learned with great glee that they wouldn't reflect radar-guns. So she only gave speed-limit signs any weight when it was obvious that the limit was there for reasons of safety. At any other time—well, he'd learned his lesson on the first ride. Now he no longer watched anything, not even the passing landscape; he just closed his eyes and listened to the music in his head. There was always music in his head these days; he was only now starting to learn what it meant, instead of flying on instinct.

His stomach lurched. *Better not think about flying.*

The advantage to Bethy's driving, as he had learned when

they showed up for pre-Faire auditions and rehearsals, was that they got to the Fairesite in a reasonable length of time. Beth must have really been pouring on the gas this morning, though, because he felt her slowing down much sooner than he had expected to, and he cracked open one eye to see that she was about to turn down the gravel "back road" to the campgrounds. He relaxed, and flexed his fingers a little, one hand at a time, as she pulled onto the road, gravel crunching under the bike tires.

Kory pulled up beside them, and Eric felt the gentle touch of inquiry, mind-to-mind, the elf sent to him. *I'm okay,* he thought back. *Just a little stiff from the ride.* Now that they weren't racing along at ninety-per, he could enjoy what there was left of the drive, despite the jouncing. It was going to be a beautiful day, that much was certain. Not too surprising, really; some of Kory's kin were coming to the house-warming party, and Kory had hinted they might Do Something to ensure cooperative weather.

Convenient. Wonder if maybe I'll be able to do something like that someday. . . . With Southern California in the grip of a five-year drought with no end in sight, he'd be real tempted to tamper. . . .

But would that be right? If he mucked around with the Southern California weather, what would that do up here? Would it have consequences that would reach even farther than that? What if he inadvertently created another Dust Bowl?

He mentally shook his head. There had been a time when he wouldn't have thought about consequences, he'd have just done what he wanted to. Was this a result of being sober for more than a year, or was it something more than that?

Jesus, I'm getting responsible in my old age. Maybe it was watching Ria Llewellyn, seeing what she did to people and things by running over the top of them to get what she wanted. Strange. He loved Bethy—but there was something about Ria . . . the memories concerned with Ria, half-elven child of the renegade Perenor, were the sharpest of all of his recollections of the battle to save the elves of

Elfhame Sun-Descending. There was just something about her—

He shook the persistent memory of blue eyes away, with just a faint hint of regret. In the end, ironically enough, it had been Ria who had saved them all. She had fought her father, when it became obvious that Perenor was mad, stark, staring bonkers—and that had given Terenil and Kory their chances to strike. And it had bought Eric and Beth time to move the magic nexus of the Sun-Descending Grove from the old, destroyed Fairesite, to a new Grove in the heart of Griffith Park, a place central to every elven Grove and a place that would—at least in the foreseeable future—never fear the destructive hand of humans. *That* had freed, Awakened, and empowered the elves of the L.A. basin, who were slowly taking their lives out of holding patterns they'd been in for more than ten years.

Yeah, well, Ria's at the Happy Home at the moment, with pineapple yogurt instead of brains. That Healer-chick thinks some day she may be able to bring her out of it, but frankly, I doubt it. Not being a fan of necrophilia, I doubt there's much of Ria Llewellyn in my future.

Some of Beth's hair escaped from inside her jacket to tickle his nose, and he brushed it away with a grin. Now *that* was a distinctly odd circumstance: Beth with a full mop of dark red hair. The girl he'd broken up with just before his involvement with elves and magic started had red hair. Maureen—who, he'd heard from the grapevine, had really abysmal taste in boyfriends since. One had ordered her around and made like he was her agent until her real agent threw him out; the next one had sponged off her for six months, then disappeared; and he'd heard that the current one was a borderline psycho and leaving bruises on her, occasionally.

Yeah, well, I was no prize, either.

He'd expected the color-change on Beth to make him feel really uneasy—but it didn't. She was still Beth Kentraine, only now instead of black hair in a punk tail, she had the most glorious mane of deep red curls he'd seen outside of a movie. Like the chick in *The Abyss*, and not

like Maureen at all. It was lots of fun to play with, too—
though he could sure understand why she didn't want to
camp out on site with it to worry about. Hard to keep a
mane like that clean and unsnarled without magic helping.
And Beth Kentraine was not at all happy about using magic
in ordinary life.

They'd decided to go ahead and bring the bikes into the
parking lot, after quite a bit of discussion, and park them
in the middle of a lot of other bikes. Then Kory would work
something like the "Obi-Wan" thing on them, only it would
make people ignore the fact that they were there. So even
if the Feds were on to them, it was unlikely that they'd
try to meddle with the bikes, even if they were looking for
them. Eric hadn't quite believed in the "spell," if that was
what it was, until Kory had proved it to him—parking his
bike in the *worst* area in Chinatown, throwing the spell on
it, and walking away. They'd come back five hours later, and
there wasn't even a fingerprint on the bike.

Kory's learned a lot from his kin up here. A couple of
the other elves had been taking the Southerner under their
wings, so to speak; teaching him little things that didn't take
a lot of magical energy, but were very effective. And they
had helped him out by kenning and replicating a lot of the
raw materials they'd used in restoring the house, letting him
save his energy for harder things, like restoring the wood
and brickwork. Eric had gathered that this lot was in contact
with more elves—and even humans—out on the East Coast;
a set of elves that wanted to integrate as much as possible
into human society. They even had something to do with—
of all things—racecar driving.

More power to them. There was a hefty faction—from
what Eric had been able to make out—that were dead-set
against that. And it seemed that Perenor wasn't the only
renegade in the world, either, though fortunately there didn't
seem to be any more like him on *this* Coast. "Sheebeg,
Sheemore" all over again—only it turned out there was a
name for these renegades and they even had their own
organization of sorts. "The Unseleighe Court," that was what
Kory's cousin called it. But they seemed to keep themselves

concentrated away from Cold Iron and in areas as isolated as possible—which meant they weren't real fond of the West Coast. North Dakota, now, maybe. . . .

Eric shook himself out of his daydreams; the parking lot was just ahead, and it was time to stop worrying about the problems of the world and start thinking about the day ahead. They still had to make some money—"the old-fashioned way"—because they'd pretty much drained the cookie-jar dry setting up for the party tonight. It was gonna be slim pickings unless the hat filled well this weekend and next week.

Don't think I can handle any more miso soup and ramen noodles for a while.

There was a cluster of bikes of all sorts off to one side, huddled together like musk-oxen; Beth brought the bike to a halt just behind Kory and all three of them got off. Eric took the bags from both of them, Beth and Kory walked the bikes over to the herd and parked them; Kory passed his hand over both.

That was it; no fireworks, no flashes of light. But as the three of them moved off, a couple of other riders came up and parked their bikes right behind the steeds, blocking their egress—something that would never have happened if they'd "noticed" the bikes were in place. Eric grinned, and slung his bags over his shoulder. All was as it should be.

Including Kory; when Kory took his helmet off, there was no way of telling him from any ordinary human.

Well, any ordinary, incredibly blond, six-foot-six, hunk-of-all-time, rad babe of a human, anyway.

Pointy ears and cat-pupiled eyes had been effectively camouflaged by another tiny little spell. Kory stood out, all right—and that was a good thing. He was the most striking of the three, visually; if there was anyone still looking for them, they *wouldn't* be looking for someone that looked like Kory. That in itself should throw confusion into the pursuit. And anyone who was looking for "Beth" and "Eric" would spot Kory first; since he was a stranger to the Faire-circuit, no one would connect him to any of the regulars. Because of that, the existence of "Tom and Janice Lynn"—

who just happened to bear a superficial resemblance to "Eric Banyon and Beth Kentraine"—would be more plausible. And they would all be accepted as newcomers without too much question.

Some of their old friends, most notably a few of the Celts, folks who knew how to keep their mouths shut, were in on the ruse, but most of the Faire regulars weren't.

Beth got the passes at the Admin building with no problems and no questions asked; from there they went off to Celtic Camp (or as Eric liked to tease Ian, Keltic Kamp) to borrow a tent for a quick change. About thirty other Celts and Celt hangers-on had the same idea; the competition for space was fierce. But Beth and Eric were old hands at this; they managed to wiggle out of their leathers and into their costumes using no more than about two square feet of space. Kory undressed with sublime unselfconsciousness— but Eric did not miss the stunned expressions of those around him and the covert glances out of eyes, male and female. Clothed, Kory was a hunk. Stripped to the skivvies Beth insisted he wear in public, and he was causing a lot of people to reach for their drool-catchers.

Yeah, I don't think there's going to be too many problems with people recognizing us. He grinned as he wriggled into his leather Faire pants. *Nobody's gonna be looking at us. This is gonna be fun.*

The bike leathers and helmets went into the costume-bags; the bags went to Admin to be locked up. Beth wasn't taking any chances on someone making a try at their expensive-looking riding leathers, even if Kory *could* magic up new sets right away. For one thing, producing identical leathers within an hour of their loss would cause some serious questions to be raised, even if only the thief knew the leathers had been taken. Anybody who'd snitch some-one's personal property could be low enough to try and peddle the information of the miraculous reproducing cloth-ing to some other interested party. And if it was the Feds who snitched the suits—the cat would definitely be out of the bag.

Not a good idea.

He laced up his leather vest over the front of his silk shirt, transferred the flute to his embroidered gig-bag, and slipped outside the tent to wait for the others. Funny, the bag used to be the classiest part of his costume; now it was the shabbiest. He'd have to ask Kory if the elf had the energy to make him one to match the rest of the costume. Beth followed a moment later, trailing Kory. As they conferred for a moment, getting their bearings, one of the ultra-period Elizabethan types sashayed by, in all her black-velvet, pearl-embroidered majesty, a galleon in full sail. She paused for a moment, one eyebrow lifted.

Eric waited for the usual comment—or, more scathing, the eyebrow to lift just a bit higher, followed by a slight sniff, before the galleon sailed on. *Authenticity Nazis,* he called them, and not entirely in jest. He'd gotten used to them over the years. They'd given him no end of grief because of his careless approach to costuming; he usually shrugged and ignored them. She probably wouldn't care for the light leather breeches, or maybe the silk shirts—or even the appliqued leather vests that matched their boots. Granted, it did look a lot more like Hollywood's idea of Elizabethan than was accurate, though Kory swore he hadn't made that many changes; simply given them an older version of breeches than the silly little puff-pants that were correct. But he hoped Kory wouldn't be upset when she gave them the inevitable thumbs-down. . . .

The eyebrow remained where it was. "Quite—striking," the galleon pronounced. "Really, quite elegant." Her eyes lingered on Kory's legs, and Eric did his best not to snicker. He should have known. She was a sucker for a hunk in tight leather pants. For that, she'd probably have forgiven them if they'd worn their biker leathers. "You must be professionals," she continued. "I don't remember seeing you here last year."

"Not as a group, milady," Kory said, bowing so gracefully that the galleon flushed with pleasure. "We've been rather busy getting settled in the area. We've had some jobs Outside, but this is our first year at the Faire together."

"I'm looking forward to hearing you." The great black

construction picked up her skirts and sailed majestically on to her next appointment—Opening Parade, no doubt. Eric checked Beth out of the corner of his eye. Her mouth was twitching.

"Was that a queen?" Kory asked, politely. Beth fell apart laughing. Fortunately, the galleon was out of sight and hearing range.

Kory looked sorely puzzled, but Eric managed enough of an explanation to satisfy him as they dropped their bags at Admin—where Caitlin gave them a cheerful if harried "thumbs-up" as a welcome for them. Just Caitlin's little way of encouraging the newcomers, who were, by her very different standards, a class act. Caitlin was *not* in on the secret; Eric had wanted to tell her, but Beth voted him down. In the end, he'd had to agree, reluctantly. Caitlin knew too many people, and she might let something slip without meaning any harm.

They hit the "streets" and headed for their chosen busking-site near the tavern, hoping to get it before anyone else staked it out.

Their luck held; they reached the shelter of the trees and got themselves arranged *just* as another group arrived: a lutanist, a harpist and a mandolin player. The dark-haired harpist sighed; Beth shrugged. "Try back in a couple of hours," she said. "We'll be doing the Celtic show, and if you get here before we leave, we'll just wrap up and turn it over to you."

The harpist brightened. "Thanks!" she called, as they headed off at a brisk walk to whatever had been their second choice.

They won't be trotting like that in a couple of hours, Eric noted. He hadn't recognized any of the three players— there was a certain amount of turnover among "Rennies," and these three didn't have quite the same casual saunter of seasoned hands. Although the morning had begun cool, by noon it was probably going to be pretty warm, and most Renfaire costumes got very hot quite quickly. Heat exhaustion was a constant problem, especially among those who were new at the game. That was why he and Beth had agreed on several particular shady sites for busking, if they could get them, even though *their* costumes were a lot cooler than they looked.

He was fitting the pieces of his flute together when he was startled by a familiar voice calling his name.

"Eric? Eric Banyon?"

He came within a hair of turning; he certainly jumped a little, nervously. Then—:*Gently, Bard,*: came another voice, this one deep inside his mind, steadying him as if Kory held a comforting hand on his shoulder. :*Remember who you are. Do not react. She is coming up behind you—she is going to touch you.*:

"Eric?" A real hand touched his elbow, and he turned, carefully schooling his face into a mask of surprise and puzzlement, mixed with a bit of annoyance at familiarity from a stranger. "Jesus, Eric, did you dye your hair or some—"

She stopped and stared at him when he didn't respond. It was Kathie, of course. Kathie, who had driven him out of Texas Faire and contributed in no small way to his drinking problem. Dressed, not in one of her carefully embroidered Faire shirts and bodice-skirt combinations, but as a "traveler," one of the paying customers, in designer jeans and a halter-top.

"Like, excuse me?" he said, in a deep Valley accent. "I think you've got, like, someone else in mind, I mean, y'know?"

She looks terrible, he observed, dispassionately. She'd lost at least twenty, maybe thirty pounds; her complexion was pasty, and from the harshness of her speaking voice she'd been doing way too much grass. She had that vague, not-quite-focused look of someone who's been smoking dope for so long it's gotten to be a permanent part of her system. *Stoned and anorexic.* She stared at him with her mouth a little agape; not a pretty sight.

And I used to be in love with her. Like his reflections on the days when he'd taken that driver's test stoned, it seemed worlds away, as if it had been someone else entirely who thought he'd lost the universe and all reason for living when this woman threw him over for a chance to sleep her way into a pro band.

:It was another person, Bard,: Kory said solemnly, as Beth kept her own expression icily aloof. *:You were another person entirely. You met misfortune and grew; she met with fortune and diminished.:*

She looked prosperous enough; at least her clothing was expensive. Kathie collected herself as Eric moved enough away that her hand was no longer in contact with his arm. "Come *on*, Eric!" she said—or rather, whined. "Quit the BS! I know it's you! Y'still have the bag I gave you!"

"What?" he said, thinking quickly. "Like, this?" He pulled the embroidered gig-bag around and looked at it. "Oh, man, listen babe, I mean, I hate t'like, y'know, thrash out yer day, but like, I got this'n the flute in a pawnshop down in Pasadena." He wrinkled his lip a little, in simulated disdain for the bag and its contents. "I didn' wanna, y'know, take a really good instrument out here in the boonies." He scratched his head in an utterly *un*Eric-like gesture, and shrugged in a good imitation of the moneyed youngsters he'd watched on Rodeo Drive, when they weren't impressed with someone. Indifferent to any distress they might cause, but going through the motions. "You're like, about the fifth person t'think I was, y'know, this Eric dude. I mean, sorry babe." He shook his head. "Name's like, Tom, okay? This's, like, our first gig out here, right Jan?"

He turned to Beth, who nodded confirmation. "We're, like, twins," she lied smoothly, and smiled. It was a very cool smile, and Eric hoped she wasn't really as angry as she looked. "We've been like, a duet forever, but it's always been like, conservatory gigs, y'know? Kory like told us we oughta like try the Faire this year, when we like got him to make it a trio, you know?"

:She's not angry,: Kory chuckled mentally. *:Or rather, she was very angry with this woman a long time ago, but now she is enjoying her discomfiture.:*

And if I know my Bethy, the fact that Kath looks like hell is pretty entertaining too, he thought wryly.

Kathie looked from one to the other of them, now totally

confused. "If you're thinking of, like, Eric Banyon," Beth continued, in the same drawling Valley accent as Eric, "Somebody with the Celts told me he'd like had a major accident or something—"

"No—" Kory put in, in a voice completely without accent—very Midwestern. "His apartment blew up, and he disappeared. Somebody said he might have gotten in trouble with a drug ring or something. That's what Ian told me, anyway." He shrugged, insincerely. "Sorry. You could go talk to Ian if you can find him. He should be over with the Celts."

"Oh." Kathie backed away, slowly, her face crumpling. For one moment Eric was tempted to stop her—

:If you do, Beth will be angry at you.:

I feel sorry for her, Eric thought, as she turned and plodded away. I mean, look at her, she isn't even doing the Faire, she's a "traveler." I don't know what happened to her, but it must have been pretty awful.

:I think she came here to try and find you,: Kory warned, :And if that is true, she could be either a plant, or someone else's unwitting stalking-horse. In either case, she is dangerous to us. I begin to believe now in the wisdom of Beth's plans.:

"Stick to the script, Banyon," Beth muttered under her breath, leaning forward to adjust his collar.

"No problem, love," he replied, with a grin. "Hey, all I have to do is remember the kind of rat she was back when, and it gets kind of hard to feel too sorry for her."

"That's my boy." She smiled back. "Now, let's make some pretty music for the travelers, hmm?"

"Okay." The travelers were starting to fill the streets between the booths; Opening Parade must be over. Kory already had his bodhran out and ready; Bethy was tuning the last string on her mandolin. Pity they wouldn't allow guitars out here, but the mando had a surprisingly loud "voice," and Beth would be giving it all she had. Between the three of them, they ought to give the travelers some spirit for their money.

"Signature tune?" he suggested. Beth flashed him a smile, and Kory nodded. "Okay, Kory, lead off; Beth, in on four."

Kory got the attention of anyone within hearing distance with a rousing four-count on the hand-drum, then he and Beth jumped in with the tune that had given them their name—"Banysh Mysfortune."

They ran it through twice, but the crowd didn't look to be in quite a giving mood, so as they rounded up the "B" part on the second pass, Beth called out "Drowsy Maggie!" and Eric followed her change.

He half-closed his eyes in pleasure. *This* was the way it should be; this was what he'd missed for the past year and a half. Not that they hadn't been busking; in fact, they'd gone out to Fisherman's Wharf most days when there was any chance of catching a crowd. But this was different— the crowds in the mundane world were harder to catch and hold. Ordinary people were off on little trips of their own, and they weren't planning on taking the time to stop and listen. They didn't necessarily want to hear folk music, either. Faire-goers were ready to be entertained; they wanted to hear something they wouldn't get on the radio. That made all the difference.

There were toes tapping out there in the crowd, and heads nodding. The boothies around them were paying attention too, and that meant they were doing just fine. The galleon sailed by, on the arm of another black-clad fellow whose surfer-tan contrasted oddly with his hose and doublet. She stopped to listen, too.

"Rutland Reel!" Beth called out as they finished up "Drowsy Maggie." If Eric hadn't been playing he'd have grinned. It was really a fiddler's tune, and the fingerings were a stone bitch, but he loved it, and the supersonic pace was bound to charm some cash from the crowd. Besides, they'd arranged it so that Kory had a place for a bodhran solo in the middle, to give him and Beth a rest, and they were going to need it.

They hit the change—and exploded.

The crowd loved it. When they finished, with a flourish, and swept immediately into a bow, change rained into the hat, and one of the boothies popped out of the tavern long enough to salt the hat with a fiver. Eric raised a surprised eyebrow at her; she just grinned from under her little dried-flower wreath. "Lunch is on us, and don't you dare go anywhere else," she said. "Just do some more Fairport Convention stuff," and then she scampered back to work.

Eric looked at Beth, who chuckled. "The request line is open," she responded. "'Riverhead' into 'Gladys' Leap' into 'Wise Maid,' right off the record, just keep it trad-sounding, or the Authenticity Nazis will get us."

"Can do," he agreed, and they were off again.

By the time they were ready to break, the hat was heavy, and it wasn't all change by any means. The folk running the tavern offered beer or lemonade; Eric thought about the beer, then chose the latter. No point in spoiling a spotless record by getting drunk on his butt by accident, just because the day was hot. He hadn't been drunk since the night of despair—

That night, after Beth had told him Kory'd vanished, had been the worst night of his life. And it hadn't ended with that; he had watched his apartment going up in flames on the evening news, and had realized from a clue on the news that Perenor had been systematically killing all the potential Bards in the L.A. basin. He had grabbed for the whiskey, and something had made him stop.

That was the night he'd decided that help wasn't ever going to be found in the bottom of a bottle.

Besides, Eric Banyon had an established reputation for getting plastered at Faires. Tom Lynn should be different; another way of confusing the Feds and the Kathies.

By the time the Celtic show rolled around at 11:30, there was no doubt that they'd done the right thing, coming out here. There was more in the hat than he'd made in the best day of his life at Faire, and the day wasn't even half over yet. Beth emptied the take into the pouch she kept *under* her skirt—wise lady, she knew very well that cutpurses of the traditional kind were alive and well at Faire, though they probably wore "Motley Crue" t-shirts. Eric had lost his own pouch that way the morning after he'd awakened Kory with his music. Though he hadn't known what he'd done at the time.

They turned the spot over to the harpist and her friends, and promised the tavern people to return after the show for the lunch they'd offered. They hurried to "catch the Celtic bus" before it left without them, running hand-in-hand like three kids, laughing all the way there.

They formed up with the other musicians in a loosely-organized mob; the chief gave the signal, and they were off.

The show was more of the same, but this time there were dancers to play for, and the show-mistress was the one calling the tunes. And there were more musicians to play with, which came very near to sending Eric into a full Bardic display of his power. He pulled himself back from the brink at the very last moment, exhilarated, but a little frightened by how easy it had been to call up the magic. He held himself in, then, just a bit; keeping his power under careful rein, like a restive horse. He exerted it only twice; once to throw power to Kory, who could never have enough with all the work he had to do, and once to grab a faltering dancer and save her from throwing out her knee.

That was something he hadn't even thought of doing until he somehow sensed the accident coming, a moment before it did, and let the power run free for that brief measure of time. She never even noticed that anything was different.

But Kory did, and the warm look of approval the elf cast him made him glow inside. Magic—the important magic—wasn't all big battles, the building of palaces. Just as important was keeping things around you running smoothly. He hadn't understood that when Kory and Arvin told him, but he did now.

The show finished, and thoroughly exhausted, they headed back to the tavern for that promised meal and a chance to listen to someone else. The trio that had replaced them were good, and it was a pleasure to sit and hear music instead of producing it, at least for a little bit. Once again, Eric opted for lemonade, and this time was rewarded with Beth's glance of approval.

That sobered him. Had she been watching him, waiting for him to revert to his old, bad habits? Probably.

I wish she'd said something, he thought, a little bitterly. *But—then again, maybe I haven't had a chance to prove myself out yet, at least not in the places where all the temptation is.*

But before his mood could sour, Beth got his attention. The trio by the tavern fence was playing "Sheebeg, Sheemore," and Kory's face wore an expression of wistful sadness. Eric had a pretty good idea why. Although it was a lovely tune, Banysh Mysfortune never played it, because it always reminded Kory of how many friends he'd lost to Perenor. . . .

"Where are we going to set up next?" Eric asked, touching Kory's hand for a moment, and trying to give him something of the same support the elf had given him when he'd confronted Kathie.

Kory shook himself loose from his mood, and turned his attention to them. "Indeed," he said, "that is a good question. I'm loath to deprive those three of such a location. We are, frankly, louder than they, and it is quiet here. I do think we could afford to go elsewhere." He looked sideways at Beth. "Could we not?"

"We certainly could," she replied, an impish grin on her face. "And I have a very choice spot in mind. After all, we've had lunch; now is time for dessert!"

Eric laughed. "I might have known!" he said, and pointed an admonishing finger at her. "It's all going on your hips, and you're never gonna be able to get back in those leather pants!"

"What?" Kory asked, bewildered, looking from Beth to Eric and back again. "What? What is this about?"

"The chocolate truffle booth by the Kissing Bridge," Eric replied, shaking his head. "Beth's a closet chocoholic."

She hung her head in mock shame. "Mea culpa. But I still think we should see if the venue's free, and grab it if it is. And I promise not to overindulge. But I've earned *one,* surely?"

"All right," Eric conceded. "One. But there'd better be something there *Kory* can eat." He raised an eyebrow at the elf. "Don't forget for a second that chocolate has caffeine in it. *I* haven't."

"There is," she said confidently. "White chocolate amaretto truffles. No real chocolate at all, I checked. Or white-chocolate-dipped strawberries. Or peanut-butter fudge. Or—"

"Enough! So, we play for dessert, and then?" Kory asked.

"Then we take a break. Go back to the camp and have something with salt in it to drink." Eric was adamant on that. "We can let the newbies wear themselves out, and we can catch the dinner crowd. We've done all right, we can afford the break."

"I think you should sing a bit, Beth," Kory added reproachfully. "You haven't yet." He gave her the look Eric called "lost puppy eyes," and she made a face. But when Eric gave her a dose of his own version, she capitulated.

They left the tavern and wandered down to the Kissing Bridge. A fiddler and bodhran-player—Eric recognized Ian and one of the girls from this area he knew by sight, though not by name—were just wrapping up and glad enough to relinquish the place and claim their rewards. Evidently the other two put in a good word at the booth as they collected their goodies; the boothies nodded before Beth could even approach them and gave her the high-sign.

"So what are we up to?" Eric asked, putting out his hat.

"If I'm going to have to sing, so are you two," Beth said, with a look that told them she'd take no argument to the contrary.

Eric sighed. "Do I get to pick?" he asked plaintively.

"One," she said.

"All right." He grinned. " 'The Ups and Downs.' "

"Oh no—" she protested, but it was too late. She was stuck with a song about a girl who should have known better—and she couldn't even cry off, because the man's part was longer than hers. All *she* had to sing was the part where she complains about how he's taken advantage of her, and tricked her into thinking he'd given her his name when he hadn't.

"Be grateful I didn't pick 'Ball of Yarn,' " he said, grinning even harder. "Or worse."

She only groaned, and nodded to Kory to lead off again.

The rest of the afternoon was even better; with no money worries for the day, they joined several others whose "take" hadn't been as good, to give them a boost. Kory was even persuaded by the step-dancers to join them in an impromptu table-dance. It paid off handsomely for the girls; Kory fairly charmed the coins out of the hands of the ladies, and Eric thought once that one yuppie-type was going to stuff a bill into the waistband of his breeches, but she evidently remembered that she was at the Faire and not a Chips revue at the last moment, and put the fiver in the hat.

By the time the Faire security chased everyone out, Beth had gone to boothies three times to get the change they'd collected converted to bills, and every time she came back, her smile was broader.

When they were in another tent, changing back into their riding leathers, she whispered the total to Eric, who whistled. Even allowing for the fact that it was a three-way split, it was worlds away better than *he'd* ever done alone. Today alone was going to cover the utility bills for the month. Tomorrow might well take care of groceries for the month as well—

—and the Faire would run for the next seven weeks! That meant their take at the Wharf could be put aside, saved for leaner times, like the winter.

Last winter had been very lean; too many days of cheap noodles, too many arguments with Kory about the advisability of using magic to conjure up better food. Too many weeks wondering if they were going to be able to pay the electric bill; too many nights huddling together to save on heat. Too many times wondering if their odd menage was going to work—if Beth was going to storm out, if Kory was going to flee Underhill, or if he himself was going to give in to his temper and bludgeon one or both of them. Faire season was going to make the difference.

Faire season was going to keep them together.

Eric donned his helmet and mounted up behind Beth, his heart completely light for the first time in months. It was going to work. *They* were going to work.

And now was truly time to party!

3

My Feet Are Set for Dancing

Eric's elation lasted as long as it took them to get to the highway; then it turned into terror. He'd forgotten that the three of them were going to have to make some serious time to beat the others back to the Bay—and that Beth and Kory knew very well that all the cops were going to be babysitting the crowd pouring out of the Faire and would have no one free to see to the back roads.

He wasn't afraid they were going to break the posted limit; he *knew* they were going to shatter it. *He* was afraid they were going to break the speed of light.

He just kept his head tucked down, his legs tucked in, and held onto Beth's waist. And kept his eyes closed.

To distract himself, he replayed the Celt show in his head, trying to figure out why it was he had so nearly gone into full Bard-magic mode.

It wasn't the other musicians; that just helped after I got there. It wasn't the songs themselves; we've done them a million times. Was it the crowd?

That had something to do with it, he decided. But why *this* crowd, when they'd played for crowds just as big on the Wharf and he'd never had that happen before?

What was different about a Faire audience?

Finally, he decided there was only one thing it could be.

Attitude. The crowds on the Wharf were not looking for anything, they had no expectations, and they were not ready for the unusual. The travelers at the Faire were *expecting* things; expecting to be surprised, to be entertained, expecting to enjoy themselves with something entirely new and different. They were even willing to suspend their disbelief and pretend they had been magically transported back in time.

They were ready to believe in magic.

And that readiness to believe had helped him give them magic. He could have done all kinds of things by accident if he hadn't recognized what was happening and put a lid on it.

Christ, that's what happens with a classical audience too; they sort of put everything mundane on hold and let their imaginations go. It's just that I haven't done a concert gig in so long, I'd forgotten it. That must be why I was able to bring up those nightmare things when I was a kid.

It made him wonder what would happen if the travelers ever got wrapped up enough in something that they *did* flip over into full belief. The idea was a little frightening; he'd had trouble hanging onto the tiger's tail as it was.

But if there ever came a time that he would need that belief, and the power that came with it, well, it was a good idea to know what it could do.

They can't work magic themselves, but they can give me the power to do it. Wonder if that was why Perenor was trying to get them and the nexus under his thumb, to harness all that creative energy for his own use. . . .

That sent him back to thoughts of Ria Llewellyn. She was *not* a good person to be around if you were weaker than she was, that was for sure. She'd drain you dry, and throw away the husk with a little shrug of regret. Eric suppressed a shiver; he'd come darn close to becoming one of those used-up husks. When he'd stomped off to Ria, mad because Kory and Beth had—well—done what was natural, she'd taken him into her home. *Now* he wasn't so sure that where she'd taken him hadn't also been partly Underhill; like the old ballads where someone goes Underhill for a day, and when he comes back a year has passed, he didn't think he'd spent more than a couple of days with Ria, but it had been *months* in the real world. Time enough for the Fairesite to be bulldozed, for the nexus there to begin to fade, and for Kory to give up in despair and go off by himself to die.

And when Ria had taken him Underhill, he'd been different. He hadn't been able to compose; he'd barely been able to play, and when he did, it was with none of the "juice" he'd become accustomed to having.

Ria had been draining him; of that he was certain. No, she was not a good person to be around when you were something less than she was.

But if you were her equal—

He played with that notion a while. It was dangerous, but intriguing. She was a very sexy, very capable lady. And there was a soft side to her that he was pretty certain she hadn't let anyone see but him: a vulnerable Ria who had been hurt over and over by an indifferent mother and a manipulative father.

What if they *could* meet again as equals?

Hell, and what if a boat could fly? One is about as likely as the other. Her brain's fried, and that's the bottom line. Hopefully whatever Happy Home Elizabet has her in is careful not to hire abusive attendants. Otherwise they'd have themselves a sure-enough sex doll, 'cause she wouldn't know or care what was happening to her.

He cracked an eyelid open and took a peek; sighed with relief. They were just coming down off the mountain and San Francisco lay before them, like a jeweled crescent pin around the Bay. Kory and Beth would have to cut the speed now; they were about to hit traffic.

The lights were on when they pulled up to the house; Eric felt Beth's muscles tense under his hand, but Kory brought his steed to a halt and pulled off his helmet, shaking his hair loose. As Beth pulled up beside them, he grinned.

"'Tis Arvin, Pelindar, Treviniel, and some of the others.

They have hasted ahead to help us. Oh, and Greg is here as well, but they have chased him from the kitchen—"

"My microwave!" Beth bleated, and abandoned the bike, leaving Eric to balance it precariously from the passenger's seat. It hovered for a moment, until he could get control, fortunately. He managed to keep it from falling over, scooted forward to grab the handlebars, and got off. Kory shook his head, and led the way to the garage.

Funny how that bike kind of balanced itself for a minute. I guess my luck-factor has really kicked in today. They walked the bikes to the garage, locked them in, and came up through the gardens.

There were two elves—Eric could see their pointed ears if he looked really closely, the way he did if he suspected illusion—already in the hot tub. They waved indolently at Eric and Kory as they passed, but didn't move. By the stature and the fact that they looked like adolescents, Eric guessed that they were Low Court elves, the kind that were tied to specific oak groves and couldn't leave them without a lot of magical help from their High Court relatives. The Low Court kids—he always thought of them as kids, even though they were usually hundreds of years old, since that was what they looked like and often acted like—tended to hang out in shopping malls a lot. They'd use their magics to copy or snitch whatever hot fashion items took their fancy, replicate just enough cash to buy themselves endless meals of junk food, sneak into the movie theaters, and play video games that lasted for days. No one ever noticed them, since they looked just like all the other kids in the malls. The kids—the real, human kids—seemed to instinctively know the difference, though, and they tended to keep away from the elves.

The sole exceptions were the occasional misfits—usually girls, nerdy, bookish, and usually very lonely—who would be taken up by one or more of the elves over the course of a summer. At the end of that summer, the girl would return to school, transformed by her brief fling with magic and by the subtle touches of the elves. Sometimes they stayed misfits, sometimes they became very popular—but the end result was that they had usually found out what magic there was that lurked within them, and were much happier than they had been before.

They would never remember anything more than a summer romance with someone really incredible that centered around the mall. The elves took care that any memories more than that never stayed, and the one who had chosen the human lover would change his or her face so that it would never be recognized again.

Eric often wondered if that was what Kory had originally intended to do with him and Beth. If so, he had changed his mind at some point. And Eric got the feeling that some of his kin did not approve.

Yeah, these mixed-species marriages never work. . . .

Oh well, if they didn't approve, at least they were being civilized about it. They weren't shunning Kory or his human friends. Which was more than you could say for—oh—the average Italian-Catholic getting involved with a Lebanese-Arab.

Much less two, though the elves seemed a lot less hung up on the mathematics of sex than humans. He'd seen them going around by twos, threes, and mobs. Hell, Arvin usually had a whole harem.

He followed Kory up the stairs, into the kitchen. Beth was nowhere to be seen. Arvin was in charge of plates of little somethings that looked incredibly fattening. He was idly filling tiny cups of pastry with something from a big bowl—not touching either, of course. Eric liked Arvin, a lot. The elf looked like a dark blond version of Tim Curry, and had a wicked sense of humor. One of the Low Court elves, a gorgeous girl in full punk gear, except it was pink, was doing something with the microwave. Evidently *she* knew what she was doing; she was setting the time, putting trays of sausages in, and nuking them until they sizzled, then dropping them into a warming-pan to stay hot. She grinned saucily at Kory, who only sighed. There were two other elves Eric didn't recognize; one, a real fairy-tale princess type who looked like she wouldn't know how to file her own nails was cutting up veggies with brisk efficiency and arranging them on dip plates. A vast set of trays of cold cuts and cheese already completed bore mute testimony to her expertise. A second, another Low-Court, this one a surfer-duuuuude complete with tan, glaring Hawaiian shirt and baggies, was running the trays out to various locations in the living and entertainment rooms.

Arvin looked up from his work. "We have things well in hand," he said mildly. "Revendel and Lorilyn cleaned ere we arrived, so there is nothing of that for you to do. I sent them to soak in yon human boiling-pot. Greg is below also, making certain the outdoor speakers function still."

Eric looked around. "I can't see anything else for anyone to do," he said, gratefully, as Kory nodded agreement. "Look, I don't know how to thank you guys—"

"A trifle." Arvin dismissed his thanks with a wave of his hand. "Enough that you have built us a trysting and dancing ground below." His eyes glittered wickedly. "And we *shall* be using it, take heed."

"Just don't take it into the street and scare the neighbors' kids," Eric advised. "Okay? Kory, we might as well get a quick shower and change."

"Aye. The mob will be here soon." Kory tossed his helmet into the air, where it promptly disappeared, and ran up the stairs. Eric put his away more mundanely, and followed.

Beth was already out of her clothes and into the shower; they joined her. It was a tight squeeze for three, but they'd done it before. There wasn't as much horseplay as they usually indulged in, but they were still breathless with laughter when they tumbled out, now clean, to scramble into clothes.

Kory and Eric opted for comfortable versions of their Faire outfits: soft, baggy cotton pants instead of the tight leather, and bare feet instead of boots. Beth was doing something she had seldom done before the hair-change; she was wearing a dress Kory had made for her. Soft black and silver, silky and floor-length, it looked vaguely period, but Eric couldn't pin it down to a particular style. Kory had one of those peculiar smiles when she twirled around in it, though, so Eric suspected that it was a copy of an elven design. Whatever, she looked terrific, straight out of the Kevin Costner *Robin Hood*.

The master-bedroom overlooked the front steps; the window was open to the glorious breeze coming in, and there were voices right below. Beth blew both of them a kiss and flew down the stairs to open the door as the doorbell rang.

After that, the guests began arriving in herds, and someone was always answering the door. At least half of the guests were elves, who had chosen, to keep from revealing themselves to the humans, Eric suspected, to enter the normal way rather than just popping into the garden. Most of the rest were the Faire folks who were in on the secret identities of Tom Lynn, Janice Lynn, and Kory Dell—or at least, they knew Kory Dell was a friend of theirs. No one knew about the elves' existence except Beth and Eric—even the former members of Beth's old rock-group Spiral Dance seemed to have put the Battle of Griffith Park out of their minds. There *were* other humans who knew about elves, like the bunch over on the East Coast Arvin referred to now and again—but the elves themselves had not seen fit to introduce Eric and Beth to them. Maybe they would, someday.

There were more of their Faire buddies than Eric had realized. The Celts alone filled a room. Of course, *one* Celt was perfectly capable of filling a room all by him/herself. . . .

In no time at all, the party was in full swing. There was a group in the entertainment room, laughing, talking, and munching away while cutting-edge rock played in the background. There was a second group in the living-room, watching a videotape someone had made of the Celtic show today, commenting sarcastically and making jokes. A spillover group of costumers in the kitchen were trading project rehashes, to the fascination of the punk-elf in pink. And Greg might just as well not have bothered about the ground-speakers; no one was using them. The clear spot in the garden, just big enough for dancing, held a tiny band of buskers who hadn't gotten their fill of playing during the day—and dancers who hadn't gotten their fill of dancing.

Oh—the buskers are dancing, and the dancers are busking. That explains it.

The hot tub was as full of people as it could be. Eric had a notion that the little nooks and corners made for privacy were full too, but he wasn't crass enough to check them out.

He spent the evening wandering, too restless to settle down, too full of nervous energy to stay in one place for very long. He spent some time with the crowd in the entertainment room when Arvin gave them a free show to the *Rocky Horror Picture Show* soundtrack. Small wonder Arvin didn't have to ken and replicate money! Even *here* he had people stuffing bills in his waistband. And Arvin finished the set with an even bigger harem than usual. . . .

Eric grinned and wandered off. He danced a little, played a little, talked a lot—ate quite a bit. And drank almost nothing, which surprised him. It was as if he'd lost his taste for it.

Funny, he thought, lounging back on the grass and watching Beth dance with Ian, *I never used to think it was a real party unless I'd gotten stoned, drunk, or both.* It wasn't as if there was any lack of opportunity; wine was more plentiful than soft drinks tonight, though there was nothing whatsoever with caffeine in it, as a safeguard against one of Kory's folk accidentally getting a dose. Plenty of people had brought stronger stuff, and he'd had lots of those bottles offered to him. And he knew he'd smelled the green-sweet smoke of weed from the secluded areas of the garden.

I guess I'm having too much fun. I'd hate to miss any of this by being flat on my back—or flat on my stomach; I've done that, too.

Gradually the crowd thinned; he found himself escorting people to the door and looked at his watch. He could hardly believe it when it read one a.m. But the kitchen clock agreed with it—and when he looked around, he realized that the only guests left had pointy ears and looked nowhere near ready to retire.

As if he had read Eric's mind, Arvin turned away from the pink-punk elf-girl. "Anyone not in a condition to drive

has been found a driver or has been put to bed upstairs.
Beth I sent up to bed not five minutes ago. Kory needs
but an hour or so of sleep—but *you*, mortal, will feel the
effect on the morrow if you do not seek yon waterbed."

Eric nodded reluctantly. "But—" he said, feeling as if
he ought to at least make the motions of being a host.

"*Go!*" Arvin scolded. "Kory is host enough for us!"

He left, gratefully. Beth was already asleep, in her usual
place in the middle of the king-sized waterbed. He stripped
off everything but the cotton pants and took his usual place,
on the right.

The sounds of the party—much quieter now—drifted up
through the hall and the windows. He listened to the music
for a moment, puzzled, trying to determine what record it
was, when a sudden change in key and tempo made him
smile. It wasn't a record, of course, it was elves making
music in the garden, blessing it and the house in their own
peculiar way.

He fell asleep, still smiling.

Something awakened him, though he couldn't remember what. A whisper of sound, like someone calling to him
very quietly, from very far away.

:*Bard, do you hear me?*:

"No, I don't, " he muttered to himself, trying to bury
his head beneath a pillow. "Go away."

He blinked once, looking around the dimly-lit room. Beth
was still asleep, one arm flung out towards him, her hair
in a wild tumble on the pillows. From downstairs, he could
hear quiet elven voices . . . Kory and his friends, talking
in the kitchen. Eric glanced at the clock, and winced, closing
his eyes again. *Three a.m.!*

:*Bard, do you hear me?*:

He sat up abruptly, the waterbed shifting underneath him
at the sudden movement. :*Yes, I hear you. Where are you?*:
:*Outside.*:

He moved carefully off the waterbed, trying not to
awaken Beth, and to the window. Outside, the street was
shrouded in fog. Someone was standing outside on the

sidewalk, barely visible through the mists, looking up at the house.

Several moments later, after pulling on the black silk robe that Kory had conjured for him, Eric was padding quietly down the stairs. He slipped past the elves in the kitchen and out the front door, still not certain why he didn't want to tell anyone else about the unexpected visitor. The concrete was cold and damp against his bare feet.

And the stranger was nowhere in sight.

Great, he thought. *Just what in the hell is* . . .

He noticed it then, the strange, unnatural silence that had settled over the sleeping city. Like the world was holding its breath, waiting for something to begin.

In the distance, a dog barked. And another. A flight of birds, nesting in the oak tree next to the front door, suddenly took wing, wheeling overhead and screaming shrilly.

Something . . . something's wrong . . .

He could feel it then, a low, rumbling noise that seemed to be growing louder. The ground rippled beneath his feet, rising gently like a wave, then falling. The front door began to rattle in its frame, at first quietly, then more insistently. Eric turned back to the house, took a step forward, and . . .

The earthquake hit in full force, hurling him to his knees. Everything was moving, panes of glass shattering like gunshots, the sidewalk cracking beneath his hands. Eric covered his head with his hands, trying to protect himself from a spray of flying glass as a pickup truck was shoved hard against the streetlight. With a rending crash, the house across the street ripped away from its neighbor, tilting slowly before collapsing into the next building.

As suddenly as it had begun, the rumbling ended. He could hear the wail of dozens of car alarms, but no other sound. A small aftershock rippled beneath him, then was gone.

He stood up unsteadily, and stared at the ruin of the street. Two of the houses had collapsed completely, while several others were canted at strange angles.

Something struck him in the small of his back, and he looked up to see plaster and wood falling from the fourth floor of his house into the street. The house began to fold in on itself, like a stack of cards in slow motion. He stared, too terrified to scream. Then someone shoved past him, climbing the wreckage of the house, screaming curses and prayers incoherently.

Himself.

The other Eric disappeared through a ruined window. He still stood on the street, frozen in shock. The streetlights flickered once, then went out, leaving everything in foggy shadows. A moment later, his duplicate climbed through the window, carrying an unconscious Beth. He set her down gently on the broken concrete, and immediately began mouth-to-mouth resuscitation. Blood was mixed with her long red hair, pooling on the sidewalk.

He stood there, unable to move. The other Eric slowly looked up at him, tears mixed with blood on his face. "You didn't stop it, you bastard," his other self whispered. "Kory's dead in there, a Cold Iron nail through his face, and Beth's dying . . . and you didn't do anything to stop this!" Something fluttered past the other Eric, a half-glimpsed shadow. Another, a touch of darkness, flitting past them.

He could see them now, the shadows in the fog. Night-flyers. Hundreds of them, moving down the silent street. They moved past him as though they couldn't see him, circling around the other Eric, Beth still cradled in his arms. His double yelled in pain as one of the creatures brushed against him, and swung at it, not connecting with the lithe shadow. Another slipped by, with a delicate touch to his back, his exposed face. Others gathered at the edge of sight, drifting with the fog.

I can't move—can't do anything— He tried to call a warding, something that would protect himself and the other, but the magic eluded him, just out of reach. *Dammit, Beth always told me to practice doing magic without using the flute, and I never did, and now we—and I—are going to die for it!*

The night brightened with a burst of light as the other Eric summoned a Ward, his Bard magic blossoming before him. The creatures recoiled for a moment, silhouetted by the bright light, then closed in. The light flickered once, then vanished. The shadow monsters flitted aside; for a brief moment, he could see his own dead face, blankly staring. Then the Nightflyers turned to face him, radiating malevolence, their shadow-claws reaching . . .

"Eric! Wake up! Eric, please, wake up!"

He blinked, looking up into a pair of concerned green eyes. Kory moved back so Eric could sit up, and he realized that Beth was watching him, too. "Guys, I'm okay, it was just a bad dream."

There was a frightened look in Beth's eyes, something Eric rarely ever saw. "It's the same bad dream, right?" she asked. "The same nightmare you've been having once a week for the past month." She glanced at Kory, then back at him. "Want to talk about it, Eric?"

Houses collapsing down the street, Beth's blood on his hands, the nightmare creatures closing in around him— "No, I don't want to talk about it. C'mon, it's not a big deal. Just a nightmare." He managed a laugh. "I should probably stop eating lunch at that burrito place near the Park. Their food would give anybody nightmares."

"This isn't funny, Eric!" He recognized that look in her eyes now . . . it had nothing to do with fear, it was that tough-as-nails Beth Kentraine that he knew and loved. "I'll call a doctor tomorrow. Somebody has to figure what's going on inside your head, love."

"Of what value is a human physician?" Kory asked. "Eric is a Bard, not a normal person. There should be nothing wrong with him that he cannot cure himself."

"We're talking about something wrong up here, Kory—" Beth tapped the side of her head. "Humans have special doctors for that kind of thing. Psychiatrists. And even magic isn't good for that kind of stuff . . . remember Perenor? He was crazy-psycho, a real nut case. His magic didn't help him there."

Kory's eyes widened in horror. "Eric isn't like Perenor! He could never be like Perenor!"

"I didn't mean he was like Perenor, just that it's the same kind of thing."

"I don't want to talk to a shrink," Eric protested. "Beth, it's just a bad dream!"

"A bad dream that you've had for over a month!"

"Look, I've talked to enough shrinks in my life, okay? I don't want to see another one, ever."

"Eric, I love you. I don't want you to have to go to a psych. But something's wrong, and you have to do something about it."

"No shrinks," Eric repeated stubbornly.

"We'll talk about this in the morning," Beth said, matching his stubbornness.

"Beth . . ." Kory began hesitantly. "You say this is a human thing, but could this have something to do with Eric's magic? Some Bards have the ability to look into the future, or to call to others from the past . . ."

His own eyes, staring and lifeless— "Kory. It's only a dream. Maybe Beth's got the right idea, maybe I'm nutso, but it's still only a dream."

"But Kory could be right." Beth sat up suddenly. "Eric, have you ever used your Bardic magic to look into the future?"

"Bethy, I've only been a Bard for a year! Give me a break!"

She gave him a look. "Well, you could give it a try," she said. "Take a look into next week and see if it turns out like your dream."

Oh God, I hope not. "Okay, okay, I'll try it, if only so you won't sign me up at the local psycho ward. Now, I think we all could use some more sleep, right?"

He lay there in the darkness, listening to Beth's quiet breathing, the waterbed shifting as Kory turned over onto his side.

I can't be seeing the future, he thought. *That can't be what's going to happen to us. San Francisco destroyed, Nightflyers everywhere, all of us dead . . .*

I won't let that happen.

In his mind, he thought about a particular melody, light and airy: "Southwind." A gentle tune, one that had always reminded him of quiet pleasures and warm evenings with friends. Good memories. That was the tune he would use to look into the future.

He could hear the lilt of the melody, adding just a touch of ornamentation at the end of the B part, a little trill to wind back into the melody. He imagined the way his fingers would press on the flute keys, the exact timing of his breath.

"Oh, what the hell," he muttered, moving carefully so he wouldn't wake Beth or Kory. "I'll never be able get back to sleep tonight anyhow."

4

A Moonlight Ramble

Once upstairs, he retrieved his flute from its stand, then moved quietly down the stairs and out into the garden. There was one place that he loved most in Kory's garden, a small stand of birch trees that circled a grassy area in a ring.

Eric sat down under the leafy trees, which had been scrawny saplings until two months ago, when Kory had "convinced" them to grow more quickly.

As always, he had the same sense that he had felt that night, years back, in the old oak grove at the destroyed Southern Fairesite, that feeling of magic lying just beneath the surface, woven into everything around him.

Just enough moonlight shone through the night fog to reflect off the flute as he brought it to his lips. It was his favorite kind of San Francisco night, the city finally quiet and sleeping as the fog swirled through it. Little tendrils of fog moved around the trees; he could taste the fog, thick and damp, as he breathed in the night air. And over all of it was the sense of belonging; this place was his, this was his home.

He'd never felt that before, not during his childhood or all the years of traveling. Now, in the perfect stillness, he played for himself and for the sleeping city.

He frowned at the first note he played: flat, and very thin. He adjusted the flute accordingly, and played another note, clear and vibrant, followed by the first few notes of "Southwind."

The tune unfolded before him, lilting notes fading into each other. He concentrated on the tune, on the coldness of the flute's metal against his fingers, on the way his lips shaped each note. After a few moments, the world faded from around him, and he was alone with the music, playing out his soul to the birch trees that bent closer to hear him.

All right, he thought, *now let's take a look Elsewhere.*

He began weaving that into the tune, the future that he wanted to see, letting the dancing notes build it out of moonlight and fog. Suddenly, it was there, shimmering before him.

Ria Llewellyn?

She stared at him, an image of mist and fog. Behind her, he could see the outline of a motel room, neon signs flickering beyond the window. Her eyes were bright with astonishment, and more than a little fear. He followed her look to the other side of the room, where he saw . . . himself, wearing a pair of silk pajamas and looking more than a little bewildered.

Eric was surprised, too. Too surprised to keep playing, he missed a note, then another. The image of Ria vanished instantly as he lost the thread of the melody, swirling back into the fog.

He sat back, his fingers clenched tightly around the flute. Then, hesitantly, he brought up the flute again and began to play.

This time, he didn't blindly reach out for whatever image would appear. Note by note, he built the idea, gathering in the moonlight as a canvas. Then he sat back and looked at what he had created.

A hospital room. Seated by the window, an elderly woman in a red silk dressing gown, staring out through the darkened glass. No, not an elderly woman; a blond woman in her thirties, her face drawn and pale, motionless, giving the impression of great age. Her eyes never moving, she gazed intently through the glass—at nothing. An empty courtyard.

The blue eyes never wavered, only blinking occasionally. He could hear someone moving through the room, the sounds of someone walking closer. "Time to be in bed, Miz Llewellyn," an older man's voice said, and then the orderly was helping her stand, walking with her back to the bed. He tucked her under the blanket, then moved out of sight. A moment later, the click of a door closing. And the blond woman was now staring at the ceiling, her eyes never moving, the expression on her face never changing.

Eric drew back from the image, horrified. *It isn't fair! She was cruel and manipulative, but she never deserved this!*

But if the other image was also a Far-Seeing, then maybe eventually she'll be okay. Maybe eventually she'll get past what happened to her at Griffith Park.

But if that was a True Seeing, and she does recover— —then what in the hell am I doing in a motel room with Ria Llewellyn?

Okay, okay. Better not worry about that right now. Concentrate on what I saw in the bad dream . . . let's see if you have any basis in reality, little nightmare . . .

The images of Ria faded back into the mists, as Eric began playing the tune again. Slowly, focusing all his concentration on the image, he called out into the night, trying to reach the future he'd seen in his dreams, over and over again. Then, suddenly, he saw it, the images spread out before him.

A desolate landscape of San Francisco, the streets dark and deserted, buildings half-collapsed, shattered. He stood at the corner of Market and Castro, near the entrance to the subway station. It was a part of the city that he'd walked through many times, especially with Kory . . . Korendil loved to walk through the Castro District. Kory's cousin Arvin, the dancer, lived only a few blocks away.

Now, the streets were empty of any sign of life . . . not a human being, or a bird, or stray cats, or even insects. Only broken glass, and wrecked cars, and the occasional shadow flickering in the moonlight.

No, not shadows, he thought. *Nightflyers.* Quietly, trying not to draw any attention to himself, Eric moved down the street, past the movie theater and the bookstores, wondering what else he could find here. There was nothing, no sign of life, no clue as to why this had happened.

He stepped over the corpse of a young blond child, lying on the sidewalk, and towards a newsstand. He looked around for a newspaper, wanting to see the date printed on it, and then stopped short. He turned, very slowly, and looked back at the corpse.

Tiny shadows were flickering over it, barely visible against the boy's pale skin. Eric reached down and lifted one of the shadows, the nearly-insubstantial creature feeling like damp tissue paper against his skin. It was tiny, not quite the size of his palm, but already he could see the distinctive billowing-cloak form of a Nightflyer.

Jesus, these things can breed!

He dropped it quickly, brushing off his hand. The shadow bounced against the concrete, then drifted back to the corpse, hovering over the dead boy's eyes. Shivering, Eric turned away.

A Nightflyer was floating directly in front of him.

Eric brought his flute up to his lips, desperately thinking of anything he could use against the creature. He was about to launch into the first notes of "Banysh Mysfortune," when the shadow-monster stepped back several paces. In a strange, almost courtly gesture, it bowed to him, then faded from sight. Eric stared at where the creature had stood, and blinked in astonishment.

In the next moment, he was seated in the garden again, the fog coiling around the trees beside him. Eric buried his face in his hands, trying to think.

It's going to happen. Something is going to destroy the city, and these things are going to take over, and all of us are going to die, and my future self yelled at me for not preventing it, and one of those monsters bowed to me! Dammit, none of this makes any sense!

Kory was waiting at the back door as he trudged back

through the garden. "I could not sleep," the elf said. "Your magic awakened me."

"Sorry about that," Eric muttered, heading towards the doorway. Kory caught his hand as he walked past. "Eric, what is wrong? Why won't you tell us what you have dreamed?"

I can't tell him that it's just a dream. Not anymore. "Kory, do you believe that a mage can see the future? Not just imagine it, but really see it?"

Kory nodded. "Of course. It is a very difficult spell, but I have known several elven lords who could look into the future."

"And if you see it, does that mean it's going to happen?"

"I don't know. I don't think so. Lord Terenil . . ." Kory's voice caught slightly on the name of his former lord and mentor, killed two years ago. "Terenil said that he could see the different paths that lie ahead, that there were always several futures before him. That the future was like the wind, but something that could change without warning. He said that it was dangerous to look too often into the future, because that might make one future, the one that you perceived, more likely than the others."

"That makes sense," Eric said, sitting down on the porch stairs. "Kory, I—I don't know what to do. I think I've seen the future, and it's awful. Really bad. I don't know what I can do about it."

"Do you wish to tell me about it?"

Beth, lying dead in his arms . . . "No, not really. Let's just say that it's really awful, and I sure don't want to see it turn into reality. What can we do to change it?"

Kory gave him a troubled look. "Perhaps we should talk with someone else, another mage, to find out whether or not this was a True Seeing. We could cross over to the Faerie Court of Mist-Hold, and talk with the Queen. Or talk with some of Beth's friends, the human witches and healers. Beth said that Elizabet and her apprentice, Kayla, would be in the city this weekend. We could skip the Faire today, call them and ask their advice."

"That's a better idea than calling a shrink, that's for sure.

Especially if this is magic-related." Beth plunked herself down on the steps next to them.

"You too, huh?" Eric grimaced.

"Yeah, it's tough to sleep when neither of you are in the waterbed. Even tougher than when you snore, Eric."

"Thanks a lot!"

"Well, it's four a.m., and I certainly won't be able to go back to sleep. What do you guys want to do for a few hours until sunrise?"

They all smiled at each other.

"Hot tub!"

The three musicians walked into the cafe, musical instruments slung on straps and in hand. One of the waiters gave them a peculiar look, probably wondering why three scruffy street musicians were walking into his restaurant. Elizabet and Kayla were waiting for them, already seated at one of the window tables.

Eric slid into the seat next to Kayla. "A new pair of safety pins, kid?" he asked, looking at the pair she wore instead of earrings. They matched perfectly with her torn t-shirt, black leather jacket, and studded armbands.

The girl gave him with a wicked look. "It's my way of getting Elizabet to buy me a new pair of earrings."

The older healer laughed, ruffling Kayla's short brown punked-out hair. "This girl is a never-ending source of joy to me. I'm very glad you crossed my path that night, child." She looked at Kory, Beth, and Eric. "Perhaps you would want to order breakfast? Everything at this cafe is quite good. We've been eating here every morning during the conference."

"How's the conference going?" Beth asked.

"Reasonably well. Any time you gather more than a hundred Wiccans together into one building, there will undoubtedly be chaos. But I believe we are accomplishing something. Just yesterday, we worked on a formal contract of apprenticeship, so that the other witches won't necessarily have to adopt their students, as I have with Kayla."

A waiter took their order, then hurried away. Beth waited

until he was out of earshot, then leaned forward, her elbows on the table. "Liz, I mentioned this over the phone . . . we're here because of a problem. Eric has been having a lot of nightmares lately."

Elizabet stirred her coffee. "Both Kayla and I are experienced at healing traumas and emotional problems, though Kayla's turning out to be better at that than I am. She's done very well with Ria Llewellyn in these last few months."

"How is Ria?" Eric asked neutrally.

"Some days, she's better than others," Kayla replied. "Sometimes she's almost lucid. A few weeks ago, she gave me this." She lifted a small amulet from where it rested on her t-shirt, tugging the necklace over her head and handing it to Eric.

He looked at it closely, wondering where he had seen something like this before. It was a small circle carved out of some kind of translucent rock, maybe a geode, with the outline of a shadowy mountain drawn out of the colors of the rock.

"I'm not certain what it is, but it's unusual," Eric said. "It might be magical, I can't tell."

Kory leaned over to look at it, puzzled. "It looks like one of the mountains in the Faerie Realm," he said thoughtfully. "One of the distant mountains, near the edge of the Lands Underhill."

Eric handed it back to Kayla. "It's probably harmless, but I'd be careful with it, anyhow. Why did Ria give it to you?"

"I don't know. She was nearly catatonic for days afterwards, and then couldn't remember it when I asked her about it. Sometimes I feel like she'll never get better . . ."

"You're doing fine, child." Elizabeth smiled reassuringly at her protégé. "Some healings just take longer than others." She glanced at Eric. "Tell us more about these nightmares, Eric. Are they all the same dream?"

He nodded. "Mostly the same. They're mostly about earthquakes." *And Nightflyers, those shadow-demons that I summoned accidentally several years ago. First at that concert, and then at Ria's, and now in my dreams . . . why do those damn things keep turning up in my life? It's like I have some weird affinity for them, somehow.*

The Nightflyer, bowing to him . . .

"And last night, after we talked about how this could be a precognitive dream, I tried to look into the future. And I saw the same thing as in my dreams, except this time I was awake." He stared down into his cup of coffee. "I'm afraid that I might be seeing the real future, that this is what's going to happen to us."

"What can we do about this?" Kory asked. "If this is a true future that Eric is seeing, we will want to do everything we can to prevent it from becoming reality."

Elizabet thought about it for a minute. "Kayla's very sensitive. If Eric looked into the future again, while she was near him, she might be able to determine if this is a fantasy that Eric is creating in his own mind, or something real."

Eric glanced at the young healer, wondering if he really wanted the punkette kid in his mind.

The girl grinned, showing teeth. "Don't worry, Bard. I'll be gentle."

"Thanks a lot," he muttered.

"We should try this as soon as possible," Elizabet continued. "Maybe tonight."

"There's something else wrong, isn't there?" Beth asked.

Elizabet grimaced, just a little. "Yes, unfortunately. Eric isn't the only one who's had problems with nightmares lately. Several of the Wiccans at the conference have had the same problem. Not dreams about earthquakes, but other things. Kat and Lisa had a similar nightmare, about being hunted by some kind of shadow-creature."

Eric's fingers tightened around his coffee mug.

Beth was quiet for a long moment. "Eric, how soon do you want to do this? We really need to get some rest so we can hit the Embarcadero, or we'll miss the business lunch crowd."

"Okay." He sat back in his chair. "Tomorrow night."

∽   ∽   ∽

Monday, they were standing in the Embarcadero plaza across from the Italian fast-food place where two dozen gray-wool "suits" were busily chowing down on pizza slices.

Beth scanned the crowd, and pointed to a corner with some benches next to it. "How 'bout that one, guys?"

Kory began unpacking the instruments. Eric just stood there for a moment, looking very tired, before he opened his flute case and began to fit the pieces together. Beth couldn't blame him for being tired, considering what had been happening lately. She just hoped that Kayla and Elizabet could do something for him. Maybe some caffeine would help. "Guys, I'm in desperate need of coffee. You too, Eric?"

He nodded blearily.

"Sparkling water for me," Kory said, looking up from where he was seated on the bench, rubbing the bodhran to tighten the drumhead. "The French brand, please."

Elves, she thought. *If we're not careful, Kory'll be the first yuppie elf in history.*

She headed over to the closest food stand, glancing around at the crowd as she stood in line. A shiny new Mercedes, pale blue and with dark-tinted windows, was parked on the street nearby. A blond man in a blue business suit—*the expensive kind,* Beth thought—stood with another man, staring down at a map spread out over the hood of the car. He looked up and saw her watching him. A moment later, he walked up to her, smiling shyly.

"Excuse me, miss?" the man asked. "Could you show me the best way to get to the Japan Center from here? I have a map in my car, but the one-way streets are so confusing. . . ."

"Sure, not a problem." She walked to the curb, where the man's friend was puzzling over a map spread out on the hood of their Mercedes. "Probably the best way is to go straight up to Van Ness, then over to Geary—"

Something hit her hard, in the small of her back, and she fell into the open car door, landing on the back seat. A split-second later she heard the door slam shut, and the sound of the car's engine starting. The interior of the car was very dark, and smelled of new leather and strange chemicals. Something cold and metallic pressed against the back of her neck, and she froze, not daring to breathe. Very slowly, she turned to stare down the barrel of a small pistol, only inches from her face.

The blond man shook the pistol at her like a teacher admonishing a naughty child. "Please, don't bother screaming. No one will hear you outside the car. Now, if you'll just sit back and relax, everything will be fine."

They're right, the barrel of a gun looks awfully huge when you're staring down into it. "If you guys think you're kidnapping me to get a ransom," Beth whispered, "you are in for a big surprise. Why are you doing this?"

"We're not interested in money," the blond man said, and Beth felt the car lurch out into traffic. "Please, don't ask any more questions." He sat back, the pistol resting in his hands.

Beth edged away from him, until her back was pressed against the car door. She glanced down at her watch, noting the time. *Think like a hostage, Kentraine. Be smart. Figure out everything you can about these bastards. Knowledge is power.*

Power. . . .

She tried to calm herself, to concentrate, imagining that long-haired too-handsome face, imagining him seated on the plaza bench, probably already wondering why it was taking her so long to get two cups of coffee and Perrier. . . .

Eric, hear me. Eric, I'm in trouble, I don't know what's going on, but I need your help, you and Kory. Come on, Eric, listen to me. . . .

"Son of a bitch!" The pistol cracked against the side of her face. Everything went white for a moment, and she tasted blood. "You're going to sit there and do nothing and think nothing, girl," the man warned her. "Or I'll kill you."

"Bastard," she muttered, covering her face with her hands, trying not to tremble too much. The tears were harder to fight, but somehow she managed to keep from crying or shaking too much by staring down at her clenched fists in her lap, only occasionally reaching up to wipe away the blood from her mouth.

It was a small room, bare concrete walls painted white, at the end of a series of concrete corridors that led out from the silent underground parking garage. The dark-haired man in front of her was also white, wearing some kind of white laboratory coat. He frowned at her when he saw the blood on her face, and gestured for her to sit down in one of the two wooden chairs in the room. He took the other chair, sitting in front of the plain table with the laptop computer set up upon it. The blond man and his driver took up positions next to the door.

Her jaw still ached, but the pain was nothing as hot as the fury in her brain. *I don't know what in the hell is going on here, but I'm going to kill someone,* she thought. "So, schmuck, why did you bring me here?"

He smiled. "Call this a recruitment drive. We have a form here that you can sign, which'll allow us to treat you as one of the team, defining your legal rights in this situation."

She hardly believed she had heard him say that. "Team of what? Psychopaths? No thanks, slimeball."

"Or we can work out some other arrangement," he continued, as if she hadn't spoken. "But it would be much easier for us if you volunteered. Much easier for you, too."

"Or there's a third option: you can let me go, and maybe I won't send the cops and the mother of all lawsuits against you, mister," Beth said angrily.

"You won't file a lawsuit against us." The man gave her a cold, patronizing smile. "You don't even know where you are, or who I am. If we toss you back out on the street, all you'll be able to do is spin some ridiculous story about being kidnapped by government officials. And no one will believe you, of course."

"So you're a government agency?" *Christ, none of this is making any sense!*

"What is your name?" he asked, glancing down at the laptop computer on the table in front of him.

"Up yours," she replied tightly.

He shook his head. "Not a very original answer. So, tell me about yourself. What are you afraid of?"

Bastards like you. What kind of place is this, anyhow? She didn't bother to answer his question, studying the blank white concrete walls. It looked too solid to be an office building. She remembered the thin plaster walls of the television studio, and how you could hear people yelling through them at every hour of the day and night. This was more like a bunker than an office building . . . who built in concrete slabs, anyhow?

"What are you afraid of?" he repeated.

Police, handcuffs, the blood staining the walls of Phil's house like a surrealist painting . . . run away, before the Feds catch you and lock you up forever in a dark, airless cell. . . . "You know," she said in a conversational voice, "I bet I could break your nose before your goons could stop me. That would be an interesting experiment, wouldn't it?"

The man made a note on his computer, then looked up at the blond man. "Bill, please turn off that fan by the door. Yes, thank you."

She glanced at the fan, then at him. "Why did you do that?"

"It felt a little chilly in here, don't you agree? Don't worry, there's plenty of air circulation in the building." He glanced back down at his computer screen, wrote several more words.

"So, is there anything you're afraid of?" he asked again.

"Damn, it's getting stuffy in here," she muttered, glancing at the fan again. The room seemed smaller, the air already heavier, harder to breathe. . . . "Nothing. Nothing scares me. Especially not an asshole like you. Do you really think you're going to get anything out of me?"

He smiled.

"I think we're finished here, boys. We'll need to go to level 4-A next . . . call ahead to clear the hallways, I'd rather not run into another misguided Berkeley intern who doesn't understand the situation."

"But that's the Aerodynamics level, sir." One of the young thugs had a puzzled expression on his face.

So did Beth, she was sure. *Government . . . Berkeley intern . . . aerodynamics . . . it felt like we were driving for no more than an hour and a half . . . am I in the Dublin Laboratories?* She shuddered involuntarily at the thought of hundreds or thousands of nuclear weapons, possibly only hundreds of feet away from her. *Armageddon at my fingertips. But that's not all they do at the Dublin Labs. Other kinds of research, too. So why am I here? And why in the hell did these idiots kidnap me?*

She stood up slowly, wondering whether she should try to make a run for it, maybe risking getting a bullet in the back. Or maybe she should just wait and see what happened next . . . *they need me for something, hell if I know what. That's what this whole song-and-dance is about. So maybe I wait and see what they want, and then use that against them?*

It seemed like a good idea, as they walked through the empty corridors and down several flights of stairs. Until she saw their destination, the huge metal sphere crouched in a corner of a lab, covered with dials and pressure gauges.

"You're not—" she said whitely, and turned to run. Blondie caught her and she screamed, kicking him hard. He cursed and dropped her, staggering back into a table covered with glass beakers and notebooks. The other thug grabbed her before she could bolt for the door, and shoved her through the narrow metal opening. The tiny chamber reverberated as he slammed the door, spinning the bolts shut tightly. Beth screamed and pounded on the glass window until her hands ached.

All light vanished suddenly as the room outside went dark. Beth slid down the cold metal wall, huddling on the floor of the chamber.

This is insane, they can't do this to me, they can't— A low rumble and hiss of machinery began, and she could feel the air pressure increasing. She swallowed, feeling her ears pop suddenly, and closed her eyes, trying to calm herself.

This can't be happening to me. What kind of lunatic locks someone in a decompression chamber? Especially someone who's . . . claustrophobic . . . like me. . . .

Stay calm, stay calm. Don't let this get to you. They're doing this deliberately, you can't let them win. . . .

She pressed her fists against her face to stop her hands from shaking. She could feel the screams building against her tightly-closed lips. The darkness seemed to close in around her, thickening, too heavy to breathe. An invisible hand tightened around her throat, cutting off her air—

Hyperventilating. I'm hyperventilating. Have to slow down my breathing. Think, Kentraine, there's plenty of air in here, you're not going to suffocate, that's all just in your mind. . . .

Breathe. In, out. In, out. Slowly, calmly, you can do it, just concentrate on your breathing. . . .

Her breath was very loud in the tiny room, gasping for air. She was too hot, it was too hot in here; she ripped open the front of her blouse, just as the room's temperature seemed to plunge by fifty degrees. She wrapped her arms around her knees, and shivered. Nausea hit her like a wave, and she choked, losing the rhythm of her breathing.

God, please, please. . . . She gulped for air, and the panic hit her, overwhelmed her . . . she heard screaming, and recognized it as her own voice. Her stomach emptied itself suddenly, and left her choking on the taste of coffee and bile. She couldn't breathe; the darkness brightened to a checkerboard of glittering black and white, as she shook and trembled and wanted to die.

A creak of metal an eternity later, as the door opened slowly. She tried to get up, but she couldn't stand. The blond man lifted her to her feet, but her legs were trembling too much, and as he let go of her she crumpled back to the metal floor. She couldn't stop crying; she couldn't speak or scream, only cry, deep wrenching sobs that hurt her aching chest.

The dark-haired man shoved a piece of paper and a pen in front of her; she tried to pick up the pen, and dropped it, her fingers too numb to hold anything. "I'm sorry, I'm sorry," she managed between sobs, as they hauled her back to her feet and toward the door.

She couldn't remember how long she walked, gasping

and sobbing and unable to feel the floor beneath her feet. They let her fall down onto a plastic mat, in a small concrete room without a window, but it was cooler, she could feel the chilled air against her skin, not the insane darkness that had clenched her throat and ripped the air from her lungs. She lay there and cried, feeling like something was broken inside, something wrong with her heart and her head. She couldn't think, everything was too blurry and bright and terrifying. She cried and cried, huddled on the plastic, until someone turned off the light overhead, and then she began to scream again.

5

Nonesuch

"No, I didn't see where she went, no, I don't see her anywhere, and will you stop asking me that!" Eric snapped in frustration, "The answer doesn't change by asking the same thing over and over!" He walked as quickly as he could on the crowded sidewalk, craning his neck in vain for a glimpse of Beth. Kory followed him several feet behind, looking uncertainly at the pedestrians on the street.

"But why would Beth leave us here?" the elf asked plaintively.

Eric couldn't help himself; he exploded. "Jesus, Kory, I don't *know*! Stop asking these stupid questions, *okay*?" People glanced at him in startlement at his outburst, then away, quickly. Kory's eyes darkened with anger for a moment—but the moment passed, and Eric tried to put a leash on his temper, feeling ashamed of himself, but too upset to admit it. Something was wrong, something was very wrong, but he didn't know what or why, and that wrongness, coupled with Beth's disappearance, had him at a breaking-point.

"Look," he said tightly, after affronted silence from Kory, "why don't you see if you can figure out which way she went? You're the one with all the experience at—uh—hunting. Don't you have some kind of tracking ability or something?"

More silence for a moment, and he turned to see Kory staring vaguely off into space. "I think she went that way," Kory said, and pointed east.

"How did you figure that out?" Eric said, trying very hard not to snarl. If the elf knew that, why couldn't he figure out where she was exactly?

Kory shrugged helplessly. "Just an intuition. I think she's over there somewhere." Kory waved in the general direction of Oakland, Berkeley, and Alameda.

"Only two million people live in that direction, Kory!" he growled. "Can't you narrow it down a little?"

"We should start searching over there," Korendil replied, his eyes focused on the far distance. "We should search until we find her. That is what any good hunter would do."

Eric couldn't help it; Kory's simplistic "solution" brought out the sarcastic side of him with a vengeance. "Right. You want to start walking through Berkeley and Oakland? You want to go ask two million people if they've seen her? Be my guest. It should only take you about fifty years or so."

Kory gave him a level look. "Have you a better plan?"

Eric's mouth tightened. "I'm going to retrace our route and figure out where she might've gone, whether anybody saw her leave, all of that. If you want to go off on a wild goose chase across half of the Bay Area, then do it! I'm going to do this scientifically, like the cops do . . . damn shame we can't call any of them in for this."

He thought about it for another minute. "Besides," he continued, half to himself, "maybe Beth just decided to go home." But the mere idea had a false ring to it. *Without telling us. When she'd just gone to get coffee. Sure.* "You can do what you want. But I think the first thing we should do is check around here some more, then check back at the house in case she left a message, and then make a plan of action if we still haven't gotten anywhere."

Kory nodded, as if Eric had answered him, then picked up his and Beth's instrument cases and began walking away.

Eric stared at the moving crowd of business-people, wondering where to start. *She went for coffee and mineral water. That means it was one of these places here . . . maybe the donut place, or the Italian food stand . . .*

A flash of something colorful and familiar caught his eye; he looked up just in time to see Kory walk aboard a Metro bus, not fifteen feet away from him, and the door closed behind him.

"Goddammit, Kory!" Eric ran to the bus, nearly falling into the path of a speeding BMW as the bus pulled away into traffic. "Dammit, Kory, I didn't mean it!"

The bus pulled away, Kory still on it, doubtless headed for Berkeley. He gave chase for another futile minute, then gave it up as he avoided death by Beemer for a second time.

He sat down on the curb, winded, and wondered what in the hell he was going to do next. Beth missing, and Kory vanishing off to search the East Bay house by house. . . .

For one selfish moment, Eric seriously considered burying his face in his hands and crying, but that wouldn't exactly be constructive. Kory knew where he was; he knew how to get around on his own. And he could have magical resources he hadn't told either of his human partners about, maybe things he couldn't do while they were around. Maybe he would be able to kick something up if he went off on a lone hunt. And if he didn't, well, he knew Eric would be going home if he came up dry. So if Kory had gone off to hunt the way an elf could, playing a magical MacGyver, Eric had better go play Spenser Junior, boy detective.

First stop, the donut shop.

He pushed the door open, and the bell over it jangled as shrilly as his nerves. "Excuse me, miss?" he asked the young woman behind the counter. "I'm looking for someone. . . ."

"Well, you've found someone." The woman looked like she'd come straight out of a James Dean movie, pink waitress uniform and bleached, teased hair and all; she glanced at him from across a tray of fresh donuts, and smiled flirtatiously. "What can I do for you, handsome?"

He didn't answer the smile. "A friend of mine is missing. Tall gal, long red hair, very pretty . . ."

"Sorry, I don't notice the women very much. Want a

donut?" Her continuing smile suggested that he might want
to try something else instead of a donut. Eric felt the blush
beginning at his ears, and fought it, somewhat unsuccess-
fully.

"You haven't seen anyone like that?" he persisted.

The smile faded. "No, can't say I have." She turned away
from him, plainly dismissing him as a lost cause. He spoke
to her back as he pushed the door open again.

"All right. Thanks." She ignored him.

He quickly retreated from the donut shop, looking around
for other likely places. The sushi stand probably didn't sell
coffee, or the Thai shop, but the Italian place. . . .

The portly, elderly man behind the stand nodded with
recognition as Eric described Beth. "Pretty gal, long red
hair? Stacked?"

At last! "Yeah," he said eagerly, "that's her."

The old man rubbed the top of his bald head, and smiled
at him the way you'd smile at a slightly stupid child. "I don't
think you need to worry about her. She left with some
friends. I saw her talking with them on the curb, then they
all left in their car."

*Friends? A car? Why wouldn't she have come back for
us?* "What kind of car?" He couldn't believe she'd just leave
like that if it really was friends. So it had to be something
else altogether. Cops? Maybe the Feds had caught up with
her? But that didn't match the feeling of wrongness. . . .

"A nice car," the old man replied vaguely. "A really nice
car. It was blue."

Eric tried to imagine just how many "nice blue" cars
existed in the Bay Area. "Great. Thanks. You've been a real
help." *Shit.*

He turned away from the stand to ponder his next move.
*All right, think this through. Beth wouldn't just leave without
telling us where she was going. Those guys weren't friends,
no way. Besides, we don't know anybody with "nice" cars;
everybody we know drives wrecks. Maybe they were Feds,
or something worse. But what could be worse than Feds?*

He didn't want to think about that.

∽   ∽   ∽

Four hours later, he didn't want to think about anything. No sign of Beth, and no new clues other than the old man's comments about her "leaving with friends." Eric sat heavily on a bench, wondering what he was supposed to do next. Go home? But that wouldn't accomplish anything either, and it would take him away from one end of the "trail," such as it was.

At five P.M., the Embarcadero Plaza was like a sea of human beings, waves of people headed toward the parking lots, Metro, and BART stations. He lay on his back on the bench at the edge of the stream of humanity, looking up at the four tall skyscrapers and a glimpse of blue sky, and tried to come up with some tactic he hadn't tried yet.

"Excuse me, can you help me?"

He jumped in startlement. "What?"

Eric looked up to see a young, blond man in a blue suit smiling at him. Blond, handsome, but not as cute as Kory. He smiled back, without any real feeling.

The young man took a step closer. "I'm a little lost. I've got a map over here, but I don't know where I am on it exactly. Do you know how to get to—" The man gestured at his car, parked in a red zone a few feet away, with a city map spread out over the hood.

Eric froze.

A blue car. A Mercedes.

A nice blue car. Just like the one that drove away with Beth—

Eric tried to jump away and fell off the bench, landing on his hands and knees. Before the man could react, he vaulted to his feet, and took off like a sprinter towards the plaza. The blond man cursed and grabbed for him; Eric felt his hand catch and slip off the fabric of Eric's jacket.

If there had been any doubts as to the man's intentions, that move had canceled them.

Eric leaped over another bench, dodging around a trio of businesswomen and a young man selling flowers. He clutched his flute case to his chest as he ran across the plaza, trying to spot a place to hide. In the Embarcadero, there weren't very many options.

He tripped over the curb, dashing across the street as the traffic light changed to green. Drivers honked at him, then a squeal of brakes behind him caught his attention. He glanced back to see a car skid to a stop inches from the blond man, who was only a few seconds behind Eric.

He turned the corner, and then another, hearing the man's running feet close behind him . . . and stopped short, confronted by a blank wall.

A dead-end alley. Dead, just like he was going to be, if that blond guy caught up with him.

He glanced back, trying not to panic. No time to get the flute out of its case. No time for anything, in fact. Except maybe to yell for help and hope somebody paid attention.

Or to try magic-music without the flute.

He puckered up, took a deep breath, and began to whistle the first thing that came to his mind, thinking very hard about being invisible. His mind had no sense of priorities; it chose a jaunty Irish tune, "The Rakes of Mallow." He nearly lost the melody as the blond man dashed around the corner, slipping on some of the scattered garbage. The stranger quickly regained his footing, and looked around the alley.

Frowning.

His glance slid over Eric as though he wasn't there.

I'm not, really. Just part of the garbage in the alley, m'friend. Managing to calm down a little, since the trick was working, Eric whistled the B part, willing the man to give up, turn away; willing the man to see nothing.

It was a long, tense moment.

Finally the blond man obliged, a snarl of frustration on his face, walking back toward the plaza.

It was tempting to run off. Even more tempting to stay where he was—

Beth. If those men have her—

Still whistling, Eric strolled after him, simultaneously thinking about being invisible while rooting in his pocket for the stub of pencil he usually kept there. He snatched up a bit of litter as the man reached his car, then jotted

down the number of the Mercedes' license plate on the
scrap of sandwich-paper he'd caught up. The blond man
conferred with another business-suited type standing by the
car, then they both got into their vehicle and drove away.

Eric didn't stop whistling until the car turned the corner onto Market Street and disappeared into traffic.

Then he sat down on the curb and thought, very hard.
Harder than he ever had in his life. About kidnappers in
fancy cars. Kory, who was still gone after several hours. And
Bardic music, which had saved them once, back in Los
Angeles, and was probably the only thing which could save
them this time.

*God knows, I sure can't go to the San Francisco cops
over this! And where in the hell is Kory?*

Korendil, Knight of Elfhame Sun-Descending and Elfhame Mist-Hold, squire of the High Court, Magus Minor,
and Child of Danaan, stood with his arms crossed, trying
to understand the forces behind an electrical fence.

He had sensed the danger from it, and noted the way
that the grass had been carefully cleared away from it. Then,
trying to understand what was so alarming about a plain
metal fence strung with wires, he was treated to the spectacular sight of what happened when a hapless sparrow had
the bad sense to try landing on the fence.

Just as dazzling as his battle with Perenor, in a small way
. . . and with the same result for the sparrow.

It would seem that climbing this fence is not a good idea,
he thought, considering the scorched bird lying dead at his
feet. *Even if Beth is here, somewhere under the ground
ahead of me.* She was there; he was sure of it. It had been
intensely frustrating to try to make the Bard understand that
his ability to track Beth depended not so much on spell-
born magic as on the spiritual bond that the three of them
had forged. Tracing her had been like playing the child's
game of "warm—getting warmer." That was as close as he
could come.

Perhaps it was just as well that Eric had remained
behind to try human means of tracking. Without the Bard

nearby to confuse the vague tuggings in his heart, it was
easier to pinpoint Beth. He walked back toward the road
and the place where the bus driver had stopped to let
him out, and then to the guard gate. Beyond the gate,
he saw that the road led into a large parking lot, surrounded by several block-like gray buildings. "Excuse me?"
he asked politely, knocking on the glass panel of the
guardhouse at the gate.

The panel slid open, and a woman peered belligerently
out at him. She wore a uniform that Kory liked immediately, a dark blue jumpsuit with different badges pinned on
it. It was very attractive. The woman would have been, too,
if she had not been frowning. He wondered what he could
possibly have done that would so raise her ire.

"Go away, kid. Your peacenik friends aren't doing their
annual blockade of the Labs until next month." Her teeth
bared in something less like a smile than a snarl. "Unless
you want to start early. You could spend the next month
in jail, until the rest of them arrive."

He shook his head, not understanding the woman's
strange speech. "No, I am not wanting to go to jail. I'm
here looking for a friend of mine. I believe she is inside
this place."

"Hmmmph. Should have said so." The woman gave him
an odd look, but softened her frown a little. "You look so
much like one of those hippie-activists, I figured you were
here to make trouble."

"No, no trouble," Kory said earnestly. "I just want to find
my friend."

"What's your friend's name?" she asked, consulting a
printed list.

Now he was getting somewhere. "Beth. Bethany Mar-
garet Kentraine."

The woman shook her head. "Sorry, she's not on the
cleared list. Maybe she's working back at the University?
A lot of the interns get switched back and forth between
the various labs . . ."

The sense of *Bethness* was even stronger now. Why was
this woman claiming that Beth was not there? "I know she

is here," he protested. "Down there—" he pointed off in the distance.

The woman's expression hardened. "Sorry. If she's not on my list, she's not here. You'd better move along, now."

"But I have to find Beth," he told her stubbornly. He turned away from her and began walking through the tall metal gates.

"Hey, kid!" The woman called from behind him. He heard the sound of sirens going off, a shrill wailing noise. Kory kept walking.

The next sound he couldn't ignore, a loud blast of noise from directly behind him. He turned . . .

. . . and found that he was looking down the twin barrels of a shotgun.

"Back through the gate, kid," the security guard gestured with the shotgun. "No one goes into the Labs without clearance. You seem like a nice boy, but you can't go any further."

He looked over the gun into the woman's eyes, pleadingly, trying to trap her gaze. "Please, I have to find Beth. I promise I won't damage anything here—" He caught her eyes; held them with his own. Touched her mind.

:Please . . . just let me walk through.:

The woman nodded, slowly, her eyes blank and unseeing, and Kory turned away, satisfied that she would no longer impede him. He continued down the road toward one of the square, squat buildings. Several people with drawn guns ran past him, heading for the gate-house. Movies and television he had seen suggested that they were answering the alarms the woman had triggered—but the same shows also told him that if he acted as if he belonged here, rather than as an intruder, they would ignore him without the intervention of magic.

He let himself in through the double glass doors of the largest building, looking around curiously. Another human in a similar uniform to the woman was seated behind a large desk. Before the man could respond to the door opening, Kory touched his mind as well; he glanced at Kory, then back at a screen on the table, ignoring the presence of a stranger. A bright red light was flashing on his desk; he paid no more attention to it than he did to Kory.

Kory crossed the sterile, white-painted entry-hall, stopped in front of a large row of elevators, and pressed the button. He looked up as another team of blue-jumpsuited humans ran to the double glass doors, taking up odd positions near the glass. It reminded him of another one of the movies he and Eric had watched on the television, with the policemen moving in pretty, dance-like patterns through rooms and stairways, hunting for an enemy. These humans seemed to be running in the same patterns, one dashing forward and then stopping behind a desk or a potted plant, and then another running past the first one, to stop at another desk or potted plant. It would probably be a good idea to leave the area as quickly as he could. The humans would not be inclined to ignore him for much longer, and he wasn't certain he could hold all of their minds at once.

The elevator arrived with a happy DING! sound, and the doors opened. Kory stepped inside, and stopped, freezing as a primal fear chilled him through all of his veins.

Iron. Cold Iron, all around him. Not touching him, but close enough that he could feel the chill on his skin, the whisper of death in the silent metal.

He wanted to turn and run, to get as far away from this place as possible. He'd been in elevators before . . . Eric and Beth had taken him up in the elevator to the top floor of a place called The Hyatt, so they could drink wine in a restaurant and watch the sunset from a vista of windows overlooking the city. But this elevator was different, built of more solid metals, more deadly metals.

He took a deep breath, and reached for the button panel inside the elevator. He couldn't retreat; not with a lobby full of wary, angry humans behind him. And besides, all of his instincts told him he had followed the right path. *Beth is down there. I cannot leave her here. The iron will not harm me, it is hidden behind layers of plastic and other metals. I can ignore it. I can do this. I can.*

The elevator doors closed. Kory kept a tight hold on

himself, fought down his fear, and considered the array of buttons, each one with a peculiar slot next to it.

He tried to decide which one to try first. He knew Beth was on one of the lower levels, but how deep? He could spend days in this place, trying each button.

Just to get started, he pressed one button. The elevator did not move.

Odd. Elevators move to the floor you press. So why wasn't this one moving? Kory chewed his lip, and again noticed the strange slots, next to each button.

The slots were roughly the size of one of Beth's old credit cards . . . he remembered how impressed he had been by the idea of giving someone a piece of plastic and in return they would give you all kinds of clothing, boots, even food. But Beth said they couldn't use her cards anymore, the police could track them that way.

In any case, he didn't have any of Beth's credit cards with him, not now. If he needed one of those cards to make the elevator work, this might turn out to be more difficult than he thought.

Perhaps there was an easier way. . . .

He knelt and pressed his hand against the elevator floor, twitching slightly at the feel of plastic against his palm. *But not Cold Iron. I can touch this, it won't hurt me.*

He pressed harder, a magical push against the elevator floor, forcing it downward.

The elevator descended silently, and Kory closed his eyes, trying to imagine where Beth might be, trying to "reach out and touch someone," as Eric always joked, trying to find . . .

There! The elevator chimed and the doors slid open for him.

It was another featureless hallway, with a young man seated behind another desk. Kory looked at the man's badges and insignia, and decided that he did want a badge with his own picture on it. Perhaps after he and Beth left this place, they could go find someone who made those badges. . . .

"Hey, how did you get down here? Where's your security badge?" the young man blurted, as Kory approached.

The sign over the young man's desk was interesting:
Psychic Research Wing. Q Clearance Required.

Psychic . . . Kory knew he'd heard that word somewhere
before. Perhaps Beth, talking with one of her Wiccan friends.
Clearance, now that was a word he understood . . . that was
when everything was half-price at Macy's, and Beth had to
go buy clothes for herself. Together, though, the sentences
did not make much sense to him.

As Kory considered this, the youth reached under his
desk, and when his hand emerged, he held a small pistol, aimed directly at Kory with an assurance that told the
elf that the human knew how to use this thing, and use
it well.

*:Please. You should not threaten someone, especially a
warrior like myself. I do not intend you any harm. I am
seeking my friend Beth Kentraine. I know she is here,
somewhere . . . have you seen her?:*

The young man stared at him, his hand dropping, his
mouth and mind both opening like poppies in the sun. An
image appeared in Kory's mind, of a woman walking down
a hallway . . . no, barely able to walk, a stranger supporting her on either side. A door closing, and the sign 13-A
Room 12 on the wall outside it.

"Thank you," Kory said gravely, and started down the
corridor. Behind him, he heard the clatter of the pistol
falling to the ground, followed shortly by the sound of a
body landing on the plastic floor.

He carefully followed the row of signs, each labeling a
closed door. From behind one door, he could hear someone crying, as if from a very far distance. Someone was
calling out hoarsely from behind another door, the words
too faint to understand. He stopped in front of "13-A Room
12," and tried the doorknob. It refused to open. Kory
frowned, and considered the lock for a moment, then closed
his eyes, gathering his will.

Korendil was not a Great Mage, not as innately talented
as the Bard, but Terenil had taught him a few tricks, in
the years before caffeine and depression had claimed the
elven prince. Such as how to escape from a locked cell, if

necessary. But a trick for breaking out from a cell ought to work for breaking into a cell . . . He touched a fingertip to the lock, and willed the door to open, the bolts to slide back. A soft click, and he turned the knob, opening the door to look within.

It was quiet, and dark. He stepped into the small room, allowing his eyes to adjust to the darkness. Someone was huddled on the floor against the far wall, not moving.

"Beth?" he called quietly.

The figure did not move. Kory held out his hand, calling light, and a soft glow filled the room.

"Beth?"

Kory.

He was staring at her, those leaf-green eyes reflecting the light in his hand. He was so handsome . . . and so far away, outside of her skin, too far for her to touch.

She was cut off from everything, everyone, smothered in fear and darkness. Just like when she was two and she'd followed her folks out into the dig, and the trench they'd abandoned had collapsed, burying her. Dirt had filled her mouth, like this thick darkness—suffocated her, just like the darkness was doing now. One of the grad students had seen her hand and dug her out; he'd known CPR. . . .

But there was no friendly grad student here, and Kory didn't know CPR, and anyway this darkness was thicker and more treacherous than dirt.

She wanted to say something to him, but the silence within her head was too loud, drowning out everything, her thoughts, her words. Somehow he didn't seem to see it, the thick darkness pressing in all around them, closing her in, pinning her against the wall. Even with the light in his hand, she could see that the light itself was being eaten by the darkness, becoming part of the screaming in her mind that wouldn't stop, couldn't stop. She felt the tears welling up again, and wrapped her arms more tightly around her knees, trying not to cry.

He knelt next to her, touching her face. With another surge of horror, she realized that she couldn't feel his hand, couldn't feel anything. All of her body was numb, lifeless. She was dead, only her heart hadn't figured that out yet; it was still beating somehow, a wild, erratic rhythm.

I need to tell him about the darkness, Beth thought, desperately. *I need to tell him about how the room is pressing against my skin, that there's no air to breathe, no way to escape.*

She opened her mouth to tell him, and the voice screaming in her mind filled the room with sound, and it wouldn't stop, it wouldn't let her go. . . .

"Beth?"

She was staring at him, not saying anything. Something was wrong. He didn't understand. She should be glad to see him; he'd come to take her away: Why was she looking at him that way, and not speaking? She recognized him, he knew that, but why wouldn't she say anything?

She was sitting strangely, too, all curled up against the wall. He'd never seen Beth sit like that . . . usually she sprawled out on a couch, or draped herself over a chair like one of the stray cats he occasionally brought into the house for milk and conversation. He saw that she was trembling as she tightened her arms around her knees.

Hesitantly, he reached to touch her face, a gentle caress. Her eyes stared at him, unblinking. She didn't smile or laugh the way she usually did, when his fingers brushed against the ticklish spot on her neck.

Something was very, very wrong.

Then she began to say something, and Kory smiled in relief. If she would just tell him what was wrong, then he could do something—

She screamed.

The shriek pierced Kory like a knife. Panic closed his throat as he tried to calm her and got no reaction, not even recognition in her eyes. He didn't know what to do, if there was anything he could do . . . the sound seemed wrenched out of Beth's throat, ending in deep sobs that shook her entire body.

He did the only thing he could think of. He sat down

on the cold plastic floor beside her, and held her until her body stopped shaking, and she closed her eyes.

He thought she might be asleep. At least she wasn't screaming. But if she woke again, with that animal-like fear filling her eyes—what was he going to do?

He wished desperately that Eric was with him, to help him understand what was happening to Beth, to help him figure out how to help her.

One thing was certain . . . Beth was sick. This wasn't like the other human sicknesses he had seen, with Eric lying in bed for several days, his nose very red, and coughing frequently. Or the time that Beth had lost her voice; she'd only been able to speak in a funny hoarse voice that made all of them laugh. He knew those sicknesses; even elves were touched with Winter Sickness, though very rarely.

. This was something different. He'd never seen one of the Folk with this kind of sickness, unable to talk or move. Even the friends that he'd lost to Dreaming, they had just slipped away into a last sleep, never to awaken. Beth's sickness was something he didn't understand, something he'd never seen before. She needed a healer, like Elizabet or Kayla—

But the first thing he had to do was take her from this strange place with their clearances and too many guns, and back to San Francisco. Once back at home, with Eric, the Bard might be able to help her—or they could go fetch the healers.

A good plan of action.

But before he could move, the door slammed shut. Kory looked up, then stood up carefully, trying not to awaken Beth. He crossed to the door, trying the lock.

It wouldn't open. He glanced down at the orb of light in his hand, and sent it into the lock, to open the door for him again.

Nothing happened.

"Damn, that's impressive," a voice on the other side of the door said thoughtfully.

Kory glared at the door and the unseen person behind it. Without eye-contact, he would not be able to get the human on the other side to help him. Rage burned in his heart as he realized that this must be the person who had put her here in the first place—perhaps even the person who had given her this illness. *I must get out of here, now! Beth is hurt, sick, and no one is going to keep us locked up!*

He hurled his will at the door, a magical blast that should've broken the door in two.

Nothing happened.

Beyond furious, Kory flung himself at the door, pounding on it with both hands. After several seconds of futile effort, he stepped back, considering the situation.

A sound from Beth, and he turned. She was lying on her side, crying again, and hitting her fist against the floor. He knelt swiftly beside her and caught her hand, afraid that she would injure herself, and pulled her gently into his lap. He tightened his arms around her, truly afraid for the first time since they had left Los Angeles. For the first time since he had awakened in the Grove, he was alone and helpless.

Eric, something is very wrong with Beth, and we cannot leave this room, and I do not know what to do. . . .

Warden Blair hid a smile and listened to Smythe babble. The security guard was sweating, now, and Blair enjoyed making people sweat. "No, sir, I can't explain what happened. Yes, you're correct, he didn't hit me physically, but something knocked me out. I don't know whether he had a gas canister concealed on his person, or it was some new kind of weapon, or . . ."

"Enough with the excuses, Smythe," Blair said tersely. "So, this is the sequence of events . . . Wildmann at the gate reports a Caucasian male intruder, long blond hair and green eyes, roughly age twenty-five. She says that he is polite to her, but tries to walk into the installation. She hits the red button, fires a warning shot, pulls the shotgun on him, and he vanishes, right in front of her eyes. Just disappears into thin air. Somehow he gets into this building, lobby security reports nothing, and he gets past the elevator security system as well. Then the guy waltzes in here, you can't stop him, he breaks into one of the rooms . . . which sets off the alarm, something you weren't capable of doing . . ." Smythe flinched visibly. " . . . and then Harris locks him in there, with one of our patients, using the new security system."

"Well, if he pulled some kind of trick on Wildmann, then maybe that's what he did to me," Smythe said faintly.

"Or maybe you and Wildmann are both equally incompetent." Blair pointed at his office door. "Get out of here, Smythe. Go find something useful to do, like collect unemployment."

The young man's eyes widened. "You can't fire me!"

"I just did." He touched his intercom button. "Harris, please come to my office immediately."

The young man clenched his jaw and spoke through his teeth. "If you fire me, Blair, I'll go to the newspapers. I have a friend at the *Chronicle,* they'd love to hear about this project. I know that not all of the patients are here voluntarily, I know that you tricked some of them into signing the consent forms, some of these people aren't mentally competent enough to sign a consent form—"

"Don't bother," Blair said, cutting off the torrent of threats. "If you talk to the press, you'll be in more trouble than you can possibly imagine." Blair leaned forward, elbows on his desk, narrowed his eyes, and smiled. "Keep this in mind, Smythe. I can find you. Anywhere. You know that's the truth. If you try and sabotage this project, I'll find you. And I'll bring Mabel with me, or one of the others. You remember what Mabel did to Dr. Richardson, right? You were the one to find him, as I remember."

Smythe's face was as pale as the whitewashed concrete walls of Blair's office. "All that blood from his nose and mouth . . . she didn't just kill him, I could see his brains oozing out through his ears . . . you wouldn't do that to someone, sir!"

Blair's smile widened.

A knock on the door interrupted them. "Come in," Blair said, enjoying the sight of the young man's bloodless face. Harris walked in, glancing curiously at Smythe.

"Escort Mr. Smythe out of the complex," Blair said quietly. "He is no longer employed with Project Cassandra."

"Of course, sir."

Smythe swallowed awkwardly, and spoke. "I'm not scared of you, Blair. You—you wouldn't do that deliberately to someone."

Blair met his eyes and held them. "Do you really want to find out?" he said softly.

After a moment, the young man broke eye-contact and shook his head. Blair noticed with satisfaction that his hands were shaking as well. Harris walked him out, closing the office door behind him.

Blair leaned back in his chair, propping his feet on his desk. *Idiots,* he thought. *I'm surrounded by incompetent idiots. Even Harris, who lost that kid today in San Francisco. He still can't explain how the kid got out of a dead-end alley. Fools.*

Then he smiled, thinking about his latest . . . patient. *Someone who can get through our top security systems, show up thirteen levels underground in a complex that's supposed to be impervious to the best terrorists and foreign agents in the world . . . I want to take this one apart. I want to find out what he can do, find out how to use him.*

I'll need a good leash on this one, though. Probably the girl; that seems to be what brought him in here in the first place. She's useless to me right now, anyhow. And she may be ruined completely—I underestimated the effects of her claustrophobia.

And then there's the other boy. He registered even higher, a bright light shining in the darkness of San Francisco. We'll get him, too.

I'll prove to those bastards at DoD that we can do it. All of them that said I was a crackpot, that this could never work . . . they'll see. When I show them someone who can walk through security systems like they don't exist, or someone can ditch a top military agent like Harris in less than ten seconds, they'll believe me then . . . they'll have to believe me.

Still smiling, Blair shoved his chair away from the desk and left his office, walking down the corridor to meet his newest acquisition.

6

The Hanged Man's Reel

"Kory? Beth?"

Eric stood in the front hallway, burdened with two armfuls of musical instruments, hoping against hope that the next thing he'd hear would be a resounding "Eric, you're home!" from Beth, followed by a hug from Kory and a kiss from Beth. Then they'd all laugh about the weird events of the day, and probably still be laughing as they piled into the bubbling hot tub. . . .

Only silence greeted him.

He walked down the hallway and into the kitchen, sitting down at the table and burying his face in his hands. He looked up longingly at the bottle of Black Bush on the counter, then away.

No. No whiskey. I've got to think, to figure this out—

It had gone so bad, so quickly. Now he didn't know what to do. He'd envisioned disasters, figuring that their good luck was too good to last, but there'd always been things like . . . Kory falling off a ladder while fixing the roof. Beth, slipping on the wet deck near the hot tub. Himself, setting the kitchen on fire while trying to make pancakes. But not this, never this.

His first impulse was to run. They'd kept a small amount of cash in the house for just that reason, in case the cops came knocking at their door one afternoon and they had to run fast. He could catch the night bus out of town with that money, be out of California and into Oregon by daybreak, and he'd be out of reach of the local cops. Except that blond man hadn't acted like a cop—a local cop would've flashed a badge and slapped a pair of handcuffs on him before he could blink, and hauled him away in a black-and-white . . .

That expensive blue car. Policemen don't drive Mercedes. In any case, he couldn't leave Beth and Kory behind. Two years ago, sure, not a problem, but not now. They were the closest damn thing he had for family, and he wouldn't abandon them.

The lyrics from a Faire song drifted across his thoughts: "No, nay, never . . . no, nay, never, no more, will I play the Wild Rover, no, never, no more . . ."

And I won't, Eric thought. *They're depending on me. I won't let them down.*

Except how in the hell am I supposed to help them? I don't know where they are, what could've happened to them . . .

What can I do?

He wanted to scream, or cry.

Instead, he set his flute case on the table, and opened it.

The flute lay there quietly against the crushed velvet, no hint of anything that had happened before reflected in the silvery metal. No sign of dragons, or elven sorcerers, or shadow-demons called up from the darkness . . . no hint of anything, in fact, just a simple musical instrument waiting to be played upon. Eric quickly fitted the pieces together, and played a quiet note, a long A tone. He slid down a mournful minor scale, then into a run of arpeggios. It was hard to concentrate, when his mind kept slipping back to Beth and Kory, and the dark fears that he kept suppressing, holding at bay—*I'll find them. They're out there, somewhere. I'm a Bard, I can use the magic, I can do it. I'll find them.*

Then he began to play "Planxty Powers," an old O'Carolan tune, one that the Irish bard had composed in honor of Fanny Powers, perhaps his lover, certainly his friend. The tune brought back a rush of memories to Eric, of sitting around on haybales at the Renaissance Faire, drinking mulled wine and playing music with friends. Of the first time he'd met Beth; how she'd flashed her ankles at him while dancing a strathspey in the Scottish show, then asked him to teach her that strathspey tune, so she could play along on her ocarina.

And Kory . . . how he'd come home late from the Southern Faire, to find an elf living in his apartment . . . those earnest green eyes, asking him to help. . . .

I won't fail you, pal. I'll find you . . . I'll find you. . . .

The music wove itself into strands of light around him, bright sparkles reflecting off the kitchen windows. He called it closer, and the light danced around him. Within it, he searched for them, calling up images of Kory and Beth, casting his vision out further and further into the city around him . . .

The light became a glow, with him encased at the heart. A softly glowing sphere, that showed him flitting images of the life of the city beyond; places they had been, places they had touched. The park, dark and mostly deserted now, shadows filling the space below the trees. The BART station near the house, as bright as the park was dark, trains pulling up to the platform in uncanny silence. The wharf, bustling with tourists. The Castro district, bustling with . . . a different kind of life. The Embarcadero, the Pig and Whistle where they sometimes played, the Opera House. . . .

All of the scenes, flitting silently in, then out of focus, as his heart searched the city below for the people he loved.

Now the scenes were unfamiliar, and a little less focused; streets, houses, lawns. . . .

Buildings, tall ones, like offices, but with a more closed-in look.

A corridor—

He caught a glimpse of Beth, and concentrated, trying to see exactly where she was. It was difficult, holding the melody and the magic, delicately reaching. . . .

"Beth! Bethy, can you hear me?"

∾   ∾   ∾

Blair smiled at the young boy seated next to the closed door to Room 12. Harris stood next to the door, an intense blue-eyed watchdog. "How are you doing, Timothy?" he asked.

"Just fine, Mr. Blair," the boy replied. "The bad man inside, he's stopped trying to get out. I guess he's figured out that I won't let him."

"Good work, Timothy." Blair nodded to Harris, who gently moved the boy away from the door. "Now let's talk with this new fellow. Timothy, don't open the door unless you hear my voice, okay?"

"You bet, Mr. Blair."

Harris checked his handgun in its shoulder holster, and opened the door quickly, scanning the room before stepping aside to let Blair enter the room.

The newest acquisition to the Project was seated on the floor next to the red-haired woman. The woman seemed to be asleep, but even across the room, Blair could still sense the turmoil in her mind. The blond man looked up at Blair with eyes burning with fury.

That's right, little fellow, Blair thought. *Hate me. Give me a handle to use on you, a window into your thoughts. Let's see what you're afraid of. . . .*

:You think to imprison me, a Knight of the Seleighe Court? And now you try to entrap my mind! I'll kill you first, bastard!:

Blair couldn't understand all of that . . . *what in the hell is a Seelie Court?* . . . but he certainly understood the way the young man launched himself from the floor, hands reaching for Blair's throat.

Harris intercepted easily, hurling the kid against the wall. Harris always made it look so easy. Years of practice, Blair thought, a little enviously. Harris was used to the difficult ones, the ones that tried to fight before they settled down to become a useful part of the Project.

Harris crossed to where the woman was slumped against the wall. Grabbing her long hair with one hand, he drew his handgun with the other, pressing it lightly against her temple. The woman flinched once at the touch of the metal against her face, but otherwise was completely unaware of anything happening around her.

The young man moved painfully from where he had fallen onto the concrete floor. A trickle of blood slid from his mouth; he ignored it, looking up at Blair and Harris with eyes filled with hatred.

"Now, let's talk," Blair said calmly, sitting down on the bare concrete floor. "I don't think I need to explain Harris' role in this, do I? Behave yourself and be a good boy, and tell me what I want to know, and nothing will happen to your friend. Understand?"

:Never, Unseleighe scum. I will kill you and leave your bodies lying for the forest creatures to feed upon, I will curse your names for a thousand years, I will laugh as your blood pools at my feet, I will do anything to kill you, even brave the touch of Cold Iron itself.:

Blair blinked, astonished at the clarity of the young man's thoughts. "I don't think you understand your situation," he said slowly. "You aren't in any position to—"

He stopped short. The key—the kid had given him the key without even realizing it! Admittedly, it was the strangest phobia he'd ever heard of in his life, but it was a lock-hold he could use. . . .

"I'll be back in a minute, Harris," he said thoughtfully, and left the room.

At the end of the hallway, in the new construction area, he found what he was looking for. It took a little improvisation with a pair of handcuffs and some wire, but then he had what he needed.

Of course, he didn't understand why the kid was so afraid of certain kinds of metal, but that didn't matter. The fears themselves were unimportant; it was the effect of the fears upon the subject that was so valuable. He walked back into Room 12, and held out the contraption with a smile. The kid's eyes widened.

Blair moved cautiously toward the young man, handcuffs ready in one hand. Suddenly everything happened very fast; the kid knocked the handcuffs out of Blair's hand, making a dash for the door; Harris dropped the handgun and tackled him from behind, wrestling with him until Blair could snap the modified handcuffs onto his wrists.

The kid screamed, a long gut-wrenching wail of despair, as the wire wrapped around the handcuffs touched his bare wrists. Then he fainted.

Well, it wasn't exactly the response Blair had wanted, but it was a good start. He'd never seen such an immediate physiological reaction to a mental aberration, but that didn't matter. It just meant that it would be easier to work with the kid, later.

Then he saw the pistol, lying on the floor next to the woman. She was staring at it, uncomprehending. Her hand twitched, moved toward the handgun. . . .

"STOP!" Blair shouted at the top of his voice.

The woman jerked her hand back, clutching her hands to her mouth. She began to cry again.

Harris, breathing hard, reached down to pick up the pistol. "Sorry, boss," he said. "Next time, I'll be more careful."

"You'd better be," Blair said tersely. "We can't afford any more mistakes." He glanced at the unconscious blond boy. "We'll start with him in the morning."

The image faded. He reached out his hand, through the layers of light, as Beth's face disappeared into the shadows.

Eric set down the flute. *So much for magic,* he thought. *After all's said and done, it can't help me find my friends.*

He tried to think of another plan of action . . . maybe calling the cops? It would mean some awkward questions to answer, and possibly a lot of trouble over Phil's death, but the more he thought about that, he decided it was worth the risk. Sure, they might have found some physical evidence that he and Beth were at Phil's house after he was killed, but the odds that they could conjure up some proof that he and Beth were the killers . . . *not too damn likely,* he thought. *It's worth the risk.*

His hand was reaching for the phone, and it hit him a split-second later.

Fire and ice, burning upward from his wrists, an unbelievable pain that knocked him out of the chair. He didn't feel the impact against the floor, but lay there, gasping for breath. Then Kory's voice, screaming in his mind—

:*Eric, help me!*:

A flurry of images, too fast for Eric to recognize. The pain ripped through him, an agony that went on and on, not stopping. . . .

Darkness.

Eric curled into a ball on the floor, tasting blood where he'd bitten his tongue. For several long seconds, all he could do was lie there and breathe. Then the realization hit him.

Kory. That was Kory. Somehow he made me feel what he was feeling, somehow he . . .

Oh, Christ, is he dead? Could someone have gone through . . . whatever that was . . . and survived? He could be dying right now!

He took several deep breaths, closing his eyes and concentrating on the images that had flashed through his mind.

Beth, huddled in the corner of a room, illuminated by witchlight . . . what is wrong with her, why won't she speak to me?

A pair of handcuffs, wrapped with some kind of wire. . . .

A woman at a gate, refusing to let him pass. A sign on the gate, black words printed on white . . . Dublin Laboratories. Authorized personnel only.

Eric sat up abruptly, his fists clenched. "Kory, what in the hell were you doing in the Dublin Labs?"

He remembered joining some Faire friends for the yearly protest, sitting in the street in front of the gate until the cops showed up to take them away. The armed guards, the electric fence, the ground beyond the fence was probably filled with land mines, for all he knew. . . .

He thought about the impossibility of breaking into the Labs to rescue them . . . *for God's sake, they build nuclear bombs there! The place has the best security in the world, millions of armed guards! How am I supposed to get them out of a place like that?*

What in the hell are Kory and Beth doing in a place like that?

He sat there, breathing unsteadily, wondering what he was supposed to do next. A single-handed assault on the Dublin Labs just didn't seem like a good plan. If he had a personal army, maybe he'd have a chance. But alone . . .

No. He wasn't alone. They had friends in San Francisco, good friends who would help them out. Especially when he told them what Kory had told him, just before their "connection" had been cut. The Mist-Hold Elves, sure, they'd help in a second.

If Kory was still alive. . . .

He forced himself to relax. Panicking wouldn't solve anything. He began dialing.

Five minutes later, he'd listened to eight answering machine messages, two unanswered ringing phones, and one "This number is out of service, and there is no new number" message.

What a great night for this, he thought sourly. *Everyone's out at the Forty-Niners game. Terrific. Couldn't the Bad Guys have picked something other than a Monday night for their kidnapping and attempted murder?*

He dialed the last number on his list, the Holiday Inn near Pier 39. After two rings, someone picked up the phone.

"Elizabet?" Kayla asked. Even across the phone lines, Eric could tell instantly that she was crying.

"Kayla, this is Eric. What's wrong?"

The girl spoke all in a rush. "Elizabet went downstairs to buy a stupid newspaper, she didn't come back, it's been over two hours, the stupid local cops say that's too soon to file a missing person report, I'm all alone in this stupid city and I know something's wrong, I *know* it—"

"Whoa, slow down!" Eric tried to kick his mind into overdrive. *Three disappearances in one day? A coincidence? Not bloody likely.* "Elizabet's not the only one who's disappeared today." He quickly described the events of the day, and the images Kory had sent to him, and the unbelievable pain he'd felt at the same time.

"That sounds bad," Kayla said seriously, gulping down

her tears, and getting herself under tight control. "I don't know too much about elven physiology, just what Elizabet and I learned after that fight at Griffith Park . . . I don't think Cold Iron is immediately fatal, not unless it breaks the skin. I'm not certain about that. Elves are so weird, it's hard to say. One of the L.A. elves told us about how long-term exposure to Cold Iron is deadly, but I think he said it took a couple days to kill someone."

Eric realized he had been holding his breath, and reminded himself to keep breathing. "Thank God. So Kory's probably still alive."

"Yeah, but he must be in a world of hurt." Kayla's voice was tight. "Cold Iron apparently triggers all of the nerve synapses continuously during the time of exposure. It's like having your hand stuck permanently in an electrical socket. Really weird. Elizabet has always wanted to know more about it, since we're doing a lot of work with the L.A. elven community now, but we can't exactly do experiments with it, y'know? All of our information is secondhand, and usually hundreds of years old."

"You'd better start at the beginning, Kayla. When exactly did Elizabet disappear? And did you see anyone suspicious around Elizabet today?" *Like two guys in suits, driving a pale blue Mercedes?*

"Okay, okay." He heard the sound of her blowing her nose on the other end of the phone line. "Elizabet and I spent all day at the conference. It was great, I met this priestess from Mendocino who loves Oingo Boingo's latest album as much as I do . . . anyhow, we came directly back to the hotel after the last discussion ended. I didn't see anyone following us or anything like that when we were walking back."

"Anyone suspicious at the conference?" he asked, waiting for the payoff.

"Well . . . yes. These three guys showed up right as we were about to break for the night. They were wearing business suits, so they stood out like sore thumbs against all of us."

Bingo.

"Did you see their car? Was it a blue Mercedes?" he asked, breathlessly.

"No, they were still hanging around the conference when we left, asking questions of various people." Kayla's voice took on a harder tone. "So, Eric, what's your plan? What are we going to do?"

Plan? You mean, I'm supposed to have a plan? Eric suppressed an impulse to blither insanely and spoke quietly instead. "We'll get them back, of course."

"How?"

"First, I'm coming over to your hotel to get you. Don't open the door for *anyone*," he said, wondering if Kayla was on their list, whoever *they* were. "I'll be over there as soon as I can."

He hung up the phone, thinking fast. Bus service in San Francisco was one of the best in the world, but the buses would stop running in another couple hours.

If only he had a car. . . .

But he did have transportation. Two motorcycles. In the garage.

Except he didn't know how to ride a motorcycle.

Except these motorcycles were really elvensteeds, old friends of Kory's that had agreed to live with them and pretend to be motorcycles. They were Faerie horses, they just looked like motorcycles. At least, that was what Kory said.

He slung his flute case under one arm, grabbed two helmets from the hall closet, and headed to the garage. Inside, the two motorcycles sat tamely. Kory had sent the two bikes—horses—back over to the Faerie Court that morning (since they didn't like Earth-style horse feed, or so they said), so at least they were well-fed. Or fully fueled, depending on how you thought about it.

"Listen, horses," Eric said awkwardly. "I have to ask a favor of you. Kory and Beth are missing, and I need to find them. I don't know how to ride either horses *or* motorcycles, so you'll have to get me there. I gotta get over to the Holiday Inn at Pier 39 and get Kayla, 'cause they have Elizabet too. Are you willing?"

For an answer, the bright red and gold motorcycle's engine coughed into life, revving loudly. A moment later, the other bike followed suit.

"Uh, thanks. I appreciate it." He lifted the garage door, then sat gingerly on the red bike, stuffing the flute case into the tank bag and fastening the spare helmet onto the seat clip. "Hey, you," he called to the black and silver bike, "You'll just have to follow us, okay? We need to get Kayla before anything else. She may be in danger too, I don't know."

The black bike's headlight flashed once. Eric assumed that meant an affirmative, but he wasn't certain.

"All right, then," he muttered. "Time for the cavalry to come to the rescue."

The bike sat motionless for a long second, and Eric began to wonder whether or not this was going to work. Then the bike kicked itself into gear, popped the clutch, and vaulted out of the garage so fast that Eric nearly fell off. A split-second later, the black bike followed them into the street.

It's just a horse, Eric thought dizzily, as the bike weaved through the cars, heading straight down Geary toward the Pier. *It's just a horse. And it's only doing . . . eighty-five miles an hour. In a thirty-five zone. Oh my God.*

Eric tried to look calm, tried to look like he was actually controlling the bike and knew what he was doing, but after the third high-velocity skidding turn around a corner, he gave up and wrapped his arms around the tank bag, holding on for dear life. The bike made a noise between an engine cough and a chuckle, and accelerated through a red light and into another high-speed left turn. Eric closed his eyes and refused to open them.

The wail of a police siren forced him to look up. One of San Fran's finest was right on their tail. The two bikes swerved through another right turn, heading due west off Van Ness up into one of the hilltop residential areas. *We're going in the wrong direction!* Eric thought, glancing back as the police car followed them up the hill. The bikes zigzagged through a small series of streets, then turned north again. Eric's heart and stomach both leaped into his throat as he realized they were heading straight for a large stone stairway leading back down into the city below.

With all lights off. As if that made any difference.

"No, don't!" he yelled involuntarily as the bike leaped up onto the sidewalk and then down the stairs. The police car screamed to a stop at the sidewalk behind them. The bike bounced down the stairs, jolting Eric with every one, and skidded to a stop at the bottom of the stairway. It revved its engine, waiting for the black bike to reach the street beside it.

The rest of the ride to Pier 39, thank God, was totally uneventful.

Eric left the bikes parked on the street near the hotel's back entrance, and hurried up the stairs to Kayla's room. He knocked on the door, then knocked again. "Hey, Kayla!" he called, suddenly afraid that he might not have gotten there in time.

The door opened suddenly, and a small hand reached out, grabbed him by the wrist, and yanked him into the room. Kayla quickly shut and locked the door.

"They're out there," the girl said quietly, her back against the door. "Three guys in business suits. They don't have a warrant, so I wouldn't open the door for them."

"Smart thinking, Kayla. Was one of them a young, blond, muscular guy?" Eric asked.

"No. All older men, in their forties or fifties. They weren't the same guys I saw earlier today at the conference."

"We'd better assume they all work for the same company." Eric walked to the window, looking down. "It's a big drop, do you think you can do it? Or do you want to risk going through the hotel?"

She bit her lip, but looked not only determined, but eager. "Of course I can do it. How are we going to get away, though? Did you bring a car?"

Eric thought about the two motorcycles, now parked sedately in the motel lot. "Uh, no, not exactly."

She shrugged. "Well, let's get moving, Bard. Hallway or window?"

"Let's try the hallway first," he said. He opened the hotel room door, glancing down the corridor.

Three men in business suits. Not ten feet away from his nose. Eric slammed the door shut.

"Then again, the window is probably a better idea." He picked up a chair, advancing on the window. "Stand back, kid, this'll probably make a real mess."

"No shit, Sherlock." Kayla stood next to the door, and visibly flinched as someone pounded on it hard from the other side.

Eric swung the chair hard against the glass. It shattered loudly, almost loud enough to hide the sound of two someones slamming themselves against the hotel room door. The door buckled, but held.

"Come on, kid!" Kayla ran toward him, as a gunshot echoed from the corridor outside. One of the three men kicked the door open, just as Eric grabbed Kayla and dived through the window.

They fell haphazardly toward the street below. Somehow he had managed to pucker up and begin to whistle a descending melodic minor scale as they exited—in the final quarter second, their tumble slowed to a high deceleration, but impact-less landing.

The motorcycles rolled up beside them a moment later, engines rumbling.

Kayla blinked and stared at the riderless bikes.

"It's okay, they're friends." Eric climbed onto the red bike. "Just hang on real tight, okay? They don't slow down for turns."

"Hey, I've never fallen off a bike in my life," Kayla said, seating herself on the black bike. "Except maybe if you count that time up in Wrightwood . . . SHIT!" The black motorcycle made a strange noise, something that sounded vaguely like a horse's whinny, as it accelerated out of the parking lot. Eric glanced once at the speedometer as the bikes headed toward the Bay Bridge, and wished he hadn't. *Can't they wait to do ninety miles an hour until we're at least on the freeway?*

"What now?" Kayla whispered, staring at the huge flood-light-illuminated area beyond the guard gate.

"I don't know," Eric replied. *What we need is an army,* he thought. *The U.S. Cavalry coming over the hill.*

It never works out like this in the movies. You never see the hero crouching in the dirt, trying to figure out a plan that won't get him killed. Usually the hero just walks right in, guns blazing, and rescues everyone. Wish I could do that.

Dammit, I'm a Bard! I should be able to do something! Everyone always treats me like I can do anything; all the elves are so sickeningly respectful toward me, even a lot of Beth's Wiccan friends. They all think I'm hot stuff. He remembered meeting Kory's cousin, the exotic dancer, and how the elf had bowed so courteously to him when Kory introduced him as "Eric, the Bard—"

Another flash of memory: standing amid the ruins of Castro Street, and the shadow-creature bowing to him—

It hit him like flash of light, the sudden realization of what he could do.

I need an army. So I'll call an army.

I can do it, he thought. *I've done it before, it's so easy. And they'll answer me, they always have. I can summon an army of them and make them obey me. Nothing can stand against them, nothing can kill them, no guns or explosives or anything. I can bring them here, control them, and use them against my enemies.*

But my dream, with the Nightflyers taking over the city . . . is it because of me, because of what I'm thinking of doing right now?

No. I can control them, keep them from killing anyone. I kept that one from hurting Ria, right?

I'll have to risk it. I don't have any choice.

He took his flute from the case, and played a quiet set of arpeggios, warming up.

Kayla grinned. "I knew you'd think of something, Eric!" she crowed. "What are you going to do, fly us over the gate or something?"

"Better than that," he muttered. "I'm calling the cavalry."

There was no Irish tune that he could use for this. But he knew exactly the tune to play. "Danse Macabre."

The first notes were deceptively soft, the calm before the storm. Then the violin solo, the notes hammering down like nails in a coffin, followed by the melody, faster and harsher . . .

He could feel it starting around him, the gathering of tension in the air, whispers of sound beyond normal human hearing. The shadows on the grass, visibly darkening as he played, slowly rising from the ground. Fingers of cold ran down his back, but he ignored them, concentrating on the music.

"Eric, what in the hell are you doing?" Kayla looked around in alarm at the thickening shadows around them.

A wild flurry of notes, and they encircled him, drifting shapes that danced with the wind. He called to them, and they answered, laughing silently as he brought them to him, one by one. When he finally let the flute fall away from his lips, they floated before him, a huge shadow-army awaiting his command.

While he was caught up in the music, he'd been fearless; now he saw them, and he was terrified.

Chills ran down his spine—a cold born of fear that he'd gotten himself into something he could not get out of again. He'd had trouble controlling *one* Nightflyer—whatever had made him think he could control an army?

Did he control them? Or were they controlling him? Had they used him to bring them here?

Kayla crouched beside him, visibly pale and trembling. He wanted to say something to calm her, but he could feel his Nightflyers testing his power over them, tugging at their leashes, and he knew what would happen if they escaped his control, even for a moment.

No choice. He was in it; he'd have to finish it. There were only two ways to get out of this one. A winner, or Nightflyer-dessert. He stood up, and started toward the front gate. "*Now* we're going to rescue them," he said, with *far* more confidence than he felt, his shadow-troops adrift behind him.

7

A Maid in Bedlam

"W-wait a minute," Kayla stammered, pulling at his sleeve. "Wh-what if they get away from you?" Her eyes were big and round and her face pale in the faint light that reached them from the lab parking lots.

He started to brush her off, a little drunk with sheer power, with the intoxication of controlling so many of the creatures—

But doubt set in immediately; did he *really* control them? Sure, they came when he called, but was that control? Could he really keep them from doing something they wanted and he didn't? And what would happen when they were out of his sight? He recalled the Nightflyer of his vision bowing to him with a shudder. Was that what had happened in that glimpse of the future? Would he lose control of his army?

Would they somehow destroy the city? A chill ran up his back and he shivered at the memory of the dream— and that waking-dream of his vision.

He surveyed the horde of Nightflyers, shadows against the shadows. There was nothing to suggest he was not the one in control, at least for now. He swallowed once, and told himself that he wouldn't lose control of them—because he didn't dare.

But that meant that there was no more time for

441

hesitation. Right now, this moment, they were his completely. If he waited a moment longer, they might not be. But he needed time to think!

Very well, he'd buy himself some time.

He was operating on pure instinct here, but the elves had told him, time and time again, that he could trust those instincts. He followed his impulse and froze them in their places with a brief, chilling run, pitched a little sharp with his nervousness. The notes bit like acid, but they did the job; the Nightflyers stopped moving, completely, giving him the unsettling impression that he was watching a movie on freeze-frame.

Now what?

He stared at them, while he made up his mind exactly what he wanted from these creatures. One of the themes that occurred over and over in the stories of encounters with the supernatural was "be careful what you ask for." There should be no "loopholes" in what he demanded of the monsters, no way that they could obey his orders and still follow their own wishes. He needed them to create as much havoc in there as possible. But only within the confines of the labs; he couldn't afford to let even one escape, not if that vision was true and the things could breed.

A fence; that was what he needed. A way to confine them to the grounds of the labs. But something like that would take more magic than he had by himself. He needed some help, and time was trickling away: time that Kory couldn't afford. By himself, he was a battery, and his charge was running out; he needed a wall-socket, or better yet, a generator—

The nexus!

Every elven community on this side of Underhill centered about a nexus, a place where the fabric between the worlds had been pierced, and the result stabilized to permit magical energy to pass into the human world. Sometimes a nexus had been created, often it occurred naturally. All of the greatest, most populous communities centered on a correspondingly powerful nexus. Elfhame Mist-Hold in San Francisco was no exception.

The magical forces the elves used could also be used, with varying success, by humans with the proper talents.

Humans such as Bards, for instance.

No sooner thought of than tapped; he'd *created* a nexus once, with the help of Spiral Dance. He certainly knew how that wellspring of magical energy looked and felt like, how it acted. Though he'd never actually been there, he knew where the major nexus here in the San Francisco area was; he couldn't *not* know, such things were magnets to him. He had only to remember what the magic felt like and *reach*—

The energy responded to his touch before he was ready for it.

He lost the world for a moment, engulfed in a tidal wave of power; it surged up around him in a flood of golden light and sweet music, capturing him and spinning him around like a bit of cork in a whirlpool.

Dizzy and disoriented, he fought his way back to himself only by concentrating on the metal flute still clenched in his hands. His eyes weren't working properly; instead of seeing his real surroundings, he Saw the power, swirling around him, gold and amber, lemon and umber. After a moment he blinked, and found himself back on the hillside above the labs, still facing the army of shadowy Nightflyers. They hadn't moved, so however shaken he'd been, his momentary lapse of control hadn't affected the hold he had on them.

And Kayla still stared at him, her hand clutching his sleeve, so although it felt as if hours had passed, it couldn't have been more than a few seconds. The only songs he could think of on the spur of the moment that involved fences were all cowboy ballads—

Well, whatever worked.

Although the Nightflyers had been immobilized, he sensed that they were aware of what was going on. Now that he had tapped into the nexus-magic, he felt their excitement—and their hunger—centered on him. Suddenly he had gone from "commander" to "prime rib special." It was not the most comfortable feeling in the world. Hurriedly, he called up the first "fence" tune that came to mind,

spinning the power into a boundary around the lab complex, following the fence and roofing it over as well.

They were not·pleased with that—he felt a sullen glow
of dull anger emanating from them; a sickly heat that irri-
tated rather than comforted. But before they reacted further, he directed their attention to the complex, creating
a dazzling little bubble of energy, moving it to dance for
a moment just above the gatehouse, then popping it.

Their reaction was not what he had expected. He lost
their interest entirely. Except for the control he still held
over them, he might just as well be one of the rocks on
the hillside. There was something down there that he
couldn't sense—something that the Nightflyers wanted,
badly. If they had been hungry when they felt him tap the
power of the elves' nexus, they were ravenous now. And
he had been demoted from "prime rib" to "leftover veggies."

Well, whatever it was, if it occupied their attention, that
was fine with him. The less attractive he looked to them,
the better. And if it was a "who," rather than a "what"—

Conscience twinged for a moment, but he thought of the
brief glimpse he'd had of Beth, the pain he'd felt from Kory.
And he told himself that anybody who worked in a place
that would kidnap and torture people, damn well deserved
what he was going to get when the Nightflyers found him!
They tugged at their restraints, eager to be off; he checked
the barriers between the lab and the outside world one more
time and found them solid.

Time for one last precaution. He emitted a burst of
power, and they turned back to him, like so many dark rags
snapping in a high wind.

"There's some people down there," he said, slowly, thinking the words as he said them and hoping they would get
the sense of them. "They look like this—"

He pictured Beth, Kory, and Elizabet, spinning images
of them out of the dusk and fog and faint starlight. Beside
him, Kayla relaxed marginally. The Nightflyers stirred,
impatiently. They cared nothing for these images; not when
there was something waiting for them that they found much
more intriguing.

He called their wandering attention back to the images. *"Don't touch them,"* he said forcefully, impressing his will on them—

—or trying, anyway.

"Don't touch them," he said again. "Don't hurt them, don't frighten them. Leave them alone. Or else—" He didn't know what to threaten them with, so he left it at that. Evidently they didn't realize that, or they didn't care, for he felt their preoccupied assent. They strained to get at whatever it was that was so attracting them, and after a moment to let their tension build, he released them.

They streamed towards the labs, and he and Kayla trailed in their wake. Kayla clung to his arm, silent—Eric kept his apprehension and doubts to himself. Sure, he and Kayla saw the Nightflyers—but what about ordinary people? Could the monsters affect them as well? Would they be able to get rid of the guards, like the muscle-bound gorilla in the little glass-enclosed booth at the gate?

He got his answer immediately, as a pair of them swarmed the lighted gatehouse, flowing into it and filling it with an impenetrable darkness. When they flowed out again, there was no sign of the man who had been inside. Eric averted his eyes as he and Kayla passed; guilty, and not sure whether or not he should be. God only knew what the Nightflyers had done to the guard, a man who hadn't done Eric any harm, who might not have any connection with what had been done to Beth and Kory. He couldn't even remember if Dublin Labs used rent-a-cops on their gates, or real company employees. . . .

"What—what did they do?" Kayla whispered, nervously, staying right with him, glancing at the silent gatehouse out of the corner of her eye. There was nothing moving in there. Whatever the Nightflyers had done, it had been permanent.

His fault.

"I don't know," he admitted, as his feeling of guilt and sickness increased. He wished that there had been another choice, something else he could have done. Now he knew what the "sorcerer's apprentice" felt like, unleashing a power he didn't really understand and wasn't entirely certain he controlled. A power that just might turn on him if it wasn't satisfied.

Kind of like riding the tiger. Don't get thrown off, and don't get off if it's hungry. And try not to look when it eats someone else, someone who never did you any harm. Eric, you're a real louse, you know that?

Kayla shivered, and he hugged her shoulders, glad of the human warmth of her. They went about a hundred yards further in, then Kayla tugged him to a stop. "I th-think we'd better stay here," she stammered. "Th-the others have to come this way to get out. If-if we k-keep going, w-we might miss them."

If we keep going, we're going to have to look at what the monsters are doing in there, he thought—but nodded, and let her tug him off the sidewalk, into the shelter of a crescent of bushes and trees. Ahead of them, inside those formidable buildings, the Nightflyers were looking for something. Whether or not they found it, they would be encountering more people in those halls and buildings; people who would probably meet the same fate as the guard. Death? Worse than death? He was beginning to hate himself, beginning to wish he had *thought* before he'd done anything. People were always telling him that— "Eric, why don't you think before you jump in?" Well, this time he'd jumped in, like always, only people were going to die.

Yeah, but they're people who grabbed Beth and Kory and tortured them! They've probably done things like that to lots of people! I mean, God only knows what they do in there—maybe they're testing nerve gas on street people, grabbing winos for drug testing—

But did that give him the right to act the way they did?

Fiercely he told his conscience to *shut up,* and followed his army.

There would be no walls and barriers to hide the Nightflyers' victims in there. And he didn't want to see them.

Maybe it was wrong of him to avoid witnessing the results of his work. Certainly it was cowardly. He wasn't going to rationalize that fact away, but he also wasn't going to watch what they were doing. And if he didn't have to see the victims afterwards, he wasn't going to. What was the point? It wouldn't make him feel worse than he did now, just sicker, at a time when he couldn't afford any weakness.

What he *was* going to do, however, was to stand here with Kayla, keep tapping into that nexus of elven power, and keep those walls standing tall and strong between his personal horrors and the outside world. No matter how many or few innocents there were inside this complex, the ones outside it were all innocent, at least of doing anything to him.

One by one, the lights shining from the windows of the buildings began to dim, and he and Kayla shivered together, avoiding the shadows beneath the trees.

Elizabet sat quietly in the corner of her cell, ignoring the outside world—which at the moment was a generous ten foot by ten foot cube. She kept her concentration turned completely inward, carefully regulating her heart-rate and brain-wave patterns so that it would appear that she was semi-conscious, terrified into near-catatonia as her captors seemed to want.

Be fair, now, she chided herself. There was only one of her captors that wanted her prostrate with fear. That repellent man, the one calling himself Warden Blair, who was clearly the one in charge. She had seen his type before. *Forty going on nine. Nasty little man.* This was the first time she'd been in the power of someone of that type, but she had a fair idea of what to expect. Brilliant, ruthless, sociopathic.

Leader of a group of those like him, he would carefully collect them; he would cultivate them, set himself up as a substitute father-figure, and collect blackmail material on them so that if they actually began to think for themselves, they could be threatened and would never dare leave his employ. Elizabet had most often encountered these little pods of psychopaths in the sciences. They were usually involved in the hard sciences: physics, computer sciences, and math. But they occurred in the "softer" sciences too, as Warden Blair's little cabal proved.

They had been nasty little children, no doubt of it; the kind that tortured and tormented other kids' pets and hid in books and laboratories. Later, they joined Mensa in college and went into psychology not to discover themselves but to find out how best to stick knives into the souls of those they considered inferior to themselves. They tended to be mostly boys; girls in general were more connected to society than boys, even when abused. That was certainly the case here; in fact, she hadn't seen any women here in anything but strictly subordinate roles. This "project" of Blair's was a kind of boy's club in many ways, where females were still "icky," still "the enemy"—for there wasn't a one of these men that had grown emotionally beyond the age of nine. That was probably why the little-boy psychics that backed up the guards here worked for Warden Blair so readily. He was one of them; their pack-leader, their Peter Pan. And it explained why he was so eager to destroy her mental stability. A man like Blair would not tolerate a strong, independent woman anywhere about him. Any woman in his "project" would have to be reduced to the status of nonperson.

Well, none of that got her free of this place. And thinking about him made her angry. Anger disturbed her equilibrium, and if she wasn't careful, that would give her away to the monitors. She was certain that there *were* monitors. They hadn't attached any wires to her, but she had no doubt that every bodily and mental function that could be monitored was being watched. In this ultra-secret complex there must be a great many technological breakthroughs available to the scientists that the general public wouldn't see for a decade or more.

Being duped into captivity had been her first and last mistake. After the initial shock and the drug they'd used on her had worn off—which was long before the car she was in reached the lab complex—she was ready and wary, feigning a fear and confusion she did not feel.

She suspected they had been relying heavily on the drug to keep her disoriented. They must not have ever had a healer with as high a drug tolerance as she had, and she had no intention of letting them know how quickly their narcotics wore off, how little they affected her. If they did, they'd drug her again, and she intended to retain her advantage.

Warden Blair had revealed more to her about himself than he dreamed, and certainly she had given very little away to him. His open questions about what frightened her, for instance—so clumsy even a CIA operative would have been ashamed. Even if he'd had someone with telepathic skills monitoring her, the chances that a telepath could penetrate her mind to read more than she allowed him to see were slim to none. She let him think that she was afraid of the dark; a simple phobia, and being left in total darkness was no hardship to her. And it was pitifully obvious from Blair's clumsy threats that he had no notion just how extensive her personal contacts were—nor how high up they reached. She had favors owed to her by some fairly high-powered lawyers and private investigators—not to mention Ria Llewellyn's still-loyal second-in-command—and when she failed to return from this conference, there were going to be several people asking awkward questions. People it would be difficult to shut up. People with money, political influence, or both.

Warden Blair was going to discover he'd taken the wrong "holdover hippie"—that was one of the kindest things he'd called her when she failed to give him any real answers to his questions. Interesting that his intelligence was so poor; either he wasn't relying on government sources, or someone was withholding information from him. Was that happening at the source, or in his own organization? She rather hoped it was the former; attempts to probe her files should set off alarms that would alert some of her friends—and her friends' friends—to the fact that Warden Blair was showing an unhealthy interest in her. Add that to her turning up missing, and the FBI might come calling, asking Dr. Blair some very awkward questions.

With luck, they'd demand to inspect the premises. There were others here besides herself; she'd sensed them as she cautiously explored the confines of her prison. She didn't dare go further than that; her telepathy was not all that strong, and she could not know if who she touched was a friend and fellow prisoner or one of Blair's tame psychics.

Of course, waiting for official help was going to take time, and time was critical for some of her patients. If she could manage it, she should try for an escape on her own. She knew that she must be in a sub-basement of some kind; that was frustrating, since it meant that even if she won free of her cell, getting to the outside was going to be very difficult. On the other hand, she was middle-aged, female, and black—and if she could find a cleaning-woman's smock, she could probably scrub her way to freedom. *No one ever looks at janitors. Particularly not black women janitors.*

The more she thought about it, the more appeal that idea had. The only problem with it was that left the others she had sensed still locked away.

Could she walk away and leave them there? They didn't have influential friends; it was just a matter of accident that she did. Her own influential friends would be unlikely to move very energetically on behalf of other nebulous captives on her word alone—they would be unlikely to move if their own interests weren't involved. She didn't know names, faces—if she couldn't actually cite the names of people known to be missing, Blair could say she was crazy, deny that there was any such thing going on here. It couldn't be that hard to hide a few dozen people; not with all the government facilities that must be available to him.

Miserable little lizard, she thought bitterly. How soon would it be before Blair's flunkies caught Kayla? That was a thought that truly chilled her. If this were Los Angeles, she wouldn't have worried; Kayla's extensive street-side connections made her impossible to catch on her home turf. But this wasn't Los Angeles, and Kayla hadn't had the time to make those connections here. She was essentially trapped in her hotel room, unless she had the wits to call Beth Kentraine for help—

She was also a minor, whose guardian had vanished. She could be charged with anything and "arrested," taken into "protective custody," and no one would make any complaints.

Except Kayla herself. Which wouldn't change a thing.

But even as she thought of Kayla—Kayla in Blair's hands—*something* changed. As real as a storm-front, as full of potential, and as difficult to pin down without the proper instruments, the passing of this "change-front" raised goose-flesh on her arms and brought all of her senses to alert. Elizabet wasn't a precognitive, but she was at least a little sensitive in every extrasensory area.

Something had just happened, out there, outside the walls of this lab. Something that changed everything, that negated every calculation, every plan. And unless she was very much mistaken, all hell was about to break loose. Her Gram used to say, "When devil walk, people should hide."

It certainly felt like devils were walking.

Be damned to Blair's monitors. If this was as big as it felt, it wouldn't matter what the monitors recorded. Blair was about to have a surprise. Fire, flood, earthquake, or something she couldn't even guess at—these labs were going to experience catastrophe. If there was enough confusion, she would be able to walk right out. She gave up her pretense of catatonia in favor of the tightest barriers she could raise, and sheltered behind them. Waiting.

Something told her that the wait wasn't going to be long.

Dr. Susan Sheffield watched the needle of the seismo-graph with one eye, and the rest of the instruments with the other. One of her techs followed the countdown silently, lips moving. When he reached zero, he clutched involun-tarily at the edge of the desk, even though the probabil-ity of them actually *feeling* anything, even if this run was successful, was less than half a percent.

Unless, of course, by pure coincidence, they had cho-sen the moment Mother Nature had picked for a shake to run Poseidon.

Nothing happened of course. It would take several minutes for Poseidon to vibrate this little faultlet loose, even under the best of circumstances. They'd only picked it because it ran directly under the Dublin Labs property, one of hundreds of little cracks coming from the San Andreas.

"Ia, Shub-Niggurath," muttered Frank Rogers, her partner.

"Say what?" she replied, without removing her attention from the instruments. Oh, they'd record whatever happened, but *if* it happened, she wanted to see it.

"Lovecraft," he told her. "Howard Phillips. Horror writer. Shub-Niggurath was one of his Elder Gods—the 'Black Goat of the Woods With a Thousand Young.' I was thinking the San Andreas is like that—Big Mama Nasty with a thousand little nasties spawned from her. The little nasties wouldn't matter squat if Mama wasn't there to back them up."

"Yeah, well if Poseidon works today, we'll have a way to lasso Mama," she said. "And we'll have the data to prove it."

Just at that moment, the needle jumped—tracking the course of a quakelet on the scrolling paper. "Shut it off!" she yelled, as she sprinted over to the bank of other geological instruments. The tech threw the switch and shut Poseidon down as she and Frank frantically took sight-readings in case any of the recording monitors might possibly have failed. Every reading Sue took made her feel like cheering more. Finally Frank let out a whoop. "Hot *damn!*" he yelled, waving his clipboard. "Come look at this one!"

The rack of crude sensors was entirely dead. As it should be; they measured nothing—only registered electrical flow across pairs of contacts set all along the faultline at varying depths. That they were all dead meant that the contacts were no longer touching.

Which meant the fault had moved, easing stress. Quietly, infinitesimally, without so much as a beaker shaking. And along the *entire* faultline.

Poseidon was an array of devices that were the sonic equivalent of a laser: coherent sound. What Frank and Susan had proposed was that if a Poseidon line could be set up along a fault under stress—like the San Andreas—low-frequency, coherent soundwaves could trigger tiny quakelets along the entire length, for as long and as often as it took to ease stress along the faultline. So far it had worked well enough to warrant a bigger proposal, taking the project out of the stage of pure research and into the stage of attempted application. The Big One everyone dreaded might never happen now. . . .

And the pinheaded holdover hippies that picketed every month might be persuaded that there was *legitimate* research going on here. Susan was getting damned tired of running a gauntlet once a month, and wondering if this time *she* would be the one who'd have to spend hours getting red paint off her car.

Not that there wasn't a military application to Poseidon— but Frank had agreed with her to destroy the figures and any reference to their other finding. That one single Poseidon CSAA (coherent sound amplification array) placed at a point of maximum stress *could* trigger a "Big One." *She* was far more right-wing than Frank, and she didn't want that information in the hands of the military. All it took was one nut . . . and unlike radioactives, CSAAs didn't require any equipment that couldn't be bought on the open market—nor did they need bombers or ICBMs to deliver them. Just a good power-source.

And earthquakes didn't discriminate between civilian and military targets. In fact, civilians were far more likely to be the victims; the technology that made military structures hardened against nuclear attacks also made them earthquake-resistant.

No—the military didn't need to know about Poseidon.

"You know, I just had a horrible thought," Frank said, turning toward her with a look of stark terror on his face.

"What?" she asked, alarmed.

"Remember when they put through that law about fault-line disclosure, and all those scumbag real-estate scammers couldn't sell their fault-line property?" he moaned. "You realize we're about to make those parasites *rich?*"

She sighed and started to make a snappy comeback— when the hair on the back of her neck started to rise.

Warden Blair rarely left his lab complex between seven in the morning and midnight; about the only thing that could lure him outside the walls was the prospect of another pickup.

The walls of his office were studded with television monitors, one for every cell in the complex. Most of them were uninteresting; the occupants were asleep or drugged unconscious. One of the catches from today, a black woman, was one of those—the only thing that made her interesting was that she had passed out in the corner of her cell, wedged into a sitting position. *Stubborn bitch.*

She'd been worse than that red-haired piece; she hadn't been anything less than polite, but she'd been just as adamant in refusing to give him any information at all and in refusing to sign up on the project. She'd stared at him and answered—when she answered at all—in words of one syllable, as if she was speaking to a particularly dense child. When he refused to answer any of her questions, she gave him a look of disgust and disdain—exactly like the one his ninth-grade teacher had given him when she discovered the frog he was dissecting was still alive.

Bitch. The word applied both to Mrs. Bucher and this hag. They both made him feel like a naughty little boy without saying a word. Well, it was too late to do anything about Mrs. Bucher, but this old bag was going to find out she was sneering at the wrong man. Maybe he'd turn Bobbie loose on her . . . when Bobbie got done, she'd be a lot more cooperative.

The other new catches, now—they were much more interesting. The man was, anyway. They'd finally had to take the cuffs off him a half an hour ago; all the devices they had monitoring vital signs went into red-alert. Heart rate was way above the safe line, brain-scan showed seizure conditions and unbearable pain. Blair had never seen so severe a psychosomatic reaction—especially not to something as nonsensical as physical contact with metal.

Now the young man huddled in the corner, head sheltered in his arms. The attendants reported that there were burn marks two inches wide circling each wrist.

So, he not only had a new type of psychic, he had someone who could reproduce stigmata-type marks. He'd been wanting to get his hands on a stigmatic for some time—the problem was every single genuine stigmatic was protected by a horde of Catholic stooges.

Once he got his hand on the third member of that little gypsy trio, and the kid who'd been with the old bat, he'd have *quite* a little stable. More than enough to impress—

The monitors went blank. All of them, at the same time.

For a moment, he stared at them, unable to believe that his state-of-the-art, triply redundant equipment had just failed on him.

No—it *couldn't* have failed on him. Someone out there had pulled the plug on his office.

He surged to his feet, suffused with rage. Whoever that someone was, he was going to pay—

He headed for the door, but before he took more than two steps, something came through it.

Through the *closed* door.

Something dark, shadowy. And very big. But transparent, and his mind dismissed it as a projection or an illusion. One or two of his stable were quite adept at creating projections, and if something had gone wrong with the equipment, the electronic fields that kept them from sending their creations outside their cells might also have malfunctioned.

He was quite certain it was harmless. Until he touched it.

Then he screamed with pain and shock—screamed even louder as it enveloped him, sure that one of his men would break down the door and save him. But his men had troubles of their own. . . .

He continued to scream for a very long time.

8

Hame, Hame, Hame

Kory huddled for a long time in the shelter of his folded arms, waiting for the pain to ebb, waiting for his body to recover from the shock of prolonged contact with the Death Metal. Physical shock was not the only thing he had to recover from; his mental processes had undergone similar damage. He did not understand these humans, the ones who had imprisoned him. Oh, abstractly he had known that there were humans who were sick, mentally unbalanced—but he had never encountered any himself. Until now. Until he had touched the thoughts of the man called Warden Blair.

In some ways, he was as shaken by his encounter with Warden Blair's mind as he was by what had been done to him. Never before had he encountered a person who so desired the pain and degradation of others; who thrived on it as anyone else would thrive on love and praise.

Even Perenor was not so twisted—he was ruthless, and he thought of humans as no better than animals, but he would never have done to them what this man has done. He used people, but he did not go out of his way to hurt any save those he felt had hurt him. Even me, he only set to sleep in the Grove. Even Terenil, he sought only to kill. This man is like the Unseleighe, and I do not understand them either.

Blair devoted himself to inflicting pain, humiliation, specialized in reducing his fellow humans to groveling, weeping nonentities. And then, he would take every opportunity to reinforce what he had done to them, keeping them ground beneath his foot.

He hated everyone; he hated and despised those beneath him, he hated and feared those above him, and he hated and wanted to dispose of his equals. If there was anything that Warden Blair cared for besides himself, Kory had not seen it.

What he was doing to those in his power was only a pale shadow of what he *wanted* to do to them. What he had already done—sometimes with the aid of his former captives—was horrifying. And not only did he feel no remorse, he regretted that he dared not take his activities as far as he would like.

What he had done to Beth—that was typical of him. It was by no means representative of the depths to which he had already gone. Warden Blair had killed, both directly and indirectly, although he himself had never dirtied his hands with anything so direct as a blade or one of the humans' guns.

That he left to men he had hired for the purpose. This was something else Kory could not understand: to hire someone for the purposes of assassination. But then, he had never understood humans or Unseleighe who made that their practice.

Once or twice, Warden Blair had found it necessary to deal death personally—but when he did, it was assassination of another sort, through the intermediary of poison. As a scientist, he had access to many poisons, several that mimicked perfectly ordinary illnesses.

And his only regret was that he had not been there to witness and enjoy the death, when it came. He routinely dispatched in this way those he had captured who proved to be too much trouble. He was already considering such an end for Beth, should she continue to resist him.

Beth— Despite his own weakness and pain, he crawled to her on his hands and knees, to gather her up in his arms and hold her. Now that he knew what Blair was like, and what the human had done to Beth, he knew that there was only one way to reach her. She would not trust anything coming from outside her—but she might trust a mind-to-mind link. She had erected shields to hold others out, but she would not have held them against him.

He held her close, shut out the pain of his body, the cold of the cell, and focused himself inward. Inward to seek outward. Inward for control, so that he might have the stability to forget himself and look into Beth's mind and heart.

He sent out a questing tendril of thought; encountered her shields, and called softly to her. *:Beth—Bethy, my lady, my friend, my love—:*

The shields softened a little. He touched the surface of her thoughts, and did not recoil from what he found there— a chaos of fear—and old memories, more potent for being early ones. *Can't breathe—choking—strangling—the air going, the walls falling in—*

Her shields softened further and he passed them by. He countered her illusions with nothing more than his presence, knowing now what fear it was that held her prisoner. *:Your lungs are filled, the air is fresh and pure. I am with you, and I will not let the walls close in. Bethy, you are not alone.:*

She finally sensed his presence in her mind, and grasped for him with the frantic strength of one who was drowning. He stood firm, holding against her tugging, vaguely aware that she confused him with someone else, some other rescuer. That was fine. If she had been rescued before, she would be the readier to believe that she was being rescued again.

:I am here. I will help you to safety, my love. Do not let yourself despair.:

She clung to him, mentally and physically. He felt her thoughts calming; found the place where her fear originated and fed back upon itself. That gave *him* something to work on; he caught the fear and held it, sensed that she was listening to him now, and knew who he was.

:There is air to breathe,: he told her silently, calmly. *:This is only a room. If the blackguard stops the air, I will start it again. If he changes it, I will protect you. I have sent word to the Bard; he is working to free us.:* That last, he was unsure of. He knew that he had briefly touched Eric, and that Eric knew what kind of danger they were in, but whether or not Eric knew where they were, and could do anything about it—that was another question altogether. He was only one man. He had the magic of the greatest Bards at his beck and call, but could that magic prevail against one such as Blair? He had imprisoned an elven warrior, even though he did not seem to know what it was he had captured. Could Bardic magic be strong enough to counter what this man could do when elven magic could not?

But the elf pushed his own doubts into the background. He must keep his thoughts positive. Beth needed them, needed him to be strong and with no doubts.

Just as she had been strong and without doubts for him, when he had despaired of saving his people, his Elfhame, himself.

How long he held her, he was not certain. Only that after a timeless moment, she reached up and touched his cheek with a shaking hand.

"K-Kory?" she whispered hoarsely. "Kory—I—"

He raised his head—and something in the quality of the atmosphere told him that there was something very different about the place, something that had changed in the past few moments. Something was very wrong.

"Kory?" Her own arms tightened about him, and he felt her shivering. "Kory, something's wrong—there's something out there—"

"I know," he whispered. He sought to identify what he sensed as he held her. It wasn't Unseleighe; it wasn't anything from Underhill at all, either from the ordered Seleighe side, or the chaos of the Unseleighe lands. It wasn't human spirits . . . or human magic. But it was somehow connected with humanity.

Its evil was human evil, that same evil that lived in Warden Blair. It was that shadowy horror that Beth sensed, that made her shiver and forget her fear of being buried alive. There were things worse than death, and in the darkness of their cell, Kory knew that he and Beth sensed one of those things brushing them with its regard.

It examined them, minutely, as he held his breath.

And passed them by.

Kory let out the breath he had been holding in. Then he realized something else that was not as it had been: the silence. While the room they were in was supposedly sound-proof, elven senses were sharper than human, and the sounds of footsteps, conversation, and other noises leaked across the threshold of the door. There had been sound out there in the corridor; there no longer was.

Cautiously, he created a mage-light; it lit Beth's face with a faint bluish glow from the palm of his hand. Her eyes were round and wide with fear, her face drawn and blood-less. Whatever he sensed from the being outside their door, she was more sensitive to it. He had hesitated to create the light, for fear it would attract the attention of the thing that had examined them, but nothing happened.

He considered his options, and the continuing silence in the hallway beyond. And he considered his own strength, which was nearly spent.

This would be the last attempt at magic he could make without a great deal of rest and recuperation. Once he had finished a final attempt on the lock, their only recourses at escape would have to be purely physical. On the other hand, what did he have to lose? If what he and Beth sensed was truly out there, prowling the corridors of Warden Blair's stronghold, the human had a great deal more to worry about than keeping his victims penned. Whatever magery had countered his own, it might be gone now.

He sent the ball of light into the mechanism of the lock, as he had before; exerting his will upon the stubborn mechanism to make it yield. This time, however, he was rewarded by the faint clicking of the tumblers. And no one on the other side of the door relocked it.

He freed himself from Beth's clutching hands, stood up shakily. She started to protest, stopped herself as he moved carefully across the darkened room to the door. He waited for a moment with his hand on the handle, extending his weary senses out beyond the metal of the heavy portal, feeling nothing in the immediate vicinity. He turned the handle, carefully; the door opened smoothly and quietly.

The hallway beyond was deserted—and curiously ill-lit, as if some of the lights had failed. Beth joined him at the door, hunched over, as if by making herself smaller, she could elude the attention of whatever was out there, human or nonhuman. Kory looked cautiously around the doorframe; there was still nothing to be seen in the hall; there wasn't even a human behind the desk-console at the end of it. He frowned; surely that was wrong. Shouldn't there be one of those uniformed humans with badges there at all times?

He stepped out into the corridor and motioned Beth to follow. She was still crouched by the wall, staring up at him. "Beth, we must leave here now. That creature could return."

"I can't," she whispered. "I can't move, I can't feel my legs."

He moved back to her, helping her to stand. She leaned against his shoulder. He could feel her trembling, and tightened his arm around her waist. "Can you walk?" he asked.

"I think I can," she said faintly, then spoke stronger. "Of course I can walk. No twisted little government shithead is going to get that victory over me. I'm walking out of here *right now.*"

Kory couldn't keep the smile off his face. This was the Beth that he knew, the human woman that he loved.

They slipped into the hallway, backs flat to the wall. Still, there was nothing to be seen anywhere in the hall, and nothing to be heard. Only an empty, echoing silence.

When they reached the desk-console, Kory stopped and peered over the edge of it. He was half-afraid that he would find a body there; that was the way it always worked in the human television shows. But to his immense relief, there was no body; there was nothing, in fact. Only a half-eaten sandwich and a can of cola, beneath row after row of darkened squares of glass, which he recognized, after a moment, as small television sets.

Beth peeked over the edge and frowned at those. Before he could stop her, she poked at some of the buttons beneath the nearest, but nothing changed.

"Are those supposed to do something?" he ventured.

"The ready-light is on. These should be working." Beth touched another button, with no visible result. "These video screens should show the insides of the cells, but they're not working at all."

"You understand these things?" he asked, amazed. This console was more complicated than the most intricate sorcery he had ever attempted. Something that could allow you to Farsee into the cells . . . *In the cells.* . . . "Beth, my lady," he said urgently. "Other cells—think you that we were the only captives here?"

Her head snapped up; her eyes met his. "No," she replied, slowly. "No, we couldn't have been. That creep knew how to break people too well—he *had* to have had practice." She began searching among the buttons and switches for something, cursing softly to herself when she could not find it, then snapped her fingers and pulled out a drawer. There was another, smaller bank of labeled buttons there, as well, besides pencils, sticks of gum, erasers, loose bullets.

"Got it," she said in satisfaction. She pushed two buttons in succession; one marked "Emergency Override," the second under a piece of masking tape with the words "cell doors" written on it, labeled "Mass Unlock."

She hesitated for another moment, then looked up at Kory. "If this system is anything like the one on the psych ward that I worked on, the unlock key won't work unless there's a real emergency—like a fire. And we're just lucky that there *is* a manual override to the computer-driven system. We're gonna have to manufacture an emergency."

Her words meant very little to him; he seized on the ones he did understand. "If we wish to release other prisoners, there must be a fire?" he asked. She nodded. "Very well then. There will be a fire."

Even exhausted, fire-making was a child's skill for any of the Folk. He stepped back along the corridor to their empty cell and considered the contents. There was bedding on the bunk, padding on the walls, all flammable. It would do.

He closed his eyes, and sent power into the cell. The bedding ignited with a *whoosh;* the padding took a moment longer, but within a heartbeat, it too was in flames.

Alarms sounded immediately; the lights in the corridor flickered and failed, and new, red lights came on. In the cell itself, water began to spray from the ceiling.

Since it did not suit Beth's plans to have the fire extinguished, he gave the copper pipe leading to the fixture a brief mental twist, blocking it. The spray of water died, and the fire continued to blaze merrily.

Far down the corridor, now, he heard people screaming, pounding on doors, and the sounds of some of those doors slamming open. He trotted back to the console, very pleased with himself.

"Will that suit—" he began, when Beth grabbed his hand and began sprinting down the hall, towards a sign over which blazed the words "Emergency Exit."

The feeling of something very old and very evil passing outside her door made every hair on Elizabet's body stand straight on end. She wasn't sure what to make of it; whatever was out there, it didn't match any horror she had ever encountered. But then, she hadn't encountered many really nasty things in her life; she had spent her time on the magics of life, not death.

Whatever it was, it passed her by as she held her breath, waiting for it to sense her and attack.

When she was certain it wasn't going to come back again, she let her breath out in a long sigh.

But what was that—thing? Another of Blair's little friends? Or was it something that Blair had attracted without knowing what he was doing? If so, he was in for a shock, especially if it was looking for him.

She decided that she was better off not moving for a while. No telling what the thing was hunting—and she was certain that it was a hunter; had an unmistakably predatory feeling about it. No telling how it hunted, either. If by sound, then her best bet was to stay quiet. Let Blair and his flunkies make all the noise and attract it.

But it was very hard to remain motionless, silent, sitting in the gloom of her cell, wondering if the thing was going to come back.

Another thought occurred to her after a moment: was this another of Blair's little ideas, something designed to make her more cooperative?

That almost seemed more likely than that it was something Blair had attracted.

If it is, I'm not going to let one haunt spook me into playing footsie with that creep, she told herself, a little angrily. *It's going to take more than a bogeyman to frighten me!*

An earthquake or a fire, now—trapped down here in a locked room in a sub-basement—

As if someone was reading her mind, fire alarms screamed out into the darkness all up and down the corridor—red emergency lights came on in her cell, startling her as much as the alarms.

She got herself to her feet, cursing middle age and the slowing of her reflexes. She ran for her door, praying that there was an emergency override on the locks in case of catastrophe—and that someone had been compassionate enough to use it. Which, given the kind of people who worked for Blair, was not a "given."

She emerged into the corridor with a half-dozen others, equally frightened, equally bewildered. She sniffed the air; no smoke on this level, but that didn't mean there wasn't a fire somewhere above or below.

One thing was obvious: there wasn't a single uniformed guard or one of Blair's suited goons among the milling, frightened people in the corridor. Whatever had happened—they'd been presented with an opportunity to escape.

"Get the rest of the doors open!" she shouted, taking charge. "Then let's get out of here!"

A woman with aggressively butch-cut hair whirled and stared at her, while the others stopped and gaped—perhaps wondering if she was one of them, or one of the enemy. The woman sized her up, then nodded, and began flinging doors open along the left-hand side of the corridor. Elizabet did the same on the right, until they were all open, the occupants either joining the rest in flight, or remaining huddled in the red-lit interior of the cells. Half of Elizabet wanted to run in there and coax them out as a few of the others were trying to do—

But the sensible half said that their window of escape might be closing at any moment. She had patients to care for, and a ward out there, waiting, probably frantic with fear.

She turned and ran for the emergency stairs.

The Nightflyer directed the steps of her host's body downwards, as the lights went to red and strange howling noises split the air. She—or it; Nightflyers were all hermaphroditic females, neuter until breeding conditions were encountered. Sometimes she thought of herself as both. One level down was something very important; something so important that her host hated the people who worked upon it with a passion undimmed by the fact that he was dead.

The Nightflyer sensed that this thing had something to do with whether or not the Breakthrough would be made. The music-maker was part of it, of course, and she was the ForeRunner, who would breach the barrier between the Waking and Nightmare Realms, but the Breakthrough itself would not occur unless some great outpouring of Waking fear gave her the energy needed to cast the bridge across the barrier and hold it open.

She was not precognitive in the sense that humans understood the word; she sensed the future in a myriad of pathways. That *this* object had the potential to make something happen, and *that* human knew the key to an event.

As now. The music-maker had the potential to bring the Breakthrough, even though it meant that the Nightflyers who answered the call would be forced to obey him. Potential future pathway: one Nightflyer would find a host. Potential future pathway: that host might lead her to something instrumental to the Breakthrough. At the moment, it appeared that Nightflyer would be her.

Down. That was the direction of the highest potential futurepath—and she followed the potential as a compass-needle follows a magnet.

There were a half-dozen white-coated humans coming up, fleeing in panic; she ignored them. They had nothing to do with her, or the potentials of the moment. At the bottom of the steps, she paused and tried the door. It opened to her touch, but not on a corridor of rooms, as she had found on the level above. This door opened on a single large room, filled with a maze of complicated devices. Blair's memory told her that this had been a storage area, until "Project Poseidon" came and did something, and found it perfect for their needs. What those needs were, Blair did not know. He only knew—the memories dimming as the body cooled—that he hated these people for taking even an unused part of "his" building, and for using money that could also have been "his."

Sounds from the other side of a wall of machines told the Nightflyer that there was still someone here. This might be a complication, or it might be another advantage. While it was in a host body, it could not kill quickly and efficiently, as it could when it was in its natural form—though to take a host, as only it could do, it did not kill quickly *or* quietly.

But while it was in a host, it also could not be compelled to return by the music-maker. Therefore it was remaining in the host, however uncomfortable and inconvenient that might be.

She moved, slowly, into a hiding place among the machines. She was not used to the way this body worked as yet, but she sensed a possibility with the as-yet unseen human, and it would require stealth to make use of the new potential that was unfolding. The human must not guess that she was there.

She wedged the body between two machines and beneath a table, in a way that would have been painful for the original occupant. Once there, she concentrated on reaching outward to that other human's mind. There was something that the human was doing that was important. . . .

The human, a male, had remained behind to perform a task of securing machines, despite a danger that he perceived. The Nightflyer sensed something beneath the surface of his concerns, and probed deeper.

There was relief there, that the machines could not be used as weapons, for only he and one other knew of that capability.

The potentials flowered, powerful and clear. This was the information she sought.

Quickly, she absorbed it all; the machines, how they worked, and how a single one of them could be used to trigger a massive earthquake. It took the Nightflyer a moment to comprehend just how massive an earthquake—and precisely what that meant to her.

At that moment, it took great control to keep from bolting from her hiding place, and taking one of the machines then and there. But she did not have the means to power or control one. She watched the human's thoughts as he locked down the equipment, then fled like the others; and she contemplated what she had learned.

One of the machines was directed very near one of the points that would trigger a major quake. Near enough, in fact, that the humans here had hesitated to use it for this experiment, and in the end, took a chance that the experiment would fail rather than take the greater risk.

She could go out now, and manually re-aim the machine. The fire and the escape of her host's captives would cause a great stir—she could use that and her host's high status to order this building sealed before the humans learned of her meddling. Then she could return to this level, and use the re-aimed machine.

And then, all she need do would be to wait.

Potential crystalized. This was a good plan, with high probability of success.

She squeezed her host's body out of its hiding place, and set to work.

∾   ∾   ∾

Kory supported Beth as she stumbled and nearly fell; there was something very odd about the absence of guards and Warden Blair's men. Was that strangeness connected with the evil creature he had sensed outside their door?

Suddenly, without warning, a shape out of nightmare loomed up in front of them, blocking their path. Kory knew it the moment it appeared, although he could not put a name to the thing. It was the creature—or one like it— that he had sensed outside their door.

And it loomed above the body of one of the guards, mantling shadowy wings over it, as if it were a great bird of prey.

Beth stifled a gasp; Kory backed carefully away from the thing. It did not move, apparently intent over its victim. After a few seconds, it drifted away, sliding through a half-opened doorway.

Well, now they knew where the guards had gone.

He glanced at Beth, and saw that she was standing motionless, her back pressed against the wall, still staring at the spot where the guard had lain. "Beth, we must leave here—" he whispered urgently to her.

"Can't you feel it?" she whispered back to him. "They're all around us, hidden in the shadows. They're so close, I can feel them brushing against my skin, stealing the air we're breathing. We'll suffocate here, as the walls fall in around us, and the shadows will eat our souls . . ."

"No!" He gathered witchlight in his hand, casting light into every corner of the corridor. "There's nothing around us, Beth. We're close to the exit, just another doorway and some stairs. I know Eric is out there, I can feel he's close to us"—*And so can anyone else within five hundred leagues, my friend the Bard is shining like a torch tonight*— "Lean on me, love, and we'll walk out of here together."

Her hand tightened on his, and he half-carried her past the place where the guard had died. He saw another Emergency Exit sign with a feeling of relief, and herded Beth toward it. As they reached it, a flood of people appeared coming from the other direction, and crowded into the door with them. There were a great many more people in this building than he would have judged, and it seemed as if all of them had chosen to bolt into the staircase he and Beth had taken.

That was not so bad—many people would provide confusion and cover, in which they could escape.

And more victims for that—creature?

Was *that* something Eric had called, in an effort to free them? If so—could the Bard control something like that? Or had he taken on more than he knew?

Kory could only hope that the Bard knew what he was doing, as he and Beth let the press of humans carry them up the stairs and into the free night air.

Eric and Kayla waited as patiently as they could for something to happen. There didn't seem to be much going on out there, though, and Eric began to wonder if he'd made a really bad choice of weapons. Maybe he should have gone to the police after all—or the media—

The Nightflyers had all headed towards one building; he and Kayla watched them drift inside, not all of them by means of doors or windows. A few of them seemed to be able to pass right through solid walls if they wanted to; something that did not bode well for his sleeping habits for a while. From the look on Kayla's face, he had the feeling the same was true for her.

But since they had entered the building, it looked like business as usual from the outside. Those shadows drifting across lighted windows—they could just as easily be late workers as his otherworldly creatures. No one came running out of there, screaming or otherwise—

Alarms sounded, shattering the silence, startling both of them into shrieks, which fortunately were drowned in the klaxon-horns. He grabbed Kayla and hauled her back, deeper into the shadows, as she tried to bolt for the building.

She couldn't have heard him unless he yelled, but his meaning was plain enough: they needed to stay where they were.

As armed security guards appeared from other parts of the lab complex, racing towards the building in question, Eric noticed that the lights in the windows had all turned red. *Is that some kind of emergency lighting? Did the Nightflyers finally do something that triggered an alarm?*

The front doors burst open as guards took up defensive positions—and were promptly overwhelmed by the rush of frantic people streaming out of the building. Some wore white lab coats, but only about half; the rest were in ordinary street clothes. Some looked injured; there were groups of two and three helping each other along. There were a lot more of them than Eric would have expected; evidently there was a lot of work going on at night. He peered through the confusion, hoping, fearing—

And spotted a pair of familiar heads as a knot of people passed under a sodium-vapor light, ignoring the guard who tried to stop them. One blond—one red—

"Elizabet!" Kayla squirmed out of his grip and sprinted away, and he didn't even try to stop her this time, assuming that the confusion would cover her. He made a dash of his own for *his* two targets; brushed aside a guard whose bewildered expression told him there was something odd about the situation, and threw his arms around the two who were supporting each other.

There was no time for greetings, though; he swept them from an embrace into a stumbling trot, heading for the gate. No one moved to stop them—no one made a move to stop *anyone* who was trying to leave.

At some point between the place where he caught Kory and Beth, and the entrance, Kayla and Elizabet joined them, making a group too formidable for anyone to trifle with. At the entrance, Eric guided them all off to the side, shoving Kory and Beth ahead of him. "I've got transportation," he said to Elizabet, "but there's something I have to take care of back there. You guys go back to the house—I think it's safe, I don't think those goons knew where we live. I'll catch BART back home."

Elizabet looked as if she wanted to object, but finally nodded, tersely. "Neither Beth nor Kory look as if they're in a fit state to be left alone," she said. "And knowing what happened to me—we'll stay with them. Kayla, I think Beth may need you the more. I'll stay with Kory."

Eric nodded his thanks, and left them heading in the direction of the bikes. He turned, and went back to the edge of the fence.

Now to put the genie back into the bottle. If I can. . . .

9

Beauty in Tears

The creature glided slowly in her direction. Dr. Susan Sheffield crouched further into the corner, watching as *something* slid past the tall yellow barrels.

The scientist in her noted calmly that the creature seemed to be comprised of different light intensities, which shifted as it moved. No, not variable light intensities, but rather the absence of light. As it floated through the air, it—absorbed? deflected?—light waves, creating the shadowy framework. It also seemed to be slightly confused by the heavy metals disposal canisters. Possibly the contained radioactivity, or maybe the metals themselves? No way to know, not without some extensive testing. . . .

The other part of her mind was too numb to think, too horrified to consider anything but screaming. But she knew that making a single noise would be fatal. She'd seen one of these *things* kill Frank, and the new lab tech, the boy whose name she could never remember. At least, she hoped they were dead.

The creature inched closer, blotting out the last of the light. She was too terrified to scream; she closed her eyes, wishing she could at least *know* what had killed her. . . .

A faint sound pierced her terror, a sound that she felt resonating beneath her skin, even though the room was completely silent. A melody, strange and alluring, calling to her, calling. . . .

She opened her eyes again, to see the creature still floating in the air before her. It began to move away, drifting toward the stairway. Without thinking about it, she moved after it, following it up the stairs. The music seemed to be saying something to her, something too important to ignore, even with the shadows of death moving through the hallways around her.

She followed the creature up the long flights of stairs, through the emergency exit and toward the main lobby. Other shadow-monsters joined them in this strange trek, drifting past her through the white metal railings.

Something stopped her by the door, though; a silhouetted human figure, standing near the doorway, staring at something beyond. A moment later, she recognized him— Warden Blair, the project manager of the team down on Level 13, one of the "sealed" floors. He stood very close to the doorway, his fingers clenched white on the lintel, as though trying to hold himself back from a force that was pulling him through the door.

She stood there for a moment, as the creatures drifted past her, coiling around her ankles and swirling her skirt around her knees. Beyond, she could see the floodlit area beyond the glass doors. Standing beyond the doors was a young man with long dark hair, playing a flute. As she watched, the shadow-monsters drifted toward the young man, gathering before him, a shifting dark cloud.

Blair turned and saw her. She recoiled at the look in his eyes . . . *there's nothing human there, a corpse has more emotion in its eyes* . . . and stepped back, though the music still tugged her forward.

Those inhuman eyes fixed on her face, lit with a strange hunger. Blair let go of the doorjamb, and reached out a clawlike hand toward her.

Susan dove past him, into the dimly-lit lobby. Her hand slapped the door release knob by the side of the glass doors, and she slammed into the doors shoulder-first, falling through to the concrete steps outside. She glanced back;

there was no sign of Blair in the shadowy lobby. Now she didn't have to worry about a homicidal maniac . . . instead, she had two hundred of those deadly creatures gathered on the asphalt not quite fifteen feet in front of her.

No problem, she thought crazily, and fainted.

All right, Eric. You get one try at this; don't screw it up. He took a deep breath, and looked out at the gathered assemblage of Nightflyers on the pavement. *I can handle this. It's just like conducting the high school orchestra back home.*

Except that the kids in the school orchestra weren't going to eat me alive if I made a mistake. . . .

The Nightflyers waited patiently. Eric could sense that they were watching him, waiting for . . . something.

For me. They're waiting for me to make a decision, to lead them. The image of the Nightflyer in the ruined city flashed through Eric's mind, the creature bowing to him as if to a great lord, a leader.

That's what I could be to these guys. A leader. He imagined himself at the head of the unliving army, sweeping through the countryside and righting all wrongs . . . no more wars, not when there wasn't a conventional army on the planet that could fight against his troops. No more crime, no drug-wars in the streets of the city . . . no one dying of violence, no one at all, ever again.

Except when these Nightflyers get hungry and need to find a dinner somewhere.

Then again, maybe all of that wouldn't be such a good idea after all. . . .

Eric shuddered, bringing himself back to the present. He saw that the crowd of Nightflyers had moved closer to him while he'd been daydreaming, and now were hovering only a few feet away, almost close enough to touch. *Get your act together, Eric, and get rid of these guys before you end up as the Blue Plate Special yourself.*

He brought his flute up to his lips, and began playing a slow slipjig, "The Boys of Ballysadare"—a tribute to fallen soldiers, young boys killed in a battle nearly forgotten in the mists of history—one by one, the Nightflyers faded from view, like shadows touched by bright sunlight. Eric felt sweat running down his skin, as he realized just how many of the creatures he had summoned, and still had left to banish.

One of the Nightflyers drifted very close to him as it faded away, the shadow-wings brushing against his skin, a touch colder than ice. He held onto his concentration like a shield, willing the monsters to go away, return to that strange place from which he'd called them. Only a few left, he saw as he began playing the A part of the tune again, only a few . . . one of his fingers, damp with sweat, slipped on the smooth metal key of the flute, and the remaining Nightflyers surged forward toward him. He caught up the thread of the melody again, holding them at bay until the last one was gone, and he was alone in the parking lot.

Eric slid down to his knees on the asphalt, the flute clutched in his nerveless hands. The adrenaline charge hit him a split-second later, his heart pounding too fast, hands shaking with the realization of how close he'd been to death. *Next time, maybe I'll just call in the Marines instead.*

He managed to stand up somehow. Fortunately, he was still alone . . . no, he wasn't. He saw an older woman, dark-haired and wearing a laboratory coat over her clothes, slumped on the pavement a split-second later, and hurried to her. Eric knelt beside her, checking her throat for a pulse.

At his touch, the dark-haired woman opened her eyes and blinked at him. "It's okay," he said quickly. "It's all over."

She sat up slowly, looking around the parking lot. In her eyes, Eric recognized the same look of total shock that he'd seen in the eyes of the Los Angeles elves, after the battle in the park.

"Do you have a car?" he asked. "I'll help you get home."

She nodded, not speaking.

He helped her to her feet. She leaned against his shoulder, walking unsteadily. As they approached a blue Suzuki jeep, parked alone beneath one of the floodlights, she silently handed the car keys to Eric. Well, he knew in theory what to do. As Eric drove the jeep out of the Dublin Labs parking lot, weaving like a drunkard, the woman looked back once at the brightly-lit laboratory complex and began to cry.

Beth held tightly to Kory as the motorcycle banked through the turn from Van Ness onto Geary Street, accelerating through the pools of light and shadows cast by the streetlights. Something bothered her about the moving shadows, the way they glided past the motorcycle and disappeared behind them.

The faerie motorcycle braked delicately into a right turn, heading up their street and toward the only lit house . . . *of course Eric forgot to turn off the lights in the garage when he left the house,* she thought and smiled. *Figures. I just hope he remembered to lock the front door—*

They pulled up into the driveway, the bike courteously switching off its own headlight. She slid off the motorcycle and nearly lost her balance, grabbing onto Kory for support.

"I'm okay," she muttered, then repeated the words louder for Kory's benefit. A moment later, the second motorcycle pulled into the driveway, and Elizabet and Kayla followed them to the front door.

Inside, the house was warm and dark. Beth felt her way carefully through the darkness, turning on lights as she went. She continued into the kitchen and the living-room, making sure that all the lights were switched on. She caught the curious looks from Elizabet and Kayla as she went into the dining room to turn on the light in that room. When all of the first floor of the house was brightly lit, she rejoined them in the living room, slumping into her favorite chair, a Papa-san with a fat pillow-seat.

"Do you want something to drink?" she asked, remembering to be a good hostess. "Some tea or coffee?"

Kayla shook her head. Beth noticed that Elizabet was giving her apprentice a different kind of odd look.

"Is anything wrong, Beth?" the older woman asked, watching her intently.

"No, not at all. I'm just glad we're home. Are you sure you wouldn't like anything to drink?" She stood up, walking to the wooden cabinet by the fireplace. "Well, if no one else wants anything, I think I'd like something." She reached for the bottle of Stolichnaya, and realized for the first time that her hands were shaking.

Elizabet stood up, and took the bottle from Beth's hand. "I don't think that would be a good idea, Beth," the healer said firmly.

Without even thinking about it, Beth slapped her across the face.

She brought her hand up to her mouth, suddenly horrified by what her hands had done. "I'm sorry, I didn't mean to . . . I . . ." To her horror, she burst into tears.

Beyond Elizabet, she could see Kory, staring at her. "I'm okay, I'm okay," she said, angrily wiping the tears from her eyes.

"I think you need some rest," Elizabet said, taking her by the arm. Something about that touch, it seemed too familiar to her . . . she glanced at Elizabet's face, and saw her handsome dark features melt, changing into something else . . . a man's face, a man wearing a business suit, smiling at her with that look of a little boy with a new toy, he was going to take her apart like a clock and toss all of her gears and wheels across the floor. . . .

She shoved Blair away from her, sending him falling back against the cabinet, and turned to run. Kayla was blocking her path, though . . . why was the little healer kid trying to help Warden Blair? Kayla said something that Beth couldn't hear, and then the world went very bright, the white light blotting out everything else. *Very strange,* she thought as the light washed over her and carried her away.

Susan stretched, not wanting to open her eyes. *What an awful dream,* she thought, remembering her nightmare. *Wish I'd gotten more sleep. It's going to be hell, trying to run the computer data on that test run, if I'm half-asleep and can't think straight. . . .*

She switched on the light on the nightstand, and heard a strange noise from the kitchen. She sat up abruptly. *Burglars!*

She reached for her bathrobe, then suddenly realized that she was still wearing her clothes from the day before, the lab coat and skirt and blouse and pantyhose, sans her lab shoes. Quietly, she moved through the hallway, pausing to pick up a heavy marble bookend from the table near the window.

She took a deep breath, hefted the reassuring weight of the bookend in her hand, and looked into the kitchen.

A handsome dark-haired young man stood in her kitchen, staring in perplexity at her espresso machine, which was currently spraying hot water into the air.

The man from my nightmare last night. . . .

"I'm really sorry," the young man said, gesturing at the hot water on the countertop and floor. "I didn't mean to wake you up or make all this mess, I just wanted some coffee before I went home."

"This machine is very temperamental," she said, recovering enough from her surprise to grab a potholder and use it to twist the machine's spigot several times. The flow of hot water ceased, and a stream of fresh coffee began to pour sedately into the waiting pot. "Give it a few seconds, and it'll be ready."

"I'm sorry if I startled you," he said after an awkward silence. "I would've left last night, but by the time we got to your place, I'd already missed the last BART home. I slept on your couch . . . I hope you don't mind."

No, not at all, I love having figments of my imagination stay over for breakfast.

Not imagination. That wasn't a dream last night. It was real, all of it was real. . . .

Either that, or I've gone mad.

He took down a mug from the shelf above the espresso machine, and poured himself a cup of coffee, as Susan stared at him.

"Okay, kid," she said in her best lab manager's voice, the one that worked so well on the obnoxious young interns from Cal Berkeley. "I want some answers, right now. What happened last night at the labs?"

"It was . . . it was a mistake," he said, staring at his coffee mug. "I shouldn't have done it, I know that now, but I couldn't think of anything else to do, and I thought Kory was dying . . . I could've lost control of them, and not banished them all . . . Christ knows what those things would've done if that had happened."

Her voice sharpened. "*What* did you do?"

He looked up at her, an odd expression in his eyes. "I called them. You saw them, you were right there on the lawn. I brought them there, and let them go. What happened in there?"

This kid . . . he thinks he caused what happened last night, whatever that force . . . those creatures . . . were, that came into the Labs. And maybe he's right, because I saw them gathering around him in the parking lot, as though he was calling them back.

She heard herself describing what she had seen in a calm, detached voice, the one she used to read papers at conferences. "Those things . . . killed a lot of people in the Labs. I don't know how many. But Frank is dead, and that boy, and God knows how many other people."

"Excuse me, please," he said faintly, and made a dash for the bathroom down the hall. Through the open door, she could hear him being quickly and violently ill.

She stood there alone, trying to gather her thoughts. She felt unnaturally calm, distant from this insanity that had suddenly engulfed her life. *It's called shock, Susan,* she thought.

Several minutes later, he returned to the kitchen, and took a quick swallow of coffee. There was a different look in his eyes, something she couldn't identify.

"Who are you? What's your name?" she asked.

He glanced up at her, a wary expression in his eyes. "Maybe . . . maybe I'd better leave now."

She stood between him and the only door out. "Not until you answer my questions, kid."

He looked as if he was going to say something else, then shook his head, pursed his lips, and whistled a brief sequence of notes, something she recognized as the beginnings of an Irish tune called "Whiskey Before Breakfast," and . . .

. . . and she blinked at the sudden bright sunlight pouring through the kitchen window. Her back was aching, as though she'd been standing on her feet too long; she looked over at the clock above the espresso machine, and blinked again.

Ten a.m.? I've been standing here like this for two hours?

And she realized something else: she was alone in the kitchen. There was no sign of the strange young man, or where he'd gone, only a half-filled coffee mug left on the kitchen counter.

The choice was to go home or call home; he only had change for one. Eric sat on the BART bench, staring at his clenched hands in his lap. He could see it now, in his mind's eye . . . the Nightflyers gliding into the building, leaving nothing alive behind them. He knew he could've seen it before it had happened, if he'd bothered to think about the consequences of his actions.

What did they do? How many people did they kill, when I let them into that complex?

Something small and shadowy whispered in the back of his mind: *We will tell you, if you let us come back . . . Bring us back, bring us back . . .*

"No!" he said violently, loudly enough that the other passengers on the subway looked up at him. He leaned his head against the glass, closing his eyes to shut out the rest of the world.

No, I won't bring you back, he silently said in the direction of that shadowy voice. *No dice. I know what you are now, and I'll never do that again, never.*

The image of the Nightflyer bowing to him in the ruined streets of San Francisco hit him like a fist, a mental sending that was as clear and sharp as a memory.

You have/will/are helping us, the voice continued. *Help us again. Lead us, bring us back . . .*

With a sudden clarity, Eric saw the Nightflyers, poised around him, but just beyond reach . . . just beyond a veil, thin and shimmering, that was all that stood between the waking world and the realm of nightmares. He understood their way of thinking in all times at once, past/future/present, and how they hungered for all things human and living. And how they needed him, needed someone or something to break through that thin veil and bring them into the real world. He could feel their slow and patient thoughts, simmering evil that was completely inhuman, and how they had watched him—since he was a child, they'd known he would be a Bard someday (if he lived that long) and would be able to aid them . . . waiting for a moment, a Breakthrough, when the Special Ones could get through.

Well, you're going to be waiting a hell of a lot longer than that! he thought to the waiting throng. *Because I'm not doing it!*

Not evil, not us, the voice said quietly across the void between the two worlds. *But different, and in need of your masses of humanity to survive . . . we need you, as you needed us. . . .*

Eric reached out blindly with his thoughts and shoved, hard, until he no longer heard the voice, and he was alone again in his own head, with no whispering evil by his side. Like a sleepwalker, he left the BART train at the Powell Street Station to change to a Metro bus, and then to step down from the bus and walk up the hill to their house. Even from the end of the street, he saw the two motorcycles parked in the driveway, and felt a weight, that he hadn't known he was carrying, lift away from him. Knowing that Beth and Kory were home, knowing that they were all right, he couldn't keep a smile from his face. Until he remembered again what he had done to bring them home.

The front door was unlocked, and he let himself in, hanging his jacket from one of the hooks near the door. He heard someone in the kitchen, and his nose filled with the smell of fresh sausage and eggs frying. The smell awoke the sour taste in his mouth again, and the twisting sensation in his stomach. He decided that maybe he'd skip breakfast, just for today.

Kayla walked quickly out of the kitchen, carrying a plate of food and a glass of milk—she stopped short at seeing Eric in the hallway, a strange expression on her face. After a split-second, Eric recognized it as fear.

She gave him a lopsided smile. "Hey, Bard! Glad to see you made it home all right. You sure look terrible."

He swallowed hard. "Kayla, is everyone okay? Where are Beth and Kory?"

"Kory's fine," Kayla said. "But you'd better talk to my boss about Bethany. Everyone's upstairs right now."

She looked fine last night . . . well, maybe not fine, but okay. Not bleeding or anything. What could've happened after they left for San Francisco?

The exhaustion finally hit him, as Eric started up the stairs. An accumulation of terror, too much magic, too little sleep, and no food . . . the world began to turn white around him, and he grabbed the bannister for support. Kayla caught him and helped him sit down; everything was too blurry, moving too fast around him.

"You're not in very great shape, either," the young healer observed clinically.

"It's been one hell of a night," Eric said, hoping that he wasn't going to be physically sick again. That would've been the perfect ending to a thoroughly awful night. And it had started out with such an adrenaline rush as he'd realized just how much power he had as a Bard, how he could summon his own personal army of demons and rescue his friends, and no one could stop him. . . .

And God knows how many people I killed last night, it's my fault, it's all my fault. . . .

Kayla's hand rested on his shoulder, and he felt the dizziness pass, and a wave of . . . something . . . wash over him instead. Suddenly he felt a little better, as the nausea faded away. "Thanks," he said.

"Not a problem," the kid replied. "That's what Elizabet calls the Kayla Patented Jump-start, perfect for those bad magical hangover mornings. You kind of overdid it last night, Bard."

"Don't you think I know it," he muttered, his face in his hands.

"Eric!"

He looked up quickly, to see Kory vaulting down the stairs towards him. The blond elf caught him up in a

bearhug, then held him at arm's length, his eyes searching Eric's face. "You look terrible, my friend."

"I know, I know. Nothing that some sleep won't cure."
He stood up slowly, and glanced upstairs. "Is Beth okay?"

Kory's face fell. "I do not understand this at all. This
must be a human thing, because I have never seen an elf
suffer from this illness."

"Is she awake? Is she—." Eric moved past Kory, heading for the bedroom door. He stopped in the open doorway.

Beth was sitting up in bed, wearing her usual sweatshirt,
her dark red hair falling loose over her shoulders. Even from
the doorway, he could see that something was different,
though he couldn't tell exactly what. It wasn't just the way
she was sitting so quietly, or the tired look in her eyes . . .
it was in the tilt of her head, the way she sat . . . something was different, and Eric already knew that he didn't
like it.

She looked up and saw him, and her eyes brightened.
"You look terrible," she said softly, smiling at him.

"I know, love." He sat down on the bed next to her,
caught her hand and brought it to his lips. "You look kinda
awful yourself."

"I'm glad to see you back, Eric," Elizabet's warm voice
spoke from across the room. Eric saw the older woman for
the first time, seated in the warm sunlight in the window
seat. "We were all worried about you."

"Nothing I couldn't handle," he said, trying to sound
nonchalant. *Nothing I couldn't handle . . . badly*, he thought.
*Nothing I couldn't handle without getting a lot of people
killed.*

"Will you be all right without me for a few minutes,
Beth?" the healer asked. "I need to talk to Eric."

"Yeah, sure." Beth waved away any concerns.

"I'll send Kayla in to keep you company," she said, and
called downstairs to her apprentice, who ran up the stairs
a couple seconds later, giving her mentor a pseudo-military
salute before sitting down in the window seat that Elizabet
had just vacated.

Eric followed Elizabet out of the room, out into the garden. The woman sat down wearily on the grass. "How are you doing, Eric? You look tired and stressed out, but not too much worse than that."

"I'm okay," he said cautiously, sitting down next to her. "What's going on with Beth?"

Elizabet hesitated. "It's a little difficult to explain. What do you know about mental illness, Eric?"

"Not much." *Not much more than three years with the expensive shrinks my mother hired could teach me. That I wasn't nuts, but I had to give them the answers they wanted to hear.*

"Well, without knowing exactly what happened to Beth last night, all I can guess is that she's suffering from an affective disorder of some kind—possibly a variation of post-traumatic stress disorder. In layman's terms, I'd call it extreme shock and the beginnings of a nervous breakdown. Definitely that . . . she cried for three hours last night without stopping. But she won't talk about it—without adequate information, there's no way to know what's really going on." She stretched, rubbing her eyes. "I'll need to get some sleep soon, or I won't be much use to anyone." She sat up, giving Eric a curious look. "Kory said something about how Beth thought she couldn't breathe, last night in the labs. Do you know anything about that?"

He thought about that for a minute. "No, not really. But . . . Beth's claustrophobic. And they were underground; I'm guessing there weren't any windows down there. Could that have caused this?"

"A normal claustrophobia attack wouldn't cause anything this severe. I'd expect to see high anxiety levels, possibly some fairly serious psychosomatic reactions, but not anything like this. It could've caused the elevated metabolic levels she was showing last night, but not any of these continuing effects."

"What about physical damage?" He had to ask. He had to. "Was she raped?"

The healer shook her head. "No, definitely not. Any damage is completely mental and emotional. But something happened to her in those labs which she won't talk about yet, and that something is what triggered all of this. And it happened before all of those . . . creatures . . . showed up at the labs. By the way, I'd like to talk to you about that," she added, giving him a very penetrating look.

He flushed. "Later," he said.

"All right." She accepted that, as she accepted most things, from elves to frightened runaways. "Listen, I need to get some sleep soon. Will you sit with Beth for the next few hours? I don't want to leave her alone for too long."

"Is there any particular reason why?" he asked, concerned.

"I'd—I'd rather not say. Just keep an eye on her, all right?"

Without even thinking about it, Eric reached out to touch the woman's thoughts. Genuine fear for Beth hit him for the first time, reading the thought that was uppermost in the healer's mind. "Do you think Beth is suicidal?"

Elizabet nodded slowly. "It's possible. That's why we're not going to leave her alone right now. I'd rather not take the risk."

He felt an icy touch inside, a cold ball of fear that wouldn't go away. "I'll stay with her."

They walked back inside the house. Upstairs, Beth was asleep, the lines of tension no longer visible in her face. He took over Kayla's place in the window seat, settling down on the pillows. He leaned back against the sun-warmed wood, feeling the terrors from last night washing away, being replaced by new terrors.

He had never expected this, never thought this could happen. Beth had always been the strongest of them all, the most determined, the one who refused to turn away from a fight. He couldn't imagine a Beth that wasn't strong-willed and outspoken, vibrant and always laughing. The concept of a Beth who was so quiet and pale, who cried for three hours without stopping, he couldn't believe that this had happened, that this was real.

He had been so afraid for Kory, knowing that something awful was happening to him, that he might've been dying, that he hadn't even thought that something worse could be happening to Beth. Now Kory was fine, and Beth was the one who had been badly hurt, and hurt in a way that he didn't understand.

And himself . . . the only word that he could think of to label himself was *monster*. Without even thinking of the consequences, he'd summoned the Nightflyers and turned them loose, killing God knows how many people in those labs. He was a monster, as much as any Nightflyer—and they knew it, those strange intelligent shadow-creatures from across the veil of dreams, and they saw him as their leader, one of their demonic horde. . . .

And somewhere in the back of his mind was a strange feeling telling him that now, when there should be nothing left to do but heal, this wasn't the end of it, a little prescient touch that things were only going to get worse. . . .

10

Off She Goes

"I'm not insane, I'm not expendable, and I'm not going." Susan sat back with her arms folded, glaring at her boss. "The Poseidon Project is at a critical stage right now, and there's no way in hell that I'm going off to some FBI summer camp to be grilled by psychiatrists for six weeks. If I go now, with Frank and Dave missing, we'll lose weeks. If you cart me off, we'll lose months. Maybe more. With all the cuts going on, we might even lose the budget for the project, and that's insane." As an afterthought, and with a glance at the tape recorder on the table, she added, "Sir."

Colonel Steve O'Neill had an uncharacteristically exasperated look on his face. "Your opinion is noted, Susan," he said dryly. "But I'm up against a wall right now. The boys Upstairs want to know what happened here last night, and so far you're the only living witness who can still speak in complete sentences."

"What about Warden Blair?" she asked, remembering her strange encounter with the scientist in the stairwell. "*He* was there. I think the cause of it was on his floor. What's more, he's just as sane as I am. However sane that is. Why not get him to speak his piece?"

"I've been told to keep my hands off of Dr. Blair," the colonel said grimly. "But if this goes on much longer without any rational reasons for what happened, they won't have any choice." He sat down across from her. "Susan, can't you just give me a better explanation of what happened here? This story of floating shadow-monsters just isn't going to fly in Washington, and you know that."

She grimaced. "What rationale are they giving right now, Colonel?" "Rationale" was not the first word that came to her mind. She wanted to say "fairy tale," but the tape was still running.

He shrugged. "So far, the only explanations are mass hysteria and some kind of mass hallucination, combined with the kidnapping, defection, or mislaying of fourteen Lab employees. Once the alarms went off, everyone headed down their safe routes to leave the building. The ones who didn't are either completely *non compos mentis* or missing. I think the Agency boys are still searching the lower levels, in the hopes of finding more of those people." He shook his head. "The current theory is that some kind of toxin might've escaped from one of the sealed rooms and gotten into the air vents, though we all know that can't happen, because of the security design."

She refrained from snorting. *Nerve gas, you mean. Or an air-borne hallucinogen. And sealed-room protocol doesn't mean squat when you're dealing with people who might have been hit with it themselves and have just gone off on their own private trip to Oz. And sealed-room protocol won't work with something so new the filters can't catch it. A micromolecule, or a virus, maybe. But you can't say that, because of the tape.*

The colonel continued, blithely unaware of what she was thinking. "So they're saying it could've been deliberate, but there are only ten or fifteen people with security access to all levels, and they're all accounted for. Another theory is mass food poisoning, but that really doesn't hold water, either. So far no one is talking about the Japanese, or terrorists, but that can't be far behind. This whole thing is giving me an awful headache," he concluded, rubbing his temples.

"At least you weren't here last night," Susan said quietly.

"I keep wishing I'd kept to an earlier plan of going to the San Francisco Opera with some friends last night, instead of running the data correlation tests." She allowed herself a single outburst of anger—in part, to help cover her grief. "Why can't you just put down what *I* saw to a mass hallucination, if you won't believe me?"

The colonel wasn't going to be sidetracked, even though she had given him a decent out. "All right, Susan. Let's go over it one more time, just to see if there's anything we missed. You were in your office, waiting for the computer to run the comparison tests on the last experiment . . ."

She nodded, wearily. "It was our first verified successful run. We recorded an energy release with a Richter equivalent of zero point nine, just enough to tap the needles on the seismograph. If all hell hadn't broken loose afterward, I would've been at your office door at eight a.m. this morning, waving test result printouts at you and screaming wildly. Happily, but wildly." *Why didn't I go watch Tosca fling herself off a bloody building? Why couldn't we have run the tests this morning?* But she knew why: because she'd been too excited, too impatient . . . nothing could've convinced her to leave the lab at that point. Finding the exact resonant frequency for that rock stratum and pinpointing the fault . . . no, leaving the lab at that point would've been inconceivable.

The colonel nodded. "After the test, what happened?"

She continued her recitation. Same words, for the benefit of those who would be listening to the tape, hunting for discrepancies. "Frank started to power down all the machines, and that new lab tech, Dave, was helping him with that. That's when the alarms went off. I knew we couldn't leave, not until all the equipment was secured, so I told them to keep working, that we'd still have time to clear the building." She could feel her hands trembling, and fought back tears. "I wish I could go back in time and tell them to get the hell out, screw the equipment. So we were still in there when that first *thing* came through the doorway, oozing right around a closed door. It opened up in front of us, going from a thin shadow to a huge billowing shape.

I don't think Frank even had time to blink, it just fell over him and he screamed, and then he was gone. The kid and I were standing there in shock, and it drifted toward him next, moving slower. I threw something heavy at it, I can't remember what—probably an oscilloscope or something. That fell right through it, but it paused long enough for both of us to get to the door."

If I'd gone to listen to an aging diva play an hysterical diva, they'd still be alive.

She heard a rising note of hysteria in her voice and quelled it. "In the hallway, I saw Mira Osaka from Dr. Siegel's team, just sitting on the floor and staring at her hands, like something was wrong with them. I tripped over her—that's when the creature killed Dave, it just slid over him like a wave. He was screaming, and I was trying to get free from Mira, because she'd grabbed onto my wrists. I think I hit her, trying to get away, and then the thing was coming after me. It seemed to ignore Mira. I made it into a storeroom, and it followed me in, but couldn't find me in there. I don't know why. Then it suddenly turned and left, and I followed it out, and that's where I saw the guy with long dark hair, the one who was in my apartment this morning."

Colonel O'Neill reached over and switched off the tape recorder. "We have to talk, off the record. You know what'll happen if I give this tape to the FBI, don't you? They'll listen to it for five minutes, and then cancel your clearance. I don't want that to happen." He glanced down at the tape recorder. "All right, this is what we're going to do. Susan, you're going to tell me that story again, and it isn't going to include anything about shadow-monsters or people disappearing into thin air. Or a hippie in your apartment. I'll rewind the tape, as a friend and someone who wants you *on* that damn project, and you give me the edited version three times. Here's what happened. The alarms went on. You tried to get out of there, Mira was in the hallway, you didn't see what happened to Frank and Dave. They just never came out of the lab." He paused for a moment, as if in thought. "And while the Feds are going over this report,

I'll send someone over to your apartment to dust for fingerprints. If we get any that aren't yours, I have private accesses to the national print banks. People who owe me favors. Maybe we can find this mysterious long-haired boy, and when we do, we can get some better answers to all of this out of him instead of you."

She was stunned. "Steve . . . that's *illegal.*"

"I know, I know." He shrugged. "Call it a command decision. I'm not going to let this sink your career, not when you're so close to doing something meaningful on this project. You're a good scientist, Susan. In all senses of the word."

She slumped a little, relief making her want to cry again. "Have I ever told you how glad I am that you were assigned to helm this project? I've been so afraid of the military applications of this, but you've always had the view that we could use this to help people, not kill them. Thank you for that, Steve. Thank you for having ethics."

"Not a problem." He smiled. "When we're done here, take the rest of the day off, Susan. Medical leave. Go shopping, go into the city, do anything you want. Just don't go home for a few hours, okay? Now, go to the lady's room. Have a cry. Come back here and we'll do the tape, then you take the day off."

"Okay. Thanks, Bossman." She stood up to leave, and impulsively hugged him.

Colonel O'Neill smiled at Susan as she left the room, then his face went flat and impassive as the door closed, as though he was only a puppet, with no puppeteer to animate his movements. That was how he felt, when he thought about it . . . when he was given the license to think about it. Like he was watching a puppet show from within his own mind, seeing himself move across a stage. All he could feel was that strange feeling of distance, of emptiness, as though all of this was happening to someone else. He thought he ought to be terrified, but he couldn't be, because the emptiness left no room for anything else in his mind, even fear.

A few moments later, he glanced at his watch, then rose from his chair and walked briskly down the hallway. Beyond another door, Warden Blair sat silently at a computer console, not even bothering to look up as O'Neill entered the room.

"Did she believe you?" Blair asked.

"I think so," the colonel replied woodenly. "At least, she said she wouldn't go back to her apartment, so I shouldn't have any problems sending a team over there to scout for prints and fibers. Maybe we'll find her mystery boy, maybe not."

Blair shook his head. "The boy doesn't matter—my people can follow him like a lighthouse beacon, anywhere in the city. What matters is that there is no interference with this project, at least for several days. And that no harm comes to your Dr. Susan Sheffield for those several days. After that, she won't matter at all. In fact, you'll probably need to kill her. Do you understand?"

"Of course." Something shifted in the emptiness of his thoughts, at the idea of harming Susan. *I . . . I don't want to do that,* he realized.

Blair continued, coldly, with calculation. "I can't control her, not without damaging her ability to complete the project. We'll need her technical expertise to complete the Breakthrough, the work that she hasn't completed yet." Blair seemed to be speaking more to himself than to O'Neill.

For a moment, O'Neill felt that strange emptiness lifting from his mind, the fog clearing slightly. His fingers strained, touched the flap of the holster at his belt, the .45 automatic nestled within. It was so difficult, harder than anything he'd ever done . . . he unsnapped the flap, wrapped his fingers around the grip, tensing. . . .

"Don't do that," Blair said absently, and Colonel O'Neill screamed inside, in fury and hopelessness, as his disobedient fingers rebuttoned the holster flap, then clenched into a fist in his lap. "I still need your services, Colonel," the thing that had been Warden Blair said in a serious tone. "I can't let you kill yourself yet. And as far as killing me . . . if this body dies, I'll simply take yours instead. Keep that thought in mind, if you think you might be able to break free."

"I'll . . . kill you," O'Neill said in a strained voice. "Don't know . . . what you are, but I'll kill you."

He felt Blair's attention focus on him, pressing down upon him like a great weight. It was more difficult to think, more difficult to focus on a single thought—he clutched desperately at the hatred, the last emotion being slowly stripped away from him.

But he couldn't fight it; it was like fighting the tide, or the turning of the planet. When it was over, there was only a small part of him left, locked deep beneath the waves of emptiness. A tiny scrap, able only to watch and weep, without acting.

Something like a smile passed over Blair's lips. "Much better. Now, your next assignment . . . I need competent laboratory personnel to replace the lost Poseidon Project team members, so we can reschedule the project. Despite the presence of the Federal officers, we should be able to resume work sometime tomorrow."

"I'll take care of it," O'Neill heard his own voice say, and he rose to leave the room.

"I'm sure you will, Colonel," Blair said, smiling.

I've seen that kid before, I know I have, Susan thought, walking past the opulent displays at Macy's and into the women's shoes department. *That handsome face, the long dark hair . . . I know him, I know that I know him. . . .*

She paused in front of a display of sequined shoes, momentarily distracted by the thought of finding shoes to match her favorite black sequin dress. *Attack sequins. Guaranteed to stop traffic.* Shopping was excellent trauma therapy, a new idea for medical treatment, she thought, eying the sequined shoes and then deciding to pass on them, at least for now.

In the next department, she considered a new British trenchcoat, perfect for foggy San Francisco mornings. It looked like a good buy, especially with the matching scarf;

a warm and comfortable coat, as comfortable as an old
friend.

*Hands in the pockets of her old coat, listening to flute
music, surprisingly lovely and unexpected. . . .*

And connected with that boy, somehow.

Susan shook her head, trying to remember. A concert
. . . no, she would've been wearing better clothes, probably her black wool wrap over a dress, not the old worn
jacket with holes in the pockets. But if it wasn't a concert, where would she have heard him play music before
. . . where?

She paid for the new coat, and left with the package
under her arm, back toward the parking lot. The wind had
picked up, swirling leaves around her feet as she crossed
the street. Near the parking lot attendant's booth, a gray-
haired man with his cap on the ground was singing Gershwin
to the street, mostly ignored by the pedestrians. And that
was when it came to her.

A street musician! That boy is a street musician!

Elation hit her in an adrenaline rush; she laughed out
loud, and began to think back of all the times she'd seen
street musicians in San Francisco, the different corners and
tourist areas and business districts . . . down near the Pier,
maybe? Or Ghiradelli Square? Maybe at the cable car station, where the crowds of tourists waited in endless lines
to ride the cable cars? Fog, cold, wind . . . where would
she find those at an hour when she wouldn't be at the lab?

"Now the quest begins," she said under her breath.
Unlocking her car, she sat down in the driver's seat and
reached for the stack of maps in the glove compartment.
With a map of San Francisco spread out in front of her,
she plotted out the best approach to the Pier area, then
folded up the map and started her car, carefully backing
out of the parking lot and into the late morning traffic.

*Maybe this is crazy. Maybe I'm searching for someone
who's nothing more than a hallucination . . . maybe we all
really were poisoned by the cafeteria meatloaf last night at
the labs, and I only imagined the guy. Then again, maybe
he's real . . . and if he's real, he's the answer to all of this.*

If I can find him, the bastard who's responsible for what happened to Frank and Dave and all those others, then maybe I won't be afraid to go back to the Labs anymore, afraid to go home to a silent apartment and afraid of trying to sleep tonight . . . afraid those things are going to come back for the one that got away.

At first, her quest seemed hopeless—on a chilly San Francisco morning, very few street musicians were at the Square or Pier 39. She asked at the Pier management office whether they might have a list of the musicians who regularly played there, and had to listen to a serious-eyed woman take ten minutes to explain that except for the performers who did shows on the small stage at the center of the Pier, they had no way of tracking the street musicians.

She stopped at Pier 45 for a quick lunch, then went back to Ghiradelli Square for another attempt. This time she hit paydirt: a quartet of musicians playing wild Celtic music for a small crowd. She waited until a lull in the music, then asked them about her mysterious musician.

"Sounds like someone I've seen at the Renaissance Faire, last few weekends," the male guitar-player said. "He's not a regular, but I've seen him there with some friends."

"You were just watching the red-haired girl," one of his female companions teased him. "He was with a woman with bright red hair," the musician informed Susan. "And another man, a blond hunk of a guy. I'd bet they'll be back at the Faire on Saturday."

Saturday . . . too many days away, by Susan's reckoning. "Do you have any idea where I could find him before the weekend?"

"Try the Embarcadero," the man suggested. "I think I saw him there once, playing for the business lunch crowd."

Susan thanked them politely, and headed back to her car. She drove back to the Embarcadero, within walking distance of where she'd started this odd trek, parked and walked to the open plaza.

Too late for the lunch crowd, she realized as she walked up the concrete steps. The plaza was mostly deserted except for businessmen apparently hurrying to meetings and such stuff, and the food stands were obviously shutting down for the afternoon.

She asked the proprietor of a hot dog stand about the street musician, and was rewarded with the man's big smile. "Oh, yes. Beth and Eric and Kory. They're going to play for my daughter's wedding next month." The man fished in his wallet, and pulled out a ragged business card with a number scribbled on the back. "This is their phone number. They live somewhere off Geary Street, maybe on the top of the hill near Broderick? Anyhow, here's the number."

If they take my clearance away, maybe I have a future as a detective, she thought, smiling. "Thank you," she said, writing down the phone number and the street information. *Anyhow, that's enough detective work for one day,* she decided. *Now it's time for combat shopping. . . .*

She made it home before the afternoon traffic began, the long slow trek of cars going across the Bay from the city, in time to see the last of O'Neill's cleanup crew leaving her apartment.

"Find anything interesting, boys?" she asked.

The youngest of the colonel's agents gave her a shy grin, and his superior chivvied him out of the apartment, nodding once to Susan.

She sat down on the couch and thought about the impossible, and what had happened last night. Suddenly she was consumed with the desire to know more, to find out what O'Neill and the other honchos had discovered while she was merrily spending money at Macy's.

Five minutes later, she was on her way back to the office. The gate guard checked her I.D. more carefully than she usually did, but let her pass in without any problems. She was on her way to O'Neill's office when two business-suited Federal agents caught her by the elbows and escorted her in another direction.

"Gentlemen, please!" she said, extracting her elbows.

"Sorry, ma'am, but it's very urgent," one of them said, as they escorted her down to one of the lowest levels in the building, and left her at an office door.

She shrugged, knocked, and walked inside.

And stopped short, seeing her boss and Warden Blair seated in front of her. Together.

"Ah, Dr. Sheffield," Blair said, looking up from a stack of papers. "We weren't expecting you until tomorrow morning. Good, we can talk now."

"We're making some changes in the project," O'Neill said awkwardly. "Because we're so shorthanded now as a result of last night's . . . incident, Dr. Blair is going to be supervising the project, as well as bringing some of his own personnel onto our team."

She was speechless for a moment, then found her voice again. "He's *what?* You can't do that, Bossman!"

"I don't think you understand, Dr. Sheffield." Blair gave her a cold smile. "I'm your boss now. I will be supervising this project, with Colonel O'Neill's assistance."

She frowned, and decided to dig her heels in. "Like hell you are. There's no paperwork on this, no clearance from DoD, nothing. I'm not handing anything over to you, mister, not without the correct paperwork."

"Susan." That was Steve, in the conciliatory tone she remembered from too many late night arguments. "The paperwork will follow in a few days. But since we're so close to getting some genuine results on the project, I thought it best to bring Dr. Blair in immediately."

"We *have* genuine results already, Steve! We don't need this idiot to help us!" She leaned forward, speaking earnestly. "Steve, don't do this to me, please. It's been our project, ever since Day One. This—whatever else he is—he's *not* a geologist or a geophysicist, he's a *psychiatrist.* He not only doesn't have the authority, he doesn't know the Richter scale from a musical scale! Why don't you just bring in Jane Goodall to supervise us, while you're at it?"

"I don't have any control over this situation," Steve said, not meeting her eyes.

Who's jerking your chain, Colonel? she thought bitterly. "I won't be a part of this, Steve. I'll quit. And I'm not bluffing, you know I'll do it." She looked up into Blair's eyes, wanting nothing more than to slap that contemptuous look on his face, and suddenly remembered . . .

. . . recoiling at the look in his eyes, knowing there was nothing human there, a corpse without emotion . . . stepping back, though the music still tugged her forward. Those inhuman eyes, lit with a strange hunger . . .

This is insane, she thought. *He's just a scientist, not a demon. There are no such things as demons, and I'm not sitting across from one.*

But inside, deep down in her gut, she *knew.* "You're one of them," she whispered, more to herself than out loud.

"One of what, doctor?" Blair's eyes followed her intently.

"Excuse me," she said, hoping she could get out of the room without being physically ill. Now she could see it clearly, the shadow behind his eyes, the emptiness where a human being's mind should have been. She made it to the door, but Blair's voice stopped her.

"Think about your job security," he said. "Think about your clearance. Think about that story the colonel taped about the floating shadow-monsters, Dr. Sheffield. I found that story of yours to be absolutely fascinating, and I'm sure the State Board of Mental Health will, too. If you quit this project, I'll make sure they hear of it."

"Go screw yourself," she said with dignity, so angry that she was fighting back tears, and slammed the door behind her.

Two cups of coffee later, the problem wasn't any easier to solve. She had considered assault and battery, intent to cause grievous bodily harm, aggravated assault, assault with a deadly weapon, and various other physical options. She'd also considered exorcism, remembering the emptiness looking back at her from within Warden Blair's eyes. She'd also considered just saying the hell with it and running away, so far that they couldn't find her, and never coming back. Or just leaving, period. She dismissed the threat of siccing the Mental Health Board on her; they didn't have time to chase after one middle-aged scientist, no matter who Blair thought he knew. They were too busy with child-abusers and serial killers. With her credentials, she could be back in work in a European lab within days. Or better yet, the Japanese; they had a vested interest in this, and they had lots and lots of lovely multicolored yen to spend on it. If she wanted to run away.

But I don't want to run. I want someone to explain what in the hell happened last night at the labs, and I want someone to pay for it, whoever caused the deaths of all of those people. I don't believe in mass hallucination, or the food poisoning theory. I want to know that those creatures can't exist, and that there's a logical explanation for all of this, so I can go home and fall asleep without being terrified of dreaming.

And I want to know why Blair's eyes make my skin crawl. . . .

She took the scrap of paper out of her purse, with the few words written on it: "Eric, Beth, Kory. Geary and Broderick." And a phone number with it. She considered the piece of paper, and also considered a third cup of coffee, but decided that it was too much of a good thing.

"I could find them," she said out loud. "I could."

She thought about it, and wondered whether she was just going to escape from the tigers by leaping off the cliff. Blair terrified her, but at least he hadn't killed anyone, at least not in front of her. The long-haired boy, he'd *controlled* those creatures. At least, he said he controlled them.

But then she remembered his shy awkwardness in her apartment that morning, and thought: *A mass murderer shouldn't blush because he's spilling hot water on a counter.*

Maybe he could explain all of this to her, help her find the answers. She wanted that more than anything—to know, to understand.

To find out for certain that she wasn't insane.

And she thought about San Francisco, and the layout of the streets. On Geary and Broderick, there wouldn't be that many houses to check. She could find them, just by walking the area.

She left a dollar on the counter for the coffee, and headed back to her car. During that hour-long drive, she contemplated the insanity that had taken over her life. And beneath it all was the tiny doubt . . . what if it really was just a hallucination? Or insanity?

Or what if it all was real?

It was early evening, and the last light was fading as the fog slowly rolled in over the city. Eric had been up in the window seat, trying to read a book, or at least had stared at the first ten pages for the last several hours, but without any success. It was too difficult to push the dark thoughts from his mind.

It had all happened too fast, much too fast. One day he'd just been Eric Banyon, comfortable in his old life, and then all of this Bard insanity had begun. Suddenly he was a Bard, and had more magic at his disposal than he ever could have imagined in his dreams. A *lot* of magic—sometimes he could sense it within him, a waiting pool of pure light, and he knew that he'd only touched the edges of it, that there was so much further he could go. Summoning the Nightflyers had been so easy, he could've called thousands more of them without straining himself. He'd frozen that scientist lady in her tracks without even thinking about it, just a reflexive grab for magic with a quick whistled musical phrase.

It was too easy, and too powerful. He remembered how high he'd been, summoning his demon army, drunk on the raw power of it.

How am I supposed to live with this? He thought about the other example of overwhelming magical power he'd seen, the insane elven mage Perenor. And his sorceress daughter, Ria. No, Ria hadn't been insane—somehow she'd learned to live with her abilities, at least to the point of not being a physical menace to the city she lived in. He was sure she'd never lost control . . . *well, except for maybe that one argument we had, back at her house in Beverly Hills. But she was really angry at the time.* . . .

How had she managed that level of control? How did anyone manage it, when you had the raw power singing inside you, calling out to be used?

If that lady wasn't catatonic in a hospital in L.A., I might want to ask her about that, Eric thought. The idea of asking Ria Llewellyn for anything appalled him, but it made sense, in a strange way. In a way, she was the only one who could understand what was happening to him, this terror of the sheer magnitude of his magical abilities. *Absolute power corrupts absolutely, and I've got a damn near infinite supply of absolute power,* he thought grimly.

"Hey, Eric."

He looked up instantly, to see Beth smiling faintly at him from the waterbed. He was at her side a moment later. "How are you feeling?"

She had a kind of fragile look to her, and an odd expression in the back of her eyes he didn't like. "Okay, I guess. Kinda thirsty. Is there anything to drink around here?"

"I'll get you a glass of water." He was halfway to the door when a scream ripped through the air.

Beth was staring at her hands, then looked up wildly at him. "Eric, my hands, they're bloody, they're covered with blood!"

"No, Beth—"

"Everything's moving . . . the walls are cracking . . . I can feel the floor giving way . . . Eric, we've got to get out of here!" She clutched at his hands. "No, they're waiting for you outside, they'll kill you! I can see them, you'll carry me out the window and they'll be waiting, waiting . . ."

Elizabet and Kayla burst into the room. "You're dead, you're all dead!" Beth wailed, and burst into tears. A split-second later, Kayla touched her very lightly on the temple. Eric could feel the burst of magic, an electrical crackle across his skin. Beth relaxed back onto the pillows, no longer screaming but still crying softly. Eric looked up as Kory leaped into the room, dripping wet from the hot tub or shower.

Eric wanted to scream himself, or cry. Instead, he moved away to let Elizabet and Kayla get closer to Beth. Kory was staring at Beth with horrified eyes, and Eric knew exactly how he felt.

At that exact moment, someone rang the doorbell downstairs. "I'll get it," Eric volunteered, and headed downstairs.

He felt he couldn't take another second of that blank look in Beth's eyes. What nightmare had she just lived through, hallucinating it right in front of him?

It hit him suddenly, like a brick between the eyes—it was *his* nightmare that she'd just seen, the earthquake destroying the house . . .

His feet continued down the stairway, independent of the turmoil in his mind. The doorbell rang again, and he felt a momentary irritation for whoever it was on the other side of the door—didn't they know that his world was crashing down around him?

It has to be the door-to-door Bible salesmen. Only they have timing this bad.

Susan reached for the doorbell again. This was the four-teenth house she'd tried—she had been keeping count—and so far no one matched her descriptions. No one even knew anyone fitting the description that was living on this street. She stepped back in surprise as the door opened suddenly.

The long-haired young man from her worst nightmare stood in front of her, blinking.

There was a long moment of total silence, as the young man stared at her.

"Well," she said at last, impatiently, "aren't you going to invite me in?"

11

Two Fair Maids

"Bard!" Kory came clattering down the stairs behind him before he could think to do anything, even to slam the door in the woman's face. "Eric, Elizabet wants—"

Eric turned to stop him, but it was too late. Kory jumped the last couple of steps, and skidded to a halt behind him. He stared at the woman from the labs with his eyes gone big and round with surprise.

Slit-pupiled, green cat-eyes. Situated between pointed ears.

Kory was not wearing his human guise. Of course he wasn't; he was tired, worried, and among friends on his home ground. He didn't have to think about keeping up an illusion.

Eric did not need to turn to know that the woman was staring at Kory with the same look of astonishment on her face as Kory was wearing.

Oh shit. As if things weren't bad enough. Before he could even move, however, *she* had forced the issue, pushing past him and closing the door. Then she leaned her back against it so that the only way to get her out would be to forcibly pry her off the door, get it open, and *then* throw her out. No doubt, with her kicking and screaming every step of the way.

He backed up a step. She stared defiantly into his eyes. "I want some answers," she said firmly, "And I want them now. *Who* are you, *what* are you, what did you do back at the labs, *why* did you do it, and *how?* And in God's name, what were those things you called up?" She moved her gaze slightly to meet Kory's for a moment. "Your type, I know, or at least I think I do. I grew up on Tolkien. I've read my Celtic myths. Provided I'm not currently hallucinating all of this, locked up in a little cell. You're either an elf, or I'm seriously ready for a jacket with extra-long sleeves. I don't know what the hell you're doing here, but if I can believe in shadow-monsters that kill people, I can believe in elves, no problem."

Kory drew himself up to his full height and put on all of his dignity. The loose shirt and jeans he wore somehow became the raiment of a prince, and Eric got the fleeting impression of a coronet encircling his head. "I am Korendil, Champion of Elfhame Sun-Descending, Knight of Elfhame Mist-Hold." He placed one long hand on Eric's shoulder. "This is my friend and brother, Bard Eric. If you have aught to challenge him with, you must also challenge me."

Eric didn't know whether to laugh or cry or both. Bethy was upstairs falling apart, this crazy woman had tracked him down and wanted to know what he had been doing at the labs—and now Kory was issuing formal challenges. It was just too much.

He blinked away dizziness. "I—" he began, and his throat closed up. Then his mind went blank.

All three of them stood there staring at each other like a cluster of dummies in a store window, until the sound of someone clearing her throat politely from above them made them all turn. Elizabet stood at the head of the stairs, with Kayla perched, a round-eyed gargoyle, at her feet. Both healers were watching all three of them like Jane Goodall and Dianne Fosse examining a trio of strange primates with unexpected behavior patterns.

"Would someone like to tell me what is going on here?" Elizabet asked.

Before Eric could get his mind and mouth to work, or even his body unfrozen, the lab woman looked up and addressed the healer as the person in charge. "I am Dr. Susan Sheffield," she said, taking an aggressive stance, feet slightly apart, hands on hips. "I work at Dublin Labs—and last night—"

"All hell broke loose," Kayla offered brightly. The woman favored the kid with a glare that had even Kayla shrinking back.

"Last night," the woman repeated tightly, "I watched some kind of shadow thing kill my research assistant and my partner. They told me today that anyone else that didn't get out when the alarms went off is either dead or crazy." She half-turned to glare accusingly at Eric. "And *he* told me it was all *his* doing."

She stabbed a finger at Eric, who shrank away from her, wishing he could melt into the wall. Wishing he could undo everything and go back to the night of the party. Back when things were simpler.

Kayla had gone very pale and quiet; Elizabet looked from the woman to Eric and back again, then nodded, as if making up her mind.

"I think we need some tea," she said, decisively. She descended the stairs like the Queen of England, as Eric repressed the urge to giggle insanely. Instead he followed meekly in her wake, preceded by the lab woman and trailed by Kory and Kayla.

His mind went blank again for a moment. Somehow he found himself sitting at the kitchen table with the rest, a cup of tea in his hands that he did not remember pouring. He sipped it. Chamomile. Just the thing for nerves. He wanted a drink . . . and he knew he didn't dare get one. One drink wouldn't be enough, and how many would it take before the Nightflyers started whispering to him again? And how many more before they started to sound like his best friends? Back when he'd been drinking, he'd thought a lot of rotten people were his best friends. . . .

"I think you should know, before you make any more accusations, that two of us were unwilling 'guests' in Dublin

Labs last night," Elizabet said, watching Susan Sheffield over the rim of her teacup. The scientist narrowed her eyes, looking skeptical. "There is a third victim of detention asleep upstairs right now, suffering severe post-traumatic stress syndrome. If this were someplace like Iraq or South America, I would have said she'd been tortured." At the scientist's look of shock, she added smoothly, "But of course, this is the United States, and nothing like that ever happens here. Does it?"

Susan Sheffield opened her mouth as if to say something, then closed it. Elizabet followed up on her advantage. "And of course, since this is the United States, no one kidnaps middle-aged health professionals from conferences on the psychic, ties them up, shoots them full of sodium amytal, and drags them off to a sub-basement at Dublin Labs. Do they?" Elizabet didn't wait for Dr. Sheffield to answer. She rolled up one of her sleeves with clinical detachment, displaying rope burns around each wrist and a bruise the size of a golf ball on her bicep, a bruise with a needle-mark clearly in the center. "He really was awful, too," she remarked. "I'm surprised that he didn't break the needle off in my arm. But then, I wasn't cooperating."

"How did you—what did you—"

She rolled her sleeve down again. "I told you, I was a health professional; I'm a licensed psychiatric therapist. As it happens, I've gotten jabbed with a needle meant for someone else from time to time in the course of my job. I never thought that would turn out to have been such a good thing. Lucky for me, I've gotten accidental trank doses so many times that my tolerance is pretty high. Otherwise, when the alarms went off, I might have been one of the ones I had to leave behind in the cells."

"Others?" Susan said sharply. "Cells? What others? What cells?"

"The cells on the thirteenth floor below the ground," Kory put in, shaking back his hair. He leaned forward earnestly. "The cells where the evil man put Beth when he took her from us, and where he also put me and tortured me with Cold Iron. I swear to you upon my honor that he did this." He displayed his own wrists, which up until this moment had been hidden in the long cuffs of his soft silk shirt. Eric gulped and averted his eyes, and beside him he heard Susan Sheffield gasp. As well she might. It looked for all the world as if someone had been working Kory's wrists and lower arms over with red-hot wires.

Eric's hands tightened around his cup, as his own wrists burned and throbbed in sympathy. *That was what I Saw,* he realized, suddenly, *when I tried to reach him with the Bardic magic. That was what I felt. They* were *hurting him, and the Cold Iron might have killed him if the pain didn't turn him crazy.*

"Level thirteen?" the scientist asked, licking her lips nervously as Kory covered his wrists again. Her eyes had gone from skeptical to wary. Eric had the feeling that the reference to this thirteenth floor hadn't taken her entirely by surprise. "But thirteen is a sealed level, it's the one just above mine. That's—that's Warden Blair's labs, the Cassandra Project! How did you get in there? Nobody gets in there! I mean, I know he has about four times the number of lab people than anyone else, but—you aren't lab people—"

Both Kory and Elizabet nodded, but it was Elizabet who spoke. "We didn't 'get in,' we were brought in. Our charming host called himself Dr. Blair," she said calmly, outwardly unmoved by the display of Kory's burns. "And I would guess that when the alarm went off, there were about a dozen of us who got out of our cells—our *locked, monitored* cells— and escaped. There were at least as many who didn't, who were either too broken, too cowed, or too frightened to run. Or, possibly, too crazy."

"He said that there were fourteen lab people missing," the scientist said, as if to herself. Then her gaze sharpened as it fell on Eric. "But what about *him* and his pet monsters? What's he got to do with this?"

Eric's wits finally came back, and he straightened up, looking back at her with all the defiance he had left. "I knew that my friends were locked up in Dublin Labs, lady—high-tech, Fed stuff in there—and everything pointed to the Feds taking them. What was I supposed to do, call the cops and tell them to go arrest some Feds, or maybe write my representative in Congress? Was I supposed to just let them rot in there? Look what they did to Kory! I had to get them out!" He swallowed once, then continued. "So I used the only weapon I could think of. It wasn't a good choice, but I didn't know that then. I didn't know what they'd do, I didn't know that they'd manage anything worse than scaring people. I thought—I don't know what I thought. I know that I didn't think there'd be anyone innocent in there." He dropped his eyes, then, to stare at his hands and the cup in them. "I thought everybody in there would have to know what was going on, would have to be bad guys. *I* don't know what goes on in a place like that! I'm just a musician."

The scientist started laughing, a note of hysteria in her voice. "Just a musician. *Just* a musician! Playing Pied Piper to a bunch of man-killing monsters and you're *just* a musician!"

For a moment, Eric thought that Elizabet might slap the woman to bring her out of her hysterics—but when he looked up, the healer just pursed her lips at him and shook her head slightly.

Susan passed from hysterical laughter to soft weeping within a few moments; sobbing into her hands, crying with a peculiarly helpless tone to her voice. Elizabet left her alone for that, too, until she got herself under control, and wiped her eyes with a paper napkin. Then she looked up at Elizabet, and when she spoke, her voice was steady.

"I could believe just about anything of Warden Blair before today," she said steadily. "And now, after this afternoon—I *can* believe he'd do anything. The man was as cold as a snake, and had about as much moral sense."

"Do you have any idea what Warden Blair did there?" Elizabet asked urgently. "I have a very traumatized woman upstairs. If I have some idea what might have happened to her, I might be able to help her."

Susan Sheffield pursed her lips. "I know he had a lot of equipment," she said, finally. "He was supposed to be running some kind of psych project. That was what rumor said, anyway. But he had all kinds of equipment that he'd scrounged from all over the labs that no psych project would need. Colonel Steve likes to use mythological names for our projects, names that kind of have something to do with the project itself. Like, mine is 'Poseidon,' because it's got to do with earthquakes, and Poseidon was the god of the sea and earthquakes."

"Poseidon, the earth-shaker," Elizabet muttered. "But 'Cassandra'—that was the prophetess of Troy, the one doomed both to speak the truth of what would come and never be believed." She pondered a moment. "Could it be that he was attempting to collect psychics for some kind of *government work*? Seeing the future, perhaps?"

The scientist shrugged. "He was popularly thought of as a real nut-case; nobody who had ever met him wanted to work on his projects. As I said, I could believe about anything of him. And—" She paused and her face paled. "And some of the people who quit his project had—bad luck. Pretty bizarre bad luck, really. . . . I'd never thought about it before, I guess nobody did, but it was things like the intern kids getting kicked out of their grad programs or being forcibly transferred to other universities. I remember one kid in tears, because they'd told him to either quit or go to Anchorage. And we sure never saw them around the labs anymore."

Elizabet snapped her fingers in front of the woman's eyes, startling her. "You were going to tell me something about the equipment Blair has," she said firmly.

"Weird stuff," the scientist said faintly. "Oh, a decompression chamber, for one thing; that had been sitting in the corner of *my* space since I'd gotten my floor and I was just as glad to see it go upstairs—but what would a psych project need with something like that? And one day one of my grad students came back giggling that the dumpster from his floor was full of boxes from—" she blushed crimson "—from, ah, one of those—ah—'adult toy stores.' You know—"

"Pornshops," Elizabet said crisply. The woman flushed again.

"Yes, well, this one is supposed to be really popular with the—ah—'leatherboys.' The ones who like to tie each other up. Handcuffs, restraints, and gags, according to my lab kid." She rubbed her cheeks, and averted her gaze. "There were lots of boxes. So many that Charlie asked me if Blair was planning on holding a party. A 'black tie-down party for thirty,' he said."

"Hmm." Elizabet seemed lost in thought, and asked the next question absently. "What did you mean, earlier, when you said that you would believe just about anything of Blair before today?"

Susan's flush vanished, and her face went dead-white. "Today—today when I saw Warden Blair, he wasn't the same man at all. Oh, outwardly he looked the same, but—the snake that used to be on the thirteenth floor was someone I wouldn't have trusted without all the cards on my side of the table, but he was still someone I understood. I've seen his type before. But today—he's changed, and I can't read him at all. I think he *would* do anything."

Eric had a horrible, sinking feeling, the feeling as if he *almost* knew something. And that when he found out what it was, he was going to be really afraid. Not that he wasn't afraid now, but—

Suddenly Susan Sheffield seemed to wake up, and she stared at Elizabet as if the healer had just sprouted horns and wings. "What am I doing, talking to you like this? You don't have clearances, you don't have any right to know *anything* about the labs. I came here to get you to answer *my* questions, not the other way around!" She shoved her chair back and stood up, angrily. Eric distinctly heard Kayla mutter *damn*. "I'm getting out of here, and when I do, I'm calling Colonel Steve and letting him know I found you."

But Kory was between her and the door, instantly. She looked up at him, surprised, probably wondering how he had gotten there so fast.

"We shall not imprison you, my lady," the elf said gravely, "but we cannot allow you to do that."

Susan's response to that was a quick knee to Kory's groin.

Eric heard something like a muffled *clank*. Then *she* bent over double, clutching her knee and moaning.

Kayla giggled. "All that and endurance too," she said with a grin. Elizabet glared at her, but she kept on grinning.

Kory remained in the doorway, shaking his head sorrowfully. "I am very sorry, my lady," he said over Kayla's snickering, "but I have seen those television programs also."

Elizabet rose, graceful and unhurried, and got the scientist back over to a chair. But instead of placing her hands on Susan's knee and doing something about the pain as Eric had expected, she sat back in her own chair.

:*Why isn't she helping?:* he asked Kory silently, forming the words carefully in his mind. This telepathy thing was still new to him and it didn't come easily. Nor was it of any use much outside of normal vocal range. A different kind of speech, was all, and if he wanted to talk to someone on the other side of town, he might as well use the telephone; it was a lot more reliable.

:*I believe because she has no strength to waste and wishes to save it for Bethany,:* Kory replied the same way.

"Gentlemen," Elizabet said after a moment, while the woman massaged her maltreated knee, "why don't you go into the other room for a moment. And Kayla, go sit with Beth. I think Susan and I should talk together a little. You can watch the door from there easily enough."

Kayla started to protest, but a look from Elizabet quelled her. She got up sulkily, and left with a look of disgust at being excluded. Eric and Kory followed.

Kayla clattered noisily up the staircase; so noisily that it had to be on purpose. Eric waited until Kayla was up the stairs before saying anything.

"Kory, Elizabet needs to know what happened to Beth, right?" he asked, flinging himself down into a chair. Kory seated himself on the couch, across from him. "Not just what *happened* to her, but what went on inside her head."

The elf nodded, slowly, his blond curls looking a lot more wilted than Eric was used to seeing. "I believe so."

This is taking a lot out of him. Me, too. "And *we* need some serious reinforcements." He scratched his head. "Look,

I tried to get through to your relatives when you got caught, and I couldn't reach them. But I was using the phone— *you've* got to have some way of getting to them, you know, elvishly. Right?"

Kory glanced warily at the kitchen door as the voices on the other side of it rose for a moment. "I can contact my cousins, yes," he replied. "And at nearly any time or place. But—why need we reinforcements? Are we not safe again, and together? Have we not defeated the evil men? Once Bethany is well—"

"Is the guy that kidnapped you dead?" Eric countered. "You just heard that woman say he's still around. As long as *he's* around, we aren't safe." He ran his hands through his hair distractedly, trying to think of all the angles. Plotting was not his forte. It should be Beth doing this, not him. "Shit, we aren't safe now, if he knows where we live. I'm only hoping that he doesn't, that the reason he took Beth in broad daylight was because he doesn't know who we really are and where we live. I dunno, he was picking up psychics, maybe he's got some kind of psychic sonar that zooms in on people like Elizabet and us. Maybe that's how he found us. I hope so. 'Cause if he knows where we live, we're in deep kimchee."

At Kory's look of bewilderment, he shook his head. "Let me see if I can explain this right. Remember—ah—*Die Hard* 2?" The elf was an insatiable consumer of action films, good, bad, and terrible, and with his magic, if they didn't have the cash, it was easy enough for him to sneak into theaters with his Low Court cousins, so it was a safe bet that he had seen the movie and he would recall it.

If the film industry had more fans as devoted as Kory, Hollywood would have nothing to worry about.

"Remember how the bad guys had friends in with the good guys?"

"The special army team; yes, I remember." Kory frowned. "I think I catch your meaning. While those who are honorable would condemn Warden Blair's actions, they are prevented from knowing about them by friends of Blair's who have been corrupted by him."

"Pretty close," Eric said, relieved. Fortunately for them all, Kory became less naive about the human world with every day, particularly where human failings were concerned. *Hooray for Hollywood.*

"And these same corrupt men have the resources to find us again," the elf brooded. "This is an ill thing. I believe I must call the others. Arvin above all will know what to do."

"Good. Excellent. How soon do you think they can be here?"

Kory pondered for a moment. "Bard Eric, would you say this is an emergency?"

He gave a thought to what the elves might consider an "emergency." His peril and Beth's—not a chance. They were human, and important only to Kory. But Kory—

"Yeah, I'd say so," he replied. "Tell Arvin that the human had you captured and bound with Cold Iron—that he's going to come after you again—and that once he has you it would only be a matter of time before he figured out what you are. That means humans—*in the government*—would know all about elves. And *that* would mean that none of you would be safe outside of Underhill." He smiled a little to himself; Arvin might well be indifferent to the fates of Kory's pet humans, but he *adored* living in human society and he'd go mad from boredom in the carefully controlled world of Underhill. That would bring him around soon enough—

"You might tell him that given this set of humans, they might even figure a way for themselves to actually get into Underhill," he added. "They're scientists, and once a scientist knows that something is possible, they find ways to do it."

Put that in your little leprechaun pipe and smoke it, Arvin.

"I shall do that," Kory replied, a certain grim delight on his face. "I think I can have at least a dozen or two here within the hour, with that to fling at them."

That was good news. "Okay, you take care of that. I'm going upstairs. By the time they get here, I may have some idea what's going on with Bethy." He vaulted up out of his chair and sprinted for the stairs, noting absently as he passed the kitchen door that the murmur of voices sounded less angry and more—anxious.

And maybe Elizabet's getting through to the scientist-lady. I sure hope so. I don't want to have to wipe her mind clean of what happened at the labs and anything to do with us.

This Bardic magic stuff was getting messier all the time. Seemed as if every time he used it to fix something, he had to use it again to fix what the fix had messed up, and then fix the problems that the fix to the fix had brought up.

Why couldn't things be simple, like in one of those awful Role Adventure Escape books? Just find the Magic Talisman and poof, all the crayon-box dragons would roll over on their backs. . . .

He paused at the door to the bedroom and peeked inside. Beth was asleep, but he doubted it was anything other than magic-induced sleep. Kayla looked up as the door creaked, surveying him warily from her perch in the window.

And just find the Wand of Wizardly Wonder, wave it, and everyone is healed of everything. Including death. He shook his head a little unhappily. *I could do with one of those right now. And not just for Bethy.*

"Kayla?" he whispered, easing himself into the room. "You're gonna have to spot for me. Kory's calling in some kind of elven SWAT team to back us, and I'm going to try to find out what happened to Bethy, since she won't tell us."

The kid's expression sharpened with interest, until she looked like an alert little fox. "What are you gonna do, Bard?"

He grimaced ruefully. "Wish I knew. Oh, I have a plan— I'm gonna try and get inside her head. But once I'm in there, well, I dunno what's gonna happen. So you'll have to play it by ear. Sorta put a lifeline on me and haul me out if something goes wrong, okay? You're better at this than Elizabet is."

"Jeez, you don't ask for much, do you?" the kid muttered. Then, louder, "Okay, I'll do what I can. But—shit, Bard,

I don't know what I'm doing here. So don't sue me if I mess it up."

"If we both mess it up, kid, there isn't gonna be anything to sue." This was going to be dangerous for Kayla—not so dangerous as it was for him—but she could get hurt and he hoped the healer kid realized it. From the expression on her face, she did. From the expression on her face, she also had no plans to try and back out.

Kayla gritted her teeth. "I know," Kayla said grimly.

He settled himself on the bed next to Beth, one hand covering one of hers. What should he use to key on? There weren't any Celtic songs about mind-reading. . . .

Oh, of course. Gordon Lightfoot. Perfect. He closed his eyes, and hummed the first few bars—and Felt the power take hold of him.

"Okay," he muttered, "let's get this over with."

He came up out of his trance with a scream.

And he found himself the center of an audience. Kayla he had expected, and maybe Kory—but the tiny room was full of bodies, human and elven. His eyes went first to Elizabet—and, to his immense relief, he saw a pale-faced, round-eyed Susan Sheffield crowded in beside her. Kory stood on the other side of the scientist, and the rest were jammed in however.

He checked the elves first, and they were equipped for mayhem. Elegant, but definitely no one was going to mess with them. Knives long enough to qualify as swords hung at many sides; the elf he had last seen dressed in pink-punk style was still in pink, but it was a catsuit, and she had a bandolier of throwing knives across her chest. One end of a *bo* staff peeked over the heads of those on the right side, and were those arrows on the left?

So they'd taken the threat seriously. Good. They'd better. The threat was a serious one. He hadn't been throwing bull when he'd told that stuff to Kory. Odds were nine-to-one it was true.

"Well?" Elizabet said, as he struggled into a sitting position—not an easy feat on a waterbed.

"Remember what you said about torture?" he asked the healer, who frowned and nodded. "Well, that's what he did. Somehow he figured out that Bethy's a claustrophobe; there's nothing in Beth's memory of how he did it, but I'm guessing maybe he used her reactions to questions and had a lie-detector on her. Then he locked her in that damn decompression chamber in the dark, and started increasing the pressure." He snarled as he spoke, and the scientist whitened a little further. "Real clever, too. Torture without leaving marks. Wonder what he'd have done to you, Elizabet?"

Kayla was livid, and holding her anger well; much better than he had expected she would. "That's probably what I was for, boss," she said to Elizabet, who nodded. "He was gonna snatch me, and tell you to cooperate or he'd take me apart and not be too careful about putting me back together. I almost wish that son of a bitch would let me get within a few feet of him, guards or no guards. . . ."

"There's more," he told them, "but right now, the only thing that's pertinent is that she's got the phobia mixed up with my precognitive dream about the Big One. The one we were kinda talking about. It's pretty clear, and there's Nightflyers mixed up in that one, too. That gonna give you enough to work on?"

"That should give me enough to break her out," Elizabet told him. "Once I've got her out of this hallucination-cycle she's in, and talking, the rest will come."

He heaved a sigh of relief, and rolled to the edge of the bed. Several sets of hands helped him up, and he staggered with fatigue as he got to his feet. Kory caught and held him, and he looked up into the friendly, worried, elven face he knew so well. "I have a nice nervous breakdown coming," he said conversationally. "I've earned it, and I'm by-God going to take it as soon as this mess is over. But right now—we've got things to take care of. Is Arvin in here, somewhere?"

"Here, Bard," said a voice at the back, somewhere near the *bo* staff.

"Okay, let's all of us get out of here and let Kayla and

Elizabet do their thing. I've got something that involves all of the rest of us." He looked straight at Susan Sheffield. "You, especially."

"Me?" She looked confused and apprehensive, and probably would have backed away from him if there hadn't been so many people.

"Yeah, you, and that Home for Deranged Scientists you work at. Let's move it on out of here." He nodded at the door, and let the tide of the others carry him down the stairs and to the living-room.

Once there, the "audience" arranged itself around him in a semicircle; Arvin wordlessly handed him a glass of Gatorade, which he downed with gratitude. His head hurt, he was ready to drop, and he wanted to sleep for a week. He could have used one of Kayla's jump-starts, but she was busy with something more important.

Christ, I haven't felt this bad since my last hangover.

And yet, he was calm for the first time in weeks, maybe months, because now he had some answers. He wasn't crazy, his dream was a warning, not a hallucination. And he wasn't—entirely—to blame for what the Nightflyers had done. He had been their tool, and there was some blame there; he had allowed himself to be deceived and that was something he was never going to forget. But others had been their tools as well, and one of them was standing awkwardly beside the sofa.

"You said your project had something to do with earthquakes, right?" he said to Susan Sheffield. She nodded uncomfortably. "So what's it all about? And what's going on with it right now?"

"I can't tell you that—" she began. He interrupted her with a downward slash of his hand.

"Damn your clearance crap anyway!" he spat, and she winced away from him. Arvin looked impressed. "All right. *I'll* tell you."

His time in trance hadn't been spent entirely in Beth's mind. And it hadn't been at all under his conscious control. Someone, or something, had guided and impelled his vision. Maybe it had only been his subconscious, which had always been better at putting two and two together than he was. Maybe it had been his conscience, which had lately been pretty good at making him face up to the facts, no matter how unpleasant they were.

Whatever it was, once he'd seen in Bethy's memory what she had been put through, his trance had taken a different turn without him thinking about it. He had leapt into an omniscient point of reference right over Warden Blair's shoulder, and fast-forwarded to the Nightflyer invasion.

He knew a lot now. He knew that Warden Blair wasn't Warden Blair anymore—and hence, the change that Dr. Sheffield had noticed. And he knew what Project Poseidon was.

"You built yourself an earthquake machine down there, didn't you?" he said to Susan, whose eyes widened with shock. "Not one to *read* them; one to make them. I don't suppose you worried much about the implications of that."

"That's all I thought about! It's meant to trigger microquakes, to relieve stress along faultlines," she said defensively. "It's going to help people, to save lives—"

"Yeah, but your project's in Warden Blair's hands, lady," he countered as she blanched. "And by the way, I wouldn't go back to my apartment right now if I were you. He told that Colonel Steve of yours to send you a little reception committee after that unscheduled visit you made to the office this afternoon. He got worried, and he wants to make sure he has your services for as long as he needs them."

Her face went paper-white, then flushed. "You'd better be telling the truth," she said angrily, "because I have a way of checking that."

He spread his hands and arched his eyebrows. "Be my guest. Check on it. I'd rather you did that than walk into an enemy ambush."

"I need the phone." She changed her challenging gaze to Kory, who moved politely out of the way of the phone on the wall—but stayed within grabbing distance of her in case she tried anything.

She dialed a number, which must have been answered on the first ring. "Hi, Betty, it's Susan. Listen, I was supposed to have a cleaning crew over this afternoon, are they there yet?" She listened for a moment, and her angry flush paled to white again, though her voice remained steady. "Well, good, Betty, that's terrific. Yes, they certainly are handsome young men. Yes, they're bonded, that's why I let the firm have a key. No, they'll probably be there a while; they're cleaning everything. That project's coming to a head, and the place is a pigpen. Thanks Betty, I just wanted to be sure they'd gotten there. No, thanks, I'll probably be working late. Bye."

She hung up, and when she turned to Eric, her hands were shaking. "A nosy, elderly neighbor can be a wonderful thing, sometimes," she said, with a false little laugh.

"Yeah," he replied.

She made her way carefully to the sofa, and sat down on it. *How much else do I tell her?* he wondered, watching her. For all the profound shocks she'd had, she was coping pretty well. Encountering Nightflyers, death, Bardic magic, elves, and betrayal all in forty-eight hours could put quite a strain on the brain. . . . But he needed her input.

Okay. He might as well go for the whole thing. "You said that you'd noticed something weird about Blair the last time you saw him?" he asked carefully. "I mean, weirder than usual."

"The lights were on, but nobody was home," she said without a second thought. "Or—no, somebody was home, all right, but it wasn't human—"

She stopped, suddenly, and he saw her putting all the facts together in the way her brow creased and her eyes widened. "One of those things," she gasped. "One of those horrible shadow things took him over, like in The Exorcist! Didn't it?"

He nodded, while all of the elves except Kory looked puzzled. *Great. Kory didn't tell them how I sprung him. That's not going to make them real happy with me, even if it isn't a direct threat to them. Yet.*

"Right," he said wearily. "And *that* is what's in charge of your project. In charge of something that can trigger the

Big One, instead of preventing it. And just what do you think it's going to do with something like that?"

He thought for a moment that she might faint, she grew so white, but she recovered.

"All right," she said, slowly. "All right. I believe you. For whatever I'm worth, you've got me on your side. Now what?"

"Now you sit there for a minute," he told her, and turned to the others, taking a deep breath.

Okay, kids, it's story-time with Uncle Eric. Got a lot of catching up to do, and a short time to do it in. "When you last saw our heroes, they were recovering from the big party," he began. "This is what happened when you all left them—"

12

Tom O'Bedlam (Reprised)

Eric waited in sick suspense when he finished his narrative. He more than halfway expected the elves—Arvin in particular—to jump all over him for the way he'd handled the Nightflyers. And he definitely expected them to be on his case for bringing them across in the first place. But they weren't and they didn't. And in a way, their actual reaction surprised him more than anything else.

Silence for a moment, then thoughtful nods. Susan looked sick, though—and more than a little afraid of him. Well, he didn't blame her for either reaction. Kory laid a comforting hand on his shoulder, and he covered it with his. That was one thing he could count on, anyway. Kory would stand by him, no matter how boneheaded he'd been, and help him fix what he'd done wrong.

"Ye didna do too badly, Bard," one of the more stiff-necked, High Court types said grudgingly. "I canna say that any of us would have acted differently."

He couldn't have been more amazed if they'd handed him the Congressional Medal of Honor. "But—" he stammered, "but—I screwed up! I did everything wrong that you could think of! It's my fault there's one of them playing around in Blair's body right now!"

But it was Arvin, not Kory, who leapt to his defense. "No

one," Arvin said fiercely, "no one in all the history that we know, has ever brought more than one of the Nightflyers over from the chaos of the Primal Plane where nightmares are. *No one.* Not even the Unseleighe. How could you know what they would do? We don't!" He looked down at Eric broodingly, no longer the careless, light-minded, exotic dancer. That persona was gone, shed as easily as shedding a costume. Arvin was a Warrior now—capital "W"—and looked it. Lightweight armor, short sword, hair tied back in a businesslike braid.

He'd shown up on the doorstep ready for a fight. "Oh, there are some few things you might have done differently, had you not been so weary and so concerned for the others."

"Like?" he prompted.

Arvin shrugged. "You should have counted the evil beasties before you sent them out; if you had been a practiced sorcerer you would have known to control them with binding spells to harm no one who was not directly involved with the abductions. And yet—that might not have been enough; they might be clever enough to find loopholes in binding spells. There is some fault resting with us, even."

Arvin and Kory both glanced over at another High Court warrior—Eric finally recalled his name as "Dharinel," and that he was one of the Mist-Hold elves that did not approve of Kory's liaison with humans. He didn't much approve of humans in general, as far as that went; he avoided coming out from Underhill as much as he could. Eric had only met him once or twice, at the time when Kory had introduced them to the Mist-Hold court, and once at a gathering of Arvin's. And he had shown up on their doorstep only once: to lecture Kory on his duty, and to find himself escorted politely to the door.

Dharinel nodded sourly in agreement with Arvin's last statement. "Korendil wished us to teach you, Bard," he said with obvious unhappiness. "Because he is only a Magus Minor, and knew nothing of the Bardic Powers or how strong you would or could become. I opposed that training. One Taliesen, I felt, was enough, especially in these days when no one believes in magic. If the humans had lost their magic, that was to the good. Or so I thought. Now, it seems, events have proved me wrong."

Well, don't apologize or anything.

"If we all survive this, Bard, we will see to your proper training," Arvin said firmly. "I will make certain that High Lord Dharinel takes care of that *personally*." The veiled glance he threw at the other elf implied a whole lot more than Eric understood.

What am I, some kind of counter in a game of elven politics? was his first thought, and *what does he mean, "if we survive?"* was his second.

"If?" he said, swallowing. "What's with this 'if' stuff? You know something I don't?"

"The reason that you could not reach me when Kory was first taken," Arvin said, his expression grim, "was that we had Seers of our own who had experienced some disturbing visions of late. Visions of the earth shaking hereabouts; of terrible death of humans. And yes, of a horde of some shadowy creatures that we *thought* might be Nightflyers. Only we were not certain; in fact, it seemed far more likely that they were some creation of our Unseleighe kindred. And there were those of us—" he cast a resentful glance at Dharinel "—who were of the opinion that it did not matter if disaster overtook the humans here. But that was before this morning."

Dharinel did not—quite—snarl. "My own sister—who is a Seer—undertook to Foresee if this great disaster could have any impact upon those of us Underhill. We had no reason to think that it would, of course, none whatsoever. But she is a cautious creature, and felt it might be worth the effort. That was when she Saw that the energies of the quake would close off the accesses here to the Elfhame, stranding any who were here in your world, and isolating them from the rest of us. Bad enough, that—but worse would come. For the creatures we had seen were Nightflyers in their dozens, but worse, they were breeding on the misery and death following the quake, breeding in the newly dead bodies. The breeding Nightflyers, growing stronger and more cunning, would find a way to prey upon the elvenkind so stranded, taking Low Court first, then High. And then—driven by hunger for the new prey—then they would break across the barriers themselves, and pour into Underhill."

Arvin nodded, and Eric whistled in mingled surprise and dismay. He knew that Nightflyers could kill; he hadn't known they could kill elves.

"That discovery is what had us isolated from you," Arvin said. "We were in conference, trying to discover what we could do to prevent such a catastrophe. Now, perhaps, we know."

"It's a quake that starts it all, right?" Susan Sheffield asked in a quiet voice. Dharinel and Arvin turned as one, as if they had forgotten she was there.

"That is what the visions seem to tell us," Arvin said carefully. "Of course, as with all visions of the future, the picture is unclear, often distorted. The future is uncertain and many things can work to change it."

"You think Blair might go ahead and run your machines without you?" Eric asked. "I mean, can he? Don't you have to be there or something? Isn't everything, like, secret? You keep what you're doing in code and in hidden notebooks?"

She smiled faintly. "Sorry kid," she said regretfully. "This isn't the late-late show. These days, especially if you're doing research on a government grant, you have to keep clear instructions and up-to-the-minute protocol, in case you get hit by a truck—or—or get 'compromised' as Steve likes to say—and somebody else has to pick up where you left off."

She shook her head, thinking of all the regs she had to follow—not for the sake of good science necessarily, but to keep her grants. She had never guessed how much of her life would be tied up in bureaucratic crap. "You've got to be ready for inspections, and be ready to prove you can do what you say you can. There's only so much grant money and lots of people want it. Especially Teller's boys, and he still has clout, the old bastard." She shrugged. "It wouldn't be easy for someone to crack my computer protections, but anybody with a higher access priority than mine—like Colonel Steve—is going to be able to bypass those." She smiled wanly. "I hope you've got a guest room. I think I'm going to need it."

"So as soon as they figure out that you aren't coming home to your apartment, we can bet on Blair having his hands on your stuff." Eric sighed and buried his face in his hands. "God, I wish we had Bethy in one piece. She's so much better at this real-world strategy stuff than I am. There's so many things to try and think of—"

"I think," Kory said, slowly, "that there are only two questions that should concern us at the moment. How soon will it take the Blair-creature to learn how to operate your mechanisms—and how long will it take for him to make the earthquake happen when he does?"

She was awake. And—not in a street full of bodies, nor a chamber with walls closing in on her. That was an improvement—at least for as long as it lasted.

Beth kept her eyes tightly closed, and took in the evidence of her other senses. Was she hallucinating again, or sane, however temporarily? Or worse—still a captive? Sound—the murmur of voices from downstairs, and the faint sounds of traffic from outside. Scent—the green of the garden on a gentle breeze. Touch—the crisp feel of sheets on her body, the soft cotton of the quilt Karen had given them under her hands, and the faintly undulating warmth of the waterbed.

I'm home. I'm safe. There's no earthquake, no monsters, and no mad scientist. . . .

She waited, holding her breath, for all of that to change. It always had. Only this time she held her breath until she couldn't stand it anymore—and it didn't.

"You might as well open your eyes, Beth Kentraine," said a voice she knew. "Because I know very well that you're awake."

"Elizabet!" Her lids flew open without any urging on her part, and she sat straight up, making the waterbed slosh. Elizabet sat on one padded railing, while Kayla perched on the other. Both of them watching her.

Doesn't that kid ever just sit somewhere? It's like she's

only there for a second before she decides to take off for somewhere else.

"What happened?" she asked, not sure what she meant.

"Ah." Elizabet's dark brow arched upwards. "That is what I wanted to ask you. What happened to you in the lab complex? Every time I attempted to ask you—well, you were most uncooperative."

"I'd—rather not talk about it," Beth faltered.

But Elizabet leaned over and seized her wrist, forcing her to look into the healer's eyes. "I do not really care that you would rather not talk about it, girl," the healer said fiercely, enunciating each word with care. "You have work to do that you can't do as walking wounded, and if you *don't* talk about what happened, I can't do anything for you!"

Beth wanted to deny that she needed any help—but the trembling, hollow place inside her told her that she did need it, and needed it badly. At any moment, she could find herself on that street, or in that tiny room. There would be no predicting it. She would never be able to sleep, waiting for nightmares; never be able to sit within four walls, waiting for them to crush her. The spells would return, throwing her back into horror with little or no warning. And she knew it.

What had been a simple phobia, easily dealt with, had become a mental cancer eating at her sanity.

She took a deep breath, and clenched her fists in the fabric of the quilt. "Some goons grabbed me on the street and shoved me into a car. I don't know where they took me, at least, I didn't until we broke out—Dublin Labs, right? All I knew was they got me into this place that was like some kind of prison."

Elizabet nodded. "Then what?"

"There was a man," she said, slowly. "Probably the same one who nabbed you. He—he wanted me to sign some papers, sort of check myself into whatever program he was running."

"He said the same to me. We think he was collecting psychics," Elizabet said, giving Beth a moment to steel herself against what she must deal with next.

"Well, I told him to go stuff it," she said. "He—didn't like that; I guess he likes people being afraid of him and it really pissed him off that I wasn't. He kept asking me questions, and he—he turned off the ventilation."

The mere memory was enough to make her sweat. But then Kayla touched her other hand—

And suddenly, it wasn't quite so bad. The feeling of edge-of-panic was still there, but not so bad. She licked her lips and continued.

"Then—I thought he might rough me up, but he didn't. He had his goons drag me around and shove me into a decompression chamber. And he—he turned off the lights—and—"

I can't! she thought, panic rising to choke her throat shut. *I can't, I can't talk about it, I—* The walls were closing in; they were going to collapse on her, she saw them moving, leaning down, about to topple—

Kayla touched her wrist again, and Elizabet did the same on the other side—hardly felt at all amid the wave of fear and panic that had washed over her.

And then—the fear was gone. Mostly, anyway. There was still sweat on her forehead, and running coldly down her spine, and her stomach was full of new-hatched butterflies, but the walls weren't moving, and she could breathe again.

She blinked in amazement, then stared at the two healers, knowing they had done something, but not sure what it was that they had done to her. "How in *hell* did you do that?" she demanded. "I was about to go into a full-bore claustrophobia attack! How in hell did you stop it?"

Kayla shrugged, and Elizabet simply smiled. "Half of our work was done for us," the older woman said. "Eric exercised some of his own powers to find out what had happened to you—and when we went to work on you while you were still unconscious, we discovered that he had already half-healed you. Without even realizing it, I suspect. That may be why the poor child looks like a puppy's favorite rag right now."

She seemed to remember something—in the depths of the worst of her nightmares—a strain of melody. An old

Shaker hymn, "Simple Gifts." And even now, as she thought of the melody, she felt a calm descending over her, and new strength coming to her.

The same one she and Eric had used to heal Kory when they thought that they had almost lost him.

A melody that she had followed out of nightmare and into ordinary fear—out of madness and into sanity.

"Am I cured?" she asked, incredulously. "I mean, am I—"

Elizabet shook her head. "You're still claustrophobic, and the only way you're going to get over that is going to be through a few months of desensitization training. I'll put you in touch with a therapist who's also a Wiccan. But for now, Kayla and I have put a layer of mental floss between you and the memories, that *should* get you through the next few days or weeks."

"Now," Kayla said firmly, "about the *other* problem. The nightmare—"

The images rose up before her, terrifying and nauseating. Wrecked buildings. Bodies in the street. Her hands covered in blood—only they weren't her hands, because she was dead, on the ground in front of herself, and there were these horrible shadow-creatures everywhere—

"It's not a nightmare," Kayla said, again putting that insulating touch between her and the memory. "It's real, I mean, it *will* be real, unless we can do something."

Beth shook her head. "Huh?" she replied cleverly.

"What Kayla is trying to say is that it isn't a dream," Elizabet told her, with her dark face shadowed by even darker thoughts. "What you experienced just now—and what you were locked into—was Eric's vision of the future. Remember, that was the nightmare you all came to talk to me about. It wasn't something that came out of some kind of mental imbalance, it was a true glimpse of a possible future. But it's not just a vision only he has had; not anymore. There were some other folks at the conference that had dreams that sounded like his."

"Yeah, and that's not all," Kayla put in. "Here's a hot news flash; your friends with the pointed ears have seen the same thing, too."

"Which means?" she asked, her mouth drying with a different kind of fear altogether.

Elizabet folded her arms as if she felt a breath of chill not even the warmth of the room could dispel. "That it becomes more and more probable with every hour that the vision is soon to become the reality. *Soon.* Within days, maybe even hours." She nodded at the door to the bedroom. "There's a war council going on downstairs right now to try and figure out what—if anything—we can do."

She waited, watching Beth with the same kind of patient expectation that a top sergeant has when he calls for volunteers from a crack unit.

What the hell do I know about those shadow-things? Or about earthquakes, either? I wouldn't be any help—

Unless she knows something she isn't telling me. . . .

Ah hell. It's Eric and Kory down there, trying to play leader. Kory makes a great knight-errant, but he's not exactly a team player. And Eric can't even plan a grocery run.

God help us, the two of them together are worse. . . .

She recalled only too well the times she had sent them out after simple staples, flour, eggs, milk, and toilet paper— and they had come back with pretty candles, macadamia brittle ice-cream, and Brussels sprouts. Not a roll of toilet paper or an egg in sight.

Men. Can't live with 'em, and you can't get a new operating system.

"All right," she said, reluctantly. "I guess I'd better get downstairs before they start looking for someone to sell 'em magic beans."

Elizabet just smiled.

The creak of the stairs made Eric look up, expecting to see Elizabet or the punk. Instead—

"Bethy!" He leapt up from his seat on the couch, vaulted the elf in the pink cat-suit, and rushed for the stairs. Beth's red hair was straggly and damp with sweat and tears; her face pale and thinner. But the smile on that face, though weak, was genuine. And the eyes held no fear, no ghost of insanity.

Kory was right behind him, but the elf had other ideas than his simple hug. He scooped Beth up in his arms, carried her the rest of the way down the stairs, and placed her gently in the chair he had vacated. Eric plodded back down to his own seat, feeling vaguely upstaged.

There was nothing wrong with Beth's mind, which further relieved him; they caught her up with what had been going on in less than a half an hour. She took it all in and asked two or three intelligent questions before sitting back with a frown of thought on her face.

"Shit. We are in a world of trouble." She shook her head and looked straight at Susan Sheffield. "You're taking this all very well."

The scientist sighed. "Either I'm crazy, in which case anything I say or do isn't going to matter squat, or I'm not crazy, in which case I'd damned well better do something to help, if I can." She smiled faintly. "I never was a political activist; I figured on trying to make things better by actually doing something instead of going out and getting my face on TV and my name on somebody's shit-list. Looks like it's time to ante up, doesn't it?"

"You will," Beth said grimly, "as soon as I figure out where you can be useful. But I have to admit, I'm really kind of surprised that you aren't freaking out over this Tolkien-fan's wet-dream, here." She waved her hand at the elves; Eric nodded. That was one question *he* wanted an answer to.

Susan Sheffield blushed. "I—ah—oh, shit, this isn't going to sound any crazier than anything else. I've seen you elves before. And not in a fantasy book either."

She glanced over at the one in pink. "I've seen—I remember seeing—her, in particular. And a really good-looking kid that isn't in this room, a kid right out of a beach movie. Except, of course, that he had those eyes and ears."

There was a chorus of *"What?"* Arvin looked amazed; Dharinel outraged.

Dharinel was the first to recover. He did not turn on Susan but rather on the young elven girl. "You!" he thundered, his face darkening with anger. "How—"

"Don't get your pantyhose in an uproar, Oberon," Susan said, fearlessly—or maybe stupidly—interrupting the tirade before it got started. "It happened a long time ago, when I was a kid; one summer vacation. About fifteen, skinny, nerdy—if there was a contest for 'least popular,' I'd have won it. *You* said you wanted me to call you 'Gidget,'" she finished, nodding at the pink-clad elf.

Dharinel stared at Susan with his mouth dropping open. *I guess that no one's ever talked back to him before,* Eric thought, holding back a grin. "Gidget?" he said. *"Gidget?"*

The elf blushed. "It seemed like a cute name at the time," she said apologetically. She turned to Susan, and stared at her. "Thirty summers ago, roughly?" she asked, frowning. "Would you have been . . . the math scholar? The one going to Yale? And you only wore black, right? You read nothing but math and fantasy, you watched no television except educational, you had a black cat, and wanted to be a witch so that you could curse the cheerleaders with terrible acne and bad hair for a weekend."

Susan's face lit up. "You remembered! I didn't think you would! What *is* your name, anyway?"

"Melisande," the girl replied. "I never use it with humans." She grinned. "I remember you as much for the fact that you simply wanted the pretty girls to experience what you were enduring as anything else. Despite the fact that they constantly made fun of you, all you wanted was justice, not revenge. That was actually charmingly forgiving of you."

It was Susan's turn to blush.

"But how on earth did you remember *us?*" Melisande asked. "After your magic summer, you mortals aren't supposed to recall a thing!"

Susan made a face. "A combination of luck and sheer stupidity," she said. "I started smoking in college, which was stupid, and I went to a fellow psych student to get him to hypnotize me to make me stop, which was even dumber. *He* was interested in previous-life regression, God help me." She shook her head. "Well, he didn't get Bridey Murphy, but I woke up without needing cancer-sticks, and remembering my fifteenth summer without the blurs around the important parts. It wouldn't have happened if he'd been more competent and ethical, and a little less eager to get a story about himself in *Rolling Stone* and usher in the Age of Aquarius."

Dharinel seemed a little more appeased, if a little puzzled by some of Susan's terminology. Melisande sighed with relief. "Part of the forgetting is to keep you from breaking your hearts over us," the young elven girl said. "You will grow up. We remain teenagers forever."

"I never thought about it that way. I just figured it was infatuation on my part, and whatever on his. Anyway," Susan continued, "I spent ten years thinking I'd hallucinated it all. Then I realized that it didn't matter. I'd had a wonderful summer, you gave me confidence that let me ignore the cheerleaders that fall, you taught me all about the differences between lust and love, and love and sex."

"A not inconsiderable set of lessons," Elizabet observed from the staircase.

Susan nodded. "When I finally got to Yale, what I learned from you elves even kept me from doing anything horribly stupid. I didn't start drugs, I didn't buy into the Hari Krishnas or the Moonies. I did two minor, stupid things: I started smoking, then I went to an idiot to find a way to quit." She shrugged. "So there it is. Now I know you are real. And it still doesn't make any difference. I still had that summer. And I'm enough of a scientist to know that there are plenty of things in the universe that are weirder and harder to explain than elves and magic."

"'There are more things in heaven and earth, Horatio,'" Elizabet murmured.

"Exactly." Susan spread her hands. "There it is, friends. Now that we have the question of my sanity settled, is there anything we can do to stop Blair from creating Nevada beachfront property out of Northern California?"

"None of us are scientifically trained," Beth reminded them, as Eric nodded vigorously. "Susan, is there any way of you getting in there and sabotaging that stuff? Or maybe coaching us and getting some of us in?"

"Same as a snowball in hell," the scientist said frankly. "After the little war you had in there? There isn't going to be a cockroach in there without an I.D. badge, and they'll be running every one of them through the scanner to make sure the badges and stats match."

The elves looked baffled; Beth explained to them the concepts of "I.D. badges," "computer records," and the types of objects their magic could not duplicate to them, while Eric thought of another question. "Susan, is there any way you can tell from out here if Blair's turned that thing on? And when he does—how much time do we have?"

She closed her eyes and sucked on her lower lip for a moment, thinking. "I couldn't tell from outside the lab without a lot of really specialized equipment," she said. "I really couldn't. As for how much time we have, that's theoretical. I mean, we only just proved we can trigger micro-quakes—but—"

"But?" he prompted. Stray bits of PBS science programs ran through his brain. Something about simulations. . . . "Come on, you have to have run some computer modeling on this before you started!"

"We did," she hesitated. "Theoretical. Purely theoretical, and we really didn't want anyone to *think* about the possibility of using Poseidon as a weapon. Instead of using the array at the point where the fault-creep is hanging up, on a line on either side of that place, you use it at the greatest area of stress, and just increase that stress until it *has* to break loose." She began spouting techno-babble at him; he stayed patient for a while, and finally she calmed down and returned to speech ordinary mortals could understand. "The computer says—well, it would take some time to set it up, but then you could kick the machines to trigger a quake in maybe an hour, maybe less. Maybe not less, because it'll take some time to build up that kind of stress. Not much more, though. At least, that's what the computer says." She shrugged. "You know what they say about computers: garbage in, garbage out. We were right on when it came to the micro-quake and stress reduction stuff. I would say, since the major-quake stuff is based on the same

model, it would be just as accurate. But I won't swear to
it."

"Uh-huh." He rubbed his eyes. "I assume they're going
to have to do something different with the equipment—I
mean, this isn't a Godzilla movie where everything's in a
van. How long do you think it'd take them to get everything set up?"

That took her by surprise. "To trigger the quake?
They'd have to move the sound probes, reposition them.
Get clearances from landowners and permits—well, maybe
not that—"

Eric smiled thinly. "Yeah, they can probably bluff for at
least twenty-four hours, provided they don't have to set one
up in the barrio. Or someplace where it's likely to get
stripped for parts two minutes after it hits the ground."

Susan grimaced. "Yeah. Wish they did; our problems
would take care of themselves. They'll have to recalibrate.
Figure he can get an unlimited number of goons to go do
the setup, where I had to make do with me, Frank, and
one lab kid—so it'll take him—a day. Maybe less." She
suddenly straightened. "Wait a minute—that's how we'd
know they're going to start!"

"If they move the equipment!" Eric was elated, and the
elves all turned to see what had gotten him so excited.

He explained quickly, and as soon as Susan finished
drawing a rough map of where the probes were, Melisande
left to recruit a team of Low Court "kids" who would keep
watch on the probes. Dharinel cautioned her against inter-
fering with the probes or the new placements.

"We do not know what the creature may have protecting these instruments," the warrior said, gravely. "They are
probably at least partially steel, which means that you would
not be able to affect them magically. My guess would be—
were *I* he, and did I know that Susan might have gone
renegade—that he will have a human at each of them."

Melisande tossed her pink hair scornfully. "And what can
a human do to us?" she asked.

"Little," Dharinel replied, giving her a look. "But the
creature may well be able to armor its agents against your

magic and illusions, and their *steel-jacketed bullets* can do much."

Melisande blanched.

As well she might. Steel—Cold Iron in any form—had disastrous effects on elven physiology. Even a fragment of a bullet might well kill one, though the marksman managed only to wound.

Storming the gates is going to be right out.

Pretty obvious that Dharinel—who had apparently been appointed their war-leader by default—had already dismissed that idea out of hand. He might prefer to stay Underhill, but he wasn't stuck back in the Middle Ages like some of the Underhill crowd. He knew modern ways, and modern weapons, and he did not underestimate humans.

Okay, they'd have some notion of when Blair was going to rev up the engines. That would buy them time to do something. What, he had no idea. They probably couldn't cut the power to the probes. They probably couldn't subvert the guards. No way they'd be able to get inside the labs. Now if there was just something that they could do about the energy the probes would be putting out. . . .

Wait a minute. It's energy. Elves play around with energy a lot. I've seen 'em change electricity into magic power— oh, they don't do it well but they can! And I've seen Kory hold a lightbulb in his hands and make it work just for kicks. Can we feed that energy back on itself, or maybe—maybe turn it into something else?

Maybe ordinary humans couldn't—but Bardic magic seemed to have a lot to do with energy manipulation, just like the elves, might be able to work a conversion of one kind of energy to another.

"Who's the best mage here?" he asked aloud. Every pair of elven eyes looked from him to Dharinel.

Dharinel seemed less than pleased to be singled out.

Great. Figures. The one elf here who hates my guts. Could be worse, I guess. Could be Perenor.

Dharinel looked at him warily, but nodded his head. "I am," he said simply. "I can work with you, Bard. This is more important than my animosity."

Thanks, Laughing Boy. He gestured, and Dharinel followed him into the kitchen. Eric gestured at the chairs, and Dharinel assumed a seat as if it were a throne.

Welcome, Your Highness, to my humble kitchen.

He dug into the fridge and poured them both big glasses of Gatorade, then got out the pretzels. Elves, he had learned, loved pretzels. Maybe it was the salt.

Dharinel took one, gingerly, and raised an eyebrow in unspoken question.

"Relax, my lord," Eric said wearily. "I don't have any assumptions, and at this point, I have no pride. I'm a half-taught bonehead, and you're going to have to cram tensor physics into me in less than a day."

"Ah." Dharinel glanced out the window at the setting sun, then bit his pretzel in half. And managed something amazingly like a smile. "I believe it is going to be a long night."

Hey, this might work. This just might work. He relaxed minutely. "Yes, my lord—but maybe it isn't going to be as long as I thought."

13

The Boys of Ballysadare

Melisande hugged the ground, ignoring the damp of fog and the dew soaking her clothing. She needed no spells of deception, no magic at all, to disguise herself; only ability. She held herself so utterly still that birds had winged in to feed within reach of her hand. It had been a long, long time since Melisande had used her skills as a warrior, but old habits were easy to take up again.

Gone were the pink hair, the Spandex bodysuit. Those, oddly enough, *were* the garb of a kind of warrior, but not the kind she was now. She had surveyed the ground of her chosen lookout point, above the green, flat lawns of Dublin Labs, and had created her camouflage accordingly.

Her hair was now a dull yellow-brown, blending with the weeds about her. Her clothing was of the same mottled coloration: gray, yellow, and brown. Her skin was hidden under gloves and mask of thin silk that blended with the rest; she had considered paint, and rejected it as too itchy and too likely to wipe off, had considered changing her skin, but rejected *that* as terribly conspicuous if she had to walk among humans. It was easy to hide the ears and the eyes; it would be a great deal harder to hide camo-colored skin.

She had cast spells of confusion to fool the eye of the humans who might be on guard against intruders, but Beth,

Susan, and Bard Eric had all spoken of machinery that might watch—machines that could detect scent as a hound, or the heat of a body as a snake.

So she had dealt with those, as well; her body was the same temperature as the ground she lay on, and her scent was that of a cat's. She only hoped that there were no other subtle machines to befool.

Below her was one of the probes Susan Sheffield said must be moved. There were a dozen more of them, all told. A dozen and one, to be precise. Somehow Melisande found that number appropriate.

Not evil, she reminded herself. *In fact, Susan meant for them to serve a good purpose. It is the one who uses them that is evil.*

There were elven watchers over all of them, although Susan was not sure which of the "array" would be repositioned. Melisande thought that this one was likely; for one thing, it was on Lab property, and there would be no attention paid when someone came to move it. For another— she had a hunch. Elven hunches were not to be taken lightly.

How long until the Nightflyer creature decided that Susan Sheffield was not to return? And then how long would it be before it decided to act on its own? There was no way of knowing. Melisande had decided that she would wait, no matter how long it took—but she had some doubts about the patience of the others. Some of them, anyway.

Light-minded. Now they are afeared, but when the fear wears off, so will their interest. Too many distractions. It is hard for some of them to believe in the FarSeeing, when there have been so few things in the human world that could ever affect us.

So she had taken up this first outpost herself, to be sure that at least one watcher would remain in place.

There were other things that troubled her. Before she left the Bard's home, there had been some discussion of *how* the Blair-human—before he became a Nightflyer's host—had found Beth, Eric, and the human healers. Melisande was not terribly interested, until Susan had speculated on more machines, and that had caught Dharinel's attention for fair. The two of them had conferenced, with Dharinel becoming more animated than Melisande had ever seen him before. They came at last to the conclusion that there must be machines that could see the thoughts that moved from mind to mind, the energies of the healer—and, yes, most probably the powers of magic.

The very thought of that made Melisande shudder. Machines that had the same ability to See as the Gifted! Worse, machines that could do so for the benefit of humans who were otherwise blind to magic and all that it meant.

That meant, that in addition to everything else, Dharinel and the others must needs construct the tightest shieldings they had ever created for each of the watchers—and for the humans as well. The healers, Eric, and Beth were shielded so tightly that they no longer existed to Melisande's inner Eye—and on the chance that there might be some subtle telltale on Susan, she had been shielded as well. It would do them little good to discover that the Blair-creature could track them and know where they were, or if it would actually *want* to find the elves. It would accomplish nothing if, with all their careful planning, the Blair-creature found and took Bard Eric.

The younger healer, Kayla, had gone out into the city to try to collect other humans with the Gifts. These, Dharinel had determined, would be needed for later work.

It was a complicated plan they had made; it relied on the abilities of humans and elves, on humans and elves working together. Melisande only hoped that it was not too complicated to succeed.

Their plans were further complicated by their inability to speak mind-to-mind through the shields, which must remain in place until the last minute. So when a man came for this probe, Melisande would have to leave her watchpost, go to the BART station, and take the humans' transportation to their headquarters. She could not even ride her elvensteed-motorcycle. Dharinel had ruled that the elvensteeds, being creatures of purest magic, had too much potential for being easily detected.

Wait—there was something moving below.

Melisande checked her shields and peered through the foggy gray of early morning. Was it a grounds-keeper? Sexless in its muddy brown coverall, it—no, he—towed a trash barrel upon wheels behind him. . . .

Then the snout of a high-powered rifle poking out of the open top of the barrel told her that this was no gardener. And as he moved across the grass towards the probe, she smiled in satisfaction.

When he reached it, and began to load it into his barrel, she inched backwards to slither down the side of the hill.

Six rings. Seven. Eight. "Damn," Elizabet swore quietly, hanging up the phone. The house seemed terribly quiet with Eric and most of the elves gone. Occasional car noises filtered up from the street, and Elizabet tried not to listen too closely for the sound of one stopping outside. The elves had pledged that they were safe. She had to believe that.

"No answer?" Kayla asked with a grimace. She had accepted the elves' assurance with no question. Elizabet wished she had her apprentice's faith.

"No answer." Elizabet stared off into the distance, her lips compressed into a tight line. *No answer—but most of them were at the conference. Most of them were already paranoid—and what happened there must have simply proven to them that their worst fears were a reality.* "Not that I blame them. After what happened to us, I wouldn't be answering my phone either."

Kayla drew a neat line through the last name on the list. "Yeah. Answer the phone and there could be a car outside your door five minutes later. Teach, we got a problem," she said. "We've got three—count 'em, three—psis contacted so far. The rest, everybody from the conference, changed their numbers in the last day and got unlisted ones, aren't answering, or just plain disappeared. Now what? Where are we gonna find anybody on this short a notice?"

Elizabet shook her head, feeling suddenly tired. *I can't*

feel tired. I don't have time to feel tired. "I don't know," she said frankly. "I'm fresh out of ideas."

Kayla blinked, then licked her lips. "I got one," she offered. She had that look about her that told Elizabet she was probably not going to like the idea, that this was something that a child shouldn't be doing. On the other hand— they were rapidly running out of choices.

Elizabet spread her hands. "I'm open to any suggestion at this point." *Just make this one a reasonable one. Something that might work.*

"Well—" Kayla took a deep breath. "You know I'm pretty street-smart. And you know I know how to find people when I want to."

In fact, Kayla's ability to find people was quite uncanny. She knew somehow when people who were pretending to be out were at home; she even knew when people who were out could be expected back, usually coming within ten minutes of their actual return. It wasn't precognition as Elizabet recognized it; it certainly wasn't anything like clairvoyance, for there was no vision involved. Just a "hunch"—one that had served Kayla well when she had been pilfering apartments for food and small amounts of cash. It was astonishing how few people locked their windows even in a city the size of Los Angeles.

"You're street-smart in L.A.," Elizabet reminded her. "This is San Francisco; you don't know the territory." *And I don't want you out on the street; you're a child, and children are terribly easy to snatch when the abductor is an adult and looks official. Flash some kind of badge, say the child is a truant or a runaway. . . .*

"Okay, I don't know this area," Kayla admitted, "but Sandy—Melisande, I mean—she does. She's got the entire BART schedule in her head. And her Grove's way up on one of the hills, so she can even go into Oakland, Berkeley—basically wherever BART can take her. So we had this idea. I know what the real high-psis around here look like, at least the ones that showed up at the conference. And I kind of picked up on things like, where they work, what their neighborhoods are like, so I could probably track them down if they're still around. And they probably remember me. So—"

"You and Melisande want to go hunting, is that it?" At Kayla's eager nod, Elizabet sighed. "A pair of teenagers."

Kayla's face fell. "What's wrong with that? We can take care of ourselves!"

"But who would believe you?" Elizabet asked gently. "Honey, if I didn't have the same Gifts, I probably wouldn't—"

"They'll believe me," said a low, tired voice from the doorway.

They both looked up to see Beth leaning against the doorframe. "Not only that," the singer continued, "but I probably know some of them myself. As far as that goes, I would bet that I know some high-psis that didn't go to your conference for one reason or another, and we could go track them down."

Kayla looked their patient over with a critical eye. "Are you sure you're up to this?" she asked, as Elizabet opened her mouth to protest, then shut it again.

Beth nodded, then smiled thinly. "Even if I wasn't, we don't have much choice, do we?" she pointed out. "It's either that, or those of us who can, run for the East. I imagine we could get into safe territory before the quake hit, even on motorbikes."

"Run out while we still have a chance to stop this thing? Leaving the people and elves who can't escape to face those—things?" Kayla snarled. "I don't think so."

"The visions all depend on Eric being there," Beth pointed out. "They all show him *here*, as the instigator. At least, the ones we know about do. . . ."

"But they're getting worse, not better." Kayla shook her head. "That's what Sandy says. The elves haven't told us much detail about theirs; maybe they don't show Eric. The only details we know came from Eric; and me and Elizabet have been putting him too far under to dream when he sleeps, so he's not getting them anymore. Which means, I bet, that it wouldn't matter if Eric was here or not. Hell, he's done his gig. They don't need him; I bet they've got some other way of coming over without him calling them. If they did need him, you can bet that bastard Blair would be on him like flies on—"

"Kayla," Elizabet said warningly.

"Yeah, well, he would." Kayla frowned. "So I don't think we got a choice. I think we gotta stop this if we can. And the only way we know of is Eric's plan."

"I don't think we have a choice either," Beth admitted. "I just wanted to hear somebody else say it." She pulled her hands out of her pockets; one of them held a bit of shiny covered elastic. She put her hair into a tail and nodded at the older healer. "So, am I sufficient chaperone for the two delinquents? Think I can keep them out of trouble?"

"You'll do," Elizabet admitted tiredly. Kayla bounced up out of her chair and stopped only when Elizabet held up a restraining hand. "We have three for the circle—plus you, Beth, and me. Eric won't be in the circle; he can't be, since he's the channel. The elves will be working their own magics. That means we *have* to have no less than seven more. I'd personally like more than that, in case we have some last minute cancellations."

One corner of Beth's mouth twitched, as if she was trying not to smile. "The classical thirteen? I thought you didn't subscribe to traditional ways."

"I don't," Elizabet snapped, "but out of the six we have so far, three of us *do*. Belief is a powerful weapon."

Beth reacted to Elizabet's unusual burst of temper by straightening and looking a little livelier. *Like a tired cop that just heard the Chief growl,* Elizabet thought. *As if she figures if I have enough left to snarl with, she should, too. Good—that was the reaction I hoped to get.*

Or maybe it was the reminder of how powerful belief *was.* Belief, after all, had helped them make it through the last one. . . .

Belief, and the unlikely combination of Eric and a plan.

The Bard is growing up, I think. Nowhere near so feckless these days.

"In that case," Beth replied, "let's see if we can't find

you a few more believers." She nodded at Kayla. "Come on, kid. Let's go collect Sandy and hit the road."

Elizabet dropped her hand, and Kayla bounded to Beth's side.

Kayla let Beth take over; it didn't matter who played leader, and Beth knew San Fran better than Kayla, though not as well as Sandy. The two of them headed out the back way into the garden, Beth in the lead, figuring to look for Melisande there first. Anytime Kayla didn't know where to look for one of the elves, but knew the elf in question was somewhere around, she always checked the garden right off.

They didn't have to look far; she was sitting in one of the little bowers, with her knees tucked up under her chin, watching—something. She sat so quietly she could have been a garden gnome—if anyone made them with pink hair. She had changed back to her pink punk look as soon as she got back to the gathering.

Come to think of it, somewhere someone probably does. Only they're in cutesy peasant costumes, not pink Spandex.

When they got a little nearer, they saw what it was that Melisande stared at so intently. An early rose, the same color as her hair and Spandex tights and miniskirt. Small, but perfect, with dew on its velvet petals, straight out of a honey-sweet greeting card.

"I always loved roses," she said, sadly and softly, as they neared. "They won't grow Underhill—did you know that? They won't grow without true sun." There was something about her; something resigned and wistful. . . .

That was when it hit Kayla: Sandy expected to die. In fact, now that she thought about it, at least half the elves gathered here had the same attitude Sandy did. Now that the probes had been moved, they expected to die; all of the Low Court elves and many of their High Court cousins. Of the High Court elves, only Kory and Dharinel seemed reasonably confident that this save could be pulled off.

I bet they figure we can't hold up our end. Huh. We did it before, we can do it again. You bet.

"Yeah, well, it'll still be here in a couple of days," she said. "From the look of it, you'll have a whole bush full of flowers you can admire. Right now, you'n me'n Beth have got some tracking to do. Beth figures she knows where some of the witches around here live."

"Not all witches," Beth corrected. "Or at least, that's what they'll tell you. They run the spectrum from ultra-Christian to the absolute opposite. But they're all psychic and they're strong, and I'm pretty sure once they hear what we're up against, they'll be willing to work together. At least, I hope so. There's a lot of rivalry and a couple of feuds we'll have to deal with."

Kayla heard an unspoken undercurrent and asked, sharply, "What's the catch?"

Beth shook her head and sighed. "The catch, me dear young child, is that most of these people range from—ah—eccentric, to pure, unadulterated out-there. I'm hoping they're enough in touch with the planet to believe they can't vibrate their way out of this one without help. But—honey, these people are the nuts and flakes in the bowl of granola."

"Great," Kayla replied as flippantly as she could manage, while Sandy got to her feet. "In that case, it'll be just like a family reunion. Everybody got change for the BART?"

Beth rubbed her temples and tried not to snap. Behind her, Kayla and Sandy stood in respectful silence.

"But the Universe is a friendly place, dear," Sister Ruth chided gently. "You simply haven't *communicated* properly with these entities. I'm sure that once you talk to them, they'll understand that they mustn't hurt anyone when they come over to Our Side."

Right. And Ted Bundy is a real sweetheart, once you get to know him. Ruthie, you'd sign Charlie Manson's parole petition. But Beth didn't allow a shadow of her real feelings to show on her face—or get past her defenses. Sister Ruth had an erratic, but unfortunately accurate, ability to read people—and this was not the time to let her read what Beth thought of her "the Universe is a friendly place" drivel.

"Once we have the time, we'll do that—" she promised

glibly. "In fact, I don't see any reason why we can't put you in charge of the project. You're so *good* at communicating with the non-human spirit-entities."

Sister Ruth beamed with pride, but Beth continued before she could say anything and get off on her own Cosmic Muffin tangent. She did not need the guided tour to the spirit-world to get in the way of the real business. "Right now, though—unless we can stop this quake before it starts, we *won't* have the time. In fact," she continued grimly, "the visions of the future that we've been granted show most of us dead. Including me. The entities aren't the real problem, Ruth, the quake is. According to the seer I've consulted, it's the quake that kills most of the people."

Sister Ruth frowned slightly, and Beth knew she'd inadvertently tripped another button. *Oh gods. Karma. Karma and predestination.* She hurried on, keeping Ruth from getting off on the "no one dies until it is time" kick. *How do I get out of this one? Ah—I know.*

"Sister Ruth, please remember, this *isn't* a natural quake. It's being created, by those military men over in Dublin Labs." She paused to let that sink in. "I know. I was there; I saw the machine. It's no more natural than if one of them dropped a bomb on the city. These people in Dublin Labs have no compunction about cutting everyone's karma short."

Yeah, and you signed on every petition to close them down since the sixties, whether or not you knew what it was about.

Sister Ruth hesitated a moment. "Dublin Labs? Oh dear. Oh my . . . they do horrible things in there. And I know that what we ignorantly call Good and Evil are just parts of the Cosmic Balance—and I'm sure that there may be a place even for people like *that* in the Balance—but they do *horrid* things in there, cutting up poor little bunnies and white mice. Making those awful nuclear bombs and lasers. Taking over our minds with Rays. And there is such a thing as Free Will . . . one can choose to be Wrong Minded. . . ."

"I'm sure that's exactly what they've done," Beth said firmly. "Really, Sister Ruth, it's your duty to help us stop them so that they learn the lesson that not all their machines and power can prevail against the Cosmic Balance. It's the kind of lesson they really need to learn."

Dear gods, I hope I'm making all the right noises, she thought frantically. *She's about a dozen bricks short of a full load, but she's really powerful—one reason why nothing's ever actually hurt her. And we need her.*

"We need you, Sister Ruth," she pleaded. "I can't tell you how much. You'll have to work with a few people you may not agree with—but do you know, I think your wonderful example in this hour of crisis may be just what they need to see the Light. Jeffrey Norman, for instance—you just might be the one to show him the Cosmic Way with your shining leadership."

The simultaneous appeal to vanity, responsibility, and the opportunity to show up some of the people she despised most in the psychic community was too much for Sister Ruth to resist. She agreed to come, with much simpering and disavowal of her own powers.

Second verse, same song.

New setting though; instead of ruffles and flowered cotton, she and her crew were surrounded by red velvet and black leather. Instead of potted plants and birdcages full of budgies, there was a microcomputer and a sleek, hi tech stereo. Instead of genteel, gentle middle-class, the place reeked of money.

Instead of an overweight myopic woman in a flowered caftan, they made their pitch to a goateed, middle-aged cynic in leather jeans. Black, of course. Like his sofa and chairs.

"Look, Jeff, you've got a choice," Beth said rudely. "You can help us—or you can watch everything you own go down in a pile of rubble."

Although Jeff—a self-proclaimed Satanist—sat back on his leather sofa with his hands laced casually behind his head, not all the control he *thought* he had over himself kept his body from tensing up. Nor did it keep him from glancing at some of the more expensive appointments of his living-room out of the corner of his eye.

"How long did you say we have?" he asked cautiously,

and Beth could almost see the little wheels turning in his head, as he tried to calculate how much stuff he could load into a trailer before the zero hour.

"Under forty-eight hours at this point," she said honestly. "I don't know if you've ever tried to rent a trailer or a truck on short notice, but it isn't easy. The things are usually booked pretty well in advance. You could probably waste about twenty-four of those hours just trying to find one."

Now she could tell that he was trying to figure how big a bribe it would take to rent a truck out from under someone.

"Besides," she continued, "you've got a lot sunk into this condo. I know you think your insurance will pay for it—" she leaned forward, intently "—but let me clue you in on a little fact of life. Insurance companies are in the biz to make money, not lose it. And the last couple years have been real bad for insurance companies. Lots of disasters." Now it was *her* turn to lean back, and spread her hands wide. "We're talking a Richter nine or even ten quake here. With a disaster of that magnitude, the city is gonna be flat. Every vision we've seen has shown major damage to every building in sight. From the looks of things, you wouldn't even be able to rescue more than a couple of suitcases worth of clothing. I'll tell you right now—*that insurance company of yours will declare bankruptcy before they pay out.* They all will. They can't *afford* losses like that. Maybe the Feds will bail them out— but after all the Savings and Loan bailouts and the hurricanes and tornadoes and floods, I wouldn't count on getting more than ten cents on the dollar. And that's a fact, Jack."

She watched his face pale for a moment, watched a tic pulse in his cheek as he calculated odds. He had *sold* insurance at one point in his life. He sometimes joked that this was how he had become a Satanist in the first place. From selling insurance to selling your soul wasn't that big a step. . . .

Actually he became a Satanist partially because it suits his cynical, hedonistic attitude, and partially because it's a good way to part fools from their cash. As witness this condo.

He didn't like the numbers his own calculations were coming up with; Beth read that in the narrowing of his eyes. Finally he leaned forward, took an oversized deck of cards from the handcarved ebony box on the teakwood table between them, and called upon his court of last resort. As he shuffled them, his hands trembled a little.

"I hate to admit it, but I couldn't figure why all my readings kept telling people to get out of town this week," he said, half to himself.

But he is high-psi. I'll give him that. His clients may be fools, but he does give them what they overpay for.

Like most psychics, Jeff was a little *too* good; he couldn't read for himself, for what he wanted to see would skew the reading off the true. And he was too proud to go to someone else for a reading. Which was probably why he'd missed seeing the quake for himself.

He stopped shuffling, evened up the pack, and laid out the cards; the Tower of Destruction occupied a prominent place. Swords were everywhere, most reversed—including the Princess. It was the single most negative reading Beth had ever seen with any Tarot deck, much less the Crowley.

So even if he runs—which is what I bet he was asking— he's screwed to the wall.

"Shit." He picked up the cards of the Crowley deck carefully, and put it back in its little ebony shrine. Only then did he look back up at her.

"All right," he said with resignation. "When and where? And what do you want me to bring?"

The sun set over the Bay, dull red in a cloudy sky, leaving them still on the hunt; one short of a full thirteen, with no spares or backups. Beth trudged wearily down into the BART station, with Kayla and Sandy trailing behind.

She stood staring at the map for a while, her eyes fixed on the YOU ARE HERE spot without really seeing it. Behind her, elf and human fidgeted restlessly in the way of teenage young.

Was I ever that young? She thought back to endless, sullen hours of playing the same tapes over and over at ear-shattering volume while native diggers cast quizzical glances at her while they followed her parents' direction. Or squirming in stiff wooden seats while one or the other read papers to an audience of fossils stiffer than the seats, when all *she* wanted was a chance to get out of there and Shop in Civilization.

Yeah, I guess I was.

"Okay, guys," she said finally. "I've got an idea. It's a long-shot, but there's two groups meeting tonight over at UC that tend to attract high-psis. Some of our missing persons probably belong to one or the other. One advantage is that both groups bring bodies in from off-campus. The other is that the devotees of both tend to be fanatic about their hobbies."

"What is the disadvantage?" Melisande asked. "We know you by now. You never state an advantage without there being a disadvantage."

Beth shrugged. "Only the usual with hobbyists. They tend to take their hobby a little too seriously. That's why they meet on the same night; the *real* fanatics on both sides don't want their members to 'waste their time' with the rival group's activities."

Melisande sighed. "Like Jeff and Sister Ruth."

"Exactly." Now that she'd decided to take the plunge into the wilds of Berserkely, Beth wanted to get it over with and get out of there. "Are you game?"

"Lead on, McDuff," Kayla replied, gesturing grandly. The train to the campus area pulled up, just as she straightened. "See? The gods are smiling upon us."

"I sure hope so," Beth muttered, and ran for the train.

"See anyone you recognize?" Beth asked Kayla, as the young healer took a slightly more aggressive stance, and Melisande tried to shrink behind both of them.

There were fifty-odd people in the room, and most of them wore expressions of faint hostility. They also wore creative variations on medieval and Rennaissance clothing.

Except for the half-dozen Costuming Nazis, who wore completely *authentic* clothing, and expressions of complete hostility.

"They probably figure we're from the Women's Lib meeting down the hall," Kayla observed, absently. "Uh-yeah. The guy in the green and black tights with the great ass, the woman that looks like a Rose Parade float, and the chick with the pregnant guitar. They were all at the conference."

"Sandy?" Beth asked. The elf peeked out from behind her shoulder. "The young man in the particolored hose, the woman in the Elizabethan farthingale, and the girl with the lute."

"They're all strongly Gifted," the elf assured her. "And imperfectly shielded." She squinted a little. "Unless I'm greatly mistaken, the woman and the young man are related. And I *think* I see a Celtic knotwork embroidery pattern on the woman's gown that used to be used as an identifying agent among the devotees of the Old Religion about twenty or twenty-five years ago."

"Oh really?" Beth's eyes narrowed, but she couldn't make out anything special amid all the decoration on the gown. "If you're right, we might have hit paydirt." She turned her attention back to the speaker on the dais. "I think they're going to break for refreshments in a bit. We'll move in then. Sandy, you try for the lute-girl; Kayla, you take the guy and I'll take the Architectural Monument."

They waited, patiently, enduring the glares from the mortally offended, until the Seneschal finally ran out of wind. When people began leaving their seats, Kayla and Beth headed for the woman and the young man, while Melisande took a lateral to intercept the musician before she could join the others who were gathering in a corner.

"Hi," Beth said cautiously, as she stepped in front of the farthingale, forcing the woman to stop. "You don't know me—but you do know a friend of mine. Her name is Elizabet—"

"And she's the teacher of that charming and obstinate little child who's trying to back my son into a corner," the woman said, with a faint smile. "Since you don't have that nasty 'desperately mundane' look of those goons that were lurking about the conference, I assume you must be all right. Or has Elizabet sent you to warn me about them?"

"Uh—sort of." Out of the corner of her eye, Beth watched the lute-girl shaking her head violently at whatever Melisande had told her. Her face was white, and her hands clutched the neck of the lute like a life-line. "Listen, this is awfully complicated, and well—"

"I know just the place." The woman waved at her son, who nodded at Kayla and gestured at her to precede him with full High Court grace.

Wonder if there's a touch of elven blood in there somewhere?

All three of them followed the woman out into the hall, to a little alcove with a pair of loveseats. The farthingale needed one all by herself; the son took up a seat on the arm of the sofa, and Kayla and Beth took the other seat.

"By the way, I'm Marge Bailey. Which was *not* the name I used for the conference, if you're interested." The woman smiled again, this time wryly. "Call me paranoid if you like, but I've always had a suspicion that some day some government goons would show up at one of these things and start taking names and addresses. So I only use the SCA post office box, and one of my old persona names."

Beth grimaced. "Just offhand, I'd say that this time your caution was entirely appropriate. . . ."

Fifteen minutes later, Marge and her son Craig were pale with shock, and Beth was dry-mouthed and talked out. She nodded to Kayla, who took over.

"We've got a plan," she said. "We think we can head this thing off. But we need—"

"A circle," Marge interrupted, leaning forward, her eyes afire with intensity. "A circle. The kind the witches of England gathered in to thwart the Armada."

"Wow!" Kayla went round-eyed. "I didn't know that! Yeah, that's exactly what—"

"When and where?" Craig said. "We'll be there; Dad'll come, and maybe we can get a couple of others." He took a deep breath. "We knew something wasn't right; we've been getting signs for weeks. But none of us are real good at prediction. That's why we went to the conference in the first place; we figured if there was anyone who'd know what was up, he'd show up there."

Beth felt a great weight lift from her shoulders. This was her thirteenth body—and one, maybe two spares. "Mount Tam—if you've been up there, you know the place. As soon after sunset as you can manage."

Marge nodded. "No problem. Did you plan on checking the Paper-gamer's Club meeting for some more recruits?"

This time it was Beth's turn to be surprised. "Uh, yes. Why?"

Marge chuckled. "Because my husband's in there. Ask someone to find Chuck Bailey for you; he'll round up the couple of gamers with—ah—esoteric talents. That should save you some time."

Beth didn't know quite what to say. "Marge—thank you. I think you just bought us our chance at making this work."

Marge shook her head. "Well, I grew up reading old J.R.R. and the Norse sagas—I always wanted to be Galadriel, the Ringbearer or another Beowulf. You know what they say about being careful what you ask for." She recovered some of her color, and managed a weak chuckle. "I suspect you've had a time convincing some of the others to get involved."

Beth nodded. "I'm still not sure why you agreed so easily."

This time Marge Bailey laughed out loud. "My dear Beth, it's really quite simple. I may be crazy, but there's one thing that I'm not."

"What's that?" Kayla asked.

"Stupid." Marge rose majestically. "I'd better get back before the others think you've recruited me for your biker gang. And we will see you tomorrow night."

"With the proverbial bells on," Craig added, as a dejected Melisande approached from the door of the meeting room. "Listen, I know Mom. This is going to work. If she can make the Kingdom Seneschal back down and *apologize* for screwing up the demo we had for the science fiction fans at ConDiego, that earthquake hasn't got a chance."

14

The Light in the Window

Eric's head was spinning from everything that had happened, and all the concentrated magic lore that Dhariel had rammed between his ears. He leaned against the cold glass in the window seat, wishing he could wake up, pretend that it was just a nightmare, that all of this would go away and never trouble his thoughts again.

It didn't matter to him that the elves thought his actions were justified. It was the look of horror in Dr. Sheffield's eyes that kept coming back to haunt him, that look that said one word:

Murderer.

So he'd sat quietly through the remainder of the war conference, as an amazingly recovered Beth and the others left on their various errands. No one had noticed as he slipped away from the gathering of elves in the living-room, continuing a discussion of whether or not the humans should carry firearms, or if the magical firepower would be enough.

The war plan seemed straightforward enough: gather the elves and the human magical/psychic talent of the Bay Area to use in case the earthquake device was triggered prematurely, to try and redirect the energy wave. Meanwhile, an elven hit squad would deal with Blair himself and destroy the machine and the other equipment in Dr. Susan's lab, so it couldn't be used again, at least not until they were *certain* that Blair was no longer a threat.

A great plan. Except that he remembered the security levels of that laboratory complex, and could guess what it'd be like with increased paranoia about a breakout. Translation of that formula: someone, or more than likely several someones, in that elven assault team were going to die.

He couldn't deal with that thought. There were too many deaths in his memory and on his conscience: the elven warriors lying still and lifeless in Griffith Park, Dr. Sheffield's colleagues.

Death follows me like a watchdog.

Maybe it didn't have to be that way. He thought about alternatives. Like running away. They could still do it— gather their friends and run.

But then something else intruded. Not a memory, but a vision.

San Francisco in ruins, the Nightflyers gliding noiselessly through the streets, drifting over the corpses lying on the cracked sidewalks . . .

No. He couldn't leave, not now. But maybe he could arrange things so that no one else was in danger. *I started this whole mess; I can finish it. Just me, alone.*

"Eric?"

He looked up to see Kayla standing in the doorway. She walked in and sat down on the edge of the waterbed. "Back already?" he asked.

She stretched like a cat, and yawned. "Look at the clock, Bard. It's after midnight. Everyone's downstairs, still making war plans, but I wanted to do something other than that for a few minutes."

He glanced at the clock involuntarily, surprised at how much time had passed. It seemed like just a few minutes ago that the others had left on their various quests. "Did you have much luck?"

"Oh, yeah. We'll have a United Wiccan Liberation Front to go up on Mount Tam tomorrow, no problem." She yawned again. "Wish I could understand all this Wiccan witchcraft stuff. Doesn't make any sense to me . . . what good is magic that you can't see?"

He blinked at that. "What do you mean, that you can't see?"

She gave him a tired but wicked grin, and held out her hands. Faint traceries of blue light appeared on her hands, brightening and moving in flickering patterns over her skin. "Elizabet taught me how to work without showing off, as she put it." The fine blue lines faded away as suddenly as they appeared. "But this Wiccan stuff, you just kinda pray and hope something happens. At least, that's how it seems to me."

"Me, too." Eric thought about his own magic, that quiet pool of—something—that he drew upon with his music. "But it seems to work."

"Sometimes. I've seen Elizabet cuss a mean streak 'cause it didn't, though." She grinned and sprawled out on the waterbed. "I prefer the kind of magic that I can do. I know it'll work, every time." Her face clouded. "Well, almost every time," she said in a low tone.

The girl's calm seemed nearly supernatural to Eric. *How does the kid manage it?* he wondered. *All I can think about is how many people are probably going to get killed tomorrow, and she seems so calm. Maybe she doesn't know enough to be afraid.* "Are you scared of what's going to happen tomorrow?" Eric asked.

The kid shrugged. "Yeah. A little. I hope it'll be quick and easy, but I know it probably won't turn out that way. But that's my job, to make sure everyone gets out okay." She gave him an odd look. "Hey, Bard, don't you want to be in on the war conference downstairs? They could probably use your input."

He shook his head. "They've got half the army of Middle Earth down there, they don't need me."

"What's eating you, Bard?"

He glanced up to meet her wry dark eyes. "Is it that obvious?"

"Only to someone standing within five miles of you. Up close, it's even more obvious."

He looked out at the street, at the cold glow of the streetlights. "What do you think it is, kid? Do you think I'm used to killing people? Fourteen people died in those labs the other night, and a lot more could die, and it's all because of me, because of what I did. Knowing that doesn't make me feel like dancing in the park, y'know?"

"I know. I was there, remember?" Kayla's voice was quiet. "It was scary, Eric. I didn't know what you were going to do, but I knew this much—you weren't in control. That's why those—*things*—went on a killing rampage through the building."

Cold settled around his heart. "Are you scared of me, Kayla?"

She didn't answer for a long moment. "I don't know. Maybe." A flash of a grin, her teeth bright against the dimness in the room. "All I can say for certain, Eric, is that life is never boring when you're around."

"Thanks," he said grimly. "Welcome to another war zone, kid. Sorry, I didn't intend to screw up your San Francisco vacation this way."

"Hey, I already saw a war before that mess in Griffith Park, thank you very much." There was an odd catch in her voice . . . Eric saw something strange in her face, a shadow of an old pain.

"I never heard about that." It occurred to Eric how little he knew about this girl, other than the fact that she was Elizabet's apprentice.

She spoke quietly. "It was in L.A. I was running wild on the streets—this was before Elizabet adopted me. Things got a little hot between two street gangs, and I was caught in the middle—see, they both wanted me, and I didn't want any part of either of them. So I played 'em against each other. A lot of people died in that one, too, Bard. And you could say it was my fault, sure." She clenched her hands into fists, staring down at them, then looked up at him, her eyes bright. "I think it's a curse we have to deal with, Eric. We're different, unusual . . . you have to learn how to deal with it."

"How do you deal with it?"

She grinned. "I try not to hurt people, unless I want to. I try not to do anything that's unethical, or will put some-one else into danger. I just try very hard."

Not put anyone else in danger. . . .

"What would you say," he asked, choosing his words carefully, "if I said I had a solution to this situation that didn't involve a lot of people risking their lives in a major assault on the Dublin Labs?"

"I'd say I'd like to hear more about it," Kayla answered cautiously.

"I think it might be possible for me to slip myself and maybe one other person into the labs, undetected. Then we could go down to the level with that earthquake gizmo, take a couple sledgehammers to the machinery, and get out of there again." *Well, getting out would probably be a lot more difficult, but . . .*

"It's a better idea than taking fifteen people in there, guns blazing. I can handle the heavy magic, you can make sure . . ." *Make sure that I don't kill anyone else by acci-dent . . .* "Make sure that my back is covered, and that no civilians get hurt this time."

"That's very true." She gave him a sidelong glance. "You keep surprising me, Bard. I never know what to expect with you." Her voice took on a more businesslike tone. "I'm guessing that you don't want the others to know about this, since they'd definitely try to stop you."

He blushed. "Well, yes."

"It sure beats watching Elizabet go back into that place," the kid said, apparently thinking out loud. "I don't want her to go back there, ever. Not after . . ." Her voice wavered a little. "Not after what those bastards did to Bethany Kentraine. I don't want to risk that happening to Elizabet."

He licked dry lips and considered the other half of the unlikely pairing. "You two go really far back, don't you?"

Kayla gave him a little half-smile. "She saved my life, and then gave me a real life, off the streets. And a future. I'm not going to let some monster outtake from the movie *Aliens* play with her mind, no way." She rubbed her hands together. "So, Bard, what's the plan? Go there ahead of the crowd tomorrow, beat the rush?"

"Yeah, we'd have to. Probably leave here in the middle of the morning, so we don't have to fight the traffic, too."

"Good plan, good plan." Kayla stretched again, and stood up. "I probably should go get some sleep, if we're going to do this tomorrow for sure. G'night, Bard."

One moment an ancient, the next moment a kid. "Good night, Kayla."

The kid left the room. Eric turned back to the window and the view of the street beyond. *It could work*, he thought. *It could work, and I wouldn't have to watch Beth and Kory die, like in my nightmare.*

He much preferred risking only his own life, not others. Though taking a seventeen-year-old kid along was an idea that still made him twitch . . . he needed her, though. If only to make sure that he didn't go nuts and kill off most of the city.

He could feel them in the back corners of his mind, a shadow of drifting blackness. The faint whispering, the voices calling to him . . .

:*Do you hear us, Bard?*:

:*Go to hell*,: he thought at them. :*Get lost. Get out of my brain. Take a hike.*: He mentally pushed them away, with about as much success as someone trying to push a shadow with their hands. The whispering drew closer, echoing in his mind. He shoved at them again, feeling the creatures drift through his mental hands again.

Then, annoyed, he closed his eyes and called light, surrounding and filling himself with incandescent illumination. The world seemed to explode with light, searing the inside of his eyelids. It was too bright to see, but still he increased the light, filling his thoughts with it, pouring it into every corner of his mind. "Chew on that, scum," he whispered to himself, hoping it would work. If it didn't, he'd probably have to get used to having this evil Greek Chorus lurking in his brain—an awful thought, that. He crossed his fingers and held onto that image of pure light within his mind.

The whispering Nightflyers scattered with a strange skittering noise, vanishing off . . . somewhere, he didn't know where. But they were gone, which was a relief. He grinned, feeling a little more confident for the first time in days.

Still smiling, he headed downstairs to join the others.

Kayla rolled over on the sofa bed, pulling the blanket tighter over her to ward off the chill of the attic room. Sleep was a great idea, but somehow it didn't seem to be in the cards, at least not for tonight. Too many thoughts, plans, running through her mind . . . too many memories.

Hey, I already saw a war. . . .

No magic in that war, not like this—no elves in bright armor, no Wiccans, no cheerful Bard Eric with a simmering magical presence that she could sense from miles away. None of that magical stuff, just a darkened room in Los Angeles with half a dozen dying boys lying on the torn mattresses and the bare floor. . . .

I don't want to think about this, I don't . . .

The smell of blood as she worked, trying to save one boy's life, then another . . . the colors of pain and terror, knowing that if she failed, she'd probably die as well . . . Carlos standing in the doorway, watching her with that terrifying cold gaze of his, watching as she tried to work harder and faster, as everything blurred around her and she couldn't stop, couldn't escape from the pain, feeling her own life fading away with each passing moment. . . .

Don't think about it, don't torture yourself. It's over, you survived, it won't happen again.

Unless she lost control again. What if they went into the Labs tomorrow and all hell broke loose? She wasn't worried about catching a bullet herself—there were ways to avoid that, if you knew the bullet was coming—but she envisioned a hallway of wounded people, herself moving from person to person, caught up again in that nightmare of not being able to stop, not being able to disengage, to pull herself back and keep a little life energy for herself, watching her own life drain away into the bodies of those she healed.

She thought about warning Eric, telling him that this could happen. That she didn't know any way of stopping it, once it started, unless someone else intervened. The first time, the intervention had been because Ramon didn't know not to touch her when she was working, and that had cast her out of the endless cycle, kept her from killing herself. Next time, she might not be so lucky.

And she had been lucky, so far. Just the fact that Elizabet had found her, and had helped her escape from Carlos, that had been pure luck. If Elizabet hadn't been in the neighborhood, close enough to sense Kayla's near brush with death, she would never have returned to try and track down the "little powerhouse" she'd detected.

In another lifetime, without that luck, Kayla probably would've stayed with Carlos and his gang, stayed until one day when Carlos couldn't protect her anymore and someone else had tried to "acquire" her instead. And that she probably wouldn't have survived. Not with Carlos having made it very clear that he'd rather kill her than lose her.

But that's over with, over and done. I don't have to worry about Carlos, not anymore. Now we have some other minor problems to deal with. . . .

Eric wasn't talking about it, but she knew something was wrong. He wasn't quite as . . . obvious . . . about his problems as Bethany, but there was something going on there, under the surface. She'd considered trying to "read" him without letting him detect it, and decided it was too risky. After a stunt like that, he'd never trust her again, and with good reason. It had taken Elizabet several months, but she'd finally convinced Kayla that listening in on people's thoughts without their knowledge was unethical. Tacky, like peeping through someone's window blinds.

So she hadn't taken the direct approach of just looking to see what was bothering the Bard. But she could tell it was something. There was that way that he'd look away, as if listening to something that no one else could hear. Very strange, and rather disturbing.

Still, he's my best chance for solving this situation without Elizabet getting killed. I don't think he's going to completely "lose it," at least not in the next few days. After that, though, all bets are off.

Beth was the one that Kayla didn't want to trust right now. She knew how fragile that "patch" was, the only thing that was keeping Bethany Kentraine from a long downward slide into insanity. What that bastard Blair had done—Kayla's fingers tightened into a fist, remembering—was inhuman. To deliberately try to break another person's mind . . .

They'd stop him. They would. He wouldn't be allowed to do that to another human being, ever. Whatever was animating his body, Nightflyer or otherwise, Eric would get rid of it. She wasn't too certain how that would happen, but she did have confidence in Eric on that count.

She just hoped that Elizabet would understand. Sure, this was dangerous, what they were planning to do, but it was something that had to be done. And Eric was right—better two people, alone, than a whole army trying to infiltrate that security complex. A neat, clean surgical operation.

But Elizabet would be very . . . angry . . . when she found out that they'd gone off on their own. Kayla reconsidered; maybe this wasn't such a good idea, after all. . . .

What the hell. She'd survived life on the street, and Carlos, and a street war in Los Angeles . . . she'd survive this, just fine.

She smiled, clutching that thought to her like the warm blankets, and drifted off to sleep.

Korendil, Champion of Elfhame Sun-Descending, Knight of Elfhame Mist-Hold, sat in the living-room of his San Francisco home and tried to pay attention to the conversation around him, without much luck. His thoughts were elsewhere, not on the war council that he had called and that he should be concentrating upon.

"Kory, what do you think about the main entrance? Should we try to draw the guards out with a distraction, or just have Eric go in and do some kind of mass hallucination on them? Kory?"

He shook himself out of his reverie, and nodded at Beth. "A distraction is best, milady," he said.

Distractions were all he could think of now. Once, he'd known exactly what his life should be, the life of a near-immortal elven warrior, but then he'd been distracted—distracted by a lovely dark-haired woman named Beth, and a handsome young man with all the powers of an ancient Bard. Because of them, his life had changed, and he had changed, into someone that he would not have recognized many years ago.

They were mortal. That thought could never leave him a moment's peace now. Dharinel had asked him that, in a quiet moment tonight when they were alone in the kitchen, refilling their glasses with dark red wine. "Why do you care so much for these humans?"

Kory had only smiled, knowing there was no answer he could give to the elven lord that the other would understand.

He was bound to them, by choice and by love. He could not imagine living without Beth's warm laugh, or the slow smile that often lighted Eric's face.

And how will I live without them, a scant hundred years from now?

That was the thought that terrified him, that he would have to watch them grow old, as humans do. It was a thought that he had not shared with either of them, not knowing what he could say.

There were answers, of course. He could ask them to join him Underhill, journeying across the veil between worlds into the elven realms where time moved slowly, if at all. But somehow, he didn't think they would accept that offer. Life in Faerie was a quiet and unchanging existence, nothing like the unpredictable life in the human world. He wasn't certain that he, himself, could return Underhill without longing for the human realms. That was why so many of his kind had chosen to live here, among the mortals. Beth had once described his inability to sit still as being "stir crazy"—somehow, he suspected that phrase also described how he would feel after several years of life in Faerie.

Until these last two days, the thought of his friends' mortality had not haunted him so. But seeing Beth so ill, with

a human malady unknown to elvenkind, had brought home
the differences between himself and his friends. Without
warning, without explanation, they could be taken from him,
simply because of their nature: they were human.

*Then again, all of us could die tomorrow, fighting this
demon-creature that wishes to destroy this entire city.*

Worry about this in another ten years, Korendil, he told
himself.

For tomorrow, you concentrate on surviving a battle.

"Korendil, do you have any opinion on that?"

He looked up, realizing that everyone was watching him,
waiting for a reply, and shrugged. "Decide as you see fit,"
he said, and stood. "I will be back shortly."

Outside the house, standing in the garden, he breathed
in the night air, letting the moonlight wash over him.
Through the open door, he could hear the arguments over
strategy and tactics continuing.

Beth yawned again, and rubbed at her aching eyes.
Enough already. "Guys, I can't keep my eyes open anymore;
I'm going to call it a night. Susan, we've set up the other
bed in the office for you, whenever you want to get some
sleep."

Susan Sheffield also looked exhausted, but she only
nodded. "Not just yet," she said. "I'm used to late nights
at the office . . . but I probably ought to get some sleep
soon."

"I'll probably be up in a little while," Eric said.

Beth headed wearily up the stairs. It had been a very
strange, surreal evening—long discussions of magic and
battle, the best methods for infiltrating the complex, and
how to link with the Mount Tam witches. Throughout the
evening, Eric had been strangely quiet, not contributing
much to the discussion.

*Probably still in shock over what's happened in the last
few days.*

She hoped he'd get over it, and quickly. Their plans
depended on him, and his Bardic abilities. If he couldn't
do the job . . .

She stripped off her shirt and jeans, and pulled on an old caftan, climbing into the large waterbed. The bed squished beneath her, rocking slightly, a gentle rhythm . . .

. . . the floor tilting beneath her, everything vibrating and shaking as long cracks zigzagged down the walls, plaster falling onto her . . .

Beth grabbed onto the edge of the bed for support, fingers whitening. She felt as though she was teetering on the edge of a dark chasm, hearing the screams of lost souls echoing up from below her. *That way lies madness.* She closed her eyes and concentrated on breathing slowly in through her nose, out through her mouth. The whirlwinds caught at her, trying to pull her down, but she held on tightly to the bed, refusing to let go.

After a long moment, the storm died away, leaving her alone again on the bed with only an echo of distant noise in her head.

She buried her face in her hands, as the tears silently leaked from her eyes. She wanted to scream from terror and frustration, and bit her lip instead.

She'd never thought this could happen to her. She'd always thought of herself as tough, independent, able to deal with anything. Except that it wasn't true—now she knew that it had never been true. Now she knew just how fragile her reality was, and what lurked out beyond the edges of sanity.

There was no way to understand this, to guess when she'd recover from it. Maybe she'd linger on this line between madness and waking for years. Maybe she'd never recover. That thought was the most terrifying of all—to continue this nightmare existence for the rest of her life. She remembered Ria Llewellyn's face after that terrible morning at Griffith Park, the awful blankness of a body without a mind, someone lost in the depths of insanity that now threatened her. She couldn't imagine herself that way, alive but not living. Trapped within her own mind, her own nightmares. It was inconceivable.

I'd rather die.

The more she thought about it, the more certain she

became of that idea: better not to live, not this way. Just the thought of trying to sleep tonight, knowing what nightmares awaited her, was more than she could bear. She crossed to the bathroom door, taking two Tylenol-with-Codeine pills from the medicine cabinet. That would work as well as sleeping pills, at least for tonight. She slid back into bed, pulling the covers tightly around her.

The fear was like a fist around her heart; despite her exhaustion, she didn't want to close her eyes, even for a moment. She knew what waited for her in the darkness.

To live like this, for years . . . maybe forever . . .

Well, tomorrow we're heading into a major fight. A lot of things can happen in a fight. Maybe I won't have to worry about this anymore.

She didn't want to die. But she wasn't too certain that she really wanted to live, either. She could feel the tenuous wall between herself and the terrors coiled beneath her, and knew that they were waiting to drag her down, bury her alive. That wall was so thin and fragile, it could break at any moment.

She knew she didn't want to live this way.

Tomorrow, they would try to save the city. She and Eric and Kory and their friends, Elizabet and Kayla, the elves of Mist-Hold, the San Francisco witches. She had a responsibility to them to help them in any way she could, and she knew she wouldn't shirk that responsibility. Somehow she would hold herself together, until the Poseidon Project equipment was destroyed, and Warden Blair was no longer a danger to anyone, and San Francisco was safe.

But afterwards . . .

15

Frosty Morning

The house was very quiet at 8 a.m., no sounds except for the faint noise of cars driving past, half a block away. Eric sat in the kitchen staring down into a mug of coffee that had been warm once, maybe an hour ago.

"You're up early," Dr. Sheffield said from behind him. He turned quickly. The lady scientist, wearing one of Beth's bathrobes, walked into the kitchen and sat down on one of the other chairs next to him.

"There's more coffee in the pot," Eric offered.

"Thanks." She reached across the table for a clean mug and the coffee pot. "Did you get much sleep?"

"No." He shook his head. "Too much to think about. All of this happened so fast—things used to be so easy for us. Uncomplicated. No problems, not in the last couple years. . . ."

"You mean, you don't usually go around summoning monsters and consorting with elves?"

He smiled. "Consorting with elves, sure. All the time. Summoning monsters, not if I can avoid it." The smile faded. "I didn't want to . . . to do what I did, at the Labs. But you know that, right?"

She didn't answer at first, swirling the coffee in her mug. "Friends of mine are dead or brain-dead because of you,

mister. I can't say I could ever forgive you for that. But
what Blair was doing, it was illegal and evil. Even if he
hadn't gotten hold of my project, he probably would've
graduated to some more extensive levels of cruelty eventually. I've read enough on psychopathic sadists to know that
they never stop until they're arrested or dead. Fourteen
people died that night at the Lab . . . yeah, and we don't
know how many people 'disappeared' under Dr. Blair's
tender care." She shook her head. "The man was already
sick and dangerous, and the truth is that even without the
Poseidon Project, if Blair continues unchecked, he'll beat
that record of fourteen eventually if he hasn't already. Just
a matter of time."

Eric's mouth opened; he closed it again.

"Besides, it's not like the Lab people don't know that
they're at risk, always. Working at the Labs, you know you're
a target. It's one of the first places a nuclear would hit, if
we ever got into that kind of war, and it's a constant target for terrorists. Those scum probably think of all the plu-
tonium in that complex and can't stop drooling." She took
another long swallow from the mug. "And then there's the
possibility that something could go wrong from the inside,
that some Lab technician could press the wrong switch and
the entire place could go up in smoke. Colonel Steve—my
boss—he thought that what happened with the monsters
could've been an internal accident, that all of us were
hallucinating from a chemical accident or something like
that. So you know you're a target when you work there,
in more ways than one." She stared down into the mug.
"It's just when it happened, when something did go wrong,
somehow I wasn't expecting it. I mean, I was expecting some
lunatic guys with automatic rifles, not an army of monsters."

"Sorry about that," Eric said sourly. "Next time, I'll leave
the demon army at home and bring a squad of terrorists
instead."

She gave him a sharp but steady look. "There won't be
a next time, kid, because you and your army of Tolkien fans
are going to get it right the first time. That's why I'm still
here, instead of taking off in the middle of the night and

heading for Sheboygan until all of this is over. I'm going to make sure you do it right."

"We'll try." *She's a good lady, Susan Sheffield. She didn't deserve this. It's the least I can do to make sure that she doesn't get hurt.*

He looked up and around, wondering where Kayla was. She ought to get up soon; they'd need to head out as soon as the morning traffic was over. He set his coffee mug down, and refilled it from the pot.

The mug rattled once on the table, then again, more insistently. The windows began to vibrate, one window swinging open. He could feel the ground moving beneath him, gentle swells that felt like floating on the tides of the ocean, close enough to shore to feel the motion of the waves.

"Oh shit, is that . . . ?" Eric turned to Susan Sheffield. The rattling noise ceased, as suddenly as it had begun.

Susan drank some coffee. Eric could see the unsteadiness of her hand as she lifted the mug. "Well, it could be natural. But—"

"But you don't think so."

She shook her head. "I'd say he's testing the engines, so to speak. Calibrating the probes. He's moving faster than I had expected . . . still, it'll take him a fair amount of time to calibrate the system, if he wants to do it right the first time. He has my notes and all my project files to work from, but Frank and I were the only ones who really lived with the system. He'll have to absorb a lot of information very quickly. And the physical calibration, even with the system computers to plot the resonance intersection points, that'll take time."

"How long?" Eric asked.

She was quiet for a few seconds, thinking about it, before she answered. "Definitely all day. Maybe by sometime tomorrow, if he works through the night. He might be able to do something tonight, but if he rushes too much, an improperly triggered earthquake could destroy the probes and he'd have to start over with the recalibration."

"Maybe we should've destroyed the probes ourselves, last night."

Susan shrugged. "Wouldn't have mattered that much. There's a roomful of them back at the Labs, though most of them still need some assembly work. We could've slowed him down a little, but not much. Maybe an hour or two. That's why I didn't suggest it at the time. What we need to do is stop Blair, not the project. In fact, I'm hoping we can do that without damaging the project equipment or laboratories—it'd sure be nice not to have to sacrifice most of my last two years' work tonight."

Kayla vaulted into the kitchen, still wearing a long flannel nightgown. It looked strange on her, now that Eric was so used to her leather clothing and studded jewelry. "Was that a real earthquake?" she asked.

"Just Warden Blair warming up the engines," Eric said. "Shouldn't you, like, get dressed or something?"

"Oh, yeah." She dived back through the doorway, and they could hear her feet pounding up the stairs.

"She's a good kid," Susan observed. "Why are you letting her get involved in this mess?"

Eric thought of Kayla after the battle in Griffith Park, soaked in blood up to her elbows, and tried to remember that this lady didn't know them, didn't know anything about them and what they'd already been through together. "She's very important. Kayla is a healer, a genuine 'lay on hands and fix what's broken' healer. If anyone gets hurt during this fight, it'll probably be Kayla who saves their lives."

"But she's just a kid!" Susan protested.

"She'll do fine. I'm more worried about the flaky Wiccans that Beth dug out of the woodwork, to be honest. From what she was saying, some of those people need to consult a crystal ball before they can tie their shoelaces in the morning. I'm not so worried about the elves; they believe in the danger and know what they're fighting for." *But with luck, none of them will need to go anywhere near the labs. I started this mess, and I'll deal with it.* "But I don't need to tell you about elves, you know enough about them already."

"I'd rather not talk about that," she said.

That was something of a surprise. "Why not? I thought

you had a good experience with the Misthold elves that summer."

"I did." She looked up to meet his gaze. "But then it ended, and they left me." She stood up abruptly. "Well, I'm going to shower and get dressed. I'm not certain what kind of clothes one is supposed to wear to Armageddon, but I'll see if I can borrow something from your friend Beth."

She set her mug down in the sink before leaving the room. Eric contemplated pouring another cup of coffee, and wondered if adding a shot of whiskey to it would help clear the blurriness from his mind. *Probably not,* he decided.

He'd never been a morning person, ever. Morning was that awful thing that happened every day before noon, something to avoid if possible, endure if not. But today he had a schedule to keep, if he wanted to keep his friends out of danger as well as the rest of San Francisco.

Maybe a little more caffeine would help. . . .

"Hey, pour me one of those," Kayla said, sliding onto the chair recently vacated by Susan Sheffield.

"It'll stunt your growth, kid," Eric said, pouring her the last cup of coffee in the pot.

"Hell, I'm tall enough already. So, are you ready? Did you eat breakfast?"

"I never eat breakfast," he said grimly. "Breakfast is for people who wake up before lunch."

"Look, Bard, you have to take care of yourself. You're about to go burn a lot of magical energy, you need something to replace it." Kayla hopped off the chair and began rummaging through the refrigerator. "How does scrambled eggs and toast sound?"

"Awful."

"I can add some cheese and salsa, if you want."

"That's worse. Kayla, make whatever you want for breakfast. I'll stick with coffee, thanks."

"Better to watch your nutrition. That's what Elizabet always tells me. Well, it's your funeral, Bard." There was an awkward silence between them. "I didn't mean it quite that way, Eric," Kayla said after a moment. "I'll cook up some eggs, and then we can get out of here."

"Right. I'll get my things together."

He headed upstairs, quietly opening the bedroom door. Beth and Kory were still asleep. He took his flute case from the top of the dresser, and slipped it into his gig-bag. His leather wallet was lying on the window seat; he checked to make sure that he had his BART card in the pocket for the subway fare, and change for the bus, enough for Kayla and himself. There was a ten-dollar bill with the BART card—*maybe Kayla and I can stop for lunch at Gordo's Burritos in Berkeley after we save the world*, he thought with a wry smile.

On the other hand, Kayla knew how to drive. Maybe they should take Beth's elven steed.

A last look at the waterbed: Kory, sleeping with his arm flung out wide, as relaxed in sleep as he always was when awake. Beth, frowning slightly in her sleep. He knelt and kissed her gently, careful not to wake her. *I might never see them again.* The thought was like a physical pain. He hurried downstairs to where Kayla was waiting, already wearing her black leather jacket and boots.

"Listen, Eric," she said, a little hesitantly. "There's something I need to tell you . . . I don't know how to say this, exactly, but . . . you're kinda visible. I can see it, and I know the elves can, too. I'd bet the bad guys could see you that way as well, so I thought you might want to do something about it."

"I don't understand," he said.

"It's a little difficult to explain . . . you kinda . . . glow, a little. Well . . . more than a little. You glow a lot, to be honest. When I close my eyes, I can still see you."

This was a bad time for a joke. Or maybe it wasn't a joke. "Are you serious?"

She nodded vigorously. "Scout's honor, Bard. You look like a neon light at five hundred feet."

He thought about that for a minute. "Okay. Let me try something." He closed his eyes and reached inside, to that still pool of power within him. With an odd mental twist, he switched it off, like a light switch, or like opening the floodgates and letting it all pour out instantly.

The wooden floor was pressed against his cheek. That was the first conscious thought that registered, that and the fact that Kayla's hands were bright with a pale blue light. He sat up slowly, waves of dizziness washing over him.

"Don't *do* that, Eric!" The threads of light faded from Kayla's hands. "Jesus, you scared me! You stopped your heart. Are you okay now?"

He nodded, not quite trusting himself to speak. *I can just see the headlines in the newspapers—"Bard Commits Suicide Out of Sheer Stupidity."* He took a deep breath. "Let me try that again."

This time, he moved more carefully into that pool of light, and the light slowly dimmed away, leaving a pool of shadows instead. He opened his eyes again, relieved to see that he was still alive. "Did that work?" he asked.

Kayla closed her eyes. "Yes," she said after a moment. "Looks good, Bard." She helped him to his feet, then hesitated. "Oh, almost forgot." She darted into the kitchen, reappearing a few seconds later. "I left them a note," she explained. "I've told them that we've gone out shopping for supplies, and told them to wait for us. Maybe we can be finished with this before they realize where we've gone."

"Yeah, sure." *You're being very optimistic about this, Kayla,* he thought. *I'd guess that you're as scared as I am, but you're even better at not showing the fear. If you can be this calm once we're inside the Labs, maybe we'll survive this after all.* "All right," he said. "Let's go."

Kory rolled over in bed, then sat up abruptly. Something was wrong, very wrong. . . .

It took him several seconds to figure it out. Nothing was wrong with him, and there were no enemies in sight, nothing more unusual than the sounds of traffic outside the window. Beth was still asleep, curled up in a ball next to him. Eric was . . .

Eric was missing.

Not just missing, but completely gone. Usually he could just think about Eric and know where he was. The touch of Bardic magic was unmistakable. Even when he had been captive in the tunnels of the Dublin Labs, it had only taken a small effort to reach out and find Eric, to touch him across all the distance of the city and the Bay.

Now he couldn't sense anything. No Bardic magic, no Eric—He cast out his thoughts in a widening ring, searching . . .

Nothing.

Kory fought against the cold terror that wrapped itself around his heart. "Don't panic, don't panic," he whispered to himself, and shook Beth awake.

"Wha—Kory?" She blinked, propping herself up on one elbow. "Is something wrong?"

"Do you know where Eric is?"

"He's not asleep . . . ?" She glanced at the alarm clock. "It's ten a.m. and Eric's already out of bed? Amazing!"

"He's gone, Beth. I can't find him anywhere."

She sat up. "You mean, you can't find him magically? Are you sure?"

He nodded. "He is not in the city, as far as I can tell. I should know where he is, but I cannot find him."

"Is he . . . ?" There was a question in her eyes that Kory did not want to answer.

"I—I do not think so. At least, I should feel that, as well. The death of a Bard . . . we would know it, I am certain of that. It would leave a mark upon the bones of the land." *Unless he was taken far away before they killed him, perhaps to the realm of those shadow-monsters. . . .*

"So either someone is hiding him from us, or Eric went AWOL." Beth was suddenly all business, pulling on her bathrobe and slippers. "If this is Eric Banyon's idea of a joke, I'm going to kill him. Can you tell where he was last, before he disappeared?"

"I don't know. *I don't know.*"

He concentrated, imagining the Bard's handsome features, remembering his laughter, the intense look on his face as he played an ancient Irish air. . . . "Downstairs," he said firmly. "In the hallway, very close to the front door. That's where Eric vanished."

"The front room? But that doesn't make any sense—If

someone had come through the front door and attacked him, Eric should've made enough noise to awaken everyone in the house." She was out of bed and running downstairs before Kory could say anything else. He followed her a moment later, to find her standing near the front door, staring at the floor, then she looked up at the row of hooks where they always hung their jackets and coats. "No sign of a scuffle down here. And Eric took his leather jacket. If he'd been kidnapped, he wouldn't have done that."

Elizabet, sleepy-eyed, walked out from the kitchen. "Are they back yet?" she asked.

"What?" Kory asked.

"Kayla and Eric. They left a note saying that they were going to get some supplies. . . . Can't imagine what they're doing, unless Kayla wanted to get some extra first aid supplies. I thought they might be back by now."

Beth shook her head, a thoughtful frown on her face. "I think I've figured this out—they took off early, leaving a note so we wouldn't worry about them, and Eric makes sure that we can't track him magically . . . where do you think they are right now, Elizabet?"

The older woman smiled wryly, her white teeth very bright against her dark skin. "Kayla isn't someone who'd run away from a fight, so I know they didn't just run for the hills—I'd guess they're on their way across the Bay to the Dublin Labs right now, wouldn't you?"

"That's what I think, too." Rage smoldered in her eyes. "Damn it, Eric Banyon, you are such a twit! How could he do this?"

"Perhaps because he did not wish any of us to risk our lives," Kory said. Beth and Elizabet both turned to look at him. "I had thought about doing something similar," he confessed, "but decided that I would probably not be able to succeed on my own."

"And Eric, on the other hand, thinks he can do anything!" Beth clenched her hands into fists. "Okay, okay. Here's what we do. I'll call the psychic team, get them to head over to Mount Tam and start ASAP. The rest of us, and the elven assault team, will head over to the Labs and save Eric from his own stupidity. I can't believe he dragged Kayla into this, too!"

"That doesn't surprise me," Elizabet said. "You don't know Kayla quite as well as I do. By the way, has anyone seen Susan this morning?"

Maybe this isn't the best idea I've had in a long time, Susan thought. *But I'm not going to be a bystander anymore. This is my project that some insane nut is trying to pervert into a killing machine, and maybe I can stop this without anyone getting killed—crazy human witches, elves or whatever other refugees from fantasy they can drag in.*

It was that thought that had sparked her flight from the house on Broderick Street: the image of Melisande, lying dead with several .45 auto bullets in her, her blood soaking the white linoleum floors of the Dublin Labs. *Not if I have anything to say about it.*

As she expected, the traffic driving east along the Bay Bridge wasn't too bad at this hour of morning. In the other direction, she could still see the "parking lot" of cars, inching their way into the city. It was a beautiful morning, with the last of the fog already burned away by the bright sunshine. She navigated the freeway interchange through Oakland, glancing involuntarily at the cleared area off to the right that had once been the double-decker Nimitz Freeway. *This is what I'm going to prevent,* she vowed silently. *That's why I fought to do the Poseidon Project, so that this would never happen again. Now I'm going to stop the inhuman bastard who wants to use my project for destruction.*

It was a simple plan, what she was going to do. If she could get to Colonel Steve without being intercepted by Blair or any of his people, she knew she could convince him. Steve was ethical, no matter what Blair was. No amount of double-talking would get Blair out of this. Just the physical evidence, the fact that Blair was moving the probes and recalibrating the equipment to trigger a major quake—five minutes in the lab, explaining what was going on to the colonel, and all of this would be over. Lab security would arrest Blair, she'd deactivate the machinery, and that would be the end of it.

The only tricky part was getting to Steve without alerting Blair. But she had a plan for that, too. . . .

With luck this would work, because she had no intention of trusting that flaky dark-haired boy and his neurotic girlfriend. The elves she trusted, of course, but she couldn't understand the overwhelming belief they had in their "Bard." *He screwed things up royally before, didn't he?* No, what she was doing was risky, but safer than the other options. And she wouldn't have to watch Sandy die.

She turned on the radio, and punched the button to bring up the local talk radio channel. The station announcer was talking about the morning's earthquake, and another very minor one that had hit ten minutes ago—*right while I was driving across the Bridge,* she thought. *Terrific.* But the announcer assured everyone that there was nothing to worry about, the seismologists at Cal Tech had said that the faults were just releasing a little pressure, there was no chance of a major quake.

She smiled humorlessly at that, and drove a little faster.

A half hour later, she braked to a stop at the guard gate at the Labs, flashing her I.D. to the security officer. She parked in the underground lot, leaving the car doors unlocked and the keys in the ignition. She knew she didn't have to worry about car thieves, not in this complex. And there was a high possibility she might want to leave in a hurry.

Her first stop was the cafeteria on the second floor. There was a small dining room off the main area, which had a telephone in it. She strolled past the security officers, staying away from the elevators that descended into the underground laboratories. At this hour, the hallways were mostly deserted. Still, she breathed a sigh of relief when she walked through the cafeteria doors.

The cafeteria was empty. She guessed that all the personnel were in the kitchen, preparing for the lunch crowd. A few seconds later, she was standing next to the telephone. She dialed Steve's extension and listened to the ringing tone. *Come on, Steve, pick up your phone!*

A click, then she heard his voice. "Colonel O'Neill, Poseidon Project."

"Steve, this is me. Are you alone?"

"Susan, where are you? Are you all right?" His voice sounded concerned.

"I'm okay. Listen, we have to talk, right now. Where's Warden Blair? Is he in the lab?"

"No, he's organizing the cleanup on Level Thirteen. Where have you been, Susan? Security said you never went home, you've been missing for twenty-four hours . . ."

"I'll explain later. Meet me in my lab, in five minutes. And please, don't tell Blair or any of his people, all right?"

She waited, wondering how that security-overconscious mind was taking what she'd just said.

"Okay. I'll be there ASAP, Susan."

She hung up the phone, and hurried to the closest stairs. Ten minutes later, she was in her lab.

For a moment, as she stepped through the doorway, it felt as though all of the events of the last two days had been only a nightmare. Maybe, if she wished for it hard enough, Frank and Dave would walk back in the door, ready to help her set up the next test run. But no, there was the oscilloscope she'd thrown at the monster, broken and dented; someone had placed it back upon the worktable.

No time for funk, not now. She moved quickly, making sure that the computer workstation was up and running, then loaded the Poseidon simulation program. She set it to run a simulation based on current test run parameters, and waited impatiently as the numbers scrolled past on the screen. The screen cleared, then began to build the three-dimensional fractal landscape of the Bay Area, pinpointing the exact trigger point of the quake and the widening circles of area of effect and potential energy release levels.

"Son of a bitch!"

Until now, I wasn't certain. It could've just been an evil fantasy, a delusion that Warden Blair wanted to destroy the city.

Now it's laid out in front of me in full-color graphics . . .

As she'd guessed from the elven scouts' reports, the

Poseidon device was aimed at the San Andreas fault, directly beneath Hollister. And the potential energy readings were off the scales, somewhere beyond 10.0 on the Richter.

He'll wipe the entire Bay Area off the map. Hell, the effects would destroy the Labs as well! How did he plan on surviving it?

The answer came to her a moment later, in a memory of the shadow-monsters drifting through the hallways of the Labs. Shadow-monsters that wouldn't care if the complex crumpled in on itself, burying level upon level in rumbling death. She remembered the alien intelligence behind Blair's eyes. *He looks human, but he isn't.*

"Susan?"

She turned quickly, to see Colonel Steve walking toward her. "Steve, thank God! Listen, we probably don't have much time . . . Blair is planning to use the project as a weapon, with San Francisco as his first test case. I have proof of this—he's moved the probes off our test run coordinates and set them to trigger a major quake. Let me show you the computer simulation . . . it displays exactly where he was going to trigger the quake."

He smiled. "It's okay, Susan. I know."

Shock froze her mind and her body—but her mouth kept going.

"But you haven't arrested Blair yet?" Surely this was just a sting. Surely Steve had something planned.

He didn't answer, only standing there, looking at her. There was something strange about Steve's face. She hadn't seen it at first, but now it was visible to her . . . lines of tension that hadn't been there before. No, not just the lines in his face . . . it was in his eyes, a cold blankness, an alien intelligence that was staring back at her. . . .

If she'd seen this before she'd met the elves, the musician, she'd have assumed she was the crazy one. Not now.

God, no. Not Steve. Please, this can't be happening, this can't be real. . . .

She had to get out of here, before this insanity consumed her as well. That was her one thought, that if Blair could

do—whatever it was that he'd done—to Steve, it was only
a matter of time until she was changed into something like
him: a walking and talking human being with an alien's
thoughts peering out from within her eyes. . . .

But Steve was between her and the door. And Steve had
a gun.

"This goes too fast," she whispered, sitting down on one
of the wooden lab stools with a thump.

*I am stuck. If he has Steve, and Steve has me—he has
me. It's over.* "So, Steve, what happens now?" she asked
conversationally, looking up at him.

He seemed momentarily taken aback. "I—I don't know,"
he said uncertainly. "I'm supposed to keep you here, until
Blair tells me what to do. I wish—I wish you hadn't come
back, Susan. For a little while, I thought you were safe,
safely far away from this."

"I could've been, if I'd had any brains." *What's going
on inside his head?* she wondered. "Steve, can't you just
let me walk out of here?"

"Can't—can't do that." He shook his head, as if to clear
it. "He won't let me." His hand twitched next to the pistol holster on his hip.

"I see." Her glance fell upon the broken oscilloscope on
the table next to her. The thought occurred to her that while
the oscilloscope had been useless against a nightmare creature, it might be significantly more applicable against a
human being. Especially if she swung it hard enough. "Steve,
is that Blair out in the hall?"

Steve's glance swung toward the open door. "No, I can
feel where he is, he's still on the thirteenth—"

The oscilloscope crashed into his chest. Steve made an
odd choking sound, and stumbled backwards into another
lab table. A split-second later, Susan was out the door and
running down the corridor.

She heard Steve's voice from behind her, furious. "Susan!
Stop or I'll shoot!"

He won't shoot me, she thought, *any more than I
could've hit him in the head with the 'scope. I couldn't kill
him, and I know he won't—*

The noise of the gun firing was very loud in the narrow corridor.

Something slammed into her back, a sudden pain like her body had been set on fire. The shock threw her forward against the wall; a second shock, a moment later, as she landed hard on the floor. Everything was very bright, very white . . . she tried to move, to get up and run, but somehow nothing seemed to be working right in her body anymore, everything was numb with pain and her legs just wouldn't move at all.

She heard footsteps approaching, and Steve's voice whispering, "I'm sorry, Susan . . . "

I can't forgive you, Steve, she wanted to whisper back to him, but the whiteness engulfed her before she could say a word.

16

Soldier's Joy

"So, Eric, what's the plan?" Kayla asked, looking at the gate of the Dublin Laboratories, a hundred yards ahead of them.

He shook his head, frowning. "I'm still trying to figure it out. Give me a minute, okay?"

He'd been thinking about this during the motorcycle ride across the Bay, and still couldn't think of a good plan that included both of them surviving this experience. "All right, here's what we do. I'm going to cast a spell over both of us, so that we'll be nearly invisible. I'll do myself first, so you can tell me whether or not it's working. Then we'll just walk in there, take a crowbar to Dr. Sheffield's machine, and walk back out again."

Kayla tilted her head to one side. "Susan will hate you for that, Eric."

He snorted. "Well, tough for her. Better that than watching all of San Francisco slide into the ocean. And after that, we can take our time dealing with Warden Blair. I was thinking that we could follow him home later, and find out whether he's a man or—or a demon wearing someone's body like a set of clothing."

Kayla shivered. "I know this sounds crazy, but I hope he really is a Nightflyer. Then maybe you can just banish

582

the Nightflyer, and we won't have to kill him. I don't want to kill anybody," she concluded, wistfully.

"I don't want to either, kid," Eric said seriously. He brought his flute to his lips, playing an experimental scale. Next to them, the parked motorcycle made an odd sound, almost a horse's whinny. Kayla stepped back from it hastily.

"Don't worry," Eric said. "Those elven horse-bikes are mostly friendly. I think that one has an awful sense of humor, though." He played another scale, then tucked the flute under his arm, rubbing his hands together briskly.

"Is something wrong?" Kayla asked, concerned.

"It's just cold out here. My fingers are stiff." He lifted the flute again and played a run of arpeggios. "That's better." He began playing "Banysh Mysfortune," slowly at first, then building in speed and intensity, concentrating on the thought: *I'm invisible, I'm unseen, I'm the wisp of melody that drifts past, unnoticed.* After playing through the A,B, and C parts twice, he ended the tune and looked over at Kayla curiously. "So, did anything happen?"

She couldn't quite meet his eyes. "Oh, yeah. You're still there, but I can't look at you, not really. It's like my eyes keep sliding off of you, it's very hard to keep trying to look at you. I think it'll work."

"Good." He ran through the melody again, this time focusing his thoughts on Kayla. When he finished, it was exactly as she had described . . . he could see her, but she was very difficult to look at. *Not bad. Maybe I'm starting to get the hang of this whole magic business.* "Let's walk in, calmly and quietly," he said. "No hurry at all. Just stroll past the guards and into the building."

"I'm with you, Bard." She grinned at him. "How 'bout going for beer and pizza after this?"

"Aren't you a little young to drink?"

She shrugged. "Alcohol can't do anything for me. I just like the taste of beer. Don't you?"

He sighed, and they started down the road toward the gate. As he had hoped, the man at the gate barely glanced at them. They received an identical lack of response from the receptionist in the lobby, and walked past what looked like a military SWAT team. . . .

A SWAT team!, Eric's mind screamed silently, but he kept walking.

Dr. Susan's directions had been very specific: take the stairs to the third level, walk down the corridor to the stairway connecting to the lower levels, continue down to the bottom level, turn left onto the main corridor, follow that to the end, turn right, then go into the fourth door on the right.

The third level was deserted, not even a security guard in sight. They continued down to the last level and were halfway down the main corridor when Kayla stopped him, her hand on his arm. "Something's wrong," she whispered. "There's someone . . . oh shit, it's Susan!" She vaulted into a run, and Eric ran after her. He turned the corner a split-second after she had, and stopped short at the sight of a tall man in a military uniform, carrying a bloody and unconscious Dr. Susan Sheffield.

Too many things happened at once: the man dropped Susan onto the floor, reaching for the pistol holstered at his side; Kayla screamed something incoherent and leaped at him; Eric desperately whistled a single shrill note—the noise of the magic and gunshot blended together. The Bardic magic caught the man and lifted him off his feet to slam against the wall, as if hit by a giant fist. He landed in an unconscious heap next to Susan.

Gunshot . . . he missed me, did he hit . . . ?

Kayla staggered backwards against him. He caught her; his flute clattered on the floor. He saw the bullet hole in her leather jacket, and felt the warmth of her blood, dripping down her back and onto his arm. She coughed suddenly, bright red blood running down her chin.

"Oh my God, kid . . ."

"Bastard . . . got a lung . . ." Kayla whispered, so faint that he could barely hear her. He could hear a strange whistling noise as she breathed. "Set me down next to Susan . . . need to be close enough to touch her . . ."

"No! Kayla, heal yourself first!"

"I've got . . . a few seconds . . . she doesn't . . . do it, Eric!"

He carefully set her down next to Susan's unconscious body. She rested her hand on Susan's shoulder, closing her eyes. Eric felt the magic in the air, as blue lines coiled and twisted over Kayla's outstretched hand. He held her other hand, her blood slick against his palm, watching her face furrowed in concentration.

Suddenly, the blue light faded.

Eric reached desperately with his own magical senses. Susan was still alive; he could see the magical light that was her life, growing brighter and brighter. But Kayla . . . he couldn't find her at first, even though he knew he was still holding her hand. She had poured all her energy into saving Susan, leaving none for herself. . . .

Wait a minute!

He caught a pale thread, held onto it. Fed it with his own magic, until Kayla moved against him, struggling feebly. Then he poured everything he could into her, giving her the power she needed to heal herself. The world dimmed around him, and he knew he was dangerously close to pouring all of his own life force into Kayla, exactly what she had done to Susan.

Kayla's hand tightened around his own. He opened his eyes and looked at her, to see a faint smile on her face. "We . . . we aren't doing so great today, are we, Bard?" she whispered.

"Yeah, I know," he whispered back.

"You're doing worse than you think," a man's voice said from behind him. Eric turned quickly, to see three drawn pistols aimed at him. Though he had never met Warden Blair, he recognized that cold smile from Beth's memories.

"Oh, hell," Eric said, wondering how fast he could call his Bardic magic. Before he could even pucker his lips to whistle, a pistol barrel caught him on the side of the face, and the world exploded into darkness.

He awakened to an aching headache, and a feeling like his arms were being pulled out of their sockets. When he

tried to move, he realized why: his arms were handcuffed
behind him. He opened his eyes, wondering why he was
still alive.

Kayla was lying on the floor near him, also handcuffed.
And Susan, on the other side of the room, apparently still
unconscious. They were in a room that Eric remembered
from Susan's descriptions: the laboratory that contained the
Poseidon computers. Two business-suited young men stood
near the door, watching him intently. He saw the handguns
stuck into their waistbands, and decided against trying to
leap at them with his hands cuffed behind his back. Probably
the world's stupidest idea. Then again, coming here with
just Kayla now seemed like the world's stupidest idea, too.

He whispered Kayla's name, and was rewarded by seeing her eyes open, then slowly focus on him. She was very
pale, blood still smeared across her face. "Eric? You okay?"

"Yeah, I think so. Just an awful headache, and everything's
a little blurry. You?"

"I'm okay. Susan . . ." He saw tears begin to roll down
her cheeks, mixing with the drying blood. "That bastard shot
Susan in the spine. I saved her life, but even if we make
it out of here, she'll be paralyzed."

"Keep quiet, both of you," one of their guards said
roughly.

Okay, so we will. He fought against the exhaustion that
threatened to overwhelm him, and whispered to her in that
silent speech that Kory had taught him.

:*Kayla, can you hear me?*:

She twitched visibly, then nodded.

:*How long was I out?*: he asked.

A moment later, he heard her voice answer silently to
him. :*Maybe an hour, hour and a half. I don't know. I've
been mostly out of it until just a few minutes ago . . . I
feel weak as a kitten right now . . . .*: A pause, then she
continued. :*You saved my life, Eric. I could feel everything
slipping away, it was like I was drowning, sliding under
the surface, and then you pulled me back.*:

:*Hey, no problem,*: he answered. :*Let's concentrate on
getting out of here, now. Susan needs a hospital, and you*

don't look so great yourself. Is there anything else I need to know before I bust us out of here?:

She nodded slightly. *:Blair was in here a few minutes ago, doing something with the computers. He left with that military guy, the one who shot me. I pretended like I was out cold. When they left, I looked through the door . . . I don't think there are any other guards except for these two guys.:*

:Good. I'll see what I can do to these guys, then we'll trash the place and leave.: Eric sat up, looking closely at the two men near the door. A simple Irish melody to make them sleepy, like "My Darling Asleep"—that might do the trick—

He held back another wave of exhaustion that threatened to drag him under, and whistled the first couple measures, watching the two men closely to see if there was any effect. If they were Nightflyer-possessed, like Warden Blair, his magic might not have any effect on them.

One of the men yawned. Eric continued the melody, not pausing until both men were slumped against the wall, one of them snoring loudly.

He stood up unsteadily, realizing for the first time how much he usually used his hands for balance, and headed to the two men. Fumbling in their pockets with his hands handcuffed behind him was awkward, but he found what he was hoping for—the handcuff key. He managed to unlock his own cuffs, then unfastened Kayla's and Susan's. Susan didn't move at all when he removed the cuffs; she looked awful, very pale and breathing shallowly. As Kayla sat up and rubbed her wrists, Eric crossed to the computer console and cursed quietly.

"What's wrong?" Kayla asked, moving to stand behind him.

"I think Blair already triggered the quake, when he was in here before. It says that the energy level is rising several percent points a second. We stop it from getting worse, but the fault is already getting ready to blow. Damn!" Eric looked around for something handy, and picked up a metal box, some kind of weird machinery with a broken green glass screen, that was lying on the floor. As he was about to swing it into the computer console, he heard Susan Sheffield's voice. "Eric, wait . . ."

He turned to see her trying to sit up, and giving up a moment later to lie helplessly on the floor. "Help me up," she said. "I'll stop the program."

Eric and Kayla exchanged a glance, then together they lifted her. Kayla winced and Eric saw the blood drain from her face, but she didn't say anything about her own pain. Together, they moved Susan to the computer console, holding her up so she could use the keyboard. She typed several commands quickly, watching the screen intently, then nodded. "Okay. It's done."

They lowered her back to the floor; she lay there for a moment before speaking, pain fighting with terror on her face. "It reached sixty-five percent before I crashed the program," she said weakly. "That's a very bad earthquake, I don't know exactly how bad. The resonance will take thirty minutes to build, maybe a few minutes more than that, depending on how well he aimed the probes, and then it'll release the faultline." She pointed at a small cardboard box on one of the shelves. "Eric, get that for me."

"Susan, are you . . . ?"

"I'm okay. Just do this, quickly."

He took it down from the shelf and opened the box. Inside was a small electronic device with a crude switch built into it, something he didn't recognize, and a computer disk.

"Put the disk in that computer and type GOODBYE, please. Now the electromagnet—walk over to that wall that has the tape backups and switch it on. If you move it next to every box of tape, that'll erase everything." She managed a smile as Eric followed her instructions. "Welcome to the wonderful world of computer destruction, kids. That disk had a specialized worm virus on it that'll keep the main computers down for hours, and it'll destroy all the pertinent data about my project. And you're wiping clean all of our data backups. Blair won't be able to do anything with the system for quite a while." She frowned. "I programmed that virus in case the military decided to play games with the project. I never thought I'd ever actually use it."

"Good planning, though," Kayla murmured.

Susan nodded, closing her eyes. Kayla knelt painfully next to her, placing one hand on her shoulder. After a moment, she looked up at Eric.

"We can't move her again. I don't know how bad the neurological damage is, but moving her again could kill her."

"Can't you—" He gestured helplessly. "Can't you just heal the damage?"

Kayla shook her head. "All I do is convince the cells to heal themselves faster. Nerve cells won't regenerate that way."

"You—you'd better get out of here," Susan whispered. "The quake's coming—you don't have much time—leave me here, just go—"

"Susan, we can't!" Kayla protested.

"Please—don't die because of me—"

"Come on, Kayla." Eric took her by the arm, moving toward the door. "She's right. We can't do anything for her, not now." He opened the door, and stopped short.

A familiar-looking man in a military uniform, with a familiar-looking .45 automatic handgun in his hand, stared back at him.

Eric shut the door.

Thinking quickly, he grabbed the broken machine on the floor, turning with it just as the man kicked the door open. Eric didn't hesitate. Ten pounds of high-tech metal crashed into the man's face. The gun dropped to the floor; Kayla retrieved it before the man could recover. She held it aimed at his chest as he straightened slowly, wiping the blood from his nose.

"Okay, slimeball," Kayla said, clicking the safety off the pistol. "Start talking."

He only stared at her blankly.

Eric hoped the man couldn't see what he so clearly could— Kayla's bravado was skin-deep. She could barely hold onto the gun, and he wasn't certain whether she could fire it, either. *If he makes a break for it, she'd better shoot him,* Eric thought, *'cause I'm sure as hell not going to be able to wrestle this guy down to the ground. And I don't think she'll be able to shoot him.* He felt the bruise swelling on the side of his face, and distantly wondered whether he had a concussion. Then he decided it didn't matter, not with the world about to crash down around them sometime in the next half hour.

No . . . the next twenty-five minutes, now.

The man was still standing, not speaking.

Eric saw it first, before Kayla did. "He has Nightflyer eyes," he said aloud, wondering what they could do with the man now.

"Please—don't kill him—" Susan's voice was weaker. "He was a friend of mine, once."

Eric thought about it, how he would summon a Night-flyer *out* of someone's body, instead of from—from wherever it was that Nightflyers came from.

"Whatever you're going to do, Eric," Kayla said, not wavering the aim of the pistol, "get moving with it. The clock is ticking, remember?"

"Right." He saw where someone had kicked his flute underneath one of the computers, and picked it up quickly. He began playing the first notes of the solo from "Danse Macabre," focusing on what lurked behind the man's pale blue eyes.

Something materialized between them—a thin shadow, smaller and less opaque than any of the other Nightflyers he had seen. *A baby Nightflyer,* he realized with a start. Without missing a beat, he slid into the A part from "Banysh Mysfortune," and the Nightflyer faded from view.

The man blinked, then stared at Eric. His pale blue eyes suddenly filled with tears. He walked past Kayla, completely ignoring the pistol in her hands, and knelt next to Susan. "Susan, I'm sorry, oh God, I'm so sorry . . ."

Kayla glanced at Eric, the pistol still clenched in her hand, obviously uncertain what to do. Eric gave her an "Okay" handsign. "He's okay now. I'm sure of it."

Susan's voice was very thin, strained. "Steve, you have to get out of here. This whole place could collapse in a few minutes . . ."

"Then I'm taking you with me." His voice was firm. For a moment, Eric saw what kind of man Steve used to be, before his own nightmare of the Nightflyers had begun.

"No, you can't move her, she's—" Kayla began.

"I've decided I don't want to die down here," Susan whispered, closing her eyes. "Take me out into the sunlight, Steve."

"We'll have to go out by one of the emergency exits," Steve said. "There's a major firefight going on in the upper levels—some crazy people dressed in medieval armor shooting it out with security."

"That sounds like the rest of our team," Kayla said. "Where did you say they were right now?"

"Upstairs, level three. But you can't—" He glanced down at the .45 automatic in Kayla's hand. "Then again, maybe you can," he said.

"Get Susan out of here," Eric said. "She needs immediate medical attention. Spine injury."

The military man looked around the laboratory, then took a metal cart covered with research material, shoving the papers and books onto the floor, and then with Eric's help carefully lifted Susan onto it. "Good luck," he said to Eric and Kayla.

Susan whispered a goodbye as they left the room.

"Good luck is right," Kayla said, turning to Eric. "What in the hell are we going to do against an army of security officers? How much time do we have left, anyhow?"

"God knows. Maybe twenty minutes." He thought about it quickly. "If we can get to the others, there might be some kind of magic we can do to stop the quake. I don't know. But we'll need an army to get to them. And I know where we can get one."

"Eric—" Kayla's eyes widened in sudden understanding and horror. "No way. You're not going to do that again."

"It's the only solution I can think of."

"Eric, if you lose control of them again, we're all dead!"

He met her eyes squarely. "Kayla, I already have enough deaths on my conscience. I won't make any mistakes this time. I promise."

Kayla still looked very uncertain, but she nodded. "All right. I won't stop you." She stepped back from him, clicking the safety on the pistol and shoving it into her waistband.

He brought the flute to his lips, and began to play the classic melody that he now privately thought of as the "Yo, Nightflyers, want to come hang out over here?" tune. "Danse Macabre."

He felt it starting around him, the whispers of sound, the cold wind touching the back of his neck.

The shadows on the floor lengthened, darkening and rising to surround him. This time, he held onto them tightly, knowing what would happen if he lost control now. They whirled around him, fast-moving shapes that circled and laughed silently.

He held them with the music, weaving an image of what would happen to them if they disobeyed him—dissolution, oblivion. The Nightflyers silently wailed with anger and fear, but the deadly whirlwind of shadows slowed to drift quietly around him.

"Forward, march," Eric muttered, catching his breath for a moment. His shadow troops floated behind him as he and Kayla started down the corridor toward the stairway.

The anti-terrorist team commander, Captain Brown, tried once again to convince the scientist to go back upstairs, where it was safe, and get out of the area of fire. Warden Blair shook his head, not explaining his real reason for wanting to be so close to the gunfight.

When they die, my children will feast on their death-agonies, he/it thought. There was so much potential here, and all of the futurepaths wove together at this point, screaming "Breakthrough, Breakthrough!" to his alien senses. In the next few minutes, all futurepaths would join into a single one, with no more chance of failure. And his children would sweep out over the city, glorying in the life-energies that were theirs for the taking.

He blinked suddenly, sensing something different. There were others of his kind, very close. He did not understand it—he had not brought them across the veil between worlds, and he knew there were no others of his kind here, except for his first child that now possessed Colonel O'Neill. That had been the easiest solution to the problem of Colonel O'Neill, since direct control by Blair had been very tiring, and dangerous as well.

Ah, that was it, he decided. Though it was risky to reproduce so young, his child must have used the life force of the music-maker and the other human to create others.

One of the other officers reported in to his captain, taking the same time to reload his assault rifle. "They're still holed up behind the barricade down the hall, sir. We have them covered from both sides, but so far we haven't managed to advance. No change in status."

"Tear gas?" the captain asked.

"Didn't seem to have any effect the first time, sir. We can try it again, if you want."

The captain shook his head. "No, keep working closer down the hallway. Get close enough to spray the area, and that'll be it. We don't need to risk any of our people trying to take these lunatic terrorists alive."

"Can I go closer to see the action?" Blair asked, trying not to sound too eager.

"No, sir, you cannot. You're already too close to our operations, and you really should leave the area." The captain looked up suddenly, down the hallway behind them. "What in the hell is that?"

Nightflyers, drifting toward them. Blair gloried in the sight, knowing that the moment was at hand.

Except . . .

Except there were two humans walking with his kindred, and one of them was the music-maker. Alive, and playing music that he could feel, even at this distance. He was *controlling* the Nightflyers, bending them to his will, and Blair could feel the tenuous strains of that music touching the edges of his mind, trying to force him to submit.

He made a snap decision, and ran in the other direction, leaving the humans to deal with the problem for him. From the end of the hallway, he could hear the music-maker's voice:

"Hi. You have three seconds to get the hell out of our way, or else."

And the sound of a human's scream of pain, though Blair could sense no death-agony. Only unconscious, not dead. Then he was among the other human soldiers, trapped between them and the elven warriors behind the barricade, and realized that he had nowhere else to run.

"So far, so good," Eric murmured, leaving two of his demon army to guard the disarmed captain and his unconscious soldier. Kayla knelt next to the sprawled soldier's body, one hand on his wrist, then looked up. "He's okay, Eric."

"All right, let's go." He gave the captain a serious look. "Don't try to run, okay? If you stay put, my demons will disappear and let you go, after I've rescued my friends. Understand?"

"I'm not stupid," the captain said flatly.

Eric and Kayla half-ran down the hallway, the Nightflyers following behind them. *This is going easier than I thought,* Eric decided. *If we can disarm the rest of the soldiers like that, maybe we will survive all of this . . . at least until the Big One shakes loose from the faultline. Minutes. All we have is minutes.*

17

Anima Urbis: Mount Jam

Lord Dharinel, Magus Major and one-time Warleader of the elven court of Mist-Hold, did not believe in giving up.

However, at the moment, he did not see many alternatives.

They were trapped in this rabbit warren of concrete and Cold Iron, caught between two opposing forces who were armed with the best human weaponry the elvenlord had ever seen. After the initial startled clash, where the elven swords had done quite well at close range against the human guns—one rifle, sliced cleanly in half, was still on the floor near his feet—the humans had withdrawn to use their ranged weapons more efficiently. Dharinel had cast magical wards against the gunfire for as long as he had the strength, while young Korendil organized the others into building a barricade out of office equipment that was heavy enough to withstand bullets.

Now they were trapped within it, as the humans hesitated to approach within range of the swords, and the elves could not venture out beyond it, out of fear of the superior firepower. Their own ranged weapons, the bows, were all but useless in these cramped hallways. They required exposing too much of the bearer—and shots clattered uselessly off the walls and ceiling as often as not.

Dharinel fumed, impatient to end this stalemate. He strode to where Korendil crouched near the open edge of the barricade, ignoring the dizziness that made his steps unsteady—an aftereffect of too much magical channeling. "What shall we do now, young knight?" he asked tersely.

Korendil looked up, his eyes bright. "An excellent question, my lord. Perhaps if one of us charged them, to draw them out into the open . . ."

"I would not wager good odds for that first warrior's survival," Dharinel said thoughtfully. "No, we are not ready for a move that desperate yet. Korendil, go attend your human friends. I will watch for any further attacks of poisoned smoke, and deflect them from us."

"My lord." Korendil bowed slightly, and went to where the two human women were seated near the wall, very close to each other.

That was something Dharinel still could not understand— he enjoyed living in the human world, for many reasons, but he could not understand how Korendil had woven his life so thoroughly with humans. Humans were so . . . fragile. Such as the human woman with pale skin and dark red hair, who even now shuddered and cried from the effects of some incomprehensible human illness. Claustrophobia, that was the word that the dark-skinned woman had said, but the word meant nothing to him.

Still, it was Korendil's life, and however he wished to spend his time was his business. Though Dharinel privately wondered how much time any of them had left now, with the bullets singing overhead every few seconds.

He turned back to watch their enemies, around a corner of the barricade, and his eyes widened.

The human guards were walking around the corner, hands raised in the air. He recognized that as a common gesture of surrender from all the movies young Arvin had shown him. Behind them was a roiling mass of darkness, moving toward them.

What . . . It was herding them. None of them wanted to touch it. It wasn't more poisoned smoke, for it moved with purpose.

Then he saw the individual shapes within the darkness, and he realized in surprised horror that it was an army of shadow-demons.

And beside them, playing music, a faint Irish melody that he now heard over the clattering of arms, was the Bard.

"The Bard!" Dharinel shouted elatedly, then was momentarily annoyed at himself for that display of unseemly emotion. The other elven warriors gathered around the barricade, and Korendil and the two human women joined them, peering around the pile of overturned desks and cabinets.

"The Bard, the Bard!"

The Bard saw them and smiled, though he continued to concentrate on playing the melody. The dark-haired human child walked beside him for a moment, then dashed past, heading toward the others at the barricade. The older human woman caught up the child in a hug, pausing only to wipe tears from her eyes.

Dharinel also saw someone else, and it was a sight that heated his blood with quick anger. Warden Blair, described to him by the human scientist and seen in the memories of young Korendil, walking with the other captured human guards. Warden Blair, the man who was responsible for all of this.

Warden Blair, who alone of his contemporary humans had captured and held an elf—and who might come to realize what he had done. Warden Blair, the most dangerous human to elves to walk the waking earth.

With a start, Dharinel realized that Blair was the target of the Bard's melody-magic, that Eric was using his music to keep the Nightflyer-possessed human under his control.

Not bad, the elven lord thought grudgingly. *Perhaps this Bard is all that Korendil has said he could be, not merely a powerful child gifted with too much magic for his own good. He seems to have overcome this situation easily enough.*

Perhaps one of the captured human guards had that same thought at the same moment. Because, before the Bard could react, the human guard broke from the ranks of captured soldiers and leaped at him. Startled, the Bard turned too quickly, and the guard's closed fist connected with a large darkened bruise on the Bard's temple.

The Bard fell like a poleaxed horse. A moment later, his flute clattered to the floor, rolling to a stop several feet away.

A stunned silence descended upon the corridor. Dharinel saw the guard blink in surprise at his unexpected success, then turn toward the shadow-demons, as if suddenly realizing that the Bard had been the only one preventing the monsters from harming him.

The demons surged forward, and that guard was the first casualty, caught for a brief moment with his mouth open in a silent scream as the monsters descended upon him.

Dharinel brought up magical wards an instant later, though he knew that he could only hold them for a few minutes. Fighting against a single demon, he might give himself even odds in that kind of battle—against a horde of them, he knew they had no chance. And what of the others? Some of them had only the thinnest of defenses. Had the crisis foretold in all the visions begun?

The demons rose slowly, leaving nothing behind from their first victim, ignoring Warden Blair and the other guards to drift toward the unconscious Bard.

Of course, Dharinel thought, even as he fought to bring up a ward over the Bard's body as well. *The Bard, the only one who can control and banish them, he will be their main target. Only then will they turn to feed upon us*

The Bard braced himself with one hand, painfully levering himself up to glare at the demons.

No wards, no shieldings. Nothing between him and the horde.

"Get lost," the young man said hoarsely, and Dharinel felt the rush of magic pouring from the human. His jaw dropped in disbelief, and he did not even try to close his mouth.

Like standing in the full desert sun—or beneath a pounding waterfall—now his shields were shunting some of that incredible power away, rather than warding against the demons. He noticed out of the corner of his eye that some of the lesser mages had ducked down behind the barricade to avoid being overwhelmed by the profligate strength of the young human's magic.

The Bard hadn't used the crutch of music this time, only focusing his will upon the creatures; his will, and the power that he now controlled, Dharinel sensed, with a sure if heavy-handed touch.

Silently, the mass of demons faded from view.

The young man slumped back against the floor, not moving.

Dharinel let out a breath he hadn't realized he was holding. The other human soldiers, as if recognizing how narrowly they had just escaped death, looked at one another, saw no officers among them, and took off running in the other direction, quickly disappearing around the corner.

Warden Blair stood alone, glancing from the unconscious body of the Bard to the elven warriors behind the barricade.

Korendil was the first over the barricade, vaulting over an overturned desk with a sword in hand.

Blair moved quickly, and even as Korendil ran toward him, placed one hand on the Bard's unconscious body. Korendil skidded to a halt, sensing that there was more here than met the eye, and poised, sword ready, but posture betraying uncertainty.

"Harm me," a voice hissed from the human's mouth, a voice that had the lifeless tones of the demon within it, no longer even pretending to be human, "and I will eat his soul before I die."

Can't we ever do something like this according to plan? Beth Kentraine asked herself, still not quite understanding how they'd gotten themselves into *this* situation.

She was still unsteady on her feet, shaking from the claustrophobia attack. Elizabet had managed to stave off part of it, but just walking down the hallways of this place had brought back all of the living nightmares. Just remembering that the decompression chamber was here, several floors below her. . . .

I'm not going to lose it now. I'm not.

She heard the shouts of "The Bard!" and fought her way to her feet—saw Eric leading an army of the shadow-things, and let out a cry of her own. She staggered to the barrier, but by the time she got to the barricade the situation had changed.

The thing in Blair's body—she didn't know how she recognized that he wasn't the same scum she had faced, but she knew it with complete certainty—held Eric's life beneath his hand. Kory faced him, sword in hand, but too far away to strike before the thing killed Eric. If anyone else moved, she had no doubt that the creature would strike.

Stalemate.

Suddenly she knew what she could do, what *only* she could do. She was the only one with the contacts, the training, and most importantly, the knowledge. She was the only one that Blair would not see as a threat, because he had already reduced her to nothing. And she greatly doubted that he would understand what she was doing.

The demon within Warden Blair was going to kill Eric in another few seconds, unless she did something, unless she . . .

. . . reached out to the impromptu coven of witches and psychics, reaching for the mind and heart of the woman she related to best: Marge Bailey, who had been made impromptu leader of the circle on Mount Tam.

They were singing and holding hands, those crazy thirteen people—Marge and Chuck and their son, Jeff and Sister Ruth, a wild long-haired singer who was into more political and religious fringe groups than Beth could count, seven more who Beth only knew as casual acquaintances but who had come through when they were needed. Even Jeff, who was pouring everything he had into this—even Sister Ruth, who was calling up a tower of light and fire. And Beth heard a faint echo of the words, something about Mount Tam, and all of this like being back in Viet Nam, with the battle coming soon . . .

. . . reached further, to the circle of power that they had been building for the last hour, and caught hold of it. The magical energy coiled down to her, making her skin tingle.

Unbelievable. Intoxicating. Riding the whirlwind, roping the lightning.

She wanted to laugh, half-drunk with the power of it, but fought for a last measure of self-control. *This must be how Eric feels, when he's controlling that unwieldy but ridiculously powerful Bardic talent of his.* She struggled with it; after a moment it seemed to recognize her and came tamely to her hand, the wild stallion willing to bear her because it pleased him.

She pushed her way past the elves, walking slowly toward Warden Blair. Permitting him to see what a tasty little chocolate eclair of Power she was—but not permitting him to see the trap behind the bait.

"Beth!" Kory called, and she glanced back at him.

He looks terrified. I bet he's afraid that I'm trying to commit suicide.

Am I?

Good question. Wish I knew the answer.

Something cold pressed against the back of Eric's neck, a touch of ice. The cold sensation dragged him up from a tangled web of pain and exhaustion, as effective as a sharp slap in the face.

Oh, please, I don't want anybody else to hit me in the face again today, he thought blearily. *I can still taste blood from the last time . . . can't I just go back to sleep now?*

He took a deep breath, about to open his eyes . . . and froze, all senses gone to red-alert.

There was a Nightflyer right next to him. An uncontrolled, full-grown, very hungry—he could sense that without even opening his eyes—and very deadly Nightflyer, not even six inches away from him.

He knew he was closer to death than he had ever been in his life. In fact, he *should* have been dead, but the thing wasn't doing anything, other than keeping one hand (hand?) on the back of his neck. That was what he had felt—a human hand with a Nightflyer on the other end, going through that hand to touch . . . something of his. *The source of my magic? My soul?* Whatever it was, it made him want to scream, that icy touch that cut through him to his most private self. *Warden Blair,* he realized a split-second later.

Warden Blair, and whatever is inside of him.

Calmly, calmly, he thought. *Don't want the thing to sense that I'm awake, or that I'm going to blast it into Eternity if I get half a chance. . . .*

Oh bravado.

The problem was that if he gathered any of his Bardic magic, that thing would know it in the same instant, and probably kill him a second later. He knew how fast it could strike, having seen too many Nightflyer killings in his own memory and through Beth's. Maybe it was only fate, justice, that this be how he died—after having caused so many other deaths, to be served up as the Blue Plate Special to a hungry alien monster.

"Hungry, are you?" someone said, not far away from him. Eric nearly replied, *No, it's the beastie that's hungry, not me!* when he recognized Beth's voice, strained and tired.

He opened his eyes without even thinking about it.

Beth stood a few feet away, holding out her hands to Warden Blair, aglow with power. Behind her, he saw the pale faces of the elven assault team, Kory in the forefront.

"Come here, you slimy son of a bitch," Beth coaxed, a wild look in her eyes. "Don't you want me? I know you do. Here I am, I'm all yours, come and get me. Yummy, yummy, little monster."

Eric blinked, trying to reconcile the Beth standing in front of him with the Beth that he knew so well. She glittered to his magical senses, inhumanly bright with life energy, more than he'd ever seen in a single person before.

There was no doubt that the Nightflyer/Blair was drawn to that, as irresistibly as a moth to the flame. The monster yearned towards her, most of his attention off Eric.

Too bad his hand wasn't.

"You thought you'd bury us, didn't you?" Beth continued. "Bury us down in the dark with the monsters, with the walls screaming and the air too thick to breathe?

Everything's burning, and all my life is on fire because of you. You're crazy, did you know that? You're as crazy as the human you took; you're infected with him, reduced to his level, just a bastard, just a . . ."

Blair's hand left Eric's neck. He straightened and took a step toward Beth as she spoke, and another.

"No, Bethy, don't!" Eric shouted, calling up his own power and knowing that Blair would strike before he could.

Just before Blair touched her, Beth swung her fist and connected hard on the man's jaw.

Eric Saw it then, what she'd been hiding behind her glittery, enticing surface: the instantaneous flow of magical energy from Beth, combined with the power gathered by the coven on Mount Tam, slamming down with a rushing magical roar like a triumphant orchestral chord.

Blair staggered back, silhouetted in lightless black, only a dark shape of a man with the tall cloak-like wings of a Nightflyer.

Held for one timeless instant, a moth against an arc-light. A hungry moth, that had met something it couldn't eat. The Nightflyer tried to separate from Blair to save itself. Too late.

That blackened figure suddenly shattered into a thousand shards, clattering metallically on the floor around Beth with an odd musical ring.

Of Blair, there was nothing left, nothing at all.

The black pieces that had been the Nightflyer dissolved an instant later, a hundred thin trickles of dark smoke that rose slowly and faded away.

"Bastard," Beth concluded, rubbing the knuckles of her hand. "Damn, that hurt. You'd think I could've remembered how to hit somebody from all those Shotokan Karate lessons." She looked down at Eric. "Hey, Eric, you okay?"

He found his voice. "Oh yeah, sure. How 'bout you?"

"I'm . . . I'm fine . . ." She staggered, nearly falling; Kory was beside her a half-second later. She gave him a wan smile as he held her for a few seconds until she could stand unaided. "We're still alive. What a concept."

Together, they helped Eric stand up—both Eric and Beth leaning on Kory, the only one of the three of them who seemed able to stand on his own two feet without assistance. Eric leaned into their embrace, too wiped out to do anything more than hold onto them, as the elves gathered around them, silent and respectful.

We aren't done yet. Shit.

"Uh . . ." He tried to gather his thoughts, which was a remarkably difficult task at the moment. "Listen, guys, we have to get out of here . . . Blair set up the quake before we could stop him, it's going to hit any second now."

He saw panic in the human eyes, calculation in the elven, as they tried to figure out how much of the original vision might still come to pass.

"We have to stop it," Kayla said. "Dr. Susan said it'd be a major quake, very bad. She thought it could collapse this complex; what would it do to the rest of the city?"

"We can't stop an earthquake," Beth said, shaking her head. "Do you know how much energy is released in a quake? It makes an atomic weapon look like a bottle bomb. We can't stop that. Nothing can stop that!"

"Not—not stop it," Eric said, wishing that his eyes would allow him to focus on his friends. Beth was still a vague blur, and looking at the elves was even worse. "Deflect it. Send part of it south, L.A. can handle a small quake. Send the rest of it out to sea, where there's nothing for a few thousand miles; a tsunami probably wouldn't hit the Orient or Hawaii from here. I hope."

"Even if it did they'd have hours of warning," Kayla said. "Plenty of time to evacuate."

"It's worth a try." Elizabet looked around at the elves, then back at Eric. "What can we do to help?"

"The Bard can gather all the energy we can give," Dharinel said firmly. "Ours, and the circle's."

Beth closed her eyes for a moment. "They're still going strong," she said. "I don't think they even noticed when I took out Blair."

"I believe in his abilities now," Dharinel said, with a nod towards Eric. "Perhaps our power, with the human witches, will be enough."

Oh God, is it up to me again?

He picked up his flute and sat down unsteadily, Beth and Kory next to him. He closed his eyes, gathering his thoughts, trying to think how in the hell he was going to do this. Not without music, that was for sure.

Next time, I just want to call in the U.S. Cavalry. Or figure out a solution and send it FedEx to Washington D.C. I hurt too much to do this. . . .

Like a distant echo, he heard the Mount Tam group singing. The melody was unfamiliar to him, but powerful, and he followed their lead, breaking away after several measures into an improvised counter-melody. He felt the magic brightening around him, and let his mind drift down, following the near-musical resonances of the Poseidon device to where the resonances gathered and built upon each other, far below the city of Hollister, many miles away.

He quailed when he saw what he faced. It was impossible. He saw the weight of the forces at play, far beneath the surface, and knew that there was no way their group could affect those vast pressures. It was completely impossible. In another few seconds, the pressure would build to the breaking point and smash the entire Bay Area with a rippling wave of destruction. . . .

And he Saw the devastation that would bring; no Nightflyers this time, but whole neighborhoods flattened, people dead and dying. High-rise buildings breaking out in fires, trapping those who had survived inside the swaying structures.

The face of Warden Blair, laughing. The man and the monster.

No! This is my city, my home. I'm not going to let that bastard win!

He reached out, in a way that he'd never thought to try before, to touch the others in the building around him, not just the elves and his friends, but the few remaining guards and personnel that hadn't been evacuated. Carefully, not wanting to hurt them, he drew power from them as well, then reached out further, drawing in as many of the people of the city of Dublin as he could reach—

More, farther, the people of the cities along the East

Bay, across the Bay to San Francisco, south to San Jose. People, people, the huge sprawling, brawling megacomplex of people, as diverse as any place on the face of the earth.

The city. The city itself was alive, had a soul, the soul of millions of people that lived in it and loved it and wouldn't live anywhere else. And that soul had power as well. The power was deeper, more akin to the force building within the fault—and perhaps it would touch that force in a way nothing else could.

He cast the power down as quickly as he drew it, forcing the energies in the faultline to dissipate harmlessly outward, gently releasing the pressure from the merging continental plates. It was a fragile balancing act—

And a deadly one; it frightened him, knowing that if he faltered and held onto any of it for more than an instant, it would destroy him, a giant hand swatting a fruit-fly. Too much, too quickly . . . he felt caught in a vise, trapped between the pressures of the faultline and the searing magic that he channeled, suspended between the live wires of a million volts of electricity. There was no way to know whether this would work—to pause for a moment, even to check the faultline, would overset him, and he would lose his balance and his life.

Something . . . shifted . . . in the fault, and he felt it in his own bones—the rising wave of energy, the earthquake arcing out in all directions from the epicenter—he cast away the last of the magic that he was channeling, and yelled, "Hang on! Here it comes!"

The floor rippled underneath him, then vibrated sharply. He felt the rumbling turning his insides to water as the floor rolled beneath him, like a boat on stormy seas. He held onto Kory and Beth and waited for his nightmare to become reality, for the walls to crack and tumble down like the houses of San Francisco in his dream.

Suddenly, it was over. The hallway trembled one last time with a faint aftershock, then everything was quiet and calm again.

It's . . . it's over? Eric asked himself, looking around. The elves and humans were staring at each other in disbelief.

"That—that was it?" Elizabet asked in an unbelieving tone. "That's *all*?"

"I guess so," Eric said, surprise in his voice.

"It worked." Kayla grinned at him, and shot her fist ceilingward. "Yes! It worked! We did it! Yeah! Way to go, Eric!"

"Th-thanks," he said. It was hard to breathe for some weird reason, and every muscle in his body seemed to be twitching. He thought about standing up and decided against it, just as everything tilted around him.

"Eric?" Kayla's voice sounded very far away. "Eric, you okay?"

"Fine," he tried to answer, but for some reason his voice didn't seem to be working right, either.

"What is wrong with him?" he heard Korendil ask in alarm.

Eric felt the magic in Kayla's hands, though he couldn't seem to focus his eyes well enough to see the pale blue light that he knew was flickering over her hands. Kayla's voice sounded closer, stronger. "Yeah. There's just a hell of a lot of energy running through this guy, and it kind of overloaded his nervous system. At least, that's what it feels like—touching him felt like sticking my hand in an electrical socket."

What an image. Eric thought of the commercial possibilities: Bard-O-Matic Fluorescent Light, just add magic. Barderator, take him on your camping trip and bring all your appliances. Compu-Bard, plug in your computer and use him as the backup power source.

Maybe he'd do better just to lie there and not worry about it. He felt terrible, and lying on the floor did seem like the best idea, at least for the next few minutes. This "saving the world" business wasn't all it was cracked up to be, and certainly didn't seem to be a very survivable hobby.

He lay there, half-awake or half-asleep, the healing energy warm and calming. He could almost breathe easily again, which felt marvelous. Other than that, he hurt too much to move.

Next time, he decided, *we'll just call Chuck Norris and the Delta Force. Or maybe Arnie. Or better yet, the IRS.*

ჰა   ჰა   ჰა

Kayla straightened at last, and Korendil breathed a sigh
of relief. The Bard was barely conscious, but he was no
longer shivering or so deathly pale. The young healer, on
the other hand, looked tired and drawn, not much better
than her patient. She stood up unsteadily, muttering some
human curse under her breath. "Can we go home now?"
she asked plaintively, and fainted.

Kory caught her easily, and the older healer was at his
side a moment later, pressing fingertips to the young girl's
wrist and checking beneath her closed eyelids a moment
later. "Someday she'll learn," Elizabet murmured, then spoke
louder. "She's all right, just exhausted."

"We'd best leave this place before other guards arrive,"
Dharinel said. He gestured at two of his warriors, one who
lifted Eric easily, the other who took Kayla from Kory's arms.
"Help your other friend, Korendil," the elven mage said
quietly, glancing at Beth.

Kory walked closer to Beth, who was standing very still,
her eyes distant. "Milady Beth, please walk with me," he
said, taking her hand. She did not answer, but followed
beside him as the group began to retrace their steps out
of this underground maze.

They had survived. That was the first and foremost
thought in his mind, that though many had been wounded
in the battle, either in body or in spirit—he glanced at Beth,
who walked woodenly, eyes downcast—they had all survived,
against all odds. Healing would come with time, at least
for the physical damage. For the wounds of spirit, he had
no way of understanding what would happen.

Beth had been hurt that way, as seriously as a sword cut
to the vitals, and it was only now something that he was
beginning to understand.

She had survived; how long until she could be healed?

18

The Pleasures of Home

Kory had thought he would never again feel as terrible as he had the day he had gone off to the bulldozed Fairesite to die. He learned differently in the next few moments.

No sooner did they reach the parking lot unmolested, than reaction set in.

Physically, while he was not wounded, he was as exhausted as it was possible to be and still remain on his feet. He had a headache from a blow one of the soldiers had dealt him on the head, combined with the unaccustomed exercise of feeding Eric with mage-energy. No, not a headache; the word was not adequate for what he was enduring. There was someone standing on top of his head with spiked shoes, while driving stakes into both eyesockets, as a third person pulled every muscle in his neck and shoulders tight and tied knots in them.

Emotionally, he was a wreck. There were the minor worries, of course, about what would happen to Susan, to Kayla. And he fretted about Eric, who looked as bad as Kory felt. He was sick with fear for Beth, who had not emerged from her silence in all the long walk to the parking lot.

And there was the old fear, driven home yet again by this series of brushes with death. *Humans. They are so fragile, so easily hurt. And they die so soon. I love them, and in a few short years they will leave me forever. . . .*

Elizabet took one look at them all, and ordered them into her car, turning to face the waiting elvensteeds with the kind of look Kory associated with training dogs.

"You two," she said sternly. "Go home. Go *directly* home. Invisibly. No excursions. No frightening the police. Got that?"

The bikes flickered their lights, and Kory got the impression of great disappointment. "Wait a moment," he said, and they canted their wheels in his direction with a sense of anticipation.

"The humans are still in circle up on Mount Tam," he pointed out. "Perhaps they could take Melisande and Arvin there to thank them, and let them know what has occurred? The countryside is a bit rough for conventional vehicles."

Elizabet nodded. "That's reasonable," she said. "And a good idea. The others should recognize Sandy, at least. Once she kills the ears and eyes. All right, go on, then."

Recognizing that the older healer had taken charge of the war-party, Lord Dharinel nodded to the two, who leapt onto the bikes and roared off into the darkness.

"With your permission, Lady Elizabet," he said, bowing, his voice only a *little* ironic, "the rest of my people and I will go home Underhill or to our Groves. We have rest and healing to accomplish."

So they did; while Kory was unwounded, that was not true of many of the others. None of the wounds were life-threatening, but many were serious, and while they had lost no one, the unspoken message was that it had been a very near thing.

Elizabet nodded, the irony in her gesture carefully gauged to exactly match that in Lord Dharinel's voice. "If we could help you, we would," she said. "As it is—"

"As it is you are fully as weary as we, having paid your portion in full, unstinted measure," Dharinel replied. "We have somehow averted many tragedies this night, coming forth relatively unscathed. I come to the conclusion that there is value in working with mortals."

Elizabet's smile widened a little, making her look like a cat with a bowl of cream and a bowl of tuna in front of her—and a canary feather at one corner of her mouth. But, "Thank you, my lord," was all she wisely said.

Dharinel, just as wise, bowed again, and led his forces out into the darkness, over the grass hills, away from the roads. Elizabet turned her attention back to her captives.

"You three in the back," she ordered. "Kayla, you in the front. *Passenger* side."

For once Kayla didn't object. She simply got in and leaned back against the seat with a sigh that spoke more of exhaustion than disappointment at being unable to drive.

Kory helped Eric in at one door, then got Beth installed in the middle of the bench seat. This was a newer car; mostly not of metal, and the bits of Cold Iron in the framework and engine were not enough to cause him discomfort.

He waited for one of the other four to say something after Elizabet took her place in the driver's seat, but no one did. There was a bit of a stir back at the building they'd just left, but it never got as far as the parking lot. Finally, after they got past the gate guard without incident, he leaned back and closed his eyes, with no further distractions to keep him from his troubles.

Beth stared at the patch of road between Elizabet's and Kayla's shoulders, and flexed mental muscles to see if they still hurt.

They did.

She *hadn't* gone into screaming hysterics when the quake hit; that in itself was something of a miracle. She wasn't certain that she believed it even now. She still walked that tightrope between sanity and the abyss; it wouldn't take much to shove her over. Not much at all, actually.

A room with no ventilation, a little commuter plane. An elevator.

A closet.

She'd never been weak. Eric and Kory always counted on *her* to be the strong one. How could she still face them like this, knowing that if they needed her, she might be falling apart?

In a state of numbed pain, she climbed the stairs to the house, then up to their room. She didn't even remember getting out of the car. She flung herself down on the waterbed and stared up at the high ceiling. After a while Kory and Eric came and sat on the rails beside her.

So, she wasn't so strong anymore, and now they knew it. What if they decided to arrange things so that they *wouldn't* need to count on her?

That's what really hurts, doesn't it, Kentraine? The idea that they might be able to live just fine without you?

One short step to the abyss. How could she live like that for the rest of her life? How could she live her life within the limits of a phobia?

She wanted to cry, but the tears were all gone.

I can't live like this, she thought. *I can't—*

Then don't, said the little voice in her head that always prodded her when she started thinking something really stupid. Like now. *Don't live like that. You aren't the only one in the world with claustrophobia, you know. Other people have gotten help.*

Yes, but— she wailed silently, her eyes closed against the two faces bent over hers in concern and fear. *But—*

But you're afraid to admit that you have weaknesses, Kentraine, the little voice continued without remorse. *Why don't you ask those two to help you and see what happens?*

But what if they don't want to?

But what if they do? the voice answered, then fell silent.

She opened her eyes. They were still there, faces still twisted with fear, eyes bright—

"You know," she said, conversationally, a catch in her voice telling her that if she wasn't careful, she'd break down and weep after all, "you two look really funny when you're about to cry. Your faces get all red and your eyes get narrow and squinched up—"

She reached out while they were still trying to think of an answer to that and snagged their supporting arms, tumbling them into bed on either side of her.

"I've—got a problem," she said, pulling the words out of pain. "That claustrophobia thing. It's kind of a big problem, and I don't know how long it's gonna take to get over it. If I can."

"Then we work around it," Eric said promptly. "We'll see what we can do to make it better, and meanwhile we'll work around it. So if we can't take the BART some days, so what? We'll bike it, or walk. Stairs instead of elevators. Outdoor gigs. We'll manage."

"You say that now—" she began. Kory interrupted her.

"We say that for always," he replied firmly. "You do not abandon a part of you because it is sick. You help it to heal, as best it can. And if you limp, where's the harm? What," he concluded, mockingly, "did you think that all tales ended in wedding the perfect princess? What a bore if they did—"

"And what a bore to be perfect!" Eric finished.

She looked from one to the other, and finally, with a flood of relief, believed them.

"I love you two," she said, hugging them as tightly as she could. "Kiss me, you fools."

CODA

The park was a good place to sit and read on a week-day during school hours. The only children around were toddlers. Not terribly noisy. Peaceful—and the closest she got to hiking, now.

"Nice lookin' rig you got there, li'l lady," drawled a pseudo-Texan voice.

Dr. Susan Sheffield looked up from the book she had been reading, and was blinded momentarily by the sun. When she could see again, she found she was surrounded by three people she hadn't thought she'd ever meet again.

"Thanks," she said, patting the side of the wheelchair. "I'm still trying to get used to the way people either try to pretend they aren't watching you, or try to pretend that Ahsera isn't here."

Eric smiled shyly. "I thought that might have been an elvensteed. I didn't think wheelchairs were supposed to hold mage-glow."

"Elvenpony, actually," she replied, relieved to be able to talk about it. Colonel Steve thought Ahsera was just a really high-tech chair—but then she never let him in the apartment, where the pony could raise or lower itself, or take any con-figuration at all to help her through her day. "Not as bright as an elvensteed—about the candlepower of a chimp, I think, without the tendency to get mad and throw feces."

"Are you getting around all right?" Beth asked. Susan took an appraising look of her own, and saw the scars of mental wounds still healing.

"As well as I can," she replied honestly. "What can I tell you? Some days I'm pretty bitter, but you know what George Burns says: living like this isn't so bad when you think about the alternative." She sighed. "And I have Ahsera here—who helps me get along pretty well in private. Colonel Steve pulled strings and got me a telecommute job at JPL. I work from my apartment."

"No more Poseidon?" Beth asked, with a shudder she could not repress.

"I sent the kernel to the Japanese," Susan said, still angry at how her vision had been perverted. "To someone I know and trust. He has a good team, and *they* don't think of earthquakes as weapons. They're going to have to go back to square one, but I think they might do better than we did. I've conferenced with some of their people, not specifically mentioning what happened here, but suggesting a terrorist scenario, and they're going to build a fail-safe into it, right from the start." She shrugged. "The package has been hedged around with so many conditions, it looks like a Hollywood contract. When they get a working model, it goes public *immediately*, and then to an international committee to watchdog it. Anybody with faults gets the probes, and the committee will make sure no faults ever build up enough stress for a quake. It's going to take them years to get where we were. And in between, quakes are still going to kill people. I can't help that. *That* is what I'm bitter about."

Eric sat down on his heels so that his face was level with hers. "So what would have been better?" he asked. "For you to have completed the project and then have *real* terrorists take it over and hold a whole *country* hostage? What would Poseidon have done in Turkey, with all those mud houses? Or one of the Slovakian republics? What if someone had taken it and used it on his *own* people— behave and do what I want, or you get a quake?"

"I'd thought about that," she admitted. "Fewer casualties the way it happened. . . ."

"But even one is too many." He straightened. "Just so you know I feel the same way."

"We did not wish to disturb you or cause you any pain," Korendil said carefully, "but Arvin said you might wish to speak with us now. Perhaps more than once."

She thought of all the elves, scatterbrained as they often seemed to be, who had rallied around her to keep her from going crazy these past few months. Arvin being the ringleader of them all—

He had *not* been the Prince Charming of her adolescent fantasy summer—in fact, when she saw him, she hardly recognized Lirylel anymore. Tastes changed . . . and he was still a teenager. But Arvin, now—intelligent, well-read, fun to be around—

—not a bad choice for a casual lover, good friend, occasional pupil. She wasn't ready for any kind of commitment of course, and if and when she made one, it was going to be with a *human*. But Arvin was a shoulder when she needed one, a cheerleader when she needed one, and he was quite inventive in the bedroom. By the time he got done experimenting, she'd have an entire repertoire ready for a steady customer. . . .

"Yeah," she said, finally. "I think I'd like to see you guys once in a while. If you wouldn't mind inviting me over to your place, that is. *Mine* doesn't have a hot tub."

Kory smiled, Beth sighed in relief, and Eric gave her the high-sign. "You're on," Eric said. "How about Saturday? We're hosting an elven full moon party. Ahsera would be right at home. We're having Greek carry-out." He lowered his voice, enticingly. "And homemade baklava."

It had been a *long* time since she'd had Greek food. The hospital hadn't allowed her anything but bland with lots of fiber.

"Is Arvin invited?" she asked.

"We invited him, but he said he didn't want to come without you," Beth replied, with a ghost of a grin. "I don't know what you're doing to him. His harem is down to less than a dozen."

Susan threw back her head and laughed, long and hard, earning startled glances from the nannies around her.

They probably think handicapped people shouldn't have any fun, she thought, but without bitterness this time.

"All right, I'll tell him tonight it's a date." She stretched a little. "Do I bring anything?"

"Retsina if you can find it," Beth said firmly. "Ouzo if you can't. Only a little—a little of that stuff goes a long way. Two bottles, max. We never get anywhere near liquor stores without a zillion instruments to carry."

Susan smiled. They hadn't patronized her by telling her "nothing," and hadn't insulted her by asking for something too simple. She'd have to go looking for Retsina, if only in the yellow pages, and either send someone out to pick it up for her, or get it herself.

"I'll take care of it," she promised, both herself and them. "Don't worry about it."

Eric grinned as the other two nodded. "I won't."

Somehow she got the feeling that they meant that the words applied to more than a simple bottle of wine.

For that matter, so did she.